TOLSTOY'S SHORT FICTION

REVISED TRANSLATIONS
BACKGROUNDS AND SOURCES
CRITICISM

A NORTON CRITICAL EDITION

TOLSTOY'S SHORT FICTION

REVISED TRANSLATIONS
BACKGROUNDS AND SOURCES
CRITICISM

Edited and with revised translations by

MICHAEL R. KATZ

MIDDLEBURY COLLEGE

W • W • NORTON & COMPANY • *New York* • *London*

Copyright © 1991 by W. W. Norton & Company, Inc.

Printed in the United States of America.

First Edition

Library of Congress Cataloging-in-Publication Data
Tolstoy, Leo, graf, 1828–1910.
[Short stories. English. Selections]
Tolstoy's short fiction / Leo Tolstoy ; edited and with revised
translations by Michael R. Katz.
p.   cm. — (A Norton critical edition)
"Revised translations, backgrounds and sources, criticism."
Includes bibliographical references.
1. Tolstoy, Leo, graf, 1828–1910—Translations, English.
2. Tolstoy, Leo, graf, 1828–1910— Criticism and interpretation.
I. Katz, Michael R.   II. Title.
PG3366.A13K38   1990
891.73'3—dc20   89-25580
ISBN 0-393-96016-1

W. W. Norton & Company, Inc., 500 Fifth Avenue, New York, N.Y. 10110
www.wwnorton.com

W. W. Norton & Company Ltd., Castle House, 75/76 Wells Street,
London W1T 3QT

6 7 8 9 0

Contents

Preface

This volume of *Tolstoy's Short Fiction* is intended to supplement and amplify the existing Norton Critical Editions of Tolstoy's two master-pieces. I have selected what I consider to be the best prose works of early and late Tolstoy, that is, before *War and Peace* (from 1854 to 1859) and after *Anna Karenina* (from 1886 to 1905). Not everyone will agree with my selections: each reader is entitled to have his or her personal favorites.

A word about the translations: both Norton Critical Editions use the versions by Louise and Aylmer Maude. The Maudes lived in Russia, knew Tolstoy intimately, and shared a genuine appreciation of his ideas. And Tolstoy admired their work. Again, each reader is likely to have a preferred version of individual works. After considerable thought I came to share the view expressed by Henry Gifford in an essay included in this volume, namely that in general the Maudes' translations are the soundest we have. I have chosen to edit and annotate their versions to render them more readable and more accessible to an American audience.[1]

Following the fictional texts, the section entitled Backgrounds and Sources contains Tolstoy's curious first literary endeavor, *A History of Yesterday* (1851), and his autobiographical fragment, *Memoirs of a Madman* (1884). These are accompanied by an excerpt from Tolstoy's diary for the year 1855 and a selection of his letters dating from 1858 to 1895.

The section of Criticism includes essays written from 1904 to 1989. It contains excerpts from Russian critics, as well as examples of the best Anglo-American scholarship on Tolstoy's work. The final item, "At the Tolstoy Museum," is a splendid short story by the late American author Donald Barthelme and is intended to provide a grain of salt (or a clean white handkerchief).

A Chronology of Tolstoy's Life and Work and a Selected Bibliography have been appended to acquaint the reader with basic facts and to provide suggestions for further study.

I wish to express my gratitude to Stephen Baehr, Robert Belknap, Reginald Christian, George Gibian, Henry Gifford, Richard Gustafson,

---

1. The exceptions are "Family Happiness," which was translated by J. D. Duff, and "Alyosha the Pot," which was translated by S. A. Carmack.

Robert Louis Jackson, Gary Jahn, Gary Saul Morson, and Kathleen Parthé for their suggestions of texts and essays to be included in this volume.

My work is dedicated to the memory of my former teacher, the Countess Darya Andreevna de Keyserlingk.

The Texts of
TOLSTOY'S
SHORT FICTION

Translations by Louise and Aylmer Maude†
Revised by Michael R. Katz

† "Family Happiness" was translated by J. D. Duff. "Alyosha the Pot" was translated by S. A. Carmack.

Sevastopol in December†

Early dawn is just beginning to color the horizon above Sapun Hill. The dark blue surface of the sea has already thrown off the gloom of night and is only awaiting the first ray of the sun to begin sparkling merrily. A current of cold misty air blows from the bay; there is no snow on the hard black ground, but the sharp morning frost crunches under your feet and makes your face tingle. Only the distant, incessant murmur of the sea, occasionally interrupted by the reverberating boom of cannon from Sevastopol, infringes the stillness of the morning. All is quiet on the ships. It strikes eight bells.

On the north side the activity of day is gradually beginning to replace the quiet of night: some soldiers with clanking muskets pass to relieve the guard, a doctor is already hurrying to the hospital, and a soldier, having crept out of his dug-out, washes his weather-beaten face with icy water and then turning to the reddening horizon says his prayers, rapidly crossing himself; a creaking Tartar cart drawn by camels crawls past on its way to the cemetery to bury the blood-stained dead with which it is loaded almost to the top. As you approach the harbor you are struck by the peculiar smell of coal-smoke, manure, dampness, and meat. Thousands of different objects are lying in heaps by the harbor: firewood, meat, gabions, sacks of flour, iron, and so on. Soldiers of various regiments, some carrying bags and muskets and others empty-handed, are crowded here together, smoking, quarrelling, and hauling heavy loads onto the steamer which lies close to the wharf, its funnel smoking. Private boats crowded with all sorts of people—soldiers, sailors, merchants, and women—keep arriving at the landing stage or leaving it.

"To the Grafskaya, your Honour? Please get in!" two or three old salts offer you their services, getting out of their boats.

You choose the one nearest to you, step across the half-decayed carcass of a bay horse that lies in the mud close to the boat, and pass on towards the rudder. You push off from the landing stage; around you is the sea, now glittering in the morning sunshine. In front of you the old sailor, in his camel-hair coat, and a flaxen-haired boy silently and steadily ply the oars. You gaze at the enormous striped ships scattered far and wide over the bay, at the ships' boats that move about over the sparkling azure like small black dots, at the opposite bank where the handsome light-colored buildings of the town are lit by the rosy rays of the morning sun, at the foaming white line by the breakwater and around the sunken vessels, the black tops of whose masts here and there stand mournfully out of the water, at the enemy's fleet looming on the crystal horizon of the sea, and at the foaming and bubbling wash of the oars. You listen

†This piece was first published in 1855.

to the steady sound of voices that reaches you across the water and to the majestic sound of firing from Sevastopol, which seems to be growing more intense.

It is impossible for some feeling of heroism and pride not to penetrate your soul at the thought that you, too, are in Sevastopol, and for the blood not to run faster in your veins.

"Straight past the *Kistentin*,[1] your Honor!" the old sailor tells you, turning round to verify the direction towards the right in which you are steering.

"And she's still got all her guns!"[2] says the flaxen-headed boy, examining the ship in passing.

"Well, of course. She's a new one. Kornilov lived on her," remarks the old seaman, also looking up at the ship.

"Look where it's burst!" the boy says after a long silence, watching a small white cloud of dispersing smoke that has suddenly appeared high above the South Bay accompanied by the sharp sound of a bursting bomb.

"That's *him* firing from the new battery today," adds the old seaman, calmly spitting on his hand. "Now then, pull away, Mishka! Let's get ahead of that long-boat." And your skiff travels faster over the broad swell of the road-stead, gets ahead of the heavy long-boat laden with sacks, unsteadily and clumsily rowed by soldiers, and making its way among all sorts of boats moored there is made fast to the Grafsky landing.

Crowds of grey-clad soldiers, sailors in black, and gaily dressed women throng noisily about the quay. There are women selling buns, Russian peasants with samovars shouting, "Hot sbiten!,"[3] and on the very first steps lie rusty cannon-balls, bombs, grape-shot, and cannon of various sizes. A little farther on is a large open space where some enormous beams are lying, together with gun carriages and sleeping soldiers. Horses, carts, cannon, green ammunition wagons, and stacked muskets stand there. Soldiers, sailors, officers, women, children, and tradespeople are moving about; carts loaded with hay, sacks, and casks are passing, now and then a Cossack, a mounted officer, or a general in a vehicle. To the right is a street closed by a barricade on which some small guns are mounted in embrasures and beside which sits a sailor smoking a pipe. To the left is a handsome building with Roman figures engraved on its frontage and before which soldiers are standing with blood-stained stretchers. Everywhere you will see the unpleasant indications of a war camp. Your first impressions will certainly be most disagreeable: the strange mixture of camp-life and town-life—of a fine town and a dirty bivouac—is not only ugly but looks like horrible disorder: it will even seem that every one is scared, in a commotion, at a loss as to what to

---

1. That is, the vessel *Constantine*.
2. Guns were removed from most of the ships for use on fortifications.

3. A hot drink made with treacle and lemon, or honey and spice.

do. But look more closely at the faces of these people moving around you and you will get a very different impression. Take for instance this convoy soldier muttering something to himself as he goes to water those three bay horses, and doing it all so quietly that evidently he will not get lost in this motley crowd, which does not even exist as far as he is concerned, but will do his job, be it what it may—watering horses or hauling guns—as calmly, self-confidently, and unconcernedly as if it were all happening in Tula or Saransk. You will read the same thing on the face of this officer passing by in immaculate white gloves, on the face of the sailor who sits smoking on the barricade, on the faces of the soldiers waiting in the portico of what used to be the Assembly Hall, and on the face of that girl who, afraid of getting her pink dress muddy, is jumping from stone to stone as she crosses the street.

Yes, disenchantment certainly awaits you on entering Sevastopol for the first time. You will look in vain in any of these faces for signs of disquiet, perplexity, or even enthusiasm, determination, or readiness for death—there is nothing of the kind. What you see are ordinary people quietly occupied with ordinary activities, so that perhaps you may reproach yourself for having felt undue enthusiasm and may doubt the justice of the ideas you had formed of the heroism of the defenders of Sevastopol, based on the tales and descriptions, sights and sounds, and heard from the North Side. But before yielding to such doubts, go to the bastions and see the defenders of Sevastopol at the very place of the defense, or better still, go straight into that building opposite which was once the Sevastopol Assembly Rooms and in the portico of which stand soldiers with stretchers. There you will see the defenders of Sevastopol and you will see terrible and lamentable, solemn and amusing, but astounding and soul-elevating sights.

You enter the large Assembly Hall. As soon as you open the door you are struck by the sight and smell of forty or fifty amputations and most seriously wounded cases, some in cots but most on the floor. Do not trust the feeling that checks you at the threshold; it is the wrong feeling. Go on, do not be ashamed of having come to *look* at the sufferers; do not hesitate to go up and speak to them. Sufferers like to see a sympathetic human face, like to speak of their sufferings and hear words of love and sympathy. You pass between the rows of beds and look for a face less stern and full of suffering, which you feel you can approach and speak to.

"Where are you wounded?" you inquire hesitatingly and timidly of an emaciated old soldier who is sitting up in his cot and following you with a kindly look as if inviting you to approach him. I say "inquire timidly" because, besides strong sympathy, sufferings seem to inspire dread of offending, as well as great respect for him who endures them.

"In the leg," the soldier replies, and at the same moment you yourself notice from the fold of his blanket that one leg is missing above the knee. "Now, thank God," he adds, "I am ready to leave the hospital."

"Is it long since you were wounded?"

"Well, it's over five weeks now, your Honor."

"And are you still in pain?"

"No, I'm not in any pain now; only when it's bad weather I seem to feel a pain in the calf. Otherwise, it's all right."

"How were you wounded?"

"It was on the Fifth Bastion, your Honor, at the first *bondbarment*. I trained the gun and was stepping across to the next embrasure, when *he* hits me in the leg, just as if I had stumbled into a hole. I look—and the leg is gone."

"Do you mean to say you felt no pain the first moment?"

"Not much, only as if something hot was shoved against my leg."

"And afterwards?"

"Not much afterwards except when they began to draw the skin together, then it did seem to smart. The chief thing, your Honor, is *not to think*; if you don't think it's nothing much. It's most because a man thinks."

At this moment a woman in a grey striped dress with a black kerchief tied round her head comes up to you and joins your conversation with the sailor. She begins telling you about him, his sufferings, the desperate condition he was in for four weeks, and how when he was wounded he stopped his stretcher-bearers so that he could see a volley fired from our battery; and how the Grand Duke spoke to him and gave him twenty-five rubles, and how he had told them he wanted to go back to the bastion to teach the young ones, if he could not fight any longer. As she says all this in one breath, the woman keeps looking first at you, then at the sailor, who having turned away is picking lint on his pillow as if not listening; her eyes shine with a peculiar rapture.

"She's my missus, your Honor!" he remarks with a look that seems to say, "You must excuse her. It's a woman's way to talk nonsense."

Now you begin to understand the defenders of Sevastopol and for some reason begin to feel ashamed of yourself in the presence of this man. You want to say too much, to express your sympathy and admiration, but you can't find the right words and are dissatisfied with those that occur to you, so you silently bow your head before this taciturn and unconscious grandeur and firmness of spirit—which is ashamed to have its worth revealed.

"Well, may God help you to get well soon," you say to him, and turn to another patient who is lying on the floor apparently awaiting death in unspeakable torment.

He is a fair-haired man with a puffy pale face. He is lying on his back with his left arm thrown back in a position that indicates cruel suffering. His hoarse breathing comes with difficulty through his parched, open mouth, his leaden blue eyes are rolled upwards, and what remains of his bandaged right arm is thrust out from under his tumbled blanket. The oppressive smell of mortified flesh assails you even more strongly, and the feverish inner heat in all the sufferer's limbs seems to penetrate you too.

"Is he unconscious?" you ask the woman who follows you and looks at you kindly as at someone akin to her.

"No, he can still hear, but not well." She adds in a whisper, "I gave him some tea to drink today—what if he is a stranger, one must have pity—but he hardly drank any of it."

"How do you feel?" you ask him.

The wounded man turns his eyes at the sound of your voice but neither sees nor understands you. ·

"My heart's on fire," he mumbles.

A little farther on you see an old soldier who is changing his shirt. His face and body are reddish brown and as gaunt as a skeleton. Nothing is left of one of his arms. It has been amputated at the shoulder. He sits up firmly; he is convalescent, but his dull, heavy look, his terrible emaciation, and the wrinkles on his face show that the best part of this man's life has been consumed by his suffering.

In a cot on the opposite side you see a woman's pale, delicate face, full of suffering, a hectic flush suffusing her cheek.

"That's the wife of one of our sailors: she was hit in the leg by a bomb on the 5th,"[4] your guide will tell you. "She was taking her husband's dinner to him at the bastion."

"Amputated?"

"Yes, cut off above the knee."

Now, if your nerves are strong, go in at the door to the left; there they bandage and operate. You will see doctors with pale, gloomy faces, and arms red with blood up to the elbows, busy at a bed on which a wounded man lies under chloroform. His eyes are open and he utters, as if in delirium, incoherent but sometimes simple and pathetic words. The doctors are engaged on the horrible but beneficent work of amputation. You will see the sharp curved knife enter healthy white flesh; you will see the wounded man come back to life with terrible, heart-rending screams and curses. You will see the doctor's assistant toss the amputated arm into a corner, and in the same room you will see another wounded man on a stretcher watching the operation, and writhing and groaning not so much from physical pain as from the mental torture of anticipation. You will see ghastly sights that will rend your soul; you will see war not with its orderly beautiful and brilliant ranks, its music and beating drums, its waving banners, its generals on prancing horses, but war in its real aspect of blood, suffering, and death. . . .

On coming out of this house of pain you will be sure to experience

4. The first bombardment of Sevastopol.

a sense of relief; you will draw deeper breaths of the fresh air and rejoice in the consciousness of your own health. Yet the contemplation of those sufferings will have made you realize your own insignificance, and you will go calmly and unhesitatingly to the bastions.

"What matters the death and suffering of so insignificant a worm as I, compared to so many deaths, so much suffering?" But the sight of the clear sky, brilliant sun, beautiful town, open church, and soldiers moving in all directions will soon bring your spirit back to its normal state of frivolity, its petty cares and absorption in the present. You may meet the funeral procession of an officer as it leaves the church, the pink coffin accompanied by waving banners and music, and the sound of firing from the bastions may reach your ears. But these things will not bring back your former thoughts. The funeral will seem a very impressive military pageant, the sounds very beautiful warlike sounds, and neither to these sights nor to these sounds will you attach the clear and personal sense of suffering and death that came to you in the hospital.

Passing the church and the barricade you enter that part of town where everyday life is most active. On both sides of the street hang signboards of shops and restaurants. Tradesmen, women with bonnets or kerchiefs on their heads, dandified officers—everything speaks of the firmness, self-confidence, and security of the inhabitants.

If you care to hear the conversation of army and navy officers, enter the restaurant on the right. There you are sure to hear them talk about last night, about Fanny, about the affair of the 24th,[5] about how costly and badly served the cutlets are, and about which of their comrades have been killed.

"Things were awfully bad at our place to-day!" a fair, beardless little naval officer with a green knitted scarf round his neck says in a bass voice.

"Where was that?" asks another.

"Oh, in the Fourth Bastion," answers the young officer, and at the words "Fourth Bastion" you will certainly look more attentively, even with a certain respect at this fair-complexioned officer. The excessive freedom of his manner, his gesticulations, and his loud voice and laugh, which had appeared to you impudent before, now seem to indicate that peculiarly combative frame of mind noticeable in some young men after they have been in danger, but all the same you expect him to say how bad the bombs and bullets made things in the Fourth Bastion. Not at all! It was the mud that made things so bad. "One can scarcely get to the battery," he continues, pointing to his boots, which are muddy even above the calves. "And I have lost my best gunner," says another, "hit right in the forehead." "Who's that? Mitukhin?" "No . . . but am I ever to get my veal, you rascal?" he adds, addressing the waiter. "Not Mi-

5. The Battle of Inkerman.

tukhin but Abramov—such a fine fellow. He was out in six sallies."

At another corner of the table sit two infantry officers with plates of cutlets and peas before them and a bottle of sour Crimean wine called "Bordeaux." One of them, a young man with a red collar and two little stars on his cloak, is talking to the other, who has a black collar and no stars, about the Alma affair. The former has already been drinking and the pauses he makes, the indecision in his face—expressive of his doubt of being believed—and especially the fact that his own part in the account he is giving is too important and the thing is too terrible, show that he is diverging considerably from the strict truth. But you do not care much for stories of this kind which will long be current all over Russia; you want to get to the bastions quickly, especially to that Fourth Bastion about which you have been told so many different tales. When anyone says: "I am going to the Fourth Bastion" he always betrays a slight agitation or too marked an indifference; if anyone wishes to chaff you, he says: "You should be sent to the Fourth Bastion." When you meet someone carried on a stretcher and ask, "Where from?" the answer usually is, "From the Fourth Bastion." Two quite different opinions are current concerning this terrible bastion: that of those who have never been there and who are convinced it is a certain grave for any one who goes, and that of those who, like the fair-complexioned midshipman, live there and who when speaking of the Fourth Bastion will tell you whether it is dry or muddy, cold or warm in the dug-outs, and so forth.

During the half-hour you have spent in the restaurant, the weather has changed. The mist that spread over the sea has gathered into dull grey moist clouds which hide the sun, and a kind of dismal sleet showers down and wets the roofs, pavements, and soldiers' overcoats.

Passing another barricade you go through some doors to the right and up a broad street. Beyond this barricade the houses on both sides of the street are unoccupied: there are no sign-boards, the doors are boarded up, and the windows are smashed. A corner of the wall is knocked down and a roof is broken in. The buildings look like old veterans who have borne much sorrow and privation; they even seem to gaze proudly and somewhat contemptuously at you. On the road you stumble over cannon-balls that lie about, and into holes made in the stony ground by bombs and now full of water. You meet and overtake detachments of soldiers, Cossacks, officers, and occasionally a woman or a child; only it will not be a woman wearing a bonnet, but a sailor's wife wearing an old cloak and soldiers' boots. After you have descended a little slope farther down the same street you will no longer see any houses, only ruined walls amid strange heaps of bricks, boards, clay, and beams; before you, up a steep hill, you see a black untidy space cut up by ditches. This space you are approaching is the Fourth Bastion. . . . Here you will meet still fewer people and no women at all; the soldiers walk briskly by, there are traces of blood on the road, and you are sure to meet four soldiers carrying a stretcher and on it a pale yellow face and a blood-stained overcoat. If you ask, "Where is he wounded?" the bearers, without looking at you, will answer crossly, "in the leg" or "in the arm" if the man is not severely wounded; or else they will remain sternly silent if no head is raised on the stretcher and the man is either dead or seriously wounded.

The whiz of a cannon-ball or bomb near by impresses you unpleasantly as you ascend the hill, and the meaning of the sounds is very different from what it seemed to be when they reached you in the town. Some peaceful and joyous memory will suddenly flash through your mind; self-consciousness begins to supercede the activity of your observation: you are less attentive to all that is around you and a disagreeable feeling of indecision suddenly seizes you. But silencing this despicable little voice that has suddenly made itself heard within you at the sight of danger—especially after seeing a soldier run past you laughing, waving his arms and slipping downhill through the yellow mud—you involuntarily expand your chest, raise your head higher, and clamber up the slippery clay hill. You have climbed only a little way before bullets begin to whiz past you to the right and left, and you will perhaps consider whether you had not better proceed inside the trench which runs parallel to the road; but the trench is full of such yellow stinking mud, more than knee deep, that you are sure to choose the road, especially as *everybody* else does. After walking a couple of hundred yards you come to a muddy place much cut up, surrounded by gabions, cellars, platforms, and dug-outs, on which large cast-iron cannon are mounted and cannon-balls lie piled in orderly heaps. It all seems placed without any plan, aim, connection, or order. A group of sailors is sitting in the battery; in the middle of the open space, half sunk in mud, lies a shattered cannon; there a foot-soldier is crossing the battery, drawing his feet with difficulty out of the sticky mud. Everywhere, on all sides and all about, you see fragments of bombs, unexploded bombs, cannon-balls, and various traces of an encampment, all sunk in the wet, sticky mud. You think you hear the thud of a cannon-ball not far off and you seem to hear different sounds of bullets all around, some humming like bees, some whistling, and some rapidly flying past with a shrill screech like the string of some instrument. You hear the dreadful boom of a shot that sends a shock through you and seems most terrible.

"So this is Fourth Bastion! This is that awful, truly dreadful spot!" So you think, experiencing a slight feeling of pride and a strong feeling of suppressed fear. But you are mistaken, this is not the Fourth Bastion yet. This is only Yazonovsky Redoubt—a comparatively safe and not at all dreadful place. To get to the Fourth Bastion you must turn to the right along that narrow trench where a foot-soldier has just passed, stooping down. In this trench you may again encounter men with stretchers, perhaps a sailor or a soldier with a spade. You will see the mouths of mines, dug-outs into which only two men can crawl, and Cossacks of the Black Sea battalions changing their boots, eating, smoking their pipes, and, in short, living their lives. Again you will see the same stinking mud, traces of camp life and cast-iron refuse of every shape and size. When you have gone about three hundred steps more you will come out at another battery—a flat space with many holes, surrounded with gabions filled with earth and cannons on platforms, and the whole thing walled in with earthworks. Here you may see four or five soldiers playing cards under shelter of the breastworks, and a naval officer, noticing that you are a stranger and inquisitive, will be pleased to show you his "household" and everything that interests you. This officer sits on a cannon rolling a yellow cigarette so composedly, walks from one embrasure to another so quietly, talks to you so calmly and with such an absence of affectation that in spite of the bullets whizzing around you more often than before, you yourself grow cooler, question him carefully, and listen to his stories. He will tell you (but only if you ask) about the bombardment on the 5th of October; he will tell you that only one gun of his battery remained usable and only eight gunners of the crew were left; nevertheless he fired all his guns the next morning, on the 6th. He will tell you how a bomb dropped into one of the dugouts and knocked over eleven sailors; from an embrasure he will show you the enemy's batteries and trenches which are not more than seventy-five to eighty-five yards distant. I am afraid, though, that when you lean out of the embrasure to have a look at the enemy, the whiz of the flying bullets will hinder you from seeing anything; but if you do see anything, you will be very surprised to find that this whitish stone wall—which is so near you and from which puffs of white smoke keep bursting—is the enemy: *he*, as the soldiers and sailors say.

It is even likely that the naval officer, from vanity or merely for a little recreation, will wish to show you some firing. "Call the gunner and crew to the cannon!" Fourteen sailors—their hob-nailed boots clattering on the platform, one putting his pipe in his pocket, another still chewing a rusk—will quickly and cheerfully man the gun and begin loading. Look carefully into these faces and note the bearing and carriage of these men. In every wrinkle of that tanned face with its high cheekbones, in every muscle, in the breadth of those shoulders, the thickness of those legs in their enormous boots, in every movement, quiet, firm, and deliberate, can be seen the chief characteristics of Russian strength—simplicity and obstinacy.

Suddenly the most fearful roar strikes not only your ears but your whole being and makes you shudder all over. It is followed by the whistle of the departing ball, and a thick cloud of powder-smoke envelops you, the platform, and the black figures of the sailors. You will hear various comments made by the sailors concerning this shot of ours and you will notice their animation, evidence of a feeling you might not have expected: a feeling of animosity and thirst for vengeance which lies hidden in each man's soul. You will hear joyful exclamations: "It's gone right into the embrasure! It's killed two, I think. . . . There, they're carrying them off!" "Now *he's* riled and will send one this way," some one remarks; and indeed, soon after, you will see a flash and some smoke; the sentinel standing on the breastwork will call out "Ca-n-non!" and then a ball will whiz past you and bury itself in the earth, throwing out a circle of stones and mud. The commander of the battery will be irritated by this shot and will give orders to fire another cannon and another; the enemy will reply in like manner, and you will experience interesting sensations and see interesting sights. Again the sentinel will call "Cannon!" and you will experience the same sound and shock, and mud will be splashed around as before. Or he will call out "Mortar!" and you will hear a regular and rather pleasant whistle—which it is difficult to connect with the thought of anything dreadful—of a bomb; you will hear this whistle coming nearer and faster towards you. Then you will see a black ball, feel the shock as it strikes the ground, and will hear the ringing explosion. The bomb will explode into whizzing and shrieking fragments, stones will rattle in the air, and you will be bespattered with mud.

At these sounds you will experience a strange feeling of pleasure mingled with fear. At the moment you know the shot is heading towards you, you are sure to imagine it will kill you; but a feeling of pride will support you and no one will know about the knife that cuts at your heart. But when the shot has flown past without hitting you, you revive and are seized, though only for a moment, by an inexpressibly joyful emotion; you feel a peculiar delight in the danger—in this game of life and death—and wish the bombs and balls were to fall nearer and nearer to you.

But again the sentinel in his loud gruff voice shouts "Mortar!" Again a whistle, a fall, an explosion; mingled with this last you are startled by a man's groans. You approach the wounded sailor just as the stretchers are brought. Covered with blood and dirt he presents a strange, scarcely human appearance. Part of his breast has been torn away. For the first few moments only terror and the kind of feigned, premature look of suffering, common to men in this state, appear on his mud-spattered face, but when the stretcher is brought and he himself lies down on it on his healthy side, you notice a change in his expression. His eyes shine more brightly, his teeth are clenched, he raises his head with difficulty, and when the stretcher is lifted he stops the bearers for a moment and turning to his comrades says with effort, in a trembling voice, "Forgive me, brothers!"[6] He wants to say more, something pa-

6. "Forgive me" and "farewell" are related terms in Russian. "Farewell" (*prostcháyte*) can also mean "forgive." The form used here (*prostite*) primarily means "forgive me." Compare the hero's last words in "The Death of Ivan Ilych."

thetic, but only repeats, "Forgive me, brothers!" At this moment a sailor approaches him, places a cap on the head the wounded man holds up towards him, and then placidly swinging his arms returns quietly to his cannon.

"That's the way it is with seven or eight men every day," the naval officer remarks to you, answering the look of horror on your face; then he yawns as he rolls another yellow cigarette.

So now you have seen the defenders of Sevastopol where they are defending it, and somehow you return with a tranquil heightened spirit, paying no heed to the balls and bombs whose whistle accompanies you all the way to the ruined theater. The principal thought you have brought away with you is a joyous conviction of the strength of the Russian people, and this you have gained not by looking at all those traverses, breastworks, cunningly interlaced trenches, mines, cannon, one after another, of which you could make nothing, but from the eyes, words, and actions—in short from seeing what is called the "spirit"—of the defenders of Sevastopol. What they do is all done so simply, with so little effort, that you feel convinced that they could do a hundred times as much. . . . You understand that the feeling which motivates them is not that petty ambition or forgetfulness which you yourself experienced, but something more powerful, which has made them able to live so quietly under the flying cannon balls, exposed to a hundred chances of death besides the one all men are subject to—and this amid conditions of constant toil, lack of sleep, and dirt. Men could not accept such terrible conditions of life for the sake of a cross, or promotion, or because of a threat: there must be some other and higher motive.

It is only now that the tales of the early days of the siege of Sevastopol are no longer beautiful historical legends for you, but have become realities: tales of the time when it was not fortified, when there was no army to defend it, when it seemed a physical impossibility to retain it, yet there was not the slightest idea of abandoning it to the enemy—of the time when Kornilov, that hero worthy of ancient Greece, making his rounds of the troops, said, "Men, we will die, but we will not surrender Sevastopol!" Our Russians, incapable of phrase-making, replied, "We will die! Hurrah!" You will recognize in the men you have just seen those heroes who gladly prepared for death and whose spirits did not flag during those dismal days, but rose instead.

Evening is closing in. Just before setting, the sun emerges from behind grey clouds that covered the sky and suddenly lights up with its bright red glow the purple clouds, the greenish sea with ships and boats rocking on its broad even swell, the white buildings of the town, and people moving in the streets. The sound of some old tune played by a military band on the boulevard is carried across the water and mingles strangely with the sound of firing on the bastions.

Sevastopol in May†

1

Six months have passed since the first cannon-ball went whistling from
the bastions of Sevastopol and threw up the earth of the enemy's entrenchments. Since then bullets, balls, and bombs by the thousand
have flown continually from the bastions to the entrenchments and from
the entrenchments to the bastions, and above them the angel of death
has hovered unceasingly.

Thousands of human ambitions have had time to be mortified, thousands to be gratified and extended, thousands to be lulled to rest in the
arms of death. What numbers of pink coffins and linen palls! And still
the same sounds from the bastions fill the air; the French still look from
their camp with involuntary trepidation and fear at the yellowish earth
of the bastions of Sevastopol and count the embrasures from which the
iron cannon fiercely frown; as before, through the fixed telescope on
the elevation of the signal-station the pilot still watches the bright-
colored figures of the French, their batteries, tents, and columns on the
green hill, and the puffs of smoke that rise from the entrenchments; as
before, crowds of men, with an even greater variety of desires, stream
with the same ardor from many parts of the world to this fatal spot. But
the question the diplomats failed to resolve still remains unresolved by
powder and blood.

2

A regimental band was playing on the boulevard near the pavilion in
the besieged town of Sevastopol, and crowds of women and military
men strolled along the paths enjoying themselves. The bright spring sun
had risen in the morning above the English entrenchments, had reached
the bastions, then the town and the Nicholas Barracks, shining with
equal joy on all, and was now sinking into the distant blue sea which,
rocking with an even motion, glittered with silvery light.

A tall infantry officer with a slight stoop, putting on a presentable
though not very white glove, passed through the gate of one of the small
sailors' houses built on the left side of Morskaya Street and gazing
thoughtfully at the ground climbed the hill towards the boulevard. The
expression on his plain face did not reveal much intellectual power, but
rather good-nature, common sense, honesty, and an inclination to re-
spectability. He was not well built and seemed rather shy and awkward
in his movements. His cap was nearly new; a gold watch-chain showed
from under his thin cloak of a rather peculiar lilac shade, and he wore

†This piece was first published in 1855.

trousers with foot-straps and clean, shiny calf-skin boots. He might have been a German (except that his features indicated his purely Russian origin), an adjutant, or a regimental quartermaster (but in that case he would have worn spurs), or an officer transferred from the cavalry or the Guards for the duration of the war. He was in fact an officer who had transferred from the cavalry, and as he climbed the hill towards the boulevard he was thinking of a letter he had received from a former comrade now retired from the army, a landed proprietor in the government of T—— ———, and of his good friend, the pale, blue-eyed Natasha, that comrade's wife. He recalled a part of the letter where his comrade wrote:

"When we receive the *Invalide*,[1] Pupka" (so the retired Uhlan called his wife) "rushes headlong into the hall, seizes the paper, and runs with it to a seat in the arbor or the drawing-room in which, you remember, we spent such pleasant winter evenings when your regiment was stationed in our town—and she reads of *your* heroic deeds with an ardor you cannot imagine. She often speaks of you. 'There now,' she says, 'Mikhaylov is a *darling*. I am ready to smother him with kisses when I see him. He is fighting on the bastions and is sure to receive a St. George's Cross, and then they'll write about him in the papers,' etc., etc. I am beginning to be quite jealous of you."

In another place he wrote: "The papers reach us very late, and though there are plenty of rumors one cannot believe them all. For instance, those young ladies with music you know of were saying yesterday that Napoleon has been captured by our Cossacks and sent to St. Petersburg, but you can imagine how much of this I believe. One fresh arrival from Petersburg tells us for certain (he is a capital fellow, sent by the Minister on special business—and now there is no one in town who can't think what a *resource* he is to us), that we have taken Eupatoria so that the French are cut off from Balaclava, and that we lost two hundred men in the affair and the French, as many as fifteen thousand. My wife was in such raptures that she *celebrated* all night and said that a presentiment had assured her that you distinguished yourself in that affair."

In spite of the words and expressions I have purposely italicized, and the whole tone of the letter, Lieutenant-Captain Mikhaylov thought with an inexpressibly melancholy pleasure about his pale-faced provincial friend and how he used to spend evenings with her in the arbor, talking *sentiment*. He thought of his kind comrade the Uhlan: how the latter used to get angry and lose when they played cards in the study for kopecks and how his wife used to laugh at him. He recalled the friendship these people had for him (perhaps he thought there was something even more on the side of his pale-faced friend): these people and their surroundings flitted through his memory in a wonderfully sweet, joyously

---

1. The Army and Navy Gazette.

rosy light and, smiling at the recollection, he put his hand on the pocket where this *dear* letter lay.

From these recollections Lieutenant-Captain Mikhaylov involuntarily passed to dreams and hopes. "How surprised and pleased Natasha will be," he thought as he passed along a narrow side-street, "when she reads in the *Invalide* of my being the first to climb on the cannon, and my receiving the St. George! I ought to be made a full captain on that former recommendation. Then I may easily become a major this year by seniority, because so many of our fellows have been killed and no doubt many more will die during this campaign. Then there'll be more fighting and I, as a well-known man, shall be entrusted with a regiment . . . then a lieutenant-colonel, the order of St. Anna . . . a colonel" . . . and he was already a general, calling on Natasha, the widow of his comrade (who would be dead by that time according to his daydream), when the sounds of the music on the boulevard reached his ears more distinctly, a crowd of people appeared before his eyes, and he realized that he was on the boulevard and still only a lieutenant-captain in the infantry.

3

He went first to the pavilion, beside which stood the band with soldiers of the same regiment acting as music-stands and holding the music books open, while around them clerks, cadets, nannies, and children formed a circle, looking on rather than listening. Most of the people who were standing, sitting, and strolling round the pavilion were naval officers, adjutants, and white-gloved army officers. Along the broad boulevard walked officers of all kinds and women of all sorts—a few of the latter in hats, but the greater part with kerchiefs on their heads, and some with neither kerchiefs nor hats—but there was not a single old woman among them—all were young. Lower down, in fragrant alleys shaded by white acacias, isolated groups sat or strolled.

No one was particularly glad to meet Lieutenant-Captain Mikhaylov on the boulevard, except perhaps Captain Obzhogov of his own regiment and Captain Suslikov who shook his hand warmly; but the former wore camel-hair trousers, no gloves, and a shabby overcoat, and his face was red and perspiring, and the latter shouted so loud and was so free and easy that one felt ashamed to be seen walking with him, especially by those white-gloved officers—to one of whom, an adjutant, Mikhaylov bowed, and might have bowed to another, a Staff officer whom he had met twice at the house of a mutual acquaintance. Besides, what was the fun of walking with Obzhogov and Suslikov when as it was he met them and shook hands with them six times a day? Was this what he had come to hear *the music* for?

He would have liked to accost the adjutant whom he had bowed to

and talk with those gentlemen, not that he wanted Obzhogov and Suslikov and Lieutenant Pashtetsky and others to see him talking to them,
but simply because they were pleasant people who knew all the news
and might have told him something.

But why is Lieutenant-Captain Mikhaylov so afraid and unable to
muster the courage to approach them? "Supposing they don't return my
greeting," he thinks, "or merely bow and go on talking among themselves
as if I were not there, or they simply walk away and leave me standing
among the aristocrats?" The word aristocrats (in the sense of the highest
and most select circle of any class) has recently gained great popularity
in Russia, where one would think it ought not to exist. It has made its
way to every part of the country, and into every level of society that can
be reached by vanity—and to what conditions of time and circumstance
does this pitiful propensity not penetrate? You find it among merchants,
officials, clerks, officers—in Saratov, Mamadishi, Vinnitsa, in fact wherever men are to be found. And since there are so many men, and
consequently much vanity, in the besieged town of Sevastopol, aristocrats
are to be found here too, though death hangs over everyone, aristocrat
or not.

To Captain Obzhogov, Lieutenant-Captain Mikhaylov was an aristocrat, and to Lieutenant-Captain Mikhaylov, Adjutant Kalugin was an
aristocrat, because he was an adjutant and intimate with another adjutant. To Adjutant Kalugin, Count Nordov was an aristocrat, because
he was aide-de-camp to the Emperor.

Vanity! vanity! vanity! everywhere, even on the brink of the grave and
among men ready to die for a noble cause. Vanity! It seems to be the
characteristic feature and special malady of our time. How is it that
among our predecessors no mention was made of this passion, as of
small-pox and cholera? How is it that in our time there are only three
kinds of people: those who, considering vanity an inevitable fact and
therefore justifiable, freely submit to it; those who regard it as a sad but
unavoidable condition; and those who act unconsciously and slavishly
under its influence? Why did the Homers and Shakespeares speak of
love, glory, and suffering, while the literature of today is an endless story
of snobbery and vanity?

Twice the lieutenant-captain passed irresolutely by this group of aristocrats, but drawing near them for the third time he made an effort and
walked up to them. The group consisted of four officers: Adjutant Kalugin, Mikhaylov's acquaintance, Adjutant Prince Galtsin, who was
rather an aristocrat even for Kalugin himself, Lieutenant-Colonel Neferdov, one of the so-called two hundred and twenty-two society men
who, being on the retired list, re-entered the army for this war; and
Cavalry-Captain Praskukhin, also of the "two hundred and twenty-two."
Luckily for Mikhaylov, Kalugin was in splendid spirits (the general had
just spoken to him in a very confidential manner, and Prince Galtsin

who had arrived from Petersburg was staying with him), so he did not think it beneath his dignity to shake hands with Mikhaylov, which was more than Praskukhin did, though he had often met Mikhaylov on the bastion, had more than once drunk his wine and vodka, and even owed him twelve and a half rubles lost at cards. Not yet being well acquainted with Prince Galtsin he did not like to appear acquainted with a mere lieutenant-captain of the infantry. So he only bowed slightly.

"Well, Captain," said Kalugin, "when will you be visiting the bastion again? Do you remember our meeting at the Schwartz Redoubt? Things were lively, weren't they, eh?"

"Yes, very," said Mikhaylov, and he recalled how, when making his way along the trench to the bastion, he had met Kalugin walking bravely along, his sabre clanking smartly.

"My turn's tomorrow by rights, but we have an officer ill," continued Mikhaylov, "so—"

He wanted to say that it was not his turn, but since the Commander of the 8th Company was ill and only the ensign was left, he felt it his duty to go in place of Lieutenant Nepshisetsky and would therefore be at the bastion that evening. But Kalugin did not hear him out.

"I feel sure that something is going to happen in a day or two," he said to Prince Galtsin.

"How about today? Will anything happen today?" Mikhaylov asked shyly, looking first at Kalugin and then at Galtsin.

No one replied. Prince Galtsin only puckered up his face in a curious way and looking over Mikhaylov's cap said after a short silence: "Fine girl that, with the red kerchief. You know her, don't you, Captain?"

"She lives near my lodgings; she's a sailor's daughter," answered the lieutenant-captain.

"Come, let's take a good look at her."

Prince Galtsin gave one of his arms to Kalugin and the other to the lieutenant-captain, being sure he would confer great pleasure on the latter by so doing, which was really quite true.

The lieutenant-captain was superstitious and considered it a great sin to amuse himself with women before going into action, but on this occasion he pretended to be a *roué*, which Galtsin and Kalugin evidently did not believe and which greatly surprised the girl with the red kerchief, who had more than once noticed how the lieutenant-captain blushed when he passed her window. Praskukhin walked behind them, and kept touching Prince Galtsin's arm and making various remarks in French, but as four people could not walk abreast on the path he was obliged to go alone until, on the second round, he took the arm of a well-known brave naval officer, Servyagin, who came up and spoke to him, also being anxious to join the aristocrats. And the well-known hero gladly passed his honest muscular hand under the elbow of Praskukhin, whom everybody, including Servyagin himself, knew to be no better than he should be. When, wishing to explain his acquaintance with this sailor, Praskukhin whispered to Prince Galtsin—who had been in the Fourth Bastion the day before and seen a shell burst at some twenty yards' distance—considering himself no less courageous than the newcomer, and believing that many reputations are obtained by luck, paid not the slightest attention to Servyagin.

Lieutenant-Captain Mikhaylov found it so pleasant to walk in this company that he forgot the nice letter from T—— and his gloomy forebodings at the thought of having to go to the bastion. He remained with them till they began talking exclusively among themselves, avoiding his eyes to show that he might leave, and at last walked away from him. All the same the lieutenant-captain was contented, and when he passed Cadet Baron Pesth—particularly conceited and self-satisfied since the previous night, when for the first time in his life he had been in the bomb-shelter of the Fifth Bastion and had consequently become a hero in his own estimation—he was not at all hurt by the suspiciously haughty expression with which the cadet saluted him.

4

But the lieutenant-captain had hardly crossed the threshold of his lodgings before very different thoughts entered his head. He saw his little room with its uneven earth floor, its crooked windows, the broken panes mended with paper, his old bedstead with two Tula pistols and a rug (showing a lady on horseback) nailed to the wall beside it, as well as the dirty bed of the cadet who lived with him, with its cotton quilt. He saw his servant Nikita, with his rough greasy hair, get up from the floor scratching himself, he saw his old cloak, his everyday boots, a little bundle tied in a large handkerchief ready for him to take to the bastion, from which peeked a bit of cheese and the neck of a bottle containing vodka—and he suddenly remembered that he had to go with his company to spend the whole night at the lodgements.

"I shall certainly be killed tonight," he thought. "I know it. And there's really no need for me to go—I offered to do so of my own accord. It always happens that the one who offers gets himself killed. And what is the matter with that confounded Nepshisetsky? He may not be ill at all, and they'll kill me because of him—they're sure to. Still, if they don't kill me I shall certainly be recommended for promotion. I saw how pleased the regimental commander was when I said: 'Let me go if Lieutenant Nepshisetsky is ill.' If I'm not made a major then I'll get the Order of Vladimir for sure. Why, I am going to the bastion for the thirteenth time. Oh dear, the thirteenth! What an unlucky number! I am sure to be killed. I know it . . . but somebody had to go: the company can't proceed with only an ensign. Supposing something were to happen. . . . Why, the honor of the regiment, the honor of the army, is at stake.

It is my *duty* to go. Yes, my sacred duty. . . . But I have a presentiment."

The lieutenant-captain forgot that it was not the first time he had felt this presentiment: to a greater or lesser degree he had it whenever he was going to the bastion. He did not know that before going into action everyone has such forebodings more or less strongly. Having calmed himself by appealing to his sense of duty—which was highly developed and very strong—the lieutenant-captain sat down at the table and began writing a farewell letter to his father. Ten minutes later, having finished his letter, he rose from the table, his eyes wet with tears, and, repeating mentally all the prayers he knew, he began to dress. His rather tipsy and rude servant lazily handed him his new cloak—the old one which the lieutenant-captain usually wore at the bastion hadn't yet been mended.

"Why isn't my cloak mended? You do nothing but sleep," said Mikhaylov angrily.

"Sleep indeed!" grumbled Nikita, "I do nothing but run about like a dog the whole day, and when I get tired I can't even go to sleep!"

"I see you are drunk again."

"It's not at your expense, so don't you complain."

"Hold your tongue, you idiot!" shouted the lieutenant-captain, ready to strike the man.

Already upset, he now lost all his patience and felt hurt by the rudeness of Nikita, who had lived with him for the last twelve years and whom he was fond of and even spoilt.

"Idiot? Idiot?" repeated the servant. "And why do you, sir, abuse me and call me an idiot? You know in times like these it isn't right to abuse people."

Recalling where he was about to go, Mikhaylov felt ashamed.

"But you know, Nikita, you would try anyone's patience!" he said mildly. "You may leave that letter to my father on the table where it is. Don't touch it," he added blushing.

"Yes sir," said Nikita, becoming sentimental under the influence of the vodka he had drunk, as he said, at his own expense, and blinking with an evident inclination to weep.

But on the porch, when the lieutenant-captain said, "Good-bye, Nikita," Nikita burst into forced sobs and rushed to kiss his master's hand, saying, "Good-bye, sir," in a broken voice. A sailor's widow who was also standing on the porch could not, as a woman, help joining in this tender scene and began wiping her own eyes on her dirty sleeve, saying something about people who, though they were gentlefolk, took such sufferings upon themselves while she, poor woman, was left a widow. And she told the tipsy Nikita for the hundredth time about her sorrows: how her husband had been killed in the first *bondbarment*, and how her little hut had been shattered (the one she lived in now was not her own), and so on. After his master was gone Nikita lit his pipe, asked the landlady's little girl to get him some vodka, very soon left off crying, and even had a quarrel with the old woman about a pail of his he said she had smashed.

"But perhaps I shall only be wounded," mused the lieutenant-captain as he drew near the bastion with his company when twilight had already begun to fall. "But where, and how? Here or here?" he said to himself, mentally passing his chest, stomach, and thighs in review. "Supposing it's here' (he thought of his thighs) 'and goes right round. . . . Or goes in here with a piece of a bomb, then it will be all over."

The lieutenant-captain passed along the trenches and reached the lodgements[2] safely. In perfect darkness he and an officer of the Engineers set the men to their work, after which he sat down in a pit under the breastwork. There was little firing; now and again there was a lightning flash on our side or *his*, and the brilliant fuse of a bomb formed a fiery arc on the dark, star-speckled sky. But all the bombs fell far beyond or far to the right of the lodgement where the lieutenant-captain sat in his pit. He drank some vodka, ate some cheese, smoked a cigarette, said his prayers, and felt inclined to sleep for a little while.

5

Prince Galtsin, Lieutenant-Colonel Neferdov, and Praskukhin—whom no one had invited and to whom no one spoke, but who still stuck with them—went to Kalugin's to tea.

"But you did not finish telling me about Vaska Mendel," said Kalugin, when he had taken off his cloak and sat in a soft easy chair by the window unbuttoning the collar of his clean starched shirt. "How did he get married?"

"It was a joke, my boy! . . . *Je vous dis, il y avait un temps, on ne parlait que de ça à Pétersbourgh*,"[3] said Prince Galtsin, laughing as he jumped up from the piano-stool and sat down near Kalugin on the window-sill, "a splendid joke. I know all about it."

And amusingly, cleverly, and with animation, he told a love story which, as it has no interest for us, we will omit.

It was noticeable that not only Prince Galtsin but each of these gentlemen who established themselves, one on the window-sill, another with his legs in the air, and a third by the piano, seemed quite different people now from what they had been on the boulevard. There was none of the absurd arrogance and haughtiness they had shown towards the infantry officers; here among themselves they were natural, and Kalugin and Prince Galtsin in particular showed themselves very pleasant, cheerful, and good-natured young men. Their conversation was about their Petersburg fellow officers and acquaintances.

2. Intrenchment consisting of a trench and a parapet formed on an occupied position to maintain it against recapture.

3. "I tell you, at one time it was the only thing talked of in Petersburg."

"What of Maslovsky?"

"Which one—the Uhlan, or the Horse Guard?"

"I know them both. The one in the Horse Guards I knew when he was a boy just out of school. But the eldest—is he a captain yet?"

"Oh yes, long ago."

"Is he still fooling around with that gipsy?"

"No, he has dropped her. . . ." And so on in the same vein.

Later on Prince Galtsin went to the piano and gave an excellent rendition of a gipsy song. Praskukhin, chiming in though uninvited, sang a second and did it so well that he was invited to continue, and this delighted him.

A servant brought tea, cream, and biscuits on a silver tray.

"Serve the prince," said Kalugin.

"Isn't it strange to think that we're in a besieged town," said Galtsin, taking his tea to the window, "and here's a *pianerforty*, tea with cream, and a house such as I should really be glad to have in Petersburg?"

"Well, if we hadn't even that much," said the old and always dissatisfied lieutenant-colonel, "the constant uncertainty we are living in—seeing people killed day after day and no end to it—would be intolerable. And to have dirt and discomfort added to it—"

"But our infantry officers live at the bastions with their men in bombproofs and eat the soldiers' soup," said Kalugin, "what about them?"

"What about them? Well, though it's true they don't change their shirts for ten days at a time, they are heroes all the same—wonderful fellows."

Just then an infantry officer entered the room.

"I . . . I have orders . . . may I see the Gen . . . his Excellency? I have come with a message from General N.," he said with a timid bow.

Kalugin rose and without returning the officer's greeting asked with an offensive, affected, official smile if he would not be so kind as to wait, and without asking him to sit down or taking any further notice of him he turned to Galtsin and began speaking French, so that the poor officer left alone in the middle of the room did not in the least know what to do with himself.

"It is a matter of the utmost urgency, sir," he said after a short silence.

"Ah! Well then, please come with me," said Kalugin, putting on his cloak and accompanying the officer to the door.

"*Eh bien, messieurs, je crois que cela chauffera cette nuit,*"[4] said Kalugin when he returned from the general's.

"Ah! What is it—a sortie?" asked the others.

"That I don't know. You will see for yourselves," replied Kalugin with a mysterious smile.

4. "Well, gentlemen, I think there will be warm work to-night."

"And my commander is at the bastion, so I suppose I must go too," said Praskukhin, buckling on his sabre.

No one replied, it was his business to know whether he had to go or not.

Praskukhin and Neferdov left to go to their appointed posts.

"Good-bye gentlemen. *Au, revoir!* We'll meet again before the night is over," shouted Kalugin from the window as Praskukhin and Neferdov, stooping on their Cossack saddles, trotted past. The tramp of their Cossack horses soon died away in the dark street.

"*Non, dites-moi, est-ce qu'il y aura véritablement quelque chose cette nuit?*"[5] asked Galtsin as he lounged in the window-sill beside Kalugin and watched the bombs that rose above the bastions.

"I can tell *you*, you see . . . have you been to the bastions?" (Galtsin nodded, though he had only been once to the Fourth Bastion.) "You remember just in front of our lunette there is a trench"—and Kalugin, with the air of one who without being a specialist considers his military judgement very sound, began, in a rather confused way and misusing technical terms, to explain the position of the enemy, our own, and the plan of intended action.

"But I say, they're firing away at the lodgements! Oho! I wonder if that's ours or *his?* . . . Now it's burst," they said, as they lounged on the window-sill looking at the fiery trails of bombs crossing one another in the air, at flashes that lit up the dark sky for a moment, at puffs of white smoke, and listened to the more rapid reports of the firing.

"*Quel charmant coup d'œil! a?*"[6] said Kalugin, drawing his guest's attention to the really beautiful sight. "Do you know, you sometimes can't distinguish a bomb from a star."

"Yes, I thought that was a star just now and then saw it fall . . . there! it's burst. And that big star—what do you call it?—looks just like a bomb."

"Do you know I am so used to these bombs that I am sure when I'm back in Russia I shall fancy I see bombs every starlit night—one gets so used to them."

"But hadn't I better go out with this sortie?" said Prince Galtsin after a moment's pause.

"Nonsense, my dear fellow! Don't think of such a thing. Besides, I won't let you," answered Kalugin. "You will have plenty of opportunities later on."

"Really? You think I need not go, eh?"

At that moment, from the direction in which these gentlemen were looking, amid the boom of the cannon came the terrible rattle of musketry, and thousands of little fires flaming up in quick succession flashed all along the line.

5. "No, tell me, will there really be anything to-   6. "What a charming sight, eh?"
night?"

"There! Now that's the real thing!" said Kalugin, "I can't keep cool when I hear the sound of muskets. It seems to seize my very soul, you know. There's a *hurrah!*" he added, listening intently to the distant and prolonged roar of hundreds of voices—"Ah—ah—ah"—which came from the bastions.

· "Whose *hurrah* was it? Theirs or ours?"

"I don't know, but it's hand-to-hand fighting now, since the firing has ceased."

At that moment an officer followed by a Cossack galloped under the window and alighted from his horse at the porch.

"Where are you from?"

"From the bastion. I want the general."

"Come along. Well, what's happened?"

"The lodgements have been attacked—and occupied. The French brought up tremendous reserves—and attacked us—we had only two battalions," said the officer, panting. He was the same one who had been there that evening, but though he was now out of breath, he walked to the door with full self-possession.

"Well, have we retreated?" asked Kalugin.

"No," replied the officer angrily, "another battalion came up in time— we drove them back, but the colonel was killed and many other officers. I have orders to ask for reinforcements."

And saying this he went with Kalugin to the general's, where we shall not follow him.

Five minutes later Kalugin was already on his Cossack horse (again in the semi-Cossack manner which I have noticed that all adjutants, for some reason, seem to consider the proper thing) and rode off at a trot towards the bastion to deliver some orders and await the final result of the affair. Prince Galtsin, under the influence of that oppressive excitement usually produced in a spectator by proximity to an action in which he is not engaged, went out and began pacing up and down the street aimlessly.

6

Soldiers passed carrying the wounded on stretchers or supporting them under their arms. It was quite dark on the street, lights could be seen here and there, but only in the hospital windows or where some officers were still up. From the bastions came the thunder of cannon and the rattle of muskets, and flashes kept on lighting up the dark sky as before. From time to time the thud of hoofs could be heard as an orderly galloped past, the groans of a wounded man, the steps and voices of stretcher-bearers, or the words of some frightened women who had come out onto their porches to watch the cannonade.

Among the spectators were our friend Nikita, the old sailor's widow with whom he had again made friends, and her ten-year-old daughter.

"O Lord! Holy Mary, Mother of God!" said the old woman, sighing as she looked at the bombs flying across from side to side like balls of fire; "What horrors! What horrors! Ah! Oh! Even during the first *bond-barment* it wasn't like this. Look where the accursed thing has just burst over our house in the outside of town."

"No, that's further; they keep tumbling into Aunt Irene's garden," said the girl.

"And where, oh where, is my master now?" drawled Nikita, who was not quite sober yet. "Oh! You don't know how I love that master of mine! I love him so that if he were killed in a sinful way, which God forbid, would you believe it, granny, after that I don't know what I wouldn't do to myself! I don't! . . . My master is that sort of man, there's only one word for it. Would I exchange him for one of them, playing cards? What are they? Ugh! There's only one word for it!" concluded Nikita, pointing to the lighted window of his master's room, to which, in the absence of the lieutenant-captain, Cadet Zhvadchevsky had invited Sub-Lieutenants Ugrovich and Nepshisetsky—the latter suffering from a nervous tic—and where he was celebrating in honor of a medal he had received.

"Look at the stars! Look how they're rolling!" the little girl broke the silence that followed Nikita's words as she stood gazing at the sky. "Another one's rolled down. What is it a sign of, mother?"

"They'll smash our hut altogether," said the old woman with a sigh, leaving her daughter's question unanswered.

"As we were going there today with uncle, mother," the little girl continued in a sing-song tone, becoming loquacious, "there was such a b-i-g cannon-ball inside the room close to the cupboard. It must have smashed in through the passage and right into the room! Such a big one—you couldn't lift it."

"Those who had husbands and money all moved away," said the old woman, "and there's the hut, all that was left me, and now that's been smashed. Just look at *him* blazing away! The fiend! . . . O Lord! O Lord!"

"And just as we were going out, a bomb comes fly-ing, and suddenly bur-sts and co-o-vers us with dust. A bit of it nearly hit me and uncle."

7

Prince Galtsin met more and more wounded men, carried on stretchers or walking supported by others who were talking loudly.

"Up they sprang, friends," said the bass voice of a tall soldier with two guns slung from his shoulder, "up they sprang, shouting 'Allah! Allah!'[7] climbing one over another. You kill one and another appears, you can't do anything; no end of 'em—"

7. Our soldiers fighting the Turks have become so accustomed to this cry of the enemy that they now always say that the French also shout "Allah!" [*Tolstoy's note*].

But at this point in the story Galtsin interrupted him.

"You are from the bastion?"

"Yes, your Honor."

"Well, what happened? Tell me."

"What happened? Well, your Honor, such a force of 'em poured down on us over the rampart, it was all over. They quite overpowered us, your Honor!"

"Overpowered? . . . But you repulsed them?"

"How could we repulse them when *his* whole force came on, killed all our men, and no re'forcements were given us?"

The soldier was mistaken, the trench had remained ours; but it's a curious fact, which anyone may notice, that a soldier wounded in action always thinks the affair is lost and imagines it to have been a very bloody fight.

"How's that? I was told they had been repulsed," said Galtsin irritably. "Perhaps they were driven back after you left? Is it long since you came away?"

"I've come straight from there, your Honor," answered the soldier; "it's hardly possible. They must have kept the trench; *he* quite overpowered us."

"Aren't you ashamed to have lost the trench? It's terrible!" said Galtsin, provoked by such indifference.

"But if strength is on their side . . ." muttered the soldier.

"Ah, your Honor," began a soldier from a stretcher which had just come up to them, "how could we help giving up when *he* had killed almost all our men? If we'd had the strength we wouldn't have given it up, not on any account. But as it was, what could we do? I stuck one, and then something hits me. Oh-h! Steady, lads, steady! Oh!" groaned the wounded man.

"Really, there seem to be too many men returning," said Galtsin, again stopping the tall soldier with the two guns. "Why are you retiring? You there, stop!"

The soldier stopped and took off his cap with his left hand.

"Where are you going, and why?" shouted Galtsin severely, "you scoun—"

But having come close up to the soldier, Galtsin noticed that no hand was visible beneath the soldier's right cuff and that the sleeve was soaked in blood to the elbow.

"I'm wounded, your Honor."

"Wounded? How?"

"Here. Must have been with a bullet," said the man, pointing to his arm, "but I don't know what struck my head here," and bending his head he showed the matted hair at the back stuck together with blood.

"And whose is this other gun?"

"It's a French rifle I took, your Honor. But I wouldn't have come away if it weren't to lead this fellow—he may fall," he added, pointing to a soldier who was walking a little in front leaning on his gun and painfully dragging his left leg.

Prince Galtsin suddenly felt horribly ashamed of his unjust suspicions. He felt himself blushing, turned away, and went to the hospital without either questioning or watching the wounded men any more.

Having pushed his way through the porch among the men who had come on foot and the bearers who were carrying in the wounded and bringing out the dead, Galtsin entered the first room, gave a look round, and involuntarily turned back and ran out into the street: it was too terrible.

8

The large, lofty, dark hall, lit up only by four or five candles with which the doctors examined the wounded, was quite full. Yet the bearers kept bringing in more wounded—laying them side by side on the floor which was already so packed that the unfortunate patients were jostled together, staining one another with their blood—and going out to fetch more wounded. The pools of blood visible in the unoccupied spaces, the feverish breathing of several hundred men, and the perspiration of the bearers with stretchers filled the air with a peculiar, heavy, thick, fetid mist, in which the candles burnt dimly in different parts of the hall. Various groans, sighs, death-rattles, now and then interrupted by shrill screams, filled the room. Nurses with quiet faces, expressing no empty feminine tearful pity, but active practical sympathy, stepped across the wounded with medicines, water, bandages, and lint, flitting among the blood-stained coats and shirts. The doctors, kneeling with rolled-up sleeves beside the wounded, by the light of candles their assistants held, examined, felt, and probed their wounds, heedless of the terrible groans and entreaties of the sufferers. One doctor sat at a table near the door and at the moment Galtsin came in was already entering No. 532.

"Ivan Bogaev, Private, Company Three, S—— Regiment, *fractura femuris complicata!*" shouted another doctor from the end of the room, examining a shattered leg. "Turn him over."

"Oh, fathers! Oh, you're our fathers!" screamed the soldier, beseeching them not to touch him.

"*Perforatio capitis!*"

"Simon Neferdov, Lieutenant-Colonel of the N—— Infantry Regiment. Have a little patience, Colonel, or it's quite possible I shall give up!" said a third doctor, poking about with some kind of hook in the unfortunate colonel's skull.

"Oh, don't! Oh, for God's sake be quick! Quick! Ah——!"

"*Perforatio pectoris* . . . Sebastian Sereda, Private . . . what regiment? You needn't write that: *moritur*. Take him away," said the doctor, leaving the soldier, whose eyes turned up and in whose throat a death-rattle already sounded.

About forty stretcher-bearers stood at the door waiting to carry the bandaged to the wards and the dead to the chapel. They looked at the scene before them in silence, broken now and then by a heavy sigh.

9

On his way to the bastion Kalugin met many wounded, but knowing by experience that in action such sights have a bad effect on one's spirits, he did not stop to question them; on the contrary, he tried not to notice them. At the foot of the hill he met an orderly galloping back from the bastion.

"Zobkin! Zobkin! Wait a bit!"

"Well, what is it?"

"Where are you from?"

"The lodgements."

"How are things there?"

"Oh, awful!"

And the orderly galloped on.

In fact, though there was now little small-arm firing, the cannonade had recommenced with fresh heat and persistence.

"Ah, that's bad!" thought Kalugin with an unpleasant sensation, and he too had a presentiment—a very ordinary thought, the thought of death. But Kalugin was ambitious and blessed with nerves of steel—in a word, he was what is called brave. He did not yield to the first feeling but began to nerve himself. He recalled how an adjutant, Napoleon's he thought, having delivered an order, galloped with a bleeding head full speed to Napoleon. "*Vous êtes blessé?*"[8] asked Napoleon. "*Je vous demande pardon, sire, je suis mort*,"[9] and the adjutant fell from his horse, dead.

That seemed to him very fine, and he pictured himself for a moment in the role of that adjutant. Then he whipped his horse, assuming a still more dashing Cossack seat, looked back at the Cossack who, standing up in his stirrups, was trotting behind, and rode quite gallantly up to the spot where he had to dismount. Here he found four soldiers sitting on some stones smoking their pipes.

"What are you doing there?" he shouted at them.

"We carried off a wounded man and sat down to rest a bit, your Honor," said one of them, hiding his pipe behind his back and taking off his cap.

"Rest, indeed! . . . To your places, march!"

And he went up the hill with them through the trench, meeting wounded men at every step.

---

8. "Are you wounded?"   9. "Pardon me, sire, I am dead."

After ascending the hill he turned to the left and a few steps farther on found himself quite alone. A splinter of a bomb whizzed near him and fell into the trench. Another bomb rose in front of him and seemed headed straight at him. He suddenly felt frightened, ran a few steps at full speed, and lay down flat. When the bomb burst a considerable distance away he felt exceedingly annoyed with himself and rose, looking round to see if anyone had noticed his action, but no one was near.

But once fear has entered the soul it does not easily yield to any other feeling. He, who always boasted that he never even stooped, now hurried along the trench almost on all fours. He stumbled, and thought, "Oh, it's awful! They'll kill me for sure!" His breath came with difficulty, and perspiration broke out over his whole body. He was surprised at himself but no longer strove to master his feelings.

Suddenly he heard footsteps in front. Quickly straightening himself up he raised his head and boldly clanking his sabre went on more deliberately. He felt himself quite a different man. When he met an officer of the Engineers and a sailor, and the officer shouted to him to lie down, pointing to a bright spot which grew brighter, approached more swiftly, and came crashing down close to the trench, he only bent a little, involuntarily influenced by the frightened cry, and then went on.

"That's a brave one," said the sailor, looking quite calmly at the bomb and with an experienced eye deciding at once that the splinters could not fly into the trench. "He won't even lie down."

It was only a few steps across open ground to the bomb-proof shelter of the bastion commander when Kalugin's mind again became clouded and the same stupid terror seized him: his heart beat more violently, blood rushed to his head, and he had to make an effort to force himself to run to the bomb-proof.

"Why are you so out of breath?" asked the general, when Kalugin had reported his instructions.

"I walked very fast, your Excellency!"

"Won't you have some wine?"

Kalugin drank a glass and lit a cigarette. The action was over; only a fierce cannonade continued from both sides. In the bomb-proof sat General N——, commander of the bastion, and six other officers among whom was Praskukhin. They were discussing various details of the action. Sitting in this comfortable room with blue wall-paper, a sofa, a bed, a table with papers on it, a wall-clock with a lamp burning before it, and an icon—looking at these signs of habitation, at the beams more than two feet thick that formed the ceiling, and listening to the shots that sounded faint here in the shelter, Kalugin could not understand how he had twice allowed himself to be overcome by such unpardonable weakness. He was angry with himself and longed for danger in order to test his nerve once more.

"Ah! I'm glad you are here, Captain," he said to a naval officer with a big moustache who wore a staff-officer's coat with a St. George's Cross and who had just entered the shelter and asked the general to give him some men to repair two embrasures of his battery which had become blocked. When the general had finished speaking to the captain, Kalugin said: "The commander-in-chief told me to ask if your guns can fire case-shot into the trenches."

"Only one of them can," said the captain gloomily.

"All the same, let's go and see."

The captain frowned and gave an angry grunt.

"I've been standing out there all night and have come in to get a bit of rest—couldn't you go alone?" he asked. "My assistant, Lieutenant Kartz, is there and can show you everything."

The captain had already been in command of this, one of the most dangerous batteries, more than six months. From the time the siege began, even before the bomb-proof shelters were constructed, he had lived continuously on the bastion and had a great reputation for courage among the sailors. That is why his refusal so struck and surprised Kalugin. "So much for reputation," he thought.

"Well then, I'll go alone if I may," he said in a slightly sarcastic tone to the captain, who paid no attention to his words.

Kalugin did not realize that whereas he had spent some fifty hours all in all at different times on the bastions, the captain had lived there for six months. Kalugin was still motivated by vanity, the wish to shine, the hope of reward, of gaining a reputation, and the charm of running risks. But the captain had already lived through all that: at first he had felt vain, had shown off his courage, had been fool-hardy, had hoped for rewards and reputation, had even gained them, but now all these incentives had lost their power over him and he saw things differently. He fulfilled his duty exactly, but quite understanding how much the chances of life were against him after six months at the bastion, he no longer ran risks without serious need. So the young lieutenant who had joined the battery a week ago and was now showing it to Kalugin, with whom he vied in leaning out of embrasures uselessly and climbing out on the banquette,[1] seemed ten times braver than the captain.

Returning to the shelter after examining the battery, Kalugin came upon the general in the dark who, accompanied by his staff officers, was going to the watch-tower.

"Captain Praskukhin," he heard the general say, "please go to the right lodgement and tell the second battalion of the M—— Regiment to cease their work, leave the place, and quietly rejoin their regiment in reserve at the foot of the hill. Do you understand? Lead them yourself to the regiment."

"Yes, sir."

---

1. An elevated earthen footbank running along the inside of a parapet or trench.

Praskukhin started at full speed towards the lodgements.

The firing was now becoming less frequent.

10

"Is this the second battalion of the M—— Regiment?" asked Praskukhin, having run to his destination and coming across some soldiers carrying earth in sacks.

"It is, your Honor."

"Where is the Commander?"

Mikhaylov, thinking that the commander of the company was being asked for, got out of his pit; taking Praskukhin for a commanding officer, he saluted and approached him.

"The general's orders are . . . that you . . . should go . . . quickly . . . and above all quietly . . . back—no, not back, but to the reserves," said Praskukhin, looking askance in the direction of the enemy's fire.

Having recognized Praskukhin and figured out what was wanted, Mikhaylov dropped his hand and passed on the order. The battalion became alert, the men took up their muskets, put on their cloaks, and set out.

No one can imagine without experiencing it the delight a man feels when, after three hours' bombardment, he leaves so dangerous a spot as the lodgements. During those three hours Mikhaylov, who more than once and not without reason had thought his end was near, had had time to accustom himself to the conviction that he would certainly be killed and that he no longer belonged to this world. But in spite of that he had great difficulty in keeping his legs from running away with him when, leading the company with Praskukhin at his side, he left the lodgement.

"*Au revoir!*" said a major with whom Mikhaylov had eaten bread and cheese in the pit under the breastwork and who was remaining at the bastion in command of another battalion. "I wish you a good journey."

"And I wish you a successful defense. It seems to be getting quieter now."

But scarcely had he uttered these words before the enemy, probably observing the movement in the lodgement, began to fire more frequently. Our guns replied and heavy firing recommenced.

The stars were high in the sky but shone feebly. The night was pitch dark, only flashes of the guns and bursting bombs made things around suddenly visible. The soldiers walked quickly and quietly, involuntarily outpacing one another; only their measured footsteps on the dry road were heard besides the incessant roll of the guns, the ringing of bayonets when they struck one another, a sigh, or the prayer of some poor soldier: "Lord, O Lord! What does it all mean?" Now and again the moaning of a man who was hit could be heard, and the cry, "Stretchers!" (In the company Mikhaylov commanded artillery fire alone carried off twenty-six men that night.) A flash on the dark and distant horizon, the cry, "Can-n-on!" from the sentinel on the bastion, and a ball flew buzzing above the company and plunged into the earth, making stones fly.

"Why the devil are they so slow?" thought Praskukhin, continually looking back as he marched beside Mikhaylov. "I'd really better run ahead. I've delivered the order. . . . But no, later they might say I'm a coward. What will be will be. I'll stay beside him."

"Now why is he walking with me?" thought Mikhaylov on his part. "I have noticed over and over again that he always brings bad luck. Here it comes, I think, straight for us."

After they had gone a few hundred paces they met Kalugin, who was walking briskly towards the lodgements clanking his sabre. He had been ordered by the general to find out how the works were progressing. But when he met Mikhaylov he thought that instead of going there himself under such terrible fire—which he was not ordered to do—he might as well find out all about it from an officer who had been there. And having heard from Mikhaylov full details of the work and walked a little way with him, Kalugin turned off into a trench leading to the bomb-proof shelter.

"Well, what news?" asked an officer who was eating his supper there all alone.

"Nothing much. It seems that the affair is over."

"Over? How so? On the contrary, the general has just returned to the watch-tower and another regiment has arrived. Yes, there it is. Listen! Muskets again! Don't go—why should you?" added the officer, noticing that Kalugin made a movement.

"I certainly ought to be there," thought Kalugin, "but I have already experienced a great deal today: the firing is awful!"

"Yes, I think I'd better wait for him here," he said.

And in fact about twenty minutes later the general and the officers who were with him returned. Among them was Cadet Baron Pesth but not Praskukhin. The lodgements had been retaken and occupied by us.

After receiving a full account of the affair, Kalugin, accompanied by Pesth, left the bomb-proof shelter.

11

"There's blood on your coat! You don't mean to say you were in a hand-to-hand fight?" asked Kalugin.

"Oh, it was awful! Just imagine—"

And Pesth began to relate how he had led his company, how the company-commander had been killed, how he himself had stabbed a Frenchman, and how if it had not been for him we should have lost the day.

This tale was based on fact: the company-commander had been killed and Pesth had bayoneted a Frenchman, but in recounting the details the cadet invented and bragged.

He bragged unintentionally, because during the whole affair he had been in a fog and was so bewildered that all he remembered of what had happened seemed to have happened somewhere, at some time, to somebody. Naturally he tried to recall the details in a light advantageous to himself. What really occurred was this:

The battalion which the cadet had been ordered to join for the sortie stood under fire for two hours next to some low wall. Then the battalion-commander in front said something, the company-commanders became active, the battalion advanced from behind the breastwork, and after going about a hundred paces stopped to form into company columns. Pesth was told to take his place on the right flank of the second company.

Quite unable to realize where he was and why he was there, the cadet took his place and involuntarily holding his breath while cold shivers ran down his back he gazed into the dark distance expecting something dreadful. He was not so frightened however (for there was no firing) as he was disturbed and agitated at being in the field beyond the fortifications.

Again the battalion-commander in front said something. Again the officers spoke in whispers passing along the order, and the black wall, formed by the first company, suddenly sank out of sight. The order was to lie down. The second company also lay down and in doing so Pesth hurt his hand on a sharp prickle. Only the commander of the second company remained standing. His short figure brandishing a sword moved in front of the company and he spoke incessantly.

"Pay attention, lads! Show them what you're made of! Don't fire, but give it to them with the bayonet—the dogs!—when I cry 'Hurrah!' Pay attention, that's the main thing! We'll let them see who we are. We won't disgrace ourselves, eh lads? For our father the Tsar!"

"What's your company-commander's name?" Pesth asked a cadet lying near him. "How brave he is!"

"Yes, he always is, in action," answered the cadet. "His name is Lisinkovsky."

Just then a flame suddenly flashed up right in front of the company, which was deafened by a resounding crash. High up in the air stones and splinters clattered. (Some fifty seconds later a stone fell from above and severed a soldier's leg.) It was a bomb fired from an elevated stand, and the fact that it reached the company showed that the French had noticed the column.

"You're sending us bombs, are you? Wait till we get at you, then you'll taste a three-edged Russian bayonet, damn you!" said the company-commander so loud that the battalion-commander had to order him to hold his tongue and not make so much noise.

After that the first company got up, then the second. They were ordered to aim bayonets and the battalion advanced. Pesth was in such a fright that he could not make out in the least how long it lasted, where he went, or who was who. He went on as if drunk. Suddenly a million fires flashed from all sides, and something whistled and clattered. He shouted and ran somewhere, because everyone else shouted and ran. Then he stumbled and fell over something. It was the company-commander, who had been wounded at the head of his company, and who taking the cadet for a Frenchman had seized him by the leg. Then when Pesth had freed his leg and got up, someone else ran against him from behind in the dark and nearly knocked him down again. "Run him through!" someone else shouted. "What are you stopping for?" Then someone seized a gun and stuck it into something soft. "*Ah Dieu!*" came a dreadful, piercing voice and Pesth only then understood that he had bayoneted a Frenchman. A cold sweat covered his whole body; he trembled as in a fever and threw down his musket. But this lasted only a moment; the thought immediately entered his head that he was a hero. He seized his musket again, and shouting "Hurrah!" ran with the crowd away from the dead Frenchman. Having run twenty paces he came to a trench. Some of our men were there with the battalion-commander.

"And I killed one!" said Pesth to the commander.

"You're a fine fellow, Baron!"

12

"Do you know Praskukhin was killed?" asked Pesth, while accompanying Kalugin on his way home.

"Impossible!"

"It's true. I saw him myself."

"Well, good-bye . . . I must be off."

"This is splendid!" thought Kalugin, as he came to his lodgings. "It's the first time I have had such luck when on duty. It's first-rate. I am alive and well and shall certainly get an excellent recommendation and am sure of a gold sabre. And I really deserve it."

After reporting what was necessary to the general he went to his room, where Prince Galtsin, long since returned, sat awaiting him, reading a book he had found on Kalugin's table.

It was with extraordinary pleasure that Kalugin found himself safe at home again, and having put on his nightshirt and got into bed he gave Galtsin all the details of the affair, telling them very naturally from a point of view where those details showed what a capable and brave officer he, Kalugin, was (which it seems to me it was hardly necessary to allude to, since everybody knew it and had no right or reason to question it, except perhaps the deceased Captain Praskukhin who, though he had considered it an honor to walk arm in arm with Kalugin, had privately told a friend only yesterday that though Kalugin was a first-rate fellow, "between you and me, he was not awfully eager to go to the bastions").

Praskukhin, who had been walking beside Mikhaylov after Kalugin had slipped away from him, had scarcely begun to revive a little on approaching a safer place, than he suddenly saw a bright light flash up behind him and heard the sentinel shout "Mortar!" and a soldier walking behind him say: "That's heading straight for the bastion!"

Mikhaylov looked round. The bright spot seemed to have stopped at its zenith, in the position which makes it absolutely impossible to define its direction. But that only lasted a moment: the bomb, coming faster and faster, nearer and nearer, so that the sparks of its fuse were already visible and its fatal whistle audible, descended towards the center of the battalion.

"Lie down!" shouted someone.

Mikhaylov and Praskukhin lay flat on the ground. Praskukhin, closing his eyes, only heard the bomb crash down on the hard earth close by. A second passed which seemed like an hour: the bomb had not exploded. Praskukhin was afraid. Perhaps he had played the coward for nothing. Perhaps the bomb had fallen far away and it only seemed to him that its fuse was fizzling close by. He opened his eyes and was pleased to see Mikhaylov lying immovable at his feet. But at that moment he caught sight of the glowing fuse of the bomb which was spinning on the ground not a yard off. Terror, cold terror excluding every other thought and feeling, seized his whole being. He covered his face with his hands.

Another second passed—a second during which a whole world of feelings, thoughts, hopes, and memories flashed before his imagination.

"Whom will it hit—Mikhaylov or me? Or both of us? And if it's me, where? In the head? Then I'm done for. But if it's in the leg, they'll cut it off (I'll certainly ask for chloroform) and I may survive. Perhaps only Mikhaylov will be hit. Then I will tell how we were walking along side by side and how he was killed and I was splashed with his blood. No, it's nearer to me . . . it will be me."

Then he remembered the twelve rubles he owed Mikhaylov, remembered a debt in Petersburg that should have been paid long ago, and the gipsy song he had sung that evening. The woman he loved rose in his imagination wearing a cap with lilac ribbons. He remembered a man who had insulted him five years ago and whom he had not yet paid back. And yet, inseparable from all these and thousands of other recollections, the present thought, the expectation of death, did not leave him for an instant. "Perhaps it won't explode," and with desperate decision he resolved to open his eyes. At that instant a red flame pierced through the still closed lids and something struck him in the middle of his chest with a terrible crash. He jumped up and began to run, but stumbling over his own sabre that got between his legs he fell on his side.

"Thank God, I'm only bruised!" was his first thought, and he was about to touch his chest with his hand, but his arms seemed tied to his sides and he felt as if a vice were squeezing his head. Soldiers flitted past him and he counted them unconsciously: "One, two, three soldiers! And there's an officer with his cloak tucked up," he thought. Then lightning flashed before his eyes and he wondered whether the shot was fired from a mortar or a cannon. "A cannon, probably. And there's another shot and more soldiers—five, six, seven. . . . They all pass by!" He was suddenly seized with fear that they would crush him. He wished to shout that he was hurt, but his mouth was so dry that his tongue clove to the roof and a terrible thirst tormented him. He felt a wetness about his chest and this sensation made him think of water, and he longed to drink even what it was that made him feel wet. "I suppose I hit myself in falling and made myself bleed," he thought; and giving way more and more to fear lest the soldiers who kept flitting past might trample him, he gathered all his strength and tried to shout, "Take me with you!" but instead of that he uttered such a terrible groan that the sound frightened him. Then some red fires began dancing before his eyes and it seemed to him that the soldiers put stones on top of him. The fires danced less and less, but the stones they put on him pressed more and more heavily. He made an effort to push off the stones, stretched, and then saw, heard, and felt nothing more. He had been killed on the spot by a bomb-splinter which had struck him in the middle of his chest.

13

When Mikhaylov dropped to the ground on seeing the bomb he too, like Praskukhin, lived through an infinitude of thoughts and feelings in the two seconds that elapsed before the bomb burst. He prayed mentally and repeated, "Thy will be done." And at the same time he thought, "Why did I enter the army? Why did I join the infantry and take part in this campaign? Wouldn't it have been better to have remained with the Uhlan regiment at T—— and spent time with my friend Natasha? And now here I am . . ." and he began to count, "One, two, three, four," deciding that if the bomb burst at an even number he would live, but if at an odd number, he would be killed. "It's all over, I'm dead!" he thought when the bomb burst (he did not remember whether it was at an odd or even number) and he felt a blow and a cruel pain in his head. "Lord, forgive me my trespasses!" he muttered, folding his hands. He rose but fell on his back senseless.

When he came to, his first sensations were that of blood trickling down his nose, and the pain in his head which had become much less violent. "That's my soul passing," he thought. "What will it be like *there?* Lord, receive my soul in peace. . . . Only it's strange," thought he, "that while dying I should hear the steps of soldiers and the sounds of firing so distinctly."

"Bring stretchers! Eh, the captain has been hit!" shouted a voice above his head, which he recognized as that of the drummer Ignatyev.

Someone took him by the shoulders. With an effort he opened his eyes and saw above him the sky, some groups of stars, and two bombs racing one another as they flew over him. He saw Ignatyev, soldiers with stretchers and guns, the embankment, trenches, and suddenly he realized that he was not yet in the other world.

He had been slightly wounded in the head by a stone. His first feeling was almost one of regret: he had prepared himself so well and so calmly to go *there* that the return to reality, with its bombs, stretchers, and blood, seemed unpleasant. The second feeling was unconscious joy at being alive; the third was a wish to get away from the bastion as quickly as possible. The drummer tied a handkerchief round his commander's head and taking his arm led him towards the ambulance station.

"But why and where am I going?" wondered the lieutenant-captain when he had recollected his senses. "My duty is to remain with the company and not leave it behind—especially," whispered a voice, "as it will soon be out of range of the guns."

"Don't worry about me, my lad," said he, drawing his hand away from the attentive drummer. "I won't go to the ambulance station: I'll stay with the company."

And he turned back.

"It would be better to have it properly bandaged, your honor," said Ignatyev. "It's only in the heat of the moment that it seems like nothing. Mind it doesn't get worse. . . . And just see what hectic work it is here. . . . Really, your honor—"

Mikhaylov stood for a moment undecided and would probably have followed Ignatyev's advice had he not reflected how many severely wounded there must be at the ambulance station. "Perhaps the doctors will smile at my scratch," thought the lieutenant-captain, and in spite of the drummer's arguments he returned to his company.

"And where is the orderly Praskukhin, who was with me?" he asked when he met the ensign who was leading the company.

"I don't know. Killed, I think," replied the ensign unwillingly.

"Killed? Or only wounded? How is it you don't know? Wasn't he going with us? And why didn't you carry him away?"

"How could we, under such fire?"

"But how could you do such a thing, Mikhail Ivanych?" asked Mikhaylov angrily. "How could you leave him thinking he was still alive? Even if he's dead his body ought to have been carried away."

"Alive indeed; I tell you I went up and saw him myself!" said the ensign. "Excuse me. . . . It's hard enough to collect our own. There, those villains are at it again!" he added. "They're sending up cannon-balls now."

Mikhaylov sat down and lifted his hands to his head, which ached terribly when he moved.

"No, it is absolutely necessary to go back and fetch him," he said. "He may still be alive. It is our *duty*, Mikhail Ivanych."

Mikhail Ivanych did not answer.

"O Lord! Just because he didn't bring him back at the time, soldiers will have to be sent out alone now . . . how can I possibly send them under this terrible fire? They may be killed for nothing," thought Mikhaylov.

"Lads! Someone will have to go back to fetch the officer who was wounded out there in the ditch," said he, not very loudly or peremptorily, for he felt how unpleasant it would be for the soldiers to carry out this order. And he was right. Since he had not named any one in particular, no one came forward to obey the order.

"And after all he may be dead already. It isn't worth exposing men to such danger uselessly. It's all my fault, I ought to have seen to it. I'll go back myself and find out whether he is alive. It is my *duty*," said Mikhaylov to himself.

"Mikhail Ivanych, you lead the company, I'll catch up with you," he said, and holding up his cloak with one hand while with the other he kept touching a small icon of St. Metrophanes that hung round his neck and in which he placed great faith, he ran quickly along the trench.

Having convinced himself that Praskukhin was dead, he dragged himself back panting, holding the bandage that had slipped from his head, which was beginning to ache very badly. When he overtook the battalion it was already at the foot of the hill and almost beyond the range of the shots. I say "almost," for a stray bomb reached them every now and then.

"Tomorrow I had better go and be entered at the ambulance station," thought the lieutenant-captain, while a medical assistant, who had turned up, was bandaging his head.

14

Hundreds of bodies, which a couple of hours before had been men full of various lofty or trivial hopes and wishes, were lying with fresh blood-stains on their stiffened limbs in the dewy, flowery valley which separated the bastions from the trenches and on the smooth floor of the mortuary chapel in Sevastopol. Hundreds of men with curses or prayers on their parched lips, crawled, writhed, and groaned, some among the dead in the flowery valley, others on stretchers, or beds, or on the blood-stained floor of the ambulance station. Yet the dawn broke behind the Sapun hill, the twinkling stars grew pale, and the white mists spread from the dark roaring sea just as on other days, and the rosy morning glow lit up the east, long streaks of red clouds spread along the pale-blue horizon, and just as in the old days the sun rose in its power and glory, promising joy, love, and happiness to all the awakening world.

15

Next evening the Chasseurs' band was playing again on the boulevard, and officers, cadets, soldiers, and young women again promenaded round the pavilion and along the side-walks under the acacias with their sweet-scented white blossoms.

Kalugin was walking arm in arm with Prince Galtsin and a colonel near the pavilion and talking about last night's affair. The main theme of their conversation, as usual in such cases, was not the affair itself, but the part each of the speakers had taken in it. Their faces and the tone of their voices were serious, almost sorrowful, as if the losses of the previous night had touched and saddened them all. But to tell the truth, as none of them had lost any one very dear to him, this sorrowful expression was only an official one they considered it their duty to exhibit.

Kalugin and the colonel in fact, though they were first-rate fellows, were ready to see such an affair every day if they could gain a gold sword and be made major-general each time. It is all very well to call some conqueror a monster because he destroys millions to gratify his ambition, but go and ask any Ensign Petrushev or Sub-Lieutenant Antonov on their conscience, and you will find that everyone of us is a little Napoleon, a petty monster ready to start a battle and kill a hundred men merely to get an extra medal or one-third additional pay.

"No, I beg your pardon," said the colonel. "It began first on the left side. I was there myself."

"Well, perhaps," said Kalugin. "I spent more time on the right. I went there twice: first to look for the general, and then just to see the lodgements. It was hectic there, I can tell you!"

"Kalugin ought to know," said Galtsin. "By the way, V—— told *me* today that you were quite a man—"

"But the losses, the losses are terrible!" said the colonel. "In my regiment we had four hundred casualties. It is astonishing that I'm still alive."

Just then the figure of Mikhaylov, with his head bandaged, appeared at the end of the boulevard walking towards these gentlemen.

"What, are you wounded, captain?" asked Kalugin.

"Yes, slightly, with a stone," answered Mikhaylov.

"*Est-ce que le pavillon est baissé déjà?*"[2] asked Prince Galtsin, glancing at the lieutenant-captain's cap and not addressing anyone in particular.

2. "Is the flag (of truce) lowered already?"

"*Non, pas encore,*"[3] answered Mikhaylov, wishing to show that he understood and spoke French.

"Do you mean to say the truce continues?" asked Galtsin, politely addressing him in Russian and thereby (so it seemed to the lieutenant-captain) suggesting: "It must be difficult for you to have to speak French, so hadn't we better simply . . ." and with that the adjutants walked away.

.The lieutenant-captain again felt exceedingly lonely, just as he had the day before. After bowing to various people—some of whom he did not wish to join and others of whom he did not dare to join—he sat down near the Kazarsky monument and smoked a cigarette.

Baron Pesth also turned up on the boulevard. He mentioned that he had been at the parley and had spoken to the French officers. According to his account one of them had said to him: "*S'il n'avait pas fait clair encore pendant une demi-heure, les ambuscades auraient été reprises,*"[4] and he replied, "*Monsieur, je ne dis pas non, pour ne pas vous donner un démenti,*"[5] and he told how pat it had come out, and so on.

But though he had been at the parley he had not really managed to say anything in particular, though he much wished to speak with the French ("for it's awfully pleasant to speak to those fellows"). He had paced up and down the line for a long time asking the Frenchmen near him: "*De quel régiment êtes-vous?*"[6] and had got his answer and nothing more. When he went too far beyond the line, the French sentry, not suspecting that "this soldier" knew French, abused him in the third person: "*Il vient regarder nos travaux, ce sacré———.*"[7] In consequence of which Cadet Baron Pesth, finding nothing more to interest him at the parley, rode home, and on his way back composed the French phrases he now repeated.

On the boulevard Captain Zobov was talking very loud, and Captain Obzhogov, the artillery captain who never curried favor with anyone, was there too, in a dishevelled condition, as well as the cadet who was always fortunate in his love affairs, and all the same people as yesterday, with the same motives as always. Only Praskukhin, Neferdov, and a few others were missing, and hardly anyone remembered or thought about them, though there had not yet been time for their bodies to be washed, laid out, and put into the ground.

16

White flags are hung out on our own bastions and on the French trenches, and in the flowery valley between them lie heaps of mangled corpses without boots, some clad in blue and others in grey, which

---

3. "No, not yet."
4. "Had it remained dark for another half hour, the ambuscades would have been recaptured."
5. "Sir, I will not disagree, lest I lie."

6. "What regiment do you belong to?"
7. "He's come to look at our works, the damned ———."

workmen are removing and piling onto carts. The air is filled with the smell of decaying flesh. Crowds of people have poured out from Sevastopol and from the French camp to see the sight, and with eager and friendly curiosity draw near to one another.

Listen to what these people are saying.

Here, in a circle of Russians and Frenchmen who have collected round him, a young officer, who speaks French badly but sufficiently to be understood, is examining a guardsman's pouch.

"*Eh sussy, poor quah se waso lié?*"[8]

"*Parce que c'est une giberne d'un régiment de la garde, monsieur, qui porte l'aigle impérial.*"[9]

"*Eh voo de la guard?*"[1]

"*Pardon, monsieur, du 6-eme de ligne.*"[2]

"*Eh sussy oo ashtay?*"[3] pointing to a cigarette-holder made of yellow wood, in which the Frenchman was smoking a cigarette.

"*A Balaclava, monsieur. C'est tout simple en bois de palme.*"[4]

"*Joli,*"[5] replies the officer, guided in his remarks not so much by what he wants to say as by the French words he happens to know.

"*Si vous voulez bien garder cela comme souvenir de cette rencontre, vous m'obligerez.*"[6] . . . .

And the polite Frenchman puts out his cigarette and presents the holder to the officer with a slight bow. The officer gives him his, and all present, both French and Russian, smile and seem pleased.

Here is a bold infantryman in a pink shirt with his cloak thrown over his shoulders, accompanied by other soldiers standing near him with their hands folded behind their backs and with merry inquisitive faces. He has approached a Frenchman and asked him for a light for his pipe. The Frenchman draws at and stirs up the tobacco in his own short pipe and shakes a light into that of the Russian.

"*Tabac boon?*" asks the soldier in the pink shirt, and the spectators smile. "*Oui, bon tabac, tabac turc,*" says the Frenchman. "*Chez vous autres tabac—Russe? Bon?*"[7]

"*Roos boon,*" says the soldier in the pink shirt while the onlookers shake with laughter. "*Fransay* not *boon. Bongjour, mossier!*" and having exhausted his whole stock of French at once, he slaps the Frenchman on the stomach and laughs. The French also laugh.

---

8. "And what is this bird tied for?"
9. "Because this is a cartridge pouch of a guard regiment, monsieur, and bears the Imperial eagle."
1. "And do you belong to the Guards?"
2. "No, monsieur, to the 6th regiment of the line."
3. "And where did you buy this?"

4. "At Balaclava, monsieur. It's only made of palm wood."
5. "Very pretty."
6. "If you will keep it as a souvenir of this meeting you will be doing me a great favor."
7. "Yes, good tobacco, Turkish tobacco. . . . You have Russian tobacco. Is it any good?"

"Ils ne sont pas jolis ces b——— de Russes,"[8] says a Zouave[9] among
the French.

"De quoi est-ce qu'ils rient donc?"[1] asks another with an Italian accent,
a dark man, coming up to our men.

"Coat boon," says the cheeky soldier, examining the embroidery of
the Zouave's coat, and everybody laughs again.

"Ne sors pas de ta ligne; à vos places, sacré nom!"[2] cries a French
corporal, and the soldiers separate with evident reluctance.

And here, in the midst of a group of French officers, one of our
young cavalry officers is gushing. They are talking about some Count
Sazonof, *"que j'ai beaucoup connu, monsieur,"* says a French officer
with only one epaulette. *"C'est un de ces vrais comtes russes, comme
nous les aimons."*[3]

"Il y a un Sazonoff, que j'ai connu," says the cavalry officer, *"mais
il n'est pas comte, à moins que je sache, un petit brun de votre âge à
peu près."*[4]

*"C'est ça, monsieur, c'est lui. Oh! que je voudrais le voir, ce cher
comte. Si vous le voyez, je vous prie bien de lui faire mes compliments—
Capitaine Latour,"*[5] he said, bowing.

*"N'est-ce pas terrible la triste besogne que nous faisons? Ça chauffait
cette nuit, n'est-ce pas?"*[6] said the cavalry officer, wishing to maintain
the conversation and pointing to the corpses.

*"Oh, monsieur, c'est affreux! Mais quels gaillards vos soldats, quels
gaillards! C'est un plaisir que de se battre avec des gaillards comme eux."*[7]

"Il faut avouer que les vôtres ne se mouchent pas du pied non plus,"[8]
said the cavalry officer, bowing and imagining himself very agreeable.

But enough.

Let us look instead at this ten-year-old boy in an old cap (probably
his father's), with shoes on his stockingless feet and nankeen trousers
held up by one brace. At the very beginning of the truce he came over
the entrenchments and has been walking around the valley ever since,
looking with dull curiosity at the French and at the corpses that lie on
the ground and gathering blue flowers with which the valley is strewn.

---

8. "They are not handsome, these d——
Russians."
9. A soldier belonging to an infantry group in the
French army organized in Algeria, noted for their
exceptional courage.
1. "What are they laughing about?"
2. "Don't leave your ranks; to your places, damn
it!"
3. "Whom I knew very intimately, monsieur. He
is one of those real Russian counts of whom we
are so fond."
4. "I am acquainted with a Sazonoff, but he is
not a count, as far as I know—a small dark man,

about your age."
5. "Just so, monsieur, that is he. Oh, how I should
like to meet the dear count. If you should see him,
please be so kind as to give him my regards—
Captain Latour."
6. "Isn't it terrible, this sad duty we are engaged
in? It was hectic work last night, wasn't it?"
7. "Ah, monsieur, it is terrible! But what fine fellows your men are, what fine fellows! It is a pleasure to fight with such fellows!"
8. "It must be admitted that yours are no fools
either."

Returning home with a large bunch he holds his nose to escape the stench that is borne towards him by the wind and stopping near a heap of corpses, he gazes for a long time at a terrible headless body that lies nearest to him. After standing there for some time he draws nearer and touches the stiff outstretched arm of the corpse with his foot. The arm trembles a little. He touches it again more boldly; it moves and falls back to its old position. The boy gives a sudden scream, hides his face in his flowers, and runs towards the fortifications as fast as his legs can carry him.

Yes, there are white flags on the bastions and trenches but the flowery valley is covered with dead bodies. The glorious sun is sinking towards the blue sea, and the undulating blue sea glitters in the golden light. Thousands of people crowd together, look at, speak to, and smile at one another. And these people—Christians professing the one great law of love and self-sacrifice—on seeing what they have done do not immediately fall repentant on their knees before Him who has given them life and placed in the soul of each a fear of death and a love of the good and the beautiful and they do not embrace like brothers with tears of joy and gladness.

The white flags are lowered, the engines of death and suffering are sounding again, innocent blood is flowing, and the air is filled with moans and curses.

There, I have said what I wished to say this time. But I am seized by an oppressive doubt. Perhaps I ought to have left it unsaid. What I have said perhaps belongs to that class of evil truths that lie unconsciously hidden in the soul of each man and should not be uttered lest they become harmful, as the dregs in a bottle must not be disturbed for fear of spoiling the wine. . . .

Where in this tale is the evil that should be avoided, and where the good that should be imitated? Who is the villain and who the hero of my story? All are good and all are bad.

Not Kalugin, with his brilliant courage—*bravoure de gentilhomme*[9]—and the vanity that influences all his actions, not Praskukhin, the empty harmless fellow (though he fell in battle for his faith, monarch, and fatherland), not Mikhaylov with his shyness, nor Pesth, a child without firm principles or convictions, can be either the villain or the hero of this tale.

The hero of my tale—whom I love with all the power of my soul, whom I have tried to portray in all its beauty, who has been, is, and always will be beautiful—is Truth.

---

9. A gentleman's bravery.

Three Deaths†

A *Tale*

I

It was autumn. Two vehicles were going along the highway at a quick trot. In the first sat two women: a lady, thin and pale, and a maidservant, plump, rosy, and shining. The maid's short dry hair escaped from under her faded bonnet and her red hand in its torn glove kept pushing it back in fits and starts; her full bosom, covered by a woollen shawl, breathed health, her quick black eyes watched the fields as they glided past the window, glanced timidly at her mistress, and then restlessly scanned the corners of the carriage. In front of her nose dangled her mistress's bonnet, pinned to the luggage carrier and on her lap lay a puppy; her feet were raised on the boxes standing on the floor and just audibly tapped against them to the creaking of the coach-springs and the clatter of the window panes.

Having folded her hands on her knees and closed her eyes, the lady swayed feebly against the pillows placed at her back, and, frowning slightly, coughed inwardly. On her head she had a white nightcap, and a blue kerchief was tied round her delicate white throat. A straight line receding under the cap parted her light brown, extremely flat, pomaded hair, and there was something dry and deathly about the whiteness of the skin of that wide parting. Her features were delicate and handsome, but her skin was flabby and rather sallow, though there was a hectic flush on her cheeks. Her lips were dry and restless, her scanty eyelashes had no curl in them, and her cloth travelling coat fell in straight folds over a sunken breast. Though her eyes were closed her face bore an expression of weariness, irritation, and habitual suffering.

A footman, leaning on the arms of his seat, was dozing on the box. The mail-coach driver, shouting lustily, urged on his four big sweating horses, occasionally turning to the other driver who called to him from the calèche[1] behind. The broad parallel tracks of the wheels spread themselves evenly and fast on the muddy, chalky surface of the road. The sky was grey and cold and a damp mist was settling on the fields and road. It was stuffy in the coach and there was a smell of Eau-de-Cologne and dust. The invalid drew back her head and slowly opened her splendid dark eyes, which were large and shining.

"Again," she said, nervously pushing away with her beautiful thin hand an end of her maid's cloak which had lightly touched her foot, and her mouth twitched painfully. Matresha gathered up her cloak with

---

†This piece was first published in 1859.
1. A light, low-wheeled carriage with an adjustable top or hood.

both hands, rose on her strong legs, and seated herself farther away, while her fresh face grew scarlet. The lady, leaning with both hands on the seat, also tried to raise herself so as to sit up higher, but her strength failed her. Her mouth twisted, and her whole face became distorted by a look of impotent malevolence and irony. "You might at least help me! . . . No, don't bother! I can do it myself, only don't put your bags or anything behind me, for goodness' sake! . . . No, it's better not to touch me since you don't know how to!" The lady closed her eyes and then, quickly raising her eyelids, glared at the maid again. Matresha, looking at her, bit her red lower lip. A deep sigh rose from the invalid's chest and turned into a cough before it was completed. She turned away, puckered her face, and clutched her chest with both hands. When the coughing fit was over she closed her eyes once more and continued to sit motionless. The carriage and calèche entered a village. Matresha stretched out her thick hand from under her shawl and crossed herself.

"What is it?" asked her mistress.

"A post-station, madam."

"I'm asking why you crossed yourself."

"There's a church, madam."

The invalid turned to the window and began to cross herself slowly, looking with large wide-open eyes at the big village church her carriage was passing.

The carriage and calèche both stopped at the post-station and the invalid's husband and doctor stepped out of the calèche and went up to the coach.

"How are you feeling?" asked the doctor, taking her pulse.

"Well, my dear, how are you—not too tired?" asked the husband in French. "Wouldn't you like to get out?"

Matresha, gathering up the bundles, squeezed herself into a corner so as not to interfere with their conversation.

"Nothing much, about the same," replied the invalid. "I won't get out."

After standing there a while her husband went into the station-house, and Matresha, too, jumped out of the carriage and ran on tiptoe across the mud and in at the gate.

"If I feel ill, it's no reason for you not to have lunch," said the sick woman with a slight smile to the doctor, who was standing at her window.

"None of them cares at all about me," she added to herself as soon as the doctor, having slowly walked away from her, ran quickly up the steps to the station-house. "They are well, so they don't care. Oh, my God!"

"Well, Edvard Ivanovich?" said the husband, rubbing his hands as he met the doctor with a merry smile. "I have ordered the lunch-basket to be brought in. What do you think about it?"

"A splendid idea," replied the doctor.

"Well, how is she?" asked the husband with a sigh, lowering his voice and lifting his eyebrows.

"As I told you: it is impossible for her to reach Italy—God grant she gets as far as Moscow, especially in this weather."

"But what are we to do? Oh, my God, my God!" and the husband hid his eyes with his hand. "Bring it here!" he said to the man who had brought in the lunch-basket.

"She ought to have stayed home," said the doctor, shrugging his shoulders.

"But what could I do?" rejoined the husband. "You know I used every possible means to get her to stay. I spoke of the expense, of our children whom we had to leave behind, and of my business affairs, but she would not listen to anything. She is making plans for life abroad as if she were in good health. To tell her about her own condition would be to kill her."

"But she is dead already—you must know that, Vasily Dmitrich. A person can't live without lungs, and new lungs won't grow. It is sad and difficult, but what is to be done? My business and yours is to see that her end is made as peaceful as possible. A priest is needed for that."

"Oh, my God! Think about me, having to remind her about her will. Come what may I can't tell her that, you know how good she is . . ."

"Still, try to persuade her to wait till the roads are fit for travel," said the doctor, shaking his head significantly, "or something bad may happen on the journey."

"Aksyusha, hello Aksyusha!" yelled the station-master's daughter, throwing her jacket over her head and stamping her feet on the muddy back porch. "Come let's take a look at the Shirkin lady: they say she is being taken abroad for chest trouble, and I've never seen what consumptive people look like!"

She jumped onto the threshold, and seizing one another by the hand the two girls ran out of the gate. Checking their pace, they passed the coach and looked in at the open window. The invalid turned her head towards them but, noticing their curiosity, frowned and turned away.

"De-arie me!" said the station-master's daughter, quickly turning her head. "What a wonderful beauty she must have been, and see what she's like now! It's dreadful. Did you see, did you, Aksyusha?"

"Yes, how thin!" Aksyusha agreed. "Let's go and look again, as if we were going to the well. See, she turned away, and I didn't see her. What a pity, Masha!"

"Yes, and what mud!" said Masha, and they both ran through the gate.

"Evidently I look terrible," thought the invalid. "If only I could get abroad quicker. I would soon recover there."

"Well, my dear, how are you?" said her husband, approaching her, still chewing.

"Always the same question," thought the invalid, "and he himself is eating."

"So-so," she murmured through her closed teeth.

"You know, my dear, I'm afraid you'll get worse travelling in this weather, and Edvard Ivanovich says so too. Don't you think we'd better turn back?"

She remained angrily silent.

"Perhaps the weather will improve and the roads be fit for travel; you will get better meanwhile, and then we will all go together."

"Excuse me. If I had not listened to you for so long, I should now at least have reached Berlin, and have been quite well."

"What could be done, my angel? You know it was impossible. But now if you stay another month you would get better, I will have finished my business, and we could take the children with us."

"The children are well, but I am not."

"But do understand, my dear, that in this weather if you should get worse on the road. . . . At least you would be at home."

"What of being at home? . . . To die at home?" answered the invalid, flaring up. But the word "die" evidently frightened her, and she looked imploringly and questioningly at her husband. He hung his head and was silent. The invalid's mouth suddenly widened like a child's, and tears rolled down her cheeks. Her husband hid his face in his hand-kerchief and silently stepped away from the carriage.

"No, I will go on," said the invalid, and lifting her eyes to the sky she folded her hands and began whispering incoherent words: "Oh, my God, what is it all for?" she said, and her tears flowed faster. She prayed long and fervently, but her chest ached and felt as tight as before; the sky, the fields, and the road were just as grey and gloomy, and the autumnal mist fell, neither thickening nor lifting, and settled on the muddy road, the roofs, the carriage, and the sheepskin coats of the drivers, who talking in their strong cheerful voices were greasing the wheels and harnessing the horses.

II

The carriage was ready but the driver still tarried. He had gone into the drivers' room at the station. It was hot, stuffy, and dark in there, with an oppressive smell of baking bread, cabbage, sheepskin garments, and humanity. Several drivers were sitting in the room, and a cook was busy at the oven, on the top of which lay a sick man wrapped in sheepskins.

"Uncle Fyodor! I say, Uncle Fyodor!" said the young driver, entering the room in his sheepskin coat with a whip stuck in his belt, and addressing the sick man.

"Why do you want Fyodor, you lazybones?" asked one of the drivers. "There's your carriage waiting for you."

"I want to ask for his boots; mine are quite worn out," answered the young fellow, tossing back his hair and straightening the mittens tucked in his belt. "Is he asleep? I say, Uncle Fyodor!" he repeated, walking over to the oven.

"What is it?" answered a weak voice, and a lean face with a red beard looked down from the oven, while a broad, emaciated, pale, and hairy hand pulled up the coat over the dirty shirt covering his angular shoulder. "Give me a drink, lad. . . . What do you want?"

The lad handed him up a dipper with some water.

"Well, you see, Fyodor," he said, stepping from foot to foot, "I expect you don't need your new boots now; won't you let me have them? I don't suppose you'll be walking about any more."

The sick man, lowering his weary head to the shiny dipper and immersing his sparse drooping moustache in the turbid water, drank feebly but eagerly. His matted beard was dirty, and his sunken clouded eyes had difficulty in looking up at the lad's face. Having finished his drink he tried to lift his hand to wipe his wet lips, but could not do so, and rubbed them on the sleeve of his coat instead. Silently, and breathing heavily through his nose, he looked straight into the lad's eyes, collecting his strength.

"But perhaps you promised them to someone else?" asked the lad. "If that's so, it's all right. The worst of it is, it's wet outside and I have to go about my work, so I said to myself: 'Suppose I ask Fyodor for his boots; I expect he doesn't need them.' If you need them yourself—just say so."

Something began to rumble and gurgle in the sick man's chest; he doubled up and began to choke with an abortive cough in his throat.

"Need them indeed!" the cook snapped unexpectedly so as to be heard by the whole room. "He hasn't come down from the oven in over a month! Hear how he's choking—it makes me ache inside just to hear him. What does he want with boots? They won't bury him in new boots. And it was high time long ago—God forgive me the sin! See how he chokes. He ought to be taken into the other room or somewhere. They say there are hospitals in town. Is it right that he should take up the whole corner?—there's no more to be said. I've no room at all, and yet they expect cleanliness!"

"Hello, Sergey! Come along and take your place, the nobles are waiting!" shouted the drivers' overseer, looking in at the door.

Sergey was about to go without waiting for a reply, but the sick man, while coughing, let him understand by a look that he wanted to give him an answer.

"Take my boots, Sergey," he said when he had mastered the cough and rested a moment. "But listen. . . . Buy a stone for me when I die," he added hoarsely.

"Thank you, uncle. I'll take them, and I'll buy a stone for sure."

"There, lads, you heard that?" the sick man managed to utter, and bent double again and began to choke.

"All right, we heard," said one of the drivers. "Go and take your seat, Sergey, there's the overseer running back. The Shirkin lady is ill, you know."

Sergey quickly pulled off his unduly large, dilapidated boots and threw them under a bench. Uncle Fyodor's new boots just fitted him, and having put them on, he went to the carriage with his eyes fixed on his feet.

"What fine boots! Let me grease them," said a driver, who held some axle-grease in his hand, as Sergey climbed onto the box and gathered up the reins. "Did he give them to you for nothing?"

"Why, are you envious?" Sergey replied, rising and wrapping the skirts of his coat under his legs. "Off with you! Gee up, my beauties!" he shouted to the horses, flourishing the whip, and the carriage and calèche with their occupants, portmanteaux, and trunks rolled rapidly along the wet road and disappeared in the grey autumnal mist.

The sick driver was left on the top of the oven in the stuffy room and, unable to relieve himself by coughing, turned with an effort onto his other side and became silent.

Till late in the evening people came in and out of the room and dined there. The sick man made no sound. When night came, the cook climbed up onto the oven and stretched over his legs to get her sheepskin coat down.

"Don't be cross with me, Nastasya," said the sick man. "I shall soon leave your corner empty."

"All right, all right, never mind," muttered Nastasya. "But what is it that hurts you? Tell me, uncle."

"My whole inside has wasted away. God knows what it is!"

"I suppose your throat hurts when you cough?"

"Everything hurts. My death has come—that's how it is. Oh, oh, oh!" moaned the sick man.

"Cover up your feet like this," said Nastasya, drawing his coat over him as she climbed down from the oven.

A night-light burnt dimly in the room. Nastasya and some ten drivers slept on the floor or on benches, snoring loudly. The sick man groaned feebly, coughed, and turned around on the oven. Towards morning he grew quite quiet.

"I had a queer dream last night," said Nastasya the next morning, stretching herself in the dim light. "I dreamt that Uncle Fyodor got down from the oven and went out to chop wood. 'Come, Nastasya,' he says, 'I'll help you!' and I say, 'How can you chop wood now?', but he just seizes the axe and begins chopping quickly, so that the chips fly all about. 'Why,' I say, 'haven't you been ill?' 'No,' he says, 'I am well,' and he swings the axe so fast that I was quite frightened. I gave a cry and woke up. I wonder whether he's dead! Uncle Fyodor! I say, Uncle Fyodor!"

Fyodor did not answer.

"True enough he may have died. I'll go and see," said one of the drivers, waking up.

The lean hand covered with reddish hair that hung down from the oven was pale and cold.

"I'll go tell the station-master," said the driver. "I think he's dead."

Fyodor had no relatives: he was from some distant place. They buried him the next day in the new cemetery beyond the wood, and Nastasya went on for days telling everybody about her dream, and about having been the first to discover that Uncle Fyodor was dead.

III

Spring had come. Rivulets of water coursed down the wet streets of the city, gurgling between lumps of frozen manure; the colors of people's clothes as they moved along the streets looked vivid and their voices sounded shrill. Behind garden-fences the buds on trees were swelling and their branches were just audibly swaying in the fresh breeze. Everywhere transparent drops were forming and falling. . . . The sparrows chirped and fluttered awkwardly with their little wings. On the sunny side of the street, on the fences, houses, and trees, everything was in motion and sparkling. There was joy and youth everywhere in the sky, on the earth, and in the hearts of men.

In one of the main streets fresh straw had been strewn on the road before a large, important house, where the invalid who had been in such a hurry to go abroad lay dying.

At the closed door of her room stood her husband and an elderly woman. On the sofa a priest sat with bowed head, holding something wrapped in his stole. In a corner of the room the sick woman's old mother lay on an invalid chair weeping bitterly: beside her stood one maidservant holding a clean handkerchief, waiting for her to ask for it; another was rubbing her temples with something and blowing under the old lady's cap onto her grey head.

"Well, may Christ help you, dear friend," the husband said to the elderly woman who stood near him at the door. "She has such confidence in you and you know how to talk to her so well; persuade her as well as you can, my dear—go to her." He was about to open the door, but her cousin stopped him, pressing her handkerchief several times to her eyes and giving her head a shake.

"Well, I don't think I look as if I had been crying now," she said and, opening the door herself, went in.

The husband was in great agitation and seemed quite distracted. He walked towards the old woman, but still several steps away from her he turned back, walked about the room, and went up to the priest. The priest looked at him, raised his eyebrows to heaven, and sighed: his thick, greyish beard also rose as he sighed and then came down again.

"My God, my God!" said the husband.

"What can be done?" said the priest with a sigh, and again his eyebrows and beard rose and fell.

"And her mother is here!" said the husband almost in despair. "She won't be able to bear it. You see, loving her as she does . . . I don't know! If you would only try to comfort her, Father, and persuade her to go away."

The priest got up and went to the old woman.

"It is true, no one can appreciate a mother's heart," he said—"but God is merciful."

The old woman's face suddenly twitched all over, and she began to hiccup hysterically.

"God is merciful," the priest continued when she grew a little calmer. "Let me tell you of a patient in my parish who was much worse off than Mary Dmitrievna, and a simple tradesman cured her in a short time with various herbs. That tradesman is still in Moscow. I told Vasily Dmitrich—we might try him. . . . At any rate it would comfort the invalid. To God all is possible."

"No, she won't live," said the old woman. "God is taking her instead of me," and the hysterical hiccuping grew so violent that she fainted.

The sick woman's husband hid his face in his hands and ran out of the room.

In the passage the first person he met was his six-year-old son, who was running full speed after his younger sister.

"Won't you order the children to be taken to their mamma?" asked the nurse.

"No, she doesn't want to see them—it would upset her."

The boy stopped a moment, looked intently into his father's face, then gave a kick and ran on, shouting merrily.

"She pretends to be the black horse, Papa!" he shouted, pointing to his sister.

Meanwhile in the other room the cousin sat down beside the invalid, and tried by skilful conversation to prepare her for the thought of death. The doctor was preparing some medicine at another window.

The patient, in a white dressing gown, sat up in bed supported all round by pillows, and looked at her cousin in silence.

"Ah, my dear friend," she said, unexpectedly interrupting her, "don't attempt to prepare me! Don't treat me like a child. I am a Christian. I know it all. I know I don't have long to live, and know that if my husband had listened to me sooner I would now have been in Italy and perhaps—no, certainly—would have been well. Everybody told him so. But what can be done? Evidently this is God's wish. We have all sinned heavily. I know that, but I trust that in God's mercy everybody will be forgiven, probably all will be forgiven. I try to understand myself. I have many sins to answer for, dear friend, but then how much I have had to suffer! I try to bear my sufferings patiently . . ."

"Shall I call the priest, my dear? You will feel even more comfortable after receiving communion," said her cousin.

The sick woman bent her head in assent.

"God forgive me, sinner that I am!" she whispered.

The cousin went out and signalled with her eyes to the priest.

"She is an angel!" she said to the husband, with tears in her eyes. The husband burst into tears; the priest went into the next room; the invalid's mother was still unconscious, and all was silent there. Five minutes later he came out again, and after taking off his stole, straightened out his hair.

"Thank God she is calmer now," he said, "and wishes to see you."

The cousin and the husband went into the sick-room. The invalid was weeping silently, gazing at an icon.

"I congratulate you, my dear,"[2] said her husband.

"Thank you! How well I feel now, what inexpressible sweetness!" said the sick woman, and a soft smile played on her thin lips. "How merciful God is! Is He not? Merciful and all powerful!" Again she looked at the icon with eager entreaty, her eyes full of tears.

Then suddenly, as if she remembered something, she beckoned to her husband to come closer.

"You never want to do what I ask . . ." she said in a feeble and dissatisfied voice.

The husband, craning his neck, listened to her humbly.

"What is it, my dear?"

"How many times have I said that these doctors don't know anything; there are simple women who can heal and who cure. The priest told me . . . there is also a tradesman . . . Send for them!"

"For whom, my dear?"

"O God, you don't want to understand anything!" . . . And the sick woman's face puckered and she closed her eyes.

The doctor came and took her hand. Her pulse was beating more and more feebly. He glanced at the husband. The invalid noticed that gesture and looked round in fear. The cousin turned away and began to cry.

"Don't cry, don't torture yourself and me," said the patient. "Don't take the last of my tranquillity away from me."

"You're an angel," said the cousin, kissing her hand.

"No, kiss me here! Only dead people are kissed on the hand. My God, my God!"

---

2. It was customary in Russia to congratulate people who had received communion.

That same evening the patient became a corpse, and the body lay in a coffin in the music room of the large house. A deacon sat alone in that big room reading the psalms of David through his nose in a monotonous voice. A bright light from the wax candles in their tall silver candlesticks fell on the pale brow of the dead woman, on her heavy wax-like hands, on the stiff folds of the pall which brought out in awesome relief her knees and toes. The deacon read on monotonously without understanding the words, and in the quiet room the words sounded strange and died away. Now and then from a distant room came the sounds of children's voices and the patter of their feet.

"Thou hidest thy face, they are troubled," said the psalter. "Thou takest away their breath, they die and return to their dust. Thou sendest forth thy spirit, they are created: and thou renewest the face of the earth. The glory of the Lord shall endure for ever."

The dead woman's face looked stern and majestic. Neither in her clear cold brow nor in her firmly closed lips was there any movement. She seemed all attention. But had she understood those solemn words even now?

IV

A month later a stone chapel was being erected over the grave of the deceased woman. On the driver's tomb there was still no stone, and only the light green grass sprouted on the mound which served as the sole token of the past existence of a man.

"It will be a sin, Sergey," said the cook at the station-house one day, "if you don't buy a stone for Fyodor. You kept saying 'It's winter, it's winter!' but why don't you keep your word now? You know I witnessed it. He has already come back once to ask you to do it; if you don't buy him a stone, he'll come again and choke you."

"But why? I'm not backing out of it," replied Sergey. "I'll buy a stone just as I said I would, and pay a ruble and a half for it. I haven't forgotten, but it has to be fetched. When I happen to be in town I'll buy one."

"You might at least put up a cross—you ought to—or else it's really wrong," interposed an old driver. "You know you're wearing his boots."

"Where can I get a cross? I can't cut one out of a log."

"What do you mean, can't cut one out of a log? You take an axe and go into the forest early, and there you can cut one. Cut down a young ash or something like that, and you can make a cross . . . you may have to treat the forester to some vodka; but one can't afford to treat him for every trifle. When I broke my splinter-bar and went and cut a new one, nobody said a word."

Early in the morning, as soon as it was daybreak, Sergey took an axe and went into the woods.

A cold white cover of dew, which was still falling untouched by the sun, lay on everything. The east was growing imperceptibly brighter, reflecting its pale light on the vault of heaven still veiled by a covering of clouds. Not a blade of grass below, nor a leaf on the topmost branches of the trees, stirred. Only occasionally a sound of wings amid the brush, or a rustling on the ground, broke the silence of the forest. Suddenly a strange sound, foreign to Nature, resounded and died away at the out-skirts of the forest. Again the sound was heard, and rhythmically repeated at the foot of the trunk of one of the motionless trees. A tree-top began to tremble in an unusual manner, its sap-filled leaves whispered some-thing, and the robin who had been sitting in one of its branches fluttered twice from place to place with a whistle, and jerking its tail sat down on another tree.

The axe at the bottom gave off a more muffled sound, moist white chips scattered on the dewy grass and a slight creaking was heard above the sound of the blows. The tree, shuddering in its whole body, bent down and quickly rose again, vibrating with fear on its roots. For an instant all was still, but the tree bent again, a crashing sound came from its trunk, and with its branches breaking and its boughs hanging down, it fell with its crown on the damp earth.

The sounds of the axe and the footsteps were silenced. The robin whistled and flitted higher. A twig which it brushed with its wings shook a little and then with all its foliage grew still like the rest. The trees flaunted the beauty of their motionless branches still more joyously in the newly cleared space.

The first sunbeams, piercing the translucent cloud, shone through and spread over earth and sky. The mist began to quiver like waves in the hollows, the dew sparkled and played on the verdure, the transparent little clouds grew whiter, and hurriedly dispersed over the deepening azure vault of the sky. The birds stirred in the thicket and, as though bewildered, twittered joyfully about something; the sap-filled leaves whis-pered gladly and peacefully on the treetops, and the branches of those that were living began to rustle slowly and majestically over the dead and prostrate tree.

Family Happiness†

Part I

I

We were in mourning for my mother, who had died during the autumn, and I spent all that winter alone in the country with Katya and Sonya.

Katya was an old friend of the family, our governess who had brought

†This piece was first published in 1859.

us all up, and I had known and loved her since my earliest recollections. Sonya was my younger sister. It was a dark and sad winter which we spent in our old house of Pokrovskoe. The weather was cold and so windy that snowdrifts reached higher than the windows; the panes were almost always dimmed by frost, and we seldom walked or drove anywhere throughout the winter. Our visitors were few, and those who came brought no cheerfulness or happiness to the household. They all wore sad faces and spoke softly, as if they were afraid of waking someone; they never laughed, but sighed and often shed tears as they looked at me and especially at little Sonya in her black frock. The feeling of death clung to the house; the air was still filled with the grief and horror of death. My mother's room was kept locked; and whenever I passed it on my way to bed, I felt a strange uncomfortable impulse to look into that cold empty room.

I was seventeen then; and in the very year of her death my mother was intending to move to Petersburg, in order to take me into society. The loss of my mother was a great grief to me; but I must confess to another feeling behind that grief—a feeling that though I was young and pretty (so everybody told me), I was wasting a second winter in the solitude of the country. Before the winter ended, this sense of dejection, solitude, and simple boredom increased to such an extent that I refused to leave my room, open the piano, or take up a book. When Katya urged me to find some occupation, I said that I did not feel up to it; but in my heart I said, "What good is it? What is the good of doing anything, when the best part of my life is being wasted like this?" And to this question, tears were my only answer.

I was told that I was growing thin and losing my looks; but even this failed to interest me. What did it matter? For whom? I felt that my whole life was bound to go on in the same solitude and helpless dreariness, from which I had no strength and even no wish to escape. Towards the end of winter Katya became anxious about me and determined to make an effort to take me abroad. But for this money was needed, and we hardly knew how our affairs stood after my mother's death. Our guardian, who was to come and clear up our position, was expected any day.

In March he arrived.

"Well, thank God!" Katya said to me one day, when I was walking up and down the room like a shadow, without occupation, without a thought, and without a wish. "Sergey Mikhaylych has arrived; he has sent to inquire about us and intends to come here for dinner. You must rouse yourself, dear Mashechka," she added, "or what will he think of you? He was so fond of you all."

Sergey Mikhaylych was our near neighbor, and, though a much younger man, had been a friend of my father's. His coming was likely to change our plans and make it possible to leave the country; I had also grown up in the habit of love and regard for him. When Katya begged me to rouse myself, she rightly guessed that it would give me special pain to appear to disadvantage before him, more than before any other of our friends. Like everyone in the house, from Katya and his god-daughter Sonya down to the helper in the stables, I loved him out of old habit; he also had a special significance for me, owing to a remark which my mother had once made in my presence. "I should like you to marry a man like him," she said. At the time this seemed to me strange and even unpleasant. My ideal husband was quite different: he was to be thin, pale, and sad; Sergey Mikhaylych was middle-aged, tall, robust, and always, as it seemed to me, in good spirits. But still my mother's words stuck in my mind; and even six years before this time, when I was eleven, and he still addressed me in the familiar form,[1] played with me, and called me by the pet-name of "violet"—even then I sometimes asked myself in a fright, "What *shall* I do, if he suddenly wants to marry me?"

Before our dinner, to which Katya made an addition of sweets and a dish of spinach, Sergey Mikhaylych arrived. From the window I watched him drive up to the house in a small sleigh; but as soon as it turned the corner, I hastened to the drawing-room, meaning to pretend that his visit was a complete surprise. But when I heard his tramp and loud voice and Katya's footsteps in the hall, I lost patience and went to meet him myself. He was holding Katya's hand, talking loud, and smiling. When he saw me, he stopped and looked at me for a time without bowing. I was uncomfortable and felt myself blushing.

"Can this be really you?" he said in his plain decisive way, walking towards me with his arms apart. "Is so great a change possible? How grown-up you are! I used to call you 'violet,' but now you are a rose in full bloom!"

He took my hand in his own large hand and pressed it so hard it almost hurt. Expecting him to kiss my hand, I bent towards him, but he only pressed it again and looked straight into my eyes with the old firmness and cheerfulness in his face.

It was six years since I had seen him last. He was much changed— older and darker in complexion; now he wore whiskers which did not become him at all. But much remained the same—his simple manner, the large features of his honest open face, his bright intelligent eyes, his friendly, almost boyish, smile.

Five minutes later he had ceased to be a visitor and had become the friend of us all, even of the servants, whose visible eagerness to wait on him proved their pleasure at his arrival.

He behaved quite unlike the neighbors who had visited us after my mother's death. They had thought it necessary to be silent when they

---

1. That is, uses the informal *ty* instead of the formal *vy*.

sat with us, and to shed tears. He, on the contrary, was cheerful and talkative, and said not a word about my mother, so that this indifference seemed strange to me at first and even improper on the part of so close a friend. But I understood later that what seemed indifference was sincerity, and I felt grateful for it. In the evening Katya poured out tea, sitting in her old place in the drawing-room, where she used to sit during my mother's lifetime; Sonya and I sat near him; our old butler Grigory had hunted out one of my father's pipes and brought it to him; he began to walk up and down the room as he used to do in past days.

"How many terrible changes there are in this house, when one thinks of it all!" he said, stopping in his walk.

"Yes," said Katya with a sigh; and then she put the top on the samovar and looked at him, quite ready to burst out crying.

"I suppose you remember your father?" he said, turning to me.

"Not clearly," I answered.

"How happy you would have been together now!" he added in a low voice, looking thoughtfully at my face above the eyes. "I was very fond of him," he added in a still lower tone, and it seemed to me that his eyes were shining more than usual.

"And now God has taken her too!" said Katya; and at once she laid her napkin on the teapot, took out her handkerchief, and began to cry.

"Yes, the changes in this house are terrible," he repeated, turning away. "Sonya, show me your toys," he added after a little while and went off to the parlor. When he had gone, I looked at Katya with eyes full of tears.

"What a splendid friend he is!" she said. And, though he was no relation, I did really feel a kind of warmth and comfort in the sympathy of this good man.

I could hear him moving about in the parlor with Sonya, and the sound of her high childish voice. I sent in tea to him there; I heard him sit down at the piano and strike the keys with Sonya's little hands.

Then came his voice—"Marya Alexandrovna, come here and play something."

I liked his easy behavior to me and his friendly tone of command; I got up and went to him.

"Play this," he said, opening a book of Beethoven's music at the *adagio* of the "Moonlight Sonata." "Let me hear how you play," he added, and went off to a corner of the room, carrying his cup with him.

I somehow felt that with him it was impossible to refuse or to say beforehand that I played badly: I sat down obediently at the piano and began to play as well as I could; yet I was afraid of criticism, because I knew that he understood and enjoyed music. The *adagio* suited the remembrance of past days evoked by our conversation at tea, and I believe I played it fairly well. But he would not let me play the *scherzo*. "No," he said, coming up to me; "you don't play that right; don't go on; but the first movement was not bad; you seem to be musical." This moderate praise pleased me so much that I even blushed. I felt it pleasant and strange that a friend of my father's, and his contemporary, should no longer treat me like a child but speak to me seriously. Katya now went upstairs to put Sonya to bed, and we were left alone in the parlor.

He talked to me about my father, and about the beginning of their friendship and the happy days they had spent together, while I was still busy with lesson-books and toys; and his talk put my father before me in quite a new light, as a man of simple and delightful character. He also asked me about my tastes, what I read and what I intended to do, and gave me advice. The man of mirth and jest who used to tease me and make me toys had disappeared; here was a serious, simple, and affectionate friend, for whom I could not help feeling respect and sympathy. It was easy and pleasant to talk to him; and yet I felt an involuntary strain also. I was anxious about each word I spoke: I wished so much to earn for my own sake the love which had been given me already merely because I was my father's daughter.

After putting Sonya to bed, Katya joined us and began to complain to him of my apathy, about which I had said nothing.

"So she never told me the most important thing of all!" he said, smiling and shaking his head reproachfully at me.

"Why tell you?" I said. "It is tiresome to talk about, and it will pass." (I really felt now, not only that my dejection would pass, but that it had already passed, or rather had never existed.)

"It is a bad thing," he said, "not to be able to endure solitude. Can it be that you are a young lady?"

"Of course, I am a young lady," I answered, laughing.

"Well, I can't praise a young lady who is alive only when people admire, but as soon as she is left alone, collapses and finds nothing to her taste—one who is all for show and has no resources in herself."

"You have a flattering opinion of me!" I said, just for the sake of saying something.

He was silent for a little. Then he said: "Yes; your likeness to your father means something. There is something in you . . . ," and his kind attentive look again flattered me and made me feel a pleasant embarrassment.

I noticed now for the first time that his face, which initially gave one the impression of high spirits, also had an expression peculiar to himself—bright at first and then more and more attentive and rather sad.

"You ought not to be bored and you cannot be," he said; "you have music, which you appreciate, books, study; your whole life lies before you; now or never is the time to prepare for it and save yourself future regrets. A year from now it will be too late."

He spoke to me like a father or an uncle, and I felt that he kept a constant check upon himself, in order to keep on my level. Though I was hurt that he considered me as inferior to himself, I was pleased that he thought it necessary to try to be different for me alone.

For the rest of the evening he talked about business with Katya.

"Well, good-bye, dear friends," he said. Then he got up, came towards me, and took my hand.

"When shall we see you again?" asked Katya.

"In the spring," he answered, still holding my hand. "I shall go to Danilovka now" (this was another property of ours), "look into things there and make what arrangements I can; then I will go to Moscow on business of my own; in the summer we shall meet again."

"Must you really be gone so long?" I asked, feeling terribly grieved. I had really hoped to see him every day, and felt a sudden shock of regret, and a fear that my depression would return. My face and voice must have made this plain.

"You must find more to do and not get depressed," he said; I thought his tone too cool and unconcerned. "I shall put you through an examination in spring," he added, letting go my hand and not looking at me.

When we saw him off in the hall, he put on his fur coat in a hurry and avoided looking at me. "He is going to a great deal of trouble for nothing!" I thought. "Does he think me so anxious that he should look at me? He is a good man, a very good man; but that's all."

That evening, however, Katya and I sat up late, talking, not about him but about our plans for the summer, and where we should spend next winter and what we should do then. I had ceased to ask that terrible question—what is the good of it all? Now it seemed quite plain and simple: the proper object of life was happiness, and I promised myself much happiness ahead. It seemed as if our gloomy old house had suddenly become full of light and life.

II

Meanwhile spring arrived. My old dejection passed and gave place to the unrest which spring brings with it, full of dreams, vague hopes and desires. Instead of living as I had done at the beginning of winter, I read and played the piano and gave lessons to Sonya; but I also went into the garden and wandered alone through the avenues, or sat on a bench there; Heaven knows what my thoughts, wishes, and hopes were at such moments. Sometimes at night, especially if there was a moon, I sat by my bedroom window till dawn; sometimes, when Katya was not watching, I stole out into the garden wearing only a cloak and ran through the dew as far as the pond; and once I went all the way to the open fields and walked right round the garden all alone at night.

I find it difficult now to recall and understand the dreams which filled my imagination. Even when I *can* recall them, I find it hard to believe that my dreams were like that: they were so strange and so remote from life.

Sergey Mikhaylych kept his promise: he returned from his travels at the end of May.

His first visit to us was in the evening and quite unexpected. We were sitting on the veranda, preparing for tea. By this time the garden was all green, and the nightingales had taken up their quarters for the duration of St. Peter's Fast in the leafy borders. The tops of the round lilac bushes had a sprinkling of white and purple—a sign that their flowers were ready to open. The foliage of the birch avenue was transparent in the light of the setting sun. In the veranda there was shade and freshness. The evening dew was sure to be heavy in the grass. Out of doors beyond the garden the last sounds of day were audible, as was the noise of sheep and cattle, as they were driven home. Nikon, the half-witted boy, was driving his water-cart along the path outside the veranda, and a cold stream of water from the sprinkler made dark circles on the mould round the stems and supports of the dahlias. On our veranda the polished samovar shone and hissed on the white table-cloth; there were crackers, biscuits, and cream on the table. Katya was busy washing the cups with her plump hands. I was too hungry after bathing to wait for tea, and was eating bread with thick fresh cream. I was wearing a gingham blouse with loose sleeves, and my hair, still wet, was covered with a kerchief. Katya saw him first, even before he entered.

"Sergey Mikhaylych!" she cried. "Why, we were just talking about you."

I got up, meaning to go and change my dress, but he caught me just by the door.

"Why stand on such ceremony in the country?" he said, smiling at the kerchief on my head. "You don't mind the presence of your butler, and I'm really the same as Grigory is." But I felt then that he was looking at me in a way quite unlike Grigory's, and I was uncomfortable.

"I shall come back at once," I said as I left them.

"But what's wrong?" he called out after me; "it's just the dress of a young peasant woman."

"How strangely he looked at me!" I said to myself as I quickly changed clothes upstairs. "Well, I'm glad he's come; things will be more lively." After a look in the mirror I ran gaily downstairs and onto the veranda; I was out of breath and did not disguise my haste. He was sitting at the table, talking to Katya about our affairs. He glanced at me and smiled; then he went on talking. From what he said it appeared that our affairs were in splendid shape: it was now possible for us, after spending the summer in the country, to go either to Petersburg for Sonya's education, or abroad.

"If only you would go abroad with us—" said Katya; "without you we shall be quite lost there."

"Oh, I should like to go around the world with you," he said, half in jest and half in earnest.

"All right," I said; "let's start off and go around the world."

He smiled and shook his head.

"What about my mother? What about my business?" he said. "But that's not the question just now: I want to know how you have been spending your time. Not depressed again, I hope?"

When I told him that I had been busy and not bored during his absence, and when Katya confirmed my report, he praised me as if he had a right to do so, and his words and looks were kind, as they might have been to a child. I felt obliged to tell him, in detail and with perfect frankness, all my good deeds, and to confess, as if I were in church, any that he might disapprove of. The evening was so fine that we stayed on the veranda after tea was cleared away; the conversation interested me so much that I did not notice how we ceased by degrees to hear any sound of the servants indoors. The scent of flowers grew stronger and came from all sides; the grass was drenched with dew; a nightingale struck up in a lilac bush close by and then stopped on hearing our voices; the starry sky seemed to sink lower over our heads.

It was growing dark, but I did not notice it till a bat suddenly and silently flew in beneath the veranda awning and began to flutter round my white shawl. I shrank back against the wall and nearly cried out; but just as silently and swiftly the bat dived out from under the awning and disappeared in the half-darkness of the garden.

"How fond I am of this place of yours!" he said, changing the conversation; "I wish I could spend all my life here, sitting on this veranda."

"Well, then do!" said Katya.

"That's all very well," he said, "but life won't sit still."

"Why don't you marry?" asked Katya; "you would make an excellent husband."

"Because I like sitting still?" and he laughed. "No, Katerina Karlovna, it's too late for you and me to marry. People have long ceased to think of me as an eligible man, and I am even surer of it myself; I declare I have felt quite comfortable since the matter was settled."

It seemed to me that he said this in an unnaturally persuasive way.

"Nonsense!" said Katya; "a man of thirty-six pretending that he's too old!"

"Too old indeed," he went on, "when all one wants is to sit still. For a man who's going to marry that's not enough. Just you ask her," he added, nodding at me; "people of her age should marry, while you and I rejoice in their happiness."

The sadness and constraint latent in his voice was not lost upon me. He was silent for a little, and neither Katya nor I spoke.

"Well, just imagine," he went on, turning a little on his seat; "suppose that by some misfortune I married a girl of seventeen, Masha, if you like—I mean, Marya Alexandrovna. The example is a good one; I am glad it turned up; there couldn't be a better one."

I laughed; but I could not understand why he was so glad, or what it was that had just turned up.

"But tell me honestly, with your hand on your heart," he said, turning as if playfully to me, "wouldn't it be a misfortune for you to unite your life with that of an old worn-out man who only wants to sit still, whereas Heaven knows what wishes are seething in that heart of yours?"

I felt uncomfortable and was silent, not knowing how to answer him.

"I'm not making you a proposal, you know," he said, laughing; "but am I really the kind of husband you dream about when walking alone in the avenue at twilight? It would be a misfortune, would it not?"

"No, not a misfortune," I began.

"But a bad thing," he ended my sentence.

"Perhaps; but I may be mistaken . . ." He interrupted me again.

"There, you see! She is quite right, and I am grateful to her for her frankness, and very glad to have had this conversation. And there is something else to be said"—he added: "for me too it would be a very great misfortune."

"How strange you are! You have not changed in the least," said Katya, and then left the veranda, to order supper to be served.

When she had gone, we were both silent and all was still around us, but for one exception. A nightingale, which had sung last night in fitful snatches, now flooded the garden with a steady stream of song, and was soon answered by another from the valley below, which had not sung till that evening. The nearer bird stopped and seemed to listen for a moment, and then broke out again still louder than before, pouring out his song in piercing long-drawn cadences. There was a regal calm in the birds' voices, as they floated through the realm of night which belongs to those birds and not to men. The gardener walked past to his quarters in the greenhouse, and the noise of his heavy boots grew fainter and fainter along the path. Someone whistled twice sharply at the foot of the hill; then all was still again. The rustling of leaves could just be heard; the veranda awning flapped; a faint perfume, floating in the air, came down on the veranda and filled it. I felt the silence was awkward after what had been said, but I did not know what to say. I looked at him. His eyes, bright in the half-darkness, turned towards me.

"How good life is!" he said.

I sighed, I don't know why.

"Well?" he asked.

"Life is good," I repeated after him.

Again we were silent, and again I felt uncomfortable. I could not help thinking that I had wounded him by agreeing that he was old; I wished to comfort him but did not know how.

"Well, I must say good-bye," he said, rising; "my mother expects me for supper; I have hardly seen her all day."

"I meant to play you the new sonata," I said.

"That must wait," he replied; and I thought that he spoke coldly. "Good-bye."

I felt even more certain that I had wounded him, and was sorry. Katya and I went to the steps to see him off and stood for a while in the open, looking along the road where he had disappeared from view. When we ceased to hear the sound of his horse's hoofs, I walked round the house to the veranda, and again sat looking into the garden; all I wished to see and hear, I still saw and heard for a long time in the dewy mist filled with the sounds of night.

He came a second time, and a third; the awkwardness arising from that strange conversation passed away entirely, never to return. During that whole summer, he came two or three times a week; I grew so accustomed to his presence, that, when he failed to come for some time, I missed him and felt angry with him, and thought he was behaving badly in deserting me. He treated me like a boy whose company he liked, asked me questions, invited the most cordial frankness on my part, gave me advice and encouragement, or sometimes scolded and checked me. But in spite of his constant effort to keep on my level, I was aware that behind the part of him which I could understand there remained an entire region of mystery, into which he did not consider it necessary to admit me; and this fact did much to preserve my respect for him and his attraction for me. I knew from Katya and from our neighbors that he had not only to care for his old mother with whom he lived, and to manage his own estate and our affairs, but was also responsible for some public business which was the source of serious worries; but what view he took of all this, what were his convictions, plans, and hopes, I could not in the least find out from him. Whenever I turned the conversation to his affairs, he frowned in a way peculiar to himself and seemed to imply, "Please stop! That is no business of yours"; and then changed the subject. This hurt me at first; but I soon grew accustomed to confining our talk to my affairs, and felt this to be quite natural.

There was another thing which displeased me at first and then became pleasant to me. This was his complete indifference and even contempt for my personal appearance. Never by word or look did he imply that I was pretty; on the contrary, he frowned and laughed, whenever the word was applied to me in his presence. He even liked to find fault with my looks and tease me about them. On special days Katya liked to dress me in fine clothes and arrange my hair effectively; but my finery met only with mockery from him, which pained kind-hearted Katya and disconcerted me at first. She had made up her mind that he admired me; she could not understand how a man could help wishing a woman whom he admired to appear to the utmost advantage. But I soon understood what he wanted. He wished to make sure that I had not a trace of affectation. When I understood this I was really quite free from affectation in the clothes I wore, or the arrangement of my hair, or my movements; but a very obvious form of affectation took its place—an affectation of simplicity, at a time when I could not yet be really simple. That he loved me, I knew; but I did not yet ask myself whether he loved me as a child or as a woman. I valued his love; I felt that he thought me better than all other young women in the world, and I could not help wishing him to go on being deceived about me. Without wishing to deceive him, I did so, and I became better myself while deceiving him. I felt it a better and worthier course to show him the good points of my heart and mind than of my body. My hair, hands, face, ways— all these, whether good or bad, he had appraised at once and knew so well, that I could add nothing to my external appearance except the wish to deceive him. But he did not know my mind and heart, because he loved them, and because they were in the very process of growth and development; and on this point I could and did deceive him. How easy I felt in his company, once I understood this clearly! My unwarranted bashfulness and awkward movements completely disappeared. Whether he saw me from in front, or in profile, sitting or standing, with my hair up or down, I felt that he knew me from head to foot, and I fancied, he was satisfied with me as I was. If, contrary to his habit, he had suddenly said to me as other people did, that I had a pretty face, I believe that I should not have liked it at all. On the other hand, how light and happy my heart was when, after I had said something, he looked hard at me and said, hiding emotion under a mask of banter:

"Yes, there *is* something in you! you are a fine girl—that I must tell you."

And for what did I receive such rewards, which filled my heart with pride and joy? Merely for saying that I felt for old Grigory in his love for his little granddaughter; or because the reading of some poem or novel moved me to tears; or because I liked Mozart better than Schulhoff.[2] And I was surprised at my own quickness in guessing what was good and worthy of love, when I certainly did not know then what *was* good and worthy to be loved. Most of my former tastes and habits did not please him; a mere look of his, or a twitch of his eyebrow was enough to show that he did not like what I was trying to say; and I felt at once that my own standard was changed. Sometimes, when he was about to give me a piece of advice, I seemed to know beforehand what he would say. When he looked in my face and asked me a question, his very look would draw out of me the answer he wanted. All my thoughts and feelings of that time were not really mine: they were his thoughts and feelings, which had suddenly become mine and passed into my life and lighted it up. Quite unconsciously I began to look at everything with different eyes—at Katya, the servants, Sonya, myself,

---

2. Julius Schulhoff (1825–98) was a piano virtuoso and a composer of music for the salon.

and my occupations. Books, which I used to read merely to escape boredom, now became one of the chief pleasures of my life, merely because he brought me the books and we read and discussed them together. The lessons I gave to Sonya had been a burdensome obligation which I forced myself to go through from a sense of duty; but, after he was present at a lesson, it became a joy to me to watch Sonya's progress. It used to seem an impossibility to learn a whole piece of music by heart; but now, when I knew that he would hear it and might praise it, I would play a single movement forty times over without stopping, till poor Katya stuffed her ears with cotton, while I was still not weary of it. The same old sonatas seemed quite different in their expression, and came out quite changed and much improved. Even Katya, whom I knew and loved like a second self, became different in my eyes. I now understood for the first time that she was not in the least bound to be the mother, friend, and slave that she was to us. Now I appreciated all the self-sacrifice and devotion of this affectionate creature, and all my obligations to her; and I began to love her even better. It was he too who taught me to take quite a new view of our serfs and servants and maids. It is an absurd confession to make—but I had spent seventeen years among these people and yet knew less about them than about strangers whom I had never seen; it had never once occurred to me that they had their affections and wishes and sorrows, just as I had. Our garden and woods and fields, which I had known for so long, suddenly became new and beautiful to me. He was right in saying that the only certain happiness in life is to live for others. At the time his words seemed strange to me, and I did not understand them; but by degrees this became my conviction, without thinking about it. He revealed to me a whole new world of joys in the present, without changing anything in my life, without adding anything except himself to each impression in my mind. All that had surrounded me from childhood without saying anything to me, suddenly came to life. The mere sight of him made everything begin to speak and press for admittance to my heart, filling it with happiness.

Often during that summer, when I went upstairs to my room and lay down on my bed, the old unhappiness of spring with its desires and hopes for the future gave place to a passionate happiness in the present. Unable to sleep, I often got up and sat on Katya's bed, and told her how perfectly happy I was, though now I realize that this was quite unnecessary, as she could see it for herself. But she told me that she was quite content and perfectly happy, and kissed me. I believed her—it seemed to me so necessary and just that everyone else should be happy. But Katya could think of sleep too; and sometimes, pretending to be angry, she drove me from her bed and went to sleep, while I turned over and over in my mind all that made me so happy. Sometimes I got up and said my prayers over again, praying in my own words and thanking God for all the happiness he had given me.

All was quiet in the room; there was only the even breathing of Katya in her sleep, and the ticking of the clock by her bed, while I turned from side to side and whispered words of prayer, or crossed myself and kissed the cross round my neck. The door was closed and the windows shuttered; perhaps a fly or gnat hung buzzing in the air. I felt a wish never to leave that room—a wish that dawn might never come, that my present frame of mind might never change. I felt that my dreams and thoughts and prayers were live things, living there in the dark with me, hovering about my bed, standing over me. Every thought was his thought, and every feeling his feeling. I did not yet know that this was love; I thought that things might go on like this forever, and that this feeling involved no consequences.

III

One day when the corn was being carried, I went with Katya and Sonya to our favorite seat in the garden, in the shade of the lime-trees and above the valley, beyond which the fields and woods lay open before us. It was three days since Sergey Mikhaylych had been to see us; we were expecting him, all the more because our bailiff reported that he had promised to visit the harvest-field. At two o'clock we saw him ride on to the rye-field. With a smile and a glance at me, Katya ordered peaches and cherries, of which he was very fond, to be brought; then she lay down on the bench and began to doze. I tore off a crooked flat lime-tree branch, which made my hand wet with its juicy leaves and moist bark. Then I fanned Katya with it and went on with my book, breaking off from time to time, to look at the field-path along which he must come. Sonya was making a dolls' house at the root of an old lime-tree. The day was sultry, still, and steamy; clouds were gathering and growing blacker; all morning a thunderstorm had been threatening, and I felt restless, as I always did before thunder. But by afternoon the clouds began to part, the sun sailed out into a clear sky, and only in one quarter was there a faint rumbling. A single heavy cloud, appearing above the horizon and mingling with dust from the fields, was rent from time to time by pale zigzags of lightning which ran down to the ground. It was clear that for to-day the storm would pass off, with us at all events. The road beyond the garden was visible in places, and we could see a procession of high creaking carts moving slowly along it with their load of sheaves, while the empty carts rattled at a faster pace to meet them, with legs swaying and shirts fluttering in them. The thick dust neither dispersed nor settled down—it stood still beyond the fence, and we could see it through the transparent foliage of the garden trees. A little farther off, in the yard, the same voices and creaking of wheels were audible; the same yellow sheaves that had moved slowly past the fence were now flying aloft, and I could see the oval stacks gradually rising higher, and their conspicuous pointed tops, and the laborers swarming upon them. On the dusty field in front more carts were moving and more yellow sheaves were visible; the noise of the carts, with the sound of talking and singing, came to us from a distance. At one side the bare stubble, with strips of fallow covered with wormwood, came more and more into view. Lower down, to the right, the pretty dresses of the women were visible, as they bent down and swung their arms to bind the sheaves. Here the bare stubble looked untidy; but the disorder was cleared by degrees, as the handsome sheaves were arranged at close intervals. It seemed as if summer had suddenly turned to autumn before my eyes. The dust and heat were everywhere, except in our favorite nook in the garden; everywhere in this heat and dust and under the burning sun, laborers carried on their heavy task with talk and noise.

Meanwhile Katya slept so sweetly on our shady bench, beneath her white cambric handkerchief, the juicy black cherries glistened so temptingly on the plate, our dresses were so clean and fresh, the water in the jug was so bright with rainbow colors in the sun, and I felt so happy! "How can I help it?" I thought; "am I to blame for being so happy? And how can I share my happiness? How and to whom can I surrender myself and all my happiness?"

By this time the sun had sunk behind the tops of the birch avenue, the dust was settling on the fields, the distance became clearer and brighter in the slanting light. The clouds had dispersed altogether; I could see through the trees the thatch of three new corn-stacks. The laborers came down off the stacks; the carts hurried past, evidently for the last time, with a loud noise of shouting; the women, with rakes over their shoulders and straw-bands in their belts, walked home past us, singing loudly; still there was no sign of Sergey Mikhaylych, though I had seen him ride down the hill long ago. Suddenly he appeared upon the avenue, coming from a quarter where I was not looking for him. He had walked round by the valley. He came quickly towards me, with his hat off and radiant with high spirits. Seeing that Katya was asleep, he bit his lip, closed his eyes, and advanced on tiptoe; I saw at once that he was in that peculiar mood of unwarranted merriment which I always delighted to see in him, and which we called "wild ecstasy." He was just like a schoolboy playing truant; his whole figure, from head to foot, breathed content, happiness, and boyish frolic.

"Well, young violet, how are you? All right?" he asked in a whisper, coming up to me and taking my hand. Then, in answer to my question, he replied "Oh, I feel splendid to-day, like a boy of thirteen—I want to play horses and climb trees."

"Is it wild ecstasy?" I asked, looking into his laughing eyes, and feeling that his "wild ecstasy" was infecting me.

"Yes," he answered, winking and checking a smile. "But I don't see why you need hit Katerina Karlovna on the nose."

With my eyes on him I had gone on waving the branch, without noticing that I had knocked the handkerchief off Katya's face and was now brushing her with the leaves. I laughed.

"She will say she was awake all the time," I whispered, as if not to awake Katya; but that was not my real reason—it was only that I liked to whisper to him.

He moved his lips in imitation of me, pretending that my voice was too low for him to hear. Catching sight of the dish of cherries, he pretended to steal it, and carried it off to Sonya under the lime-tree, where he sat down on her dolls. Sonya was angry at first, but he soon made his peace with her by starting a game, to see which of them could eat cherries faster.

"If you like, I will send for more cherries," I said; "or let us go ourselves."

He took the dish and set the dolls on it, and the three of us started for the orchard. Sonya ran behind us, laughing and pulling at his coat, to make him surrender the dolls. He gave them up and then turned to me, speaking more seriously.

"You really are a violet," he said, still speaking softly, though there was no longer any fear of waking anybody; "when I came to you out of all that dust and heat and toil, I positively smelt violets at once. But not the sweet violet—you know, that early dark violet that smells of melting snow and spring grass."

"Is the harvest going well?" I asked, in order to hide the happy agitation his words produced in me.

"First-rate! Our laborers are always splendid. The more you know them, the better you like them."

"Yes," I said; "before you came I was watching them from the garden, and suddenly I felt ashamed to be so comfortable myself while they were so hard at work, and so . . ."

He interrupted me, with a kind but grave look: "Don't talk like that, my dear; it's too sacred a matter to talk about lightly. God forbid that you should use fine phrases about it!"

"But it's only to *you* I say this."

"All right, I understand. But what about those cherries?"

The orchard was locked, and no gardener was to be seen: he had sent them all off to help with the harvest. Sonya ran to fetch the key. But he would not wait for her: climbing up a corner of the wall, he raised the net and jumped down on the other side.

His voice came over the wall—"If you want some, give me the dish."

"No," I said; "I want to pick for myself. I shall fetch the key; Sonya won't find it."

But suddenly I felt that I must see what he was doing there and what he looked like—that I must watch his movements while he supposed that no one saw him. Besides just then I was simply unwilling to lose sight of him for a single minute. Running on tiptoe through the nettles to the other side of the orchard where the wall was lower, I climbed on an empty cask, till the top of the wall was on a level with my waist, and then leaned over into the orchard. I looked at the gnarled old trees, with their broad dented leaves and the ripe black cherries hanging straight and heavy among the foliage; then I pushed my head under the net, and from under the knotted bough of an old cherry-tree I caught sight of Sergey Mikhaylych. He evidently thought that I had gone away and that no one was watching him. With his hat off and his eyes shut, he was sitting on the fork of an old tree and carefully rolling into a ball a lump of cherry-tree gum. Suddenly he shrugged his shoulders, opened his eyes, muttered something, and smiled. Both words and smile were so unlike him that I felt ashamed of myself for eavesdropping. It seemed to me that he had said, "Masha!" "Impossible," I thought. "Darling Masha!" he said again, in a lower and more tender voice. There was no possible doubt about the two words this time. My heart beat hard, and such a passionate joy—illicit joy, as I felt—took hold of me, that I clutched at the wall, fearing to fall and betray myself. Startled by the sound of my movement, he looked around—he dropped his eyes instantly, and his face turned red, even scarlet, like a child's. He tried to speak, but in vain; again and again his face positively flamed up. Still he smiled as he looked at me, and I smiled too. Then his whole face grew radiant with happiness. He had ceased to be the old uncle who spoiled or scolded me; he was a man on my own level, who loved and feared me as I loved and feared him. We looked at one another without speaking. But suddenly he frowned; the smile and light in his eyes disappeared, and he resumed his cold paternal tone, just as if we were doing something wrong and he was repenting and calling on me to repent.

"You had better get down, or you'll hurt yourself," he said; "and fix your hair; just think what you look like!"

"What makes him pretend? what makes him want to hurt me?" I wondered in my vexation. And the same instant brought an irresistible desire to upset his composure again and test my power over him.

"No," I said; "I mean to pick for myself." I caught hold of the nearest branch and climbed to the top of the wall; then, before he had time to catch me, I jumped down on the other side.

"What foolish things you do!" he muttered, flushing again and trying to hide his confusion under a pretense of annoyance; "you might really have hurt yourself. But how do you mean to get out of this?"

He was even more confused than before, but this time his confusion frightened rather than pleased me. It infected me too and made me blush; avoiding his gaze and not knowing what to say, I began to pick cherries though I had nothing to put them in. I reproached myself, I repented for what I had done, I was frightened; I felt that I had lost his good opinion forever by my folly. Both of us were silent and embarrassed. From this difficult situation Sonya rescued us by running back with the key in her hand. For some time we both addressed our conversation to her and said nothing to each other. When we returned to Katya, who assured us that she had never been asleep and was listening all the time, I calmed down, and he tried to drop into his fatherly patronizing manner again, but I was not taken in by it. A discussion which we had had some days before came back clear before me.

Katya had been saying that it was easier for a man to be in love and declare his love than for a woman.

"A man may say that he's in love, and a woman can't," she said.

"I disagree," he said; "a man has no business to say, and can't say, that he's in love."

"Why not?" I asked.

"Because it can never be true. What sort of a revelation is it, that a man is in love? A man seems to think that whenever he says the word, something will go pop!—some miracle will occur, signs and wonders, with big guns firing at once! In my opinion," he went on, "whoever solemnly utters the words 'I love you' is either deceiving himself or, even worse, deceiving others."

"How then is a woman to know that a man is in love with her, unless he tells her?" asked Katya.

"That I don't know," he answered; "every man has his own way of telling things. If the feeling exists, it will come out somehow. When I read novels, I always fancy the crestfallen look of Lieutenant Strelsky or Alfred,[3] when he says, 'I love you, Eleanora,' and expects something wonderful to happen at once; yet no change at all takes place in either of them—their eyes, noses and their whole selves remain exactly as they were."

Even then I had felt that this banter covered something serious that had reference to me. But Katya resented his disrespectful treatment of the heroes in novels.

"You're never serious," she said; "but tell me truthfully, have you never told a woman that you loved her?"

"Never, and never gone down on one knee," he answered, laughing; "and I never will."

I now recalled this conversation, and reflected that there was no need for him to tell me that he loved me. "I know he loves me," I thought, "and all his attempts to seem indifferent will not change my opinion."

He said little to me throughout the evening, but in every word he said to Katya and Sonya and in every look and movement of his I saw love and felt no doubt of it. I was only annoyed and sorry for him, that he thought it necessary still to hide his feelings and feign coldness, when

---

3. These references cannot be identified.

it was all so clear, and when it would have been so simple and easy to
be boundlessly happy. But my jumping down to him in the orchard
weighed on me like a crime. I kept feeling that he would cease to respect
me and was angry with me.

After tea I went to the piano, and he followed me.

"Play something for me—it is long since I heard you," he said, coming
up to me in the parlor.

"I was just going to," I said. Then I looked straight in his face and
said quickly, "Sergey Mikhaylych, you're not angry with me, are you?"

"What for?" he asked.

"For not obeying you this afternoon," I said, blushing.

He understood me: he shook his head and made a grimace, which
implied that I deserved a scolding but that he was unable to give it.

"So it's all right, and we're friends again?" I said, sitting down at the
piano.

"Of course!" he said.

In the drawing-room, a large lofty room, there were only two lighted
candles on the piano, the rest of the room remaining in half-darkness.
Outside the open windows the summer night was bright. All was silent,
except when the sound of Katya's footsteps in the unlighted parlor was
heard occasionally, or when his horse, which was tied up under the
window, snorted or stamped his hoof on the burdocks that grew there.
He sat behind me, where I could not see him; but everywhere—in the
half-darkness of the room, in every sound, in myself—I felt his presence.
Every look, every movement of his, though I could not see them, found
an echo in my heart. I played a sonata of Mozart's which he had brought
me and which I had learnt in his presence and for him. I was not
thinking at all of what I was playing, but I believe I played it well, and
thought he was pleased. I was conscious of his pleasure, and conscious
too, though I never looked at him, of his gaze fixed on me from behind.
Still moving my fingers mechanically, I turned around quite involuntarily and looked at him. The night had grown brighter, and his head
stood out on a background of darkness. He was sitting with it propped
on his hands, and his eyes shone as they gazed at me. Catching his
look, I smiled and stopped playing. He smiled too and shook his head
reproachfully at the music, urging me to go on. When I stopped, the
moon had grown brighter and was riding high in the heavens; the faint
light of the candles was supplemented by a new silvery light which came
in through the windows and fell on the floor. Katya called out that it
was really too bad—that I had stopped at the best part of the piece, and
that I was playing badly. But he declared that I had never played so
well; then he began to walk about the rooms—through the drawing-
room to the unlighted parlor and back to the drawing-room again, and
each time he looked at me and smiled. I smiled too; I even wanted to
laugh with no reason; I was so happy at something that had happened

that day. Katya and I were standing by the piano; each time he vanished through the drawing-room door, I started kissing her in my favorite place, the soft part of her neck under the chin; and each time he came back, I made a solemn face and barely refrained from laughing.

"What's the matter with her to-day?" Katya asked him.

He only smiled at me without answering; he knew what was the matter with me.

"Just look what a night it is!" he called out from the parlor, where he had stopped by the open French window looking into the garden.

We joined him; it really was such a night as I have never seen since. The full moon shone above the house and behind us, so that we could not see it, and half the shadow, thrown by the roof and pillars of the house and by the veranda awning, lay slanting and foreshortened on the gravel-path and the strip of turf beyond. Everything else was bright and saturated with the silver of the dew and the moonlight. The broad garden-path, on one side of which the shadows of the dahlias and their supports lay aslant, all bright and cold, and shining on the uneven gravel, ran on till it vanished in the mist. Through the trees the roof of the greenhouse shone bright, and a growing mist rose from the valley. The lilac-bushes, already partly leafless, were all bright to the center. Each flower was distinguishable, and all were drenched with dew. In the avenues light and shade were so mingled that they looked, not like paths and trees but like transparent houses, swaying and moving. To our right, in the shadow of the house, everything was black, indistinguishable, and uncanny. But all the brighter for the surrounding darkness was the top of a poplar, with a fantastic crown of leaves, which for some strange reason remained there close to the house, towering into the bright light, instead of flying away into the dim distance, into the retreating dark-blue of the sky.

"Let's go for a walk," I said.

Katya agreed, but said I must put on my galoshes.

"I don't want them, Katya," I said; "Sergey Mikhaylych will give me his arm."

As if that would prevent me from wetting my feet! But to the three of us this seemed perfectly natural at the time. Though he never used to offer me his arm, I now took it of my own accord, and he saw nothing strange in it. We all went down from the veranda together. That whole world, that sky, that garden, that air, were different from those that I knew.

We were walking along an avenue, and it seemed to me, whenever I looked ahead, that we could go no farther in the same direction, that the world of the possible ended there, and that the whole scene must remain fixed for ever in its beauty. But still we moved on, and the magic wall kept parting to let us in; still we found the familiar garden with trees and paths and withered leaves. And we really were walking along paths, treading on patches of light and shade; a withered leaf really was crackling under my foot, and a live twig brushing my face. And that really was he, walking steadily and slowly at my side, carefully supporting my arm; that really was Katya walking beside us with her creaking shoes. And that must be the moon in the sky, shining down on us through motionless branches.

But at each step the magic wall closed up again behind us and in front; I ceased to believe in the possibility of advancing farther—I ceased to believe in the reality of it all.

"Oh, there's a frog!" cried Katya.

"Who said that? and why?" I thought. But then I realized it was Katya, and that she was afraid of frogs. Then I looked at the ground and saw a little frog which gave a jump and then stood still in front of me, while its tiny shadow was reflected on the shining clay of the path.

"You're not afraid of frogs, are you?" he asked.

I turned and looked at him. Just where we stood there was a gap of one tree in the lime-avenue, and I could see his face clearly—it was so handsome and so happy!

Though he had asked about my fear of frogs, I knew that he meant to say, "I love you, my dear!" "I love you, I love you" was repeated by his look, by his arm; the light, the shadow, and the air all repeated the same words.

We had gone all around the garden. Katya's short steps had kept up with us, but now she was tired and out of breath. She said it was time to go in; I felt very sorry for her. "Poor thing!" I thought; "why does not she feel as we do? why aren't we all young and happy, like this night and like him and me?"

We went in, but it was a long time before he went away, though the cocks had crowed, and everyone in the house was asleep; his horse, tethered under the window, snorted continually and stamped his hoof on the burdocks. Katya never reminded us of the hour, and we sat talking of the merest trifles and not thinking of the time, till it was past two. The cocks were crowing for the third time and dawn was breaking when he rode away. He said good-bye as usual and made no special allusion; but I knew that from that day on he was mine, and that I should never lose him. As soon as I had confessed to myself that I loved him, I took Katya into my confidence. She rejoiced in the news and was touched by my telling her; but she was actually able—poor thing!—to go to bed and sleep! For me, I walked for a long, long time about the veranda; then I went down to the garden, where, recalling each word, each movement, I walked along the same avenues through which I had walked with him. I did not sleep at all that night, and saw sunrise and early dawn for the first time in my life. Never again did I see such a night and morning. "But why doesn't he tell me plainly that he loves me?" I thought; "what makes him invent obstacles and call himself old, when everything is so simple and splendid? What makes him waste this golden time which may never return? Let him say 'I love you'—say it in plain words; let him take my hand in his, bend over it and say 'I love you.' Let him blush and look down before me; then I will tell him all. No! not tell him, but throw my arms round him and press close to him and weep." But then a thought came to me—"What if I am mistaken and he doesn't love me?"

I was startled by this fear—God knows where it might have led me. I recalled his embarrassment and mine, when I jumped down to him in the orchard; my heart grew very heavy. Tears gushed from my eyes, and I began to pray. A strange thought occurred to me, calming me and bringing with it hope. I resolved to begin fasting that day, to take Communion on my birthday, and on that same day to be betrothed to him.

How this result would come to pass I had no idea; but from that moment I believed and felt sure it would be so. The dawn had come and the laborers were getting up when I went back to my room.

IV

Since the Feast of the Assumption fell in August, no one in the house was surprised by my intention to fast.

During the whole week he never once came to see us; but, far from being surprised, vexed, or made uneasy by his absence, I was glad of it—I did not expect him until my birthday. Each day during that week I got up early. While the horses were being harnessed, I walked in the garden alone, turning over in my mind the sins of the day before, and considering what I must do today, so as to be satisfied with my day and not spoil it by a single sin. It seemed so easy then to abstain from sin altogether; only the slightest effort seemed necessary. When the horses came around, I got into the carriage with Katya or one of the maids, and we drove to church two miles away. While entering the church, I always recalled the prayer for those who "come unto the Temple in fear of God," and tried to get into just that frame of mind when mounting the two grass-grown steps up to the building. At that hour there were not more than a dozen worshippers—household servants or peasant women keeping the Fast. They bowed to me, and I returned their bows with studied humility. Then, with what seemed a great effort of courage, I went myself and got candles from the man who kept them, an old soldier and an Elder; I placed the candles before the icons. Through the central door of the altar-screen I could see the altar-cloth which my mother had made; on the screen were two angels which had seemed so big when I was little, and the dove with a golden halo which had fascinated me long ago. Behind the choir stood the old battered font, where I had been christened myself and had stood as godmother to so many of the servants' children. The old priest came out, wearing a cope made of the pall that had covered my father's coffin; he began to read in the same voice that I had heard all my life—at services held in our house, at Sonya's christening, at memorial services for my father, and at my mother's funeral. The same old quavering voice of the deacon rose in the choir; and the same old woman, whom I could remember at every service in that church, crouched by the wall, fixing her streaming eyes on an icon in the choir, pressing her folded fingers against her faded kerchief, and muttering with her toothless gums. These objects were no longer merely curious to me, merely interesting from old recollections—each had become important and sacred in my eyes and seemed charged with profound meaning. I listened to each word of the prayers and tried to suit my feeling to it; and if I failed to understand, I prayed silently that God would enlighten me, or made up a prayer of my own in place of what I had failed to catch. When the penitential prayers were repeated, I recalled my past life, and that innocent childish past seemed so black to me when compared to the present brightness of my soul, that I wept and was horrified at myself; but I felt that all those sins would be forgiven, and that if my sins had been even greater, my repentance would be all the sweeter. At the end of the service when the priest said, "The blessing of the Lord be upon you!" I seemed to feel an immediate sensation of physical well-being, of a mysterious light and warmth that instantly filled my heart. The service over, the priest came and asked me whether he should come to our house to say Mass, and what hour would suit me; I thanked him for the suggestion, intended, as I thought, to please me, but said that I would come to church instead, walking or driving.

"Is that not too much trouble?" he asked. And I was at a loss for an answer, fearing to commit a sin of pride.

After Mass, if Katya was not with me, I always sent the carriage home and walked back alone, bowing humbly to all who passed, and trying to find an opportunity of giving help or advice. I was eager to sacrifice myself for someone, to help in lifting a fallen cart, to rock a child's cradle, to yield the path to others by stepping into the mud. One evening I heard the bailiff report to Katya that Simon, one of our serfs, had come to beg some boards to make a coffin for his daughter, and a ruble to pay the priest for the funeral; the bailiff had given what he asked. "Are they as poor as that?" I asked. "Very poor, Miss," the bailiff answered; "they have no salt for their food." My heart ached to hear this, and yet I felt a kind of pleasure too. Pretending to Katya that I was merely going for a walk, I ran upstairs, got out all my money (it was very little, but it was all I had), crossed myself, and started off alone, through the veranda and the garden, on my way to Simon's hut. It stood at the end of the village, and no one saw me as I went up to the window, placed the money on the sill, and tapped on the pane. Someone came

out, making the door creak, and called to me; but I hurried home, cold
and shaking with fear like a criminal. Katya asked where I had been and
what was the matter with me; but I did not answer, and did not even
understand what she was saying. Everything suddenly seemed so petty
and insignificant. I locked myself up in my own room, and for a long
time walked up and down alone, unable to do anything, unable to think,
unable to understand my own feelings. I thought about the joy of the
whole family, and about what they would say of their benefactor; I felt
sorry that I had not given them the money myself. I also thought of
what Sergey Mikhaylych would say, if he knew what I had done; I was
glad to think that no one would ever find out. I was so happy, and felt
myself and everyone else so bad, and yet was so kindly disposed to myself
and all the world, that the thought of death came to me as a dream of
happiness. I smiled and prayed and wept, and felt at that moment a
burning passion of love for all the world, myself included. Between
services I used to read the Gospel; the book became more and more
intelligible to me, and the story of that divine life simpler and more
touching; the depths of thought and feeling I found in studying it became
more awful and impenetrable. On the other hand, how clear and simple
everything seemed to me when I rose from the study of this book and
looked again on life around me and reflected on it! It was so difficult,
I felt, to lead a bad life, and so simple to love everyone and be loved.
All were so kind and gentle to me; even Sonya, whose lessons I had not
broken off, was quite different—trying to understand and please me and
not to anger me. Everyone treated me as I treated them. Thinking over
my enemies, of whom I must ask pardon before confession, I could only
remember one—one of our neighbors, a girl, whom I had made fun of
in company a year ago, and who had ceased to visit us. I wrote to her,
confessing my fault and asking her forgiveness. She replied that she
forgave me and wished me to forgive her. I cried for joy over her simple
words, and saw in them, at the time, a deep and touching feeling. My
old nurse cried, when I asked her to forgive me. "What makes them all
so kind to me? what have I done to deserve their love?" I asked myself.
Sergey Mikhaylych would come into my mind, and I thought about
him for a long time. I could not help it, and I did not consider these
thoughts sinful. But my thoughts of him were quite different from what
they had been on the night when I first realized I loved him: he seemed
to me now like a second self, and became a part of every plan for the
future. The inferiority which I had always felt in his presence had
vanished entirely: I felt myself his equal, and could understand him
thoroughly from the moral elevation I had reached. What had seemed
strange in him was now quite clear to me. Now I could see what he
meant by saying that to live for others was the only true happiness, and
I agreed with him entirely. I believed that our life together would be
endlessly happy and untroubled. I looked forward, not to foreign travel

or fashionable society or display, but to a quite different scene—quiet family life in the country, with constant self-sacrifice, constant mutual love, and constant recognition in all things of the kind hand of Providence.

I carried out my plan of taking Communion on my birthday. When I came back from church that day, my heart so swelled with happiness that I was afraid of life, afraid of any feeling that might impinge on that happiness. We had hardly left the carriage for the steps in front of the house, when there was a sound of wheels on the bridge, and I saw Sergey Mikhaylych drive up in his well-known trap. He congratulated me, and we went together to the parlor. Never since I had known him had I been so much at my ease with him and so self-possessed as on that morning. I felt in myself a whole new world, out of his reach and beyond his comprehension. I was not conscious of the slightest embarrassment in speaking to him. He must have understood the cause of this feeling; he was tender and gentle beyond his wont and showed a kind of reverent consideration for me. When I headed for the piano, he locked it and put the key in his pocket.

"Don't spoil your present mood," he said, "you have the sweetest of all music in your soul just now."

I was grateful for his words, and yet I was not quite pleased at his understanding too easily and clearly what ought to have been an exclusive secret in my heart. At dinner he said that he had come to congratulate me and also to say good-bye; tomorrow he must go to Moscow. He looked at Katya as he spoke; but then he stole a glance at me, and I saw that he was afraid he might detect signs of emotion on my face. But I was neither surprised nor agitated; I did not even ask whether he would be away long. I knew he would say this, and I knew that he would not go. How did I know? I cannot explain that to myself now; but on that memorable day it seemed that I knew everything that had been and would be. It was like a delightful dream, when all that happens seems to have happened already and to be quite familiar; it will all happen over again, and one knows that it will happen.

He meant to go away right after dinner; but, as Katya was tired after church and went to lie down for a little, he had to wait until she woke up in order to say good-bye to her. The sun shone into the drawing-room, and we went out to the veranda. When we were seated, I began at once, quite calmly, the conversation that was bound to fix the fate of my heart. I began to speak, no sooner and no later, but at the very moment when we sat down, before our talk had taken any turn or color that might have hindered me from saying what I meant to say. I cannot tell myself where it came from—my coolness, determination, and preciseness of expression. It was as if something independent of my will was speaking through my lips. He sat opposite me with his elbows resting on the rails of the veranda; he pulled a lilac-branch towards him and stripped the leaves off it. When I began to speak, he let the branch go and leaned his head on one hand. His attitude might have shown either perfect calmness or strong emotion.

"Why are you going?" I asked, significantly, deliberately, and looking straight at him.

He did not answer at once.

"Business!" he muttered at last and dropped his eyes.

I realized how difficult he found it to lie to me, especially in reply to such a frank question.

"Listen," I said; "you know what to-day is to me, how important for many reasons. If I question you, it is not to show an interest in your affairs (you know that I have become intimate with you and fond of you)—I ask you this question, because I *must* know the answer. Why are you going?"

"It is very hard to tell you the true reason," he said. "During this week I have thought much about you and about myself, and have decided that I must go. You understand why; and if you care for me, you will ask no questions." He put up a hand to rub his forehead and cover his eyes. "I find it very difficult. . . . But you will understand."

My heart began to beat fast.

"I cannot understand you," I said; "I *cannot! You* must tell me; in God's name and for the sake of this day tell me what you please, and I shall hear it with calmness," I said.

He changed his position, glanced at me, and again drew the lilac-twig towards him.

"Well!" he said, after a short silence in a voice that tried in vain to seem steady, "it is a foolish matter and impossible to put into words; I feel the difficulty, but I will try to explain it to you," he added, frowning as if in bodily pain.

"Well?" I said.

"Just imagine the existence of a man—let us call him A—who has left youth far behind, and of a woman whom we may call B, who is young and happy and has seen nothing as yet of life or the world. Family circumstances of various kinds brought them together; he grew to love her as a daughter, and had no fear that his love would change its nature."

He stopped, but I did not interrupt him.

"But he forgot that B was so young, that life was still all a game to her," he went on with a sudden swiftness and determination, without looking at me, "and that it was easy to fall in love with her in a different way, and that this would amuse her. He made a mistake and was suddenly aware of another feeling, as heavy as remorse, making its way into his heart, and he was afraid. He was afraid that their old friendly relations would be destroyed, and he made up his mind to go away before that happened." As he said this, he began to rub his eyes again with a pretense of indifference, and to close them.

"Why was he afraid to love differently?" I asked very softly; but I restrained my emotion and spoke in an even voice. He evidently thought I was not serious, for he answered as if he were hurt.

"You are young, and I am not. You want amusement, while I want something different. Amuse yourself, if you like, but not with me. If you do, I shall take it seriously; then I shall be unhappy, and you will repent. That is what A said," he added; "however, this is all nonsense; but you understand why I am going. Let's not continue this conversation. Please!"

"No! no!" I said, "we must continue it," and tears began to tremble in my voice. "Did he love her, or nòt?"

He did not answer.

"If he did not love her, why did he treat her as a child and pretend to her?" I asked.

"Yes, A behaved badly," he interrupted me quickly; "but it all came to an end and they parted friends."

"This is horrible! Is there no other ending?" I said with great effort, and then felt afraid of what I had said.

"Yes, there is," he said, showing a face full of emotion and looking straight at me. "There are two different endings. But, for God's sake, listen to me quietly and don't interrupt. Some say"—here he stood up and smiled with a look that was heavy with pain—"some say that A lost his head, fell passionately in love with B, and told her so. But she only laughed. To her it was all a joke, but to him it was a matter of life and death."

I shuddered and tried to interrupt him—to say that he must not dare speak for me; but he stopped me, laying his hand on mine.

"Wait!" he said, and his voice shook. "The other story is that she took pity on him, and fancied, poor child, from her ignorance of the world, that she really could love him, and so consented to be his wife. And he, in his madness, believed it—believed that his whole life could begin anew; but she herself saw that she had deceived him and he had deceived her. . . . But let us drop the subject finally," he ended, clearly unable to say anymore; then he began to walk up and down in silence before me.

Though he had asked that the subject should be dropped, I saw that his whole soul was hanging on my answer. I tried to speak, but the pain in my heart kept me silent. I glanced at him—he was pale and his lower lip trembled. I felt sorry for him. With a sudden effort I broke the bonds of silence which had held me fast, and began to speak in a low inward voice, which I feared would break every moment.

"There is a third ending to the story," I said, and then paused, but he said nothing; "the third ending is that he did not love her, but hurt her, hurt her, and thought that he was right; then he left her and was actually proud of himself. You have been pretending, not I; I have loved you since the first day we met, loved you," I repeated, and at the word "loved" my low inward voice changed, without my own intention, to a wild cry which frightened even me.

He stood pale before me, his lip trembled more and more violently, and two tears stood upon his cheeks.

"It's wrong!" I almost screamed, feeling that I was choking with angry tears. "Why do you do it?" I cried, and got up to leave him.

But he would not let me go. His head was resting on my knees, his lips were kissing my trembling hands, and his tears were falling on them. "My God! if I had only known!" he whispered.

"Why? why?" I kept on repeating, but in my heart there was happiness, happiness which had now come back, after almost departing for ever.

Five minutes later Sonya was rushing upstairs to Katya and proclaiming all over the house that Masha intended to marry Sergey Mikhaylych.

V

There were no reasons for putting off our wedding, and neither he nor I wished for delay. Katya, it is true, thought we ought to go to Moscow, to buy and order wedding-clothes; and his mother tried to insist that, before the wedding, he must order a new carriage, buy new furniture, and re-paper the whole house. But together we two prevailed: all these things, if they were really indispensable, should be done afterwards, and we should be married within a fortnight after my birthday, quietly, without wedding-clothes, without a party, without best men and supper and champagne, and all the other conventional features of a wedding. He told me how dissatisfied his mother was that there would be no band, no pile of luggage, no renovation of the whole house—so unlike her own marriage which had cost thirty thousand rubles; and he told of the solemn and secret consultations which she held in her store-room with her housekeeper, Maryushka, rummaging through chests and discussing carpets, curtains, and trays as indispensable conditions of our happiness. At our house Katya did just the same with my old nurse, Kuzminichna. It was impossible to treat the matter lightly with Katya. She was firmly convinced that he and I, when discussing our future, were merely talking the sentimental nonsense natural to people in our position; and that our real future happiness depended on the hemming of table-cloths and napkins and the proper cutting and stitching of under-clothing. Several times a day secret information passed between the two houses, to communicate what was going forward in each; and though external relations between Katya and his mother were most affectionate, a slightly hostile, though very subtle diplomacy was already perceptible in their dealings. I now became more intimate with Tatyana Semenovna, Sergey Mikhaylych's mother, an old-fashioned lady, strict and formal in the management of her household. Her son loved her, not merely because she was his mother: he thought her the best, cleverest, kindest, and most affectionate woman in the world. She was always kind to us and to me especially, and was glad that her son would be getting married; but when I was with her after our engagement, I always felt she wished me to understand that, in her opinion, her son might have looked higher, and that it would be as well for me to keep that in mind. I understood her meaning perfectly and thought her quite right.

During that fortnight he and I met every day. He came to dinner regularly and stayed till midnight. But though he said—and I knew he was speaking the truth—that he had no life apart from me, he never spent the whole day with me, and tried to go on with his ordinary occupations. Our outward relations remained unchanged to the very day of our marriage: we went on using the formal form of address with each other; he did not even kiss my hand; he did not seek, but even avoided, opportunities for being alone with me. It was as if he feared to yield to the harmful excess of tenderness he felt. I don't know which of us had changed; but I now felt myself entirely his equal; I no longer found in him the pretense of simplicity which had displeased me earlier; and I often delighted to see in him, not a grown man inspiring respect and awe, but a loving and wildly happy child. "How mistaken I was about him!" I often thought; "he is just such another human being like myself!" It seemed now, that his whole character was before me and that I thoroughly understood it. How simple every feature of his character was, how congenial to my own! Even his plans for our future life together were my plans, only more clearly and better expressed in his words.

The weather was inclement, and we spent most of our time indoors. The corner between the piano and the window was the scene of our most intimate talks. The candle-light was reflected on the blackness of the window near us; from time to time drops struck the glistening pane and rolled down. The rain pattered on the roof; the water splashed in a puddle under the spout; it felt damp near the window; but our corner seemed all the brighter, warmer, and happier for that.

"Do you know, there is something I have long wished to say to you," he began one night when we were sitting up late in our corner; "I was thinking of it all the time you were playing."

"Don't say it, I know all about it," I replied.

"All right! mum's the word!"

"No! what is it?" I asked.

"Well, it's this. You remember the story I told you about A and B?"

"Indeed I do! What a stupid story! Lucky that it ended as it did!"

"Yes. I very nearly destroyed my happiness by my own act. You saved me. But the main thing is that I was always telling lies then; I'm ashamed of it, and I want to have my say now."

"Please don't! you really mustn't!"

"Don't be frightened," he said, smiling. "I only want to justify myself. When I began then, I meant to argue."

"It's always a mistake to argue," I said.

"Yes, I argued badly. After all my disappointments and mistakes in life, I told myself firmly when I came to the country this year, that love was no longer for me, that all I had to do was grow old decently. So for a long time, I was unable to clarify my feeling towards you, or to discern where it might lead me. I hoped, and I didn't hope: at one time I thought you were playing with me; at another I felt sure of you but could not decide what to do. But after that evening, you remember, when we walked in the garden at night, I got alarmed: the present happiness seemed too great to be real. What if I allowed myself to hope and then failed? Of course I was thinking only of myself, for I am disgustingly selfish."

He stopped and looked at me.

"But it was not all nonsense that I said then. It was possible and right for me to have fears. I take so much from you and can give so little. You're still a child, a bud that has yet to open; you have never been in love before, and I . . ."

"Yes, do tell the truth . . .," I began, and then stopped, afraid of his answer. "No, never mind," I added.

"Have I been in love before? is that it?" he said, guessing my thoughts at once. "That I can tell you. No, never before—nothing at all like what I feel now." But a sudden painful recollection seemed to flash across his mind. "No," he said sadly; "in this too I need your compassion, in order to have the right to love you. Well, was I not bound to think twice before saying that I loved you? What do I give you? love, no doubt."

"And is that little?" I asked, looking him in the face.

"Yes, my dear, it is little to give *you*," he continued; "you have youth and beauty. I often lie awake at night from happiness, and all the time I think of our future life together. I have lived through much, and now I think I have found what is needed for happiness. A quiet secluded life in the country, with the possibility of being useful to people to whom it is easy to do good, and who are not accustomed to have it done to them; then work which one hopes may be of some use; then rest, nature, books, music, love for one's neighbor—such is my idea of happiness. And then, on the top of all that, you for a mate, and children, perhaps— what more can the heart of man desire?"

"It should be enough," I said.

"Enough for me whose youth is over," he went on, "but not for you. Life is still before you, and you will perhaps seek happiness, and perhaps find it, in something different. Now you think that this is happiness, because you love me."

"You're wrong," I said; "I have always desired just that quiet domestic life and prized it. You only say just what I have thought."

He smiled.

"So you think, my dear; but that's not enough for you. You have youth and beauty," he repeated thoughtfully.

But I was angry because he doubted me and seemed to throw my youth and beauty in my face.

"Why do you love me then?" I asked angrily; "for my youth or for myself?"

"I don't know, but I do love you," he answered, looking at me with his attentive and attractive gaze.

I did not reply and looked into his eyes involuntarily. Suddenly a strange thing happened: first I ceased to see what was around me; then his face seemed to vanish till only his eyes were left, shining over against mine; next his eyes seemed to be in my own head, and then all became confused—I could see nothing and was forced to shut my own eyes, in order to break loose from the feeling of pleasure and fear which his gaze was producing in me . . .

The day before our wedding-day, the weather cleared up towards evening. The rains which had begun in summer gave way to clear weather, and we had our first autumn evening, bright and cold. It was a wet, cold, shining world, and the garden showed for the first time the spaciousness, color, and bareness of autumn. The sky was clear, cold, and pale. I went to bed happy in the thought that to-morrow, our wedding-day, would be fine.

I awoke with the sun, and the thought that this very day . . . was somehow alarming and surprising. I went out into the garden. The sun had just risen and shone fitfully through the meager yellow leaves of the lime avenue. The path was strewn with rustling leaves, clusters of mountain-ash berries hung red and wrinkled on the boughs, with a sprinkling of frost-bitten crumpled leaves; the dahlias were black and wrinkled. The first frost lay like silver on the pale green grass and on the broken burdock plants around the house. In the clear cold sky there was not, and could not be, a single cloud.

"Can it possibly be to-day?" I asked myself, incredulous of my own happiness. "Is it possible that I shall wake tomorrow, not here but in that strange house with the pillars? Is it possible that I shall never again wait for his coming and meet him, and sit up late with Katya to talk about him? Shall I never sit with him beside the piano in our drawing-room? never see him off and feel uneasy about him on dark nights?" But I remembered that he promised yesterday to pay a last visit, and that Katya had insisted on my trying on my wedding-dress, and had said "For to-morrow." I believed for a moment that it was all real, and then doubted again. "Can it be that after to-day I shall be living there with a mother-in-law, without Nadëzha or old Grigory or Katya? Shall I go to bed without kissing my old nurse good-night and hearing her say, while she makes the sign of the cross over me out of her old custom, 'Good-night, Miss'? Shall I never again teach Sonya and play with her and knock on her wall to her in the morning and hear her hearty laugh? Shall I become from to-day someone that I myself no longer know? and is a new world, that will realize my hopes and desires, opening up before

me? and will that new world last for ever?" Alone with these thoughts
I was depressed and eager for his arrival. He came early, and it required
his presence to convince me that I should really be his wife that very
day, and the prospect ceased to frighten me.

Before dinner we walked to the church, to attend a memorial service
for my father.

"If only he were living now!" I thought as we were returning and I
leant silently on the arm of him who had been the dearest friend of the
object of my thoughts. During the service, while I pressed my forehead
against the cold stone of the chapel floor, I recalled my father so vividly;
I was so convinced that he understood me and approved my choice,
that I felt as if his spirit were still hovering over us and blessing me.
And my recollections and hopes, my joy and sadness, made one solemn
and satisfied feeling which was in harmony with the fresh still air, the
silence, the bare fields and pale sky, from which the bright but powerless
rays, trying in vain to burn my cheek, fell over all the landscape. My
companion seemed to understand and share my feeling. He walked
slowly and silently; and his face, at which I glanced from time to time,
expressed the same serious mood between joy and sorrow which I shared
with nature.

Suddenly he turned to me, and I saw that he intended to speak.
"Suppose he starts talking about some other subject than that which is
in my mind?" I thought. But he began to speak of my father and did
not even name him.

"He once said to me in jest, 'you should marry my Masha,' " he began.

"He would have been happy now," I answered, pressing the arm
closer which held mine.

"You were a child then," he went on, looking into my eyes; "I loved
those eyes then and used to kiss them only because they were like his,
never thinking they would be so dear to me for their own sake. I used
to call you Masha then."

"I want you to use the familiar form of address to me," I said.

"I was just going to," he answered; "I feel for the first time that *you
are* entirely mine"; and his calm happy gaze that drew me to him rested
on me.

We went on along the path over the beaten and trampled stubble;
our voices and footsteps were the only sounds. On one side the brownish
stubble stretched over a hollow to a distant leafless wood; across it at
some distance a peasant was noiselessly ploughing a black strip which
grew wider and wider. A herd of horses scattered under the hill seemed
close to us. On the other side, as far as the garden and our house peeping
through the trees, a field of winter corn, thawed by the sun, showed
black with occasional patches of green. The winter sun shone over
everything, and everything was covered with long gossamer spider's webs,

which floated in the air round us, lay on the frost-dried stubble, and got into our eyes, hair, and clothes. When we spoke, the sound of our voices hung in the motionless air above us, as if we two were alone in the whole world—alone under that azure vault, in which the beams of the winter sun played and flashed without scorching.

I too wished to use familiar forms to him, but I felt ashamed.

"Why *do you* walk so fast?" I said quickly and almost in a whisper; I could not help blushing.

He slackened his pace, and the gaze he turned on me was even more affectionate, cheerful, and happy.

At home we found that his mother and the inevitable guests had already arrived, and I was never alone with him again till we came out of church to drive to Nikolskoe.

The church was nearly empty: I just caught a glimpse of his mother standing up straight on a mat by the choir and of Katya wearing a cap with purple ribbons and with tears on her cheeks, and of two or three of our servants looking curiously at me. I did not look at him, but felt his presence there beside me. I attended to the words of the prayers and repeated them, but they found no echo in my heart. Unable to pray, I looked listlessly at the icons, the candles, the embroidered cross on the priest's cope, the screen, and the window, but took nothing in. I only felt that something strange was being done to me. At last the priest turned to us with the cross in his hand, congratulated us, and said, "I christened you and by God's mercy have lived to marry you." Katya and his mother kissed us, and Grigory's voice was heard, calling for the carriage. But I was only frightened and disappointed: everything was over, but nothing extraordinary, nothing worthy of the Sacrament I had just received, had taken place in myself. He and I exchanged kisses, but the kiss seemed strange and not expressive of our feeling. "Is this all?" I wondered. We left the church; the sound of wheels reverberated under the vaulted roof and the fresh air blew on my face. He put on his hat and helped me into the carriage. Through the window I could see a frosty moon with a halo round it. He sat down beside me and shut the door after him. I felt a sudden pang. His assurance seemed insulting to me. Katya called out that I should put something on my head; the wheels rumbled on the stone, then moved along the soft road, and we were off. Huddling in a corner, I looked out at the distant fields and the road flying past in the cold glitter of the moon. Without looking at him, I felt his presence beside me. "Is this all I got from the moment, of which I expected so much?" I thought; and still it seemed humiliating and insulting to be sitting alone with him, and so close. I turned to him, intending to speak; but the words would not come, as if my love had vanished, giving place to a feeling of mortification and alarm.

"Till this moment I did not believe it was possible," he said in a low voice in answer to my look.

"But I'm afraid somehow," I said.

"Afraid of me, my dear?" he asked, taking my hand and bending over it.

My hand lay lifeless in his, and the cold at my heart was painful.

"Yes," I whispered.

But at that moment my heart began to beat faster, my hand trembled and pressed his; I grew hot, my eyes sought his in the half-darkness, and all at once I felt that I did not fear him, that this fear was love—a new love still tenderer and stronger than the old. I felt that I was entirely his, and that I was happy in his power over me.

Part II

I

Days, weeks, two whole months of seclusion in the country slipped by unnoticed, as we thought then; and yet those two months comprised feelings, emotions, and happiness, sufficient for a lifetime. Our plans for the regulation of our life were not carried out at all in the way that we expected; but the reality was not inferior to our ideal. There was none of that hard work, performance of duty, self-sacrifice, and life for others, which I had pictured to myself before our marriage; there was, on the contrary, merely a selfish feeling of love for one another, a wish to be loved, a constant causeless gaiety and entire oblivion of all the world. It is true that my husband sometimes went to his study to work, or drove to town on business, or walked about attending to the management of the estate; but I saw what it cost him to tear himself away from me. He confessed later that every occupation, in my absence, seemed to him mere nonsense in which it was impossible to take any interest. It was just the same with me. If I read, or played the piano, or passed my time with his mother, or taught in the school, I did so only because each of these occupations was connected with him and won his approval; but whenever the thought of him was not associated with any duty, my hands fell by my sides and it seemed to me absurd to think that anything existed apart from him. Perhaps it was a wrong and selfish feeling, but it gave me happiness and lifted me high above all the world. He alone existed on earth for me, and I considered him the best and most faultless man on earth; so that I could not live for anything other than for him, and my one object was to realize his conception of me. And in his eyes I was the first and most excellent woman in the world, the possessor of all possible virtues; and I strove to be that woman in the opinion of the first and best of men.

He came to my room one day while I was praying. I looked around at him and went on with my prayers. Not wishing to interrupt me, he sat down at a table and opened a book. But I thought he was looking at me and looked around myself. He smiled, I laughed, and had to stop my prayers.

"Have you prayed already?" I asked.

"Yes. But you go on; I'll go away."

"You do say your prayers, I hope?"

He made no answer and was about to leave the room when I stopped him.

"Darling, for my sake, please say the prayers with me!" He stood up beside me, dropped his arms awkwardly, and began, with a serious face and some hesitation. Occasionally he turned towards me, seeking signs of approval and aid in my face.

When he came to an end, I laughed and embraced him.

"I feel as if I were ten! And you do it all!" he said, blushing and kissing my hands.

Our house was one of those old-fashioned country houses in which several generations have passed their lives together under one roof, respecting and loving one another. It was all redolent of good sound family traditions, which as soon as I entered it seemed to become mine too. The management of the household was carried on by Tatyana Semenovna, my mother-in-law, along old-fashioned lines. There was not much grace and beauty; but, from the servants down to the furniture and food, there was abundance of everything, and a general cleanliness, solidity, and order, which inspired respect. The drawing-room furniture was arranged symmetrically; there were portraits on the walls, and the floor was covered with home-made carpets and mats. In the parlor there was an old piano, with bureaus of two different patterns, sofas, and little carved tables with bronze ornaments. My sitting-room, specially arranged by Tatyana Semenovna, contained the best furniture in the house, of many styles and periods, including an old wall mirror, which I was frightened to look into at first, but came to value as an old friend. Though Tatyana Semenovna's voice was never heard, the whole household went like clockwork. The number of servants was far too large (they all wore soft boots with no heels, because Tatyana Semenovna had an intense dislike for stamping heels and creaking soles); but they all seemed proud of their calling, trembled before their old mistress, treated my husband and me with an affectionate air of patronage, and performed their duties, to all appearance, with extreme satisfaction. Every Saturday without fail the floors were scoured and the carpets beaten; on the first of every month there was a religious service in the house and holy water was sprinkled; on Tatyana Semenovna's name-day and on her son's (and on mine too, beginning from that autumn) entertainment was regularly provided for the whole neighborhood. And all this had gone on without a break ever since the beginning of Tatyana Semenovna's life.

My husband took no part in the household management; he attended only to the farm-work and the laborers, and devoted much time to this.

Even in winter he got up so early that I often woke to find him gone. He generally came back for early tea, which we drank alone together; at that time, when the worries and vexations of the estate were over, he was almost always in that state of high spirits which we called "wild ecstasy." I often made him tell me what he had been doing in the morning, and he gave such absurd accounts that we both laughed till we cried. Sometimes I insisted on a serious account, and he gave it, restraining a smile. I watched his eyes and moving lips and took nothing in: the sight of him and the sound of his voice was pleasure enough.

"Well, what have I been saying? repeat it," he would sometimes say. But I could repeat nothing. It seemed so absurd that *he* should talk to *me* of any other subject than ourselves. As if it mattered in the least what went on in the world outside! It was at a much later time that I began to understand to some extent and take an interest in his occupations. Tatyana Semenovna never appeared before dinner: she had breakfast alone and said good-morning to us by deputy. In our exclusive little world of frantic happiness a voice from the staid orderly region in which she dwelt was quite startling: I often lost my self-control and could only laugh without speaking, when the maid stood before me with folded hands and made her formal report: "The mistress bade me inquire how you slept after your walk yesterday evening; and about her I was to report that she had a pain in her side all night, and a stupid dog barked in the village and kept her awake: I was also to ask how you liked the bread this morning, and to tell you that it was not Taras who baked today, but Nikolashka who was trying his hand for the first time; and she says his baking is not at all bad, especially the biscuits: but the tea-rusks were over-baked."

Before dinner we saw little of each other: he wrote or went out again while I played the piano or read; but at four o'clock we all met in the drawing-room. Tatyana Semenovna sailed out of her own room, and certain poor and pious maiden ladies, of whom there were always two or three living in the house, made their appearance as well. Every day without fail my husband by old habit offered his arm to his mother, to escort her in to dinner: but she insisted that I should take the other, so that every day, without fail, we got stuck in the door and got in each other's way. She also presided at dinner, where the conversation, if rather solemn, was polite and sensible. The commonplace talk between my husband and me was a pleasant interruption to the formality of those entertainments. Sometimes there were squabbles between mother and son and they bantered with one another; I especially enjoyed those scenes, because they were the best proof of the strong and tender love which united the two of them. After dinner Tatyana Semenovna went to the parlor, where she sat in an armchair and ground her snuff or cut the leaves of new books, while we read aloud or went off to the piano in the morning-room. We read much together at this time, but music was our favorite and best enjoyment, always evoking fresh chords in our hearts and as it were revealing each afresh to the other. While I played his favorite pieces, he sat on a distant sofa where I could hardly see him. He was ashamed to betray the impression produced on him by the music; but often, when he was not expecting it, I rose from the piano, went up to him, and tried to detect on his face signs of emotion—the unnatural brightness and moistness of his eyes, which he tried in vain to conceal. Tatyana Semenovna, though she often wanted to take a look at us there, was also anxious to place no constraints upon us. So she always passed through the room with an air of indifference and a pretense of being busy; but I knew that she had no real reason for going to her room and returning so soon. In the evening I poured tea in the large drawing-room, and all the household met again. This solemn ceremony of distributing cups and glasses before the solemnly shining samovar made me nervous for a long time. I felt myself still unworthy of such a distinction, too young and frivolous to turn the tap of such a big samovar, to put glasses on Nikita's tray, saying "For Peter Ivanovich," "For Marya Minichna," to ask "Is it sweet enough?" and to leave out lumps of sugar for Nanny and other deserving persons. "Splendid! splendid! Just like a grown-up person!" was a frequent comment from my husband, which only increased my confusion.

After tea Tatyana Semenovna played patience or listened to Marya Minichna telling fortunes by cards. Then she kissed us both, made the sign of the cross over us, and we went off to our own rooms. We generally sat up together till midnight, and that was our best and most pleasant time. He told me stories about his past life; we made plans and sometimes even talked philosophy; but we always tried to speak softly, for fear we should be heard upstairs and reported to Tatyana Semenovna, who insisted on our going to bed early. Sometimes we grew hungry; then we stole off to the pantry, secured a cold supper by the good offices of Nikita, and ate it in my sitting-room by the light of one candle. He and I lived like strangers in that big old house, where the uncompromising spirit of the past and of Tatyana Semenovna ruled supreme. Not she only, but the servants, the old ladies, the furniture, even the pictures, inspired me with respect and a little alarm, and made me feel that he and I were a little out of place in that house and must always be very careful and cautious in our doings. Thinking it over now, I see that many things—the pressure of that unvarying routine, and that crowd of idle and inquisitive servants—were uncomfortable and oppressive; but at the time that very constraint made our love for one another still keener. Not I only, but he too, never grumbled openly at anything; on the contrary he shut his eyes to what was amiss. Dmitry Sidorov, one of the footmen, was a great smoker; every day, when we two were in the morning-room after dinner, he went to my husband's study to take tobacco from the jar; it was a sight to see Sergey Mikhaylych creeping on tiptoe to me with a face between delight and terror, and a wink and a warning forefinger, while he pointed at Dmitri Sidorov, who was quite unconscious of being watched. Then, when Dmitri Sidorov had gone away without having seen us, in his joy that all had passed off successfully, he declared (as he did on every other occasion) that I was a darling, and kissed me. At times his calm connivance and apparent indifference to everything annoyed me, and I took it for weakness, never noticing that I acted in the same way myself. "It's like a child who dares not show his will," I thought.

"My dear! my dear!" he said once when I told him that his weakness surprised me; "how can a man, as happy as I am, be dissatisfied with anything? Better to give way myself than to lay compulsion on others; of that I have long been convinced. There is no condition in which one cannot be happy; but our life is such bliss! I simply cannot be angry; to me nothing seems bad now, only pitiful and amusing. Above all—*le mieux est l'ennemi du bien.*[4] Will you believe it, when I hear a ring at the bell, or receive a letter, or even wake up in the morning, I'm frightened. Life must go on, something may change; and nothing can be better than the present."

I believed him but did not understand him. I was happy; but I took that as a matter of course, the invariable experience of people in our position, and believed that there was somewhere, I knew not where, a different happiness, not greater but different.

Two months went by and winter came with its cold and snow; in spite of his company, I began to feel lonely, that life was repeating itself, that there was nothing new either in him or in myself, and that we were merely going back to what had been before. He began to give more time to business which kept him away from me, and my old feeling returned, that there was a special department of his mind into which he was unwilling to admit me. His unbroken calmness provoked me. I loved him as much as ever and was as happy as ever in his love; but my love, instead of increasing, stood still; another new and disquieting sensation began to creep into my heart. To love him was not enough for me after the happiness I had felt in falling in love. I wanted movement and not a calm course of existence. I wanted excitement and danger and the chance to sacrifice myself for love. I felt in myself a superabundance of energy which found no outlet in our quiet life. I had fits of depression which I was ashamed of and tried to conceal from him, and fits of excessive tenderness and high spirits which alarmed him. He realized my state of mind before I did, and proposed a visit to Petersburg; but I begged him to give this up and not to change our manner of life or spoil our happiness. Happy indeed I was; but I was tormented by the thought that this happiness cost me no effort or sacrifice, though I was even

4. Better is the enemy of good.

painfully conscious of my power to face both. I loved him and saw that I was everything to him; but I wanted everyone to see our love; I wanted to love him in spite of obstacles. My mind, and even my senses, were fully occupied; but there was another feeling of youth and craving for movement, which found no satisfaction in our quiet life. What made him say that, whenever I liked, we could move to town? Had he not said so I might have realized that my uncomfortable feelings were my own fault and dangerous nonsense, and that the sacrifice I desired was right there before me, in the task of overcoming these feelings. I was haunted by the thought that I could escape from depression by a mere change from the country; at the same time I felt ashamed and sorry to tear him away, out of selfish motives, from all he cared for. So time went on, the snow grew deeper, and we remained together there, all alone and just the same as before, while outside I knew there was noise, glitter, excitement, and hosts of people suffering or rejoicing without any thought of us and our remote existence. I suffered most from the feeling that custom was petrifying our lives into one fixed shape, that our minds were losing their freedom and becoming enslaved to the steady passionless course of time. The morning always found us cheerful; we were polite at dinner, and affectionate in the evening. "It is all right," I thought, "to do good to others and lead upright lives, as he says; but there is time for that later; there are other things, for which the time is now or never." I wanted, not what I had, but a life of struggle; I wanted feeling to guide life, not life to guide feeling. If only I could go with him to the edge of a precipice and say, "One step, and I shall fall over— one movement, and I shall be lost!" then, pale with fear, he would catch me in his strong arms and hold me over the edge till my blood froze, then carry me off wherever he pleased.

This state of feeling even affected my health, and I began to suffer from nerves. One morning I was worse than usual. He had come back from the estate-office out of sorts, which was a rare thing with him. I noticed it at once and asked what was the matter. He would not tell me and said it was of no importance. I found out afterwards that the police-inspector, out of spite against my husband, was summoning our peasants, making illegal demands on them, and using threats against them. My husband could not swallow this at once; he could not feel it merely "pitiful and amusing." He was provoked, and therefore unwilling to speak to me about it. But it seemed that he did not wish to speak about it because he considered me a mere child, incapable of understanding his concerns. I turned away from him and said no more. Then I told the servant to ask Marya Minichna, who was staying in the house, to join us at breakfast. I ate my breakfast very quickly and took her to the morning-room, where I began to talk loudly to her about some trifle which did not interest me in the least. He walked about the room, glancing at us from time to time. This made me more and more inclined to talk and even to laugh; all that I said myself, and all that Marya Minichna said, seemed laughable. He went off to his study without a word and shut the door behind him. When I ceased to hear him, all my high spirits vanished at once: indeed Marya Minichna was surprised and asked what was the matter. I sat down on a sofa without answering, and felt ready to cry. "What does he have on his mind?" I wondered; "some trifle which he thinks important; but, if he tried to tell it to me, I should soon show him it was mere nonsense. But he must think I won't understand; he must humiliate me by his majestic composure, and always be in the right. But I too am in the right when I find things tiresome and trivial," I reflected; "and I want to lead an active life rather than stagnate in one spot and feel life flowing past me. I want to move forward, to have some new experience every day and every hour, whereas he wants to stand still and keep me standing beside him. How easy it would be for him to gratify me! He need not take me to town; he need only be like me and not put such compulsion on himself and regulate his feelings, but live simply. That's the advice he gives me, but he's not simple himself. That's what's the matter."

I felt tears rising and knew that I was irritated with him. My irritation frightened me, and I went to his study. He was sitting at the table, writing. Hearing my step, he looked up for a moment and then went on writing; he seemed calm and unconcerned. His look annoyed me: instead of going up to him, I stood beside his writing-table, opened a book, and began to look at it. He interrupted his writing again and looked at me.

"Masha, are you out of sorts?" he asked.

I replied with a cold look, as much as to say, "You are very polite, but what's the use of asking?" He shook his head and smiled with a tender timid air; but his smile, for the first time, drew no answering smile from me.

"What happened to you to-day?" I asked; "why did you not tell me?"

"Nothing much—a trifling nuisance," he said. "But I might tell you now. Two of our serfs went off to town . . ."

But I would not let him go on.

"Why wouldn't you tell me, when I asked you at breakfast?"

"I was angry then and should have said something foolish."

"I wanted to know then."

"Why?"

"Why do you suppose I can never help you in anything?"

"Not help me!" he said, dropping his pen. "Why, I believe that without you I couldn't live. You not only help me in everything I do, but you do it yourself. You're very wide of the mark," he said, and laughed. "My life depends on you. I'm pleased with things, only because you're there, because I need you . . ."

"Yes, I know; I'm a delightful child who must be humored and kept quiet," I said in a voice that astonished him, so that he looked up as if this was a new experience; "but I don't want to be quiet and calm; that's more in your line, and too much in your line," I added.

"Well," he began quickly, interrupting me and evidently afraid to let me continue, "when I tell you the facts, I should like to know your opinion."

"I don't want to hear them now," I answered. I did want to hear the story, but I found it so pleasant to break down his composure. "I don't want to play at life," I said, "but to live it, as you do yourself."

His face, which reflected every feeling so quickly and vividly, now expressed pain and intense attention.

"I want to share your life, to . . . ," but I couldn't go on—his face showed such deep distress. He was silent for a moment.

"But what part of my life don't you share?" he asked; "is it because I, and not you, have to bother with the inspector and with tipsy laborers?"

"That's not the only thing," I said.

"For God's sake try to understand me, my dear!" he cried. "I know that excitement is always painful; I have learnt that from the experience of life. I love you, and I can't help wanting to save you from excitement. My whole life consists of my love for you; you shouldn't make life impossible for me."

"You're always in the right," I said without looking at him.

I was vexed again by his calmness and coolness while I was conscious of annoyance and some feeling akin to penitence.

"Masha, what's the matter?" he asked. "The question is not, which of us is in the right—not at all; but rather, what grievance do you have against me? Take time before you answer, and tell me all that's in your mind. You're dissatisfied with me: no doubt you're right; but let me understand what I've done wrong."

How could I put my feeling into words? That he understood me at once, that again I stood before him like a child, that I could do nothing without his understanding and foreseeing it—all this only increased my agitation.

"I have no complaint to make of you," I said; "I'm merely bored and want not to be bored. But you say it can't be helped, and, as always, you're right."

I looked at him as I spoke. I had gained my object: his calmness had disappeared, and I read fear and pain in his face.

"Masha," he began in a low troubled voice, "this is no mere trifle: the happiness of our lives is at stake. Please hear me out without answering. Why do you wish to torment me?"

But I interrupted him.

"Oh, I know you'll turn out to be right. Words are useless; of course you're right." I spoke coldly, as if some evil spirit were speaking with my voice.

"If you only knew what you're doing!" he said, and his voice shook.

I burst out crying and felt relieved. He sat down beside me and said nothing. I felt sorry for him, ashamed of myself, and annoyed at what I had done. I avoided looking at him. I felt that any look from him at that moment must express severity or perplexity. At last I looked up and saw his eyes: they were fixed on me with a tender gentle expression that seemed to ask for pardon. I caught his hand and said,

"Forgive me! I myself don't know what I've been saying."

"But I do; and you spoke the truth."

"What do you mean?" I asked.

"That we must go to Petersburg," he said; "there's nothing for us to do here just now."

"As you please," I said.

He took me in his arms and kissed me.

"You must forgive me," he said; "for I am to blame."

That evening I played for him for a long time, while he walked about the room. He had a habit of muttering to himself; when I asked what he was muttering, he always thought for a moment and then told me exactly what it was. It was generally verse, and sometimes mere nonsense, but I could always judge his mood by it. When I asked him now, he stood still, thought an instant, and then repeated two lines from Lermontov:

> He in his madness prays for storms,
> And dreams that storms will bring him peace.[5]

"He's really more than human," I thought; "he knows everything. How can one help loving him?"

I got up, took his arm, and began to walk up and down with him, trying to keep step.

"Well?" he asked, smiling and looking at me.

"All right," I whispered. And then a sudden fit of merriment came over us both: our eyes laughed, we took longer and longer steps, and rose higher and higher on tiptoe. Prancing in this manner, to the profound dissatisfaction of the butler and astonishment of my mother-in-law, who was playing patience in the parlor, we proceeded through the house till we reached the dining-room; there we stopped, looked at one another, and burst out laughing.

Two weeks later, before Christmas, we were in Petersburg.

II

The journey to Petersburg, a week in Moscow, visits to my own relatives and my husband's, settling down in our new quarters, travel, new towns and new faces—all this passed before me like a dream. It was all so new,

5. The concluding lines of Lermontov's famous lyric "The Sail" (1832).

interesting, and delightful, so warmly and brightly lit up by his presence and his love, that our quiet life in the country seemed to me something very remote and unimportant. I had expected to find people in society proud and cold; but to my great surprise, everywhere I was received with unfeigned cordiality and pleasure, not only by relatives, but also by strangers. I seemed to be the sole object of their thoughts, and my arrival the one thing they wanted, to complete their happiness. I was also surprised to discover in what seemed the very best society a number of people acquainted with my husband, though he had never mentioned them to me; I often felt it odd and disagreeable to hear him speak disapprovingly of some of these people who seemed so kind to me. I could not understand his coolness towards them or his endeavors to avoid many acquaintances that seemed so flattering. Surely, the more kind people one knows, the better; and here everyone was kind.

"This is how we must manage, you see," he said to me before we left the country; "here we are little Croesuses,[6] but in town we shall not be rich at all. So we must not stay after Easter, or go into society, or we shall get into difficulties. For your sake too I should not wish it."

"Why should we go into society?" I asked; "we shall have a look at the theaters, see our relatives, go to the opera, hear some good music, and be ready to come home before Easter."

But these plans were forgotten the moment we got to Petersburg. I found myself at once in such a new and delightful world, surrounded by so many pleasures and confronted by such novel interests, that I instantly, though unconsciously, turned my back on my past life and its plans. "All that was preparation, a mere playing at life; but this is the real thing! And there is the future too!" Such were my thoughts. The restlessness and symptoms of depression which had troubled me at home vanished at once and entirely, as if by magic. My love for my husband grew calmer, and I ceased to wonder whether he loved me less. Indeed I could not doubt his love: every thought of mine was understood at once, every feeling shared, and every wish gratified by him. His composure, if it still existed, no longer provoked me. I also began to realize that he not only loved me but was proud of me. If we paid a visit, or made some new acquaintance, or gave an evening party at which I, trembling inwardly from fear of disgracing myself, acted as hostess, he often said when it was over: "Bravo, young lady! splendid! you needn't be frightened; a real success!" And his praise gave me great pleasure. Soon after our arrival he wrote to his mother and asked me to add a postscript, but refused to let me see his letter; of course I insisted on reading it. He had said: "You would not know Masha again, I don't myself. Where does she get that charming graceful self-confidence and ease, such social gifts combined with such simplicity, charm, and kind-

6. Croesus was the last king of Lydia (560–546 B.C.), noted for his great wealth.

liness? Everybody is delighted with her. I can't admire her enough myself, and should be more in love with her than ever, if that were possible."

"Now I know what I am like," I thought. In my joy and pride I felt that I loved him more than before. My success with all our new acquaintances came as a complete surprise to me. I heard on all sides, how this uncle had taken a special liking to me, and that aunt was raving about me; I was told by one admirer that I had no rival among Petersburg ladies, and assured by another, a lady, that I might, if I cared, lead the fashion in society. A cousin of my husband's, in particular, a Princess D., middle-aged and very much at home in society, fell in love with me at first sight and paid me compliments which turned my head. The first time she invited me to a ball and spoke to my husband about it, he turned to me and asked if I wished to go; I could just detect a sly smile on his face. I nodded assent and felt that I was blushing.

"She looks like a criminal when confessing what she wants," he said with a good-natured laugh.

"But you said we mustn't go into society, and you don't care for it yourself," I answered, smiling and looking imploringly at him.

"Let's go, if you want to very much," he said.

"Really, we'd better not."

"Do you want to? very badly?" he asked again.

I said nothing.

"Society in itself is no great harm," he went on; "but unsatisfied social aspirations are a bad and ugly business. We must certainly accept, and we will."

"To tell you the truth," I said, "never in my life have I longed for anything as much as I do for this ball."

So we went, and my delight exceeded all my expectations. It seemed to me, more than ever, that I was the center around which everything revolved, that for my sake alone this great room was lit up and the band played, and that this crowd of people had assembled to admire me. From the hairdresser and the lady's maid to my partners and the old gentlemen promenading the ballroom, all alike seemed to make it plain that they were in love with me. The general verdict formed at the ball about me and reported by my cousin, came to this: I was quite unlike other women and had a rural simplicity and charm of my own. I was so flattered by my success that I frankly told my husband I should like to attend two or three more balls during the season, and "get so thoroughly sick of them," I added; but I did not mean what I said.

He agreed readily; he accompanied me at first with obvious satisfaction. He took pleasure in my success, and seemed to have quite forgotten his former warning or to have changed his opinion.

But the time came when he was evidently bored and wearied by the life we were leading. I was too busy, however, to think about that. Even if I sometimes noticed his eyes fixed questioningly on me with a serious

attentive gaze, I did not realize its meaning. I was utterly blinded by
the sudden affection which I seemed to evoke in all our new acquaintances, and confused by the unfamiliar atmosphere of luxury, refinement, and novelty. It pleased me so much to find myself in these
surroundings not merely his equal but his superior, and yet to love him
better and more independently than before, that I could not understand
what he could object to for me in society life. I had a new sense of pride
and self-satisfaction when my entry at a ball attracted all eyes, while he,
as if ashamed to confess his ownership of me in public, made haste to
leave my side and efface himself in the crowd of black coats. "Wait a
little!" I often said in my heart, when I identified his obscure and
sometimes pitiful figure at the end of the room—"Wait till we get home!
Then you will see and understand for whose sake I try to be beautiful
and brilliant, and what it is I love in all that surrounds me this evening!"
I really believed that my success pleased me only because it enabled me
to give it up for his sake. One danger I recognized as possible—that I
might get carried away by a fancy for some new acquaintance, and that
my husband might grow jealous. But he trusted me so absolutely, and
seemed so undisturbed and indifferent, and all the young men were so
inferior to him, that I was not alarmed by this one danger. Yet the
attention of so many people in society gave me satisfaction, flattered my
vanity, and made me think that there was some merit in my love for
my husband. Thus I became more offhand and self-confident in my
behavior towards him.

"Oh, I saw you this evening carrying on a most animated conversation
with Mme N.," I said one night on returning from a ball, shaking my
finger at him. He really had been talking to this lady, who was a well-
known figure in Petersburg society. He was more silent and depressed
than usual, and I said this to rouse him.

"What's the good of talking like that, for *you* especially, Masha?" he
said with half-closed teeth and frowning as if in pain. "Leave that to
others; it doesn't suit you and me. Pretense of that sort may spoil the
true relations between us, which I hope may still come back."

I was ashamed and said nothing.

"Will it ever come back, Masha, do you think?" he asked.

"It never was spoilt and never will be," I said; and I really believed
it then.

"God grant that you're right!" he said; "if not, we ought to return
home."

But he only spoke like this once—in general he seemed as satisfied
as I was, and I was so cheerful and happy! I comforted myself too by
thinking, "If he's bored sometimes, I endured the same thing for his
sake in the country. If the relation between us has become a little
different, everything will be the same again in summer, when we'll be
alone in our house at Nikolskoe with Tatyana Semenovna."

So the winter slipped by, and in spite of our plans we stayed on over

Easter in Petersburg. A week later we were preparing to start for home; our packing was all done; my husband, who had bought things—plants for the garden and presents for people at Nikolskoe, was in a specially cheerful and affectionate mood. Just then Princess D. came and begged us to stay till Saturday, in order to be present at a reception to be given by Countess R. The Countess was very anxious to secure me, because a foreign prince, who was visiting Petersburg and had already seen me at a ball, wished to make my acquaintance; indeed this was his motive for attending the reception, and he declared that I was the most beautiful woman in Russia. All the world was to be there; in a word, it would really be too bad, if I did not go too.

My husband was talking to someone at the other end of the drawing-room.

"So you will go, won't you, Mary?" said the Princess.

"We meant to start for the country the day after tomorrow," I answered undecidedly, glancing at my husband. Our eyes met, and he turned away at once.

"I must persuade him to stay," she said, "and then we can go on Saturday and turn all heads. All right?"

"It would upset our plans; and we have already packed," I answered, beginning to give way.

"She had better go this evening and make her curtsey to the Prince," my husband called out from the other end of the room; and he spoke in a tone of suppressed irritation which I had never heard from him before.

"I declare he's jealous, for the first time in his life," said the lady, laughing. "But it's not for the sake of the Prince I urge it, Sergey Mikhaylych, but for all our sakes. The Countess was so anxious to have her."

"It depends on her entirely," my husband said coldly, and then left the room.

I saw that he was much disturbed, and this pained me. I gave no positive promise. As soon as our visitor left, I went to my husband. He was walking up and down his room, thinking, and neither saw nor heard me when I came in on tiptoe.

Looking at him I said to myself: "He is already dreaming of his dear Nikolskoe, our morning coffee in the bright drawing-room, the land and the laborers, our evenings in the music-room, and our secret midnight suppers." Then I decided in my own heart: "Not for all the balls and all the flattering princes in the world will I give up his glad confusion and tender cares." I was just about to say that I did not wish to go to the ball and would refuse, when he looked round, saw me, and frowned. His face, which had been gentle and thoughtful, changed at once to its old expression of sagacity, penetration, and patronizing composure. He would not show himself to me as a mere man, but had to be a demigod on a pedestal.

"Well, my dear?" he asked, turning towards me with an unconcerned air.

I said nothing. I was provoked, because he was hiding his real self from me, and would not continue to be the man I loved.

"Do you want to go to the reception on Saturday?" he asked.

"I did, but you disapprove. Besides, our things are all packed," I said.

Never before had I heard such coldness in his tone to me, and never before seen such coldness in his eye.

"I shall order our things to be unpacked," he said, "and I shall stay till Tuesday. So you can go to the party, if you like. I hope you will; but I won't go."

Without looking at me, he began to walk about the room jerkily, as was his habit when perturbed.

"I simply can't understand you," I said, following him with my eyes from where I stood. "You say that you never lose your self-control" (he had never really said that); "then why do you talk to me so strangely? I am ready on your account to sacrifice this pleasure, and then you, in a sarcastic tone which is altogether new, insist that I should go."

"So you make a *sacrifice!*" he put special emphasis on the last word. "Well, so do I. What could be better? We compete in generosity—what an example of family happiness!"

Such harsh and contemptuous language I had never heard from his lips before. I was not abashed, but mortified by his contempt; his harshness didn't frighten me, but made me harsh too. How could *he* speak thus, he who was always so frank and simple and dreaded insincerity in our speech to one another? What had I done that he should speak so? I really intended to sacrifice for his sake a pleasure in which I could see no harm; a moment ago I loved him and understood his feelings as well as ever. We had changed parts: now he avoided direct and plain words, and I desired them.

"You have changed considerably," I said, with a sigh. "How am I guilty before you? It's not this party—you have something else, some old grudge against me. Why this insincerity? You used to be so afraid of it yourself. Tell me plainly what you have to complain of." "What will he say?" I wondered, and reflected with some complacency that I had done nothing all winter which he could find fault with.

I went into the middle of the room, so that he had to pass close to me, and looked at him. I thought, "He will come and clasp me in his arms, and put an end to it." I was even sorry that I wouldn't have the chance to prove him wrong. But he stopped at the far end of the room and looked at me.

"Don't you understand yet?" he asked.

"No, I don't."

"Then I must explain. What I feel, and cannot help feeling, positively sickens me for the first time in my life." He stopped, evidently startled by the harsh sound of his own voice.

"What do you mean?" I asked, with tears of indignation in my eyes.

"It sickens me that the Prince admired you, and that you therefore run to meet him, forgetting your husband and yourself and your womanly dignity. You wilfully misunderstand what your want of self-respect makes your husband feel for you: you actually come to me and speak of the 'sacrifice' you're making, by which you mean—'To show myself to His Highness is a great pleasure to me, but I will "sacrifice" it.' "

The longer he spoke, the more he was excited by the sound of his own voice, which was hard and rough and cruel. I had never seen him, had never thought of seeing him, like that. The blood rushed to my heart and I was frightened; but I felt that I had nothing to be ashamed of, and the excitement of wounded vanity made me eager to punish him.

"I have been expecting this for a long time," I said. "Go on. Go on!"

"I don't know what you expected," he went on; "but I might well expect the worst, when I saw you day after day sharing the dirtiness, idleness, and luxury of this foolish society, and it has come at last. Never have I felt such shame and pain as now—pain for myself, when your friend thrusts her unclean fingers into my heart and speaks of my jealousy!—jealousy of a man whom neither you nor I know; and you refuse to understand me and offer to make a sacrifice for me—what sacrifice? I am ashamed for you, for your degradation! . . . Sacrifice!" he repeated again.

"Ah, so this is a husband's power," thought I: "to insult and humiliate a perfectly innocent woman. Such may be a husband's rights, but I will not submit to them." I felt the blood leave my face and a strange distension of my nostrils, as I said, "No! I make no sacrifice on your account. I shall go to the party on Saturday without fail."

"And I hope you enjoy it. But all is over between us!" he cried out in a fit of unrestrained fury. "You shall not torture me any longer! I was a fool, when I . . . ," but his lips quivered, and he refrained with a visible effort from ending the sentence.

I feared and hated him at that moment. I wished to say a great deal to him and punish him for all his insults; but if I had opened my mouth, I should have lost my dignity by bursting into tears. I said nothing and left the room. But as soon as I ceased to hear his footsteps, I was horrified at what we had done. I feared that the tie which had made all my happiness might really be snapped for ever; and I thought of going back. But then I wondered: "Is he calm enough now to understand me, if I stretch out my hand and look at him in silence? Will he realize my generosity? What if he calls my grief a mere pretense? Or he may feel sure that he is right and accept my repentance and forgive me with unruffled pride. Why, oh why, did he whom I so loved insult me so cruelly?"

I went to my own room, not to him, and sat there for a long time and cried. I recalled with horror each word of our conversation, and substituted different words, kind words, for those we had spoken, and added others; again I remembered the reality with horror and a feeling of injury. In the evening I went down for tea and met my husband in the presence of a friend who was staying with us; it seemed to me that a wide gulf had opened between us from that day. Our friend asked me when we were to start for home; before I could speak, my husband answered:

"On Tuesday," he said; "we have to stay for Countess R.'s reception." He turned to me: "I believe you intend to go?" he asked.

His matter-of-fact tone frightened me, and I looked at him timidly. His eyes were directed straight at me with an unkind and scornful expression; his voice was cold and even.

"Yes," I answered.

When we were alone that evening, he came up to me and held out his hand.

"Please forget what I said to you to-day," he began.

As I took his hand, a smile quivered on my lips and tears were ready to flow; but he took his hand away and sat down on an armchair at some distance, as if fearing a sentimental scene. "Is it possible that he still thinks he's right?" I wondered; and, though I was quite ready to explain and beg that we not go to the party, the words died on my lips.

"I must write to my mother and say that we have put off our departure," he said; "otherwise she will be uneasy."

"When do you think of going?" I asked.

"On Tuesday, after the reception," he replied.

"I hope it is not on my account," I said, looking into his eyes; but those eyes merely looked—they said nothing, and a veil seemed to keep them from me. His face seemed to have grown suddenly old and disagreeable.

We went to the reception, and friendly relations between us seemed to have been restored, but these relations were quite different from what they had been.

At the party I was sitting with some other ladies when the Prince came up to me, so that I had to stand up in order to speak to him. As I rose, my eyes involuntarily sought my husband. He was looking at me from the other end of the room, and now turned away. I was seized by a sudden sense of shame and pain; in my confusion I blushed all over my face and neck under the Prince's eye. I was forced to stand and listen, while he spoke, eyeing me from his superior height. Our conversation was over soon: there was no room for him beside me, and he, no doubt, felt that I was uncomfortable with him. We talked of the last ball, of where I should spend the summer, and so on. As he left, he expressed a wish to make the acquaintance of my husband, and I saw them meet and begin a conversation at the far end of the room. The Prince evidently said something about me; he smiled in the middle of their talk and looked in my direction.

My husband suddenly flushed. He made a low bow and turned away from the Prince without being dismissed. I blushed too: I was ashamed of the impression which I and, still more, my husband must have made on the Prince. Everyone, I thought, must have noticed my awkward shyness when I was presented, and my husband's eccentric behavior. "Heaven knows how they'll interpret such conduct? Perhaps they already know all about the scene with my husband!"

Princess D. drove me home, and on the way I spoke to her about my husband. My patience was at an end, and I told her the whole story of what had taken place between us owing to this unlucky party. To calm me, she said that such differences were very common and quite unimportant, and that our quarrel would leave no trace. She explained her view of my husband's character—that he had become very stiff and unsociable. I agreed, and believed that I had learned to judge him myself more calmly and more accurately.

But later when I was alone with my husband, the thought that I had sat in judgement upon him weighed like a crime upon my conscience; I felt that the gulf which divided us had grown even greater.

III

From that day there was a complete change in our life and our relations to each other. We were no longer as happy when we were alone together. To certain subjects we gave wide berth, and conversation flowed more easily in the presence of a third person. When talk turned to life in the country, or to a ball, we were uneasy and shrank from looking at one another. Both of us knew where the gulf between us lay, and seemed afraid to approach it. I was convinced that he was proud and irascible, and that I must be careful not to touch his weak point. He was equally sure that I disliked the country and was dying for social distraction, and that he must put up with this unfortunate taste of mine. We both avoided frank conversation on these topics, and each misjudged the other. We had long ceased to think each other the most perfect people in the world; each now judged the other in secret, and measured the offender by the standard of other people. I fell ill before we left Petersburg, and we went from there to a house near town, from which my husband went on alone, to join his mother at Nikolskoe. By that time I was well enough to have gone with him, but he urged me to stay on the pretext of my health. I knew, however, that he was really afraid we should be uncomfortable together in the country; so I did not insist much, and he went off alone. I felt dull and lonely in his absence; but when he came back, I saw that he did not add to my life what he had added formerly. In the old days every thought and experience weighed on me like a crime till

I had imparted it to him; every action and word of his seemed to me a model of perfection; we often laughed for joy at the mere sight of each other. But these relations had changed, so imperceptibly that we had not even noticed their disappearance. Separate interests and cares, which we no longer tried to share, made their appearance, and even the fact of our estrangement ceased to trouble us. The idea became familiar, and, before a year had passed, each could look at the other without confusion. His fits of boyish merriment with me had quite vanished; his mood of calm indulgence to all that passed, which used to provoke me, had disappeared; there was an end of those penetrating looks which used to confuse and delight me, an end of the ecstasies and prayers which we once shared in common. We did not even meet very often: he was continually absent, with no fears or regrets at leaving me alone; and I was constantly in society, where I did not need him.

There were no further scenes or quarrels between us. I tried to satisfy him, he carried out all my wishes, and we seemed to love each other.

When we were by ourselves, which we seldom were, I felt neither joy nor excitement nor embarrassment in his company: it seemed like being alone. I realized that he was my husband and no mere stranger, a good man, and as familiar to me as my own self. I was convinced that I knew just what he would say and do, and how he would look; if anything he did surprised me, I concluded that he had made a mistake. I expected nothing from him. In a word, he was my husband—that was all. It seemed to me that things must be so, as a matter of course, and that no other relations between us had ever existed. When he left home, especially at first, I was lonely and frightened and keenly felt my need of support; when he came back, I ran to his arms with joy, though two hours later my joy was quite forgotten, and I found nothing to say to him. Only at moments of quiet undemonstrative affection which sometimes occurred between us, I felt something wrong and some pain in my heart, and I seemed to read the same story in his eyes. I was conscious of a limit to tenderness, which he seemingly would not, and I could not, overstep. This saddened me sometimes; but I had no leisure to reflect on anything, and I tried to drown my regret for a change which I vaguely realized in the distractions which were always within my reach. Fashionable life, which had dazzled me at first by its glitter and flattery of my self-love, now took entire command of my nature, became a habit, laid its fetters upon me, and monopolized my capacity for feeling. I could not bear solitude, and was afraid to reflect on my position. My whole day, from late in the morning till late at night, was taken up by the claims of society; even if I stayed at home, my time was not my own. This no longer seemed either cheerful or dull; it seemed that it always had to be so, and not otherwise.

Three years passed, during which our relations to one another remained unchanged and seemed to have taken a fixed shape which could not become either better or worse. Though two events of importance in our family life took place during that time, neither of them changed my own life. These were the birth of my first child and the death of Tatyana Semenovna. At first the feeling of motherhood did take hold of me with such power, and produce in me such a passion of unanticipated joy, that I believed this would prove the beginning of a new life. But, in the course of two months, when I began to go out again, my feeling grew weaker and weaker, till it passed into mere habit and the lifeless performance of duty. My husband, on the contrary, from the birth of our first boy, became his old self again—gentle, composed, and home-loving, and transferred to the child his old tenderness and gaiety. Many a night when I went, dressed for a ball, to the nursery, to make the sign of the cross over the child before he slept, I found my husband there and felt his eyes fixed on me with a certain reproof in their serious gaze. Then I was ashamed and even shocked by my own callousness, and asked myself if I was worse than other women. "But it can't be helped," I said to myself; "I love my child, but it would bore me to sit beside him all day long; and nothing will make me pretend what I do not really feel."

His mother's death was a great sorrow to my husband; he said that he found it painful to go on living at Nikolskoe. For myself, although I mourned for her and sympathized with my husband's sorrow, I found life in that house easier and pleasanter after her death. Most of those three years we spent in town: I went to Nikolskoe only once for two months; the third year we went abroad and spent the summer at Baden.

I was then twenty-one; our financial position was, I believed, satisfactory; my domestic life gave me all that I asked of it; everyone I knew, it seemed to me, loved me; my health was good; I was the best-dressed woman in Baden; I knew that I was good-looking; the weather was fine; I enjoyed the atmosphere of beauty and refinement; in short, I was in excellent spirits. They had once been even higher at Nikolskoe, when my happiness was in myself and came from the feeling that I deserved to be happy, and from the anticipation of still greater happiness to come. That was a different state of affairs; but I did very well this summer also. I had no special wishes, hopes, or fears; it seemed that my life was full and my conscience easy. Among all the visitors at Baden that season there was no one man I preferred to the rest, or even to our old ambassador, Prince K., who was assiduous in his attentions to me. One was young, another old; one was English and fair, another French and wore a beard—to me they were all alike, but all indispensable. Indistinguishable as they were, together they made up the atmosphere which I found so pleasant. But there was one, an Italian marquis, who stood out from the rest by reason of the boldness with which he expressed his admiration. He seized every opportunity of being with me—danced with me, rode with me, and met me at the casino; and everywhere he spoke to me of my charms. Several times I saw him from my windows loitering around our hotel, and the fixed gaze of his bright eyes often troubled me, made me blush and turn away. He was young, handsome, and well-mannered; above all, by his smile and the expression of his brow, he resembled my husband, though much handsomer. He struck me by this likeness, though in general, in his lips, eyes, and long chin, there was something coarse and animal which contrasted with my husband's charming expression of kindness and noble serenity. I supposed him to be passionately in love with me, and thought of him sometimes with proud commiseration. When I tried to soothe him at times and change his tone to one of easy, half-friendly confidence, he resented the suggestion with vehemence, and continued to disquiet me by a smouldering passion which was ready at any moment to burst forth. Though I would not own it even to myself, I feared him and often thought of him against my will. My husband knew him, and treated him—even more than other acquaintances of ours who regarded him only as my husband—with coldness and disdain.

Towards the end of the season I fell ill and stayed indoors for two weeks. The first evening I went out again to hear the band, I learnt that Lady S., an Englishwoman famous for her beauty, who had long been expected, had arrived in my absence. My return was welcomed, and a group gathered around me; but a more distinguished group attended the beautiful stranger. She and her beauty were the one subject of conversation around me. When I saw her, she really was beautiful, but her self-satisfied expression struck me as disagreeable, and I said so. That day everything that had formerly seemed amusing, seemed dull. Lady S. arranged an expedition to the ruined castle for the next day; but I declined to be of the party. Almost everyone else went; my opinion of Baden underwent a complete change. Everything and everybody seemed stupid and tiresome; I wanted to cry, to end my cure, to return to Russia. There was some evil feeling in my soul, but I did not yet acknowledge it to myself. Pretending that I was not strong, I ceased to appear at crowded parties; if I went out, it was only in the morning by myself, to drink the waters; and my only companion was Mme M., a Russian lady, with whom I sometimes took drives in the nearby country. My husband was absent: he had gone to Heidelberg for a while, intending to return to Russia when my cure was over, and only paid me occasional visits at Baden.

One day when Lady S. had carried off all the company on a hunting-expedition, Mme M. and I drove to the castle in the afternoon. While our carriage moved slowly along the winding road, bordered by ancient chestnut-trees and commanding a vista of the pleasant country around Baden, with the setting sun lighting it up, our conversation took a more serious turn than had ever happened to us before. I had known my companion for a long time; but she appeared to me now in a new light, as a well-principled and intelligent woman, to whom it was possible to speak without reserve, and whose friendship was worth having. We spoke of our private concerns, our children, the emptiness of life at Baden, till we felt a longing for Russia and the Russian countryside. When we entered the castle we were still under the impression of this serious feeling. Within the walls there was shade and coolness; the sunlight played from above upon the ruins. Steps and voices were audible. The landscape, charming enough but cold to a Russian eye, lay before us in the frame made by a doorway. We sat down to rest and watched the sunset in silence. The voices now sounded louder, and I thought I heard my own name. I listened and could not help overhearing every word. I recognized the voices: the speakers were the Italian marquis and a French friend of his whom I knew also. They were talking of me and Lady S., and the Frenchman was comparing us as rival beauties. Though he said nothing insulting, his words made my pulse quicken. He explained in detail the good points of us both. I was already a mother, while Lady S. was only nineteen; though I had the advantage in hair, my rival had a better figure. "Besides," he added, "Lady S. is a real *grande dame*, and the other is nothing in particular, only one of those obscure Russian princesses who turn up here nowadays in such numbers." He ended by saying that I was wise in not attempting to compete with Lady S., and that I was completely buried as far as Baden was concerned.

"I feel sorry for her—unless indeed she takes a fancy to console herself with you," he added with a hard ringing laugh.

"If she goes away, I shall follow her"—he blurted out in an Italian accent.

"Happy man! he is still capable of a passion!" laughed the Frenchman.

"Passion!" said the other voice and then was still for a moment. "It is a necessity to me: I cannot live without it. To make life a romance is the one thing worth doing. And with me romance never breaks off in the middle; this affair I shall carry through to the end."

"*Bonne chance, mon ami!*"[7] said the Frenchman.

They turned a corner, and the voices stopped. Then we heard them coming down the steps, and a few minutes later they came upon us by a side-door. They were very surprised to see us. I blushed when the marquis approached, and felt afraid when we left the castle and he offered me his arm. I could not refuse, and we set off for the carriage, walking behind Mme M. and his friend. I was mortified by what the Frenchman had said about me, though I secretly admitted that he had only put in words what I myself felt; but the plain speaking of the Italian had surprised and upset me by its coarseness. I was tormented by the thought that, though I had overheard him, he showed no fear of me. It was hateful

---

7. "Good luck, my friend."

to have him so close; I walked quickly after the other couple, not looking at him or answering him and trying to hold his arm in such a way as not to hear him. He spoke of the fine view, the unexpected pleasure of our meeting, and so on; but I was not listening. My thoughts were with my husband, my child, my country; I felt ashamed, distressed, anxious; I was in a hurry to get back to my solitary room in the Hôtel de Bade, there to think at leisure of the storm of feeling that had just risen in my heart. But Mme M. walked slowly, it was still a long way to the carriage, and my escort seemed to loiter on purpose as if he wished to detain me. "None of that!" I thought, and resolutely quickened my pace. But it soon became unmistakable that he was detaining me and even pressing my arm. Mme M. turned a corner, and we were quite alone. I was afraid.

"Excuse me," I said coldly and tried to free my arm; but the lace of my sleeve caught on a button of his coat. Bending towards me, he began to unfasten it, and his ungloved fingers touched my arm. A feeling new to me, half horror and half pleasure, sent an icy shiver down my back. I looked at him, intending by my coldness to convey all the contempt I felt for him; but my look expressed nothing but fear and excitement. His blazing liquid eyes, right up against my face, stared strangely at me, at my neck and breast; both his hands fingered my arm above the wrist; his parted lips were saying that he loved me, and that I was all the world to him; those lips were coming nearer and nearer, those hands were squeezing mine harder and harder and burning me. A fever ran through my veins, my sight grew dim, I trembled, and the words intended to check him died away in my throat. Suddenly I felt a kiss on my cheek. Trembling all over and turning cold, I stood still and stared at him. Unable to speak or move, I stood there, horrified, expectant, even desirous. It was over in a moment, but the moment was horrible! In that short time I saw him exactly as he was—his low straight forehead (so like my husband's!) under the straw hat; the handsome regular nose and dilated nostrils; the long waxed moustache and short beard; the close-shaved cheeks and sunburnt neck. I hated and feared him; he was utterly repugnant and alien to me. And yet the excitement and passion of this strange hateful man raised a powerful resonance in my own heart; I felt an irresistible longing to surrender myself to the kisses of that coarse handsome mouth, and to the pressure of those white hands with their delicate veins and jewelled fingers; I was tempted to throw myself headlong into the abyss of forbidden delights that had suddenly opened up before me.

"I am so unhappy already," I thought; "let more storms of unhappiness burst over my head!"

He put one arm around me and bent towards my face. "Better that way!" I thought: "let sin and shame cover me over deeper and deeper!"

"*Je vous aime!*" he whispered in the voice which was so like my husband's. At once I thought of my husband and child, as creatures once precious to me who had now passed altogether out of my life. At that moment I heard Mme M.'s voice; she called to me from around the corner. I came to myself, tore my hand away without looking at him, and almost ran after her: I only looked at him after she and I were already seated in the carriage. Then I saw him raise his hat and ask some commonplace question with a smile. He little knew the inexpressible aversion I felt for him at that moment.

My life seemed so wretched, the future so hopeless, the past so black! When Mme M. spoke, her words meant nothing to me. I thought she talked only out of pity, to hide the contempt I aroused in her. In every word and every look I seemed to detect this contempt and insulting pity. The shame of that kiss burnt my cheek, and the thought of my husband and child was more than I could bear. When I was alone in my own room, I tried to think over my position; but I was afraid to be alone. Without drinking the tea which was brought me, and uncertain of my own motives, I got ready with feverish haste to catch the evening train and join my husband at Heidelberg.

I found seats for myself and my maid in an empty carriage. When the train started and the fresh air blew through the window on my face, I grew more composed and pictured my past and future more clearly. The course of our married life from the time of our first visit to Petersburg now presented itself to me in a new light, and lay like a reproach on my conscience. For the first time I clearly recalled our start at Nikolskoe and our plans for the future; and for the first time I asked myself what happiness my husband had had since then. I felt that I had behaved badly to him. "But why," I asked myself, "why did he not stop me? Why did he make pretenses? Why did he always avoid explanations? Why did he insult me? Why did he not use the power of his love to influence me? Or did he not love me?" But whether he was to blame or not, I still felt the kiss of that strange man upon my cheek. The nearer we got to Heidelberg, the clearer the picture of my husband, and the more I dreaded our meeting. "I shall tell him all," I thought, "and wipe out everything with tears of repentance; he will forgive me." But I myself did not know what I meant by "everything"; and I did not believe in my heart that he would forgive me.

As soon as I entered my husband's room and saw his calm though surprised expression, I felt at once that I had nothing to tell him, no confession to make, and nothing to ask forgiveness for. I had to suppress my unspoken grief and penitence.

"What put this into your head?" he asked. "I meant to go to Baden tomorrow." Then he looked more closely at me and seemed to be concerned. "What's the matter with you? What has happened?" he said.

"Nothing at all," I replied, almost breaking down. "I am not going back. Let's go home, to-morrow if you like, to Russia."

For some time he said nothing but looked at me attentively. Then he said, "But tell me what has happened to you."

I blushed involuntarily and looked down. There came into his eyes a flash of anger and displeasure. Afraid of what he might imagine, I said with a power of pretense that surprised myself:

"Nothing at all has happened. It was merely that I grew weary and sad by myself; I have been thinking a great deal about our way of life and about you. I have long been to blame towards you. Why do you take me abroad, when you can't bear it yourself? I have long been to blame. Let us go back to Nikolskoe and settle there forever."

"Spare us these sentimental scenes, my dear," he said coldly. "To go back to Nikolskoe is a good idea, for our money is running short; but the notion of staying there 'forever' is fanciful. I know you would not settle down. Have some tea, and you will feel better," and he rose to ring for the waiter.

I imagined all he might be thinking about me; I was offended by the horrible thoughts which I ascribed to him when I encountered the dubious and shame-faced look he directed at me. "He will not and cannot understand me." I said I would go and look at our child, and I left the room. I wished to be alone, and to cry and cry and cry . . .

IV

The house at Nikolskoe, so long unheated and uninhabited, came to life again; but much of the past was dead beyond recall. Tatyana Semenovna was no more, and now we were alone together. But far from desiring such close companionship, we even found it irksome. To me that winter was the more trying because I was in bad health, from which I recovered only after the birth of my second son. My husband and I were still on the same terms as during our life in Petersburg: we were coldly friendly to each other; but in the country each room, wall, and sofa recalled what he had once been to me, and what I had lost. It was as if some unforgiven grievance held us apart, as if he were punishing me and pretending not to be aware of it. But there was nothing to ask pardon for, no penalty to deprecate; my punishment was merely this, that he did not give his whole heart and mind to me as he used to do; but he did not give it to anyone or to anything; it was as though he no longer had a heart to give. Sometimes it occurred to me that he was only pretending to be like that, in order to hurt me, and that the old feeling was still alive in his breast; and I tried to call it forth. But I always failed: he always seemed to avoid frankness, evidently suspecting me of insincerity, and dreading the folly of any emotional display. I could read in his face and in the tone of his voice, "What's the good of talking? I know all the facts already, I know what's on the tip of your tongue, and I know that you'll say one thing and do another." At first I was mortified by his dread of frankness, but later I came to think it was rather the absence, on his part, of any need of frankness. It would never have occurred to me now, to tell him all of a sudden that I loved him, or to ask him to repeat my prayers with me or listen while I played the piano. Our relations came to be regulated by a fixed code of good manners. We lived our separate lives: he had his own occupations in which I was not needed, and which I no longer wished to share, while I continued my idle life which no longer annoyed or grieved him. The children were still too young to form a bond between us.

But spring came and brought Katya and Sonya to spend the summer with us in the country. As the house at Nikolskoe was under repair, we went to live at my old home at Pokrovskoe. The old house was unchanged—the veranda, the folding table and the piano in the sunny drawing-room, my old bedroom with its white curtains and dreams of my girlhood which I seemed to have left behind there. In that room there were two beds: one had been mine, and in it my plump little Kokosha lay sprawling, when I went at night to make the sign of the cross over him; the other was a crib, in which the little face of my baby, Vanya, peeked out from his swaddling-clothes. Often, when I had made the sign of the cross over them and remained standing in the middle of the quiet room, there suddenly rose up from all the corners, from the walls and curtains, old forgotten visions of youth. Old voices began to sing the songs of my girlhood. Where were those visions now? where were those dear old songs? All that I had hardly dared to hope for had come to pass. My vague confused dreams had become a reality, and the reality had become an oppressive, difficult, and joyless life. Everything remained the same—the garden visible through the window, the grass, the path, the very same bench above the valley, the same song of the nightingale by the pond, the lilacs in full bloom, the moon shining above the house; and yet, in everything there was such a terrible inconceivable change! Such coldness in all that might have been near and dear! Just as in old times, Katya and I sit alone quietly together in the parlor and talk about him. But Katya has grown wrinkled and pale; her eyes no longer shine with joy and hope, but express only sympathy, sorrow, and regret. We don't go into raptures as we used to, we judge him coolly; we don't wonder what we have done to deserve such happiness, or long to proclaim our thoughts to all the world. No! we whisper together like conspirators and ask each other for the hundredth time why everything has changed so sadly. Yet he was still the same man, save for the deeper furrow between his eyebrows and the whiter hair on his temples; but his serious attentive look was constantly veiled from me by a cloud. And I am the same woman, but without love or desire for love, with no longing for work and no contentment with myself. My religious ecstasies, my love for my husband, the fullness of my former life—all these now seem utterly remote and visionary. Once it seemed so plain and right that to live for others was happiness; but now it has become unintelligible. Why live for others, when life has no attraction even for oneself?

I had given up music altogether since the time of our first visit to Petersburg; now the old piano and the old music tempted me to begin again.

One day I was not well and stayed indoors alone. My husband had taken Katya and Sonya to see the new buildings at Nikolskoe. Tea was served; I went downstairs and while waiting for them to return sat down at the piano. I opened the "Moonlight Sonata" and began to play. There was no one within sight or sound, the windows were open over the garden, and the familiar sounds floated through the room with a solemn sadness. At the end of the first movement I looked round instinctively to the corner where he used to sit and listen to my playing. He was not there; his chair, long unmoved, was still in its place; through the window I could see a lilac-bush against the light of the setting sun; the freshness of evening streamed in through the open windows. I rested my elbows on the piano and covered my face with both hands; and so I sat for a long time, thinking. I recalled with pain the irrevocable past, and timidly imagined the future. But for me there seemed to be no future, no desires at all and no hopes. "Can life be over for me?" I thought with horror; then I looked up, and, trying to forget and not to think, I began playing the same movement over again. "O God!" I prayed, "forgive me if I have sinned, restore to me all that once blossomed in my heart, or teach me what to do and how to live now." There was a sound of wheels on the grass before the steps of the house; then I heard cautious and familiar footsteps pass along the veranda and cease; but my heart no longer replied to the sound. When I stopped playing the footsteps were behind me and a hand was laid on my shoulder.

"How clever of you to think of playing that!" he said.

I said nothing.

"Have you had tea?" he asked.

I shook my head without looking at him—I was unwilling to let him see the signs of emotion on my face.

"They'll be here immediately," he said; "the horse gave us trouble, and they got out on the high road to walk home."

"Let's wait for them," I said, and went out to the veranda, hoping that he would follow; but he asked about the children and went upstairs to see them. Once more his presence and simple kind voice made me doubt if I had really lost anything. What more could I wish? "He is kind and gentle, a good husband, a good father; I myself don't know what more I want." I sat down under the veranda awning on the very bench on which I had sat when we became engaged. The sun had set, it was growing dark, and a little spring rain-cloud hung over the house and garden; only behind the trees the horizon was clear, with the fading glow of twilight, in which one star had just begun to twinkle. The landscape, covered by the shadow of the cloud, seemed waiting for the light spring shower. There was not a breath of wind; not a single leaf or blade of grass stirred; the scent of lilac and bird-cherry was so strong in the garden and veranda that it seemed as if all the air was in flower; it came in wafts, now stronger, now weaker, till one longed to shut both eyes and ears and drink in that fragrance. The dahlias and rose-bushes, not yet in flower, stood motionless on the black border, looking as if they were growing slowly upwards on their white stakes; beyond the valley, frogs were making the most of their time before the rain drove them to the pond, croaking busily and loudly. Only the high continuous note of water falling at some distance rose above their croaking. From time to time the nightingales called to one another, and I could hear them flitting restlessly from bush to bush. Again this spring a nightingale had tried to build a nest in a bush under the window, and I heard her fly off across the avenue when I went onto the veranda. From there she whistled once and then stopped; she, too, was expecting rain.

I tried in vain to calm my feelings: I had a sense of anticipation and regret.

He came downstairs again and sat down beside me.

"I'm afraid they'll get wet," he said.

"Yes," I answered; and we sat for a long time without speaking.

The cloud hung down lower and lower with no wind. The air grew stiller and more fragrant. Suddenly a drop fell on the canvas awning and seemed to rebound from it; then another broke on the gravel path; soon there was a splash on the burdock leaves, and a fresh shower of big drops came down faster and faster. Nightingales and frogs fell silent; only the high note of the falling water, though the rain made it seem more distant, still went on; and a bird, which must have sheltered among the dry leaves near the veranda, steadily repeated its two unvarying notes. My husband got up to go in.

"Where are you going?" I asked, trying to keep him; "it's so pleasant here."

"We must send them an umbrella and galoshes," he replied.

"Don't trouble—it will soon be over."

He thought I was right, and we remained together on the veranda. I rested one hand upon the wet slippery rail and put my head out. The fresh rain wet my hair and neck in places. The cloud, growing lighter and thinner, was passing overhead; the steady patter of the rain gave way to occasional drops that fell from the sky or dripped from trees. Frogs began to croak again in the valley; the nightingales woke up and began to call from the dripping bushes first from one side and then from another. The whole prospect before us grew clear.

"How delightful!" he said, seating himself on the veranda rail and passing a hand over my wet hair.

This simple caress had the effect of a reproach: I felt inclined to cry.

"What more does a man need?" he said; "I am so content now that I want nothing; I am perfectly happy!"

He told me a different story once, I thought. He had said that, however great his happiness might be, he always wanted more and more. Now he is calm and contented; whereas my heart is full of unspoken repentance and unshed tears.

"I think it delightful too," I said; "but I'm sad just because of the beauty of it all. Everything is so fair and lovely outside me, while my own heart is confused, baffled, and full of vague unsatisfied longing. Is it possible that there is no element of pain, no yearning for the past, in your enjoyment of nature?"

He took his hand off my head and was silent for a little.

"I used to feel that too," he said, as though recalling it, "especially in spring. I used to sit up all night, with only my hopes and fears for company, and good company they were! But life was all before me then. Now it is all behind me, and I am content with what I have. I find life splendid," he added with such careless confidence, that I believed, whatever pain it gave me to hear it, that it was the truth.

"But is there nothing you wish for?" I asked.

"I don't ask for impossibilities," he said, guessing my thoughts. "You go and get your head wet," he added, stroking my head like a child's and again passing his hand over the wet hair; "you envy the leaves and the grass their wetness from the rain, and you would like to be the grass and the leaves and the rain. But I am content to enjoy them and everything else that is good and young and happy."

"Do you regret nothing of the past?" I asked, while my heart grew heavier and heavier.

Again he thought for a while before replying. I saw that he wished to answer with perfect frankness.

"Nothing," he said shortly.

"Not true! not true!" I said, turning towards him and looking into his eyes. "Do you really not regret the past?"

"No!" he repeated; "I'm grateful for it, but I don't regret it."

"But wouldn't you like to have it back?" I asked.

He turned away and looked out over the garden.

"No; I might as well wish to have wings. It's impossible."

"And wouldn't you alter the past? don't you reproach yourself or me?"

"No, never! It was all for the best."

"Listen to me!" I said touching his arm to make him look around. "Why didn't you ever tell me that you wished me to live as you really did? Why did you give me freedom for which I was unfit? Why did you stop teaching me? If you had wished it, if you had guided me differently, none of this would have happened!" I said in a voice that increasingly expressed cold displeasure and reproach in place of the love of former days.

"What wouldn't have happened?" he asked, turning to me in surprise.

"As it is, there's nothing wrong. Things are all right, quite all right," he added with a smile.

"Does he really not understand?" I thought; "or even worse, does he not wish to understand?"

Then I suddenly broke out. "Had you acted differently, I should not be punished now, for no fault at all, by your indifference and even contempt, and you wouldn't have taken from me unjustly all that I valued in life!"

"What do you mean, my dear?" he asked—he seemed not to understand.

"No! don't interrupt me! You have taken from me your confidence, your love, even your respect; for I cannot believe, when I think of the past, that you still love me. No! don't speak! once for all I must say what has been torturing me for so long. Is it my fault that I knew nothing of life, that you left me to learn experience for myself? Is it my fault that now, when I have gained the knowledge and have been struggling for nearly a year to come back to you, you push me away and pretend not to understand what I want? And you always do it in such a way that it is impossible to reproach you, while I am guilty and unhappy. Yes, you wish to drive me out again to that life which might rob us both of happiness."

"How did I show that?" he asked in evident alarm and surprise.

"No later than yesterday you said, and you constantly say, that I can never settle down here, and that we must spend this winter in Petersburg; I hate Petersburg!" I went on. "Instead of supporting me, you avoid all plain talk, you never say a single frank affectionate word to me. And then, when I fall utterly, you'll reproach me and rejoice in my fall."

"Stop!" he said with cold severity. "You have no right to say that. It only proves that you are ill-disposed towards me, that you don't . . ."

"That I don't love you? Don't hesitate to say it!" I cried, and the tears began to flow. I sat down on the bench and covered my face with my handkerchief.

"So that's how he understood me!" I thought, trying to restrain the sobs which choked me. "Gone, gone is our former love!" said a voice in my heart. He didn't come close or try to comfort me. He was hurt by what I had said. When he spoke, his tone was cool and dry.

"I don't know what you reproach me with," he began. "If you mean that I don't love you as I once did . . ."

"Did!" I said, with my face buried in the handkerchief, while the bitter tears fell still more abundantly.

"If so, time is to blame for that, and we ourselves. Each time of life has its own kind of love." He was silent for a moment. "Shall I tell you the whole truth, if you really long for frankness? In that summer when I first knew you, I used to lie awake all night, thinking about you, and I made that love myself, and it grew and grew in my heart. Again, in

Petersburg and abroad, in the course of horrible sleepless nights, I strove to shatter and destroy that love, which had come to torture me. I didn't destroy it, but I destroyed that part of it which gave me pain. Then I grew calm; I still feel love, but it is a different kind of love."

"You call it love, but I call it torture!" I said. "Why did you allow me to go into society, if you thought so badly of it that you ceased to love me on that account?"

"No, it was not society, my dear," he said.

"Why didn't you exercise your authority?" I went on: "why didn't you lock me up or kill me? That would have been better than the loss of all that formed my happiness. I should have been happy, instead of being ashamed."

I began to sob again and hid my face.

Just then Katya and Sonya, wet and cheerful, came out onto the veranda, laughing and talking loudly. They were silent as soon as they saw us, and went in again immediately.

We remained silent for a long time. I had had my cry and felt relieved. I glanced at him. He was sitting with his head resting on his hand; he intended to make some reply to my glance, but only sighed deeply and resumed his former position.

I went up to him and removed his hand. His eyes turned thoughtfully to my face.

"Yes," he began, as if continuing his thoughts aloud, "all of us, and especially you women, must have personal experience of all the nonsense of life, in order to get back to life itself; evidence of other people is no good. At that time you had still not got near the end of that charming nonsense which I admired in you. So I let you go through it alone, feeling that I had no right to put pressure on you, though my own time for that sort of thing was long past."

"If you loved me," I said, "how could you stand beside me and allow me to go through it?"

"Because it was impossible for you to take my word for it, though you would have tried. Personal experience was necessary, and now you've had it."

"There was much calculation in all that," I said, "but little love."

Again we were silent.

"What you said just now is severe, but true," he began, rising suddenly and beginning to walk about the veranda. "Yes, it's true. I was to blame," he added, stopping opposite me; "I ought either to have kept myself from loving you at all, or to have loved you in a simpler way."

"Let's forget it all," I said timidly.

"No," he said; "the past can never come back, never"; and his voice softened as he spoke.

"It's restored already," I said, laying a hand on his shoulder.

He took my hand away and pressed it.

"I was wrong when I said that I didn't regret the past. I do regret it; I weep for that past love which can never return. Who's to blame, I don't know. Love remains, but not the old love; its place remains, but it's all wasted away and has lost all strength and substance; recollections are still left, and gratitude; but . . ."

"Don't say that!" I broke in. "Let it all be as it was before! Surely that's possible?" I asked, looking into his eyes; but their gaze was clear and calm, and did not look deeply into mine.

Even while I spoke, I knew that my wishes and petition were impossible. He smiled calmly and gently; I thought it was the smile of an old man.

"How young you are still!" he said, "and I'm so old. What you seek in me is no longer there. Why deceive ourselves?" he added, still smiling.

I stood silent opposite him, and my heart grew calmer.

"Let us not try to repeat life," he went on. "Let us not make pretenses to ourselves. Let us be thankful that there is an end of the old emotions and excitements. The excitement of searching is over for us; our quest is done, happiness enough has fallen to our lot. Now we must stand aside and make room—for him, if you like," he said, pointing to the nurse who was carrying Vanya out and had stopped at the veranda door. "That's the truth, my dear one," he said, drawing down my head and kissing it, not a lover any longer but an old friend.

The fragrant freshness of the night rose even stronger and sweeter from the garden; the sounds and the silence grew more solemn; star after star began to twinkle overhead. I looked at him, and suddenly my heart grew light; it seemed that the cause of my suffering had been removed like an aching nerve. Suddenly I realized clearly and calmly that the past feeling, like the past itself, was gone beyond recall, and that it would be not only impossible but painful and uncomfortable to bring it back. After all, was that time really so good which seemed to me so happy? And it was all so long, long ago!

"Time for tea!" he said, and we went together into the parlor. At the door we met nanny with the baby. I took him in my arms, covered his bare little red legs, pressed him to me, and kissed him with the lightest touch of my lips. Half asleep, he moved the parted fingers of one creased little hand and opened his dim little eyes, as if looking for something or recalling something. All at once his eyes rested on me, a spark of consciousness shone in them, the little pouting lips, parted before, now met and opened in a smile. "Mine, mine, mine!" I thought, pressing him to my breast with such an impulse of joy in every limb that I found it hard to restrain myself from hurting him. I began kissing his cold little feet, his stomach and hand and head with its thin covering of down. My husband came up to me, and I quickly covered the child's face and uncovered it again.

"Ivan Sergeich!" said my husband, tickling him under the chin. But

I made haste to cover Ivan Sergeich up again. Only I had any business looking at him. I glanced at my husband. His eyes smiled as he looked at me; I looked into them with an ease and happiness which I had not felt for a long time.

That day ended the romance of our marriage; the old feeling became a precious irrecoverable remembrance; but a new feeling of love for my children and their father laid the foundation of a new life and quite a different happiness; that life and happiness have lasted to the present time.

God Sees the Truth, But Waits†

In the town of Vladimir lived a young merchant named Ivan Dmitrich Aksenov. He had two shops and a house of his own.

Aksenov was a handsome, fair-haired, curly-headed fellow, full of fun and very fond of singing. When quite a young man he had been prone to drink and was riotous when he'd had too much; but after he married he gave up drinking except now and then.

One summer Aksenov was going to the Nizhny Fair, and as he bade good-bye to his family his wife said to him, "Ivan Dmitrich, don't start out to-day; I've had a bad dream about you."

Aksenov laughed, and said, "You're afraid that when I get to the fair I'll go on a spree."

His wife replied: "I don't know what I'm afraid of; all I know is that I had a bad dream. I dreamt you returned from town, and when you took off your cap I saw that your hair was quite grey."

Aksenov laughed. "That's a lucky sign," he said. "See if I don't sell all my goods and bring you home some presents from the fair."

So he said good-bye to his family and drove away.

When he had travelled half-way, he met a merchant whom he knew, and they put up at the same inn for the night. They drank some tea together, and then went to bed in adjoining rooms.

It was not Aksenov's habit to sleep late, and, wishing to travel while it was still cool, he aroused his driver before dawn and told him to harness the horses.

Then he made his way across to the landlord of the inn (who lived in a cottage at the back), paid his bill, and continued his journey.

When he'd gone about twenty-five miles he stopped for the horses to be fed. Aksenov rested awhile in the passage of the inn, then he stepped out onto the porch and, ordering a samovar to be heated, got out his guitar and began to play.

Suddenly a troika drove up with tinkling bells and an official got out,

†This piece was first published in 1872.

followed by two soldiers. He came to Aksenov and began to question him, asking him who he was and where he came from. Aksenov answered him fully, and said, "Won't you have some tea with me?" But the official went on cross-examining him and asking him, "Where did you spend last night? Were you alone, or with another merchant? Did you see the other merchant this morning? Why did you leave the inn before dawn?"

Aksenov wondered why he was being asked all these questions, but he described all that had happened, and then added, "Why are you cross-examining me as if I were a thief or a robber? I'm travelling on business of my own, and there's no need to question me."

Then the official, calling the soldiers, said, "I'm the police-officer of this district, and I'm questioning you because the merchant with whom you spent last night has been found with his throat cut. We must search your things."

They entered the house. The soldiers and the police-officer unstrapped Aksenov's luggage and searched it. Suddenly the officer drew a knife out of his bag, crying, "Whose knife is this?"

Aksenov looked, and seeing a blood-stained knife taken from his own bag, he became frightened.

"Why is there blood on this knife?"

Aksenov tried to answer, but could hardly utter a word, and only stammered: "I—don't know—it's not mine."

Then the police-officer said, "This morning the merchant was found in bed with his throat cut. You are the only person who could have done it. The house was locked from inside, and no one else was there. Here is a blood-stained knife in your bag, and your face and manner betray you! Tell me how you killed him and how much money you stole!"

Aksenov swore he hadn't done it; that he hadn't seen the merchant after they'd had tea together; that he had no money except eight thousand rubles of his own, and that the knife was not his. But his voice was broken, his face pale, and he trembled with fear as though he were guilty.

The police-officer ordered the soldiers to bind Aksenov and to put him in the cart. As they tied his feet together and flung him into the cart, Aksenov crossed himself and wept. His money and goods were taken away from him, and he was sent to the nearest town and imprisoned there. Inquiries as to his character were made in Vladimir. The merchants and other inhabitants of that town said that in former days he used to drink and loiter about, but that he was a good man. Then the trial came: he was charged with murdering a merchant from Ryazan and robbing him of twenty thousand rubles.

His wife was in despair, and did not know what to believe. Her children were all quite small; one was still a baby at the breast. Taking them all with her, she went to town where her husband was in jail. At first she was not allowed to see him; but, after much begging, she obtained permission from the officials and was taken to him. When she saw her husband in prison-dress and in chains, shut up with thieves and criminals, she fell down and didn't recover her senses for a long time. Then she drew her children to her, and sat down near him. She told him about things at home, and asked what had happened to him. He told her all, and she asked, "What can we do now?"

"We must petition the Tsar not to let an innocent man perish."

His wife told him that she had sent a petition to the Tsar, but that it hadn't been accepted.

Aksenov didn't reply, but only looked downcast.

Then his wife said, "It was not for nothing I dreamt your hair had turned grey. You remember? You shouldn't have started out that day." And passing her fingers through his hair she said: "Vanya dearest, tell your wife the truth; was it you who did it?"

"So you, too, suspect me!" said Aksenov; hiding his face in his hands, he began to weep. Then a soldier came to say that his wife and children must go away, and Aksenov said good-bye to his family for the last time.

When they had gone, Aksenov recalled what had been said. When he remembered that his wife also had suspected him, he said to himself, "It seems that only God can know the truth; it is to Him alone we must appeal and from Him alone expect mercy."

Aksenov wrote no more petitions, gave up all hope, and only prayed to God.

Aksenov was condemned to be flogged and sent to the mines. So he was flogged with a knout, and when the wounds caused by the knout were healed, he was taken off to Siberia with other convicts.

For twenty-six years Aksenov lived as a convict in Siberia. His hair turned white as snow, and his beard grew long, thin, and grey. All his mirth disappeared; he stooped; he walked slowly, spoke little, and never laughed, but he often prayed.

In prison Aksenov learnt to make boots, and earned a little money, with which he bought *The Lives of the Saints*. He read this book when it was light enough in the prison; on Sundays in the prison-church he read the Gospel and sang in the choir, for his voice was still good.

The prison authorities liked Aksenov for his meekness, and his fellow-prisoners respected him: they called him "Grandfather" and "The Saint." When they wanted to petition the prison authorities about anything, they always chose Aksenov as their spokesman, and when there were quarrels among the prisoners they came to him to put things right, and to judge the matter.

No news reached Aksenov from his home, and he did not even know if his wife and children were still alive.

One day a fresh gang of convicts came to the prison. In the evening the old prisoners gathered around the new ones and asked them what towns or villages they came from, and what they were sentenced for. Along with the rest Aksenov sat down near the new-comers, and listened with a downcast air to what was being said.

One of the new convicts, a tall, strong man of sixty, with a closely-cropped grey beard, was telling the others what he had been arrested for.

"Well, friends," he said, "I took a horse that was tied to a sledge, and I was arrested and accused of stealing. I said I'd only taken it to get home quicker, and then had let it go; besides, the driver was a personal friend of mine. So I said, 'It's all right.' 'No,' said they, 'you stole it.' But how or where I stole it they couldn't say. I once really did something wrong, and by rights I ought to have come here long ago, but that time I wasn't found out. Now I've been sent here for nothing at all . . . Eh, but it's all lies I'm telling you; I've been to Siberia before, but I didn't stay long."

"Where are you from?" asked someone.

"From Vladimir. My family comes from that town. My name is Makar, and they also call me Semenich."

Aksenov raised his head and asked: "Tell me, Semenich, do you know anything of the merchants Aksenov, from Vladimir? Are they still alive?"

"Know them? Of course I do. The Aksenovs are rich, though their father is in Siberia: a sinner like ourselves, it seems! As for you, Gran'dad, how did you come here?"

Aksenov didn't like to speak about his misfortune. He only sighed, and said, "For my sins I've been in prison these last twenty-six years."

"What sins?" asked Makar Semenich.

But Aksenov only said, "Well, well—I must have deserved it!" He would have said no more, but his companions told the new-comer how Aksenov came to be in Siberia: how some one had killed a merchant and had put a knife among Aksenov's things, and how he'd been unjustly condemned.

When Makar Semenich heard this he looked at Aksenov, slapped his own knee, and exclaimed, "Well, that's wonderful! Really wonderful! But how old you've grown, Gran'dad!"

The others asked him why he was so surprised, and where he'd seen Aksenov before; but Makar Semenich didn't reply. He only said: "It's wonderful that we should meet here, lads!"

These words made Aksenov wonder whether perhaps this man knew who'd killed the merchant; so he said, "Perhaps, Semenich, you've heard about this affair, or maybe you've seen me before?"

"How could I help hearing? The world's full of rumors. But it's a long time ago, and I've forgotten what I heard."

"Perhaps you heard who killed the merchant?" asked Aksenov.

Makar Semenich laughed, and replied, "It must have been the one in whose bag the knife was found! If someone else hid the knife there—

'He's not a thief till he's caught,' as the saying goes. How could anyone put a knife in your bag while it was under your head? It would surely have woke you up."

When Aksenov heard these words he felt sure this was the man who'd killed the merchant. He got up and went away. All that night Aksenov lay awake. He felt terribly unhappy, and all sorts of images rose in his mind. First there was the image of his wife as she was when he parted from her to go to the fair. He saw her as if she were present; her face and eyes arose before him, he heard her speak and laugh. Then he saw his children, quite little, as they were at that time: one with a little cloak on, another at his mother's breast. Then he remembered himself as he used to be—young and merry. He remembered how he sat playing the guitar on the porch of the inn where he was arrested, and how free from all care he had been. Then he saw in his mind the place where he was flogged, the executioner, and people standing around; the chains, convicts, all twenty-six years of his prison life, and his premature old age. The thought of it all made him so wretched that he was ready to kill himself.

"And it's all that villain's doing!" thought Aksenov. And his anger was so great against Makar Semenich that he longed for vengeance, even if he himself would perish for it. He kept saying prayers all night, but could get no peace. During the day he didn't go anywhere near Makar Semenich, nor even look at him.

Two weeks passed in this way. Aksenov could not sleep at night and was so miserable that he didn't know what to do.

One night as he was walking about the prison he noticed some earth that came rolling out from under one of the shelves on which the prisoners slept. He stopped to see what it was. Suddenly Makar Semenich crept out from under the shelf, and looked up at Aksenov with a frightened face. Aksenov tried to pass without looking at him, but Makar seized his hand and told him that he had dug a hole under the wall, getting rid of the earth by putting it into his high boots and emptying it out every day on the road when the prisoners were driven to their work.

"You keep quiet, old man, and you'll get out too. If you blab, they'll flog the life out of me, but I'll kill you first."

Aksenov trembled with anger as he looked at his enemy. He drew his hand away, saying, "I have no wish to escape, and you have no need to kill me; you killed me a long time ago! And as for squealing on you— I may do so or I may not, as God directs."

The next day, when the convicts were led out to work, the convoy soldiers noticed that one or other of the prisoners emptied some earth out of his boots. The prison was searched and the tunnel was found. The Governor came and questioned all the prisoners to find out who'd dug the hole. They all denied any knowledge of it. Those who knew wouldn't betray Makar Semenich, knowing that he'd be flogged almost to death. At last the Governor turned to Aksenov, whom he knew to be a just man, and said:

"You're a truthful old man; tell me, before God, who dug the hole?"

Makar Semenich stood as if he were quite unconcerned, looking at the Governor and not so much as glancing at Aksenov. Aksenov's lips and hands trembled, and for a long time he couldn't utter a word. He thought, "Why should I protect someone who ruined my life? Let him pay for what I've suffered. But if I tell, they'll probably flog the life out of him, and maybe I suspect him wrongly. And, after all, what good would it be to me?"

"Well, old man," repeated the Governor, "tell us the truth: who's been digging under the wall?"

Aksenov glanced at Makar Semenich and said, "I cannot say, your Honor. It's not God's will that I should tell! Do what you like with me; I'm in your hands."

However much the Governor tried, Aksenov would say no more, and so the matter had to be left.

That night, when Aksenov was lying on his bed and just beginning to doze, someone came quietly and sat down on his bed. He peered through the darkness and recognized Makar.

"What more do you want of me?" asked Aksenov. "Why have you come here?"

Makar Semenich was silent. So Aksenov sat up and said, "What do you want? Go away or I'll call the guard!"

Makar Semenich bent over close to Aksenov, and whispered, "Ivan Dmitrich, forgive me!"

"What for?" asked Aksenov.

"It was I who killed the merchant and hid the knife among your things. I meant to kill you too, but I heard a noise outside; so I hid the knife in your bag and escaped through the window."

Aksenov was silent and didn't know what to say. Makar Semenich slid off the bed-shelf and knelt down upon the ground. "Ivan Dmitrich," he said, "forgive me! For the love of God, forgive me! I'll confess that it was I who killed the merchant, and now you'll be released and you can go home."

"It's easy for you to talk," said Aksenov, "but I've suffered for you these last twenty-six years. Where could I go now? My wife is dead, and my children have forgotten me. I have nowhere to go. . . ."

Makar Semenich didn't get up, but beat his head on the floor. "Ivan Dmitrich, forgive me!" he cried. "When they flogged me with the knout it wasn't as hard to bear as it is to see you now . . . but you took pity on me and didn't tell. For Christ's sake forgive me, wretch that I am!" And he began to sob.

When Aksenov heard him sobbing he, too, began to weep.

"God will forgive you!" he said. "Maybe I'm a hundred times worse than you." At these words his heart grew light and the longing for home left him. He no longer had any desire to leave prison, but only hoped for his last hour to come.

In spite of what Aksenov had said, Makar Semenich confessed his guilt. But when the order for his release came, Aksenov was already dead.

The Death of Ivan Ilych†

I

During an interval in the Melvinsky trial in the large building of the Law Court the members and public prosecutor met in Ivan Egorovich Shebek's private room, where the conversation turned to the celebrated Krasovsky case. Fedor Vasilievich fervently declared that it was not subject to their jurisdiction, Ivan Egorovich maintained the contrary, while Peter Ivanovich, not having entered into the discussion at the start, took no part in it, but looked through the *Gazette* which he had just been handed.

"Gentlemen," he said, "Ivan Ilych has died!"

"You don't say so!"

"Here, read it yourself," replied Peter Ivanovich, handing Fedor Vasilievich the paper still damp from the press. Surrounded by a black border were the words: "Praskovya Fedorovna Golovina, with profound sorrow, informs relatives and friends of the demise of her beloved husband Ivan Ilych Golovin, Member of the Court of Justice, which occurred on February the 4th of this year 1882. The funeral will take place on Friday at one o'clock in the afternoon."

Ivan Ilych had been a colleague of the gentlemen present and was liked by them all. He had been ill for some weeks with an illness said to be incurable. His post had been kept open for him, but there had been conjectures that in case of his death Alexeev might receive his appointment, and that either Vinnikov or Shtabel would succeed Alexeev. So on receiving the news of Ivan Ilych's death the first thought of each of the gentlemen present in that private room was about the changes and promotions it might occasion among themselves or their acquaintances.

"I shall be sure to get Shtabel's place or Vinnikov's," thought Fedor Vasilievich. "I was promised that long ago, and the promotion means an extra eight hundred rubles a year for me besides the allowance."

"Now I must apply for my brother-in-law's transfer from Kaluga,"

†This piece was first published in 1886.

thought Peter Ivanovich. "My wife will be very pleased, and then she won't be able to say that I never do anything for her relatives."

"I thought he would never leave his bed again," said Peter Ivanovich aloud. "It's very sad."

"But what was really the matter with him?"

"The doctors couldn't say—at least they could, but each of them said something different. When last I saw him I thought he was getting better."

"I haven't been to see him since the holidays. I always meant to go."

"Did he have any property?"

"I think his wife had a little—but it was quite unimportant."

"We shall have to go to see her, but they live so terribly far away."

"Far from you, you mean. Everything's far away from your place."

"You see, he never can forgive my living on the other side of the river," said Peter Ivanovich, smiling at Shebek. Then, still talking of the distances between different parts of the city, they returned to the Court.

Besides considerations as to possible transfers and promotions likely to result from Ivan Ilych's death, the mere fact of the death of a near acquaintance aroused, as usual, in all who heard of it the complacent feeling that, "it's he who is dead and not I."

Each one thought or felt, "Well, he's dead but I'm alive!" But the more intimate of Ivan Ilych's acquaintances, his so-called friends, could not help also thinking that now they would have to fulfil the very tiresome demands of propriety by attending the funeral service and paying a condolence call on the widow.

Fedor Vasilievich and Peter Ivanovich had been his nearest acquaintances. Peter Ivanovich had studied law with Ivan Ilych and had considered himself to be under obligations to him.

Having told his wife at dinner of Ivan Ilych's death, and of his conjecture that it might be possible to get her brother transferred to their circuit, Peter Ivanovich sacrificed his usual nap, put on his evening clothes and drove to Ivan Ilych's house.

At the entrance stood a carriage and two cabs. Leaning against the wall in the hall downstairs near the coat-stand was a coffin-lid covered with cloth of gold, ornamented with gold cord and tassels, that had been polished with metal powder. Two ladies in black were taking off their fur cloaks. Peter Ivanovich recognized one of them as Ivan Ilych's sister, but the other was a stranger to him. His colleague Schwartz was just coming downstairs, but on seeing Peter Ivanovich enter he stopped and winked at him, as if to say: "Ivan Ilych has made a mess of things—not like you and me."

Schwartz's face with his Piccadilly whiskers, and his slim figure in evening dress, as usual had an air of elegant solemnity which contrasted with the playfulness of his character and had a special piquancy here, or so it seemed to Peter Ivanovich.

Peter Ivanovich allowed the ladies to precede him and slowly followed them upstairs. Schwartz did not come down but remained where he was, and Peter Ivanovich understood that he wanted to arrange where they should play bridge that evening. The ladies went upstairs to the widow's room, and Schwartz with seriously compressed lips but a playful look in his eyes, indicated by a twist of his eyebrows the room to the right where the body lay.

Peter Ivanovich, like everyone else on such occasions, entered feeling uncertain what he would have to do. All he knew was that at such times it is always safe to cross oneself. But he was not quite sure whether one should bow while doing so. He therefore adopted a middle course. On entering the room he began crossing himself and made a slight movement resembling a bow. At the same time, as far as the motion of his head and arm allowed, he surveyed the room. Two young men—apparently nephews, one of whom was a high-school pupil—were leaving the room, crossing themselves as they did so. An old woman was standing motionless, and a lady with strangely arched eyebrows was saying something to her in a whisper. A vigorous, resolute Church Reader, in a frock-coat, was reading something in a loud voice with an expression that precluded any contradiction. The butler's assistant, Gerasim, stepping lightly in front of Peter Ivanovich, was strewing something on the floor. Noticing this, Peter Ivanovich was immediately aware of a faint odor of a decomposing body.

The last time he had called on Ivan Ilych, Peter Ivanovich had seen Gerasim in the study. Ivan Ilych had been particularly fond of him and he was performing the duty of a sick nurse.

Peter Ivanovich continued to make the sign of the cross slightly inclining his head in an intermediate direction between the coffin, the Reader, and the icons on the table in a corner of the room. Afterwards, when it seemed to him that this movement of his arm in crossing himself had gone on too long, he stopped and began to look at the corpse.

The dead man lay, as dead men always lie, in a specially heavy way, his rigid limbs sunk in the soft cushions of the coffin, with the head forever bowed on the pillow. His yellow waxen brow with bald patches over his sunken temples was thrust up in the way peculiar to the dead, the protruding nose seeming to press on the upper lip. He was much changed and had grown even thinner since Peter Ivanovich had last seen him, but, as is always the case with the dead, his face was handsomer and above all more dignified than when he was alive. The expression on the face said that what was necessary had been accomplished, and accomplished rightly. Besides this there was in that expression a reproach and a warning to the living. This warning seemed out of place to Peter Ivanovich, or at least not applicable to him. He felt a certain discomfort and so he hurriedly crossed himself once more, turned and went out the door—too hurriedly and regardless of propriety, as he himself was aware.

Schwartz was waiting for him in the adjoining room with legs spread wide apart and both hands toying with his top-hat behind his back. The mere sight of that playful, well-groomed, and elegant figure restored Peter Ivanovich. He felt that Schwartz stood above all these happenings and would not surrender to any depressing influences. His very look said that this incident of a church service for Ivan Ilych could not be a sufficient reason for infringing the order of the session—in other words, that it would certainly not prevent his unwrapping a new pack of cards and shuffling them that evening while a footman placed four fresh candles on the table: in fact, that there was no reason for supposing that this incident would hinder their spending the evening agreeably. Indeed he said this in a whisper as Peter Ivanovich passed him, proposing that they should meet for a game at Fedor Vasilievich's. But apparently Peter Ivanovich was not destined to play bridge that evening. Praskovya Fedorovna (a short, fat woman who despite all efforts to the contrary had continued to broaden steadily from her shoulders downwards and who had the same extraordinarily arched eyebrows as the lady who had been standing by the coffin), dressed all in black, her head covered with lace, came out of her own room with some other ladies, conducted them to the room where the dead body lay, and said: "The service will begin immediately. Please go in."

Schwartz, making an indefinite bow, stood still, evidently neither accepting nor declining this invitation. Praskovya Fedorovna recognizing Peter Ivanovich, sighed, went up close to him, took his hand, and said: "I know you were a true friend to Ivan Ilych . . ." and looked at him awaiting some suitable response. And Peter Ivanovich knew that, just as it had been the right thing to cross himself in that room, what he had to do here was press her hand, sigh, and say, "Believe me . . ." So he did all this and as he did it felt that the desired result had been achieved: both he and she were touched.

"Come with me. I want to speak to you before it begins," said the widow. "Give me your arm."

Peter Ivanovich gave her his arm and they went to the inner rooms, passing Schwartz who winked at Peter Ivanovich compassionately.

"That does it for our bridge! Don't object if we find another player. Perhaps you can cut in when you do escape," said his playful look.

Peter Ivanovich sighed still more deeply and despondently, and Praskovya Fedorovna pressed his arm gratefully. When they reached the drawing-room, upholstered in pink cretonne and lighted by a dim lamp, they sat down at the table—she on a sofa and Peter Ivanovich on a low pouffe, the springs of which yielded spasmodically under his weight. Praskovya Fedorovna had been on the point of warning him to take another seat, but felt that such a warning was out of keeping with her present condition and so she changed her mind. As he sat down on the pouffe Peter Ivanovich recalled how Ivan Ilych had arranged this room and had consulted him regarding this pink cretonne with green leaves. The whole room was full of furniture and knick-knacks, and on her way to the sofa the lace of the widow's black shawl caught on the carved edge of the table. Peter Ivanovich rose to detach it, and the springs of the pouffe, relieved of his weight, rose also and gave him a push. The widow began detaching her shawl herself, and Peter Ivanovich again sat down, suppressing the rebellious springs of the pouffe under him. But the widow had not quite freed herself and Peter Ivanovich got up again, and again the pouffe rebelled and even creaked. When this was all over she took out a clean cambric handkerchief and began to weep. The episode with the shawl and the struggle with the pouffe had cooled Peter Ivanovich's emotions and he sat there with a sullen look on his face. This awkward situation was interrupted by Sokolov, Ivan Ilych's butler, who came in to report that the plot in the cemetery that Praskovya Fedorovna had chosen would cost two hundred rubles. She stopped weeping and, looking at Peter Ivanovich with the air of a victim, re- marked in French that it was very hard for her. Peter Ivanovich made a silent gesture signifying his full conviction that it must indeed be so.

"You may smoke," she said in a magnanimous yet crushed voice, and turned to discuss the price of the plot for the grave with Sokolov.

While lighting his cigarette Peter Ivanovich heard her inquiring very circumstantially into the prices of different plots in the cemetery and finally decide which one she would take. When that was done she gave instructions about engaging the choir. Sokolov then left the room.

"I look after everything myself," she told Peter Ivanovich, shifting the albums that lay on the table; and noticing that the table was endangered by his cigarette-ash, she immediately passed him an ash-tray, saying as she did so: "I consider it an affectation to say that my grief prevents me from attending to practical affairs. On the contrary, if anything can—I won't say console me, but—distract me, it is seeing to everything concerning him." Once again she took out her handkerchief as if preparing to cry, but suddenly, as if mastering her feeling, shook herself and began to speak calmly. "But there is something I want to talk to you about."

Peter Ivanovich bowed, keeping control of the springs of the pouffe, which immediately began quivering under him.

"He suffered terribly during the last few days."

"Did he?" said Peter Ivanovich.

"Oh, terribly! He screamed unceasingly, not for minutes but for hours. For the last three days he screamed incessantly. It was unendurable. I cannot understand how I stood it; you could hear him three rooms away. Oh, what I have suffered!"

"Is it possible that he was conscious all that time?" asked Peter Ivanovich.

"Yes," she whispered. "To the last moment. He took leave of us a quarter of an hour before he died, and asked us to take Volodya away."

The thought of the suffering of this man whom he had known so intimately, first as a cheerful little boy, then as a schoolmate, and later as a grown-up colleague, suddenly struck Peter Ivanovich with horror, despite an unpleasant consciousness of his own and this woman's dissimulation. He saw that brow again, and that nose pressing down on the lip, and he felt afraid for himself.

"Three days of frightful suffering and then the death! Why, that might suddenly, at any time, happen to me," he thought, and for a moment felt terrified. But—he did not know how—the customary reflection at once occurred to him that this terrible thing had happened to Ivan Ilych and not to him, and that it should not and could not happen to him, and that to think that it could would be yielding to depression which he ought not to do, as Schwartz's expression plainly showed. After this reflection Peter Ivanovich felt reassured, and began to ask with interest about the details of Ivan Ilych's death, as though death was an accident natural to Ivan Ilych but certainly not to himself.

After many details of the really dreadful physical sufferings Ivan Ilych had endured (which details he learned only from the effect those sufferings had produced on Praskovya Fedorovna's nerves) the widow apparently found it necessary to get down to business.

"Oh, Peter Ivanovich, how hard it is! How terribly, terribly hard!" and she began to weep again.

Peter Ivanovich sighed and waited for her to finish blowing her nose. When she had done so he said, "Believe me . . ." and again she began talking and brought out what was evidently her chief concern with him—namely, to question him as to how she could obtain a grant from the government on the occasion of her husband's death. She made it appear that she was asking Peter Ivanovich's advice about her pension, but he soon saw that she already knew about that to the minutest detail, more even than he did himself. She knew how much could be procured from the government in consequence of her husband's death, but wanted to find out whether she could possibly extract some more. Peter Ivanovich tried to think of some means of doing so, but after reflecting for a while and, out of propriety, condemning the government for its niggardliness, said he thought that nothing more could be got. Then she sighed and evidently began to devise some means of getting rid of her visitor. Noticing this, he put out his cigarette, rose, pressed her hand, and went out into the anteroom.

In the dining-room where the clock stood that Ivan Ilych had liked so much and had bought at an antique shop, Peter Ivanovich met a priest and a few acquaintances who had come to attend the service, and he recognized Ivan Ilych's daughter, a handsome young woman. She was dressed in black and her slim figure appeared slimmer than ever. She had a gloomy, determined, almost angry expression, and bowed to Peter Ivanovich as though he were in some way to blame. Behind her, with the same offended look, stood a wealthy young man, an examining magistrate, whom Peter Ivanovich also knew and who was her fiancé, as he had heard. He bowed mournfully to them and was about to pass into the death-chamber, when from under the stairs appeared the figure of Ivan Ilych's schoolboy son, who looked extremely like his father. He seemed a little Ivan Ilych, such as Peter Ivanovich remembered when they studied law together. His tear-stained eyes had in them the look that is seen in the eyes of boys of thirteen or fourteen who are not pure-minded. When he saw Peter Ivanovich he scowled morosely and shamefacedly. Peter Ivanovich nodded to him and entered the death-chamber. The service began: candles, groans, incense, tears, and sobs. Peter Ivanovich stood looking gloomily down at his feet. He did not look at the dead man once, did not yield to any depressing influence, and was one of the first to leave the room. There was no one in the anteroom, but Gerasim darted out of the dead man's room, rummaged with his strong hands among the fur coats to find Peter Ivanovich's, and helped him on with it.

"Well, friend Gerasim," said Peter Ivanovich, so as to say something. "It's a sad affair, isn't it?"

"It's God's will. We shall all come to it some day," said Gerasim, displaying his teeth—the even, white teeth of a healthy peasant—and, like a man in the thick of urgent work, he briskly opened the front door, called the coachman, helped Peter Ivanovich into the sledge, and sprang back to the porch as if in readiness for what he had to do next.

Peter Ivanovich found the fresh air particularly pleasant after the smell of incense, the dead body, and carbolic acid.

"Where to, sir?" asked the coachman.

"It's still not too late. . . . I'll call on Fedor Vasilievich."

Accordingly he drove there and found them just finishing the first rubber, so that it was quite convenient for him to cut in.

II

Ivan Ilych's life had been most simple and most ordinary and therefore most terrible.

He had been a member of the Court of Justice, and died at the age of forty-five. His father had been an official who after serving in various ministries and departments in Petersburg had made the sort of career which brings men to positions from which by reason of their long service they cannot be dismissed, though they are obviously unfit to hold any responsible position, and for whom therefore posts are specially created, which though fictitious carry salaries of from six to ten thousand rubles that are not fictitious, in receipt of which they live on to a great age.

Such was the Privy Councillor and superfluous member of various superfluous institutions, Ilya Epimovich Golovin.

He had three sons, of whom Ivan Ilych was the second. The eldest son was following in his father's footsteps only in another department, and was already approaching that stage in the service at which a similar sinecure would be reached. The third son was a failure. He had ruined his prospects in a number of positions and was now serving in the railway department. His father and brothers, and still more their wives, not merely disliked meeting him, but avoided remembering his existence unless compelled to do so. His sister had married Baron Greff, a Petersburg official of her father's type. Ivan Ilych was *le phénix de la famille*[1] as people said. He was neither as cold and formal as his elder brother nor as wild as the younger; he was a happy mean between them—an intelligent, polished, lively and agreeable man. He had studied with his younger brother at the School of Law, but the latter had failed to complete the course and was expelled when he was in his fifth year. Ivan Ilych finished the course well. Even when he was at the School of Law he was just what he remained for the rest of his life: a capable, cheerful, good-natured, and sociable man, though strict in the fulfilment of what he considered to be his duty. And he considered his duty to be what was so considered by those in authority. Neither as a boy nor as a man was he a toady, but from early youth he was by nature attracted to people of high station as a fly is drawn to the light, assimilating their ways and views of life and establishing friendly relations with them. All the enthusiasms of childhood and youth passed without leaving much trace on him; he succumbed to sensuality, to vanity, and recently among the highest classes to liberalism, but always within limits which his instinct unfailingly indicated to him as correct.

At school he had done things which had formerly seemed to him very horrid and made him feel disgusted with himself when he did them; but later on when he saw that such actions were done by people of good position and that they did not regard them as wrong, he was not exactly able to regard them as right, but to forget about them entirely or not be troubled at all by remembering them.

Having graduated from the School of Law and qualified for the tenth rank of the civil service, and having received money from his father for his equipment, Ivan Ilych ordered himself clothes at Scharmer's, the fashionable tailor, hung a medallion inscribed *respice finem*[2] on his watch-chain, took leave of his professor and the prince who was patron of the school, had a farewell dinner with his comrades at Donon's first-class restaurant, and with his new and fashionable portmanteau, linen, clothes, shaving and other toilet articles, and a travelling rug, all purchased at the best shops, he set off for one of the provinces where, through his father's influence, he had been attached to the governor as an official for special service.

1. The phoenix of the family.   2. Look to, or regard, the end (Lat.).

In the province Ivan Ilych soon arranged as easy and agreeable a position for himself as he had enjoyed at the School of Law. He performed his official tasks, established his career, and at the same time amused himself pleasantly and decorously. Occasionally he paid official visits to country districts where he behaved with dignity both to his superiors and inferiors, and performed the duties entrusted to him, which related chiefly to the schismatics,[3] with an exactness and incorruptible honesty of which he could not but feel proud.

In official matters, despite his youth and taste for frivolous gaiety, he was exceedingly reserved, punctilious, and even severe; but in society he was often amusing and witty, always good-natured, correct in his manner, and *bon enfant*,[4] as the governor and his wife—with whom he was like one of the family—used to say of him.

In the province he had an affair with a lady who made advances to the elegant young lawyer, and there was also a milliner; and there were carousals with aides-de-camp who visited the district, and after-supper visits to a certain outlying street of doubtful reputation; and there was also some obsequiousness to his chief and even to his chief's wife, but all this was done with such a tone of good breeding that no harsh names could be applied to it. It all came under the heading of the French saying: "*Il faut que jeunesse se passe.*"[5] It was all done with clean hands, in clean linen, with French phrases, and above all among people of the best society and consequently with the approval of people of rank.

So Ivan Ilych served for five years and then came a change in his official life. The new and reformed judicial institutions were introduced, and new men were needed. Ivan Ilych became such a new man. He was offered the post of examining magistrate, and he accepted it though the post was in another province and required him to give up the connections he had formed and to make new ones. His friends met to give him a send-off; they had a group-photograph taken and presented him with a silver cigarette-case, and he set off to his new post.

As examining magistrate Ivan Ilych was just as *comme il faut*[6] and decorous a man, inspiring general respect and capable of separating his official duties from his private life, as he had been when acting as an official on special service. His duties now as examining magistrate were far more interesting and attractive than before. In his former position it had been pleasant to wear an everyday uniform made by Scharmer, and to pass through the crowd of petitioners and officials who were timorously awaiting an audience with the governor, and who envied him as with a free and easy gait he went straight into his chief's private room to have a cup of tea and a cigarette with him. But not many people had then

---

3. Old believers who rejected Patriarch Nikon's reforms in the mid-seventeenth century.
4. A good fellow.

5. Youth will have its fling.
6. As it should be, proper, fitting.

been directly dependent on him—only police officials and the sectarians when he went on special missions—and he liked to treat them politely, almost as comrades, as if he were letting them feel that he who had the power to crush them was treating them in this simple, friendly way. Then there were only a few such people. But now, as an examining magistrate, Ivan Ilych felt that everyone without exception, even the most important and self-satisfied, was in his power, and that he need only write a few words on a sheet of paper with a certain heading, and this or that important, self-satisfied person would be brought before him in the role of an accused party or a witness, and if he did not choose to allow him to sit down, would have to stand before him and answer his questions. Ivan Ilych never abused his power; on the contrary he tried to soften its expression, but the consciousness of it and the possibility of softening its effect, supplied the chief interest and attraction of his office. In his work itself, especially in his examinations, he soon acquired a method of eliminating all considerations irrelevant to the legal aspect of the case, and reducing even the most complicated case to a form in which it would be presented on paper only in its externals, completely excluding his personal opinion of the matter, while above all observing every prescribed formality. The work was new and Ivan Ilych was one of the first men to apply the new Code of 1864.[7]

On taking up the post of examining magistrate in a new town, he made new acquaintances and connections, placed himself on a new footing, and assumed a somewhat different tone. He took up an attitude of rather dignified aloofness towards the provincial authorities, but picked out the best circle of legal gentlemen and wealthy gentry living in town and assumed a tone of slight dissatisfaction with the government, of moderate liberalism, and of enlightened citizenship. At the same time, without at all altering the elegance of his toilet, he ceased shaving his chin and allowed his beard to grow as it pleased.

Ivan Ilych settled down very pleasantly in this new town. The society there, which inclined towards opposition to the governor, was friendly, his salary was larger, and he began to play *vint*,[8] which he found added considerably to the pleasure of life, for he had a capacity for cards, played good-humoredly, and calculated rapidly and astutely, so that he usually won.

After living there for two years he met his future wife, Praskovya Fedorovna Mikhel, who was the most attractive, clever, and brilliant girl of the set in which he moved, and among other amusements and relaxations from his labors as examining magistrate, Ivan Ilych established light and playful relations with her.

While he had been an official on special service he had been accustomed to dance, but as an examining magistrate it was exceptional for

---

7. Major judicial reform that followed emanci-   8. A form of bridge.
pation of the serfs in 1861.

him to do so. If he danced now, he did it as if to show that though he served under the reformed order of things, and had reached the fifth official rank, still when it came to dancing he could do it better than most people. So at the end of an evening he sometimes danced with Praskovya Fedorovna, and it was chiefly during these dances that he captivated her. She fell in love with him. At first Ivan Ilych had no definite intention of marrying, but when the girl fell in love with him he said to himself: "Really, why shouldn't I marry?"

Praskovya Fedorovna came from a good family, was not bad looking, and had a bit of property. Ivan Ilych might have aspired to a more brilliant match, but even this was good. He had his salary, and she, he hoped, would have an equal income. She was well connected, and was a sweet, pretty, thoroughly correct young woman. To say that Ivan Ilych married because he fell in love with Praskovya Fedorovna and found that she sympathized with his views of life would be as incorrect as to say that he married because his social circle approved of the match. He was swayed by both these considerations: the marriage gave him personal satisfaction, and at the same time it was considered the right thing to do by the most highly placed of his associates.

So Ivan Ilych got married.

The preparations for marriage and the beginning of married life, with its conjugal caresses, new furniture, new crockery, and new linen, were very pleasant until his wife became pregnant—so that Ivan Ilych had begun to think that marriage would not impair the easy, agreeable, pleasant and always decorous character of his life, approved of by society and regarded by himself as natural, but would even improve it. But from the first months of his wife's pregnancy, something new, unpleasant, depressing, and unseemly, from which there was no way of escape, unexpectedly showed itself.

His wife, without any reason—*de gaieté de cœur*[9] as Ivan Ilych expressed it to himself—began to disturb the pleasure and propriety of their life. She began to be jealous without cause, expected him to devote his whole attention to her; she found fault with everything, and made coarse and ill-mannered scenes.

At first Ivan Ilych hoped to escape from the unpleasantness of this state of affairs by the same easy and decorous relation to life that had served him heretofore: he tried to ignore his wife's disagreeable moods, continued to live in his usual easy and pleasant way, invited friends to his house for a game of cards, and also tried going out to his club or spending his evenings with friends. But one day his wife began upbraiding him so vigorously, using such coarse words, and continued to abuse him every time he did not fulfil her demands, so resolutely and with such evident determination not to give way till he submitted—that is,

9. Out of sheer wantonness.

till he stayed at home and was bored just as she was—that he became alarmed. He now realized that matrimony—at any rate with Praskovya Fedorovna—was not always conducive to the pleasures and amenities of life, but on the contrary often infringed both comfort and propriety, and that he must therefore entrench himself against such infringement. And Ivan Ilych began to seek means of doing so. His official duties were the one thing that imposed upon Praskovya Fedorovna, and by means of his official work and the duties attached to it he began struggling with his wife to secure his own independence.

With the birth of their child, attempts to feed it and various failures in doing so, and with the real and imaginary illnesses of mother and child, in which Ivan Ilych's sympathy was demanded but about which he understood nothing, the need of securing for himself an existence outside his family life became still more imperative.

As his wife grew more irritable and exacting and Ivan Ilych transferred the center of gravity of his life more and more to his official work, so did he grow to like his work better and became more ambitious than before.

Very soon, within a year of his wedding, Ivan Ilych had realized that marriage, though it may add some comforts to life, is in fact a very intricate and difficult affair towards which in order to perform one's duty, that is, to lead a decorous life approved of by society, one must adopt a definite attitude, just as towards one's official duties.

And Ivan Ilych evolved such an attitude towards married life. He only required of it those conveniences—dinner at home, housewife, and bed—which it could give him, and above all that propriety of external forms required by public opinion. For the rest he looked for light-hearted pleasure and propriety, and was very thankful when he found them, but if he met with antagonism and querulousness he retired at once into his separate fenced-off world of official duties, where he found satisfaction.

Ivan Ilych was esteemed a good official, and after three years was made Assistant Public Prosecutor. His new duties, their importance, the possibility of indicting and imprisoning anyone he chose, the publicity his speeches received, and the success he had in all these things, made his work still more attractive.

More children came. His wife became more and more querulous and ill-tempered, but the attitude Ivan Ilych had adopted towards his home life rendered him almost impervious to her grumbling.

After seven years' service in that town he was transferred to another province as Public Prosecutor. They moved, but were short of money and his wife did not like the place they moved to. Though the salary was higher the cost of living was greater, besides which two of their children died and family life became still more unpleasant for him.

Praskovya Fedorovna blamed her husband for every inconvenience they encountered in their new home. Most of the conversations between

husband and wife, especially as to the children's education, led to topics
which recalled former disputes, and these disputes were apt to flare up
again at any moment. There remained only those rare periods of amorousness which still came to them at times but did not last long. These
were islets at which they anchored for a while and then again set out
upon that ocean of veiled hostility which showed itself in their aloofness
from one another. This aloofness might have grieved Ivan Ilych had he
considered that it ought not to exist, but now he regarded the position
as normal, and even made it the goal at which he aimed in family life.
His aim was to free himself more and more from those unpleasantnesses
and to give them a semblance of harmlessness and propriety. He attained
this by spending less and less time with his family, and when obliged
to be at home he tried to safeguard his position by the presence of
outsiders. The chief thing however was that he had his official duties.
The whole interest of his life now centered in the official world and that
interest absorbed him. The consciousness of his power, being able to
ruin anybody he wished to ruin, the importance, even the external
dignity of his entry into court, or meetings with his subordinates, his
success with superiors and inferiors, and above all his masterly handling
of cases, of which he was conscious—all this gave him pleasure and
filled his life, together with chats with his colleagues, dinners, and
bridge. So that on the whole Ivan Ilych's life continued to flow as he
considered it should do—pleasantly and properly.

So things continued for another seven years. His eldest daughter was
already sixteen, another child had died, and only one son was left, a
schoolboy and a subject of dissension. Ivan Ilych wanted to put him in
the School of Law, but to spite him Praskovya Fedorovna entered him
at the High School. The daughter had been educated at home and had
turned out well: the boy did not learn badly either.

III

So Ivan Ilych lived for seventeen years after his marriage. He was already
a Public Prosecutor of long standing, and had declined several proposed
transfers while awaiting a more desirable post, when an unanticipated
and unpleasant occurrence quite upset the peaceful course of his life.
He was expecting to be offered the post of presiding judge in a University
town, but Happe somehow came to the front and obtained the appointment instead. Ivan Ilych became irritable, reproached Happe, and quarrelled both with him and with his immediate superiors—who became
colder to him and again passed him over when other appointments were
made.

This was in 1880, the hardest year of Ivan Ilych's life. It was then
that it became evident on the one hand that his salary was insufficient
for them to live on, and on the other that he had been forgotten, and

not only that; what was for him the greatest and most cruel injustice appeared to others as quite an ordinary occurrence. Even his father did not consider it his duty to help him. Ivan Ilych felt himself abandoned by everyone; they regarded his position with a salary of 3,500 rubles as quite normal and even fortunate. He alone knew that with the consciousness of the injustices done him, with his wife's incessant nagging, and with the debts he had contracted by living beyond his means, his position was far from normal.

In order to save money that summer he obtained a leave of absence and went away with his wife to live in the country at her brother's place. There, without his work, he experienced boredom for the first time in his life, and not only boredom but intolerable depression. He decided it was impossible to go on living this way, and that it was necessary to take energetic measures.

Having passed a sleepless night pacing up and down the veranda, he decided to go to Petersburg and bestir himself, in order to punish those who had failed to appreciate him and to get transferred to another ministry.

Next day, despite many protests from his wife and her brother, he started for Petersburg with the sole object of obtaining a post with a salary of five thousand rubles a year. He was no longer bent on any particular department, or tendency, or kind of activity. Now all he wanted was an appointment to another post with a salary of five thousand rubles, either in the administration, in the banks, with the railways in one of the Empress Marya's Institutions,[1] or even in customs—but it had to provide a salary of five thousand rubles and be in a ministry other than the one in which they had failed to appreciate him.

And this quest of Ivan Ilych's was crowned with remarkable and unexpected success. At Kursk an acquaintance of his, F. I. Ilyin, got into the first-class carriage, sat down beside Ivan Ilych, and told him about a telegram just received by the governor of Kursk announcing that a change was about to take place in the ministry: Peter Ivanovich was to be superseded by Ivan Semenovich.

The proposed change, apart from its significance for Russia, had a special significance for Ivan Ilych, because by bringing forward a new man, Peter Petrovich, and consequently his friend Zakhar Ivanovich, it was highly favorable for Ivan Ilych, since Zakhar Ivanovich was a friend and colleague of his.

In Moscow this news was confirmed, and on reaching Petersburg Ivan Ilych found Zakhar Ivanovich and received a definite promise of an appointment in his former Department of Justice.

A week later he telegraphed his wife: "Zakhar in Miller's place. I shall receive appointment on presentation of report."

1. Second wife of Paul I, Marya Fyodorovna was dowager empress during the reign of Alexander I (1801–25). She founded several charitable institutions and schools.

Thanks to this change of personnel, Ivan Ilych had unexpectedly obtained an appointment in his former ministry which placed him two stages above his former colleagues besides giving him five thousand rubles salary and three thousand five hundred rubles for expenses connected with his transfer. All his ill humor towards his former enemies and the whole department vanished, and Ivan Ilych was completely happy.

He returned to the country more cheerful and contented than he had been for a long time. Praskovya Fedorovna also cheered up and a truce was arranged between them. Ivan Ilych told of how he had been fêted by everybody in Petersburg, how all those who had been his enemies were put to shame and now fawned on him, how envious they were of his appointment, and how much everybody in Petersburg had liked him.

Praskovya Fedorovna listened to all this and appeared to believe it. She did not contradict anything, but only made plans for their life in the town to which they were going. Ivan Ilych saw with delight that these plans were his plans, that he and his wife agreed, and that, after a stumble, his life was regaining its due and natural character of pleasant lightheartedness and decorum.

Ivan Ilych had come back for a short time only, for he had to take up his new duties on the 10th of September. Moreover, he needed time to settle into the new place, to move all his belongings from the province, and to buy and order many additional things: in a word, to make arrangements as he had resolved on, which were almost exactly what Praskovya Fedorovna had also decided on.

Now that everything had happened so fortunately, and he and his wife were at one in their aims and moreover saw so little of one another, they got on together better than they had done since the first years of their marriage. Ivan Ilych had thought of taking his family away with him at once, but the insistence of his wife's brother and her sister-in-law, who had suddenly become particularly amiable and friendly to him and his family, induced him to depart alone.

So he left, and the cheerful state of mind induced by his success and by the harmony between his wife and himself, the one intensifying the other, did not desert him. He found a delightful house, just the thing both he and his wife had dreamt about. Spacious, lofty reception rooms in the old style, a convenient and dignified study, rooms for his wife and daughter, a study for his son—it might have been made to order for them. Ivan Ilych himself oversaw all the arrangements, chose the wallpapers, supplemented the furniture (preferably with antiques which he considered particularly *comme il faut*), and supervised the upholstering. Everything progressed and approached the ideal he had set himself: even when things were only half completed they exceeded his expectations. He saw what a refined and elegant character, free from vulgarity, it would all have when it was ready. On falling asleep he pictured to himself how the reception-room would look. Looking at the yet unfinished drawing-room he could see the fireplace, the screen, the bookcase, the little chairs dotted here and there, the dishes and plates on the walls, and the bronzes, as they would be when everything was in place. He was pleased by the thought of how his wife and daughter, who shared his taste in this matter, would be impressed by it. They were certainly not expecting as much. He had been particularly successful in finding, and buying cheaply, antiques which gave a particularly aristocratic character to the whole place. But in his letters he intentionally understated everything in order to be able to surprise them. All this so absorbed him that his new duties—though he liked his official work—interested him less than he had expected. Sometimes he even had moments of absent-mindedness during the court sessions, and would consider whether he should have straight or curved cornices for his curtains. He was so interested in it all that he often did things himself, rearranging the furniture, or rehanging the curtains. Once when mounting a stepladder to show the upholsterer, who did not understand, how he wanted the hangings draped, he made a false step and slipped, but being a strong and agile man he clung on and only knocked his side against the knob of the window frame. The bruised place was painful but the pain soon passed, and he felt particularly bright and well just then. He wrote: "I feel fifteen years younger." He thought he would have everything ready by September, but it dragged on till mid-October. The result was charming not only in his eyes but to everyone who saw it.

In reality it was just what is usually seen in the houses of people of moderate means who want to appear rich, and therefore succeed only in resembling others like themselves: there were damasks, dark wood, plants, rugs, dull and polished bronzes—all the things people of a certain class have in order to resemble other people of that class. His house was so like others that it would never have been noticed, but to him it all seemed to be quite exceptional. He was very happy when he met his family at the station and brought them to the newly furnished house all lit up, where a footman in a white tie opened the door into the hall decorated with plants, and when they went on into the drawing-room and the study uttering exclamations of delight. He conducted them everywhere, drank in their praises eagerly, and beamed with delight. At tea that evening, when Praskovya Fedorovna among other things asked him about his fall, he laughed, and showed them how he had gone flying and had frightened the upholsterer.

"It's a good thing I'm a bit of an athlete. Another man might have been killed, but I merely knocked myself, just here; it hurts when it's touched, but it's passing already—it's only a bruise."

So they began living in their new home—in which, as always happens, when they got thoroughly settled in they found they were just one room short—and with the increased income, which as always was just a little (about five hundred rubles) too little, but it was all very nice.

Things went particularly well at first, before everything was finally arranged and while something still had to be done: this thing bought, that thing ordered, another thing moved, and something else adjusted. Though there were some disputes between husband and wife, they were both so well satisfied and had so much to do that it all passed off without any serious quarrels. When nothing was left to arrange it became rather dull and something seemed to be lacking, but then they were making acquaintances, forming habits, and life was growing fuller.

Ivan Ilych spent his mornings at the law court and came home to dinner; at first he was generally in a good humor, though he occasionally became irritable just on account of his house. (Every spot on the table-cloth or the upholstery, and every broken window-blind string, irritated him. He had devoted so much trouble to arranging it all that every disturbance distressed him.) But on the whole his life ran its course as he believed life should do: easily, pleasantly, and decorously.

He got up at nine, drank his coffee, read the paper, and then put on his uniform and went to the law courts. There the harness in which he worked had already been stretched to fit him and he donned it without a hitch: petitioners, inquiries at the chancery, the chancery itself, and the sittings, both public and administrative. In all this the thing was to exclude everything fresh and vital, which always disturbs the regular course of official business, and to admit only official relations with people, and then only on official grounds. A man would come, for instance, wanting some information. Ivan Ilych, as one in whose sphere the matter did not lie, would have nothing to do with him: but if the man had some business with him in his official capacity, something that could be expressed on officially stamped paper, he would do everything, positively everything he could within the limits of such relations, and in so doing would maintain the semblance of friendly human relations, that is, would observe the courtesies of life. As soon as the official relations ended, so did everything else. Ivan Ilych possessed this capacity to separate his real life from the official side of affairs and not mix the two, in the highest degree, and by long practice and natural aptitude had brought it to such a pitch that sometimes, in the manner of a virtuoso, he would even allow himself to let the human and official relations mingle. He let himself do this just because he felt that at any time he could resume the strictly official attitude again and drop the human relations. And he did it all easily, pleasantly, correctly, even artistically. In the intervals between sessions he smoked, drank tea, chatted a little about politics, a little about general topics, a little about cards, but most of all about official appointments. Tired, but feeling like a virtuoso—one of the first violins who has played his part in an orchestra with precision—he would return home to find that his wife and daughter had been out paying calls, or had a visitor, and that his son had been to school, had done his homework with his tutor, and was duly learning what is taught at High Schools. Everything was as it should be. After dinner, if they had no visitors, Ivan Ilych sometimes read a book that was being widely discussed at the time, and in the evening settled down to work, that is, read official papers, compared the depositions of witnesses, and noted paragraphs of the Code applying to them. This was neither dull nor amusing. It was dull when he might have been playing bridge, but if no bridge was available it was certainly better than doing nothing or sitting with his wife. Ivan Ilych's chief pleasure was giving little dinners to which he invited men and women of good social position, and just as his drawing-room resembled all other drawing-rooms, so did his enjoyable little parties resemble all other parties.

Once they even gave a dance. Ivan Ilych enjoyed it and everything went off well, except that it led to a violent quarrel with his wife about the cakes and sweets. Praskovya Fedorovna had made her own plans, but Ivan Ilych insisted on getting everything from an expensive confectioner and ordered too many cakes. The quarrel occurred because some of those cakes were left over and the confectioner's bill came to forty-five rubles. It was a great and disagreeable quarrel. Praskovya Fedorovna called him "a fool and an imbecile," and he clutched at his head and made angry allusions to divorce.

But the dance itself had been enjoyable. The best people were there, and Ivan Ilych had danced with Princess Trufonova, a sister of the distinguished founder of the Society "Bear My Grief."[2]

The pleasures connected with his work were pleasures of ambition; his social pleasures were those of vanity; but Ivan Ilych's greatest pleasure was playing bridge. He acknowledged that whatever disagreeable incident happened in his life, the pleasure that beamed like a ray of sunshine above everything else was to sit down to bridge with good players, not noisy partners, and of course to four-handed bridge (with five players it was annoying to have to stand out, though one pretended not to mind), to play a clever and serious game (when the cards allowed it) and then to have supper and drink a glass of wine. After a game of bridge, especially if he had won a little (to win a large sum was unpleasant), Ivan Ilych went to bed in specially good humor.

So they lived. They formed a circle of acquaintances among the best people and were visited by people of importance and by young folk. In their views as to their acquaintances, husband, wife and daughter were entirely agreed, and tacitly and unanimously kept at arm's length and shook off various shabby friends and relations who, with much show of affection, gushed into the drawing-room with its Japanese plates on the walls. Soon these shabby friends ceased to obtrude themselves and only the best people remained in the Golovins' set.

2. A charitable organization patronized by the empress.

Young men courted Lisa, and Petrishchev, an examining magistrate and Dmitri Ivanovich Petrishchev's son and sole heir, began to be so attentive to her that Ivan Ilych had already spoken to Praskovya Fedorovna about it, and considered whether they should not arrange a party for them, or organize some private theatricals.

So they lived, and all went well, without change, and life flowed pleasantly.

IV

They were all in good health. It could not be called ill health if Ivan Ilych sometimes said that he had a queer taste in his mouth and felt some discomfort in his left side.

But this discomfort increased and, though not exactly painful, grew into a sense of pressure in his side accompanied by ill humor. His irritability became worse and worse and began to mar the agreeable, easy, and correct life that had established itself in the Golovin family. Quarrels between husband and wife became more and more frequent, and soon the ease and amenity disappeared and even the decorum was barely maintained. Once again scenes became frequent, and very few issues remained on which husband and wife could meet without an explosion. Praskovya Fedorovna now had good reason to say that her husband's temper was trying. With characteristic exaggeration she said he had always had a dreadful temper, and that it had needed all her good nature to put up with it for twenty years. It was true that now their quarrels were started by him. His bursts of temper always came just before dinner, often just as he began to eat his soup. Sometimes he noticed that a plate or dish was chipped, or the food was not right, or his son put his elbow on the table, or his daughter's hair was not done as he liked it, and for all this he blamed Praskovya Fedorovna. At first she retorted and said disagreeable things to him, but once or twice he fell into such a rage at the beginning of dinner that she realized it was due to some physical derangement brought on by taking food, and so she restrained herself and did not answer, but only hurried to get through dinner. She regarded this self-restraint as highly praiseworthy. Having come to the conclusion that her husband had a dreadful temper and made her life miserable, she began to feel sorry for herself; the more she pitied herself the more she hated her husband. She began to wish he would die; yet she did not want him to die because then his salary would cease. And this irritated her still more. She considered herself dreadfully unhappy just because not even his death could save her, and though she concealed her exasperation, that hidden emotion of hers increased his irritation as well.

After one scene in which Ivan Ilych had been particularly unfair and after which he had said in explanation that he certainly was irritable but that it was due to his not being well, she said that if he was ill it should be attended to, and insisted on his going to see a celebrated doctor.

He went. Everything took place as he had expected and as it always does. There was the usual waiting and the important air assumed by the doctor, with which he was so familiar (resembling that which he himself assumed in court), and the sounding and listening, and the questions which called for answers that were foregone conclusions and were evidently unnecessary, and the look of importance which implied that "if only you put yourself in our hands we will arrange everything— we know indubitably how it has to be done, always the same for every-body." It was all just as it was in the law courts. The doctor put on just the same air towards him as he himself put on towards an accused person.

The doctor said that so-and-so indicated that there was such-and-such inside the patient, but if the investigation of so-and-so did not confirm this, then he must assume this and that. If he assumed this and that, then . . . and so on. To Ivan Ilych only one question was important: was his case serious or not? But the doctor ignored that inappropriate question. From his point of view it was not the one under consideration; the real question was to decide between a floating kidney, chronic ca-tarrh, or appendicitis. It was not a question of Ivan Ilych's life or death, but one between a floating kidney and appendicitis. And that question the doctor solved brilliantly, as it seemed to Ivan Ilych, in favor of the appendix, with the reservation that should an examination of his urine give fresh indications, the matter would be reconsidered. All this was just what Ivan Ilych had himself brilliantly accomplished a thousand times in dealing with men on trial. The doctor summed it up just as brilliantly, looking over his spectacles triumphantly and even gaily at the accused. From the doctor's summation Ivan Ilych concluded that things were bad, but that for the doctor, and perhaps for everybody else, it was a matter of indifference, though for him it was bad. This con-clusion struck him painfully, arousing in him a great feeling of pity for himself and of bitterness towards the doctor's indifference to a matter of such importance.

He said nothing about it, but rose, placed the doctor's fee on the table, and remarked with a sigh: "We sick people probably pose inap-propriate questions frequently. But tell me, doctor, in general, is this complaint dangerous, or not? . . ."

The doctor looked at him sternly over his spectacles with one eye, as if to say: "Prisoner, if you will not keep to the questions put to you, I shall be obliged to have you removed from the court."

"I have already told you what I consider necessary and proper. The analysis may show something more." And the doctor bowed.

Ivan Ilych went out slowly, seated himself disconsolately in his sleigh, and drove home. All the way home he was going over what the doctor had said, trying to translate those complicated, obscure, scientific phrases into plain language and find in them an answer to the question: "Is my condition bad? Is it very bad? Or is there still nothing much wrong?" It seemed to him that the meaning of what the doctor had said was that it was very bad. Everything in the streets seemed depressing. The cabmen, the houses, the passers-by, and the shops, were dismal. His ache, this dull gnawing ache that never ceased for a moment, seemed to have acquired a new and more serious significance from the doctor's dubious remarks. Ivan Ilych now watched it with a new and oppressive feeling.

He reached home and began to tell his wife about it. She listened, but in the middle of his account his daughter came in with her hat on, ready to go out with her mother. She sat down reluctantly to listen to his tedious story, but could not stand it for very long, and her mother too did not hear him out to the end.

"Well, I'm very glad," she said. "Mind now to take your medicine regularly. Give me the prescription and I'll send Gerasim out to the pharmacy." And she went to get ready to go out.

While she was in the room Ivan Ilych had hardly taken time to breathe, but he sighed deeply when she left.

"Well," he thought, "perhaps it isn't so bad after all."

He began taking his medicine and following his doctor's orders, which had been altered after the examination of his urine. But then it seemed that there was a contradiction between the indications drawn from the examination of his urine and the symptoms that showed themselves. It turned out that what was happening differed from what the doctor had told him, and that he had either forgotten, or blundered, or hidden something from him. He could not, however, be blamed for that, and Ivan Ilych still obeyed his orders implicitly and at first derived some comfort from doing so.

From the time of his visit to the doctor, Ivan Ilych's chief occupation was the exact fulfillment of his doctor's instructions regarding hygiene and the taking of medicine, and the observation of his pain and his excretions. His chief interests came to be people's ailments and their health. When sickness, deaths, or recoveries were mentioned in his presence, especially when the illness resembled his own, he listened with considerable agitation which he tried to conceal, asked questions, and applied what he heard to his own case.

The pain did not diminish, but Ivan Ilych made efforts to force himself to think that he was better. He could do this so long as nothing agitated him. But as soon as he had any unpleasantness with his wife, any lack of success in his official work, or held bad cards at bridge, he was at once acutely aware of his disease. He had formerly borne such mishaps, hoping soon to adjust what was wrong, to master it and attain success, or make a grand slam. But now every mishap upset him and plunged him into despair. He would say to himself: "There now, just as I was beginning to get better and the medicine had begun to take effect, comes this accursed misfortune, or unpleasantness . . ." And he was furious with the mishap, or with the people who were causing the unpleasantness, for he felt that this fury was killing him but he could not restrain it. One would have thought that it should have been clear to him that this exasperation with circumstances and people aggravated his illness, and that therefore he ought to ignore unpleasant occurrences. But he drew the very opposite conclusion: he said that he needed peace, and he watched for everything that might disturb it and became irritable at the slightest infringement. His condition was rendered worse by the fact that he read medical books and consulted doctors. The progress of his disease was so gradual that he could deceive himself when comparing one day with another—the difference was so slight. But when he consulted the doctors it seemed to him that he was getting worse, even very rapidly. Yet despite this he was continually consulting them.

That month he went to see another celebrity, who told him almost the same as the first had done, but put his questions rather differently, and the interview with this celebrity only increased Ivan Ilych's doubts and fears. A friend of a friend of his, a very good doctor, diagnosed his illness again quite differently from the others, and though he predicted recovery, his questions and suppositions bewildered Ivan Ilych still more and increased his doubts. A homeopathist diagnosed the disease in yet another way, and prescribed medicine which Ivan Ilych took secretly for a week. But after this week, not feeling any improvement and having lost confidence both in the former doctor's treatment and in this one's, he became still more despondent. One day a lady acquaintance mentioned a cure effected by a wonder-working icon. Ivan Ilych caught himself listening attentively and beginning to believe that it had occurred. This incident alarmed him. "Has my mind really weakened to such an extent?" he asked himself. "Nonsense! It's all rubbish. I mustn't give way to nervous fears; having chosen a doctor must keep strictly to his treatment. That is what I will do. Now it's all settled. I won't think about it, but will follow the treatment seriously till summer, and then we shall see. From now on there must be no more wavering!" This was easy to say but impossible to carry out. The pain in his side oppressed him and seemed to grow worse and more incessant, while the taste in his mouth grew stranger and stranger. It seemed to him that his breath had a disgusting smell, and he was conscious of a loss of appetite and strength. There was no deceiving himself: something terrible, new, and more important than anything before in his life, was taking place within him of which he alone was aware. Those about him did not understand or would not understand it, but thought everything in the world was going on as usual. That tormented Ivan Ilych more than anything. He saw that his household, especially his wife and daughter who were in a perfect whirl of visiting, did not understand anything about it and were annoyed that he was so depressed and so exacting, as if he were to blame. Though they tried to disguise it he saw that he was an obstacle in their path, and that his wife had adopted a definite line in regard to his illness and kept to it regardless of anything he said or did. Her attitude was this: "You know," she would say to her friends, "Ivan Ilych can't do as other people do, and keep to the treatment prescribed for him. One day he takes his drops and keeps strictly to his diet and goes to bed in good time, but the next day unless I watch him, he suddenly forgets his medicine, eats sturgeon—which is forbidden—and sits up playing cards till one in the morning."

"Oh, come, when was that?" Ivan Ilych would ask in vexation. "Only once at Peter Ivanovich's."

"And yesterday with Shebek."

"Well, even if I hadn't stayed up, the pain would have kept me awake."

"Be that as it may you'll never get well like that, but you'll always make us wretched."

Praskovya Fedorovna's attitude to Ivan Ilych's illness, as she expressed it both to others and to him, was that it was all his own fault and was yet another of the annoyances he caused her. Ivan Ilych felt that this opinion escaped her involuntarily—but that did not make it any easier for him.

At the law courts too, Ivan Ilych noticed, or thought he noticed, a strange attitude towards himself. It sometimes seemed that people were watching him inquisitively as a man whose place might soon become vacant. Then again, his friends would suddenly begin to tease him in a friendly way about his low spirits, as if the awful, horrible, and unheard-of thing that was going on within him, incessantly gnawing at him and irresistibly drawing him away, was a very agreeable subject for jests. Schwartz in particular irritated him by his jocularity, vivacity, and *savoir-faire*, which reminded him of what he himself had been ten years ago.

Friends came to make up a set and they sat down to cards. They dealt, bending the new cards to soften them, and he sorted the diamonds in his hand and found he had seven. His partner said "No trumps" and supported him with two diamonds. What more could be wished for? It ought to be jolly and lively. They would make a grand slam. But suddenly Ivan Ilych was conscious of that gnawing pain, that taste in his mouth, and it seemed ridiculous that in such circumstances he should be pleased to make a grand slam.

He looked at his partner Mikhail Mikhailovich, who rapped the table with his strong hand and instead of snatching up the tricks pushed the cards courteously and indulgently towards Ivan Ilych that he might have the pleasure of gathering them up without the trouble of stretching out his hand for them. "Does he think I'm too weak to stretch out my arm?" thought Ivan Ilych, and forgetting what he was doing he over-trumped his partner, missing the grand slam by three tricks. And what was most awful of all was that he saw how upset Mikhail Mikhailovich was about it, but he himself did not care. And it was dreadful to realize why he did not care.

They all saw that he was suffering, and said: "We can stop if you're tired. Take a rest." Lie down? No, he was not tired at all, and finished the rubber. All were gloomy and silent. Ivan Ilych felt that he had diffused this gloom over them and was unable to dispel it. They had supper and went away; Ivan Ilych was left alone with the consciousness that his life was poisoned and was poisoning the lives of others, and that this poison did not lessen but penetrated more and more deeply into his whole being.

With this consciousness, and with physical pain besides the terror, he must go to bed, often to lie awake the greater part of the night. The next morning he had to get up again, dress, go to the law courts, speak, and write; or if he did not go out, spend those twenty-four hours a day at home each of which was a torture. And he had to live thus all alone on the brink of an abyss, with no one who understood him or pitied him.

V

So one month passed and then another. Just before the New Year his brother-in-law came to town and stayed at their house. Ivan Ilych was at the law courts and Praskovya Fedorovna had gone shopping. When Ivan Ilych came home and entered his study he found his brother-in-law there—a healthy, florid man—unpacking his bag himself. He raised his head on hearing Ivan Ilych's footsteps and looked up at him for a moment without a word. That stare told Ivan Ilych everything. His brother-in-law opened his mouth to utter an exclamation of surprise but checked himself, and that action confirmed it all.

"I've changed, eh?"

"Yes, there's been a change."

After that, try as he would to get his brother-in-law to return to the subject of his looks, the latter would say nothing about it. Praskovya Fedorovna came home and her brother went out to her. Ivan Ilych locked the door and began to examine himself in the glass, first full face, then in profile. He took up a portrait of himself taken with his wife, and compared it with what he saw in the mirror. The change was immense. Then he bared his arms to the elbow, looked at them, drew the sleeves down again, sat down on an ottoman, and grew blacker than night.

"No, no, this won't do!" he said to himself, and jumped up, went to the table, took up some law papers and began to read them, but he could not continue. He unlocked the door and went into the reception-room. The door leading to the drawing-room was shut. He approached it on tiptoe and listened.

"No, you're exaggerating!" Praskovya Fedorovna was saying.

"Exaggerating! Don't you see it? Why, he's a dead man! Look at his eyes—there's no light in them. But what's wrong with him?"

"No one knows. Nikolaevich (that was another doctor) said something, but I don't know what. And Leshchetitsky (this was the celebrated specialist) said quite the opposite . . ."

Ivan Ilych walked away, went to his own room, lay down, and began musing: "A kidney, a floating kidney." He recalled all the doctors had told him about how it detached itself and swayed about. By an effort of imagination he tried to catch that kidney and arrest it and support it. So little was needed for this, it seemed to him. "No, I'll go see Peter Ivanovich again." (That was the friend whose friend was a doctor.) He rang, ordered the carriage, and got ready to go.

"Where are you going, Jean?" asked his wife, with a specially sad and exceptionally kind look.

This exceptionally kind look irritated him. He looked at her morosely.

"I must go see Peter Ivanovich."

He went to see Peter Ivanovich, and together they went to see his friend, the doctor. He was in, and Ivan Ilych had a long talk with him.

Reviewing the anatomical and physiological details of what in the doctor's opinion was going on inside him, he understood it all.

There was something, a small thing, in the vermiform appendix. It might be all right. Only stimulate the energy of one organ and check the activity of another, then absorption would take place and everything would be all right. He got home rather late, ate his dinner, and conversed cheerfully, but for a long time he could not bring himself to go back to work in his room. At last, however, he went to his study and did what was necessary, but the consciousness that he had put something aside—an important, intimate matter which he would revert to when his work was done—never left him. When he had finished his work he remembered that this intimate matter was the thought of his vermiform appendix. But he did not give himself up to it, and went to the drawing-room for tea. There were callers there, including the examining magistrate who was a desirable match for his daughter, and they were conversing, playing the piano, and singing. Ivan Ilych, as Praskovya Fedorovna remarked, spent that evening more cheerfully than usual, but he never forgot for a moment that he had postponed the important matter of his appendix. At eleven o'clock he said good-night and went to his bedroom. Since his illness he had slept alone in a small room next to his study. He undressed and took up a novel by Zola, but instead of reading it he fell into thought, and in his imagination that desired improvement in the vermiform appendix occurred. There took place the absorption and evacuation and the re-establishment of normal activity. "Yes, that's it!" he said to himself. "One need only assist nature, that's all." He remembered his medicine, got up, took it, and lay down on his back waiting for the beneficent action of the medicine and for it to lessen the pain. "I need only take it regularly and avoid all injurious influences. I'm feeling better already, much better." He began touching his side: it was not painful to the touch. "There, I really don't feel it. It's much better already." He put out the light and turned over on his side . . . "My appendix is getting better, absorption is occurring." Suddenly he felt the old, familiar, dull, gnawing pain, stubborn and serious. There was the same familiar loathsome taste in his mouth. His heart sank and he felt dazed. "My God! My God!" he muttered. "Again, again! It will never cease." Suddenly the matter presented itself in quite a different aspect. "Vermiform appendix! Kidney!" he said to himself. "It's not a question of my appendix or my kidney, but of life and . . . death. Yes, life was there and now it is going, going and I cannot stop it. Yes. Why deceive myself? Isn't it obvious to everyone but me that I'm dying, and that it's only a question of weeks, days . . . it may happen any moment. There was light and now there's darkness. I was here and now I'm going there! Where?" A chill came over him, his breathing ceased, and he felt only the throbbing of his heart.

"When I'm not, what will there be? There'll be nothing. Then where will I be when I'm no more? Can this be dying? No, I don't want to!" He jumped up and tried to light the candle, felt for it with his trembling hands, dropped both candle and candlestick on the floor, and fell back on his pillow.

"What's the use? It makes no difference," he said to himself, staring with wide-open eyes into the darkness. "Death. Yes, death. And none of them knows or wishes to know it, and they have no pity for me. Now they are singing and playing." (He heard through the door the distant sound of a song and its accompaniment.) "It's all the same to them, but they'll die too! Fools! First me, and later them, but it'll be the same for them. And now they're merry . . . the beasts!"

Anger choked him and he was agonizingly, unbearably miserable. "It's impossible that all men have been doomed to suffer this awful horror!" He raised himself up.

"Something must be wrong. I must calm myself—I must think it all over from the beginning." He began thinking again. "Yes, the beginning of my illness: I bumped my side, but I was still quite well that day and the next. It hurt a little, then rather more. I saw doctors, there followed despondency and anguish, more doctors, and I drew nearer to the abyss. My strength grew less and I kept coming nearer and nearer; now I have wasted away and there is no light left in my eyes. I think about my appendix—but this is really death! I think of mending my appendix, and all the while here comes death! Can it really be death?" Terror seized him again and he gasped for breath. He leant down and began feeling for the matches, pressing on the stand beside the bed with his elbow. It was in his way and it hurt him, he grew furious with it, pressed on it still harder, and upset it. Breathless and in despair he fell on his back, expecting death to come immediately.

Meanwhile the visitors were leaving. Praskovya Fedorovna was seeing them off. She heard something fall and came in.

"What happened?"

"Nothing. I knocked it over accidentally."

She went out and returned with a candle. He lay there panting heavily, like a man who's run a thousand yards, and stared at her with a fixed look.

"What is it, Jean?"

"No . . . o . . . thing. I knocked it over." ("Why speak about it? She won't understand," he thought.)

Indeed she did not understand. She picked up the stand, lit his candle, and hurried away to see another visitor off. When she came back he still lay on his back, looking upwards.

"What is it? Do you feel worse?"

"Yes."

She shook her head and sat down.

"Do you know, Jean, I think we must ask Leshchetitsky to come and see you here."

This meant calling in the famous specialist, regardless of expense. He smiled malignantly and said "No." She stayed a little longer and then went up to him and kissed his forehead.

While she was kissing him he hated her from the bottom of his heart and refrained with difficulty from pushing her away.

"Good-night. I pray to God you'll get some sleep."

"Yes."

VI

Ivan Ilych saw that he was dying, and he was in continual despair.

In the depth of his heart he knew he was dying, but not only was he unaccustomed to the thought, he simply did not and could not grasp it.

The syllogism he had learnt from Kiesewetter's Logic: "Caius is a man, men are mortal, therefore Caius is mortal,"[3] had always seemed to him correct as applied to Caius, but it certainly didn't apply to himself. That Caius—man in the abstract—was mortal, was perfectly correct, but he was not Caius, not an abstract man, but a creature quite separate from all others. He had been little Vanya, with a mamma and a papa, with Mitya and Volodya, with toys, a coachman and a nanny, afterwards with Katenka and with all the joys, griefs, and delights of childhood, boyhood, and youth. What did Caius know of the smell of that striped leather ball Vanya had been so fond of? Had Caius kissed his mother's hand like that, and did the silk of her dress rustle for Caius? Had he rioted like that at school when the pastry was bad? Had Caius been in

3. J. G. Kiesewetter (1766–1819), a follower of Kant, published a textbook of logic widely used in Russian schools. Caius is Julius Caesar.

love like that? Could Caius preside at a session as he did? "Caius really was mortal, and it was right for him to die; but as for me, little Vanya, Ivan Ilych, with all my thoughts and emotions, it's altogether a different matter. It cannot be that I ought to die. That would be too terrible."

Such was his feeling.

"If I had to die like Caius I should have known it. An inner voice would have told me so, but there was nothing of the sort in me; I and all my friends felt that our case was quite different from that of Caius. And now here it is!" he said to himself. "It can't be. It's impossible! But here it is. How's this? How's one to understand it?"

He could not understand it, and tried to drive away this false, incorrect, morbid thought and to replace it by other proper, healthy thoughts. But that thought, and not only the thought but the reality itself, seemed to come and confront him.

To replace that thought he called up a succession of others, hoping to find some support in them. He tried to get back into the former current of thoughts that had once screened the thought of death from him. But strange to say, all that had formerly shut off, hidden, and destroyed his consciousness of death, no longer had that effect. Ivan Ilych now spent most of his time attempting to re-establish that old current. He would say to himself: "I will take up my duties again—after all I used to live by them." Banishing all doubts he would go to the law courts, enter into conversation with his colleagues, and sit carelessly as was his wont, scanning the crowd with a thoughtful look and leaning both his emaciated arms on the arms of his oak chair; bending over as usual to a colleague and drawing his papers nearer he would exchange whispers with him, and then suddenly raising his eyes and sitting erect would pronounce certain words and open the proceedings. But suddenly in the midst of those proceedings the pain in his side, regardless of the stage the proceedings had reached, would begin its own gnawing work. Ivan Ilych would turn his attention to it and try to drive the thought of it away, but without success. *It* would come and stand before him and look at him, and he would be petrified. The light would die out in his eyes, and he would begin asking himself again whether *It* alone was true. His colleagues and subordinates would notice with surprise and distress that he, the brilliant and subtle judge, was becoming confused and making mistakes. He would shake himself, try to pull himself together, somehow manage to bring the session to a close, and return home with the sorrowful consciousness that his judicial labors could no longer hide from him what he wanted them to hide, and could not deliver him from *It*. And what was worst of all was that *It* drew his attention to itself not in order to make him take some action, but only so that he should look at *It*, look it straight in the face: look at it and without doing anything, suffer inexpressibly.

To save himself from this condition Ivan Ilych looked for consolations—new screens—and they were found and for a while seemed to save him, but then they immediately fell to pieces or rather became transparent, as if *It* penetrated them and nothing could veil *It*.

During these last few days he would go into the drawing-room he had arranged—that drawing-room where he had fallen and for the sake of which (how bitterly ridiculous it seemed) he had sacrificed his life—for he knew that his illness originated with that knock. He would enter and see that something had scratched the polished table. He would look for the cause and find that it was the bronze ornament on an album, that had got bent. He would take up the expensive album which he had lovingly arranged, and feel vexed with his daughter and her friends for their untidiness—the album was torn here and there and some of the photographs were turned upside down. He would put it carefully in order and bend the ornament back into position. Then it would occur to him to place all those things in another corner of the room, near the plants. He would call the footman, but his daughter or wife would come to help him. They wouldn't agree, and his wife would contradict him; he would dispute and grow angry. But that was all right, for then he didn't think about *It*. *It* was invisible.

But then, when he was moving something himself, his wife would say: "Let the servants do it. You'll hurt yourself again." Suddenly *It* would flash through the screen and he would see it. It was just a flash, and he hoped it would disappear, but involuntarily he would pay attention to his side. "It just sits there as before, gnawing just the same!" He could no longer forget *It*, but could see it distinctly looking at him from behind the flowers. "What's it all for?"

"It really is so! I lost my life over that curtain as I might have done storming a fort. Is that possible? How terrible and how stupid. It can't be true! It can't, but it is."

He would go to his study, lie down, and be alone again with *It*: face to face with *It*. Nothing could be done with *It* except to look at it and shudder.

VII

How it happened it is impossible to say because it came about step by step, unnoticed, but in the third month of Ivan Ilych's illness, his wife, his daughter, his son, his acquaintances, the doctors, the servants, and above all he himself, were aware that the whole interest he had for other people was whether he would soon vacate his place, and at last release the living from the discomfort caused by his presence and be released himself from his sufferings.

He slept less and less. He was given opium and hypodermic injections of morphine, but this did not relieve his pain. The dull depression he experienced in a somnolent condition at first gave him a little relief, but only as something new; afterwards it became as distressing as the pain itself or even more so.

Special foods were prepared for him on the doctors' orders, but all those foods became increasingly distasteful and disgusting to him.

For his excretions special arrangements had to be made, and this was a torment to him every time—a torment from the uncleanliness, the unseemliness, and the smell, and from knowing that another person had to take part in it.

But it was just through this most unpleasant matter, that Ivan Ilych obtained some comfort. Gerasim, the butler's young assistant, always came to carry things out. Gerasim was a clean, fresh peasant lad, grown stout on town food, always cheerful and bright. At first the sight of him, in his clean Russian peasant costume, engaged on such a disgusting task embarrassed Ivan Ilych.

Once when he got up from the commode too weak to draw up his own trousers, he dropped into a soft armchair and looked with horror at his bare, enfeebled thighs with the muscles so sharply marked on them.

Gerasim with a firm light tread, his heavy boots emitting a pleasant smell of tar and fresh winter air, came in wearing a clean Hessian apron, the sleeves of his print shirt tucked up over his strong bare young arms; refraining from looking at his sick master out of consideration for his feelings, and restraining the joy of life that beamed from his face, he went up to the commode.

"Gerasim!" said Ivan Ilych in a weak voice.

Gerasim started, evidently afraid he might have committed some blunder, and with a rapid movement turned his fresh, kind, simple young face which just showed the first downy signs of a beard.

"Yes, sir?"

"That must be very unpleasant for you. You must forgive me. I am helpless."

"Oh, why, sir," Gerasim's eyes beamed and he showed his glistening white teeth, "what's a little trouble? It's a case of illness with you, sir."

His deft strong hands did their accustomed task, and he went out of the room stepping lightly. Five minutes later he returned as lightly.

Ivan Ilych was still sitting in the same position in the armchair.

"Gerasim," he said when the latter had replaced the freshly-washed item. "Please come here and help me." Gerasim went up to him. "Lift me up. It is hard for me to get up, and I have sent Dmitri away."

Gerasim went up to him, grasped his master with his strong arms deftly but gently, in the same way that he moved—lifted him, supported him with one hand, and with the other drew up his trousers and would have set him down again, but Ivan Ilych asked to be led to the sofa. Gerasim, without effort and without apparent pressure, led him, almost lifting him, to the sofa and placed him on it.

"Thank you. How easily and well you do it all!"

Gerasim smiled again and turned to leave the room. But Ivan Ilych felt his presence such a comfort that he did not want to let him go.

"One thing more, please move up that chair. No, the other one—under my feet. It's easier for me when my feet are raised."

Gerasim brought the chair, set it down gently in place, and raised Ivan Ilych's legs on to it. It seemed to Ivan Ilych that he felt better while Gerasim was holding up his legs.

"It's better when my legs are higher," he said. "Place that cushion under them."

Gerasim did so. Again he lifted the legs and placed them, and again Ivan Ilych felt better while Gerasim held his legs. When he set them down Ivan Ilych fancied he felt worse.

"Gerasim," he said. "Are you busy now?"

"Not at all, sir," said Gerasim, who had learnt from townspeople how to speak to gentlefolk.

"What have you still to do?"

"What have I to do? I've done everything except chop the logs for to-morrow."

"Then hold my legs up a bit higher, will you?"

"Of course I will. Why not?" Gerasim raised his master's legs higher and Ivan Ilych thought that in that position he did not feel any pain at all.

"How about the logs?"

"Don't worry about that, sir. There's plenty of time."

Ivan Ilych told Gerasim to sit down and hold his legs, and began to talk to him. Strange to say it seemed that he felt better while Gerasim held his legs up.

After that Ivan Ilych would sometimes call Gerasim and get him to hold his legs on his shoulders, and he liked talking to him. Gerasim did it all easily, willingly, simply, and with good humor that touched Ivan Ilych. Health, strength, and vitality in other people were offensive to him, but Gerasim's strength and vitality did not mortify, but soothed him.

What tormented Ivan Ilych most was the deception, the lie, which for some reason they all accepted, that he was not dying but was simply ill, and that he need only keep still and undergo treatment and then something very good would result. He knew however that do what they would nothing would come of it, only still more agonizing suffering and death. This deception tortured him—their not wishing to admit what they all knew and what he knew, but wanting to lie to him concerning his terrible condition, and wishing and forcing him to participate in that lie. Those lies—enacted over him on the eve of his death and destined to degrade this awful, solemn act to the level of their visits, their curtains, their sturgeon for dinner—were a terrible agony for Ivan

Ilych. And strangely enough, many times when they were going through their antics over him he had been within a hairbreadth of calling out to them: "Stop lying! You know and I know that I'm dying. Then at least stop lying about it!" But he had never the courage to do it. The awful, terrible act of his dying was, he could see, reduced by those around him to the level of a casual, unpleasant, almost indecorous incident (as if someone entered a drawing-room diffusing an unpleasant odor) and this was done by that very decorum which he had served his whole life long. He saw that no one felt for him, because no one even wished to grasp his position. Only Gerasim recognized it and pitied him. And so Ivan Ilych felt at ease only with him. He felt comforted when Gerasim supported his legs (sometimes all night long) and refused to go to bed, saying: "Don't you worry, Ivan Ilych. I'll get sleep enough later on," or when he suddenly became familiar and exclaimed: "If you weren't sick it would be another matter, but as it is, why should I grudge a little trouble?" Only Gerasim did not lie; everything showed that he alone understood the facts of the case and did not consider it necessary to disguise them, but simply felt sorry for his emaciated and enfeebled master. Once when Ivan Ilych was sending him away he even said straight out: "We shall all die, so why should I grudge a little trouble?"—expressing the fact that he did not consider his work burdensome, because he was doing it for a dying man and hoped someone would do the same for him when his time came.

Apart from this lying, or because of it, what tormented Ivan Ilych most was that no one pitied him as he wished to be pitied. At certain moments after prolonged suffering he wished most of all (though he would have been ashamed to confess it) for someone to pity him as a sick child is pitied. He longed to be petted and comforted. He knew he was an important functionary, that his beard was turning grey, and that therefore what he longed for was impossible, but still he longed for it. In Gerasim's attitude towards him there was something akin to what he wished for, and so that attitude comforted him. Ivan Ilych wanted to weep, wanted to be petted and cried over; then his colleague Shebek would come, and instead of weeping and being petted, Ivan Ilych would assume a serious, severe, and profound air. By force of habit he would express his opinion on a decision of the Court of Cassation[4] and would stubbornly insist on that view. This falsity around him and within him did more than anything else to poison his last days.

VIII

It was morning. He knew it was morning because Gerasim had gone, and Peter the footman had come in and put out the candles, drawn back one of the curtains, and quietly begun to tidy up. Whether it was

---

4. An appeals court for criminal cases, which was created by the judicial reform of 1864.

morning or evening, Friday or Sunday, made no difference, it was all just the same: the gnawing, unmitigated, agonizing pain, never ceasing for an instant, the consciousness of life inexorably waning but not yet extinguished, the approach of that ever dreaded and hateful Death which was the only reality, and always the same falsity. What were days, weeks, hours, in such a case?

"Will you have some tea, sir?"

"He wants things to be regular, and wishes the gentlefolk to drink tea in the morning," thought Ivan Ilych, and only said "No."

"Wouldn't you like to move onto the sofa, sir?"

"He wants to tidy up the room, and I'm in the way. I am uncleanliness and disorder," he thought, and said only:

"No, leave me alone."

The man went on bustling about. Ivan Ilych stretched out his hand. Peter came up, ready to help.

"What is it, sir?"

"My watch."

Peter took the watch which was close at hand and gave it to his master.

"Half-past eight. Are they up?"

"No sir, except Vladimir Ivanich" (the son) "who has gone to school. Praskovya Fedorovna ordered me to wake her if you asked for her. Shall I do so?"

"No, there's no need to." "Perhaps I'd better have some tea," he thought, and added aloud: "Yes, bring me some tea."

Peter went to the door, but Ivan Ilych dreaded being left alone. "How can I keep him here? Oh yes, my medicine." "Peter, give me my medicine." "Why not? Perhaps it may still do me some good." He took a spoonful and swallowed it. "No, it won't help. It's all foolishness, all deception," he decided as soon as he became aware of the familiar, sickly, hopeless taste. "No, I can't believe in it any longer. But the pain, why this pain? If it would only cease just for a moment!" And he moaned. Peter turned towards him. "It's all right. Go and fetch me some tea."

Peter went out. Left alone Ivan Ilych groaned not so much with pain, terrible though that was, as from mental anguish. Always and forever the same, always these endless days and nights. If only it would come quicker! If only *what* would come quicker? Death, darkness? . . . No, no! Anything rather than death!

When Peter returned with the tea on a tray, Ivan Ilych stared at him for a time in perplexity, not realizing who and what he was. Peter was disconcerted by that look and his embarrassment brought Ivan Ilych to himself.

"Oh, tea! All right, put it down. Only help me wash and put on a clean shirt."

Ivan Ilych began to wash. With pauses for rest, he washed his hands and then his face, cleaned his teeth, brushed his hair, and looked in the mirror. He was terrified by what he saw, especially by the limp way in which his hair clung to his pallid forehead.

While his shirt was being changed he knew that he would be still more frightened at the sight of his body, so he avoided looking at it. Finally he was ready. He drew on a dressing-gown, wrapped himself in a plaid, and sat down in the armchair to take his tea. For a moment he felt refreshed, but as soon as he began to drink the tea he was again aware of the same taste, and the pain returned too. He finished it with an effort, and then lay down stretching out his legs, and dismissed Peter.

Always the same. Now a spark of hope flashes up, then a sea of despair rages, and always pain; always pain, always despair, and always the same. When alone he had a dreadful and distressing desire to call someone, but he knew beforehand that with others present it would be still worse. "Another dose of morphine—to lose consciousness. I'll tell him, the doctor, that he must think of something else. It's impossible, impossible, to go on like this."

An hour and another pass like that. But now there's a ring at the door bell. Perhaps it's the doctor? It is. He comes in fresh, hearty, plump, and cheerful, with that look on his face that seems to say: "There now, you're in a panic about something, but we'll arrange it all for you at once!" The doctor knows this expression is out of place here, but he has put it on once and for all and can't take it off—like a man who has put on a frock-coat in the morning to pay a round of calls.

The doctor rubs his hands vigorously and reassuringly.

"Brr! How cold it is! There's such a sharp frost; just let me warm myself!" he says, as if it were only a matter of waiting till he was warm, and then he would put everything right.

"Well now, how are you?"

Ivan Ilych feels the doctor would like to say: "Well, how are our affairs?" but that even he feels this would not do, and says instead: "What sort of a night did you have?"

Ivan Ilych looks at him as if to say: "Are you really never ashamed of lying?" But the doctor does not wish to understand this question, and Ivan Ilych says: "Just as terrible as ever. The pain never leaves me and never subsides. If only something . . ."

"Yes, you sick people are always like that. . . . There, now I think I'm warm enough. Even Praskovya Fedorovna, who's so particular, could find no fault with my temperature. Well, now I can say good-morning," and the doctor presses his patient's hand.

Then, dropping his former playfulness, he begins with a most serious face to examine the patient, feeling his pulse and taking his temperature, and then begins the sounding and auscultation.

Ivan Ilych knows quite well and definitely that this is all nonsense and pure deception, but when the doctor, getting down on his knee, leans over him, putting his ear first higher then lower, and performs various gymnastic movements over him with a significant expression on his face, Ivan Ilych submits to it all just as he used to submit to the speeches of the lawyers, though he knew very well that they were all lying and knew why they were lying.

The doctor, kneeling on the sofa, is still sounding him when Praskovya Fedorovna's silk dress rustles at the door and she's heard scolding Peter for not having let her know of the doctor's arrival.

She comes in, kisses her husband, and at once proceeds to prove that she has been up a long time, and owing only to a misunderstanding failed to be there when the doctor arrived.

Ivan Ilych looks at her, scans her all over, sets against her the whiteness, plumpness, and cleanness of her hands and neck, the gloss of her hair, and the sparkle of her vivacious eyes. He hates her with his whole soul. The thrill of hatred he feels for her makes him suffer from her touch.

Her attitude towards him and his disease is still the same. Just as the doctor had adopted a certain relation to his patient which he could not abandon, so had she formed one towards him—that he was not doing something he ought to do and was himself to blame, and she reproached him lovingly for this—and now she could not change that attitude.

"You see he doesn't listen to me and doesn't take his medicine at the proper time. Above all he lies in a position that's no doubt bad for him—with his legs up."

She described how he made Gerasim hold his legs up.

The doctor smiled with a contemptuous affability that said: "What's to be done? These sick people do have foolish fancies of that kind, but we must forgive them."

When the examination was over the doctor looked at his watch, and then Praskovya Fedorovna announced to Ivan Ilych that it was of course as he pleased, but she had sent to-day for a celebrated specialist who would examine him and have a consultation with Mikhail Danilovich (their regular doctor).

"Please don't raise any objections. I'm doing this for my own sake," she said ironically, letting it be felt that she was doing it all for his sake and only said this to leave him no right to refuse. He remained silent, knitting his brows. He felt that he was surrounded and involved in such a mesh of falsity that it was hard to unravel anything.

Everything she did for him was entirely for her own sake; she told him she was doing for herself what she actually was doing for herself, as if that was so incredible he must understand the opposite.

At half-past eleven the celebrated specialist arrived. Again the sounding began and the significant conversations in his presence and in another room, about his kidneys and appendix, and the questions and answers, with such an air of importance that again, instead of the real question of life and death which now alone confronted him, the question arose of his kidney and appendix which were not behaving as they ought to and would now be attacked by Mikhail Danilovich and the specialist and forced to mend their ways.

The celebrated specialist took leave of him with a serious though not hopeless look, and in reply to the timid question Ivan Ilych, eyes glistening with fear and hope, put to him as to whether there was any chance of recovery, said that he could not vouch for it but there was a possibility. The look of hope with which Ivan Ilych watched the doctor out was so pathetic that Praskovya Fedorovna, seeing it, even wept as she left the room to hand the doctor his fee.

The gleam of hope kindled by the doctor's encouragement did not last long. The same room, the same pictures, curtains, wall-paper, medicine bottles, were all there, and the same aching suffering body, and Ivan Ilych began to moan. They gave him a subcutaneous injection and he sank into oblivion.

It was twilight when he came to. They brought him his dinner and he swallowed some beef broth with difficulty; then everything was the same again and night was coming on.

After dinner, at seven o'clock, Praskovya Fedorovna came into the room in evening dress, her full bosom pushed up by her corset, and with traces of powder on her face. She had reminded him in the morning that they were going to the theater. Sarah Bernhardt[5] was visiting town and they had a box, which he had insisted on their taking. Now he had forgotten about it and her toilet offended him, but he concealed his vexation when he remembered that he had himself insisted on their securing a box and going because it would be an instructive and aesthetic pleasure for the children.

Praskovya Fedorovna came in, self-satisfied but with a rather guilty air. She sat down and asked how he was, but, as he saw, only for the sake of asking and not in order to learn about it, knowing that there was nothing to learn. Then she went on to what she really wanted to say: she would not on any account have gone but the box had been taken and Helen and their daughter were going, as well as Petrishchev (the examining magistrate, their daughter's fiancé) and that it was out of the question to let them go alone. She would have much preferred to sit with him for a while; he must be sure to follow the doctor's orders while she was away.

"Oh, and Fedor Petrovich" (the fiancé) "would like to come in. May he? And Lisa?"

"All right."

Their daughter came in in full evening dress, her fresh young flesh exposed (making a show of that very flesh which in his own case caused so much suffering), strong, healthy, evidently in love, and impatient with his illness, suffering, and death, because they interfered with her happiness.

5. The famous French actress (1844–1923) was on tour in Russia during the winter of 1881–82.

Fedor Petrovich came in too, in evening dress, his hair curled à la Capoul,[6] a tight stiff collar around his long sinewy neck, an enormous white shirt-front and narrow black trousers tightly stretched over his strong thighs. He had one white glove tightly drawn on, and was holding his opera hat in his hand.

Following him the schoolboy crept in unnoticed, in a new uniform, poor little fellow, and wearing gloves. Terribly dark shadows showed under his eyes, the meaning of which Ivan Ilych knew well.

His son had always seemed pathetic to him, and now it was dreadful to see the boy's frightened look of pity. It seemed to Ivan Ilych that Vasya was the only one besides Gerasim who understood and pitied him.

They all sat down and again asked how he was. A silence followed. Lisa asked her mother about the opera-glasses, and there was an altercation between mother and daughter as to who had taken them and where they had been put. This occasioned some unpleasantness.

Fedor Petrovich inquired of Ivan Ilych whether he had ever seen Sarah Bernhardt. Ivan Ilych did not at first catch the question, but then replied: "No, have you seen her before?"

"Yes, in *Adrienne Lecouvreur*."[7]

Praskovya Fedorovna mentioned some roles in which Sarah Bernhardt was particularly good. Her daughter disagreed. Conversation sprang up as to the elegance and realism of her acting—the sort of conversation that is always repeated and is always the same.

In the midst of the conversation Fedor Petrovich glanced at Ivan Ilych and became silent. The others also looked at him and grew silent. Ivan Ilych was staring with glittering eyes straight before him, evidently indignant with them. This had to be rectified, but it was impossible to do so. The silence had to be broken, but for a time no one dared break it and they all became afraid that the conventional deception would suddenly become obvious and the truth become plain to all. Lisa was the first to pluck up her courage and break that silence, but by trying to hide what everybody was feeling, she betrayed it.

"Well, if we're going it's time to start," she said, looking at her watch, a present from her father, with a faint, significant smile at Fedor Petrovich relating to something known only to them. She got up with a rustle of her dress.

They all rose, said good-night, and went away.

When they had gone it seemed to Ivan Ilych that he felt better; the falsity had gone away with them. But the pain remained—the same pain and the same fear that made everything monotonously alike, nothing harder and nothing easier. Everything was worse.

6. Named after the French tenor Joseph Capoul (1839–1924), the hairstyle consisted of a part down the middle with a curl on each side of the forehead.
7. A comedy written by A. E. Scribe and E. Le-gouvé in 1849 based on the life of the eighteenth-century French actress. The title role was one of Sarah Bernhardt's most successful parts.

Again minute followed minute and hour followed hour. Everything remained the same; there was no cessation. The inevitable end of it all became more and more terrible.

"Yes, send Gerasim in here," he replied to a question Peter asked.

IX

His wife returned late at night. She came in on tip-toe, but he heard her, opened his eyes, and made haste to close them again. She wished to send Gerasim away and sit with him herself, but he opened his eyes and said: "No, go away."

"Are you in great pain?"

"Always the same."

"Take some opium."

He agreed and took some. She went away.

Till about three in the morning he was in a state of stupefied misery. It seemed to him that he and his pain were being thrust into a narrow, deep black sack, and though they were being pushed further and further in they could not be pushed to the bottom. And this, terrible enough in itself, was accompanied by suffering. He was frightened, yet wanted to fall through the sack; he struggled yet co-operated. Suddenly he broke through, fell, and regained consciousness. Gerasim was sitting at the foot of the bed dozing quietly and patiently, while he himself lay with his emaciated stockinged legs resting on Gerasim's shoulders; the same shaded candle stood there and the same unceasing pain.

"Go away, Gerasim," he whispered.

"It's all right, sir. I'll stay a while."

"No. Go away."

He removed his legs from Gerasim's shoulders, turned sideways onto his arm, and felt sorry for himself. He only waited till Gerasim had gone into the next room and then restrained himself no longer but wept like a child. He wept on account of his helplessness, his terrible loneliness, the cruelty of man, the cruelty of God, and the absence of God. "Why hast Thou done all this? Why hast Thou brought me here? Why, why dost Thou torment me so terribly?"

He did not expect an answer and wept because there was no answer and could be none. The pain grew more acute again, but he did not stir and did not call. He said to himself: "Go on! Strike me! But what is it for? What have I done to Thee? What is it for?"

Then he grew quiet and not only ceased weeping, but even held his breath and became all attention. It was as though he were listening not to an audible voice, but to the voice of his soul, to the current of thoughts arising within him.

"What do you want?" was the first clear conception capable of being expressed in words, that he heard.

"What do you want? What do you want?" he repeated to himself.

"What do I want? To live and not to suffer," he answered.

Again he listened with such concentrated attention that even his pain did not distract him.

"To live? How?" asked his inner voice.

"Why, to live as I used to—well and pleasantly."

"As you lived before, well and pleasantly?" the voice repeated.

And in his imagination he began to recall the best moments of his pleasant life. But strange to say none of those best moments of his pleasant life now seemed at all what they had seemed then—none of them except his first recollections of childhood. There, in childhood, there had been something really pleasant with which it would be possible to live, if it could return. But the child who had experienced that happiness no longer existed, it was like a recollection of somebody else.

As soon as the period began which had produced the present Ivan Ilych, all that had then seemed joys now melted away before his sight and turned into something trivial and often nasty.

The further he departed from childhood and the nearer he came to the present the more worthless and doubtful were the joys. This began with the School of Law. A little that was really good was still to be found there—there was light-heartedness, friendship, and hope. But in the upper classes there had already been fewer good moments. Then during the first years of his official career, when he was in the service of the governor, some pleasant moments occurred again: they were the memories of his love for a woman. Then all became confused and there was still less of what was good; later on again there was even less that was good, and the further he went the less there was. His marriage, a mere accident, then the disenchantment that followed it, his wife's bad breath and her sensuality and hypocrisy: then that deadly official life and those preoccupations about money, a year of it, two, ten, twenty, and always the same thing. The longer it lasted the more deadly it became. "It is as if I had been going downhill while I imagined I was going up. And that's really what it was. I was going up in public opinion, but to the same extent life was ebbing away from me. And now it's all over and there's only death.

"Then what does it mean? Why? It can't be that life is so senseless and horrible. But if it really has been so horrible and senseless, why must I die and die in agony? There's something wrong!

"Maybe I didn't live as I ought to have done," it suddenly occurred to him. "But how could that be, when I did everything properly?" he replied, and immediately dismissed from his mind this, the sole solution of all the riddles of life and death, as something quite impossible.

"Then what do you want now? To live? Live how? Live as you lived in the law courts when the usher proclaimed 'The judge is coming!' The judge is coming, the judge!" he repeated to himself. "Here he is, the judge. But I'm not guilty!" he exclaimed angrily. "What is it for?" And he ceased crying, but turning his face to the wall continued to ponder the same question: Why, and for what purpose, is there all this horror? But however much he pondered, he found no answer. And whenever the thought occurred to him, as it often did, that it all resulted from his not having lived as he ought to have done, he recalled at once the correctness of his whole life and dismissed so strange an idea.

X

Another fortnight passed. Ivan Ilych now no longer left his sofa. He would not lie in bed but lay on the sofa, facing the wall nearly all the time. He suffered the same unceasing agonies and in his loneliness pondered the same insoluble question: "What is this? Can it be that it is Death?" And the inner voice answered: "Yes, it is Death."

"Why these sufferings?" And the voice answered, "For no reason— just so." Beyond and besides this, there was nothing.

From the very beginning of his illness, ever since he had first been to see the doctor, Ivan Ilych's life had been divided between two contrary and alternating moods: either despair and the expectation of this un-comprehended and terrible death, or hope and an intently interested observation of the functioning of his organs. Before his eyes there was either a kidney or an intestine that temporarily evaded its duty, or that incomprehensible and dreadful death from which it was impossible to escape.

These two states of mind had alternated from the very beginning of his illness, but the further it progressed, the more doubtful and fantastic became the conception of his kidney, and the more real the sense of impending death.

He had but to recall what he had been three months before and what he was now, to recall with what regularity he had been going downhill, for every possibility of hope to be shattered.

Lately during that loneliness in which he found himself as he lay facing the back of the sofa, a loneliness in the midst of a populous town, surrounded by numerous acquaintances and relations, but that could not have been more complete anywhere—either at the bottom of the sea or under the earth—during that terrible loneliness Ivan Ilych had lived only in memories of the past. Pictures of his past rose before him one after another. They always began with what was nearest in time and then went back to what was most remote—to his childhood—and stopped there. If he thought of the stewed prunes that had been offered him that day, his mind went back to the raw shrivelled French plums of his childhood, their peculiar flavor and the flow of saliva when he sucked their pits; along with the memory of that taste came a whole series of memories of those days: his nanny, his brother, and their toys.

"No, I mustn't think of that. . . . It's too painful," Ivan Ilych said to himself, and brought himself back to the present—to the button on the back of the sofa and the creases in its morocco. "Morocco is expensive, but it doesn't wear well: there had been a quarrel about it. It was a different kind of quarrel and a different kind of morocco that time when we tore father's portfolio and were punished, and mamma brought us some tarts. . . ." Once again his thoughts dwelt on childhood; again it was painful and he tried to banish them and fix his mind on something else.

Then together with that chain of memories another series passed through his mind—of how his illness had progressed and grown worse. There too the further back he looked, the more life there was. There had been more of what was good in life and more of life itself. The two merged. "Just as the pain went on getting worse and worse, so my life grew worse and worse," he thought. "There's one bright spot there at the back, at the beginning of life, and afterwards all becomes blacker and blacker and proceeds more and more rapidly—in inverse ratio to the square of the distance from death," thought Ivan Ilych. And the example of a stone falling downwards with increasing velocity entered his mind. Life, a series of increasing sufferings, flies further and further towards its end—the most terrible suffering. "I'm flying. . . ." He shuddered, shifted himself, and tried to resist, but was already aware that resistance was impossible, and again with eyes tired of gazing but unable to cease seeing what was before them, he stared at the back of the sofa and waited—awaiting that dreadful fall and shock and destruction.

"Resistance is impossible!" he said to himself. "If I could only understand what it's all for! But that too is impossible. An explanation would be possible if it could be said that I've not lived as I ought to. But it's impossible to say that," and he remembered all the legality, correctitude, and propriety of his life. "At any rate that can certainly not be admitted," he thought, and his lips smiled ironically as if someone could see that smile and be taken in by it. "There's no explanation! Agony, death. . . . What for?"

XI

Another two weeks went by in this way and during that time an event occurred that Ivan Ilych and his wife had desired. Petrishchev formally proposed. It happened in the evening. The next day Praskovya Fedorovna came into her husband's room considering how best to inform him of it, but that very night there had been a change for the worse in his condition. She found him still lying on the sofa but in a different position. He lay on his back, groaning and staring fixedly straight in front of him.

She began to remind him about his medicines, but he turned his eyes towards her with such a look that she did not finish what she was saying; so great an animosity, to her in particular, did that look express.

"For Christ's sake let me die in peace!" he said.

She would have gone away, but just then their daughter came in and went to say good morning. He looked at her as he had his wife, and in reply to her inquiry about his health said dryly that he would soon free them all of himself. They were both silent and after sitting with him for a while went away.

"Is it our fault?" Lisa asked her mother. "It's as if we were to blame! I'm sorry for papa, but why should we be tortured?"

The doctor came at his usual time. Ivan Ilych answered "Yes" and "No," never taking his angry eyes from him, and said at last: "You know you can do nothing for me, so leave me alone."

"We can ease your sufferings."

"You can't even do that. Let me be."

The doctor went into the drawing-room and told Praskovya Fedorovna that the situation was very serious and that the only resource left was opium to allay her husband's sufferings, which must be terrible.

It was true, as the doctor said, Ivan Ilych's physical sufferings were terrible, but worse than the physical sufferings were his mental sufferings which were his chief torture.

His mental sufferings were due to the fact that that night, as he looked at Gerasim's sleepy, good-natured face with its prominent cheek-bones, the question suddenly occurred to him: "What if my whole life has been wrong?"

It occurred to him that what had appeared perfectly impossible before, namely that he had not spent his life as he should have done, might be true after all. It occurred to him that his scarcely perceptible attempts to struggle against what was considered good by the most highly placed people, those scarcely noticeable impulses which he had immediately suppressed, might have been the real thing, and all the rest false. His professional duties and the whole arrangement of his life and his family, all his social and official interests, might all have been false. He tried to defend all those things to himself and suddenly felt the weakness of what he was defending. There was nothing to defend.

"But if that's so," he said to himself, "and I'm leaving this life with the consciousness that I've lost all that was given me and it's impossible to rectify it—what then?" He lay on his back and began to pass his life in review in quite a new way. In the morning when he first saw his footman, then his wife, then his daughter, and then the doctor, their every word and movement confirmed the awful truth that had been revealed to him during the night. In them he saw himself—all that for which he had lived—and saw clearly that it was not real at all, but a terrible and huge deception which had hidden both life and death. This consciousness intensified his physical suffering tenfold. He groaned, tossed about, and pulled at his clothing which choked and stifled him. And he hated them on that account.

He was given a large dose of opium and became unconscious, but at noon his sufferings began again. He drove everybody away and tossed from side to side.

His wife came to him and said:

"Jean, my dear, do this for me. It can't do any harm and it often helps. Healthy people often do it."

He opened his eyes wide.

"What? Take communion? Why? It's unnecessary! However . . ."

She began to cry.

"Yes, do, my dear. I'll send for our priest. He's such a nice man."

"All right. Very well," he muttered.

When the priest came and heard his confession, Ivan Ilych was softened and seemed to feel some relief from his doubts and consequently from his sufferings, and for a moment there came a ray of hope. Again he began to think of his vermiform appendix and the possibility of correcting it. He received the sacrament with tears in his eyes.

When they laid him down again afterwards he felt a moment's peace, and the hope that he might live awoke in him once again. He began to think of the operation that had been suggested to him. "To live! I want to live!" he said to himself.

His wife came in to congratulate him after his communion, and when uttering the usual conventional words she added:

"You feel better, don't you?"

Without looking at her he said "Yes."

Her dress, her figure, the expression of her face, the tone of her voice, all revealed the same thing. "This is wrong, it's not as it should be. All you've lived for and still live for is falsehood and deception, hiding life and death from you." As soon as he admitted that thought, his hatred and agonizing physical suffering increased again, and with that suffering a consciousness of the unavoidable, approaching end. And to this was added a new sensation of grinding, shooting pain and a feeling of suffocation.

The expression of his face when he uttered that "Yes" was dreadful. Having uttered it, he looked her straight in the eye, turned his face away with a rapidity extraordinary in his weak state and shouted:

"Go away! Go away and leave me alone!"

XII

From that moment the screaming began that continued for three days, and was so terrible that one could not hear it through two closed doors without horror. At the moment he answered his wife he realized that he was lost, that there was no return, that the end had come, the very end, and his doubts were still unsolved and remained doubts.

"Oh! Oh! Oh!" he cried in various intonations. He had begun by screaming "I won't!" and continued screaming on the letter "O."

For three whole days, during which time did not exist for him, he struggled in that black sack into which he was being thrust by an invisible, irresistible force. He struggled as a man condemned to death struggles in the hands of the executioner, knowing that he cannot save himself. Every moment he felt that despite all his efforts he was drawing nearer and nearer to what terrified him. He felt that his agony was due to his being thrust into that black hole and still more to his not being able to get right into it. He was hindered from getting into it by his conviction that his life had been a good one. That very justification of his life held him fast and prevented his moving forward, and it caused him the most torment of all.

Suddenly some force struck him in the chest and side, making it even harder to breathe, and he fell through the hole and there at the bottom was a light. What had happened to him was like the sensation one sometimes experiences in a railway carriage when one thinks one is going backwards while one is really going forwards and suddenly becomes aware of the real direction.

"Yes, it was all not the right thing," he said to himself, "but that doesn't matter. The "right thing" can still be done. But what is the right thing?" he asked himself, and suddenly grew quiet.

This occurred at the end of the third day, two hours before his death. Just then his schoolboy son had crept in softly and gone up to the bedside. The dying man was still screaming desperately and waving his arms. His hand fell on the boy's head, and the boy caught it, pressed it to his lips, and began to cry.

At that very moment Ivan Ilych fell through and caught sight of the light, and it was revealed to him that though his life had not been what it should have been, it could still be rectified. He asked himself, "What is the right thing?" and grew still, listening. Then he felt that someone was kissing his hand. He opened his eyes, looked at his son, and felt sorry for him. His wife came up to him and he glanced at her. She was gazing at him open-mouthed, with undried tears on her nose and cheek and a despairing look on her face. He felt sorry for her too.

"Yes, I am making them all wretched," he thought. "They're sorry, but it'll be better for them when I die." He wished to say this, but didn't have the strength to utter it. "Besides, why speak? I must act," he thought. With a look at his wife he indicated his son and said:

"Take him away . . . sorry for him . . . and for you too. . . ." He tried to add, "Forgive me," but said "Let me through"[8] and waved his

---

8. Ivan misspeaks: he means to say *Prosti* (Forgive me), but utters the word *Propusti* (Let me through) by mistake.

hand, knowing that He whose understanding mattered would understand.

Suddenly it grew clear to him that what had been oppressing him and would not leave him was all dropping away at once from two sides, from ten sides, from all sides. He was sorry for them, he must act so as not to hurt them: release them and free himself from these sufferings. "How good and how simple!" he thought. "And the pain?" he asked himself. "What has become of it? Where are you, pain?"

He turned his attention to it.

"Yes, here it is. Well, what of it? Let it be."

"And death . . . where is it?"

He looked for his former accustomed fear of death and did not find it. "Where is it? What death?" There was no fear because there was no death.

In place of death there was light.

"So that's what it is!" he suddenly exclaimed aloud. "What joy!"

To him all this happened in a single instant, and the meaning of that instant did not change. For those present his agony continued for another two hours. Something rattled in his throat, his emaciated body twitched, then the gasping and rattle became less and less frequent.

"It is finished!" said someone near him.

He heard these words and repeated them in his soul.

"Death is finished," he said to himself. "It is no more!"

He drew in a breath, stopped in the midst of a sigh, stretched out, and died.

The Three Hermits†

An Old Legend from the Volga District

> "And in praying use not vain repetitions, as the Gentiles do: for they think that they shall be heard for their much speaking. Be not therefore like unto them: for your Father knoweth what things ye have need of, before ye ask Him."—Matt. 6.7.8.

A bishop was sailing from Archangel[1] to the Solovetsk Monastery,[2] and on the same vessel were a number of pilgrims on their way to visit the shrines at that place. The voyage was a smooth one. The wind was favorable and the weather, fair. The pilgrims lay on deck, eating, or sat in groups talking to one another. The Bishop, too, came on deck, and as he was pacing up and down, he noticed a group of men standing near the prow and listening to a fisherman, who was pointing to the sea

---

†This piece was first published in 1886.
1. Major port on the mouth of the Northern Dvina River near the White Sea.

2. Built in the fifteenth century on an island in the White Sea at the entrance of Onega Bay.

and telling them something. The Bishop stopped, and looked in the direction in which the man was pointing. He could see nothing, however, but the sea glistening in the sunshine. He drew nearer to listen, but when the man saw him, he took off his cap and was silent. The rest of the people also took off their caps and bowed.

"Don't let me disturb you, friends," said the Bishop. "I came to hear what this good man was saying."

"The fisherman was telling us about the hermits," replied one, a tradesman, rather bolder than the rest.

"What hermits?" asked the Bishop, going over to the side of the vessel and seating himself on a box. "Tell me about them. I'd like to hear. What were you pointing at?"

"Why, that little island you can just see over there," answered the man, pointing to a spot ahead and a little to the right. "That's the island where the hermits live for the salvation of their souls."

"Where's the island?" asked the Bishop. "I see nothing."

"There, in the distance, if you'll look along my hand. Do you see that little cloud? Below it, and a bit to the left, there's just a faint streak. That's the island."

The Bishop looked carefully, but his unaccustomed eyes could make out nothing but the water shimmering in the sun.

"I cannot see it," he said. "But who are the hermits that live there?"

"They are holy men," answered the fisherman. "I'd heard tell of them a long time ago, but never chanced to see them myself till the year before last."

And the fisherman related how once, when he was out fishing, he'd been stranded at night on that island, not knowing where he was. In the morning, as he wandered about, he came across an earth hut, and met an old man standing near it. Presently two others came out, and after having fed him and dried his things, they helped him repair his boat.

"What are they like?" asked the Bishop.

"One is a small man and his back is bent. He wears a priest's cassock and is very old; he must be more than a hundred, I'd say. He's so old that the white of his beard is taking on a greenish tinge, but he's always smiling, and his face is as bright as an angel's from heaven. The second is taller, but he's also very old. He wears a tattered peasant coat. His beard is broad, and of a yellowish grey color. He's a strong man. Before I had time to help him, he turned my boat over as if it were only a pail. He too is kindly and cheerful. The third is tall, and has a beard as white as snow reaching down to his knees. He's stern, with overhanging eyebrows; and he wears nothing but a piece of matting tied round his waist."

"Did they speak to you?" asked the Bishop.

"For the most part they did everything in silence, and spoke but little even to one another. One of them would just give a glance, and the others would understand him. I asked the tallest whether they had lived there for long. He frowned, and muttered something as if he were angry; but the oldest one took his hand and smiled, and then the tall one was quiet. The oldest one only said: 'Have mercy upon us,' and smiled."

While the fisherman was talking, the ship had drawn nearer to the island.

"There, now you can see it plainly, if your Lordship will please look," said the tradesman, pointing with his hand.

The Bishop looked, and now he really did see a dark streak—which was the island. Having looked at it for a while, he left the prow of the vessel. Going to the stern, he asked the helmsman:

"What island is that?"

"That one," replied the man, "has no name. There are many like that in this sea."

"Is it true that there are hermits who live there for the salvation of their souls?"

"So it's said, your Lordship, but I don't know if it's true. Fishermen say they've seen them; but of course they may only be spinning yarns."

"I'd like to land on the island and see these men," said the Bishop. "How could I manage it?"

"The ship cannot get close to the island," replied the helmsman, "but you could be rowed there in a boat. You'd better speak to the captain."

The captain was sent for and came.

"I'd like to see these hermits," said the Bishop. "Could I be rowed ashore?"

The captain tried to dissuade him.

"Of course it could be done," he said, "but we'd lose a great deal of time. And if I might venture to say so to your Lordship, the old men aren't worth your pains. I've heard it said that they're foolish old fellows, who understand nothing, and never speak a word, any more than do the fish in the sea."

"I wish to see them," said the Bishop, "and I will pay you for your trouble and the loss of time. Please let me have a boat."

There was no help for it; the order was given. The sailors trimmed the sails, the steersman put up the helm, and the ship's course was set for the island. A chair was placed at the prow for the Bishop, and he sat there, looking ahead. The passengers all collected at the prow, and gazed at the island. Those who had the sharpest eyes could presently make out the rocks on it, and then a mud hut. At last one man saw the hermits themselves. The captain brought a spyglass and, after looking through it, handed it over to the Bishop.

"It's right enough. There are three men standing on the shore. There, a little to the right of that big rock."

The Bishop took the spyglass, got it into position, and saw the three men: a tall one, a shorter one, and one very small and bent, standing on the shore and holding each other by the hand.

The captain turned to the Bishop.

"The vessel can get no closer than this, your Lordship. If you wish to go ashore, we must ask you to go in the boat, while we anchor here."

The cable was quickly let out; the anchor cast, and the sails furled. There was a jerk, and the vessel shook. Then, a boat was lowered, the oarsmen jumped in, the Bishop descended the ladder and took his seat. The men pulled at their oars and the boat moved rapidly towards the island. When they came within a stone's throw, they saw three old men: a tall one with only a piece of matting tied around his waist, a shorter one in a tattered peasant coat, and a very old one bent with age and wearing an old cassock—all three standing hand in hand.

The oarsmen pulled the boat in to the shore, and held on with the boathook while the Bishop got out.

The three old men bowed to him, and he gave them his blessing, at which they bowed still lower. Then the Bishop began to speak to them.

"I've heard," he said, "that you, godly men, live here saving your own souls and praying to our Lord for your fellow men. I, an unworthy servant of Christ, have been called, by God's mercy, to keep and teach His flock. I wished to see you, servants of God, and to do what I can to teach you, also."

The old men looked at each other smiling, but remained silent.

"Tell me," said the Bishop, "what are you doing to save your souls, and how are you serving God on this island?"

The second hermit sighed, and looked at the oldest, the very ancient one. The latter smiled, and said:

"We don't know how to serve God. We only serve and support ourselves, O servant of God."

"But how do you pray to God?" asked the Bishop.

"We pray like this," replied the hermit. "Three are ye, three are we, have mercy upon us."

When the old man said this, all three of them raised their eyes to heaven, and repeated:

"Three are ye, three are we, have mercy upon us!"

The Bishop smiled.

"You've obviously heard something about the Holy Trinity," he said. "But you don't pray correctly. You've won my affection, godly men. I see you wish to please the Lord, but don't know how to serve Him. That's not the way to pray; but listen to me, and I will teach you. I will teach you, not a way of my own, but the way in which God in the Holy Scriptures has commanded all men to pray to Him."

And the Bishop began explaining to the hermits how God had revealed Himself to men; telling them of God the Father, God the Son, and God the Holy Ghost.

"God the Son came down on earth," he said, "to save men, and this is how He taught us all to pray. Listen, and repeat after me: 'Our Father.' "

And the first old man repeated after him, "Our Father," and the second said, "Our Father," and the third said, "Our Father."

"Which art in heaven," continued the Bishop.

The first hermit repeated, "Which art in heaven," but the second blundered over the words, and the tall hermit couldn't say them properly. His hair had grown over his mouth so that he couldn't speak clearly. The very old hermit, having no teeth, also mumbled indistinctly.

The Bishop said the words again, and the old men repeated them after him. The Bishop sat down on a stone, and the old men stood before him, watching his mouth, and repeating the words as he uttered them. And all day long the Bishop labored, saying a word twenty, thirty, a hundred times over, and the old men repeated it after him. They blundered, he corrected them, and made them begin again.

The Bishop didn't stop till he'd taught them the whole of the Lord's Prayer so that they could not only repeat it after him, but could say it all by themselves. The middle one was the first to know it, and to repeat all of it alone. The Bishop made him say it again and again; at last the others could say it too.

It was getting dark and the moon was appearing over the water, before the Bishop rose to return to the vessel. When he took leave of the old men they all bowed down to the ground before him. He raised them up, and kissed each one of them, telling them to pray as he had taught them. Then he got into the boat and returned to the ship.

And as he sat in the boat and was rowed to the ship he could hear the three voices of the hermits loudly repeating the Lord's Prayer. As the boat drew near the vessel their voices could no longer be heard, but they could still be seen in the moonlight, standing as he had left them on the shore, the shortest in the middle, the tallest on the right, the middle one on the left. As soon as the Bishop had reached the vessel and got on board, the anchor was raised and the sails unfurled. The wind filled them and the ship sailed away; the Bishop took a seat in the stern and watched the island as they left. For a while he could still see the hermits, but presently they disappeared from sight, though the island was still visible. At last it too vanished, and only the sea could be seen, rippling in the moonlight.

The pilgrims lay down to sleep, and all was quiet on deck. The Bishop didn't wish to sleep, but sat alone at the stern, gazing at the sea where the island was no longer visible, and thinking about the three old men. He thought how pleased they'd been to learn the Lord's Prayer; and he thanked God for having sent him there to teach and help such godly men.

So the Bishop sat, thinking, and gazing at the sea where the island had disappeared. The moonlight flickered before his eyes, sparkling here and there upon the waves. Suddenly he saw something white and shining, on the bright path which the moon cast across the sea. Was it a seagull, or the little gleaming sail of some small boat? The Bishop fixed his eyes on it, wondering.

"It must be a boat sailing after us," he thought, "but it's overtaking us very rapidly. It was far, far away a minute ago, but now it's much nearer. It cannot be a boat, for I can see no sail; but whatever it is, it's following us and catching up."

He couldn't make out what it was. Not a boat, nor a bird, nor a fish! It was too large for a man, and besides a man couldn't be out there in the midst of the sea. The Bishop rose, and said to the helmsman:

"Look there, what is that, my friend? What is it?" the Bishop repeated, though he could now see plainly what it was—it was the three hermits running across the water, all gleaming white, their grey beards shining, approaching the ship as quickly as though it were not moving.

The steersman looked, and let go the helm in terror.

"Oh, Lord! The hermits are running after us across the water as though it were dry land!"

The passengers, hearing him, jumped up and crowded to the stern. They saw the hermits coming along hand in hand, and the two outer ones beckoning the ship to stop. All three were gliding along upon the water without moving their feet. Before the ship could be stopped, the hermits had reached it; raising their heads, all three as with one voice, began to say:

"We have forgotten your teaching, servant of God. As long as we kept repeating it, we remembered, but when we stopped saying it for a while, a word dropped out, and now it's all fallen to pieces. We can remember nothing of it. Teach us again."

The Bishop crossed himself, and leaning over the ship's side, he said:

"Your own prayer will reach the Lord, O men of God. It is not for me to teach you. Pray for us sinners."

And the Bishop bowed low before the old men; they turned and went back across the sea. And a light shone until daybreak on the spot where they were lost to sight.

The Kreutzer Sonata †

28 But I say unto you, That whosoever looketh on a woman to lust after her hath committed adultery with her already in his heart.

10 ¶ His disciples say unto him, If the case of the man be so with *his* wife, it is not good to marry.

11 But he said unto them, All *men* cannot receive this saying, save *they* to whom it is given.

†This piece was first published in 1889.

12 For there are some eunuchs, which were so born from *their* mother's womb: and there are some eunuchs, which were made eunuchs of men: and there be eunuchs, which have made themselves eunuchs for the kingdom of heaven's sake. He that is able to receive *it*, let him receive *it*.

Matthew 5 and 19

I

It was early spring, and the second day of our journey. Passengers going short distances entered and left our carriage, but three others, like myself, had come all the way with the train. One was a lady, plain and no longer young, who smoked, had a harassed look, and wore a mannish coat and cap; another was an acquaintance of hers, a talkative man of about forty, whose things looked neat and new; the third was a rather short man who kept himself apart. He was not old, but his curly hair had gone grey prematurely. His movements were abrupt and his unusually glittering eyes moved rapidly from one object to another. He wore an old overcoat, evidently from a first-rate tailor, with an astrakhan collar, and a tall astrakhan cap. When he unbuttoned his overcoat a sleeveless Russian jacket and embroidered shirt showed beneath it. A peculiarity of this man was a strange sound he emitted, something like a clearing of his throat, or a laugh begun and sharply broken off.

All along the way this man had carefully avoided making the acquaintance or entering into any conversation with his fellow passengers. When spoken to by those near him he gave short and abrupt answers; at other times he read, looked out of the window, smoked, or drank tea and ate something he took out of an old bag.

It seemed to me that his loneliness depressed him, and I made several attempts to converse with him, but whenever our eyes met, which happened often as he sat nearly opposite me, he turned away and took up his book or looked out of the window.

Towards the second evening, when our train stopped at a large station, this nervous man fetched himself some boiling water and made tea. The man with the neat new things—a lawyer as I later found out—and his neighbor, the smoking lady with the mannish coat, went to the refreshment-room to drink tea.

During their absence several new passengers entered the carriage, among them a tall, shaven, wrinkled old man, evidently a tradesman, in a coat lined with skunk fur, and a cloth cap with an enormous peak. The tradesman sat down opposite the seats of the lady and the lawyer, and immediately started a conversation with a young man who had also entered at that station and, judging by his appearance, was a tradesman's clerk.

I was sitting on the other side of the aisle and as the train was standing still I could hear snatches of their conversation when nobody was passing between us. The tradesman began by saying that he was going to his estate which was only one station farther on; then the conversation turned to prices and trade as usual and they spoke about the state of business in Moscow and then about the Nizhni-Novgorod Fair.[1] The clerk began to relate how a wealthy merchant, known to both of them, had gone on a spree at the fair, but the old man interrupted him by telling about the orgies he had been at in former times at Kunavino Fair. He evidently prided himself on the part he had played in them, and recounted with pleasure how he and some acquaintances, together with the merchant they had been speaking about, had once gotten drunk at Kunavino[2] and played such a trick that he had to tell about it in a whisper. The clerk's roar of laughter filled the whole carriage; the old man also laughed, exposing two yellow teeth.

Not expecting to hear anything interesting, I got up to stroll about the platform till the train started. At the carriage door I met the lawyer and the lady who were talking with animation as they approached.

"You won't have time," said the sociable lawyer, "the second bell will ring in a moment."

The bell did ring before I had gone the full length of the train. When I returned, the animated conversation between the lady and the lawyer was proceeding. The old tradesman sat silent opposite them, looking sternly before him, and occasionally mumbled disapprovingly as if chewing something.

"Then she plainly informed her husband," the lawyer was saying with a smile as I passed him, "that she was unable, and did not wish, to live with him since . . ."

He went on to say something I couldn't hear. Several other passengers came in after me. The guard passed, a porter hurried in, and for some time the noise made their voices inaudible. When all was quiet again the conversation had evidently turned from the particular case to general considerations.

The lawyer was saying that public opinion in Europe was occupied with the question of divorce, and that cases of "that kind" were occurring more and more often in Russia. Noticing that his was the only voice audible, he stopped his discourse and turned to the old man.

"Those things didn't happen in the old days, did they?" he asked, smiling pleasantly.

The old man was about to reply, but the train moved and he took off his cap, crossed himself, and whispered a prayer. The lawyer turned his eyes away and waited politely. Having finished his prayer and having crossed himself three times, the old man set his cap straight, pulled it

1. Nizhni-Novgorod (now Gorky) was a major port along the Volga. Each summer an important trade fair was held there.

2. Suburb of Nizhni-Novgorod.

well down over his forehead, changed his position, and began to speak.

"They used to happen even then, sir, but less often," he said. "As times are now they can't help happening. People have got too educated."

The train moved faster and faster and jolted over the joints of the rails, making it difficult to hear, but being interested I moved nearer. The nervous man with the glittering eyes opposite me, evidently also interested, listened without changing his place.

"What's wrong with education?" asked the lady, with a scarcely perceptible smile. "Surely it can't be better to marry as they used to in the old days when the bride and groom didn't even see one another before the wedding," she continued, answering not what her interlocutor had said, but what she thought he would say, in the way many ladies have. "Without knowing whether they loved, or whether they could love, they married just anybody, and were wretched all their lives. Do you think that was better?" she asked, evidently addressing me and the lawyer chiefly and least of all the old man with whom she was talking.

"They've got so very educated," the tradesman reiterated, looking contemptuously at the lady and leaving her question unanswered.

"It would be interesting to know how you explain the connection between education and matrimonial discord," said the lawyer, with a scarcely perceptible smile.

The tradesman was about to speak, but the lady interrupted him.

"No," she said, "those times have passed." But the lawyer stopped her.

"Yes, but allow the gentleman to express his views."

"Foolishness comes from education," the old man said categorically.

"They make people marry who don't love one another, and then wonder that they live in discord," the lady hastened to say, turning to look at the lawyer, at me, and even at the clerk, who had stood up and, leaning on the back of the seat, was listening to the conversation with a smile. "It's only animals, you know, that can be paired off as their master likes; human beings have their own inclinations and attachments," said the lady, with an evident desire to annoy the tradesman.

"You shouldn't talk like that, madam," said the old man. "Animals are cattle, but human beings have a law given them."

"Yes, but how is one to live with a man when there's no love?" the lady again hastened to express her argument, which probably seemed very new to her.

"They used not to talk about that," said the old man in an impressive tone. "It's only now that all this has sprung up. The least thing makes them say: 'I will leave you!' The fashion has spread even to the peasants. 'Here you are!' she says. 'Here, take your shirts and trousers and I'll go off with Vanka; his head is curlier than yours.' What can you say? The first thing that should be required of a woman is fear!"

The clerk glanced at the lawyer, at the lady, and at me, apparently suppressing a smile and prepared to ridicule or to approve the tradesman's words according to the reception they met with.

"Fear of what?" asked the lady.

"Why this: Let her fear her husband! That fear!"

"Oh, the time for that, sir, has passed," said the lady with a certain viciousness.

"No, madam, that time cannot pass. Even as she, Eve, was made from the rib of a man, so it will remain to the end of time," said the old man, jerking his head with such sternness and such a victorious look that the clerk concluded at once that victory was on his side, and laughed loudly.

"Ah yes, that's the way you men argue," said the lady unyieldingly, and turned to us. "You've given yourselves freedom but want to shut women up in a tower. No doubt you permit yourselves everything."

"No one's permitting anything, but a man doesn't bring offspring into the home; while a woman—a wife—is a leaky vessel," the tradesman continued insistently. His tone was so impressive that it evidently vanquished his listeners, and even the lady felt crushed but still she did not give in.

"Yes, but I think you'll agree that a woman is a human being and has feelings just as a man does. What is she to do then, if she doesn't love her husband?"

"Doesn't love!" said the tradesman severely, moving his brows and lips. "She'll love, have no fear!" This unexpected argument particularly pleased the clerk, and he emitted a sound of approval.

"Oh, no, she won't!" the lady began. "And when there's no love you can't enforce it."

"Well, and supposing the wife is unfaithful, what then?" asked the lawyer.

"That's not admissible," said the old man. "One has to see to that."

"But if it happens, what then? You know it does occur."

"It happens among some, but not among us," said the old man.

Everyone was silent. The clerk moved, came still nearer, and, evidently unwilling to be left behind, began with a smile.

"Yes, a young friend of ours had a scandal. It was a difficult case to deal with. It was a case of a woman who was a bad thing. She began to play the devil, while the young fellow is respectable and cultured. At first it was with one of the office-clerks. The husband tried to persuade her with kindness. She wouldn't stop, but played all sorts of dirty tricks. Then she began to steal his money. He beat her, but she only grew worse. She carried on intrigues, if I may mention it, with an unchristened Jew. What was he to do? He turned her out altogether and lives as a bachelor, while she roams about."

"Because he's a fool," said the old man. "If he'd rebuked her properly from the start and not let her have way, she'd still be living with him, have no fear! It's giving way at first that counts. Don't trust your horse in the field, or your wife in the house."

At that moment the guard entered to collect tickets for the next station. The old man surrendered his.

"Yes, the female sex must be curbed in time or else all's lost!"

"Yes, but you yourself were speaking just now about the way married men amuse themselves at the Kunavino Fair," I could not help saying.

"That's a different matter," said the old man and relapsed into silence.

When the whistle sounded the tradesman rose, got out his bag from under the seat, buttoned up his coat, and slightly lifting his cap went out of the carriage.

II

As soon as the old man had gone several voices were raised.

"A man of the old style!" remarked the clerk.

"A living *Domostroy!*"[3] said the lady. "What barbarous views of women and marriage!"

"Yes, we're far from the European understanding of marriage," said the lawyer.

"The chief thing such people don't understand," continued the lady, "is that marriage without love isn't marriage; love alone sanctifies marriage, and real marriage is only that sanctified by love."

The clerk listened with a smile, trying to store up for future use all he could of this clever conversation.

In the midst of the lady's remarks we heard, behind me, a sound like that of a broken laugh or sob; on turning around we saw my neighbor, the lonely grey-haired man with the glittering eyes, who had approached unnoticed during our conversation, which evidently interested him. He stood with his arms on the back of the seat, evidently much excited; his face was red and a muscle twitched in his cheek.

"What kind of love . . . love . . . is it that sanctifies marriage?" he asked hesitatingly.

Noticing the speaker's agitation, the lady tried to answer him as gently and fully as possible.

"True love . . . When such love exists between a man and a woman, then marriage is possible," she said.

"Yes, but how is one to understand what is meant by 'true love'?" said the gentleman with the glittering eyes timidly and with an awkward smile.

"Everybody knows what love is," replied the lady, evidently wishing to break off her conversation with him.

"But I don't," said the man. "You must define what you mean . . ."

"Why? It's very simple," she said, but stopped to consider. "Love?

3. A medieval Russian treatise that espouses very conservative views on domestic life.

Love is an exclusive preference for one person above everybody else,"
said the lady.

"Preference for how long? A month, two days, or half an hour?" said
the grey-haired man and began to laugh.

"Excuse me, we're evidently not speaking about the same thing."

"Oh, yes! Exactly the same."

"She means," interposed the lawyer, pointing to the lady, "that in
the first place marriage must be the outcome of attachment—or love,
if you please—and only where that exists is marriage sacred, so to speak.
Secondly, that marriage when not based on natural attachment—love,
if you prefer the word—lacks the element that makes it morally binding.
Do I understand you correctly?" he added, addressing the lady.

The lady indicated her approval of his explanation by a nod of her
head.

"It follows . . ." the lawyer continued—but the nervous man whose
eyes now glowed as if aflame and who had evidently restrained himself
with difficulty, began without letting the lawyer finish:

"Yes, I mean exactly the same thing, a preference for one person over
everybody else, and I'm only asking: a preference for how long?"

"For how long? For a long time; for life sometimes," replied the lady,
shrugging her shoulders.

"Oh, but that happens only in novels and never in real life. In real
life this preference for one may last for years (that happens very rarely),
more often for months, perhaps for weeks, days, or hours," he said,
evidently aware that he was astonishing everybody by his views and
pleased it was so.

"Oh, what are you saying?" "But no . . ." "No, allow me . . ." we
all three began at once. Even the clerk uttered an indefinite sound of
disapproval.

"Yes, I know," the grey-haired man shouted above our voices, "you're
talking about what's supposed to be, but I'm speaking of what is. Every
man experiences what you call love for every pretty woman."

"Oh, what you say is awful! But the feeling that's called love does
exist among people, and is experienced not for months or years, but for
a lifetime!"

"No, it does not! Even if we should grant that a man might prefer a
certain woman all his life, the woman in all probability would prefer
someone else; so it always has been and still is in the world," he said,
and taking out his cigarette-case he began to smoke.

"But the feeling may be reciprocal," said the lawyer.

"No, sir, it can't!" rejoined the other. "Just as it cannot be that in a
cartload of peas, two marked peas will lie side by side. Besides, it's not
merely this impossibility, but inevitable satiety. To love one person for
a whole lifetime is like saying that one candle will burn a whole life,"
he said, greedily inhaling the smoke.

"But you're talking all the time about physical love. Don't you acknowledge love based on identity of ideals, on spiritual affinity?" asked the lady.

"Spiritual affinity! Identity of ideals!" he repeated, emitting his peculiar sound. "But in that case why go to bed together? (Excuse my coarseness!) Or do people go to bed together because of the identity of their ideals?" he said, bursting into a nervous laugh.

"But permit me," said the lawyer. "Facts contradict you. We do see that matrimony exists, that all mankind, or the greater part of it, lives in wedlock, and many people honorably live long married lives together."

The grey-haired man laughed again.

"First you say marriage is based on love, and when I express a doubt as to the existence of a love other than sensual, you prove the existence of love by the fact that marriages exist. But these days marriages are mere deception!"

"No, allow me!" said the lawyer. "I only say that marriages have existed and do exist."

"They do! But why? They have existed and do exist among people who see in marriage something sacramental, a mystery binding them in the sight of God. Among them marriages do exist. Among us, people marry regarding marriage as nothing but copulation, and the result is either deception or coercion. When it's deception it's easier to bear. The husband and wife merely deceive people by pretending to be monogamists, while living polygamously. That's bad, but still bearable. But when, as most frequently happens, the husband and wife have undertaken the external duty of living together all their lives, and begin to hate each other after a month, and wish to part but still continue to live together, it leads to that terrible hell which makes people take to drink, shoot themselves, and kill or poison themselves or one another," he went on, speaking more rapidly, not allowing anyone to put in a word and becoming more excited. We all felt embarrassed.

"Yes, undoubtedly there are critical episodes in married life," said the lawyer, wishing to end this disturbingly heated conversation.

"I see you've found out who I am!" said the grey-haired man softly, with apparent calm.

"No, I've not that pleasure."

"It's no great pleasure. I'm that Pozdnyshev in whose life that critical episode occurred to which you alluded—the episode when he killed his wife," he said, rapidly glancing at each of us.

No one knew what to say and all remained silent.

"Well, never mind," he said with that peculiar sound of his. "However, pardon me. Ah! . . . I won't intrude on you."

"Oh, no, if you please . . ." said the lawyer, himself not knowing "if you please" what.

But Pozdnyshev, without listening to him, rapidly turned away and went back to his seat. The lawyer and the lady whispered together. I sat down beside Pozdnyshev in silence, unable to think of anything to say. It was too dark to read, so I shut my eyes pretending that I wished to go to sleep. So we travelled in silence to the next station.

There the lawyer and the lady moved into another car, having some time previously consulted the guard about it. The clerk lay down on the seat and fell asleep. Pozdnyshev kept smoking and drinking tea which he had made at the last station.

When I opened my eyes and looked at him he suddenly addressed me resolutely and irritably:

"Perhaps it's unpleasant for you to sit with me, knowing who I am? In that case I'll go away."

"Oh no, not at all."

"Well then, won't you have some tea? It's very strong."

He poured out some tea for me.

"They talk . . . and they always lie . . ." he remarked.

"What are you talking about?" I asked.

"Always about the same thing. About that love of theirs and what it is! Don't you want to sleep?"

"Not at all."

"Would you like me to tell you how that love led to what happened to me?"

"Yes, if it won't be too painful for you."

"No, it's painful for me to keep silent. Drink the tea . . . or is it too strong?"

The tea was more like beer, but I drank a glass of it. Just then the guard entered. Pozdnyshev followed him with angry eyes, and only began to speak after he had left.

III

"Well then, I'll tell you. But do you really want to hear it?"

I repeated that I did very much. He paused, rubbed his face with his hands, and began:

"If I am to tell it, I must tell everything from the beginning: I must tell how and why I married, and the kind of man I was before my marriage.

"Till my marriage I lived as everybody does, that is, everybody in our social class. I'm a landowner and a graduate of the university, and was a marshal of the gentry.[4] Before my marriage I lived as everyone does, that is, dissolutely; and while living dissolutely I was convinced, like everybody in our class, that I was living as one has to. I thought I was a charming fellow and quite a moral man. I was not a seducer, had no unnatural tastes, did not make that the chief purpose of my life as many

_____
4. A noble elected to manage the affairs and represent the interests of the gentry.

of my associates did, but I practiced debauchery in a steady, decent way for health's sake. I avoided women who might tie my hands by having a child or by attachment for me. However, there may have been children and attachments, but I acted as if there were not. And I not only considered this moral, but I was even proud of it."

He paused and gave vent to his peculiar sound, as he evidently did whenever a new idea occurred to him.

"And you know, that's the chief abomination!" he exclaimed. "Dissoluteness does not lie in anything physical—no kind of physical misconduct is debauchery; real debauchery lies precisely in freeing oneself from moral relations with a woman with whom you have physical intimacy. Such emancipation I regarded as a merit. I remember how I once worried because I'd not had an opportunity to pay a woman who gave herself to me (having probably taken a liking to me) and how I only calmed down after having sent her some money—thereby intimating that I didn't consider myself morally bound to her in any way . . . Don't nod as if you agreed with me," he suddenly shouted at me. "Don't I know these things? We all, and you too unless you're a rare exception, hold those same views, just as I used to. Never mind, I beg your pardon, but the fact is that it's terrible, terrible, terrible!"

"What's terrible?" I asked.

"That abyss of error in which we live regarding women and our relations with them. No, I can't speak calmly about it, not because of that 'episode,' as he called it, in my life, but because since that 'episode' occurred my eyes have been opened and I've seen everything in quite a different light. Everything reversed, everything reversed!"

He lit a cigarette and began to speak, leaning his elbows on his knees.

It was too dark to see his face, but, above the jolting of the train, I could hear his impressive and pleasant voice.

IV

"Yes, only after such torments as I've endured, only by their means, have I understood where the root of the matter lies—understood what ought to be, and therefore seen all the horror of what is.

"So you'll see how and when that which led up to my 'episode' began. It began when I was not quite sixteen. It happened when I still went to grammar school and my elder brother was a first-year student at the university. I had not yet known any woman, but, like all the unfortunate boys of our class, I was no longer innocent. I had been depraved two years before that by other boys. Already woman, not any particular woman but woman as something to be desired, woman, every woman, woman's nudity, tormented me. My solitude was not pure. I was tormented, as ninety-nine per cent of our boys are. I was horrified, I suffered, I prayed, and I fell. I was already depraved in imagination and in fact, but I had not yet taken the last step. I was perishing, but I had not yet laid hands on another human being. One day a comrade of my brother's, a jolly student, a so-called good fellow, that is, the worst kind of good-for-nothing, who had taught us to drink and play cards, persuaded us after a drinking bout to go *there*.[5] We went. My brother was also still innocent, and he fell that same night. And I, a fifteen-year-old boy, defiled myself and took part in defiling a woman, without understanding at all what I was doing. I had never heard from any of my elders that what I was doing was wrong, you know. And indeed no one hears it now. It's true it's in the Commandments but then the Commandments are only needed to answer the priest at Scripture examination, and even then they're not really necessary, not nearly as necessary as the commandment about the use of *ut* in conditional sentences in Latin.

"So I never heard those older persons whose opinions I respected say it was evil. On the contrary, I heard people I respected say it was good. I had heard that my struggles and sufferings would be eased after that. I heard this and read it, and heard my elders say it would be good for my health, while from my comrades I heard that it was rather a fun, exciting thing to do. So in general I expected nothing but good from it. The risk of disease? But that too had been foreseen. A paternal government saw to that.[6] It sees to the correct working of the brothels, and makes profligacy safe for schoolboys. Doctors too deal with it for a consideration. That's only proper. They assert that debauchery is good for the health, and they organize proper well-regulated debauchery. I even know some mothers who attend to their sons' health in that sense. Science sends them to brothels."

"Why do you say 'science'?" I asked.

"Why, who are doctors? Priests of science. Who deprave youths by maintaining that it's necessary for their health? They do.

"If one-hundredth of the efforts devoted to the cure of syphilis were devoted to the eradication of debauchery there wouldn't be a trace of syphilis left. As it is, efforts are made not to eradicate debauchery, but to encourage it and make it safe. That's not the point however. The point is that with me—and with nine-tenths, if not more, not only of our class but of all classes, even the peasants—this terrible thing happens that happened to me; I fell not because I succumbed to the natural temptation of a particular woman's charm—no, I was not seduced by a woman—I fell because, in the people around me, what was really a fall was regarded by some as a most legitimate function good for one's health, and by others as a very natural and not only excusable but even innocent amusement for a young man. I didn't understand that it was a fall, but simply indulged in that half-pleasure, half-need, which, as was suggested

5. That is, a brothel.   "licensed" to practice their trade.
6. Prostitutes were given medical inspections and

to me, was natural at a certain age. I began to indulge in debauchery just as I began to drink and smoke. Yet in that first fall there was something special and pathetic. I remember that at once, on the spot before I left the room, I felt sad, so sad I wanted to cry—to cry for the loss of my innocence and for my relationship with women, now sullied for ever. Yes, my natural, simple relationship with women was spoilt for ever. From that time I haven't had, and couldn't have, pure relations with women. I'd become what's called a libertine. To be a libertine is a physical condition like that of an addict, a drunkard, or a smoker. As an addict, a drunkard, or a smoker is no longer normal, so too a man who's known several women for his pleasure is not normal; he's a man perverted for ever, a libertine. As a drunkard or an addict can be recognized at once by his face and manner, so it is with a libertine. A libertine may restrain himself, may struggle, but he'll never have those pure, simple, clear, brotherly relations with a woman. By the way he looks at a young woman and examines her, a libertine can always be recognized. I had become and I remained a libertine, and it was this that brought me to ruin.

V

"Ah, yes! After that things went from bad to worse, and there were all sorts of deviations. Oh, God! When I recall the abominations I committed in this respect I'm seized with horror! And that's true of me, whom my companions, I remember, ridiculed for my so-called innocence. And when one hears about 'gilded youths,' officers, Parisians . . . ! And when all these gentlemen, and I—who have hundreds of the most varied and horrible crimes against women on our souls—when we thirty-year-old profligates, very carefully washed, shaved, perfumed, in clean linen and in evening dress or uniform, enter a drawing-room or ball-room, we are emblems of purity, charming!

"Only think about what ought to be, and what is! When in society such a gentleman comes up to my sister or my daughter, I, knowing his life, ought to go up to him, take him aside, and say quietly, 'My dear fellow, I know the life you lead, how and with whom you pass your nights. This is no place for you. There are pure, innocent girls here. Be off!' That's what ought to be; but what happens is that when such a gentleman comes and dances, embracing our sister or daughter, we're jubilant if he's rich and well-connected. Maybe after Rigulboche[7] he'll honor my daughter! Even if traces of disease remain, no matter! They're clever at curing that nowadays. Oh, yes, I know several girls in the best society whom their parents enthusiastically gave in marriage to men suffering from a certain disease. Oh, . . . the abomination of it!

7. The stage name of Marguerite Bodel, a French dancer and cabaret singer who was very popular in mid-nineteenth-century Paris.

But time will come when this abomination and falsehood will be exposed!"

He made his strange noise several times and drank some tea again. It was very strong and there was no water with which to dilute it. I felt that I was stimulated by the two glasses I had drunk. Probably the tea affected him too, for he became more and more excited. His voice grew increasingly mellow and expressive. He continually changed his position, taking off his cap and putting it on again, and his face changed strangely in the semi-darkness in which we were sitting.

"So I lived till I was thirty, not abandoning for a moment the intention of marrying and arranging for myself a most elevated and pure family life. With that purpose I observed the girls suitable for that end," he continued. "I wallowed in a mire of debauchery and at the same time was on the lookout for a girl pure enough to be worthy of me.

"I rejected many just because they were not pure enough to suit me, but at last I found one whom I considered worthy. She was one of two daughters of a once-wealthy Penza landowner who had been ruined.

"One evening after we had been out in a boat and had returned by moonlight, I was sitting beside her admiring her curls and her shapely figure in a tight-fitting jersey, I suddenly decided that it was she! It seemed to me that evening that she understood all that I felt and thought, and that what I felt and thought was very lofty. In reality it was only that the jersey and the curls were particularly becoming to her and that after a day spent near her I wanted to be still closer.

"It's amazing how complete the delusion is that beauty is goodness. A handsome woman talks nonsense, you listen and hear only cleverness. She says and does horrid things, and you see only charm. And if a handsome woman doesn't say stupid or horrid things, you persuade yourself at once that she's wonderfully clever and moral.

"I returned home in rapture, decided that she was the acme of moral perfection, and therefore she was worthy to be my wife; I proposed to her the next day.

"What a muddle it is! Out of a thousand men who marry (not only among us but unfortunately also among the masses) there's hardly one who hasn't already been married ten, a hundred, or even, like Don Juan, a thousand times, before his wedding.

"It's true as I've heard and have myself observed that nowadays there are some chaste young men who feel and know that this thing is not a joke but an important matter.

"God help them! In my time there was not one such man in ten thousand. Everybody knows this and pretends not to know it. In all the novels they describe in detail the heroes' feelings, the ponds and bushes beside which they walk, but when their great love for some maiden is described, nothing is said about what's happened to these interesting heroes before: not a word about their frequenting certain houses, or about the servant-girls, cooks, and other people's wives! If there exist such improper novels, they are not put into the hands of those who most need this information—unmarried girls.

"First we pretend to these girls that the profligacy which fills half the life of our towns, and even of our villages, does not exist at all.

"Then we get so accustomed to this pretense that at last, like the English, we ourselves really begin to believe that we're all moral people and live in a moral world. The girls, poor things, believe this quite seriously. So too did my unfortunate wife. I remember how, when we were engaged, I showed her my diary, from which she could learn something, if but a little, of my past, especially about my last *liaison*, of which she might hear from others, and about which I therefore felt it necessary to inform her.[8] I remember her horror, despair, and confusion, when she learned of it and understood it. I saw then that she wanted to give me up. Why didn't she? . . ."

He made that sound again, swallowed another mouthful of tea, and remained silent for a while.

VI

"No, after all, it's better, better like this!" he exclaimed. "It serves me right! But that's not the point—I meant to say that it's only unfortunate girls who are deceived.

"Mothers know it, especially those educated by their own husbands—they know it very well. While pretending to believe in the purity of men, they act quite differently. They know with what bait to catch men for themselves and for their daughters.

"You see it's only we men who don't know (because we don't wish to know) what women know very well, that the most exalted poetic love, as we call it, depends not on moral qualities but on physical nearness, the *coiffure*, and the color and cut of the dress. Ask an expert coquette who has set herself the task of captivating a man, which she would prefer to risk: to be convicted in his presence of lying, cruelty, or even dissoluteness, or to appear before him in an ugly and badly made dress—she will always prefer the first. She knows that we're continually lying about high sentiments, but really only want her body and will therefore forgive any abomination except an ugly, tasteless costume that's in bad style.

"A coquette knows that consciously, and every innocent girl knows it unconsciously just as animals do.

"That's why there are those detestable jerseys, bustles, and naked shoulders, arms, almost breasts. A woman, especially if she has graduated from the male school, knows very well that all the talk about elevated subjects is just talk; what a man wants is her body and all that presents

8. An autobiographical detail: Tolstoy showed his diary to his fiancée, Sonya Behrs, and she was horrified.

it in the most deceptive but alluring light, and she acts accordingly. If we only throw aside our familiarity with this indecency, which has become second nature to us, and look at the life of our upper classes as it is, in all its shamelessness—why, it's simply a brothel . . . You don't agree? Allow me, I'll prove it," he said, interrupting me. "You say that the women of our society have other interests in life than prostitutes have, but I say no, and will prove it. If people differ in the aims of their lives, by the inner content of their lives, this difference will necessarily be reflected in externals, and their externals will be different. But look at those unfortunate despised women and at our highest society ladies: the same costumes, the same fashions, the same perfumes, the exposure of arms, shoulders, and breasts, the same tight skirts over prominent bustles, the same passion for little stones, for costly, glittering objects, the same amusements, dances, music, and singing. As the former employ all means to allure, so do the latter.

VII

"Well, so these jerseys, curls, and bustles caught me!

"It was very easy to catch me for I was brought up in conditions in which amorous young people are forced like cucumbers in a hot-bed. You see our stimulating super-abundance of food, together with complete physical idleness, is nothing but a systematic excitement of desire. Whether this astonishes you or not, it's so. Why, till quite recently I didn't see anything of this myself, but now I've seen it. That's why it torments me that nobody knows this, and people talk such nonsense as that lady did.

"Yes, last spring some peasants were working in our neighborhood on a railway embankment. The usual food of a young peasant is rye-bread, kvas,[9] and onions; he keeps alive and is vigorous and healthy; his task is light agricultural work. When he goes to railway-work his rations are buckwheat porridge and a pound of meat a day. But he works off that pound of meat during his sixteen hours' wheeling barrow-loads of half-a-ton, so it's just enough for him. But we who consume two pounds of meat every day, and game, and fish and all sorts of fortifying foods and drinks—where does all that go? Into excesses of sensuality. And if it goes there and the safety-valve is open, all's well; but try and close the safety-valve, as I closed it temporarily, and at once a stimulus arises which, passing through the prism of our artificial life, expresses itself in utter infatuation, sometimes even platonic. And I fell in love as they all do.

"Everything was there on hand: raptures, tenderness, and poetry. In reality that love of mine was the result, on the one hand of her mamma's and the dressmakers' activity, and on the other, of the super-abundance

9. A traditional Russian beverage prepared from flour or dark rye bread soaked in water and malt.

of food consumed by me while living an idle life. If on the one hand there had been no boat ride, no dressmaker with her waists and so forth, and had my wife been sitting at home in a shapeless dressing-gown, and had I, on the other hand, been in circumstances normal to man—consuming just enough food to suffice for the work I did, and had the safety-valve been open—it happened to be closed at the time—I should not have fallen in love and nothing of all this would have happened.

VIII

"Well, and it so happened that everything combined—my condition, her becoming dress, and the satisfactory boat ride. It had failed twenty times but now it succeeded. Just like a trap! I'm not joking. You see nowadays marriages are arranged that way—like traps. What's the natural way? The girl is ripe, she must be given away in marriage. It seems very simple if the girl isn't ugly and there are men wanting to marry. That's how it was done in olden times. The girl was raised and her parents arranged the marriage. So it was done, and is done, among all mankind—Chinese, Hindus, Moslems, and among our own working classes; so it is done among at least ninety-nine per cent of the human race. Only among one per cent or less, among us libertines, has it been discovered that that's not right, and something new has been invented. What is this novelty? It's that maidens sit around and men walk about, as at a bazaar, choosing. The maidens wait and think, but dare not say: 'Me, please!' 'No me!' 'Not her, me!' 'Look what shoulders and other things I have!' And we men stroll around and look, and are very pleased. 'Yes, I know! I won't be caught!' They stroll about and look, and are very pleased that everything is arranged like that for them. Then in an unguarded moment—snap! He's caught!"

"Then how should it be done?" I asked. "Should the woman propose?"

"Oh, I don't know how; but if there's to be equality, let it be equality. If they've discovered that pre-arranged matches are degrading, why this is a thousand times worse! Then rights and chances were equal, but here woman is a slave in a bazaar or bait in a trap. Tell any mother, or the girl herself, the truth, that she's only occupied in catching a husband . . . oh dear! what an insult! Yet they all do it and have nothing else to do. What's so terrible is to see quite innocent poor young girls engaged on it. Again, if it were done openly—but it's always done deceitfully. 'Ah, the origin of species, how interesting!' 'Oh, Lily takes such an interest in painting! Will you be going to the exhibition? How instructive!' And the troika-drives, shows, and symphonies! 'Oh! how remarkable! My Lily is mad about music.' 'And why don't you share these convictions?' And boat rides . . . But their one thought is: 'Take me, take me!' 'Take my Lily!' 'Or try—at least!' Oh, what an abomination! What falsehood!" he concluded, finishing his tea and beginning to put away the tea-things.

IX

"You know," he began while packing the tea and sugar into his bag. "The domination of women from which the world suffers all arises from this."

"What 'domination of women'?" I asked. "The rights, the legal privileges, are on the man's side."

"Yes, yes! That's just it," he interrupted me. "That's just what I want to say. It explains the extraordinary phenomenon that on the one hand woman is reduced to the lowest stage of humiliation, while on the other she dominates. Just like the Jews: as they pay us back for their oppression by financial domination, so it is with women. 'Ah, you want us to be traders only—all right, as traders we'll dominate you!' say the Jews. 'Ah, you want us to be mere objects of sensuality—all right, as objects of sensuality we'll enslave you,' say the women. Woman's lack of rights arises not from the fact that she must not vote or be a judge—to be occupied with such affairs is no privilege—but from the fact that she's not man's equal in sexual intercourse and hasn't the right to use a man or abstain from him as she likes—isn't allowed to choose a man at her pleasure instead of being chosen by him. You say that's monstrous. Very well! Then a man mustn't have those rights either. As it is at present, a woman is deprived of that right while a man has it. And to make up for that right she acts on man's sensuality, and through his sensuality subdues him so that he chooses only formally, while in reality it's she who chooses. And once she has obtained these means, she abuses them and acquires a terrible power over people."

"But where is this special power?" I inquired.

"Where is it? Why everywhere, in everything! Go around the shops in any big town. There are goods worth millions and you cannot estimate the human labor expended on them, and look whether in nine-tenths of these shops there is anything for men. All the luxuries of life are demanded and maintained by women.

"Count all the factories. An enormous proportion of them produce useless ornaments, carriages, furniture, and trinkets for women. Millions of people, generations of slaves, perish at hard labor in factories merely to satisfy woman's caprice. Women, like queens, keep nine-tenths of mankind in bondage to heavy labor. And all because they've been debased and deprived of equal rights with men. They revenge themselves by acting on our sensuality and catch us in their nets. Yes, it all comes to that.

"Women have made themselves such an instrument for acting upon our sensuality that a man cannot consort with a woman quietly. As soon as a man approaches a woman, he succumbs to her stupefying influence and becomes intoxicated and crazy. I used to feel uncomfortable and uneasy when I saw a lady dressed up for a ball, but now I'm simply frightened and see her as something dangerous and illicit. I want to call a policeman and ask for protection from the peril, and demand that the dangerous object be removed and put away.

"Ah, you're laughing!" he shouted at me, "but it's not a joke at all. I'm sure a time will come, perhaps very soon, when people will understand this and will wonder how a society could exist in which actions were permitted which so disturb social tranquillity as those adornments of the body directly evoking sensuality, which we tolerate for women in our society. Why, it's like setting all sorts of traps along paths and promenades—it's even worse! Why is gambling forbidden while women in costumes which evoke sensuality aren't? They're a thousand times more dangerous!

X

"Well, you see, I was caught that way. I was what is called in love. I not only imagined her to be the height of perfection, but during the time of our engagement I also regarded myself as the height of perfection. You know there's no rascal who cannot, if he tries, find rascals in some respects worse than himself, and who consequently cannot find reasons for pride and self-satisfaction. So it was with me: I wasn't marrying for money—covetousness had nothing to do with it—unlike the majority of my acquaintances who married for money or connections—I was rich, she was poor. That was one thing. Another thing I prided myself on was that while others married intending to continue in the future the same polygamous life they had lived before marriage, I was firmly resolved to be monogamous after marriage, and there was no limit to my pride on that score. Yes, I was a dreadful pig and imagined myself to be an angel.

"Our engagement didn't last long. I cannot now think of that time without shame! What nastiness! Love is supposed to be spiritual and not sensual. Well, if love is spiritual, a spiritual communion, then that communion should find expression in words, in conversations, in discourse. There was nothing of the kind. It used to be dreadfully difficult to talk when we were left alone. It was the labor of Sisyphus. As soon as we thought of something to say and said it, we had to be silent again, devising something else. There was nothing to talk about. All that could be said about the life that awaited us, our arrangements and plans, had been said; what was there more? Now if we had been animals we should have known that speech was unnecessary; here on the contrary it was necessary to speak, but there was nothing to say, because we were not occupied with what finds vent in speech. Moreover there was that ridiculous custom of giving presents, vulgar gourmandizing on sweets, and all those abominable preparations for the wedding: remarks about the house, the bedroom, beds, housecoats, dressing-gowns, under-clothing, costumes. You must remember that if one married according to the injunctions of *Domostroy*, as that old fellow was saying, then feather-beds, trousseau, and bedstead are all but details appropriate to the sacrament. But among us, when out of ten who marry, there are certainly nine who not only don't believe in the sacrament, but don't even believe that what they're doing entails certain obligations—where scarcely one man out of a hundred has not been married before, and of fifty scarcely one isn't preparing in advance to be unfaithful to his wife at every convenient opportunity—when the majority regard the going to church as only a special condition for obtaining possession of a certain woman—think what dreadful significance all these details acquire. They show that the whole business is only that: a kind of sale. An innocent girl is sold to a profligate, and the sale is accompanied by certain formalities.

XI

"That's how everybody marries and that's how I married, and the much vaunted honeymoon began. Why, its very name is vile!" he hissed viciously. "In Paris I once went to see the sights, and noticing a bearded woman and a water-dog on a sign-board, I entered the show. It turned out to be nothing but a man in a woman's low-necked dress, and a dog done up in walrus skin and swimming in a bath. It was very far from being interesting; but as I was leaving, the showman politely saw me out and, addressing the public at the entrance, pointed to me and said, 'Ask the gentleman whether it is not worth seeing! Come in, come in, one franc apiece!' I felt ashamed to say it was not worth seeing, and the showman had probably counted on that. It must be the same with those who have experienced the abomination of a honeymoon and who don't disillusion others. Neither did I disillusion anyone, but I don't see why I shouldn't tell the truth now. Indeed, I think it's necessary to tell the truth about it. One felt awkward, ashamed, repelled, sorry, and above all dull, intolerably dull! It was something like what I felt when I learned how to smoke—when I felt sick and the saliva gathered in my mouth and I swallowed it and pretended it was very pleasant. Pleasure from smoking, just as from that, if it comes at all, comes later. The husband must cultivate that vice in his wife in order to derive pleasure from it."

"Why vice?" I asked. "You're speaking of the most natural human functions."

"Natural?" he replied. "Natural? No, I may tell you that I've come to the conclusion that it is, on the contrary, *un*natural. Yes, quite *un*natural. Ask any child, ask an unperverted girl.

"Natural, you say!

"It's natural to eat. Eating is, from the very beginning, enjoyable, easy, pleasant, and not embarrassing; but this is horrid, shameful, and painful. No, it's unnatural! And an unspoilt girl, as I have convinced myself, always hates it."

"But how," I asked, "would the human race continue?"

"Yes, wouldn't the human race perish?" he replied, irritably and ironically, as if he'd expected this familiar and insincere objection. "Teach abstention from child-bearing so that English lords may always gorge themselves—that's all right. Preach it for the sake of greater pleasure—that's all right; but just hint at abstention from child-bearing in the name of morality—and, my goodness, what a rumpus . . . ! Isn't there a danger that the human race may die out because they want to cease to be swine? But forgive me! This light is unpleasant, may I shade it?" he said, pointing to the lamp. I said I didn't mind; and with the haste with which he did everything, he got up on the seat and drew the woollen shade over the lamp.

"All the same," I said, "if everyone thought this the right thing to do, the human race would cease to exist."

He did not reply at once.

"You ask how the human race will continue to exist," he said, having sat down again in front of me, and spreading his legs far apart he leaned his elbows on his knees. "Why should it continue?"

"Why? If not, we shouldn't exist."

"And why should we exist?"

"Why? In order to live, of course."

"But why live? If life has no aim, if life is given us for life's sake, there's no reason for living. And if that's so, then the Schopenhauers, Hartmanns,[1] and all the Buddhists as well, are quite right. But if life has an aim, it's clear that it ought to come to an end when that aim is reached. And so it turns out," he said with noticeable agitation, evidently prizing his thought very highly. "So it turns out. Just think: if the aim of humanity is goodness, righteousness, love—call it what you will—if it's what the prophets have said, that all mankind should be united together in love, that spears should be beaten into pruning-hooks and so forth, what is it that hinders the attainment of this aim? The passions hinder it. Of all the passions the strongest, cruellest, and most stubborn is the sex-urge, physical love; therefore if the passions are destroyed, including the strongest of them—physical love—the prophecies will be fulfilled, mankind will be brought into unity, the aim of human existence will be attained, and there will be nothing further to live for. As long as mankind exists the ideal is before it, and of course not the rabbits' and pigs' ideal of breeding as fast as possible, nor that of monkeys or Parisians—to enjoy sex in the most refined manner, but the ideal of

---

1. Eduard von Hartmann (1842–1906), author of *The Philosophy of the Unconscious*, wrote a refutation of Schopenhauer's treatise *The World as Will and Idea*.

goodness attained by continence and purity. Towards that people have always striven and still strive. You see what follows.

"It follows that physical love is a safety-valve. If the present generation has not attained its aim, it has not done so because of its passions, of which sex is the strongest. And if the sex-urge endures there will be a new generation and consequently the possibility of attaining the aim in the next generation. If the next one doesn't attain it, then the one after that may, and so on, till the aim is attained, the prophecies fulfilled, and mankind attains unity. If not, what would result? If one admits that God created men for the attainment of a certain aim, and created them mortal but sexless, or created them immortal, what would be the result? Why, if they were mortal but without the sex-urge, and died without attaining the aim, God would have had to create new people to attain his aim. If they were immortal, let's grant that (though it would be more difficult for the same people to correct their mistakes and approach perfection than for those of another generation) they might attain that aim after many thousands of years, but what use would they be afterwards? What could be done with them? It's best as it is. . . . Perhaps you don't like that way of putting it? Perhaps you're an evolutionist? It comes to the same thing. The highest race of animals, the human race, in order to maintain itself in the struggle with other animals ought to unite into one whole like a swarm of bees, and not breed continually; it should bring up sexless members as the bees do; that is, again, it should strive towards continence and not towards inflaming desire—to which our whole system of life is now directed." He paused. "The human race will cease? But can anyone doubt it, whatever his outlook on life may be? Why, it's as certain as death. According to all the teaching of the Church the end of the world will come, and according to all the teaching of science the same result is inevitable.

XII

"In our world it's just the reverse: even if a man does think about continence while he's a bachelor, once married he's sure to think it no longer necessary. You know those wedding tours—the seclusion into which, with their parents' consent, the young couple go—are nothing but licensed debauchery. But a moral law avenges itself when it's violated. Hard as I tried to make a success of my honeymoon, nothing came of it. It was horrid, shameful, and dull, the whole time. Very soon I started to experience a painful, oppressive feeling. That began very quickly. I think it was on the third or fourth day that I found my wife depressed. I began asking her the reason and embracing her, which in my view was all she could want, but she removed my arm and began to cry. What about? She couldn't say. But she felt sad and distressed. Probably her exhausted nerves suggested to her the truth regarding the vileness of our relations but she didn't know how to express it. I began to question her, and she said something about feeling sad without her mother. It seemed to me that this was untrue, and I began comforting her without alluding to her mother. I didn't understand that she was simply depressed and her mother was merely an excuse. But immediately she took offense because I hadn't mentioned her mother, as though I didn't believe her. She told me she saw that I didn't love her. I reproached her with being capricious, and suddenly her face changed entirely and instead of sadness it expressed irritation; with the most venomous words she began accusing me of selfishness and cruelty. I gazed at her. Her whole face showed complete coldness and hostility, almost hatred. I remember how horror-struck I was when I saw this. 'How? What?' I thought. 'Love is a union of souls—and instead of that there's this! Impossible, this isn't she!' I tried to soften her, but encountered such an insuperable wall of cold, virulent hostility that before I had time to turn around I too was seized with irritation and we said a great many unpleasant things to one another. The impression of that first quarrel was dreadful. I call it a quarrel, but it wasn't really a quarrel, only the disclosure of the abyss that existed between us. Amorousness was exhausted by the satisfaction of sensuality and we were left confronting one another in our true relation: that is, as two egotists quite alien to each other who wished to get as much pleasure as possible each from the other. I call what took place between us a quarrel, but it wasn't a quarrel, only the consequence of the cessation of sensuality—revealing our true relations to one another. I didn't understand that this cold and hostile relation was our normal state, I didn't understand it because at first this hostile attitude was soon concealed from us by a renewal of redistilled sensuality, that is by love-making.

"I thought we had quarrelled and made up again, and that it wouldn't recur. But during that same first month of honeymoon a period of satiety soon returned; again we ceased to need one another, and another quarrel occurred. This second quarrel struck me even more painfully than the first. 'So the first one was not an accident but was bound to happen and will happen again,' I thought. I was all the more staggered by that second quarrel because it arose from such an impossible pretext. It had something to do with money, which I never grudged and could certainly not have grudged to my wife. I only remember that she gave the matter such a twist that some remark of mine appeared to be an expression of a desire on my part to dominate her by means of money, to which I was supposed to assert an exclusive right—it was something impossibly stupid, mean, and not natural either to me or to her. I became exasperated, and upbraided her with lack of consideration for me. She accused me of the same thing, and it all began again. In her words and in the expression of her face and eyes I noticed again the cruel cold hostility that had so staggered me before. Previously I had quarrelled with my brother, my friends, and my father, but there had never, I remember, been the special venomous malice which there was here. After a while this mutual hatred was screened by amorousness, that is sensuality, and I still consoled myself with the thought that these two quarrels had been mistakes and could be remedied. But then a third and a fourth followed and I realized that it was not accidental; it was bound to happen and would happen, and I was horrified at the prospect before me. At the same time I was tormented by the terrible thought that I alone lived on such bad terms with my wife, so unlike what I had expected, whereas this didn't happen between other married couples. I didn't know then that it's our common fate, but that everybody imagines, just as I did, that it's their peculiar misfortune, and everyone conceals this exceptional and shameful misfortune not only from others, but even from himself and doesn't acknowledge it.

"It began during the first days and continued all the time, increasing and growing more persistent. In the depths of my soul I felt from the first weeks that I was lost, that things had not turned out as I expected, that marriage was not only no happiness but a very heavy burden; but like everybody else I didn't wish to acknowledge this to myself (I should not have acknowledged it even now except for the end that followed) and I concealed it not only from others but from myself as well. Now I'm astonished that I failed to see my real position. It might have been seen from the fact that the quarrels began on pretexts it was impossible to remember when they were over. Our reason was not quick enough to *devise* sufficient excuses for the animosity that always existed between us. But more striking still was the insufficiency of excuses for our reconciliations. Sometimes there were words, explanations, even tears, but sometimes . . . oh! it's disgusting even now to think of it—after the most cruel words to one another, came sudden silent glances, smiles, kisses, embraces. . . . Ugh, how horrid! How is it I didn't see all the vileness of it then?"

XIII

Two new passengers entered and settled down on the farthest seats. He was silent while they were seating themselves but as soon as they had settled down he continued, evidently not losing the thread of his idea for a moment.

"You know what is vilest about it," he began, "is that in theory love is something ideal and exalted, but in practice it's abominable, swinish; horrid and shameful to mention or remember. It is not for nothing that nature has made it so disgusting and shameful. And if it is disgusting and shameful, one must understand that it is so. But here, on the contrary, people pretend that what is disgusting and shameful is beautiful and lofty. What were the first symptoms of my love? I gave way to animal excesses, not only without shame but was somehow even proud of the possibility of these physical excesses, and without in the least considering either her spiritual or even her physical life. I wondered what embittered us against one another, yet it was perfectly simple: that animosity was nothing but the protest of our human nature against the animal nature that overpowered it.

"I was surprised at our enmity to one another; yet it couldn't have been otherwise. That hatred was nothing but the mutual hatred of accomplices in a crime—both for the incitement to the crime and for the part taken in it. Was it anything but a crime when she, poor thing, became pregnant in the first month and our *swinish* connection continued? You think I'm straying from my subject? Not at all! I am telling you *how* I killed my wife. They asked me at the trial with what and how I killed her. Fools! They thought I killed her with a knife on the 5th of October. It was not then that I killed her, but much earlier. Just as they're all now killing, all, all. . . ."

"But with what?" I asked.

"That's just what's so surprising, that nobody wants to see what's so clear and evident, what doctors ought to know and preach, but are silent about. Yet the matter is very simple. Men and women are created like animals so that physical love is followed by pregnancy and then by suckling—conditions under which physical love is bad for both the woman and her child. There are an equal number of men and women. What follows from this? It seems clear, and no great wisdom is needed to draw the conclusion that animals do, namely, the need of continence. But no. Science has been able to discover some kind of leucocytes that run about in the blood, and all sorts of useless nonsense, but it cannot understand that. At least one does not hear of science teaching it!

"So a woman has only two ways out: one is to make a monster of herself, to destroy and go on destroying within herself to such a degree as necessary the capacity of being a woman, that is, a mother, in order that a man may quietly and continuously get his enjoyment; the other way out—and it's not even a way out but a simple, coarse, and direct violation of the laws of nature—practised in all so-called decent families—is that, contrary to her nature, the woman must be her husband's mistress even while she's pregnant or nursing—must be what not even an animal descends to, and for which her strength is insufficient. That's what causes nerve trouble and hysteria in our class, and among the peasants causes what they call being 'possessed by the devil'—epilepsy. You will notice that no pure maidens are ever 'possessed,' only married women living with their husbands. That's so here, and it's just the same in Europe. All the hospitals for hysterical women are full of people who have violated nature's law. Epileptics and Charcot's patients are complete wrecks, you know, but the world is full of half-crippled women.[2] Just think of it, what great work goes on within a woman when she conceives

2. Jean Martin Charcot (1825–93) was a French neurologist who founded a clinic for diseases of the nervous system.

or when she's nursing an infant. That is growing which will continue us and replace us. And this sacred work is violated—by what? It's terrible to think of it! And they carry on about the freedom and rights of women! It's as if cannibals fattened their captives to be eaten, and at the same time declared they were concerned about their prisoners' rights and freedom."

All this was new to me and startled me.

"What's one to do? If that's so," I said, "it means one may love one's wife once for two years, but men must . . ."

"Men must!" he interrupted me. "Again it's those precious priests of science who have persuaded everybody of that. Imbue a man with the idea that he requires vodka, tobacco, or opium, and all these things will be indispensable to him. It seems that God didn't understand what was necessary and therefore, omitting to consult those wizards, arranged things badly. You see matters don't tally. They've decided that it's essential for a man to satisfy his desires; then the bearing and nursing of children comes and interferes with it and hinders the satisfaction of that need. What's one to do then? Consult the wizards! They'll arrange it. And they have devised something. Oh! when will those wizards with their deceptions be dethroned? It's high time! It's come to such a point that people go mad and shoot themselves and all because of this. How could it be otherwise? Animals seem to know that their progeny continue their race, and they keep to a certain law in this matter. Man alone neither knows it nor wishes to know, but is concerned only to get all the pleasure he can. And who is doing that? The lord of nature—man! Animals, you see, only come together at times when they're capable of producing progeny, but the filthy lord of nature is at it any time it pleases him! And as if that were not sufficient, he exalts this apish occupation into the most precious pearl of creation, into love. In the name of this love, that is, this filth, he destroys—what? Why, half the human race! He converts all the women who might help the progress of mankind towards truth and goodness, for the sake of his pleasure, into enemies instead of helpmates. See what it is that everywhere impedes the forward movement of mankind. Women! And why are they what they are? Only because of that. Yes, yes . . ." he repeated several times, and began to move about, and to get out his cigarettes to smoke, evidently trying to calm himself.

XIV

"I too lived like a pig," he continued in his former tone. "The worst thing about it was that while living that horrid life I imagined that, because I did not chase after other women, I was living an honest family life, that I was a moral man and in no way blameworthy, and if quarrels occurred it was her fault and resulted from her character.

"Of course the fault was not hers. She was like everybody else—like the majority of women. She had been brought up as the position of women in our society requires, and therefore as all women of the leisured classes are brought up and cannot help being brought up. People talk about a new kind of education for women. It's all empty words: their education is exactly what it has to be in view of our unfeigned, real, general opinion about women.

"The education of women will always correspond to men's opinion about them. Don't we know how men regard women: *Wein, Weib, und Gesang,* [3] and what the poets say in their verses? Take all poetry, all painting and sculpture, beginning with love poems and nude Venuses and Phrynes, [4] and you will see that woman is an instrument of enjoyment; she is so on the Truba and the Grachevka, [5] and also at Court balls. And note the devil's cunning: if they're here for enjoyment and pleasure, let it be known that it is pleasure and that woman is a sweet morsel. But no, first the knights-errant declare that they worship women (worship her, and yet regard her as an instrument of enjoyment), and now people assure us that they respect women. Some yield their places to her, pick up her handkerchief; others acknowledge her right to occupy all positions and to take part in government, and so on. They do all that, but their outlook remains the same. She is a means of enjoyment. Her body is a means of enjoyment. And she knows this. It's just as it is with slavery. Slavery, you know, is nothing else than the exploitation by some of the unwilling labor of many. Therefore to get rid of slavery it's necessary that people shouldn't wish to profit by the forced labor of others and should consider it a sin and a shame. But they abolish the external form of slavery and arrange it so that one can no longer buy and sell slaves; they imagine and assure themselves that slavery no longer exists, and do not see or wish to see that it does, because people still want and consider it good and right to exploit the labor of others. And as long as they consider that good, there will always be people stronger or more cunning than others who will succeed in doing it. So it is with the emancipation of woman: the enslavement of woman lies simply in the fact that people desire, and think it good, to avail themselves of her as a tool of enjoyment. They liberate woman, give her all sorts of rights equal to man, but continue to regard her as an instrument of enjoyment, and so educate her in childhood and afterwards by public opinion. And there she is, still the same humiliated and depraved slave, while man is still a depraved slave-owner.

"They emancipate women in universities and in law courts, but continue to regard her as an object of enjoyment. Teach her, as she is taught among us, to regard herself as such, and she will always remain

---

3. Wine, women, and song.
4. A courtesan in ancient Greece celebrated for her beauty. She served as the model for several statues.

5. Two streets in that part of Moscow where numerous brothels were located.

an inferior being. Either with the help of those scoundrels the doctors she will prevent the conception of offspring—that is, will be a complete prostitute, lowering herself not to the level of an animal, but to the level of a thing—or she will be what the majority of women are, mentally diseased, hysterical, unhappy, and lacking all capacity for spiritual development. High schools and universities cannot alter that. It can only be altered by a change in men's outlook on women and women's way of regarding themselves. It will change only when woman regards virginity as the highest state, and does not, as at present, consider the highest state of a human being a shame and a disgrace. As long as that is not so, the ideal of every girl, whatever her education, will continue to be to attract as many men as possible, as many males as possible, so as to have the possibility of choosing.

"But the fact that one of them knows more mathematics, and another can play the harp, makes no difference. A woman is happy and attains all she can desire when she has bewitched a man. Therefore the chief aim of a woman is to be able to bewitch him. So it has been and will be. So it is during her maiden life in our society, and so it continues to be during her married life. For a maiden this is necessary in order to have choice, for the married woman in order to have power over her husband.

"The one thing that stops this or at any rate suppresses it for a time, is children, and then only if the mother is not a monster, that is, if she nurses them herself. But here the doctors again come in.

"My wife, who wanted to nurse, and did nurse the four later children herself, happened to be unwell after the birth of her first child. Those doctors, who cynically undressed her and felt her all over—for which I had to thank them and pay them money—those dear doctors considered that she must not nurse the child; and that first time she was deprived of the only means which might have kept her from coquetry. We engaged a wet nurse, that is, we took advantage of the poverty, the need, and the ignorance of a woman, tempted her away from her own baby to ours, and in return gave her a fine head-dress with gold lace. But that's not the point. The point is that during that time when my wife was free from pregnancy and from suckling, the feminine coquetry which had lain dormant within her manifested itself with particular force. And coinciding with this the torments of jealousy rose up in me with special force. They tortured me all my married life, as they cannot but torture all husbands who live with their wives as I did with mine, that is, immorally.

XV

"During the whole of my married life I never ceased to be tormented by jealousy, but there were periods when I specially suffered from it.

One of these periods was when, after the birth of our first child, the doctors forbade my wife to nurse it. I was particularly jealous at that time, in the first place because my wife was experiencing that unrest natural to a mother which is sure to be aroused when the natural course of life is needlessly violated; and secondly, because seeing how easily she abandoned her moral obligations as a mother, I rightly though unconsciously concluded that it would be equally easy for her to disregard her duty as a wife, especially as she was quite well and in spite of the precious doctors' prohibition was able to nurse her later children admirably."

"I see you don't like doctors," I said, noticing a peculiarly malevolent tone in his voice whenever he alluded to them.

"It is not a case of liking or disliking. They have ruined my life as they have ruined and are ruining the lives of thousands and hundreds of thousands of human beings, and I cannot help connecting the effect with the cause. I understand that they want to earn money like lawyers and others, and I would willingly give them half my income, and all who realize what they are doing would willingly give them half their possessions, if only they would not interfere with our family life and would never come near us. I haven't collected evidence, but I know dozens of cases (there are any number of them!) where they have killed a child in its mother's womb asserting that she could not give birth, though she's had children quite safely later on; or they've killed the mother on the pretext of performing some operation. No one reckons these murders any more than they reckoned the murders of the Inquisition, because it's supposed that it's done for the good of mankind. It's impossible to number all the crimes they commit. But, all those crimes are nothing compared to the moral corruption of materialism they introduce into the world, especially through women.

"I don't lay stress on the fact that if one is to follow their instructions, then on account of the infection which exists everywhere and in everything, people wouldn't progress towards greater unity but towards separation; for according to their teaching we all ought to sit apart and not remove the carbolic atomizer from our mouths (though now they have discovered that even that is of no avail).[6] But that doesn't matter either. The principal poison lies in the demoralization of the world, especially of women.

"To-day one can no longer say: 'You're not living right, live better.' One can't say that, either to oneself or to anyone else. If you live a bad life it's caused by the abnormal functioning of your nerves, etc. So you must go to them, and they will prescribe thirty-five kopecks worth of medicine from a pharmacist, which you must take!

"You get even worse: then more medicine and the doctor again. An excellent trick!

6. Carbolic acid was used in weak solution as an antiseptic or disinfectant.

"That however is not the point. All I wish to say is that she nursed her babies perfectly well and that only her pregnancy and the nursing of her babies saved me from the torments of jealousy. Had it not been for that, it would all have happened sooner. The children saved me and her. In eight years she had five children and nursed all except the first herself."

"Where are your children now?" I asked.

"My children?" he repeated in a frightened voice.

"Forgive me, perhaps it's painful for you to be reminded of them."

. "No, it doesn't matter. My wife's sister and brother have taken them. They wouldn't let me have them. I gave them my estate, but they didn't give them up to me. You know I'm a sort of lunatic. I have left them now and am going away. I have seen them, but they won't let me have them because I might bring them up so that they would not be like their parents, and they have to be just like them. Oh well, what's to be done? Of course they won't let me have them and won't trust me. Besides, I don't know whether I should be able to bring them up. I think not. I'm a ruin, a cripple. Still I have one thing in me. I know! Yes, that's true, I know what others are far from knowing.

"Yes, my children are living and growing up just like savages as everybody else around them. I saw them, saw them three times. I can do nothing for them, nothing. I'm now going to my place in the south. I have a little house and a small garden there.

"Yes, it will be a long time before people learn what I know. It's easy to find out how much iron and other metal there is in the sun and the stars, but anything that exposes our swinishness is difficult, terribly difficult!

"At least you listen to me, and I'm grateful for that.

XVI

"You mentioned my children. There again, what terrible lies are told about children! Children are a blessing from God, a joy! That's all a lie. It was so once upon a time, but now it's not so at all. Children are a torment and nothing more. Most mothers feel this quite plainly, and sometimes inadvertently say so. Ask most mothers of our propertied classes and they'll tell you that they don't want to have children for fear of their falling ill and dying. They don't want to nurse them if they do have them, for fear of becoming too much attached to them and having to suffer. The pleasure a baby gives them by its loveliness, its little hands and feet, its whole body, is not as great as the suffering caused by the very fear of its possibly falling ill and dying, not to speak of its actual illness or death. After weighing the advantages and disadvantages it seems disadvantageous, and therefore undesirable, to have children. They say this quite frankly and boldly, imagining that these feelings of theirs arise from their love of children, a good and laudable feeling of which they are proud. They don't notice that by this reflection they plainly repudiate love, and only affirm their own selfishness. They get less pleasure from a baby's loveliness than suffering from fear on its account, and therefore the baby they would love is not wanted. They don't sacrifice themselves for a beloved being, but sacrifice a being whom they might love, for their own sakes.

"It's clear that this isn't love but selfishness. But one hasn't the heart to blame them—mothers in well-to-do families—for that selfishness, when one remembers how dreadfully they suffer on account of their children's health, again thanks to the influence of those same doctors among our well-to-do classes. Even now, when I remember my wife's life and the condition she was in during the first years when we had three or four children and she was so absorbed in them, I'm seized with horror! We led no life at all, but were in a state of constant danger, of escape from it, recurring danger, again followed by a desperate struggle and another escape—always as if we were on a sinking ship. Sometimes it seemed to me that this was done on purpose and that she pretended to be anxious about the children in order to subdue me. It solved all questions in her favor with such tempting simplicity. It sometimes seemed as if all she did and said on these occasions was pretense. But no! She herself suffered terribly, and continually tormented herself about the children and their health and illnesses. It was torture for her and for me too, and it was impossible for her not to suffer. After all, the attachment to her children, the animal need of feeding, caressing, and protecting them, was there as with most women, but there was not the lack of imagination and reason that there is in animals. A hen is not afraid of what may happen to her chick, does not know all the diseases that may befall it, and does not know all those remedies with which people imagine they can save it from illness and death. And for a hen her young are not a source of torment. She does for them what it's natural and pleasurable for her to do; her young ones are a pleasure to her. When a chick falls ill her duties are quite definite: she warms and feeds it. And doing this she knows that she's doing all that's necessary. If her chick dies she does not ask herself why it died, or where it's gone to; she cackles for a while, and then leaves off and goes on living as before. But for our unfortunate women, my wife among them, it wasn't so. Not to mention illnesses and how to cure them, she was always hearing and reading from all sides endless rules for the rearing and educating of children, which were continually being superseded by others. This is the way to feed a child: feed it in this way, on such and such; no, not on such and such, but in this way; clothes, drinks, baths, putting to bed, walking, fresh air,—for all these things we, especially she, heard new rules every week, just as if children had only begun to be born into the world yesterday. And if a child that had not been fed or bathed in the right way or at the right time fell ill, it appeared that we were to blame for not having done what we ought.

"That was so while they were well. It was a torment even then. But if one of them happened to fall ill, it was all over: a regular hell! It's supposed that illness can be cured and that there's a science about it, and people—doctors—who know about it. Ah, but not all of them know—only the very best. When a child is ill one must get hold of the very best doctor, the one who saves lives, and then the child is saved; but if you don't get that doctor, or if you don't live in the place where that doctor lives, the child is lost. This was not a creed peculiar to her, it's the creed of all women of our class, and she heard nothing else from all sides. Catherine Semenovna lost two children because Ivan Zakharych was not called in in time, but Ivan Zakharych saved Mary Ivanovna's eldest girl, and the Petrovs moved in time to various hotels on the doctor's advice, and the children remained alive; but if they hadn't been segregated the children would have died. Another who had a delicate child moved south on the doctor's advice and saved her child. How can she help being tortured and agitated all the time, when the lives of the children for whom she has an animal attachment depend on her finding out in time what Ivan Zakharych will say! But nobody knows what Ivan Zakharych will say, and he knows least of all, for he's well aware that he knows nothing and therefore cannot be of any use, but just shuffles about at random so that people shouldn't cease believing that he knows something or other. You see, had she been wholly an animal she wouldn't have suffered so, and if she had been quite a human being she would have had faith in God and would have said and thought, as a believer does: 'The Lord giveth and the Lord taketh away. One can't escape from God.'

"Our whole life with the children, for my wife and consequently for me, was not a joy but a torment. How could she help torturing herself? She tortured herself incessantly. Sometimes when we had just made peace after a scene of jealousy, or simply after a quarrel, and thought we should be able to live, read, and think a little, we had no sooner settled down to some occupation than the news came that Vasya was sick, or Masha showed symptoms of dysentery, or Andrusha had a rash, and there was an end to our peace; it was not life any more. Where was one to drive to? For what doctor? How isolate the child? And then it's a case of enemas, temperatures, medicines, and doctors. Hardly is that over before something else begins. We had no regular settled family life but only, as I've already said, continual escapes from imaginary and real dangers. It's like that in most families nowadays, you know, but in my family it was especially acute. My wife was a child-loving and credulous woman.

"So the presence of children not only failed to improve our life but poisoned it. Besides, the children were a new cause of dissension. As soon as we had children they became the means and object of our discord, and more often the older they grew. They were not only the object of discord but the weapons of our strife. We used our children, as it were, to fight one another. Each of us had a favorite weapon among them for our strife. I used to fight her chiefly through Vasya, the eldest boy, and she fought me through Lisa. Besides that, as they grew older and their characters became more defined, it came about that they grew into allies whom each of us tried to draw to his or her side. They, poor things, suffered terribly from this, but we, with our incessant warfare, had no time to think about that. The girl was my ally, and the eldest boy, who resembled his mother and was her favorite, was often hateful to me.

XVII

"Well, and so we lived. Our relations to one another grew more and more hostile and at last reached a stage where it was not disagreement that caused hostility, but hostility that caused disagreement. Whatever she said I disagreed with beforehand, and it was just the same with her.

"In the fourth year we both came to the conclusion that we couldn't understand one another. We no longer tried to bring any dispute to a conclusion. We invariably kept to our own opinions even about the most trivial questions, especially about the children. As I now recall the views I maintained were not at all so dear to me that I could not have given them up; but she was of the opposite opinion and to yield meant yielding to her, and that I couldn't do. It was the same with her. She probably considered herself in the right towards me, and as for me I always thought myself a saint towards her. When we were alone together we were doomed almost to silence, or to conversations such as I'm convinced animals can carry on with one another: 'What's the time? Time to go to bed. What's for dinner? Where shall we go? What's in the papers? Send for the doctor; Masha has a sore throat.' We only needed to go a little beyond this impossibly limited circle of conversation for irritation to flare up. We had collisions and acrimonious words about the coffee, a tablecloth, a carriage, a lead at bridge, all things that couldn't be of any importance to either of us. In me at any rate there often raged a terrible hatred of her. Sometimes I watched her pouring out tea, swinging her leg, lifting a spoon to her mouth, smacking her lips and drawing in some liquid, and I hated her for these things as though they were the worst possible actions. I didn't notice at the time that the periods of anger corresponded quite regularly and exactly to the periods of what we called love. A period of love—then a period of animosity; an energetic period of love, then a long period of animosity; a weaker manifestation of love, and a shorter period of animosity. We didn't understand that this love and animosity were one and the same animal feeling, only at opposite poles. To live like that would have been awful had we understood our position; but we neither understood nor saw it. Both salvation and punishment for man lie in the fact that if he lives in the wrong way he can befuddle himself so as not to see the misery of his position. And this we did. She tried to forget herself in intense and hurried occupation with household affairs, busying herself with the arrangements of the house, her own and the children's clothes, their lessons, and their health, while I had my own occupations: wine, my office duties, shooting, and cards. We were both continually occupied, and we felt that the busier we were, the nastier we might be to each other. 'It's all very well for you to grimace,' I thought, 'but you've harassed me all night with your scenes, and I have a meeting.' 'It's all very well for you,' she not only thought but said, 'but I've been awake all night with the baby.' Those new theories of hypnotism, psychic diseases, and hysterics are not a simple folly, but a dangerous and repulsive one. Charcot would certainly have said that my wife was hysterical, and that I was abnormal, and he would no doubt have tried to cure me. But there was nothing to cure.

"Thus we lived in a perpetual fog, not seeing the condition we were in. And if what did happen had not happened, I should have gone on living like that to old age and should have thought, when dying, that I had led a good life. I should not have realized the abyss of misery and the horrible falsehood in which I wallowed.

"We were like two convicts hating each other and chained together, poisoning one another's lives and trying not to see it. I didn't know at the time that ninety-nine per cent of married people live in a similar hell to the one I was in and that it cannot be otherwise. I didn't know this either about others or about myself.

"It's strange what coincidences there are in regular, or even in irregular, lives! Just when the parents find life together unendurable, it becomes necessary to move to town for the children's education."

He stopped, and once or twice gave vent to his strange sounds, which were now quite like suppressed sobs. We were approaching a station.

"What's the time?" he asked.

I looked at my watch. It was two o'clock.

"You're not tired?" he asked.

"No, but you are?"

"I'm suffocating. Excuse me, I'll walk up and down and drink some water."

He went unsteadily through the carriage. I remained alone thinking over what he had said, and I was so engrossed in thought that I didn't notice when he re-entered by the door at the other end of the carriage.

XVIII

"Yes, I keep digressing," he began. "I have thought about it a great deal. I now see many things differently and want to express it.

"Well, so we lived in town. There a man can live for a hundred years without noticing that he has been dead a long time and has rotted away. He has no time to take account of himself; he is always occupied. Business affairs, social intercourse, health, art, the children's health and their education. Now one has to receive so-and-so and so-and-so, go to see so-and-so and so-and-so; now one has to go and look at this, hear this man or that woman. In town, you know, there are at any given moment one, two, or even three celebrities whom one must on no account miss seeing. Then one has to undergo treatment oneself or get someone else attended to; then there are teachers, tutors, and governesses. But one's own life is quite empty. Well, so we lived and felt less the painfulness of living together. Besides at first we had splendid occupations, arranging things in a new place, in new quarters; and we were also occupied in going from town to the country and back to town again.

"So we lived through one winter; during the next there occurred, unnoticed by anyone, an apparently unimportant event, but the cause of all that happened later.

"She was not well and the doctors told her not to have children, and taught her how to avoid it. To me it was disgusting. I struggled against it, but with frivolous obstinacy she insisted on having her own way and I submitted. The last excuse for our swinish life—children—was then taken away, and life became viler than ever.

"To a peasant, a laboring man, children are necessary; though it is hard for him to feed them, he still needs them, and therefore his marital relations have justification. But to us who have children, more are unnecessary; they are an additional care and expense, a further division of property, and a burden. So our swinish life has no justification. We either artificially deprive ourselves of children or regard them as a misfortune, the consequences of carelessness, and that's still worse.

"We have no justification. But we have fallen morally so low that we don't even feel the need of any justification.

"The majority of the present educated world devotes itself to this kind of debauchery without the least qualm of conscience.

"There's nothing indeed that can feel qualms, for conscience in our society is non-existent, unless one can call public opinion and the criminal law 'conscience.' In this case neither the one nor the other is infringed: there's no reason to be ashamed of public opinion since everybody acts in the same way—Mary Pavlovna, Ivan Zakharych, and the rest. Why breed paupers or deprive oneself of the possibility of social life? There's no need to fear or be ashamed in face of criminal law either. Those shameless hussies, or soldiers' wives, throw their babies into ponds or wells, and of course they must be put into prison, but we do it all at the proper time and in a clean way.

"We lived like that for another two years. The means employed by those scoundrel-doctors evidently began to bear fruit; she became physically stouter and handsomer, like the late beauty of summer's end. She felt this and paid more attention to her appearance. She developed a provocative kind of beauty which made people restless. She was in the full vigor of a well-fed and excited woman of thirty who is not bearing children. Her appearance disturbed people. When she passed men she attracted their notice. She was like a fresh, well-fed, harnessed horse, whose bridle has been removed. There was no bridle, as is the case with ninety-nine per cent of our women. I felt this—and was frightened."

XIX

He suddenly rose and sat down close to the window.

"Pardon me," he muttered and, with his eyes fixed on the window, he remained silent for about three minutes. Then he sighed deeply and moved back to the seat opposite mine. His face was quite changed, his eyes looked pathetic, and his lips puckered strangely, almost as if he were smiling. "I'm rather tired but I'll go on with it. We have still plenty of time, it's not dawn yet. Ah, yes," he began after lighting a cigarette, "she grew plumper after she stopped having babies, and her malady—that everlasting worry about the children—began to pass . . . at least not actually to pass, but she woke up from an intoxication, came to herself, and saw that there was a whole divine world with its joys which she had forgotten, but a world she did not know how to live in and did not understand at all. 'I mustn't miss it! Time is passing and won't come back!' So, I imagine, she thought, or rather felt, nor could she have thought or felt differently: she'd been brought up in the belief that there was only one thing in the world worthy of attention—love. She had married and received something of that love, but not nearly what had been promised and expected. Even that had been accompanied by many disappointments and sufferings, and then this unexpected torment: so many children! The torments exhausted her. Then, thanks to the obliging doctors, she learnt that it was possible to avoid having children. She was very glad, tried it, and came alive again for the one thing she knew—love. But love with a husband, befouled by jealousy and all kinds of anger, was no longer the thing she wanted. She had visions of some other, clean, new love; at least I thought she had. She began to look about her as if expecting something. I saw this and could not help feeling anxious. It happened again and again that while talking to me, as usual through other people—that is, telling a third person what was meant for me—she boldly, without remembering that she had expressed the opposite opinion an hour before, declared, though half-jokingly, that a mother's cares are a fraud, and that it's not worth while devoting one's life to children when one is young and can enjoy life. She gave less attention to the children, and less frenziedly than before, but gave more and more to herself, to her appearance (though she tried to conceal it), and to her pleasures, even to her accomplishments. Again she enthusiastically took to the piano which she had quite abandoned, and it all began from that."

He turned his weary eyes to the window again but, evidently making an effort, immediately continued once more.

"Yes, that man made his appearance . . ." he became confused and once or twice made that peculiar sound with his nose.

I could see that it was painful for him to name that man, to recall him, or speak about him. But he made an effort and, as if he had broken the obstacle that hindered him, continued resolutely.

"He was a worthless man in my opinion and according to my estimate. Not because of the significance he acquired in my life but because he really was so. However, the fact that he was a poor sort of fellow only served to show how irresponsible she was. If it had not been he, it would have been another. It had to be!"

Again he paused. "Yes, he was a musician, a violinist; not a professional, but a semi-professional semi-society man.

"His father, a landowner, was a neighbor of my father's. He had been ruined, and his children—there were three boys—had obtained positions; only this one, the youngest, had been handed over to his godmother in Paris. There he was sent to the *Conservatoire* because he had a talent for music, and he came out a violinist and played concerts. He was a man . . ." Having evidently intended to say something bad about him, Pozdnyshev restrained himself and rapidly said: "Well, I don't really know how he lived, I only know that he returned to Russia that year and appeared in my house.

"With moist almond-shaped eyes, red smiling lips, a small waxed moustache, hair done in the latest fashion, and an insipidly pretty face, he was what women call 'not bad looking.' His figure was weak though not misshapen, and he had a specially developed posterior, like a woman's, or such as Hottentots are said to have. They too are reported to be musical. Pushing himself as far as possible into familiarity, but sensitive and always ready to yield at the slightest resistance, he maintained his dignity in externals, wore buttoned boots of a special Parisian fashion, bright-colored ties, and other things foreigners acquire in Paris, which by their noticeable novelty always attract women. There was an affected external gaiety in his manner. You know, that manner of speaking about everything in allusions and unfinished sentences, as if you knew it all, remembered it, and could complete it yourself.

"It was he with his music who was the cause of it all. You know at the trial the case was put as if it was all caused by jealousy. No such thing; that is, I don't mean 'no such thing'—it was and yet it wasn't. At the trial it was decided that I was a wronged husband and had killed her while defending my outraged honor (that's the phrase they employ, you know). That's why I was acquitted. I tried to explain matters at the trial but they took it that I was trying to rehabilitate my wife's honor.

"What my wife's relations with that musician may have been has no meaning for me, or for her either. What has meaning is what I've told you about—my swinishness. The whole thing was a result of the terrible abyss between us which I've told you about—that dreadful tension of mutual hatred which made the first excuse sufficient to produce a crisis. The quarrels between us had for some time become frightful, and were all the more startling because they alternated with similarly intense animal passion.

"If he hadn't appeared there would've been someone else. If the occasion had not been jealousy it would've been something else. I maintain that all husbands who live as I did, must either live dissolutely, separate, or kill themselves or their wives as I did. If there's anybody who's not done so, he's a rare exception. Before I ended as I did, I had several times been on the verge of suicide, and she too had repeatedly tried to poison herself.

XX

"Well, that's how things were going not long before it happened. We seemed to be living in a state of truce and had no reason to infringe it. Then we chanced to speak about a dog which I said had been awarded a medal at an exhibition. She remarked, 'Not a medal, but honorable mention.' A dispute ensues. We jump from one subject to another, reproach one another, 'Oh, that's nothing new, it's always been like that.' 'You said . . .' 'No, I didn't say so.' 'Then I'm telling lies! . . .' You feel that at any moment that dreadful quarrelling which makes you wish to kill yourself or her will start. You know it will begin immediately, and fear it like fire and therefore wish to restrain yourself, but your whole being is seized with fury. She, being in the same or even in worse condition, purposely misinterprets every word you say, giving it the wrong meaning. Her every word is venomous; where she knows that I'm most sensitive, she stabs. It gets worse and worse. I shout: 'Be quiet!' or something of that kind.

"She rushes out of the room and into the nursery. I try to hold her back in order to finish what I was saying, to prove my point, and I seize her by the arm. She pretends that I have hurt her and screams: 'Children, your father is striking me!' I shout: 'Don't lie!' 'But it's not the first time!' she screams, or something like that. The children rush to her. She calms them down. I say, 'Don't pretend!' She says, 'Everything is pretending in your eyes, you would kill any one and say they were pretending. Now I've understood you. That's just what you want!' 'Oh, I wish you were dead as a dog!' I shout. I remember how those dreadful words horrified me. I never thought I could utter such terrible, coarse words, and am surprised that they escaped me. I shout them and rush into my study, sit down, and smoke. I hear her go out into the hall preparing to go away. I ask, 'Where are you going?' She doesn't reply. 'Well, to hell with her,' I say to myself, and go back to my study, lie down, and smoke. A thousand different plans of how to revenge myself and get rid of her, and how to improve matters and go on as if nothing had happened, come into my head. I think all that and go on smoking and smoking. I think of running away from her, hiding myself, going to America. I get as far as dreaming of how I'll get rid of her, how splendid that will be, and how I'll find another, an admirable woman—quite different. I shall get rid of her either by her dying or by a divorce, and I plan how it will be done. I notice that I'm getting confused and not thinking of what's necessary, and to prevent myself from perceiving that my thoughts are not to the point, I go on smoking.

"Life in the house goes on. The governess comes in and asks: 'Where is madame? When will she be back?' The footman asks whether he's to serve tea. I go to the dining-room. The children, especially Lisa who already understands, gaze inquiringly and disapprovingly at me. We drink tea in silence. She's still not come back. The evening passes, she hasn't returned, and two different feelings alternate within me. Anger because she torments me and the children by her absence which will end by her returning; and fear that she won't return but will do something to herself. I would go to fetch her, but where am I to look for her? At her sister's? But it would be so stupid to go and ask. And it's all the better: if she is bent on tormenting someone, let her torment herself. Besides, that's what she's waiting for; and next time it would be worse still. But suppose she's not with her sister but is doing something to herself, or has already done it! It's past ten, past eleven! I don't go to the bedroom—it would be stupid to lie there alone waiting—but I'll not lie down here either. I wish to occupy my mind, to write a letter or to read, but I can't do anything. I sit alone in my study, tortured, angry, and listening. It's three o'clock, four o'clock, and she's not back. Towards morning I fall asleep. I wake up, she's still not come!

"Everything in the house goes on in the usual way, but all are perplexed and look at me inquiringly and reproachfully, considering me to be the cause of it all. The same struggle still continues in me: anger that she's torturing me, and anxiety for her.

"At about eleven in the morning her sister arrives as her envoy. The usual talk begins. 'She's in a terrible state. What does it all mean?' 'After all, nothing's happened.' I speak of her impossible character and say that I haven't done anything.

" 'But, you know, it can't go on like this,' says her sister.

" 'It's all her doing and not mine,' I say. 'I won't take the first step. If it means separation, let it be separation.'

"My sister-in-law goes away having achieved nothing. I had boldly said that I would not take the first step; but after her departure, when I came out of my study and saw the children piteous and frightened, I was prepared to take the first step. I should be glad to do it, but I don't know how. I pace up and down again and smoke; at lunch I drink vodka and wine and attain what I unconsciously desire—I no longer see the stupidity and humiliation of my position.

"At about three she comes home. When she meets me she doesn't speak. I imagine that she's submitted, and begin to say that I'd been provoked by her reproaches. She, with the same stern expression on her terribly harassed face, says that she hasn't come for explanations but to fetch the children, because we can no longer live together. I begin telling her that the fault is not mine and that she provoked me beyond endurance. She looks severely and solemnly at me and says: 'Don't say any more, you'll repent it.' I tell her that I cannot stand comedies. Then she cries out something I don't catch, and rushes into her room. The key clicks behind her—she's locked herself in. I try the door, but getting no answer, go away angrily. Half-an-hour later Lisa runs in crying. 'What is it? Has anything happened?' 'We can't hear mama.' We go. I pull at the double doors with all my might. The bolt had not been firmly secured, and the two halves come open. I approach the bed, on which she is lying awkwardly in her petticoats and with a pair of high boots on. An empty opium bottle is on the table. She's brought to herself. Tears follow, and a reconciliation. No, not a reconciliation: in the heart of each of us there's still the old animosity, with the additional irritation produced by the pain of this quarrel which each attributes to the other. But one must of course finish it all somehow, and life goes on in the old way. And so the same kind of quarrel, and even worse ones, occurred continually: once a week, once a month, at times every day. It was always the same. Once I had already procured a passport to go abroad—the quarrel had continued for two days. But again there was a partial explanation, a partial reconciliation, and I did not go.

XXI

"So those were our relations when that man appeared. He arrived in Moscow—his name is Trukhachevsky—and came to my house. It was in the morning. I received him. We had once been on familiar terms and he tried to maintain a familiar tone by using non-committal expressions, but I definitely adopted a conventional tone and he submitted to it at once. I disliked him from the first glance. But curiously enough a strange and fatal force led me not to repulse him, not to keep him away,

but on the contrary to invite him to the house. After all, what could
have been simpler than to converse with him coldly, and say good-bye
without introducing him to my wife? But no, as if on purpose, I began
talking about his playing, and said I'd been told he had given up the
violin. He replied that, on the contrary, he now played more than ever.
He referred to the fact that there had been a time when I myself played.
I said I had given it up but that my wife played well. It is an astonishing
thing that from the first day, from the first hour of my meeting him,
my relations with him were such as might have been only after all that
subsequently happened. There was something strained in them: I noticed
every word, every expression he or I used, and attributed importance to
them.

"I introduced him to my wife. The conversation immediately turned
to music, and he offered to be of use to her by playing. My wife was,
as usual of late, very elegant, attractive, and disquietingly beautiful. He
evidently pleased her at first sight. Besides she was glad that she would
have someone to accompany her on the violin, which she was so fond
of that she used to engage a violinist from the theater for that purpose;
her face reflected her pleasure. But catching sight of me she understood
my feeling at once and changed her expression; a game of mutual
deception began. I smiled pleasantly to appear as if I liked it. He, looking
at my wife as all immoral men look at pretty women, pretended that he
was only interested in the subject of the conversation—which no longer
interested him at all; she tried to seem indifferent, though my false smile
of jealousy with which she was familiar, and his lustful gaze, evidently
excited her. I saw that from their first encounter her eyes were particularly
bright and, probably as a result of my jealousy, it seemed as if an electric
current had been established between them, evoking as it were an identity
of expressions, looks, and smiles. She blushed and he blushed. She
smiled and he smiled. We spoke about music, Paris, and all sorts of
trifles. Then he rose to go, and stood wearing a smile, holding his hat
against his twitching thigh and looking first at her, then at me, in
expectation of what we would do. I remember that instant because at
that moment I might not have invited him, and then nothing would
have happened. But I glanced at him and at her and said silently to
myself, 'Don't suppose that I'm jealous,' 'or that I'm afraid of you,' I
added mentally addressing him, and I invited him to come some evening
and bring his violin to accompany my wife. She glanced at me with
surprise, flushed, and as if frightened began to decline, saying that she
didn't play well enough. This refusal irritated me still more, and I insisted
on his coming. I remember the curious feeling with which I looked at
the back of his head, with the black hair parted in the middle contrasting
with the white nape of his neck, as he went out with his peculiar sprightly
gait suggestive of a bird. I could not conceal from myself that this man's
presence tormented me. 'It depends on me,' I reflected, 'to act so as to

see nothing more of him. But that would be to admit that I'm afraid of him. No, I'm not afraid of him; it would be too humiliating,' I said to myself. And there in the ante-room, knowing that my wife heard me, I insisted that he should come that evening with his violin. He promised to do so, and left.

"In the evening he brought his violin and they played. But it took a long time to arrange matters—they didn't have the music they wanted, and my wife could not play what they had without preparation. I was very fond of music and sympathized with their playing, arranging a music-stand for him and turning the pages. They played a few things, some songs without words, and a little sonata by Mozart. They played splendidly, and he had an exceptionally fine tone. Besides that, he had refined and elevated taste not at all in correspondence with his character.

"He was of course a much better player than my wife, and he helped her, while at the same time politely praising her playing. He behaved himself very well. My wife seemed interested only in music and was very simple and natural. Though I pretended to be interested in the music I was tormented by jealousy all evening.

"From the first moment his eyes met my wife's I saw that the animal in each of them, regardless of all conditions of their position and of society, asked, 'May I?' and answered, 'Oh, yes, certainly.' I saw that he'd never expected to find my wife, a Moscow lady, so attractive, and that he was very pleased. He had no doubt whatever that she was *willing*. The crux was whether that unendurable husband could hinder them. Had I been pure, I wouldn't have understood this, but, like the majority of men, I myself had regarded women in that way before I married and therefore could read his mind like an open book. I was particularly tormented because I saw without doubt that she had no other feeling towards me than a continual irritation only occasionally interrupted by habitual sensuality; but that this man—by his external refinement and novelty and still more by his undoubtedly great talent for music, by the nearness that comes of playing together, and by the influence music, especially the violin, exercises on impressionable natures—was sure not only to please, but certainly and without the least hesitation to conquer, crush, bind her, twist her round his little finger and do whatever he liked with her. I couldn't help seeing this and I suffered terribly. But for all that, or perhaps on account of it, some force obliged me against my will to be not merely polite but amiable to him. Whether I did it for my wife or for him, to show that I was not afraid of him, or whether I did it to deceive myself—I don't know, but I know that from the first I couldn't behave naturally with him. In order not to yield to my wish to kill him there and then, I had to make a great fuss over him. I gave him expensive wines at supper, went into raptures over his playing, spoke to him with a particularly amiable smile, and invited him to dine and accompany my wife again the next Sunday. I told him I would invite a few friends who were fond of music to hear him. And so it ended."

Greatly agitated, Pozdnyshev changed his position and emitted his peculiar sound.

"It's strange how the presence of that man acted on me," he began again, with an evident effort to keep calm. "I come home from the Exhibition a day or two later, enter the ante-room, and suddenly feel something heavy, as if a stone had fallen on my heart, and I cannot understand what it is. Passing through the ante-room I noticed something which reminded me of him. I realized what it was only in my study, and went back to the ante-room to make sure. Yes, I was not mistaken, there was his overcoat. A fashionable coat, you know. (Though I didn't realize it, I observed everything connected with him with extraordinary attention.) I inquire: sure enough he's there. I pass on to the dancing-room, not through the drawing-room but through the schoolroom. My daughter, Lisa, sits reading a book and the nurse sits with the youngest boy at the table, making a lid of some kind spin around. The door to the dancing-room is shut but I hear the sound of a rhythmic arpeggio and their voices. I listen, but cannot make anything out.

"Evidently the sound of the piano is purposely made to drown the sound of their voices, their kisses . . . perhaps. My God! What was aroused in me! Even to think of the beast that then lived in me fills me with horror: My heart suddenly contracted, stopped, and then began to beat like a hammer. My chief feeling, as usual whenever I was enraged, was one of self-pity. 'In the presence of the children! of their nanny!' I thought. I probably looked awful, for Lisa gazed at me with strange eyes. 'What am I to do?' I asked myself. 'Go in? I can't: heaven only knows what I should do. But neither can I go away.' Our nanny looked at me as if she understood my position. 'But it's impossible not to go in.' I said to myself, and quickly opened the door. He was sitting at the piano playing those arpeggios with his large white upturned fingers. She was standing in the curve of the piano, bending over some open music. She was the first to see or hear, and glanced at me. Whether she was frightened and pretended not to be, or whether she was not really frightened, she did not start or move but only blushed, and not at once.

" 'How glad I am that you've come: we haven't decided what to play on Sunday,' she said in a tone she would never have used with me had we been alone. This and her using the word "we" of herself and him, filled me with indignation. I greeted him silently.

He pressed my hand, and at once, with a smile which I thought distinctly ironic, began to explain that he'd brought some music to practice for Sunday, but that they disagreed about what to play: a classical, but more difficult piece, namely Beethoven's sonata for violin, or a few little pieces. It was all so simple and natural that there was nothing one could complain about, yet I felt certain that it was all untrue and that they'd agreed how to deceive me.

"One of the most distressing conditions of life for a jealous man (and everyone's jealous in our world) are certain society conventions which allow a man and woman the greatest and most dangerous proximity. You would become a laughing-stock to others if you tried to prevent such contact at balls, or the nearness of doctors to their women-patients, or of people occupied with art, sculpture, and especially music. A couple is occupied with the noblest of arts, music; this demands a certain intimacy, and there's nothing reprehensible in that. Only a stupid jealous husband can see anything undesirable in it. Yet everybody knows that it's by means of those very pursuits, especially music, that the greater part of the adulteries in our society occur. Evidently I confused them by the confusion I betrayed: for a long time I couldn't speak. I was like a bottle held upside down from which the water doesn't flow because it's too full. I wanted to abuse him and throw him out, but again I felt that I must treat him courteously and amiably. And I did so. I acted as though I approved of it all, and again because of the strange feeling which made me behave more amiably the more his presence distressed me, I told him that I trusted his taste and advised her to do the same. He stayed as long as was necessary to efface the unpleasant impression caused by my sudden entrance—looking frightened and remaining silent—and then left, pretending that it was now decided what to play next day. I was fully convinced however that compared to what interested them the question of what to play was quite unimportant.

"I saw him out to the ante-room with special politeness. (How could one do less than accompany a man who'd come to disturb the peace and destroy the happiness of a whole family?) I pressed his soft white hand with particular warmth.

XXII

"I didn't speak to her all that day—I couldn't. Proximity to her aroused such hatred of her that I was afraid of myself. At dinner in the presence of the children she asked me when I was going away. I had to go next week to the District Meetings of the Zemstvo.[7] I told her the date. She asked whether I didn't need anything for the journey. I didn't answer but sat silent at table and then went in silence to my study. Lately she never used to come to my room, especially not at that time of day. I lay in my study filled with anger. Suddenly I heard her familiar step, and the terrible, monstrous idea entered my head that like Uriah's wife, she wished to conceal the sin she'd already committed and that was why

7. Elective district council in pre-revolutionary Russia.

she was coming to me at such an unusual time.[8] 'Can she be coming to me?' I thought, listening to her approaching footsteps. 'If she's coming here, then I'm right,' and an inexpressible hatred of her took possession of me. Nearer and nearer came the steps. Is it possible that she won't pass on to the dancing-room? No, the door creaks and in the doorway appears her tall handsome figure; on her face and in her eyes a timid ingratiating look which she tries to hide, but which I see and the meaning of which I know. I held my breath for so long, I almost choked; still looking at her, I grasped my cigarette-case and began to smoke.

" 'Now how can you? I come to sit with you for a while, and you begin smoking'—and she sat down close to me on the sofa, leaning against me. I moved away so as not to touch her.

" 'I see you're dissatisfied at my wanting to play on Sunday,' she said.

" 'I'm not at all dissatisfied,' I said.

" 'As if I don't see!'

" 'Well, I congratulate you on seeing. But I only see that you behave like a coquette. . . . You always find pleasure in all kinds of vileness, but to me it's terrible!'

" 'Oh, well, if you're going to scold like a driver I'll go away.'

" 'Good, but remember that if you don't value the family honor, I value not you (to hell with you), but I value the honor of our family!'

" 'But what's the matter? What?'

" 'Go away, for God's sake go away!'

"Whether she pretended not to understand what it was about or really didn't understand, at any rate she took offense, grew angry, and didn't go away but stood in the middle of the room.

" 'You really have become impossible,' she began. 'You have a char-acter that even an angel couldn't put up with.' And as usual trying to wound me as painfully as possible, she reminded me of my conduct to my sister (an incident when, being exasperated, I said rude things to her); she knew I was distressed about it and she stung me just on that spot. 'After that, nothing from you will surprise me,' she said.

" 'Yes! Insult me, humiliate me, disgrace me, and then put the blame on me,' I said to myself, and suddenly I was seized by such terrible rage as I had never before experienced.

"For the first time I wished to give physical expression to that rage. I jumped up and went towards her; but just as I jumped up, I remembered becoming conscious of my rage and asking myself: 'Is it right to give way to this feeling?' At once I answered that it was right, that it would frighten her, and instead of restraining my fury I began inflaming it still further, and was glad it burnt yet more fiercely within me.

" 'Go away, or I'll kill you!' I shouted, going up to her and seizing her by the arm. I consciously intensified the anger in my voice as I said

8. Uriah was a Hittite captain whose beautiful wife, Bathsheba, aroused David's lust. He arranged for Uriah to die in battle and then married her (2 Samuel 11.15).

this. I suppose I appeared terrible, for she was so frightened that she didn't even have the strength to go away, but only said: 'Vasya, what is it? What's the matter with you?'

" 'Go!' I roared louder still. 'No one but you can drive me to fury. I don't answer for myself!'

"Having given free rein to my rage, I revelled in it and wished to do something still more unusual to show the degree of my anger. I felt a terrible desire to hit her, to kill her, but knew this would not do, and so to give vent to my fury I seized a paper-weight from my table, again shouting 'Go!' and hurled it to the floor near her. I aimed it very carefully past her. Then she left the room, but stopped in the doorway, and immediately, while she was still watching it (I did it so that she might see), I began snatching things from the table—candlesticks and ink-stand—and hurling them on the floor still shouting 'Go! Get out! I don't answer for myself!' She went away—and I stopped immediately.

"An hour later our nanny came to tell me that my wife was in hysterics. I went to see her; she sobbed, laughed, couldn't speak; her whole body was convulsed. She was not pretending, but was really ill.

"Towards morning she grew quiet, and we made peace under the influence of the feeling we called love.

"In the morning after our reconciliation, I confessed that I was jealous of Trukhachevsky, she was not at all confused, but laughed most naturally; so strange did the very possibility of an infatuation for such a man seem to her.

" 'Could a decent woman experience any other feeling for such a man except for the pleasure of his music? Why, if you like I'm ready never to see him again . . . not even on Sunday, though everybody has been invited. Write and tell him that I'm ill, and that's all there is to it! Only it's unpleasant that anyone, especially he himself, should imagine that he's dangerous. I'm too proud to allow anyone to think that of me!'

"And you know, she wasn't lying; she believed what she was saying. She hoped by those words to evoke contempt for him in herself and thus defend herself from him, but she did not succeed in doing so. Everything was against her, especially that accursed music. So it ended, and on the Sunday the guests assembled and again they played together.

XXIII

"I suppose it's hardly necessary to say that I was very vain: if one is not vain there's nothing to live for in our usual way of life. So on that Sunday I arranged the dinner and musical evening with considerable care. I bought the supplies myself and invited the guests.

"Towards six the visitors assembled. He came in evening dress with diamond studs that showed bad taste. He behaved in a free and easy manner, answered everything hurriedly with a smile of agreement and understanding, you know, with that peculiar expression which seems to say that all you say or do is just what he expected. I noticed everything that was not in good taste about him with particular pleasure, because it should have had the effect of tranquillizing me and showing me that he was so far beneath my wife that, as she had said, she couldn't lower herself to his level. I didn't allow myself to be jealous. In the first place I had lived through that torment and needed rest; secondly I wanted to believe my wife's assurances and did believe them. Even though I was not jealous, nevertheless I was not natural with either of them; at dinner and during the first half of the evening before the music began I still followed all their movements and looks.

"The dinner was, as dinners are, dull and pretentious. The music began fairly early. Oh, how well I remember every detail of that evening! I remember how he brought in his violin, unlocked the case, took off the cover a certain lady had embroidered for him, drew out the violin, and began tuning it. I remember how my wife sat down at the piano with pretended unconcern, under which I saw that she was trying to conceal great timidity—chiefly as to her own ability—and then the usual A on the piano began, the pizzicato of the violin, and the arrangement of the music. I remember how they glanced at one another, turned to look at the audience who were seating themselves, said something to one another, and started to play. He took the first chords. His face grew serious, stern, and sympathetic; listening to the sounds he produced, he touched the strings with careful fingers. The piano answered him. The music began. . . ."

Pozdnyshev paused and produced his strange sound several times in succession. He tried to speak, but sniffed, and stopped.

"They played Beethoven's Kreutzer Sonata," he continued.[9] "Do you know the first presto? You do?" he cried. "Ugh! It's a terrible thing, that sonata. And especially that part. In general music is a dreadful thing! What is it? I don't understand it. What is music? What does it do? And why does it do what it does? They say music exalts the soul. Nonsense, it's not true! It has an effect, an awful effect—I'm speaking about myself—but not of an exalting kind. It has neither an exalting nor a debasing effect, but it produces agitation. How can I put it? Music makes me forget myself, my real position; it transports me to some other position. Under the influence of music it seems that I feel what I don't really feel, that I understand what I don't really understand, that I can do what I cannot really do. I explain it by the fact that music acts like yawning, like laughter: I'm not sleepy, but I yawn when I see someone yawning; there's nothing for me to laugh at, but I laugh when I hear people laughing.

9. Sonata ("Kreutzer") for piano and violin, opus 47, composed 1802.

"Music carries me immediately and directly into the mental condition in which the man was who composed it. My soul merges with his and together with him I pass from one condition into another. Why this happens I don't know. You see, he who wrote, let's say, the Kreutzer Sonata—Beethoven—knew of course why he was in that condition; that condition caused him to do certain things and therefore that condition had meaning for him, but for me—none at all. That's why music only agitates and doesn't lead to any conclusion. When a military march is played soldiers march to the music and the music has achieved its object. A dance is played, I dance and the music has achieved its object. Mass has been sung, I receive Communion, and that music has reached a conclusion. Otherwise it's only agitating, and what ought to be done in that agitation is lacking. That's why music sometimes acts so dreadfully, so terribly. In China, music is a State affair. That's as it should be. How can you allow anyone who pleases to hypnotize another, or many others, and do what he likes with them? Especially when this hypnotist should be the first immoral man who turns up?

"It's a terrible instrument in the hands of any chance user! Take that Kreutzer Sonata, for instance! How can that first presto be played in a drawing-room among ladies in low-necked dresses? To hear that played, to applaud and then to eat sweets and talk about the latest scandal? Such things should only be played on certain important occasions, and then only when certain actions answering to such music are wanted; play it then and do what the music has moved you to. Otherwise an awakening of energy and feeling unsuited both to the time and place, to which no outlet is given, cannot but act harmfully. At any rate that piece had a terrible effect on me; it was as if new feelings, new possibilities, of which I had till then been unaware, had been revealed to me. 'That's how it is: not at all as I used to think and live, but that way,' something seemed to say within me. What this new thing was that had been revealed to me I couldn't explain to myself, but the consciousness of this new condition was very joyous. All those people, including my wife and him, appeared in a new light.

"After that allegro they played the beautiful, but common and un-original, andante with trite variations, and the very weak finale. Then, at the request of the visitors, they played Ernst's Elegy and a few small pieces.[1] They were all good, but did not produce even one-hundredth of the impression the first piece had. The effect of that piece formed the background for them all.

"I felt light-hearted and cheerful the whole time. I had never seen my wife as she was that evening. Those shining eyes, that severe, sig-nificant expression while she played, her melting languor, her feeble, pathetic, and blissful smile after they finished. I saw all that but did not

1. Heinrich Wilhelm Ernst (1814–65), Moravian violinist and composer of many salon pieces, fantasias, and variations.

attribute any meaning to it except that she was feeling what I felt, and that to her as well as to me new feelings, never before experienced, were revealed or, as it were, recalled. The evening ended satisfactorily and the visitors departed.

"Knowing that I had to attend the Zemstvo Meetings two days later, Trukhachevsky said on leaving that he hoped to repeat the pleasure of that evening when he returned to Moscow. From this I concluded that he did not consider it possible to come to my house during my absence, and that pleased me.

"It turned out that since I would not be back before he left town, we wouldn't see one another again.

"For the first time I shook his hand with real pleasure, and thanked him for the enjoyment he had given us. In the same way he bade a final farewell to my wife. Their leave-taking seemed to be most natural and proper. Everything was splendid. My wife and I were both satisfied with our evening party.

XXIV

"Two days later I left for the Meetings, parting from my wife in the best and most tranquil of moods.

"In the district there was always an enormous amount to do and quite a special life, a special little world of its own. I spent two long ten-hour days at the Council. A letter from my wife was brought to me on the second day and I read it there and then.

"She wrote about the children, about her uncle, about nanny, about shopping, and among other things she mentioned, as a most natural occurrence, that Trukhachevsky had stopped by, brought some music he had promised, and had offered to play again, but that she had refused.

"I didn't remember his having promised to bring any music, and thought he had taken leave for good; therefore I was unpleasantly struck by this. I was however so busy that I had no time to think about it; it was only in the evening when I had returned to my lodgings that I re-read her letter.

"Besides the fact that Trukhachevsky had called at my house during my absence, the whole tone of the letter seemed to me unnatural. The mad beast of jealousy began to growl in its kennel and wanted to leap out, but I was afraid of that beast and quickly locked him in. 'What an abominable feeling jealousy is!' I said to myself. 'What could be more natural than what she writes?'

"I went to bed and began thinking about the affairs awaiting me the next day. During those Meetings, sleeping in a new place, I usually slept badly, but now I fell asleep very quickly. As sometimes happens, you know, you feel a kind of electric shock and suddenly wake up. I awoke thinking of her, of my physical love for her, and of Trukhachevsky, and of everything happening between them. Horror and rage gripped my heart. I began to reason with myself. 'What nonsense!' I said to myself. 'There are no grounds to go on, there's nothing and there's been nothing. How can I so degrade her and myself as to imagine such horrors? He's a sort of hired violinist, known as a worthless fellow, and suddenly an honorable woman, the respected mother of a family, *my* wife. . . . What absurdity!' So it seemed to me on the one hand. 'How could it help being so?' it seemed on the other. 'How could that simplest and most intelligible thing help happening—that for the sake of which I married her, for the sake of which I have been living with her, what alone I wanted from her, and which other men including this musician must therefore also want? He's an unmarried man, healthy (I remember how he crunched the gristle of a cutlet and how greedily his red lips clung to the glass of wine), well-fed, plump, and not merely unprincipled, but evidently making it a principle to accept those pleasures that present themselves. And they have music, that most exquisite voluptuousness of the senses, as a link between them. What could make him refrain? She? But who is she? She was, and still is, a mystery. I don't know her. I only know her as an animal. And nothing can or should restrain an animal.'

"Only then did I remember their faces that evening when, after the Kreutzer Sonata, they played some impassioned little piece, I don't remember by whom, impassioned to the point of obscenity. 'How dared I go away?' I asked myself, remembering their faces. Wasn't it clear that everything had happened between them that evening? Wasn't it evident already that there was not only no barrier between them, but that they both, and she chiefly, felt a certain measure of shame after what had happened? I remember her weak, piteous, and beatific smile as she wiped the perspiration from her flushed face when I came up to the piano. Even then they avoided looking at one another, and only at supper when he was pouring some water for her, they glanced at each other with the vestige of a smile. I now recalled with horror the glance and scarcely perceptible smile I had then caught. 'Yes, it's all over,' said one voice, and immediately the other voice said something entirely different. 'Something has come over you, it can't be so,' said that other voice. It felt uncanny lying there in the dark and I struck a match, and felt a kind of terror in that little room with its yellow wallpaper. I lit a cigarette and, as always happens when one's thoughts go round and round in a circle of insoluble contradictions, I smoked, taking one cigarette after another in order to befog myself so as not to see those contradictions.

"I did not sleep all night, and at five in the morning, having decided that I could no longer continue in such a state of tension, I rose, woke the caretaker who attended me and sent him to get horses. I sent a note to the Council saying that I had been recalled to Moscow on urgent business and asked that one of the other members should take my place. At eight o'clock I got into my carriage and started home."

XXV

The conductor entered and seeing that our candle had burnt down put it out, without supplying a fresh one. The day was dawning. Pozdnyshev was silent, but sighed deeply all the time the conductor was in the carriage. He continued his story only after the conductor had gone out; in the semi-darkness of the carriage only the rattle of the windows of the moving carriage and the rhythmic snoring of the clerk could be heard. In the half-light of dawn I couldn't see Pozdnyshev's face at all, but only heard his voice becoming more excited and full of suffering.

"I had to travel twenty-four miles by road and eight hours by rail. It was splendid driving: frosty autumn weather, bright and sunny. The roads were in that condition when the wheels leave their dark imprint on them, you know. They were smooth, the light was brilliant, and the air invigorating. It was pleasant driving in the carriage. When it grew lighter and I had started home I felt better. Looking at the houses, fields, and passers-by, I forgot where I was going. Sometimes I felt that I was simply taking a drive, and that nothing was calling me back. This oblivion was peculiarly enjoyable. When I remembered where I was going, I said to myself, 'We shall see when the time comes; I must not think about it.' When we were halfway there an incident occurred which detained me and still further distracted my thoughts. The carriage broke down and had to be repaired. That break-down had a very important effect, for it caused me to arrive in Moscow at midnight, instead of at seven o'clock as I had expected, and to reach home between twelve and one, as I missed the express and had to travel by an ordinary train. Going to fetch a cart, having the carriage mended, settling in, tea at the inn, a talk with the innkeeper—all this still further diverted my attention. It was twilight before everything was ready and I started again. By night it was even more pleasant driving than during the day. There was a new moon, a slight frost, smooth roads, good horses, and a cheerful driver; as I went on I enjoyed it, hardly thinking at all of what lay before me. Perhaps I enjoyed it just because I knew what awaited me and was saying good-bye to the joys of life. But that tranquil mood, that ability to suppress my feelings, ended with my drive. As soon as I entered the train, something entirely different happened. That eight-hour journey in a railway carriage was something dreadful which I shall never forget all my life. Whether it was that having taken my seat in the carriage I vividly imagined myself as having already arrived, or that railway travel has such an exciting effect on people, at any rate from the moment I sat down on the train I could no longer control my imagination; with extraordinary vividness which inflamed my jealousy it painted incessantly, one after another, pictures of what had gone on in my absence, of how she had been false to me. I burnt with indignation, anger, and a peculiar feeling of intoxication with my own humiliation, as I gazed at those pictures, and could not tear myself away from them; I couldn't help looking at them, couldn't efface them, and couldn't help evoking them.

"That was not all. The more I gazed at those imaginary pictures the stronger grew my belief in their reality. The vividness with which they presented themselves to me seemed to serve as proof that what I imagined was real. It was as if against my will some devil invented and suggested to me the most terrible reflections. An old conversation I'd had with Trukhachevsky's brother came to mind, and in a kind of ecstasy I tore my heart with that conversation, making it refer to Trukhachevsky and my wife.

"That had occurred a long time before, but I recalled it. Trukhachevsky's brother, I remember, in reply to a question whether he frequented houses of ill-repute, had said that a decent man would not go to places where there was danger of infection and where it was dirty and nasty; besides, he could always find a decent woman. And now his brother had found my wife! 'True, she's not in her first youth, she's lost a side-tooth, and there's a slight puffiness about her; but it can't be helped, one has to take advantage of what one can get,' I imagined him to be thinking. 'Yes, it's condescending of him to take her for his mistress!' I said to myself. 'And she's safe. . . .' 'No, it's impossible!' I thought horror-struck. 'There's nothing of the kind, nothing! There aren't even any grounds for suspecting such things. Didn't she tell me that the very thought that I could be jealous of him was degrading to her? Yes, but she's lying, she's always lying!' I exclaimed, and everything began all over again. . . . There were only two other people in the carriage; an old woman and her husband, both were very taciturn, and even they got out at one of the stations and then I was quite alone. I was like a caged animal: I jumped up and went to the window, I began to walk up and down trying to speed the train up; but the carriage with all its seats and windows went jolting along in the same way, just as ours does now . . ."

Pozdnyshev jumped up, took a few steps, and sat down again.

"Oh, I'm afraid, afraid of railway carriages, I'm seized with horror. Yes, it's awful!" he continued. "I said to myself, 'I'll think about something else. Suppose I think about the innkeeper where I had tea,' and there in my mind's eye appears the innkeeper with his long beard and his grandson, a boy of the age of my Vasya! He'll see how the musician kisses his mother. What will happen in his poor soul? But what does she care? She loves . . .' and again the same thing arose in me. 'No, no . . . I'll think about the inspection of the District Hospital. Oh, yes, about the patient who complained of the doctor yesterday. The doctor has a moustache like Trukhachevsky's. How impudent he is . . . they both deceived me when he said he was leaving Moscow,' and it began again. Everything I thought about had some connection with them. I suffered dreadfully. The chief cause of the suffering was my ignorance, my doubt, and the contradictions within me: my not knowing whether I ought to love her or hate her. My suffering was of a strange kind. I felt a hateful consciousness of my humiliation and of his victory, but a terrible hatred for her. 'It will not do to put an end to myself and leave her; at least she must suffer to some extent, and at least understand that I have suffered,' I said to myself. I got out at every station to divert my mind. At one station I saw some people drinking, and I immediately drank some vodka. Beside me stood a Jew who was also drinking. He began to talk, and to avoid being alone in my carriage I went with him into his dirty third-class carriage reeking with smoke and sprinkled with shells of sunflower seeds. There I sat down beside him and he chattered a great deal and told anecdotes. I listened to him, but could not take in what he was saying because I continued to think about my own affairs. He noticed this and demanded my attention. Then I rose and went back to my carriage. 'I must think it over,' I said to myself. 'Is what I suspect true, and is there any reason for me to suffer?' I sat down, wishing to think it over calmly, but immediately, instead of calm reflection, the same thing began again: instead of reflection, only pictures and fantasy. 'How often I've suffered like this,' I said to myself (recalling former attacks of jealousy), 'and afterwards it all ended in nothing. So it may be now, yes certainly it will. I shall find her sound asleep, she will wake up, be pleased to see me, and by her words and looks I'll know that there's been nothing and that this is all nonsense. Oh, how good that would be! But no, that's happened too often and won't happen again now,' some voice seemed to say; and it began again. Yes, that was where the punishment lay! I wouldn't take a young man to a hospital for venereal diseases to knock the hankering after women out of him, but into my soul, to see the devils that were tearing it apart! What was terrible, you know, was that I considered myself to have a complete right to her body as if it were my own, and yet at the same time I felt I could not control that body, that it was not mine and she could dispose of it as she pleased, and that she wanted to dispose of it not as I wished her to. And I could do nothing either to her or to him. Like Vanka the Steward, he too could sing a song before the gallows of how he kissed the sugared lips and so forth.[2] And he would triumph. If she hasn't yet done it but wishes to—and I know that she does—it's even worse; it would be better if she had done it and I knew it, so that there would be an end to this uncertainty. I couldn't have said what it was I wanted.

2. The hero of numerous Russian folk songs, who boasts of his love for the master's wife or daughter and who pays for his bragging with his life.

I wanted her not to desire that which she was bound to desire. It was utter insanity.

XXVI

"At the last station but one, when the conductor had come to collect the tickets, I gathered my things together and went out onto the brake-platform; the consciousness that the crisis was at hand still further increased my agitation. I felt cold, and my jaw trembled so much that my teeth chattered. I automatically left the terminus with the crowd, took a cab, got in, and drove off. I rode looking at the few passers-by, the night-watchmen, and the shadows of my cab thrown by the street lamps, first in front and then behind me, and did not think of anything. When we had gone about half a mile my feet felt cold, and I remembered that I had taken off my woollen stockings in the train and put them in my satchel. 'Where's the satchel? Is it here? Yes.' And my wicker trunk? I remembered that I had entirely forgotten about my luggage, but finding that I had the luggage-ticket I decided that it was not worth while going back for it, and so continued along my way.

"Try now as I will, I cannot recall my state of mind at the time. What was I thinking? What did I want? I don't know at all. All I remember is a consciousness that something dreadful and very important in my life was imminent. Whether that important event occurred because I thought it would, or whether I had a presentiment of what was to happen, I don't know. It may even be that after what has happened all the preceding moments have acquired a certain gloom in my mind. I drove up to the front porch. It was past midnight. Some cabmen were waiting in front of the porch expecting, from the fact that there were lights in the windows, to get fares. (The lights were in our flat, in the dancing-room and in drawing-room.) Without considering why it was still light in our windows so late, I went upstairs in the same state of expectation of something dreadful, and rang. Egor, a kind, willing, but very stupid footman, opened the door. The first thing my eyes fell on in the hall was a man's cloak hanging on the stand with other outdoor coats. I ought to have been surprised but was not, for I had expected it. 'That's it!' I said to myself. When I asked Egor who the visitor was and he named Trukhachevsky, I inquired whether there was anyone else. He replied, 'Nobody, sir.' I remember that he replied in a tone as if he wanted to cheer me up and dissipate my doubts of there being anybody else there. 'So it is, so it is,' I seemed to be saying to myself. 'And the children?' 'All well, heaven be praised. In bed, long ago.'

"I couldn't breathe, and couldn't check the trembling of my jaw. 'Yes, so it's not as I thought: I used to expect a misfortune, but things used to turn out all right and in the usual way. Now it's not as usual, but all as I pictured to myself. I thought it was only my imagination, but here it is, all real. Here it all is . . . !'

"I almost began to sob, but the devil immediately suggested to me: 'Cry, be sentimental, and they'll get away quietly. You'll have no proof and will continue to suffer and doubt all your life.' My self-pity vanished immediately, and a strange sense of joy arose in me, that my torture would soon be over, that now I could punish her, get rid of her, and vent my anger. And I gave vent to it—I became a beast, a cruel and cunning beast.

" 'Don't!' I said to Egor, who was about to go into the drawing-room. 'Here's my luggage-ticket, take a cab as quick as you can and go get my luggage. Go!' He went down the passage to fetch his overcoat. Afraid that he might alarm them, I went as far as his little room and waited while he put on his coat. From the drawing-room, beyond another room, one could hear voices and the clatter of knives and plates. They were eating and had not heard the bell. 'If only they don't come out now,' I thought. Egor put on his overcoat, which had an astrakhan collar, and went out. I locked the door after him and felt eerie when I knew I was alone and must act at once. How, I didn't yet know. I only knew that now all was over, that there could be no doubt as to her guilt, and that I should punish her immediately and end my relations with her.

"Previously I had doubted and had thought: 'Perhaps it's not true after all, perhaps I'm mistaken.' But now it was no longer so. It was all irrevocably decided. 'Without my knowledge she's alone with him at night! That shows complete disregard of everything! Even worse: it's intentional boldness and impudence in crime, so that her boldness may serve as a sign of her innocence. All is clear. There's no doubt.' I only feared one thing—their parting hastily, inventing some fresh lie, and thus depriving me of clear evidence and the possibility of proving the fact. So as to catch them more quickly I went on tiptoe to the dancing-room where they were, not through the drawing-room but through the passage and nurseries.

"The boys slept in the first nursery. In the second nursery nanny moved and was about to awake; I imagined to myself what she would think when she knew all. Such pity for myself seized me at that thought, I could not restrain my tears. So as not to awaken the children, I ran on tiptoe into the passage and on into my study, where I fell sobbing on the sofa.

" 'I, an honest man, the son of my parents, who all my life have dreamt of the happiness of married life; I, a man who was never unfaithful to her. . . . And now! Five children, and she's embracing a musician because he has red lips!

" 'No, she's not a human being. She's a bitch, an abominable bitch! In the next room to her children whom she's pretended to love all her life. And writing to me as she did! Throwing herself so barefacedly on his neck! But what do I know? Perhaps she carried on with the footmen long ago, and bore the children who are considered mine!

" 'Tomorrow I should have come back and she would have met me with her fine coiffure, her elegant waist and her indolent, graceful movements.' (I imagined her attractive, hateful face), 'and that beast of jealousy would have sat in my heart forever lacerating it. What will nanny think? . . . And Egor? Poor little Lisa! She understands something already. Ah, that impudence, those lies! And that animal sensuality which I know so well,' I said to myself.

"I tried to get up but couldn't. My heart was beating so loudly that I couldn't stand on my feet. 'Yes, I'll die of a stroke. She'll kill me. That's just what she wants. What does killing mean to her? But no, that would be too advantageous to her and I will not give her that pleasure. Yes, here I sit while they eat and laugh and . . . Yes, though she was no longer in her first freshness he did not reject her. For in spite of that she's not bad looking, and above all she's not dangerous to his precious health. And why didn't I throttle her then?' I said to myself, recalling the moment when, the week before, I drove her out of my study and hurled things about. I vividly recalled the state I'd been in then; I not only recalled it, but again felt the need to strike and destroy that I'd felt then. I remember how I wished to act, and how all considerations except those necessary for action went out of my head. I entered into that condition when an animal or a man, under the influence of physical excitement at a time of danger, acts with precision and deliberation, but without losing a moment and always with a single definite aim in view.

"The first thing I did was to take off my boots and, in my socks, approach the sofa, on the wall above which guns and daggers were hung. I took down a curved Damascus dagger that had never been used and was very sharp. I drew it out of its scabbard. I remember the scabbard fell behind the sofa, and I remember thinking 'I must find it afterwards or it will get lost.' Then I took off my overcoat which I was still wearing, and stepping softly in my socks I went in there.

XXVII

"Having crept up stealthily to the door, I suddenly opened it. I remember the expression of their faces. I remember that expression because it gave me painful pleasure—it was an expression of terror. That was just what I wanted. I shall never forget the look of desperate terror that appeared on both their faces the first instant they saw me. I think he was sitting at the table, but on seeing or hearing me he jumped to his feet and stood with his back to the cupboard. His face expressed nothing but unmistakable terror. Her face too expressed terror, but there was something else besides. If it had expressed only terror, perhaps what happened might not have happened; but on her face there was, or at any rate so it seemed to me at the first moment, an expression of regret and annoyance that love's raptures and her happiness had been disturbed. It

was as if she wanted nothing but that her present happiness should not
be interfered with. These expressions remained on their faces for only
an instant. The look of terror on his changed immediately to one of
inquiry: might he, or might he not, begin lying? If he might, he must
begin at once; if not, something else would happen. But what? . . . He
looked inquiringly at her face. On her face the look of vexation and
regret changed as she looked at him (or so it seemed) to one of solicitude
for him.

"For an instant I stood in the doorway holding the dagger behind my
back.

"At that moment he smiled, and in a ridiculously indifferent tone
remarked: 'We've been making some music.'

" 'What a surprise!' she began, falling into his tone. But neither of
them finished; the same fury I had experienced the week before overcame
me. Again I felt that need of destruction, violence, and a transport of
rage, and yielded to it. Neither finished what they were saying. That
something else began which he had feared and which immediately
destroyed all they were saying. I rushed towards her, still hiding the
dagger that he might not prevent my striking her in the side under her
breast. I selected that spot from the very first. Just as I rushed at her he
saw it, and—a thing I never expected of him—he seized me by the arm
and shouted: 'Think what you're doing! . . . Help, someone! . . .'

"I snatched my arm away and rushed at him in silence. His eyes met
mine and he suddenly grew as pale as a sheet to his very lips. His eyes
flashed in a peculiar way, and—again what I had not expected—he
darted under the piano and out the door. I was going to rush after him,
but a weight hung on my left arm. It was she. I tried to free myself, but
she hung on yet more heavily and would not let me go. This unexpected
hindrance, the weight, and her touch which was loathsome to me,
inflamed me still more. I felt that I was quite mad and that I must look
frightful, and this delighted me. I swung my left arm with all my might,
and my elbow hit her straight in the face. She cried out and let go my
arm. I wanted to run after him, but remembered that it's ridiculous to
run after one's wife's lover in one's socks; and I did not wish to be
ridiculous but terrible. In spite of the fearful frenzy I was in, I was aware
all the time of the impression I might produce on others, and was even
partly guided by that impression. I turned towards her. She fell on the
couch, and holding her hand to her bruised eyes, looked at me. Her
face showed fear and hatred of me, the enemy, as a rat's does when one
lifts the trap in which it's been caught. At any rate I saw nothing in her
expression but this fear and hatred of me. It was just the fear and hatred
of me which would be evoked by love for another. I might still have
restrained myself and not done what I did, had she remained silent. But
suddenly she began to speak and to catch hold of the hand in which I
held the dagger.

" 'Come to yourself! What are you doing? What's the matter? There's been nothing, nothing, nothing. . . . I swear it!'

"I might still have hesitated, but those last words of hers, from which I concluded just the opposite—that everything had happened—called forth a reply. And the reply had to correspond to the temper to which I had brought myself, which continued to increase and had to go on increasing. Fury, too, has its own laws.

" 'Don't lie, you wretch!' I howled, and seized her arm with my left hand, but she wrenched herself away. Then, still without letting go of the dagger, I seized her by the throat with my left hand, threw her backwards, and began throttling her. What a firm neck it was . . . ! She seized my hand with both hers trying to pull it away from her throat, and as if I had only waited for that, I struck her with all my might with the dagger in the side below the ribs.

"When people say they don't remember what they do in a fit of fury, it's rubbish, falsehood. I remembered everything and not for a moment did I lose consciousness of what I was doing. The more frenzied I became the more brightly the light of consciousness burnt in me, so that I couldn't help knowing everything I did. I knew what I was doing every second. I cannot say that I knew beforehand what I was going to do; but I knew what I was doing when I did it, and I think even a little before, as if to make repentance possible and to be able to tell myself that I could stop. I knew I was hitting her below the ribs and that the dagger would enter. At the moment I did it, I knew I was doing an awful thing such as I had never done before, and one which would have terrible consequences. But that consciousness passed like a flash of lightning and the deed immediately followed the consciousness. I realized the action with extraordinary clearness. I felt, and remember, the momentary resistance of her corset and of something else, and then the plunging of the dagger into something soft. She seized the dagger with her hands, and cut them, but could not hold it back.

"For a long time afterwards, in prison when the moral change had taken place in me, I thought about that moment, recalled what I could of it, and considered it. I remembered that for an instant, only an instant, before the action I had a terrible consciousness that I was killing, had killed, a defenseless woman, my wife! I remember the horror of that consciousness and conclude from that, and even dimly remember, that having plunged the dagger in, I pulled it out immediately, trying to remedy what had been done and to stop it. I stood for a second motionless waiting to see what would happen, and whether it could be remedied.

"She jumped to her feet and screamed: 'Nanny! He's killed me.'

"Having heard the noise nanny was standing by the door. I continued to stand there waiting, not believing the truth. But the blood rushed from under her corset. Only then did I understand that it could not be remedied, and I immediately decided that it was unnecessary it should be, that I had done what I wanted and what I had to do. I waited till she fell down, and nanny, crying 'Good God!' ran to her; only then did I throw away the dagger and leave the room.

" 'I must not get excited; I must know what I'm doing,' I said to myself without looking at her and at nanny. Nanny was screaming—calling for the maid. I went down the passage, sent the maid, and went into my study. 'What am I to do now?' I asked myself, and immediately realized what it must be. On entering the study I went straight to the wall, took down a revolver and examined it—it was loaded—I put it on the table. Then I picked up the scabbard from behind the sofa and sat down there.

"I sat there for a long time. I didn't think of anything or call anything to mind. I heard sounds of bustling outside. I heard someone drive up, then someone else. Then I heard and saw Egor bring into the room my wicker trunk that he had fetched. As if anyone wanted that!

" 'Have you heard what happened?' I asked. 'Tell the yard-porter to inform the police.' He didn't reply, and went away. I rose, locked the door, got out my cigarettes and matches and began to smoke. I hadn't finished the cigarette before sleep overpowered me. I must have slept for a couple of hours. I remember dreaming that she and I were friendly together, that we had quarrelled but were making it up, there was something in the way, but we were friends. I was awakened by someone knocking at the door. 'That's the police!' I thought, waking up. 'I have committed murder, I think. But perhaps it's *she*, and nothing's happened.' There was another knock at the door. I did not answer, but was trying to solve the question whether it had happened or not. But it had! I remembered the resistance of the corset and plunging in the dagger, and a cold shiver ran down my spine. 'Yes, it has. Yes, and now I must do away with myself too,' I thought. But I thought this knowing that I would *not* kill myself. Still I got up and took the revolver in my hand. But it's strange: I remember how I'd been near suicide many times, how even that day on the railway it had seemed easy, just because I thought how it would astonish her—now I was not only unable to kill myself, but even to think of it. 'Why should I do it?' I asked myself, and there was no reply. There was more knocking at the door. 'First I must find out who's knocking. There will still be time for this.' I put down the revolver and covered it with a newspaper. I went to the door and un-latched it. It was my wife's sister, a kindly, stupid widow. 'Vasya, what's this?' and her tears began to flow.

" 'What do you want?' I asked rudely. I knew I ought not to be rude to her and had no reason to be, but I could think of no other tone to adopt.

" 'Vasya, she's dying! Ivan Zakharych says so.' Ivan Zakharych was her doctor and adviser.

" 'Is he here?' I asked, and all my animosity against her surged up again. 'Well, what of it?'

" 'Vasya, go to her. Oh, how terrible it all is!' said she.

" 'Shall I go to her?' I asked myself, and immediately decided that I must. Probably it's always done, when a husband has killed his wife, as I had—he must certainly go to her. 'If that's what's done, then I must go,' I said to myself. 'If necessary I shall always have time,' I reflected, referring to shooting myself, and I went to her. 'Now we shall have phrases and grimaces, but I won't yield to them,' I thought. 'Wait,' I said to her sister, 'it's silly to go without boots; let me put on slippers at least.'

XXVIII

"Wonderful to say, when I left my study and went through the familiar rooms, the hope that nothing had happened awoke in me again; but the smell of that doctor's nastiness—iodoform[3] and carbolic—took me aback. 'No, it had happened.' Going down the passage past the nursery I saw little Lisa. She looked at me with frightened eyes. It even seemed to me that all five children were there and all were looking at me. I approached the door; the maid opened it from inside and then she left. The first thing that caught my eye was her light-grey dress thrown on a chair and stained black with blood. She was lying on one of the twin beds (on mine because it was easier to get to), with her knees raised. She lay in a very sloping position supported by pillows, with her dressing jacket unfastened. Something had been put on the wound. There was a heavy smell of iodoform in the room. What struck me first and most of all was her swollen and bruised face, blue on part of her nose and under her eyes. This was the result of the blow with my elbow when she had tried to hold me back. There was nothing beautiful about her, but something repulsive as it seemed to me. I stopped on the threshold. 'Go up to her,' said her sister. 'Yes, no doubt she wants to confess,' I thought. 'Shall I forgive her? Yes, she's dying and may be forgiven,' I thought, trying to be magnanimous. I went up close to her. She raised her eyes to me with difficulty, one of them was black, and with some effort she said falteringly:

" 'You've got your way, killed . . .' Through the look of suffering and even the nearness of death her face had the old expression of cold animal hatred that I knew so well. 'I won't . . . let you have . . . the children, all the same. . . . My sister will take . . .'

"About the most important matter, her guilt, her faithlessness, she seemed to consider it beneath her to speak.

" 'Yes, admire what you've done,' she said looking towards the door, and she sobbed. In the doorway stood her sister with the children. 'Yes, look what you've done.'

"I looked at the children and at her bruised disfigured face, and for the first time I forgot myself, my rights, my pride, and for the first time

3. An antiseptic used for dressing wounds.

saw a human being in her. So insignificant did all that had offended me, all my jealousy, appear, and so important what I had done, that I wished to fall with my face onto her hand, and say: 'Forgive me,' but I dared not do so.

"She lay silent with her eyes closed, evidently too weak to say anymore. Then her disfigured face trembled and puckered. She pushed me away feebly.

" 'Why did it all happen? Why?'

" 'Forgive me,' I said.

" 'Forgive! That's all rubbish! . . . Only not to die! . . .' she cried, raising herself; her glittering eyes were fixed on me. 'Yes, you've had your way! . . . I hate you! Ah!' she cried, evidently already delirious and frightened at something. 'Shoot! I'm not afraid! . . . Only kill everyone . . . ! He's gone . . . ! Gone . . . !'

"After that the delirium continued all the time. She did not recognize anyone. She died towards noon that same day. Before that they'd taken me to the police-station and then to prison. There, during the eleven months I remained awaiting trial, I examined myself and my past, and understood it. I began to understand it on the third day: on the third day they took me *there* . . ."

He was going on but, unable to repress his sobs, he stopped. When he recovered himself he continued:

"I only began to understand when I saw her in the coffin . . ."

He gave a sob, but immediately continued hurriedly:

"Only when I saw her dead face did I understand all that I'd done. I realized that I had killed her; that it was my doing that she, living, moving, warm, had now become motionless, waxen, and cold, and that this could never, anywhere, by any means, be remedied. He who has not lived through it cannot understand. . . . Ugh! . . ." he cried several times and then fell silent.

We sat in silence a long while. He kept sobbing and trembling as he sat opposite me without speaking. His face had grown narrow and elongated and his mouth seemed to stretch right across it.

"Yes," he said suddenly. "Had I known then what I know now, everything would have been different. Nothing would have induced me to marry her. . . . I should never have married at all."

Again we remained silent for a long time.

"Well, forgive me. . . ." He turned away from me and lay down on the seat, covering himself up with his blanket. At the station where I had to get out (at eight o'clock in the morning) I went up to him to say good-bye. Whether he was asleep or only pretended to be, at any rate he didn't move. I touched him with my hand. He uncovered his face, and I could see he'd not been asleep.

"Good-bye," I said, holding out my hand. He gave me his and smiled slightly, but so piteously that I felt ready to weep.

"Yes, forgive me . . ." he said, repeating the same words with which he'd concluded his story.

Master and Man†

I

It happened in the 'seventies during the winter, on the day after St. Nicholas's Day.[1] There was a fête in the parish and the innkeeper, Vasily Andreevich Brekhunov, a Second Guild merchant,[2] being a church elder had to go to church, and also had to entertain his relatives and friends at home.

But when the last of them had gone at once he began to prepare to drive over to see a neighboring proprietor about a grove which he had been bargaining over for a long time. He was now in a hurry to start off, so that buyers from town might not forestall him in making a profitable purchase.

The youthful landowner was asking ten thousand rubles for the grove simply because Vasily Andreevich was offering only seven thousand. Seven thousand was, however, only a third of its real value. Vasily Andreevich might perhaps have got it down to his own price, for the woods were in his district and he had a long-standing agreement with other village dealers that no one should run up the price in another's district, but now he had learned that some timber-dealers from town meant to bid for the Goryachkin grove, and he resolved to go at once and get the matter settled. So as soon as the feast was over, he took seven hundred rubles from his strong box, added two thousand three hundred rubles of church money he had in his keeping, so as to bring the sum up to three thousand; he carefully counted the notes, and having put them into his pocket-book, made haste to start.

Nikita, the only one of Vasily Andreevich's laborers who was not drunk that day, ran to harness the horse. Though an habitual drunkard, Nikita was sober because since the day before the fast, when he'd sold off and drunk up his coat and leather boots, he'd sworn off drink and had kept this vow for two months, and was still keeping it despite the temptation of the vodka that had been drunk everywhere during the first two days of the feast.

Nikita was a peasant, about fifty years old, from a neighboring village, "not a manager" as the peasants said about him, meaning that he was not the thrifty head of a household; he lived most of the time away from home as a laborer. He was valued everywhere for his industry, dexterity,

---

† This piece was first published in 1895.
1. December 6 (old style), or December 19 (new style).
2. Russian merchants were divided into three cat-

egories or guilds depending on the amount of capital they possessed. The Second Guild was in the middle.

and strength at work, and still more for his kindly and pleasant temper. But he never settled down anywhere for long because about twice a year, or even more often, he had a drinking bout, and then besides spending all his clothes on drink, he became turbulent and quarrelsome. Vasily Andreevich himself had turned him away several times, but had afterwards taken him back again—valuing his honesty, his kindness to animals, and especially his cheapness. Vasily Andreevich did not pay Nikita the eighty rubles a year such a man was worth, but only about forty, which he gave him in irregular intervals, in small sums, and even that mostly not in cash, but in goods from his own shop and at high prices.

Nikita's wife Martha, who had once been a handsome, vigorous woman, managed the homestead with the help of her son and two daughters, and did not urge Nikita to live at home: first because she had been living for some twenty years already with a cooper, a peasant from another village who lodged in their house: and secondly because though she managed her husband as she pleased when he was sober, she feared him like fire when he was drunk. Once when he had got drunk at home, Nikita, probably to make up for his submissiveness when sober, broke open her box, took out her best clothes, grabbed an axe, and chopped all her undergarments and dresses to bits. All the wages Nikita earned went to his wife, and he raised no objection to that. So now, two days before the holiday, Martha had twice been to see Vasily Andreevich and had got from him wheat flour, tea, sugar, and a quart of vodka, the whole lot costing three rubles, and also five rubles in cash, for which she thanked him as for a special favor, though he owed Nikita at least twenty rubles.

"What agreement did we ever draw up with you?" Vasily Andreevich asked Nikita. "If you need anything, take it; you'll work it off. I'm not like others to keep you waiting, making up accounts, and reckoning fines. We deal straight-forwardly. You serve me and I won't neglect you."

And when saying this Vasily Andreevich was honestly convinced that he was Nikita's benefactor; he knew how to put it so plausibly that all those who depended on him for their money, beginning with Nikita, confirmed the conviction that he was their benefactor and did not take advantage of them.

"Yes, I understand, Vasily Andreevich. You know that I serve you and take as many pains as I would for my own father. I understand very well!" Nikita would reply. He was quite aware that Vasily Andreevich was cheating him, but at the same time he felt that it was useless to try to clear up his accounts with him or explain his side of the matter, and that as long as he had nowhere else to go he must accept what he could get.

Now, having heard his master's order to harness the horse, he went as usual cheerfully and willingly to the shed, stepping briskly and easily on his rather turned-in feet; he took down from a nail the heavy tasselled leather bridle, and jingling the rings of the bit, went to the closed stable where the horse he was to harness was standing by himself.

"What, feeling lonely, feeling lonely, you little silly?" Nikita said in answer to the low whinny with which he was greeted by the good-tempered, medium-sized bay stallion, with a rather slanting rump, who stood alone in the shed. "Now then, now then, there's time enough. Let me give you some water first," he went on, speaking to the horse just as if to someone who understood the words he was using; having whisked the dusty, grooved back of the well-fed young stallion with the skirt of his coat, he put a bridle on his handsome head, straightened his ears and forelock, and having taken off his halter, led him out to water.

Picking his way out of the dung-strewn stable, Mukhorty frisked, and making play with his hind leg, pretended that he meant to kick Nikita, who was running at a trot beside him to the pump.

"Now then, now then, you rascal!" Nikita called out, well knowing how carefully Mukhorty threw out his hind leg just to touch his greasy sheepskin coat but not to strike him—a trick Nikita much appreciated.

After a drink of cold water the horse sighed, moving his strong wet lips, from the hairs of which transparent drops fell into the trough; then standing still as if in thought, he suddenly gave a loud snort.

"If you don't want any more, you needn't drink. But don't go asking for any later," said Nikita quite seriously and fully explaining his conduct to Mukhorty. Then he ran back to the shed pulling by the rein the playful young horse, who wanted to gambol all over the yard.

There was no one else around except a stranger, the cook's husband, who had come for the holiday.

"Go and ask which sleigh is to be harnessed—the wide one or the small one—there's a good fellow!"

The cook's husband went into the house, which stood on an iron foundation and was iron-roofed, and soon returned saying that the little one was to be harnessed. By that time Nikita had put the collar and brass-studded belly-band on Mukhorty and, carrying a light, painted shaft-bow in one hand, was leading the horse with the other up to two sleighs that stood in the shed.

"All right, let it be the little one!" he said, backing the intelligent horse, which all the time kept pretending to bite him, into the shafts, and with the aid of the cook's husband he proceeded to harness him. When everything was nearly ready and only the reins had to be adjusted, Nikita sent the other man to the shed for some straw and to the barn for a drugget.[3]

"There, that's all right! Now, now, don't bristle up!" said Nikita, pressing down into the sleigh the freshly threshed oat straw the cook's

3. Piece of coarsely woven fabric.

husband had brought. "Now let's spread the sacking like this, and the
drugget over it. There, that will be comfortable sitting," he went on,
suiting the action to the words and tucking the drugget all round over
the straw to make a seat.

"Thank you, dear man. Things always go more quickly with two
working at it!" he added. And gathering up the leather reins fastened
together by a brass ring, Nikita took the driver's seat and started the
impatient horse over the frozen manure which lay in the yard, towards
the gate.

"Uncle Nikita! Uncle, Uncle!" a high-pitched voice shouted, and a
seven-year-old boy in a black sheepskin coat, new white felt boots, and
a warm cap, ran hurriedly out of the house into the yard. "Take me
with you!" he cried, fastening up his coat as he ran.

"All right, come along, darling!" said Nikita, and stopping the sleigh
he picked up the master's pale thin little son, radiant with joy, and drove
out into the road.

It was past two o'clock and the day was windy, dull, and cold, with
more than twenty degrees of frost. Half the sky was hidden by a low
dark cloud. In the yard it was quiet, but in the street the wind was felt
more keenly. The snow swept down from a neighboring shed and whirled
about in the corner near the bath-house.

Hardly had Nikita driven out of the yard and turned the horse's head
to the house, before Vasily Andreevich emerged from the high porch
in front of the house with a cigarette in his mouth and wearing a cloth-
covered sheepskin coat tightly girdled low at his waist, and stepped onto
the hard-trodden snow which squeaked under the leather soles of his
felt boots, and stopped. Taking a last puff of his cigarette he threw it
down, stepped on it, and letting the smoke escape through his moustache
and looking askance at the horse that was coming up, began to tuck in
his sheepskin collar on both sides of his ruddy face, clean-shaven except
for the moustache, so that his breath would not moisten the collar.

"See now! The young scamp is there already!" he exclaimed when
he saw his little son in the sleigh. Vasily Andreevich was aroused by
the vodka he had drunk with his visitors, so he was even more pleased
than usual with everything that was his and all that he did. The sight
of his son, whom he always thought of as his heir, now gave him great
satisfaction. He looked at him, screwing up his eyes and showing his
long teeth.

His wife—pregnant, thin and pale, with her head and shoulders
wrapped in a shawl so that nothing of her face could be seen but her
eyes—stood behind him in the vestibule to see him off.

"Now really, you ought to take Nikita with you," she said timidly,
stepping out from the doorway.

Vasily Andreevich didn't answer. Her words evidently annoyed him
and he frowned angrily and spat.

"You have money on you," she continued in the same plaintive voice. "What if the weather gets worse! Do take him, for goodness' sake!"

"Why? Do I know the road so badly that I must take along a guide?" exclaimed Vasily Andreevich, uttering every word very distinctly and compressing his lips unnaturally, as he usually did when speaking to buyers and sellers.

"Really you ought to take him along. I beg you in God's name!" his wife repeated, wrapping her shawl more closely around her head.

"There, she sticks to it like a leech! . . . Where am I to take him?"

"I'm quite ready to go with you, Vasily Andreevich," said Nikita cheerfully. "But they must feed the horses while I'm away," he added, turning to his master's wife.

"I'll look after them, Nikita dear. I'll tell Simon," replied the mistress.

"Well, Vasily Andreevich, am I to come with you?" asked Nikita, awaiting a decision.

"It seems I must humor my old woman. But if you're coming you'd better put on a warmer cloak," said Vasily Andreevich, smiling again as he winked at Nikita's short sheepskin coat, which was torn under the arms and at the back, was greasy and out of shape, frayed to a fringe around the skirt, and had endured many things in its lifetime.

"Hey, dear man, come and hold the horse!" shouted Nikita to the cook's husband, who was still in the yard.

"No, I will, I will!" shrieked the little boy, pulling his hands, red with cold, out of his pockets, and seizing the cold leather reins.

"Don't be too long dressing yourself up. Look alive!" shouted Vasily Andreevich, grinning at Nikita.

"Only a moment, Vasily Andreevich!" replied Nikita, and running quickly with his inturned toes in his felt boots, their soles patched with felt, he hurried across the yard and into the workmen's hut.

"Arinushka! Get my coat down from the stove. I'm going with the master," he said, as he ran into the hut and took down his girdle from the nail on which it hung.

The workmen's cook, who'd had a little sleep after dinner and was now getting the samovar ready for her husband, turned cheerfully to Nikita, and infected by his hurry began to move as quickly as he did; she got down his miserable worn-out cloth coat from the stove where it was drying, and began hurriedly shaking it out and smoothing it down.

"There now, you'll have a chance of a holiday with your good man," said Nikita, who from kindhearted politeness always said something to anyone he was alone with.

Then, drawing his worn narrow girdle around him, he drew in his breath, pulling in his lean stomach still more, and girdled himself as tightly as he could over his sheepskin.

"There now," he said addressing himself no longer to the cook but the girdle, as he tucked the ends in at the waist, "now you won't come undone!" And working his shoulders up and down to free his arms, he put the coat over his sheepskin, arched his back more strongly to ease his arms, poked himself under the armpits, and took down his leather-covered mittens from the shelf. "Now we're all right!"

"You ought to wrap your feet up, Nikita. Your boots are very bad."

Nikita stopped as if he had suddenly realized this.

"Yes, I ought to. . . . But they'll do like this. It isn't far!" and he ran out into the yard.

"Won't you be cold, Nikita?" said the mistress as he came up to the sleigh.

"Cold? No, I'm quite warm," answered Nikita as he pushed some straw up to the forepart of the sledge so that it would cover his feet, and stowed away the whip, which the good horse would not need, at the bottom of the sleigh.

Vasily Andreevich, who was wearing two fur-lined coats one over the other, was already in the sleigh, his broad back filling nearly its whole rounded width, and taking the reins he immediately touched the horse. Nikita jumped in just as the sleigh started, and seated himself in front on the left side, with one leg hanging over the edge.

II

The good stallion took the sleigh along at a brisk pace over the smooth-frozen road through the village, the runners squeaking slightly as they went.

"Look at him hanging on there! Hand me the whip, Nikita!" shouted Vasily Andreevich, evidently enjoying the sight of his "heir," who standing on the runners was hanging on at the back of the sleigh. "I'll give it to you! Be off to mamma, you dog!"

The boy jumped down. The horse increased his amble and, suddenly changing foot, broke into a fast trot.

The Crosses, the village where Vasily Andreevich lived, consisted of six houses. As soon as they had passed the blacksmith's hut, the last in the village, they realized that the wind was much stronger than they had thought. The road could hardly be seen. The tracks left by the runners were immediately covered by snow and the road was only distinguished by the fact that it was higher than the rest of the ground. There was a whirl of snow over the fields and the line where sky and earth met could not be seen. The Telyatin forest, usually clearly visible, now loomed up only occasionally and dimly through the driving snowy dust. The wind came from the left, insistently blowing over to one side the mane on Mukhorty's sleek neck and carrying aside even his fluffy tail, which was tied in a simple knot. Nikita's wide coat-collar, as he sat on the windy side, pressed close to his cheek and nose.

"This road doesn't give him a chance—it's too snowy," said Vasily

Andreevich, who prided himself on his good horse. "I once drove to Pashutino with him in half an hour."

"What?" asked Nikita, who could hardly hear on account of his collar.

"I say I once went to Pashutino in half an hour," shouted Vasily Andreevich.

"It goes without saying that he's a good horse," replied Nikita.

They were silent for a while. But Vasily Andreevich wished to talk.

"Well, did you tell your wife not to give the cooper any vodka?" he began in the same loud tone, quite convinced that Nikita must feel flattered to be talking with so clever and important a person as himself. He was so pleased with his jest that it did not even enter his head that the remark might be unpleasant to Nikita.

The wind again prevented Nikita's hearing his master's words.

Vasily Andreevich repeated the jest about the cooper in his loud, clear voice.

"That's their business, Vasily Andreevich. I don't pry into their affairs. As long as she doesn't ill-treat our boy—God be with them."

"That's so," said Vasily Andreevich. "Well, and will you be buying a horse this spring?" he went on, changing the subject.

"Yes, I can't avoid it," answered Nikita, turning down his collar and leaning back towards his master.

The conversation now became interesting to him and he did not wish to lose a word.

"The lad's growing up. He must begin to plough for himself, but till now we've always had to hire someone," he said.

"Well, why not take the lean-rumped one. I won't charge much for it," shouted Vasily Andreevich, feeling animated, and consequently starting on his favorite occupation—that of horse-trading—which absorbed all his mental powers.

"Or you might let me have fifteen rubles and I'll buy one at the horse-market," said Nikita, who knew that the horse Vasily Andreevich wanted to sell him would be expensive at seven rubles, but that if he took it from him, he would be charged twenty-five, and then would be unable to draw any money for half a year.

"It's a good horse. I think of your interest as my own—according to conscience. Brekhunov isn't a man to wrong anyone. Let the loss be mine. I'm not like others. Honestly!" he shouted in the voice in which he hypnotized his customers and dealers. "It's a really good horse."

"Quite so!" said Nikita with a sigh; convinced that there was nothing more to listen to, he released his collar again, which immediately covered his ear and face.

They drove on in silence for about half an hour. The wind blew sharply onto Nikita's side and arm where his sheepskin was torn.

He huddled up and breathed into the collar which covered his mouth, and was not entirely cold.

"What do you think—shall we go through Karamyshevo or by the straight road?" asked Vasily Andreevich.

The road through Karamyshevo was more travelled and was well marked with a double row of high stakes. The straight road was nearer but little used and had no stakes, or only poor ones covered with snow.

Nikita thought for awhile.

"Though Karamyshevo is farther, it's easier going," he said.

"But by the straight road, when once we get through the hollow by the forest, it's easy going—sheltered," said Vasily Andreevich, who wished to go the nearest way.

"Just as you please," said Nikita, and again let go of his collar.

Vasily Andreevich did as he had said, and having gone about half a verst came to a tall oak stake which had a few dry leaves still dangling on it, and there he turned to the left.

On turning they faced directly against the wind, and snow was beginning to fall. Vasily Andreevich, who was driving, inflated his cheeks, blowing the breath out through his moustache. Nikita dozed.

So they went on in silence for about ten minutes. Suddenly Vasily Andreevich began saying something.

"Eh, what?" asked Nikita, opening his eyes.

Vasily Andreevich didn't answer, but bent over, looking behind them and then ahead of the horse. The sweat had curled Mukhorty's coat between his legs and on his neck. He went at a walk.

"What is it?" Nikita asked again.

"What is it? What is it?" Vasily Andreevich mimicked him angrily. "There aren't any stakes to be seen! We must've got off the road!"

"Well, pull up then, and I'll look for it," said Nikita, and jumping down lightly from the sleigh and taking the whip from under the straw, he went off to the left from his own side of the sleigh.

The snow was not deep that year, so that it was possible to walk anywhere, but in places it was still knee-deep and got into Nikita's boots. He went about feeling the ground with his feet and the whip, but couldn't find the road anywhere.

"Well, how is it?" asked Vasily Andreevich when Nikita came back to the sleigh.

"There's no road this side. I must go to the other side and try there," said Nikita.

"There's something there in front. Go and have a look."

Nikita went to what had appeared dark, but found that it was earth which the wind had blown from the bare fields of winter oats and had strewn over the snow, coloring it. Having searched to the right also, he returned to the sleigh, brushed the snow off his coat, shook it out of his boots, and seated himself once more.

"We must go to the right," he said decidedly. "The wind was blowing on our left before, but now it's straight in my face. Drive to the right," he repeated with decision.

Vasily Andreevich took his advice and turned to the right, but still there was no road. They went on in that direction for some time. The wind was as fierce as ever and it was snowing lightly.

"It seems, Vasily Andreevich, that we have gone quite astray," Nikita suddenly remarked, as if it were a pleasant thing. "What's that?" he added, pointing to some potato vines that showed up from under the snow.

Vasily Andreevich stopped the perspiring horse, whose deep sides were heaving heavily.

"What is it?"

"Why, we are on the Zakharov lands. See where we've got to!"

"Nonsense!" retorted Vasily Andreevich.

"It's not nonsense, Vasily Andreevich. It's the truth," replied Nikita. "You can feel that the sleigh is going over a potato-field, and there are the heaps of vines which have been carted here. It's the Zakharov factory land."

"Dear me, how we have gone astray!" said Vasily Andreevich. "What are we to do now?"

"We must go straight on, that's all. We shall come out somewhere— if not at Zakharova, then at the proprietor's farm," said Nikita.

Vasily Andreevich agreed, and drove as Nikita had indicated. So they went on for a considerable time. At times they came onto bare fields and the runners rattled over frozen lumps of earth. Sometimes they got onto a winter-rye field, or a fallow field on which they could see stalks of wormwood, and straws sticking up through the snow and swaying in the wind; sometimes they came onto deep and even white snow, above which nothing was to be seen.

The snow was falling from above and sometimes rose from below. The horse was evidently exhausted, his hair had all curled up from sweat and was covered with hoar-frost, and he went at a walk. Suddenly he stumbled and sat down in a ditch or water-course. Vasily Andreevich wanted to stop, but Nikita cried to him:

"Why stop? We've got in and must get out. Hey, pet! Hey, darling! Gee up, old fellow!" he shouted in a cheerful tone to the horse, jumping out of the sleigh and getting stuck in the ditch himself.

The horse gave a start and quickly climbed out onto the frozen bank. It was evidently a ditch that had been dug there.

"Where are we now?" asked Vasily Andreevich.

"We'll soon find out!" Nikita replied. "Go on, we'll get somewhere."

"Why, this must be the Goryachkin forest!" said Vasily Andreevich, pointing to something dark that appeared amid the snow in front of them.

"We'll see what forest it is when we get there," said Nikita.

He saw that beside the black thing they had noticed, dry, oblong willow-leaves were fluttering, and so he knew it was not a forest but a settlement, but he did not wish to say so. And in fact they had not gone twenty-five yards beyond the ditch before something in front of them, evidently trees, appeared black, and they heard a new and melancholy sound. Nikita had guessed right: it was not a wood, but a row of tall willows with a few leaves still fluttering on them here and there. They had evidently been planted along the ditch around a threshing-floor. Coming up to the willows, which moaned sadly in the wind, the horse suddenly planted his forelegs above the height of the sleigh, drew up his hind legs also, pulling the sleigh onto higher ground, and turned to the left, no longer sinking up to his knees in snow. They were back on a road.

"Well, here we are, but heaven only knows where!" said Nikita.

The horse kept straight along the road through the drifted snow, and before they had gone another hundred yards the straight line of the dark wattle wall of a barn showed up black before them, its roof heavily covered with snow which poured down from it. After passing the barn the road turned to the wind and they drove into a snow-drift. But ahead of them was a lane with houses on either side, so evidently the snow had been blown across the road and they had to drive through the drift. And so it was in fact. Having driven through the snow they came out onto a street. At the end house of the village some frozen clothes hanging on a line—shirts, one red and one white, trousers, leg-bands, and a petticoat—fluttered wildly in the wind. The white shirt in particular struggled desperately, waving its sleeves about.

"There now, either a lazy woman or a dead one has not taken her clothes down before the holiday," remarked Nikita, looking at the fluttering shirts.

III

At the entrance to the street the wind still raged and the road was thickly covered with snow, but well within the village it was calm, warm, and cheerful. At one house a dog was barking, at another a woman, covering her head with her coat, came running from somewhere and entered the door of a hut, stopping on the threshold to have a look at the passing sleigh. In the middle of the village girls could be heard singing.

Here in the village there seemed to be less wind and snow, and the frost was less keen.

"Why, this is Grishkino," said Vasily Andreevich.

"So it is," responded Nikita.

It really was Grishkino, which meant that they had gone too far to the left and had travelled some six miles, not quite in the direction they aimed at, but towards their destination nevertheless.

From Grishkino to Goryachkin was about another four miles.

In the middle of the village they almost ran into a tall man walking down the middle of the street.

"Who are you?" shouted the man, stopping the horse, and recognizing Vasily Andreevich he immediately took hold of the shaft, went along it hand over hand till he reached the sleigh, and placed himself on the driver's seat.

He was Isay, a peasant of Vasily Andreevich's acquaintance, and well known as the principal horse-thief in the district.

"Ah, Vasily Andreevich! Where are you off to?" asked Isay, enveloping Nikita in the odor of the vodka he had drunk.

"We were going to Goryachkin."

"And look where you've got to! You should have gone through Molchanovka."

"Should have, but didn't manage it," said Vasily Andreevich, holding in the horse.

"That's a good horse," said Isay, with a shrewd glance at Mukhorty, and with a practiced hand he tightened the loosened knot high in the horse's bushy tail.

"Are you going to stay the night?"

"No, friend. I must get on."

"Your business must be pressing. And who's this? Ah, Nikita Stepanych!"

"Who else?" replied Nikita. "But I say, good friend, how are we to avoid going astray again?"

"Where can you go astray here? Turn back straight down the street and then when you come out keep straight on. Don't turn to the left. You'll come out onto the high road, and then turn to the right."

"Where do we turn off the high road? As in summer, or the winter way?" asked Nikita.

"The winter way. As soon as you turn off you'll see some bushes, and opposite them there's a way-mark—a large oak, with branches— that's the way."

Vasily Andreevich turned the horse back and drove through the outskirts of the village.

"Why not stay the night?" Isay shouted after them.

But Vasily Andreevich didn't answer and touched the horse. Four miles of good road, two of which lay through the forest, seemed easy to manage, especially as the wind was apparently quieter and the snow had stopped.

Having driven along the trodden village street, darkened here and there by fresh manure, past the yard where the clothes hung out and where the white shirt had broken loose and was now attached only by one frozen sleeve, they came again within sound of the weird moan of the willows, and again emerged on the open fields. The storm, far from ceasing, seemed to have grown even stronger. The road was completely covered with drifting snow, and only the stakes showed that they had not lost their way. But even the stakes ahead of them were not easy to see, since the wind blew in their faces.

Vasily Andreevich screwed up his eyes, bent his head down, and looked out for the markers, but trusted mainly to the horse's sagacity, letting it take its own way. The horse really did not lose the road but followed its windings, turning now to the right and now to the left and sensing it under his feet, so that although the snow fell thicker and the wind strengthened, they still continued to see marks now to the left and now to the right of them.

So they travelled on for about ten minutes, when suddenly, through the slanting screen of wind-driven snow, something black showed up which moved in front of the horse.

This was another sleigh with fellow-travellers. Mukhorty overtook them, and struck his hoofs against the back of the sleigh in front of him.

"Pass on . . . hey there . . . get in front!" cried voices from the other sleigh.

Vasily Andreevich swerved aside to pass the other sleigh. In it sat three men and a woman, evidently visitors returning from a feast. One peasant was whacking the snow-covered croup of their little horse with a long switch, and the other two sitting in front waved their arms and shouted something. The woman, completely wrapped up and covered with snow, sat dozing and bumping at the back.

"Who are you?" shouted Vasily Andreevich.

"From A-a-a . . ." was all that could be heard.

"I say, where are you from?"

"From A-a-a-a!" one of the peasants shouted with all his might, but still it was impossible to make out who they were.

"Get along! Keep up!" shouted another, ceaselessly beating his horse with the switch.

"So you're coming from a feast, it seems?"

"Go on, go on! Faster, Simon! Get in front! Faster!"

The wings of the sleighs bumped against one another, almost got jammed but managed to separate, and the peasants' sleigh began to fall behind.

Their shaggy, big-bellied horse, all covered with snow, breathed heavily under the low shaft-bow and, evidently using the last of its strength, vainly endeavored to escape from the switch, hobbling with its short legs through the deep snow which it threw up under itself.

Its muzzle, young-looking, with the nether lip drawn up like that of a fish, nostrils distended and ears pressed back from fear, kept up for a few seconds near Nikita's shoulder and then began to fall behind.

"Just see what liquor does!" said Nikita. "They've tired that little horse to death. What pagans!"

For a few minutes they heard the panting of the tired little horse and the drunken shouting of the peasants. Then the panting and the shouts died away, and around them nothing could be heard but the whistling of the wind in their ears and now and then the squeak of their runners over a windswept part of the road.

This encounter cheered and enlivened Vasily Andreevich, and he drove on more boldly without examining the markers, urging on the horse and trusting him.

Nikita had nothing to do, and as usual in such circumstances he dozed, making up for much sleepless time. Suddenly the horse stopped and Nikita nearly fell forward onto his nose.

"You know we're off the track again!" said Vasily Andreevich.

"How's that?"

"Why, there are no markers to be seen. We must have got off the road again."

"Well, if we've lost the road we must find it," said Nikita curtly; getting out and stepping lightly on his pigeon-toed feet, he started once more going about on the snow.

He walked around for a long time, first disappearing then reappearing, and finally he came back.

"There's no road here. There may be one farther on," he said, getting into the sleigh.

It was already growing dark. The snow-storm had not increased, but had also not subsided.

"If we could only hear those peasants!" said Vasily Andreevich.

"Well they haven't caught up. We must have gone too far astray. Maybe they've lost their way too."

"Where are we to go then?" asked Vasily Andreevich.

"Why, we must let the horse find its own way," said Nikita. "He'll take us right. Let me have the reins."

Vasily Andreevich gave him the reins, the more willingly because his hands were beginning to feel frozen in his thick gloves.

Nikita took the reins, but only held them, trying not to shake them and rejoicing at his favorite's sagacity. And indeed the clever horse, turning first one ear and then the other now to one side, then to the other, began to wheel around.

"The one thing he can't do is talk," Nikita kept saying. "See what he's doing! Go on, go on! You know best. That's it, that's it!"

The wind was now blowing from behind and it felt warmer.

"Yes, he's clever," Nikita continued, admiring the horse. "A Kirgiz horse is strong but stupid. But this one—just see what he's doing with his ears! He doesn't need any telegraph. He can catch the scent a mile off."

Before another half-hour had passed they saw something dark ahead of them—a wood or a village—and again stakes appeared to the right. They had evidently come out onto the road.

"Why, that's Grishkino again!" Nikita suddenly exclaimed.

And indeed, there on their left was that same barn with snow flying from it, and farther on the same line with the frozen washing, shirts and trousers, which still fluttered desperately in the wind.

Again they drove into the street and again it grew quiet, warm, and cheerful; again they could see the manure-stained street and hear voices and songs and the barking of a dog. It was already so dark that there were lights in some of the windows.

Half-way through the village Vasily Andreevich turned the horse towards a large double-fronted brick house and stopped at the porch.

Nikita went to the lighted snow-covered window, in the rays of which flying snow-flakes glittered, and knocked at it with his whip.

"Who's there?" a voice replied to his knock.

"From Kresty, the Brekhunovs, dear fellow," answered Nikita. "Just come out for a minute."

Someone moved from the window, and a minute or two later there was the sound of the passage door as it came unstuck, then the latch of the outside door clicked and a tall white-bearded peasant, with a sheepskin coat thrown over his white holiday shirt, pushed his way out holding the door firmly against the wind, followed by a lad in a red shirt and high leather boots.

"Is that you, Andreevich?" asked the old man.

"Yes, friend, we've gone astray," said Vasily Andreevich. "We wanted to get to Goryachkin but found ourselves here. We went out a second time but lost our way again."

"Just see how you've gone astray!" said the old man. "Petrushka, go and open the gate!" he added, turning to the lad in the red shirt.

"All right," said the lad in a cheerful voice, and ran back into the passage.

"But we're not staying the night," said Vasily Andreevich.

"Where will you go? You'd better stay!"

"I'd be glad to, but I must go on. It's business, and it can't be helped."

"Well, warm yourself at least. The samovar's just ready."

"Warm myself? Yes, I'll do that," said Vasily Andreevich. "It won't get darker. The moon will rise and it will be lighter. Let's go in and warm ourselves, Nikita."

"Well, why not? Let's warm ourselves," replied Nikita, who was stiff with cold and anxious to warm his frozen limbs.

Vasily Andreevich went into the room with the old man, and Nikita drove through the gate opened for him by Petrushka, by whose advice he backed the horse under the penthouse. The ground was covered with manure and the tall bow over the horse's head caught against the beam. The hens and the cock had already settled to roost there, and clucked peevishly, clinging to the beam with their claws. The disturbed sheep shied and rushed aside trampling the frozen manure with their hooves. The dog yelped desperately with fright and anger and then burst out barking like a puppy at the stranger.

Nikita talked to them all, excused himself to the fowls and assured them that he wouldn't disturb them again, rebuked the sheep for being frightened without knowing why, and kept soothing the dog, while he tied up the horse.

"Now that'll be all right," he said, knocking the snow off his clothes. "Just hear how he barks!" he added, turning to the dog. "Be quiet, stupid! Be quiet. You're troubling yourself for nothing. We're not thieves, we're friends. . . ."

"And these, it's said, are the three domestic counsellors," remarked the lad, and with his strong arms he pushed under the pent-roof the sleigh that had remained outside.

"Why counsellors?" asked Nikita.

"That's what's printed in Paulson.[4] A thief creeps up to a house—the dog barks, that means, 'Be on your guard!' The cock crows, that means, 'Get up!' The cat licks herself—that means, 'A welcome guest is coming. Get ready to receive him!' " said the lad with a smile.

Petrushka could read and write and knew Paulson's primer, his only book, almost by heart, and he was fond of quoting sayings from it that he thought suited the occasion, especially when he'd had something to drink, as today.

"That's so," said Nikita.

"You must be chilled through and through," said Petrushka.

"Yes, I am," said Nikita, and they went across the yard and passage into the house.

IV

The household to which Vasily Andreevich had come was one of the richest in the village. The family had five allotments, besides renting other land. They had six horses, three cows, two calves, and some twenty sheep. There were twenty-two members belonging to the homestead: four married sons, six grandchildren (one of whom, Petrushka, was married), two great-grandchildren, three orphans, and four daughters-in-law with their babies. It was one of the few homesteads that remained undivided, but even here the dull internal work of disintegration which would inevitably lead to separation had already begun, starting as usual among the women. Two sons were living in Moscow as water-carriers, and one was in the army. At home now were the old man and his wife, their second son who managed the homestead, the eldest who had come

4. I. I. Paulson (1825–98) was the compiler of numerous textbooks for primary schools. This is a reference to his very popular *Book for Reading*.

from Moscow for the holiday, and all the women and children. Besides these members of the family there was a visitor, a neighbor who was godfather to one of the children.

Over the table in the room hung a lamp with a shade, which brightly lit up the tea-things, a bottle of vodka, and some refreshments, besides illuminating the brick walls, which in the far corner were hung with icons on both sides of which were pictures. At the head of the table sat Vasily Andreevich in a black sheepskin coat, sucking his frozen moustache and observing the room and the people around him with his prominent hawk-like eyes. With him sat the old, bald, white-bearded master of the house in a white homespun shirt, and next to him the son home from Moscow for the holiday—a man with a sturdy back, powerful shoulders, clad in a thin print shirt—then the second son, also broad-shouldered, who acted as head of the house, and then a lean red-haired peasant—the neighbor.

Having had a drink of vodka and something to eat, they were about to drink some tea, and the samovar standing on the floor beside the brick oven was already humming. The children could be seen in the top bunks and on the top of the oven. A woman sat on a lower bunk with a cradle beside her. The old housewife, her face covered with wrinkles which extended even to her lips, was waiting on Vasily Andreevich.

As Nikita entered the house she was offering her guest a small tumbler of thick glass which she had just filled with vodka.

"Don't refuse, Vasily Andreevich, you mustn't! Wish us a merry feast. Drink it, dear!" she said.

The sight and smell of vodka, especially now when he was chilled through and tired out, was very disturbing to Nikita's mind. He frowned, and having shaken the snow off his cap and coat, stopped in front of the icons as if not seeing anyone, crossed himself three times, and bowed to the icons. Then, turning to the old master of the house and bowing first to him, then to all those at the table, then to the women who stood by the oven, and muttering: "A merry holiday!" he began taking off his outer garments without looking at the table.

"Why, you're all covered with hoar-frost, old fellow!" said the eldest brother, looking at Nikita's snow-covered face, eyes, and beard.

Nikita took off his coat, shook it again, hung it up beside the oven, and came up to the table. He too was offered vodka. He went through a moment of painful hesitation and nearly took up the glass and emptied the clear fragrant liquid down his throat, but he glanced at Vasily Andreevich, remembered his oath and the boots that he had sold for drink, recalled the cooper, remembered his son for whom he had promised to buy a horse by spring, sighed, and declined it.

"I don't drink, thank you kindly," he said frowning, and sat down on a bench near the second window.

"How's that?" asked the eldest brother.

"I just don't drink," replied Nikita without lifting his eyes but looking askance at his scanty beard and moustache and getting the icicles out of them.

"It's not good for him," said Vasily Andreevich, munching a cracker after emptying his glass.

"Well, then, have some tea," said the kindly old hostess. "You must be chilled through, good soul. Why are you women dawdling so with the samovar?"

"It's ready," said one of the young women, and after flicking with her apron the top of the samovar which was now boiling over, she carried it with an effort to the table, raised it, and set it down with a thud.

Meanwhile Vasily Andreevich was telling how he had lost his way, how they had come back twice to this same village, and how they had gone astray and had met some drunken peasants. Their hosts were surprised, explained where and why they had missed their way, said who the tipsy people they had met were, and told them how they ought to proceed.

"A little child could find the way to Molchanovka from here. All you have to do is to take the right turn from the high road. There's a bush you can see just there. But you didn't even get that far!" said the neighbor.

"You'd better stay the night. The women will make up beds for you," said the old woman persuasively.

"You could go on in the morning and it would be pleasanter," said the old man, confirming what his wife had said.

"I can't, friend. Business!" said Vasily Andreevich. "Lose an hour and you can't catch it up in a year," he added, remembering the grove and the dealers who might snatch that deal from him. "We'll get there, won't we?" he said, turning to Nikita.

Nikita didn't answer for some time, apparently still intent on thawing out his beard and moustache.

"If only we don't go astray again," he replied gloomily.

He was gloomy because he passionately longed for some vodka, and the only thing that could assuage that longing was tea and he hadn't yet been offered any.

"But we have only to reach the turning and then we can't go wrong. The road will lead through the forest the whole way," said Vasily Andreevich.

"Just as you please, Vasily Andreevich. If we're to go, then let's go," said Nikita, taking the glass of tea he was offered.

"We'll drink our tea and be off."

Nikita said nothing but only shook his head, and carefully pouring some tea into his saucer began warming his hands, the fingers of which were always swollen from hard work, over the steam. Then, biting off a tiny bit of sugar, he bowed to his hosts, said, "To your health!" and sipped the steaming liquid.

"If somebody would see us as far as the turning," said Vasily Andreevich.

"Well, we can do that," said the eldest son. "Petrushka will harness and go that far with you."

"Well, then, put in the horse, lad, and I'll be grateful to you for it."

"Oh, what for, dear man?" said the kindly old woman. "We're glad to do it."

"Petrushka, go and put in the mare," said the eldest brother.

"All right," replied Petrushka with a smile, and promptly snatching his cap down from a nail, he ran away to harness.

While the horse was being harnessed the talk returned to the point at which it had stopped when Vasily Andreevich drove up to the window. The old man had been complaining to his neighbor, the village elder, about his third son who hadn't sent him anything for the holiday though he'd sent a French shawl to his wife.

"The young people are getting out of hand," said the old man.

"And how!" said the neighbor. "There's no managing them! They know too much. There's Demochkin, who broke his father's arm. It's all from being too clever, it seems."

Nikita listened, watched their faces, and evidently would have liked to share in the conversation, but he was too busy drinking his tea and only nodded his head approvingly. He emptied one tumbler after another and grew warmer and warmer, more and more comfortable. The talk continued on the same subject for a long time—the harmfulness of a household dividing up—and it was clearly not an abstract discussion but concerned the question of a separation in that house; this separation was demanded by the second son who sat there morosely silent.

It was evidently a sore subject and absorbed them all, but out of propriety they didn't discuss their private affairs before strangers. At last, however, the old man couldn't restrain himself, and with tears in his eyes declared that he would not consent to a break-up of the family during his lifetime, that his house was prospering, thank God, but that if they separated they would all have to go begging.

"Just like the Matveevs," said the neighbor. "They used to have a proper house, but now that they've split up none of them has anything."

"And that's what you want to happen to us," said the old man, turning to his son.

The son made no reply and there was an awkward pause. The silence was broken by Petrushka, who having harnessed the horse had returned to the hut a few minutes before and had been listening all the while with a smile.

"There's a fable about that in Paulson," he said. "A father gave his sons a broom to break. At first they couldn't break it, but when they took it twig by twig they broke it easily. It's the same here," he said and gave a broad smile. "I'm ready!" he added.

"If you're ready, let's go," said Vasily Andreevich. "And as to separating, don't you allow it, Grandfather. You got everything together and you're the master. Go to the Justice of the Peace. He'll say how things should be done."

"He carries on so, carries on so," the old man continued in a whining tone. "There's no doing anything with him. It's as if the devil possessed him."

Meanwhile Nikita finished his fifth glass of tea and laid it on its side instead of turning it upside down, hoping to be offered a sixth glass. But there was no more water in the samovar, so the hostess did not fill it up for him. Besides, Vasily Andreevich was putting his things on, so there was nothing for Nikita to do except get up too, put back into the sugar-basin the lump of sugar he'd nibbled all around, wipe his perspiring face with the skirt of his sheepskin, and go put on his overcoat.

Having put it on he sighed deeply, thanked his hosts, said good-bye, and went out of the warm bright room into the cold dark passage, through which the wind was howling and where snow was blowing through the cracks of the shaking door, and from there into the yard.

Petrushka stood in his sheepskin in the middle of the yard by his horse, repeating some lines from Paulson's primer. He said with a smile:

> "The storm covers the sky in darkness
> Spinning the snowy whirlwinds
> Now it howls like a wild beast
> Then it cries like a little child."[5]

Nikita nodded approvingly as he arranged the reins.

The old man, seeing Vasily Andreevich off, brought a lantern into the passage to light his way, but it was blown out at once. Even in the yard it was evident that the snowstorm had become more violent.

"Well, some weather!" thought Vasily Andreevich. "Perhaps we may not get there after all. But there's nothing to be done. Business! Besides, we're all ready, our host's horse has been harnessed; we'll get there with God's help."

Their aged host also thought they ought not to go, but he'd already tried to persuade them to stay and hadn't been listened to.

"It's no use asking them again. Maybe my age makes me timid. They'll get there all right, and at least we'll get to bed in good time and without any fuss," he thought.

Petrushka didn't think about danger. He knew the road and the whole district so well, and the lines about "snowy whirlwinds spinning around" described what was happening outside so aptly that it cheered him up. Nikita didn't want to go at all, but he'd been accustomed not to get his own way and to serve others for so long that there was no one to hinder the departing travellers.

5. The initial stanza of a well-known lyric entitled "Winter Evening" (1825) by Russia's most famous poet, A. S. Pushkin.

V

Vasily Andreevich went over to his sleigh, found it in the darkness with difficulty, climbed in and took the reins.

"Go on in front!" he cried.

Petrushka kneeling in his low sleigh started his horse. Mukhorty, who'd been neighing for some time, now scenting a mare ahead of him started after her, and they drove out into the street. They drove again through the outskirts of the village and along the same road, past the yard where the frozen linen had hung (which, however, was no longer to be seen), past the same barn, which was now covered with snow almost up to the roof and from which snow was endlessly pouring, past the same dismally moaning, whistling, and swaying willows, and again entered into the sea of blustering snow raging from above and below. The wind was so strong that when it blew from the side and the travellers steered against it, it tilted both sleighs and turned the horses to one side. Petrushka drove his good mare in front at a brisk trot and kept shouting heartily. Mukhorty pressed after her.

After travelling so for about ten minutes, Petrushka turned round and shouted something. Neither Vasily Andreevich nor Nikita could hear anything because of the wind, but they guessed that they'd arrived at the turning. In fact Petrushka had turned to the right, and now the wind that had blown from the side blew straight in their faces, and through the snow they saw something dark on their right. It was the bush at the turning.

"Well now, God speed you!"

"Thank you, Petrushka!"

"The storm covers the sky in darkness!" shouted Petrushka as he disappeared.

"There's a poet for you!" muttered Vasily Andreevich, pulling at the reins.

"Yes, a fine lad—a true peasant," said Nikita.

They drove on.

Nikita, wrapping his coat closely about him and pressing his head down so close to his shoulders that his short beard covered his throat, sat silently, trying not to lose the warmth he'd obtained while drinking tea in the house. Before him he saw the straight lines of the shafts which constantly deceived him into thinking they were on a well-travelled road, and the horse's swaying rump with his knotted tail blown to one side, and farther ahead the high shaft-bow and the swaying head and neck of the horse with its waving mane. Now and then he caught sight of a signpost, so he knew they were still on a road and there was nothing for him to be concerned about.

Vasily Andreevich drove on, leaving it to the horse to keep to the road. But Mukhorty, though he'd had some breathing-space in the village, ran reluctantly, and seemed now and then to get off the road, so that Vasily Andreevich had to correct him repeatedly.

"Here's a stake to the right, and another, and here's a third," Vasily Andreevich counted, "and here's the forest in front," he thought, as he looked at something dark in front of him. But what had seemed a forest was only a bush. They passed it and drove on for another hundred yards but there was no fourth marker nor any forest.

"We must reach the forest soon," Vasily Andreevich thought, and animated by the vodka and the tea he didn't stop but shook the reins, and the good obedient horse responded, now ambling, now trotting slowly in the direction in which he was sent, though he knew that he was not going the right way. Ten minutes went by, but there was still no forest.

"There now, we must have gone astray again," Vasily Andreevich said pulling up.

Nikita silently got out of the sleigh and holding his coat, which the wind first wrapped closely about him and then almost tore off, he started to feel about in the snow, going first to one side, then to the other. Three or four times he was completely lost to sight. At last he returned and took the reins from Vasily Andreevich's hand.

"We must go to the right," he said sternly and peremptorily, as he turned the horse.

"Well, if it's to the right, then go to the right," said Vasily Andreevich, yielding the reins to Nikita and thrusting his freezing hands into his sleeves.

Nikita did not reply.

"Now then, friend, stir yourself!" he shouted to the horse, but in spite of the shake of the reins Mukhorty moved only at a walk.

The snow in places was up to his knees, and the sleigh moved by fits and starts with his every movement.

Nikita took the whip that hung over the front of the sleigh and struck him once. The good horse, unused to the whip, sprang forward and moved at a trot, but immediately fell back into an amble and then to a walk. So they went on for five minutes. It was dark and the snow whirled from above and rose from below, so that sometimes the shaft-bow could not be seen. At times the sleigh seemed to stand still and the field seemed to run backwards. Suddenly the horse stopped abruptly, evidently aware of something close in front of him. Nikita sprang lightly out again, throwing down the reins, and went ahead to see what had brought him to a standstill, but hardly had he made a step in front of the horse before his feet slipped and he went rolling down an incline.

"Whoa, whoa, whoa!" he said to himself as he fell, and tried to stop his fall but couldn't; he only stopped when his feet plunged into a thick layer of snow that had drifted to the bottom of the hollow.

The fringe of a snowdrift that hung on the edge of the hollow, disturbed by Nikita's fall, showered down on him and got inside his collar.

"What a thing to do!" said Nikita reproachfully, addressing the drift and the hollow and shaking the snow out from under his collar.

"Nikita! Hey, Nikita!" shouted Vasily Andreevich from above.

But Nikita didn't reply. He was too occupied shaking the snow out and searching for the whip he dropped when rolling down the incline. Having found the whip he tried to climb straight up the bank, but it was impossible to do so: he kept rolling down again. He had to go along at the foot of the hollow to find a way up. About seven yards farther on he managed with difficulty to crawl up the incline on all fours; then he followed the edge of the hollow back to the place where the horse should have been. He couldn't see either horse or sleigh, but as he walked against the wind he heard Vasily Andreevich's shouts and Mukhorty's neighing, calling him.

"I'm coming! I'm coming! What are you cackling for?" he muttered.

Only when he'd come up to the sleigh could he make out the horse, and Vasily Andreevich standing beside it looking gigantic.

"Where the devil did you vanish to? We must go back, even if only to Grishkino," he began reproaching Nikita.

"I'd be glad to get back, Vasily Andreevich, but which way are we to go? There's such a ravine here that once we get in we won't get out again. I got stuck so fast that I could hardly get out."

"What shall we do, then? We can't stay here! We must go somewhere!" said Vasily Andreevich.

Nikita said nothing. He seated himself in the sleigh with his back to the wind, took off his boots, shook out the snow that had got into them, and taking some straw from the bottom, carefully plugged a hole in his left boot.

Vasily Andreevich remained silent, as though now leaving everything to Nikita. Having put his boots on again, Nikita drew his feet into the sleigh, put on his mittens, took up the reins, and directed the horse along the side of the ravine. But they had not gone a hundred yards before the horse stopped short again. The ravine was in front of him again.

Nikita climbed out and once again trudged about in the snow. He did this for a considerable time and at last appeared from the opposite side to that from which he'd started.

"Vasily Andreevich, are you alive?" he called out.

"Here!" replied Vasily Andreevich. "Well, what now?"

"I can't make anything out. It's too dark. There's nothing but ravines. We must drive against the wind again."

They set off once more. Again Nikita went stumbling through the snow, again he fell in, again he climbed out and trudged about, and at last quite out of breath he sat down beside the sledge.

"Well, what now?" asked Vasily Andreevich.

"Why, I'm quite worn out and the horse won't go."

"Then what's to be done?"

"Why, wait a minute."

Nikita went away again but soon returned.

"Follow me!" he said, going in front of the horse.

Vasily Andreevich no longer gave orders but implicitly did what Nikita told him.

"Here, follow me!" Nikita shouted, stepping quickly to the right, and seizing the rein he led Mukhorty down towards a snow-drift.

At first the horse held back, then he jerked forward, hoping to leap the drift, but he didn't have the strength and sank into it up to his collar.

"Get out!" Nikita called to Vasily Andreevich who still sat in the sleigh, and taking hold of one shaft he moved the sleigh closer to the horse. "It's hard, brother!" he said to Mukhorty, "but it can't be helped. Make an effort! Now, now, just a little one!" he shouted.

The horse gave a tug, then another, but failed to clear himself and settled down again as if considering something.

"Now, brother, this won't do!" Nikita admonished him. "Once more!"

Again Nikita tugged at the shaft on his side, and Vasily Andreevich did the same on the other.

Mukhorty lifted his head and then gave a sudden jerk.

"That's it! That's it!" cried Nikita. "Don't be afraid—you won't sink!"

One plunge, another, and a third, and at last Mukhorty was out of the snow-drift, and stood still, breathing heavily and shaking the snow off himself. Nikita wished to lead him farther, but Vasily Andreevich, in his two fur coats, was so out of breath that he couldn't walk any farther and dropped into the sleigh.

"Let me catch my breath!" he said, unfastening the kerchief with which he'd tied the collar of his fur coat at the village.

"It's all right here. You lie there," said Nikita. "I'll lead him along." And with Vasily Andreevich in the sleigh he led the horse by the bridle about ten paces down and then up a slight rise, and stopped.

The place where Nikita had stopped was not completely in the hollow where the snow sweeping down from the hillocks might have buried them altogether, but it was still partly sheltered from the wind by the side of the ravine. There were moments when the wind seemed to abate a little, but that did not last long and as if to make up for that respite, the storm swept down with tremendous vigor and tore and whirled the more fiercely. Such a gust struck them at the moment when Vasily Andreevich, having recovered his breath, got out of the sleigh and went up to Nikita to consult him as to what they should do. They both bent down involuntarily and waited till the violence of the squall passed. Mukhorty too laid back his ears and shook his head discontentedly. As soon as the violence of the blast had abated a little, Nikita took off his mittens, stuck them into his belt, breathed onto his hands, and began to undo the straps of the shaft-bow.

"What are you doing there?" asked Vasily Andreevich.

"Unharnessing. What else is there to do? I have no strength left," said Nikita as though excusing himself.

"Can't we drive somewhere?"

"No, we can't. We'll only kill the horse. Why, the poor beast isn't himself now," said Nikita, pointing to the horse, which was standing submissively waiting for what might come, with his steep wet sides heaving heavily. "We'll have to stay the night here," he said, as if preparing to spend the night at an inn, and he proceeded to unfasten the collar-straps. The buckles came undone.

"But won't we be frozen?" inquired Vasily Andreevich.

"Well, if we are, we can't help it," replied Nikita.

VI

Although Vasily Andreevich felt quite warm in his two fur coats, especially after struggling in the snow-drift, a cold shiver ran down his back on realizing that he must really spend the night where they were. To calm himself he sat down in the sleigh and got out his cigarettes and matches.

Nikita meanwhile unharnessed Mukhorty. He unstrapped the belly-band and the back-band, took away the reins, loosened the collar-strap, and removed the shaft-bow, talking to him all the time to encourage him.

"Now come on! come on!" he said, leading him clear of the shafts. "Now we'll tie you up here and I'll put some straw down and take off your bridle. When you've had a bite you'll feel more cheerful."

But Mukhorty was restless and evidently not comforted by Nikita's remarks. He stepped first on one foot, then on another, and pressed close against the sleigh, turning his back to the wind and rubbing his head on Nikita's sleeve. Then, as if not to offend Nikita by refusing his offer of the straw put before him, he hurriedly snatched a wisp out of the sleigh, but immediately decided that it was now not the time to think of straw and threw it down; the wind instantly scattered it, carried it away, and covered it with snow.

"Now we'll set up a signal," said Nikita, and turning the front of the sleigh to the wind he tied the shafts together with a strap and set them up on end in front of the sledge. "There now, when the snow covers us up, good folk will see the shafts and dig us out," he said, slapping his mittens together and putting them on. "That's what the old folks taught us!"

Vasily Andreevich meanwhile had unfastened his coat, and holding its skirts up for shelter, struck one sulphur match after another on the steel box. But his hands trembled, and one match after another either did not kindle or was blown out by the wind just as he was lifting it up to his cigarette. At last a match did catch fire, and its flame lit up for a moment the fur of his coat, his hand with the gold ring on the bent forefinger, and the snow-sprinkled oat-straw that stuck out from under the sacking. The cigarette lit up, he eagerly took a whiff or two, inhaled the smoke, let it out through his moustache, and would have inhaled again, but the wind tore off the burning tobacco and whirled it away as it had done the straw.

But even these few puffs had cheered him up.

"If we must spend the night here, we must!" he said with decision. "Wait a bit, I'll arrange a flag as well," he added, picking up the kerchief which he'd thrown down in the sleigh after taking it from around his collar, and drawing off his gloves and standing up on the front of the sledge and stretching to reach the strap, he tied the handkerchief to it with a tight knot.

The kerchief immediately began to flutter wildly, now clinging round the shaft, now suddenly streaming out, stretching and flapping.

"See what a fine flag!" said Vasily Andreevich, admiring his handiwork and letting himself down into the sleigh. "We would be warmer together, but there isn't room enough for two," he added.

"I'll find a place," Nikita said. "But I must cover the horse first—he sweated so, poor thing. Let go!" he added, drawing the sacking from under Vasily Andreevich.

Having got the sacking, he folded it in two, and after taking off the breechband and pad, covered Mukhorty with it.

"Anyhow it'll be warmer, silly!" he said, putting the breechband and the pad back on the horse over the sacking. Then having finished that, he returned to the sleigh, and addressing Vasily Andreevich, said: "You won't need the sackcloth, will you? And let me have some straw."

Having taken these things from under Vasily Andreevich, Nikita went behind the sleigh, dug out a hole for himself in the snow, put straw into it, wrapped his coat well round him, covered himself with the sackcloth, and pulling his cap well down seated himself on the straw he'd spread out, and leant against the wooden back of the sleigh to shelter himself from the wind and snow.

Vasily Andreevich shook his head disapprovingly at what Nikita was doing, as he disapproved in general of the peasant's stupidity and lack of education, and he began to settle himself down for the night.

He smoothed the remaining straw over the bottom of the sledge, putting more of it under his side. Then he thrust his hands into his sleeves and settled down, sheltering his head in the corner of the sledge from the wind in front.

He did not wish to sleep. He lay there and thought: thought about the one thing that constituted the sole aim, meaning, pleasure, and pride of his life—about how much money he'd made and might still make, about how much other people he knew had made and possessed, and about how those others had made and were making it, and how

he, like them, might still make much more. The purchase of the Goryachkin grove was a matter of immense importance to him. By that one
deal he hoped to make perhaps ten thousand rubles. He began mentally
to reckon the value of the wood he'd inspected in autumn, and on five
acres of which he'd counted all the trees.

"The oaks will go for runners. The undergrowth will take care of
itself, and there'll still be some thirty sazhens[6] of fire-wood left on each
desyatin,"[7] he said to himself. "That means there'll be at least two
hundred and twenty-five rubles' worth left on each desyatin. Fifty-six
desyatins means fifty-six hundreds, and fifty-six hundreds, and fifty-six
tens, and another fifty-six tens, and then fifty-six fives. . . ." He saw
that it came out to more than twelve thousand rubles, but couldn't
reckon it up exactly without an abacus. "But I won't give ten thousand,
anyhow. I'll give about eight thousand with a deduction on account of
the glades. I'll grease the surveyor's palm—give him a hundred rubles,
or a hundred and fifty, and he'll reckon that there are some five desyatins
of glade to be deducted. And he'll let it go for eight thousand. Three
thousand cash down. That'll move him, have no fear!" he thought, and
pressed his pocket-book with his forearm.

"God only knows how we missed the turning. The forest ought to be
there, and a watchman's hut, and dogs barking. But the damned things
don't bark when they're wanted." He turned his collar down from his
ear and listened, but as before only the whistling of the wind could be
heard, the flapping and fluttering of the kerchief tied to the shafts, and
the pelting of the snow against the woodwork of the sleigh. He covered
up his ear again.

"If I'd known I would have stayed the night. Well, no matter, we'll
get there to-morrow. It's only one day lost. The others won't travel in
such weather." Then he remembered that on the 9th he had to receive
payment from the butcher for his oxen. "He meant to come himself,
but he won't find me, and my wife won't know how to receive the
money. She doesn't know the right way of doing things," he thought,
recalling how at their party the day before she hadn't known how to
treat the police-officer who was their guest. "Of course she's only a
woman! Where could she have seen anything? In my father's time what
was our house like? Just a rich peasant's house: just an oatmill and an
inn—that was the whole property. But what have I done during these
fifteen years? A shop, two taverns, a flour-mill, a grain-store, two farms
leased out, and a house with an iron-roofed barn," he thought proudly.
"Not as it was in Father's time! Who is talked about in the whole district
now? Brekhunov! And why? Because I stick to business. I take trouble,
not like others who lie in bed or waste their time on foolishness while
I don't sleep nights. Blizzard or no blizzard I start out. So business gets

6. Russian measure of length, equivalent to seven   7. Russian measure of land, equivalent to 2.7
feet.   acres.

done. They think money-making is a joke. No, you take pains and rack your brains! You get overtaken out of doors at night, like this, or keep awake night after night till the thoughts whirling in your head make the pillow turn," he thought with pride. "They think people get along through luck. After all, the Mironovs are now millionaires. And why? Take pains and God gives. If only He grants me health!"

The thought that he might himself become a millionaire like Mironov, who began with nothing, so excited Vasily Andreevich that he felt the need of talking to somebody. But there was no one to talk to. . . . If only he could have reached Goryachkin he would've talked to the landlord and shown him a thing or two.

"Just see how it blows! It will cover us up so deep in snow that we won't be able to get out in the morning!" he thought, listening to a gust of wind that blew against the front of the sleigh, bending it and lashing the snow against it. He raised himself and looked round. All he could see through the whirling darkness was Mukhorty's dark head, his back covered by the fluttering sacking, and his thick knotted tail; while all around, in front and behind, was the same fluctuating white darkness, sometimes seeming to get a little lighter and sometimes growing even denser.

"A pity I listened to Nikita," he thought. "We ought to have driven on. We would have come out somewhere, if only back to Grishkino and stayed the night at Taras's. As it is we must sit here all night. But what was I thinking about? Yes, God gives to those who take trouble, but not to loafers, lazybones, or fools. I must have a smoke!"

He sat down again, got out his cigarette-case, and stretched himself out flat on his stomach, screening the matches with the skirt of his coat. But the wind found its way in and put out match after match. At last he got one to burn and lit a cigarette. He was very glad that he had managed to do what he wanted, and though the wind smoked more of the cigarette than he did, he still managed two or three puffs and felt more cheerful. He leant back again, wrapped himself up, started reflecting and remembering, then suddenly and quite unexpectedly lost consciousness and fell asleep.

Suddenly something seemed to give him a push and awoke him. Whether it was Mukhorty who'd pulled some straw from under him, or whether something within him had startled him, at all events it woke him, and his heart began to beat faster and faster so that the sleigh seemed to tremble under him. He opened his eyes. Everything around him was just as before. "It looks lighter," he thought. "I expect it won't be long before dawn." But at once he remembered that it was lighter because the moon had risen. He sat up and looked first at the horse. Mukhorty still stood with his back to the wind, shivering all over. One side of the sacking, which was completely covered with snow, had been blown back, the breeching had slipped down, and the snow-covered head with its waving forelock and mane were now more visible. Vasily Andreevich leant over the back of the sleigh and looked behind. Nikita still sat in the same position in which he'd settled himself. The sacking with which he was covered, and his legs, were covered with thick snow.

"If only that peasant doesn't freeze to death! His clothes are so wretched. I may be held responsible for him. What shiftless people they are—such a lack of education," thought Vasily Andreevich, and he felt like taking the sacking off the horse and putting it over Nikita, but it would be very cold to get out and move about; moreover, the horse might freeze to death. "Why did I bring him with me? It was all her stupidity!" he thought, recalling his unloved wife, and he rolled over into his old place at the front part of the sleigh. "My uncle once spent a whole night like this," he reflected, "and was all right." But another case came to mind at once. "But when they dug Sebastian out he was dead—stiff like a frozen carcass. If I'd only stopped for the night in Grishkino all this would never have happened!"

And wrapping his coat carefully around him so that none of the warmth of the fur would be wasted but would warm him all over, neck, knees, and feet, he shut his eyes and tried to sleep again. But try as he would, he couldn't get drowsy; on the contrary he felt wide awake and animated. Again he began counting his gains and the debts owed to him, again he began bragging and feeling pleased with himself and his position; but all this was continually disturbed by a stealthily approaching fear and by the unpleasant regret that he hadn't remained in Grishkino.

"How different it would be to be lying warm on a bench!" He turned over several times in his attempts to get into a comfortable position, more sheltered from the wind; he wrapped up his legs closer, shut his eyes, and lay still. But either his legs in their strong felt boots began to ache from being bent in one position, or the wind blew in somewhere; after lying still for a short time again he began to recall the disturbing fact that he might now be lying quietly in the warm hut at Grishkino. He sat up again, turned about, muffled himself up, and settled down again.

Once he imagined that he heard a distant cock-crow. He felt glad, turned down his coat-collar and listened with strained attention; but in spite of all his efforts nothing could be heard but the wind whistling between the shafts, the flapping of the kerchief, and the snow pelting against the frame of the sleigh.

Nikita sat just as he had done all the time, not moving and not even answering Vasily Andreevich who'd addressed him a couple of times. "He doesn't care a bit—he's probably asleep!" thought Vasily Andreevich with vexation, looking behind the sleigh at Nikita who was covered with a thick layer of snow.

Vasily Andreevich got up and lay down again some twenty times. It seemed to him that the night would never end. "It must be getting near morning," he thought, getting up and looking around. "Let's have a look at my watch. It will be cold to unbutton, but if I only know that it's getting near morning, I'll feel more cheerful at any rate. We could begin harnessing."

In the depth of his heart Vasily Andreevich knew that it couldn't be near morning yet, but he was growing more and more afraid, and wished both to know and yet to deceive himself. He carefully undid the fastening of his sheepskin, pushed in his hand, and felt about for a long time before he got to his waistcoat. With great difficulty he managed to draw out his silver watch with its enamelled flower design, and tried to make out the time. He could not see anything without a light. Again he went down on his knees and elbows as he had done when he lighted a cigarette, got out his matches, and proceeded to strike one. This time he went to work more carefully, and feeling with his fingers for a match with the largest head and the greatest amount of phosphorus, lit it at the first try. Bringing the face of the watch under the light he could hardly believe his eyes. . . . It was only ten minutes past twelve. Almost the whole night was still before him.

"Oh, how long the night is!" he thought, feeling a cold shudder run down his back. Having fastened his fur coats again and wrapped himself up, he snuggled into a corner of the sleigh intending to wait patiently. Suddenly, above the monotonous roar of the wind, he clearly distinguished another new and living sound. It steadily strengthened, and having become quite clear diminished just as gradually. Beyond all doubt it was a wolf, and he was so near that the movement of his jaws as he changed his cry was carried along the wind. Vasily Andreevich turned back the collar of his coat and listened attentively. Mukhorty strained to listen too, moving his ears; when the wolf had ceased its howling he shifted from foot to foot and gave a warning snort. After this Vasily Andreevich couldn't fall asleep again or even calm himself. The more he tried to think of his accounts, his business, his reputation, his worth and his wealth, the more was he mastered by fear, and regrets that he hadn't stayed at Grishkino for the night dominated and mingled in all his thoughts.

"To hell with the forest! Things were all right without it, thank God. Ah, if we'd only stayed there for the night!" he said to himself. "They say it's drunkards that freeze," he thought, "and I've had something to drink." Observing his own sensations he noticed that he was beginning to shiver, without knowing whether it was from cold or from fear. He tried to wrap himself up and lie down as before, but could no longer do so. He couldn't stay in one position. He wanted to get up, to do something to master the gathering fear that was rising in him and against which he felt himself powerless. He again got out his cigarettes and matches, but there were only three matches left and they were bad ones. The phosphorus rubbed off them all without lighting.

"To hell with you! Damned thing! Curse you!" he muttered, not knowing whom or what he was cursing, and he flung away the crushed cigarette. He was about to throw away the matchbox too, but checked the movement of his hand and put the box in his pocket instead. He was seized with such unrest that he could no longer remain in one spot. He climbed out of the sleigh and standing with his back to the wind began to shift his belt again, fastening it lower down on his waist and tightening it.

"What's the use of lying here and waiting for death? Better mount the horse and get away!" The thought suddenly occurred to him. "The horse will move when he has someone on his back. As for him," he thought of Nikita—"it's all the same to him whether he lives or dies. What's his life worth? He won't grudge his life, but I have something to live for, thank God."

He untied the horse, threw the reins over his neck and tried to mount, but his coats and boots were so heavy that he failed. Then he clambered up in the sleigh and tried to mount from there, but it tilted under his weight, and he failed again. At last he drew Mukhorty nearer to the sleigh, cautiously balanced on one side of it, and managed to lie on his stomach across the horse's back. After lying like that for a while he shifted forward once and again, threw a leg over, and finally seated himself, supporting his feet on the loose breeching-straps. The shaking of the sleigh awoke Nikita. He raised himself, and it seemed to Vasily Andreevich that he said something.

"Listen to such fools as you! Am I to die like this for nothing?" exclaimed Vasily Andreevich. Tucking the loose skirts of his fur coat in under his knees, he turned the horse and rode away from the sledge in the direction in which he thought the forest and the forester's hut must be.

VII

From the time he'd covered himself with the sackcloth and seated himself behind the sleigh, Nikita hadn't stirred. Like all those who live in touch with nature and have known want, he was patient and could wait for hours, even days, without growing restless or irritable. He heard his master call him, but didn't answer because he didn't want to move or talk. Though he still felt some warmth from the tea he'd drunk and from his energetic struggle when clambering about in the snowdrift, he knew that this warmth would not last long and that he had no strength left to warm himself again by moving about; he felt as tired as a horse when it stops and refuses to go further in spite of the whip, and its master sees that it must be fed before it can work again. The foot in the boot with a hole in it had already grown numb, and he could no longer feel his big toe. Besides that, his whole body began to feel colder and colder.

The thought that he might, and very probably would, die that night occurred to him, but didn't seem particularly unpleasant or dreadful. It didn't seem particularly unpleasant, because his whole life had never been a continual holiday; on the contrary it was an unceasing round of toil of which he was beginning to feel weary. And it didn't seem particularly dreadful, because besides the masters he'd served here, like Vasily Andreevich, he always felt himself dependent on the Chief Master, He who had sent him into this life; he knew that when dying he would still be in that Master's power and would not be ill-used by Him. "It seems a pity to give up what one's used to and accustomed to. But there's nothing to be done, I'll get used to new things."

"Sins?" he thought, and remembered his drunkenness, the money that had gone on drink, how he'd offended his wife, his cursing, his neglect of church and the fasts, and all the things the priest blamed him for at confession. "Of course they're sins. But then, did I take them on myself? That's evidently the way God made me. Well, and the sins? Where am I to escape to?"

So at first he thought of what might happen to him that night, and then didn't return to such thoughts but gave himself up to whatever recollections came into his head by themselves. Now he thought of Martha's arrival, of the drunkenness among the workers and his own renunciation of drink, then of their present journey, of Taras's house and the talk about the breaking-up of the family, then of his own lad, of Mukhorty now sheltered under the sacking, and then of his master who made the sleigh creak as he tossed about in it. "I expect you're sorry yourself that you started out, dear man," he thought. "It would seem hard to leave a life such as his! It's not like the likes of us."

Then all these recollections began to grow confused and got mixed in his head, and he fell asleep.

But when Vasily Andreevich, getting on the horse, jerked the sleigh, against the back of which Nikita was leaning, and it shifted away and hit him in the back with one of its runners, he awoke and had to change his position whether he liked it or not. Straightening his legs with difficulty and shaking the snow off them he got up, and an agonizing cold immediately penetrated his whole body. On making out what was happening he called to Vasily Andreevich to leave him the sacking which the horse no longer needed, so that he might wrap himself in it.

But Vasily Andreevich didn't stop, but disappeared amid the powdery snow.

Left alone, Nikita considered for a moment what he should do. He felt that he hadn't the strength to go off in search of a house. It was no longer possible to sit down in his old place—it was now all filled with snow. He felt that he couldn't get warmer in the sleigh either, for there was nothing to cover himself with, and his coat and sheepskin no longer warmed him at all. He felt as cold as though he had nothing on but a shirt. He became frightened. "Lord, heavenly Father!" he muttered, and was comforted by the consciousness that he was not alone, but that there was One who heard him and would not abandon him. He gave a deep sigh, and keeping the sackcloth over his head, he got inside the sleigh and lay down in the place where his master had been.

But he couldn't get warm in the sleigh either. At first he shivered all over; then the shivering ceased and little by little he began to lose consciousness. He didn't know whether he was dying or falling asleep, but he felt equally prepared for the one as for the other.

VIII

Meanwhile Vasily Andreevich, with his feet and the ends of the reins, urged the horse on in the direction in which for some reason he expected the forest and forester's hut to be. The snow covered his eyes and the wind seemed intent on stopping him, but bending forward and constantly lapping his coat over and pushing it between himself and the cold harness pad which prevented him from sitting properly, he kept urging the horse on. Mukhorty ambled on obediently though with difficulty, in the direction in which he was driven.

Vasily Andreevich rode for about five minutes straight ahead, as he thought, seeing nothing but the horse's head and the white waste, and hearing only the whistle of the wind about the horse's ears and his coat collar.

Suddenly a dark patch showed up in front of him. His heart beat with joy, and he rode towards the object, already seeing in imagination the walls of village houses. But the dark patch was not stationary, it kept moving; it was not a village but some tall stalks of wormwood sticking up through the snow on the boundary between two fields, and desperately tossing about under the pressure of the wind which beat it all to one side and whistled through it. The sight of that wormwood tormented by the pitiless wind made Vasily Andreevich shudder, he knew not why, and he hurriedly began urging the horse on, not noticing that when riding up to the wormwood he'd quite changed his direction and was now heading the opposite way, though still imagining that he was riding towards where the hut should be. But the horse kept making towards the right, and Vasily Andreevich kept guiding it to the left.

Again something dark appeared in front of him. Again he rejoiced, convinced that now it was certainly a village. But once more it was the same boundary line overgrown with wormwood, once more the same wormwood desperately tossed by the wind and carrying unreasoning terror to his heart. But its being the same wormwood was not all, for beside it there was a horse's track partly snowed over. Vasily Andreevich stopped, stooped down and looked carefully. It was a horse-track only partially covered with snow, and could be none but his own horse's hoofprints. He had evidently gone around in a small circle. "I'll perish like that!" he thought, and not to give way to his terror he urged on the horse still more, peering into the snowy darkness in which he saw only flitting and fitful points of light. Once he thought he heard the barking of dogs or the howling of wolves, but the sounds were so faint and indistinct that he didn't know whether he heard them or merely imagined them; he stopped and began to listen intently.

Suddenly some terrible, deafening cry resounded near his ears, and everything shivered and shook under him. He seized Mukhorty's neck, but that too was shaking all over and the terrible cry grew still more frightful. For some seconds Vasily Andreevich couldn't collect himself or understand what was happening. It was only that Mukhorty, whether to encourage himself or to call for help, had neighed loudly and resonantly. "Ugh, you wretch! How you frightened me, damn you!" thought Vasily Andreevich. But even when he understood the cause of his terror he couldn't shake it off.

"I must calm myself and think things over," he said to himself, but he couldn't stop, and continued to urge the horse on, without noticing that he was now going with the wind instead of against it. His body, especially between his legs where it touched the pad of the harness and was not covered by his overcoats, was getting painfully cold, especially when the horse walked slowly. His legs and arms trembled and his breathing came fast. He saw himself perishing amid this dreadful snowy waste, and could see no means of escape.

Suddenly the horse under him tumbled into something and, sinking into a snow-drift, began to plunge and fell on his side. Vasily Andreevich jumped off, and in so doing dragged to one side the breechband on which his foot was resting, and twisted around the pad to which he held as he dismounted. As soon as he had jumped off, the horse struggled to his feet, plunged forward, gave one leap and another, neighed again, and dragging the sacking and the breechband after him, disappeared, leaving Vasily Andreevich alone on the snow-drift.

The latter pressed on after the horse, but the snow lay so deep and his coats were so heavy that, sinking above his knees at each step, he stopped breathless after taking not more than twenty steps. "The copse, the oxen, the lease-hold, the shop, the tavern, the house with the iron-roofed barn, and my heir," he thought. "How can I leave all that? What does this mean? It cannot be!" These thoughts flashed through his mind. Then he thought of the wormwood tossed by the wind, which he had twice ridden past, and he was seized with such terror that he didn't believe in the reality of what was happening to him. "Can this be a dream?" he wondered, and tried to wake up but could not. It was real snow that lashed his face, covered him and chilled his right hand from which he'd lost the glove, and this was a real desert in which he was now left alone like that wormwood, awaiting an inevitable, speedy, and meaningless death.

"Queen of Heaven! Holy Father Nicholas, teacher of temperance!" he thought, recalling the service of the day before, the holy icon with its black face and gilt frame, and the tapers which he sold to be set before that icon and which were almost immediately brought back to him scarcely burnt at all, and which he put away in the store-chest. He began to pray to that same Nicholas the Wonder-Worker to save him, promising him a thanksgiving service and some candles. But he clearly and indubitably realized that the icon, its frame, the candles, the priest, and the thanksgiving service, though very important and necessary in church, could do nothing for him out here, and that there was and could be no connection between those candles and services and his present disastrous plight. "I must not despair," he thought. "I must follow the horse's track before it's snowed under. He'll lead me out, or I may even catch him. Only I mustn't hurry, or I'll stick fast and be more lost than ever."

But in spite of his resolution to go on quietly, he rushed forward and even ran, continually falling, getting up and falling again. The horse's track was already hardly visible in places where the snow wasn't very deep. "I'm lost!" he thought. "I'll lose the track and won't catch the horse." But at that moment he saw something black. It was Mukhorty, and not only Mukhorty, but the sleigh with the shafts and the kerchief. Mukhorty, with the sacking and the breechband twisted around to one side, was standing not in his former place but nearer to the shafts, shaking his head which the reins he was stepping on drew downwards. It turned out that Vasily Andreevich had sunk in the same ravine Nikita had previously fallen into, and that Mukhorty had been bringing him back to the sleigh and he had got off his back no more than fifty paces from where the sleigh was.

IX

Having stumbled back to the sleigh Vasily Andreevich caught hold of it and for a long time stood motionless, trying to calm himself and recover his breath. Nikita was not in his former place, but something, already covered with snow, was lying in the sleigh and Vasily Andreevich concluded that this was Nikita. His terror had now quite left him, and if he felt any fear it was that the dreadful terror would return that he'd experienced when on the horse and especially when he was left alone in the snowdrift. At any cost he had to avoid that terror, and to keep it away he must do something—occupy himself with something. The first thing he did was to turn his back to the wind and open his fur coat. Then, as soon as he recovered his breath a little, he shook the snow out of his boots and out of his left-hand glove (the right-hand glove was hopelessly lost and by this time probably lying somewhere under a dozen inches of snow); then as was his custom when going out of his shop to buy grain from the peasants, he pulled his girdle low down and tightened it and prepared for action. The first thing that occurred to him was to free Mukhorty's leg from the rein. Having done that, and tethered him to the iron cramp at the front of the sleigh where he'd been before, he was going around the horse's quarters to put the breechband and pad straight and cover him with the cloth, but at that moment he noticed that something was moving in the sleigh and Nikita's head rose up out of the snow that covered it. Nikita, who was half frozen, rose with great difficulty and sat up, moving his hand before his nose in a strange manner just as if he were driving away flies. He waved his hand and said something, and seemed to Vasily Andreevich to be calling him. Vasily Andreevich left the cloth unadjusted and went up to the sleigh.

"What is it?" he asked. "What are you saying?"

"I'm dy . . . ing, that's what," said Nikita in broken speech and with difficulty. "Give what you owe to me to my lad, or to my wife, no matter."

"Why, are you really frozen?" asked Vasily Andreevich.

"I feel it's my death. Forgive me for Christ's sake . . ." said Nikita in a tearful voice, continuing to wave his hand before his face as if driving away flies.

Vasily Andreevich stood silent and motionless for half a minute. Then suddenly, with the same resolution with which he used to shake hands when making a good purchase, he took a step back and turning up his sleeves began raking the snow off Nikita and out of the sleigh. Having done this he hurriedly undid his girdle, opened out his fur coat, and having pushed Nikita down, lay down on top of him, covering him not only with his fur coat but with the whole of his body, which glowed with warmth. After pushing the skirts of his coat between Nikita and the sides of the sleigh, and holding down its hem with his knees, Vasily Andreevich lay like that face down, with his head pressed against the front of the sleigh. Here he no longer heard the horse's movements or the whistling of the wind, only Nikita's breathing. At first and for a long time Nikita lay motionless, then he sighed deeply and moved.

"There, and you say you're dying! Lie still and get warm, that's our way . . ." began Vasily Andreevich.

But to his great surprise he could say no more, for tears came to his eyes and his lower jaw began to quiver rapidly. He stopped speaking and only gulped down the risings in his throat. "Seems I was badly frightened and have gone quite weak," he thought. But this weakness was not only not unpleasant, but gave him a peculiar joy such as he had never felt before.

"That's our way!" he said to himself, experiencing a strange and solemn tenderness. He lay like that for a long time, wiping his eyes on the fur of his coat and tucking under his knee the right skirt, which the wind kept turning up.

But he longed so passionately to tell somebody of his joyful condition that he said: "Nikita!"

"It's comfortable, warm!" came a voice from beneath.

"There, you see, friend, I was going to perish. And you would have been frozen, and I should have . . ."

But again his jaws began to quiver and his eyes to fill with tears, and he could say no more.

"Well, never mind," he thought. "I know about myself what I know."

He remained silent and lay like that for a long time.

Nikita kept him warm from below and his fur coats from above. Only his hands, with which he kept his coat-skirts down around Nikita's sides, and his legs which the wind kept uncovering, began to freeze, especially his right hand which had no glove. But he didn't think of his legs or his hands but only of how to warm the peasant who was lying under him. He looked out several times at Mukhorty and could see that his back was uncovered and the sacking and breeching were lying on the snow, and that he ought to get up and cover him, but he couldn't bring himself to leave Nikita and disturb even for a moment the joyous condition he was in. He no longer felt any kind of terror.

"No fear, we won't lose him this time!" he said to himself, referring to his getting the peasant warm with the same boastfulness with which he spoke of his buying and selling.

Vasily Andreevich lay in that way for one hour, another, and a third, but he was unconscious of the passage of time. At first impressions of the snow-storm, the sleigh-shafts, and the horse with the shaft-bow shaking before his eyes, kept passing through his mind, then he remembered Nikita lying under him, then recollections of the festival, his wife, the police-officer, and the box of candles, began to mingle with these; then again Nikita, this time lying under that box, then the peasants, customers and traders, and the white walls of his house with its iron roof with Nikita lying underneath, all presented themselves to his imagination. Afterwards all these impressions blended into one nothingness. As the colors of the rainbow unite into one white light, so all these different impressions mingled into one, and he fell asleep.

He slept for a long time without dreaming, but just before dawn the visions returned. It seemed to him that he was standing by the box of tapers and that Tikhon's wife was asking for a five-kopek taper for the Church fête. He wished to take one out and give it to her, but his hands wouldn't lift, being held tight in his pockets. He wanted to walk around the box but his feet wouldn't move and his clean new galoshes had stuck to the stone floor, and he could neither lift them nor get his feet out of them. Then the taper-box was no longer a box but a bed, and suddenly Vasily Andreevich saw himself lying in his bed at home. He was lying in his bed and couldn't get up. But it was necessary for him to get up because Ivan Matveich, the police-officer, would soon call for him and he had to go with him—either to bargain for the forest or to put Mukhorty's breeching straight.

He asked his wife: "Nikolaevna, hasn't he come yet?" "No, he hasn't," she replied. He heard someone drive up to the front steps. "It must be him." "No, he's gone past." "Nikolaevna! I say, Nikolaevna, isn't he here yet?" "No." He was still lying on his bed and couldn't get up, but was still waiting. And this waiting was uncanny and yet joyful. Then suddenly his joy was completed. The one whom he was expecting came; not Ivan Matveich the police-officer, but someone else—yet it was he whom he had been waiting for. He came and called him; and it was he who'd called him and told him to lie down on Nikita. And Vasily Andreevich was glad that he had come for him.

"I'm coming!" he cried joyfully, and that cry awoke him, but when he woke he was not at all the same person he'd been when he fell asleep. He tried to get up but couldn't, tried to move his arm and couldn't, to move his leg and also couldn't, to turn his head and couldn't. He was surprised but not at all disturbed by this. He understood that this was death, and was not at all disturbed by that either. He remembered that Nikita was lying under him and that he had got warm and was alive, and it seemed to him that he was Nikita and Nikita was he, and that his life was not in himself but in Nikita. He strained his ears and heard Nikita breathing and even slightly snoring. "Nikita is alive, so I too am alive!" he said to himself triumphantly.

And he remembered his money, his shop, his house, the buying and selling, and Mironov's millions, and it was hard for him to understand why that man, called Vasily Brekhunov, had troubled himself with all those things with which he had been troubled.

"Well, it was because he did not know what the real thing was," he thought, concerning that Vasily Brekhunov. "He did not know, but now I know and know for sure. Now I know!" And again he heard the voice of the one who had called him before. "I'm coming! Coming!" he responded gladly, and his whole being was filled with joyful emotion. He felt himself free and that nothing could hold him back any longer.

After that Vasily Andreevich neither saw, heard, nor felt anything more in this world.

All around the snow still eddied. The same whirlwinds of snow circled about, covering the dead Vasily Andreevich's fur coat, the shivering Mukhorty, the sleigh, now scarcely to be seen, and Nikita lying at the bottom of it, kept warm beneath his dead master.

X

Nikita awoke before daybreak. He was aroused by the cold that had begun to creep down his back. He had dreamt that he was coming from the mill with a load of his master's flour and when crossing the stream had missed the bridge and let the cart get stuck. He saw that he had crawled under the cart and was trying to lift it by arching his back. But strange to say the cart didn't move; it stuck to his back and he could neither lift it nor get out from under it. It was crushing the whole of his loins. How cold it felt! Evidently he must crawl out. "Have done!" he exclaimed to whomever was pressing the cart down on him. "Take out the sacks!" But the cart pressed down colder and colder, and then he heard a strange knocking, awoke completely, and remembered everything. The cold cart was his dead and frozen master lying upon him. And the knock was produced by Mukhorty, who had twice struck the sleigh with his hoof.

"Andreevich! Eh, Andreevich!" Nikita called cautiously, beginning to realize the truth, and straightening his back. But Vasily Andreevich didn't answer and his stomach and legs were stiff and cold and heavy like iron weights.

"He must have died! May the Kingdom of Heaven be his!" thought Nikita.

He turned his head, dug with his hand through the snow and opened his eyes. It was daylight; the wind was whistling as before between the shafts, and the snow was falling in the same way, except that it was no longer driving against the frame of the sleigh but silently covered both sleigh and horse deeper and deeper; neither the horse's movements nor his breathing were to be heard any longer.

"He must have frozen too," thought Nikita about Mukhorty, and indeed those hoof knocks against the sleigh, which had awakened Nikita, were the last efforts the already numbed Mukhorty had made to keep on his feet before dying.

"O Lord God, it seems Thou art calling me too!" said Nikita. "Thy Holy Will be done. It's uncanny. . . . Still, a man can't die twice and must die once. If only it would come soon!"

And again he drew in his head, closed his eyes, and became unconscious, fully convinced that now he was certainly and finally dying.

It was not till noon that day that peasants dug Vasily Andreevich and Nikita out of the snow with their shovels, not more than seventy yards from the road and less than half a mile from the village.

The snow had hidden the sleigh, but the shafts and the kerchief tied to them were still visible. Mukhorty, buried up to his belly in snow, with the breeching and sacking hanging down, stood all white, his dead head pressed against his frozen throat: icicles hung from his nostrils, his eyes were covered with hoar-frost as though filled with tears, and he'd grown so thin in that one night that he was nothing but skin and bone.

Vasily Andreevich was stiff as a frozen carcass, and when they rolled him off Nikita his legs remained apart and his arms stretched out as they had been. His bulging hawk eyes were frozen, and his open mouth under his clipped moustache was full of snow. But Nikita though chilled through was still alive. When he'd been brought to, he felt sure that he was already dead and that what was taking place was no longer happening in this world but in the next. When he heard the peasants shouting as they dug him out and rolled the frozen body of Vasily Andreevich off him, at first he was surprised that in the other world peasants would be shouting in the same old way and had the same kind of body, and then when he realized that he was still in this world, he was sorry rather than glad, especially when he found that the toes on both his feet were frozen.

Nikita lay in the hospital for two months. They cut off three of his toes, but the others recovered so that he was still able to work and went on living for another twenty years, first as a farm-laborer, then in his old age as a watchman. He died at home as he'd wished, only this year, under the icons with a lighted taper in his hands. Before he died he asked his wife's forgiveness and forgave her for the cooper. He also took leave of his son and grandchildren, and died sincerely glad that he was relieving his son and daughter-in-law of the burden of having to feed him, and that now he was really passing from this life of which he was weary into that other life which every year and every hour grew clearer and more desirable to him. Whether he's better or worse off there where he awoke after his death, whether he was disappointed or found what he expected, we shall all soon learn.

Alyosha the Pot†

Alyosha was a younger brother. He was nicknamed "the Pot," because once, when his mother sent him with a pot of milk for the deacon's wife, he stumbled and broke it. His mother thrashed him soundly, and the children in the village began to tease him, calling him "the Pot." Alyosha the Pot: and this is how he got his nickname.

Alyosha was a skinny little fellow, lop-eared—his ears stuck out like wings—and with a large nose. The children always teased him about this, too, saying "Alyosha has a nose like a gourd on a pole!"

There was a school in the village where Alyosha lived, but reading and writing and such did not come easy for him, and besides there was no time to learn. His older brother lived with a merchant in town, and Alyosha had begun helping his father when still a child. When he was only six years old, he was already watching over his family's cow and sheep with his younger sister in the common pasture. And long before he was grown, he had started taking care of their horses day and night. From his twelfth year he plowed and carted. He hardly had the strength for all these chores, but he did have a certain manner—he was always cheerful. When the children laughed at him, he fell silent or laughed himself. If his father cursed him, he stood quietly and listened. And

† Translated by S. A. Carmack. Reprinted with permission of Harper and Row, Publishers, Inc. This piece was first published in 1905.

when they finished and ignored him again, he smiled and went back to whatever task was before him.

When Alyosha was nineteen years old, his brother was taken into the army; and his father arranged for Alyosha to take his brother's place as a servant in the merchant's household. He was given his brother's old boots and his father's cap and coat and was taken into town. Alyosha was very pleased with his new clothes, but the merchant was quite dissatisfied with his appearance.

"I thought you would bring me a young man just like Semyon" said the merchant, looking Alyosha over carefully. "But you've brought me such a sniveller. What's he good for?"

"Ah, he can do anything—harness and drive anywhere you like. And he's a glutton for work. Only looks like a stick. He's really very wiry."

"That much is plain. Well, we shall see."

"And above all he's a meek one. Loves to work."

"Well, what can I do? Leave him."

And so Alyosha began to live with the merchant.

The merchant's family was not large. There were his wife, his old mother, and three children. His older married son, who had only completed grammar school, was in business with his father. His other son, a studious sort, had been graduated from the high school and was for a time at the university, though he had been expelled and now lived at home. And there was a daughter, too, a young girl in the high school.

At first they did not like Alyosha. He was too much the peasant and was poorly dressed. He had no manners and addressed everyone familiarly as in the country. But soon they grew used to him. He was a better servant than his brother and was always very responsive. Whatever they set him to do he did willingly and quickly, moving from one task to another without stopping. And at the merchant's, just as at home, all the work was given to Alyosha. The more he did, the more everyone heaped upon him. The mistress of the household and her old mother-in-law, and the daughter, and the younger son, even the merchant's clerk and the cook—all sent him here and sent him there and ordered him to do everything that they could think of. The only thing that Alyosha ever heard was "Run do this, fellow," or "Alyosha, fix this up now," or "Did you forget, Alyosha? Look here, fellow, don't you forget!" And Alyosha ran, and fixed, and looked, and did not forget, and managed to do everything and smiled all the while.

Alyosha soon wore out his brother's boots, and the merchant scolded him sharply for walking about in tatters with his bare feet sticking out and ordered him to buy new boots in the market. These boots were truly new, and Alyosha was very happy with them; but his feet remained old all the same, and by evening they ached so from running that he got mad at them. Alyosha was afraid that when his father came to collect his wages, he would be very annoyed that the master had deducted the cost of the new boots from his pay.

In winter Alyosha got up before dawn, chopped firewood, swept out the courtyard, fed grain to the cow and the horses and watered them. Afterwards, he lit the stoves, cleaned the boots and coats of all the household, got out the samovars and polished them. Then, either the clerk called him into the shop to take out the wares or the cook ordered him to knead the dough and to wash the pans. And later he would be sent into town with a message, or to the school for the daughter, or to fetch lamp oil or something else for the master's old mother. "Where have you been loafing, you worthless thing?" one would say to him, and then another. Or among themselves they would say "Why go yourself? Alyosha will run for you. Alyosha, Alyosha!" And Alyosha would run.

Alyosha always ate breakfast on the run and was seldom in time for dinner. The cook was always chiding him, because he never took meals with the others, but for all that she did feel sorry for him and always left him something hot for dinner and for supper.

Before and during holidays there was a lot more work for Alyosha, though he was happier during holidays, because then everyone gave him tips, not much, only about sixty kopeks usually; but it was his own money, which he could spend as he chose. He never laid eyes on his wages, for his father always came into town and took from the merchant Alyosha's pay, giving him only the rough edge of his tongue for wearing out his brother's boots too quickly. When he had saved two rubles altogether from tips, Alyosha bought on the cook's advice a red knitted sweater. When he put it on for the first time and looked down at himself, he was so surprised and delighted that he just stood in the kitchen gaping and gulping.

Alyosha said very little, and when he did speak, it was always to say something necessary abruptly and briefly. And when he was told to do something or other or was asked if he could do it, he always answered without the slightest hesitation "I can do it." And he would immediately throw himself into the job and do it.

Alyosha did not know how to pray at all. His mother had once taught him the words, but he had forgot even as she spoke. Nonetheless, he did pray, morning and evening, but simply, just with his hands, crossing himself.

Thus Alyosha lived for a year and a half, and then, during the second half of the second year, the most unusual experience of his life occurred. This experience was his sudden discovery, to his complete amazement, that besides those relationships between people that arise from the need that one may have for another, there also exist other relationships that are completely different: not a relationship that a person has with another because that other is needed to clean boots, to run errands, or to harness horses; but a relationship that a person has with another who is in no way necessary to him, simply because that other one wants to serve him and to be loving to him. And he discovered, too, that he, Alyosha, was just such a person. He realized all this through the cook Ustinya. Ustinya was an orphan, a young girl yet, and as hard a worker as Alyosha. She began to feel sorry for Alyosha, and Alyosha for the first time in his life felt that he himself, not his services, but he himself was needed by another person. When his mother had been kind to him or had felt sorry for him, he took no notice of it, because it seemed to him so natural a thing, just the same as if he felt sorry for himself. But suddenly he realized that Ustinya, though completely a stranger, felt sorry for him, too. She always left him a pot of kasha with butter, and when he ate, she sat with him, watching him with her chin propped upon her fist. And when he looked up at her and she smiled, he, too, smiled.

It was all so new and so strange that at first Alyosha was frightened. He felt that it disturbed his work, his serving, but he was nonetheless very happy. And when he happened to look down and notice his trousers, which Ustinya had mended for him, he would shake his head and smile. Often while he was working or running an errand, he would think of Ustinya and mutter warmly "Ah, that Ustinya!" Ustinya helped him as best she could, and he helped her. She told him all about her life, how she had been orphaned when very young, how an old aunt had taken her in, how this aunt later sent her into town to work, how the merchant's son had tried stupidly to seduce her, and how she put him in his place. She loved to talk, and he found listening to her very pleasant. Among other things he heard that in town it often happened that peasant boys who came to serve in households would marry the cooks. And once she asked him if his parents would marry him off soon. He replied that he didn't know and that there was no one in his village whom he wanted.

"What, then, have you picked out someone else?" she asked.

"Yes. I'd take you. Will you?"

"O Pot, my Pot, how cunningly you put it to me!" she said, cuffing him playfully on the back with her ladle.

At Shrovetide Alyosha's old father came into town again to collect his son's wages. The merchant's wife had found out that Alyosha planned to marry Ustinya, and she was not at all pleased. "She will just get pregnant, and then what good will she be!" she complained to her husband.

The merchant counted out Alyosha's money to his father. "Well, is my boy doing all right by you?" asked the old man. "I told you he was a meek one, would do anything you say."

"Meek or no, he's done something stupid. He has got it into his head to marry the cook. And I will not keep married servants. It doesn't suit us."

"Eh, that little fool! What a fool! How can he think to do such a stupid thing! But don't worry over it. I'll make him forget all that nonsense."

The old man walked straight into the kitchen and sat down at the table to wait for his son. Alyosha was, as always, running an errand, but he soon came in all out of breath.

"Well, I thought you were a sensible fellow, but what nonsense you've thought up!" Aloysha's father greeted him.

"I've done nothing."

"What d'you mean nothing! You've decided to marry. I'll marry you when the time comes, and I'll marry you to whoever I want, not to some town slut."

The old man said a great deal more of the same sort. Alyosha stood quietly and sighed. When his father finished, he smiled.

"So I'll forget about it" he said.

"See that you do right now" the old man said curtly as he left.

When his father had gone and Alyosha remained alone with Ustinya, who had been standing behind the kitchen door listening while his father was talking, he said to her: "Our plan won't work out. Did you hear? He was furious, won't let us."

Ustinya began to cry quietly into her apron. Alyosha clucked his tongue and said "How could I not obey him? Look, we must forget all about it."

In the evening, when the merchant's wife called him to close the shutters, she said to him "Are you going to obey your father and forget all this nonsense about marrying?"

"Yes. Of course. I've forgot it" Alyosha said quickly, then smiled and immediately began weeping.

From that time Alyosha did not speak again to Ustinya about marriage and lived as he had before.

One morning during Lent the clerk sent Alyosha to clear the snow off the roof. He crawled up onto the roof, shovelled it clean and began to break up the frozen snow near the gutters when his feet slipped out from under him and he fell headlong with his shovel. As ill luck would have it, he fell not into the snow, but onto an entry-way with an iron railing. Ustinya ran up to him, followed by the merchant's daughter.

"Are you hurt, Alyosha?"

"Yes. But it's nothing. Nothing."

He wanted to get up, but he could not and just smiled. Others came and carried him down into the yard-keeper's lodge. An orderly from the hospital arrived, examined him, and asked where he hurt. "It hurts all over" he replied. "But it's nothing. Nothing. Only the master will be annoyed. Must send word to Papa."

Alyosha lay abed for two full days, and then, on the third day, they sent for a priest.

"You're not going to die, are you?" asked Ustinya.

"Well, we don't all live forever. It must be some time" he answered quickly, as always. "Thank you, dear Ustinya, for feeling sorry for me. See, it's better they didn't let us marry, for nothing would have come of it. And now all is fine."

He prayed with the priest, but only with his hands and with his heart. And in his heart he felt that if he was good here, if he obeyed and did not offend, then there all would be well.

He said little. He only asked for something to drink and smiled wonderingly. Then he seemed surprised at something, and stretched out and died.

BACKGROUNDS
AND SOURCES

LEO TOLSTOY

A History Of Yesterday†

I am writing a history of yesterday not because yesterday was remarkable in any way, for it might rather be called unremarkable, but because I have long wished to trace the intimate side of life through an entire day. Only God knows how many diverse and diverting impressions, together with the thoughts awakened by them, occur in a single day. Obscure and confused they may be, but they are nevertheless comprehensible to our minds. If they could be recorded in such a way that I myself—and others after me—could easily read the account, the result would be a most instructive and absorbing book; nor would there be ink enough in the world to write it, or typesetters to put it into print. However, let us get on with the story.

I arose late yesterday—at a quarter to ten—because I had gone to bed after midnight. (It has long been my rule never to retire after midnight, yet this happens to me about three times a week.) But there are circumstances in which I consider this a fault rather than a crime. The circumstances vary; yesterday they were as follows:

Here I must apologize for going back to the day before yesterday. But then, novelists devote whole chapters to their heroes' forebears.

I was playing cards; not from any passion for the game, as it might seem; no more, indeed, from a passion for the game than one who dances the polonaise does so from a passion for promenading. Rousseau, among other things which he proposed and no one has accepted, suggested the playing of cup-and-ball in society in order to keep the hands occupied.[1] But that is scarcely enough; in society the head too should be occupied, or at the very least should be so employed as to permit silence as well as conversation. Such an occupation has been invented: cards. People of the older generation complain that 'nowadays there is no conversation.' I don't know how people were in the old days (it seems to me that people have always been the same), but conversation there can never be. As an occupation conversation is the stupidest of inventions.—It is not from any deficiency of intelligence but from egotism that conversation fails. Everyone wishes to talk about himself or about that which interests him; however, if one person speaks while another

† An earlier edition of this translation by George L. Kline first appeared in *The Russian Review* 8 (1949). The present version has been thoroughly revised by the translator. This is the first known piece of Tolstoy's fiction, written in 1851 when he was only twenty-two. It was not published until after his death. The opening section of the narrative, the beginning of a longer work that Tolstoy planned, was inspired by an evening he spent at the home of distant relatives, Prince A. A. Volkonsky and his wife, who later served as the model for the "little princess," wife of Prince Andrei Bolkonsky, in *War and Peace*.

1. An inaccurate summary of an idea advanced by Rousseau in chapter 5 of his *Confessions* (1781).

listens, you have not a conversation but a lecture. If two people come together who are interested in the same thing, then a third person is enough to spoil the whole business: he interferes, you must try to give him a share too—and your conversation has gone to the devil.

There are also conversations between people who are interested in the same thing, and where no one disturbs them, but such cases are even worse. Each speaks of the same thing from his own viewpoint, transposing everything to his own key, and measuring everything with his own yardstick. The longer the conversation continues, the farther apart they draw, until at last each one sees that he is no longer conversing, but is preaching with a freedom which he permits only to himself; that he is making a spectacle of himself, and that the other is not listening to him, but is doing the same thing. Have you ever rolled eggs during Holy Week? You start off two identical eggs with the same stick, but with their little ends on opposite sides. At first they roll in the same direction, but then each one begins to roll away in the direction of its little end. In conversation as in egg-rolling, there are little rowboats that roll along noisily and not very far; there are sharp-ended ones that wander off heaven knows where. But, with the exception of the little rowboats, there are no two eggs that will roll in the same direction. Each has its little end.

I am not speaking now of those conversations which are carried on simply because it would be improper not to say something, just as it would be improper to appear without a necktie. One person thinks, 'You know quite well that I have no real interest in what I am saying, but it is necessary'; and the other, 'Talk away, talk away, poor soul—I know it is necessary.' This is not conversation, but the same thing as a swallowtail coat, a calling card, and gloves—a matter of decorum.

And that is why I say that cards are an excellent invention. In the course of the game one may chat, gratify one's ego, and make witty remarks; furthermore, one is not obligated to keep to the same subject, as one is in that society where there is only conversation.

One must reserve the last intellectual cartridge for the final round, when one is taking one's leave: then is the time to explode your whole supply, like a race horse approaching the finish line. Otherwise one appears pale and insipid; and I have noticed that people who are not only clever but capable of sparkling in society have lost out in the end because they lacked this sense of timing. If you have spoken heatedly and then become too bored and listless to reply, the last impression lingers and people say, 'How dull he is . . .' But when people play cards this does not happen. One may remain silent without incurring censure.

Besides, women—young ones—play cards, and what more could one wish than to sit beside a young lady for two or three hours? And if it is *that* young lady, this is more than enough.

And so I played cards. We took seats on the right, on the left, opposite—and everything was cozy.

This diversion continued until a quarter to twelve. We finished three rubbers. Why does this woman love (how I should like to finish this sentence here with 'me'!) to embarrass me?—For even if she didn't I would not be myself in her presence. It seems to me either that my hands are very dirty, or that I am sitting awkwardly, or else I am tormented by a pimple on my cheek—the one towards her. But it seems that she is in no way to blame for this: I am always ill at ease with people whom I either do not like or like very much. Why is this? Because I wish to convey to the former that I do not like them, and to the latter that I do, and to convey what you wish is very difficult. With me it always works out in reverse. I wish to be cool, but then this coolness seems overdone and to make up for it I become too cordial. With people whom you love honorably, the thought that they may think you love them dishonorably unnerves you and you become short and brusque.

She is the woman for me because she has all those endearing qualities which compel one to love them, or rather, to love her—for I do love her. But not in order to possess her. That thought never entered my head.

She has the bad habit of billing and cooing with her husband in front of others, but this does not bother me; it means no more to me than if she should kiss the stove or the table. She plays with her husband as a swallow plays with a blossom, because she is warmhearted and this makes her happy.

She is a coquette; no, not a coquette, but she loves to please, even to turn heads. I won't say coquette, because either the word or the idea associated with it is bad. To call showing the naked body and deceiving in love coquetry!—That is not coquetry but brazen impudence and baseness. But to wish to please and to turn heads is fine and does no one any harm, since there are no Werthers,[2] and it provides innocent pleasure for oneself and others. Thus, for example, I am quite content that she should please me; I desire nothing more. Furthermore, there is clever coquetry and stupid coquetry: clever coquetry is inconspicuous and you do not catch the culprit in the act; stupid coquetry, on the contrary, hides nothing. It speaks thus: 'I am not so good-looking, but what legs I have! Look! Do you see? What do you say? Nice?'—Perhaps your legs are nice, but I did not notice, because you showed them.— Clever coquetry says: 'It is all the same to me whether you look or not. I was hot, so I took off my hat.' I saw everything. 'And what does it matter to me?' *Her* coquetry is both innocent and clever.

I looked at my pocket watch and got up. It is astonishing: except when I am speaking to her, I never see her looking at me, and yet she sees all my movements.—'Oh, what a pink watch he has!' I am very much offended when people find my Bréguet watch[3] pink; it would be equally offensive if they told me that my vest is pink. I suppose I was visibly

2. The romantic hero of Goethe's epistolary novel *Die Leiden des jungen Werthers* (1774), who killed himself over his unhappy loves.

3. A fashionable pocketwatch invented by the Parisian watchmaker Abraham-Louis Bréguet (1747–1823).

embarrassed, because when I said that on the contrary it was an excellent watch, she became embarrassed in her turn. I dare say she was sorry that she had said something which put me in an awkward position. We both sensed the humor of the situation, and smiled. Being embarrassed together and smiling together was very pleasant to me. A silly thing, to be sure, but together.—I love these secret, inexplicable relationships, expressed by an imperceptible smile or by the eyes. It is not just that one person understands the other, but that each understands that the other understands that he understands him, etc.

Whether she wished to end this conversation which I found so sweet, or to see how I would refuse, or whether I would refuse, or whether she simply wished to continue playing, she looked at the figures which were written on the table, drew the chalk across the table—making a figure that could be classified neither as mathematical nor pictorial—looked at her husband, then between him and me, and said: 'Let's play three more rubbers.' I was so absorbed in the contemplation not of her movements alone, but of everything that is called *charme*—which it is impossible to describe—that my imagination was very far away, and I did not have time to clothe my words in a felicitous form. I simply said: 'No, I can't.'

Before I had finished saying this I began to regret it,—that is, not all of me, but a certain part of me. There is no action which is not condemned by some part of the mind. On the other hand, there is a part that speaks in behalf of any action: what is so bad about going to bed after midnight, and when do you suppose you will spend another such delightful evening?—I dare say this part spoke very eloquently and persuasively (although I cannot convey what is said), for I became alarmed and began to cast about for arguments.—In the first place, I said to myself, there is no great pleasure in it, you do not like her at all, and you're in an awkward position; besides, you've already said that you can't stay, and you would fall in her estimation. . . .

'*Comme il est aimable, ce jeune homme.*'[4]

This sentence, which followed immediately after mine, interrupted my reflections.—I began to make excuses, to say I couldn't stay, but since one does not have to think to make excuses, I continued reasoning with myself.

. . . How I love to have her speak of me in the third person. In German this is rude, but I would love it even in German. Why doesn't she find a decent name for me? It is clearly awkward for her to call me either by my given name or by my surname and title. Can this be because I . . .

'Stay for supper,' said her husband.—As I was busy with my reflections on the formula of the third person, I did not notice that my body, while

---

4. "How pleasant this young man is."

very properly excusing itself for not being able to stay, was putting down its hat again and sitting down quite coolly in an easy chair. It was clear that my mind was taking no part in this absurdity. I became highly vexed and was about to begin roundly reproaching myself, when a most pleasant circumstance diverted me. She very carefully drew something which I could not see, lifted the chalk a little higher than was necessary, and placed it on the table. Then she put her hands down on the divan on which she was sitting and, wiggling from side to side, pushed herself to the very back of it and raised her head—her little head, with the fine rounded contours of her face, the dark, half-closed, but energetic eyes, the narrow, sharp little nose and the mouth that was one with the eyes and always expressed something new. At this moment who could say what it expressed? There was pensiveness and mockery, and pain, and a desire to keep from laughing, dignity, and capriciousness, and intelligence, and stupidity, and passion, and apathy, and much more. After waiting for a moment, her husband went out—I suppose to order the supper.

To be left alone with her is always frightening and oppressive to me. As I follow with my eyes whoever is leaving, it is as painful to me as the fifth figure of the quadrille: I see my partner going over to the other side and I must remain alone.[5] I am sure it was not so painful for Napoleon to see the Saxons crossing over to the enemy at Waterloo[6] as it was for me in my early youth to watch this cruel maneuver. The stratagem that I employ in the quadrille I employed also in this case: I acted as though I did not notice that I was alone with her. And now even the conversation which had begun before his exit came to an end; I repeated the last words that I had said, adding only, 'So that's how it is.' She repeated hers, adding, 'Yes.' But at the same time another, inaudible, conversation began.

She: 'I know why you repeat what you have already said. It is awkward for you to be alone with me and you see that it is awkward for me,— so in order to seem occupied you begin to talk. I thank you very much for this attention, but perhaps one could say something a little bit more intelligent.'

I: 'That is true, your observation is correct, but I don't know why *you* feel awkward. Surely you don't think that when you are alone with me I will begin to say things that will be disagreeable to you? To prove that I am ready to sacrifice my own pleasures for your sake, however agreeable our present conversation is to me, I am going to speak aloud. Or else you begin.'

She: 'Well, go on!'

I was just opening my mouth to say something that would allow me

5. A sequence when the man, temporarily abandoned by his partner, is required to dance alone.
6. One of the reasons for Napoleon's defeat at Waterloo (1815) was the defection of the Saxon troops from the French ranks to the Anglo-Prussian side.

to think of one thing while saying something else, when she began a conversation aloud which apparently could continue for a long while. In such a situation the most intriguing questions are neglected because *that* conversation continues. Having each said a sentence, we fell silent, tried once more to speak, and again fell silent.

That conversation—I: 'No, it is quite impossible to talk. Since I see that this is awkward for you, it would be better if your husband were to return.'

She: (Aloud to a servant) 'Well, where is Ivan Ivanovich? Ask him to come in here.' . . . If anyone does not believe that there are such secret conversations, that should convince him.

'I am very glad that we are now alone,' I continued, speaking silently, 'I have already mentioned to you that you often offend me by your lack of trust. If my foot accidentally touches yours, you immediately hasten to apologize and do not give me time to do so, while I, having realized that it was actually your foot, was just about to apologize myself. Because I am slower than you are, you think me indelicate.'

Her husband came in. We sat for a while, had supper, and chatted. At about twelve-thirty I went home.

In the Sledge

It was spring, the twenty-fifth of March. The night was clear and still; a young moon was visible from behind the red roof of the large white house opposite; most of the snow was already gone.

Only my night sledge was at the entrance, and even without the footman's shout of 'Let's go, there!' Dmitry knew quite well that I was leaving. A smacking sound was audible, as though he were kissing someone in the dark, which, I conjectured, was intended to urge the little mare and the sledge away from the pavement stones on which the runners grated and screeched unpleasantly. Finally the sledge drew up. The solicitous footman took me under the elbow and assisted me to my seat. If he had not held me I should simply have jumped into the sledge, but as it was, in order not to offend him, I walked slowly, and broke through the thin ice which covered the puddle—getting my feet wet. 'Thank you, my friend.' 'Dmitry, is there a frost?'—'Of course, sir; we still have a bit of frost at night.'—

—How stupid! Why did I ask that?—No, there is nothing stupid about it. You wanted to talk, to enter into communication with someone, because you are in high spirits. And why am I in high spirits? Half an hour ago if I had gotten into my sledge, I wouldn't have started to talk.— Because you spoke rather well when taking your leave, because her husband saw you to the door and said, 'When will we see you again?'— Because as soon as the footman caught sight of you he jumped up and, despite the fact that he reeked of parsley, he took pleasure in serving you.—Well, I gave him a fifty-kopek piece.—In all our recollections the middle falls away and the first and last impressions remain, especially the last. For this reason there exists the splendid custom of the master of the house accompanying his guest to the door, where, most often, twining one leg about the other, the host must say something kind to his guest. Despite any intimacy of relations, this rule should not be disregarded. Thus, for example, 'When will we see you again?' means nothing, but from vanity the guest involuntarily translates it as follows: *When* means, 'please make it soon;' *we* means 'not only myself but my wife, who is also very pleased to see you'; *see you* means, 'give us the pleasure another time;' *again* means, 'we have just spent the evening together, but with you it is impossible to be bored.' And the guest carries away a pleasant impression.

It is also necessary to give money to the servants, especially in homes that are not well regulated and where not all the footmen are courteous— in particular the doorman (who is the most important personage because of the first and last impression). They will greet you and see you off as if you were a member of the family, and you translate their solici- tousness—whose source is your fifty-kopek piece—as follows: 'Everyone here loves you and respects you, therefore we try, in pleasing the masters, to please you.' Perhaps it is only the footman who loves and respects you, but all the same it is pleasant. What's the harm if you are mistaken? If there were no mistakes, there would be no . . .

'Are you crazy! . . . What the devil!'

Dmitry and I were very quietly and modestly driving down one of the boulevards, keeping to the ice on the right-hand side, when suddenly some 'chowderhead' (Dmitry gave him this name afterwards) in a carriage and pair ran into us. We separated, and only after we had gone on about ten paces did Dmitry say, 'Look at that, the chowderhead, he doesn't know his right hand from his left!'

Don't think that Dmitry was a timid man or slow to answer. No, on the contrary, although he was of small stature, clean shaven—but with a moustache—he was deeply conscious of his own dignity and strictly fulfilled his duties. His weakness in this case was attributable to two circumstances: 1) Dmitry was accustomed to driving carriages which inspired respect, but now we were driving in a small sledge with very long shafts, pulled by a very small horse, which he could hardly reach even with a whip; what is more, the horse dragged its hind legs pitifully— and all this could easily evoke the derision of by-standers. Consequently this circumstance was all the more difficult for Dmitry and could quite destroy his feeling of [self-confidence?].[7] 2) Probably my question, 'Is there a frost?' had reminded him of similar questions that I had asked him in the autumn on starting out to hunt. A hunter has something to

---

7. This word is illegible in Tolstoy's manuscript.

daydream about, and he forgets to hurl a well-timed curse at the driver who does not keep to the right-hand side. With coachmen, as with everyone else, the one who shouts first and with the greatest assurance is right. There are certain exceptions. For example, a poor droshky-driver cannot shout at a carriage; a coach—even an elegant one—drawn by a single horse can hardly shout at a four-in-hand. But then, everything depends on the nature of the individual circumstances and, most important, on the personality of the driver and the direction in which he is going. I once saw in Tula a striking example of the influence that one man can have on others through sheer audacity.

Everyone was driving to the carnival: sleighs with pairs, four-in-hands, carriages, trotters, women in wide silk coats—all drawn out in a line on the Kiev highway—and there were swarms of pedestrians. Suddenly there was a shout from a side street: 'Hold back, hold back your horses! Out of the way there!' in a self-assured voice. Involuntarily the pedestrians made way, the pairs and four-in-hands were reined in. And what do you think? A ragged cabby, brandishing the ends of the reins over his head, standing on a broken-down sledge drawn by a miserable jade, tore through with a shout to the other side, before anyone realized what was happening. Even the policemen burst out laughing.

Although Dmitry is a venturesome fellow and loves to swear, he has a kind heart and spares his poor horse. He uses the whip not as an incentive but as a corrective, that is, he doesn't spur his horse on with the whip: this is incompatible with the dignity of a city driver. But if the trotter doesn't stand still at the entrance, he will 'give him one.' I had occasion to observe this presently: crossing from one street to another our little horse was hardly able to drag us along, and I noticed from the desperate movements of Dmitry's back and arms and from his clucking that he was having difficulties. Would he use the whip? That was not his custom. But what if the horse stopped? That he would not tolerate, even though here he didn't need to fear the wag who would say, 'Feeding time, eh?' . . . Here was proof that Dmitry acted more from a consciousness of his duty than from vanity.

I thought much more about the many and varied relations of drivers among themselves, of their intelligence, resourcefulness, and pride. I suppose that at large gatherings those who have been involved in collisions recognize one another and pass from hostile to peaceable relations. Everything in the world is interesting, especially the relationships which exist in classes other than our own.

If the carriages are going in the same direction the disputes last longer. The one who was to blame attempts to drive the other away or to fall behind him, and the latter sometimes succeeds in proving to him the wrongness of his action, and gains the upper hand; incidentally, when both are going the same way, the one with faster horses has the advantage.

All of these relationships correspond very closely to the general relationships in life. The relationships of gentlemen among themselves and with their drivers in the case of such collisions are also interesting.— 'Hey there, you low-life, where do you think you're going?'—When this cry is addressed to the whole carriage, the passenger involuntarily tries to assume a serious, or cheerful, or carefree, expression—in a word, one that he did not have before. It is evident that he would be pleased if the situation were reversed. I have noticed that gentlemen with moustaches are especially sensitive to the insults sustained by their carriages.

—'Who goes there?'

This shout came from a policeman who had in my presence been very much offended by a driver this same morning. At the entrance across from his sentry-box a carriage was standing; a splendid figure of a driver with a red beard, having tucked the reins under him, and resting his elbows on his knees, was warming his back in the sun—with evident pleasure, for his eyes were almost completely closed. Opposite him the policeman walked up and down on the platform in front of his sentry-box and, using the end of his halberd, adjusted the plank which was laid across the nearby puddles.—Suddenly he seemed to resent the fact that the carriage was standing there, or else he had become envious of the driver, who was warming himself with such pleasure, or perhaps he merely wished to start a conversation. He walked the length of his little platform, peered into the side street, and then thumped with his halberd on the plank: 'Hey you, where do you think you're stopping? You're blocking the road.' The driver unscrewed his left eye a little, glanced at the policeman, and closed it again.

—'Get a move on! I'm talking to you!' No sign of life.—'Are you deaf? Eh? Move along, I said!' The policeman, seeing that there was no response, walked the length of his little platform, peered into the side street once more, and evidently was getting ready to say something devastating. At this point the driver raised himself a little, adjusted the reins under him, and turning with sleepy eyes to the policeman, said, 'What are you gawking at? They wouldn't even let you have a gun, you simpleton, and still you go around yelling at people!'

'Get out of here!'

The driver roused himself and got out of there.

I looked at the policeman. He muttered something and looked angrily at me; apparently he was annoyed that I had overheard and was looking at him. I know of nothing that can offend a man more deeply than to give him to understand that you have noticed something but do not wish to mention it. As a result I became embarrassed myself; I felt sorry for the policeman and went away.

I love Dmitry's ability to give people names on the spur of the moment; it amuses me. 'Get along, little cap! Get along, monkey suit! Get along, whiskers! Get along, washerwoman! Get along, horse-doctor! Get along, bigwig! Get along, M'sieu!' The Russian has an amazing ability to come up with a concise insult for a person he has never seen before, and not only for an individual, but for a whole social class. A member of the lower middle class is a 'catdealer,' because, it is said, they trade in catskins; a footman is a 'lapper,' a 'lickspittle'; a peasant is 'Rurick'— why, I don't know; a driver is a 'harness-eater,' etc.,—it is impossible to list them all. If a Russian quarrels with someone whom he has just met, he immediately christens him with a name which goes straight to the most sensitive point: 'crooked nose,' 'crosseyed devil,' 'thick-lipped scoundrel,' 'snubnose.' One must experience this oneself to realize how accurately such epithets always hit the sorest spot. I shall never forget the insult which I once received behind my back. A Russian said of me, 'Oh, he's a snaggle-toothed fellow!' It should be known that my teeth are extremely bad, decayed, and sparse.

At Home

I arrived at home. Dmitry hurried to climb down and open the gate, and I did the same so as to pass through the gate before him. It always happens this way: I hurry to go in because I am accustomed to do so; he hurries to drive me up to the porch because he is accustomed to that.—For a long time I couldn't rouse anyone with my ringing. The tallow candle had burned very low and Prov, my old footman, was asleep. While I rang I was thinking as follows: Why is it always repugnant to me to come home, no matter where or how I live—repugnant to see the same Prov in the same place, the same candle, the same spots on the wallpaper, the same pictures? The whole thing is positively dismal.

I am particularly tired of the wallpaper and the pictures because they have pretensions to variety, and after looking at them for two days in a row they are worse than a blank wall. This unpleasant sensation upon coming home is due, I suppose, to the fact that a man is not meant to lead a bachelor's life at the age of twenty-two.

It would be quite different if I could ask Prov as he opens the door (he has jumped up and is clumping with his boots to show that he has been listening for a long time and is wide awake): 'Is the mistress asleep?'

—'No sir, not at all, she's reading in a book'—That would be something: I should put both my hands behind her head, hold her at arm's length before me, look at her, kiss her—another look, and another kiss; and it would not be depressing to return home.

Now the only question that I can ask Prov—to show him that I have noticed that he never sleeps when I am not at home—is: 'Did anyone call?'—'No one.'—Every time I ask this question Prov answers in a pitiful voice, and I always want to say to him, 'Why do you speak in such a pitiful voice? I am very glad that no one called.' But I restrain myself; Prov might be offended and he is a man of dignity.

In the evening I usually write in my diary, my Franklin journal,[8] and my daily accounts.

Today I didn't spend anything because I haven't even a half-kopek piece left, so there is nothing to write in the account book.—The diary and the journal are another matter. I ought to write in them, but it is late; I'll put it off until tomorrow.—

I have often heard the words, 'He's a frivolous person; he lives without a goal.' I myself have often said this, and I say it not because I repeat other people's words but because I feel in my heart that this is bad and that one should have a *goal* in life.

But how is one to do this—to be a 'complete person and have a goal in life'? To set up a goal for oneself is impossible.—I have tried this many times and it does not work. One should not invent a goal, but find such a one as harmonizes with a man's inclinations, which existed previously, but of which one has just become aware. It seems to me I have found such a goal: a well-rounded education and the development of all my abilities. One of the principal means recognized for its attainment is the diary and Franklin journal. Every day I confess in my diary everything bad that I have done. I enter my weaknesses in columns in the journal—laziness, mendacity, gluttony, indecision, the desire to show off, sensuality, lack of *fierté*,[9] etc.,—all such paltry passions. I post my transgressions from the diary to the journal by placing little crosses in the columns.

As I began to undress I thought: 'Where in all this is your well-rounded education and the development of your abilities, of your virtue? Will you ever attain to virtue by this path? Where is this journal leading you?—It serves you only as an indication of your weaknesses, which have no end, and which increase every day. Even if you overcame these weaknesses you would not attain to virtue.—You are only deceiving yourself and playing with this like a child with a toy.—Surely it is not sufficient for an artist to know what things should not be done in order to become an artist. Surely one cannot accomplish anything worthwhile merely by negatively refraining from doing harm. It is not enough for the farmer to weed his field, he must till and sow. Set up rules of virtue and follow them.—It was the part of my mind which is occupied with criticism that said this.

I became thoughtful. Surely it is not enough to destroy the cause of evil in order to bring about the good. Good is positive and not negative. And it is sufficient that good is positive and evil negative for the very reason that evil can be destroyed but good cannot. Good is always in our soul and the soul is good; but evil is implanted. If there were no evil the good would develop freely. The comparison with the farmer is

8. Tolstoy kept a "journal of weaknesses" according to a system developed by Benjamin Franklin (1706–90).
9. Pride.

not valid; he has to sow and plow, but in the soul the good is already sown. The artist must practice and he will master his art, if he does not conform to negative rules, but he must [be free]¹ from arbitrariness. Practice is not necessary for the exercise of virtue—the practice is life itself.

Cold is the absence of heat. Darkness is the absence of light, evil the absence of good.—Why do we love heat, light, and good? Because they are natural. There is a cause of heat, light, and good—the sun, God; but there is no cold or dark sun, no evil God. We see light and rays of light, we seek the cause and say that there is a sun. Light and heat and the law of gravitation prove this to us. This is in the physical world. In the moral world we see good, we see its rays, we see that there is a law of gravitation of the good towards something higher, and that its source is God.—

Remove the coarse crust from a diamond and it will sparkle; throw off the envelope of weaknesses and you will find virtue. But surely it is not just these trifles, these little weaknesses which you write down in the journal that prevent you from being good? Are there not greater passions? And why is such a large number added every day: *it is either self-deception or faintheartedness*, or something of the kind. There is no lasting improvement. In many respects there is no progress at all.— Again the part occupied with criticism made this observation.

To be sure, all the weaknesses that I have written down may be reduced to three classes, but since each has many degrees they may be combined in infinite ways. 1) Pride, 2) weakness of will, 3) deficiency of intelligence.—But it is not possible to assign all weaknesses individually to a given class, for they result from a combination. The first two kinds have decreased; the last, as an independent one, can make progress only with time. For example, I lied today, and clearly without cause. I was invited to dinner. I declined and then said that I could not come because I had a lesson.—What kind?—An English lesson, I said, when I actually had gymnastics. The reasons: 1) lack of intelligence, that I failed to observe at once that it was stupid to lie, 2) lack of resolution, that I didn't make my reason for refusing explicit, 3) stupid pride, assuming that an English lesson is a better excuse than gymnastics.—

Surely virtue does not consist of correcting the weaknesses which harm you in life. It would seem in such a case that virtue is self-denial.—But that is not true. Virtue brings happiness because happiness brings virtue.—Whenever I write candidly in my diary I do not experience the least vexation toward myself for my weaknesses; it seems to me that when I avow them, they have already ceased to exist.

This is pleasant. I said my prayers and lay down to sleep. In the evening I pray better than in the morning; I understand better what I

---

1. This word is illegible in Tolstoy's manuscript.

am saying and feeling. In the evening I do not fear myself, in the morning I do—there is much before me.

Sleep in all its phases is a wonderful thing: the preparation, falling asleep, and sleep itself.—As soon as I lay down I thought, 'What a delight to wrap oneself up warmly and immediately forget oneself in sleep.' But as soon as I began to fall asleep I remembered that it is pleasant to fall asleep, and I woke up. All the pleasures of the body are destroyed by consciousness. One should not be conscious; but I was conscious that I was conscious, and I continued to be conscious, and I couldn't get to sleep. How annoying! Why did God give us consciousness when it only interferes with life?—Because moral pleasures on the contrary are felt more deeply when one is conscious of them.

Reflecting thus, I turned over onto the other side and in so doing uncovered myself. What a disagreeable sensation to uncover yourself in the dark. It always seems as if some one or something is grabbing me or something cold or hot is touching my bare leg. I covered myself up quickly, tucked the blanket in under me on all sides, covered my head and began to go to sleep. My thoughts ran as follows:

'Morpheus, enfold me in your embrace.' This is a Divinity whose priest I would willingly become. And do you remember how the young lady was offended when they said to her: *'Quand je suis passé chez vous, vous étiez encore dans les bras de Morphée.'*[2] She thought Morphée was a name like André or Malaphée. What a comical name! . . . A splendid expression, *dans les bras;* I picture to myself so clearly and elegantly the condition *dans les bras,*—and especially clearly the *bras* themselves—arms bare to the shoulder, with little dimples and creases, and a white chemise indiscreetly open.—How wonderful arms are in general, especially if they have a little dimple!—I stretched. Do you remember, Saint Thomas forbade stretching. He is like Diedrichs. We rode with him on horseback. The hunting was fine. Gelke rode beside the district police officer hallooing to the hounds, and Nalyot was doing his best, even on the frozen mud. How vexed Seryozha[3] was! He's at sister's.— What a treasure Masha[4] is—if only I could find such a wife! Morpheus would be good on a hunt, only he would have to ride naked, or else you might find a wife.—Oh, how Saint Thomas is tearing along—and the lady has already set off to overtake them all; she stretches out in vain, but then that wonderful *dans les bras.*—Here I suppose I went to sleep completely.—I dreamed that I wanted to overtake the young lady, suddenly there was a mountain, I pushed it with my hands, pushed it again—it collapsed; (I threw down the pillow) and I came home to eat. Not ready yet. Why not?—Vasily was swaggering loudly (it was the mistress of the house asking from behind the partition what the noise

2. "When I stopped to see you, you were still in the arms of Morpheus."

3. Tolstoy's brother, Sergei Nikolaevich.
4. Tolstoy's sister, Maria Nikolaevna.

was, and the chambermaid answering her; I heard this, that is why I dreamed it). Vasily came in just as everyone wanted to ask him why it wasn't ready. They saw that Vasily was in his undershirt and that there was a ribbon across his chest; I became frightened, I fell on my knees, cried and kissed his hands; it was as pleasant to me as though I were kissing her hands,—even more so. Vasily took no notice of me and asked, 'Have you loaded?' The Tula pastry-cook Diedrichs said, 'Ready!'—'Well, fire!'—They discharged a volley. (The shutter banged.)—Vasily and I started to dance the polonaise, but it was no longer Vasily, it was she. Suddenly, oh horror! I notice that my trousers were so short that my bare knees were showing. It is impossible to describe how I suffered (my bare legs became uncovered; for a long time I wasn't able to cover them up in my sleep, but finally I did). We continued dancing the polonaise and the Queen of Württemberg was there; suddenly I started to dance a Ukrainian dance. Why?—I couldn't restrain myself. Finally they brought me an overcoat and boots; but even worse: no trousers at all. It cannot be that I am awake; surely I am asleep. I woke up.—I went to sleep again.—I thought, then I could no longer think; I began to imagine things, but I imagined them connectedly and pictorially; then my imagination went to sleep; dark images remained. Then my body went to sleep too.—A dream is made up of the first and last impressions.

It seemed to me that under this blanket no one and nothing could reach me.—Sleep is a condition in which a person completely loses consciousness; but since one goes to sleep by degrees, one also loses consciousness by degrees. Consciousness is what is called the soul; but the soul is regarded as something unified, while there are as many consciousnesses as there are separate parts of a human being. It seems to me that there are three such parts: 1) mind, 2) feeling, 3) body.—1) The first is the highest and this consciousness is an attribute of cultivated people only; animals and animal-like people do not have it. It goes to sleep first. 2) The consciousness of feeling is also an exclusively human attribute; it goes to sleep next. 3) The consciousness of the body goes to sleep last and seldom completely.—Animals do not have this gradation of consciousness, nor do people when they are in such a state that they lose all consciousness—after a strong shock or when intoxicated. The consciousness of being asleep awakens one immediately.

The recollection of the time which we spend asleep does not proceed from the same source as do the recollections of real life—i.e., from memory, the ability to reproduce our impressions—but from the ability to group impressions. In the moment of awakening we unite all the impressions which we received while going to sleep and while asleep (a person almost never sleeps completely) under the influence of the impression which caused us to awaken. This process is the same as falling asleep: it proceeds by degrees, starting with the lowest faculty and ending with the highest. This takes place so rapidly that it is impossible to detect it, and being accustomed to consistency and to the form of time in which life manifests itself, we accept this aggregate of impressions as a recollection of time passed in sleep. In this way you may explain the fact that you have a long dream which ends with the circumstance that awakened you.—You dream that you are going hunting, you load your gun, flush the game, take aim, fire—and the noise which you take for the shot is the carafe which you knocked onto the floor in your sleep. Or you come to see your friend N., you wait for him, and finally a servant comes in and reports that N. has arrived; this is actually being said to you by your own servant to wake you up.

If you wish to check the adequacy of this explanation, God forbid you should believe the dreams which are told you by people who always dream something significant and interesting. These people are accustomed to draw conclusions from dreams according to the principles of fortune-telling; they have set up a certain form to which everything is reduced. They supply what is lacking from their imagination and reject anything that does not fit into this form. For example, a mother will tell you that she dreamed that her daughter flew up into the sky and said: 'Farewell, Mamma dear, I shall pray for you!' And what she really dreamed was that her daughter climbed up onto the roof and said nothing, and after she had climbed up the daughter suddenly became the cook Ivan and said, 'Don't you climb up here.'

Perhaps what they recount is made up by their imaginations from mere force of habit; if so, this is a further proof of my theory of dreams. . . .

If you wish to verify this, try it out on yourself: recall your thoughts and images at the time of going to sleep and of waking up, and if anyone watched you while you were sleeping and can tell you all the circumstances which could have produced an effect on you, you will understand why you dreamed what you did and not something else. These circumstances are so numerous, depending on your constitution, on your digestion, and on physical causes, that it is impossible to enumerate them all. But it is said that when we dream that we are flying or swimming this means that we are growing. Notice why you swim one day and fly another; recollect everything, and you can explain it very easily.

If one of those persons who are in the habit of interpreting dreams had dreamed my dream, here is how it would be told. 'I saw Saint Thomas running and running for a long time, and I said to him: "Why are you running?" and he said to me: "I am seeking the bride."—So you see, he will either get married or there will be a letter from him. . . .'

Note also that there is no chronological order to your recollections. If you will recall your dreams, you will realize that at some time in the past you actually saw what you dreamed later.—During the night you wake up several times (almost always), but only the two lower degrees of consciousness—body and feeling—are awakened. After this, feeling and body go to sleep again—and the impressions which were received at the time of this awakening join the general impression of the dream without any order or sequence. If the third, higher conceptual consciousness awoke also and afterwards went to sleep again, the dream would be divided into two parts.

Another Day [On the Volga]

I took it into my head to travel from Saratov to Astrakhan by way of the Volga. In the first place, I thought, it is better in case of bad weather to travel a longer distance rather than jolt over bad roads for seven hundred versts; besides, the picturesque banks of the Volga, the day-dreams, the danger—all this is pleasant and may have a beneficial effect. I fancied myself a poet, I called to mind my favorite characters and heroes, putting myself in their places.—In a word, I thought, as I always think when I undertake anything new, 'Only now will real life begin; until now it has been merely a paltry prelude which was hardly worth bothering about.' I know that this is nonsense. I have observed many times that I always remain the same and that I am no more a poet on the Volga than on the Voronka,[5] but I still believe, I still seek, I still wait for something. It always seems to me when I am in doubt whether to do something that a voice says: you won't really do that, you won't go there, and yet it was there that happiness was waiting for you; now you have let it escape for ever.—It always seems to me that something is about to start without me.—Although this is silly, it is the reason why I travelled by way of the Volga to Astrakhan. I used to be afraid and ashamed to act on such silly grounds, but no matter how much I examine my past life, I find that for the most part I have acted on grounds that were no less silly. I don't know how it is with others, but I am used to this, and for me the words 'trivial' and 'silly' have become words without meaning. Where are the 'important' and 'serious' grounds?

I set off for the Moscow ferry and began to stroll about among the rowboats and flat-bottomed boats. 'Are these boats taken? Is there a free one?' I asked a group of barge-haulers who were standing on the shore. 'And what does your worship require?' an old man with a long beard in a gray homespun coat and lamb's-wool hat asked me.—'A boat to Astrakhan.' 'Well, that can be managed, sir!'—

5. A stream on the grounds at Yasnaya Polyana.

LEO TOLSTOY

The Memoirs of a Madman†

20 October 1883

To-day I was taken to the Provincial Government Board to be certified. Opinions differed. They disputed and finally decided that I was not insane—but they arrived at this decision only because during the examination I did my utmost to restrain myself and not give myself away. I did not speak out, because I am afraid of the lunatic asylum, where they would prevent me from doing my mad work. So they came to the conclusion that I am subject to hallucinations and something else, but am of sound mind.

They came to that conclusion, but I myself know that I am mad. A doctor prescribed a treatment for me and assured me that if I would follow his instructions exactly everything would be all right—all that troubled me would pass. Ah, what would I not give that it might all pass! The torment is too great. In due order I will tell how and from what this medical certification came about—how I went mad and how I betrayed myself.

Up to the age of thirty-five I lived just as everybody else does; nothing strange was noticed about me. Perhaps in early childhood, before the age of ten, there was at times something resembling my present condition, but only in fits, not continually as now. Moreover, in childhood it used to affect me rather differently. For instance I remember that once when going to bed, at the age of five or six, my nanny Eupraxia, a tall thin woman who wore a brown dress and a cap and had flabby skin under her chin, was undressing me and lifting me up to put me into my cot. "I will get into bed by myself—myself!" I said, and stepped over the side of the cot.

"Well, lie down then. Lie down, Fedya! Look at Mitya. He's a good boy and is lying down already," she said, indicating my brother with a jerk of her head.

I jumped into bed still holding her hand and then let it go, kicked about under my bedclothes, and wrapped myself up. I had such a pleasant feeling. I grew quiet and thought: "I love Nanny; she loves me and Mitya; and I love Mitya, and Mitya loves me and Nanny. Nanny loves Taras, and I love Taras, and Mitya loves him. And Taras loves me and Nanny. And Mamma loves me and Nanny, and Nanny loves Mamma and me and Papa—everybody loves everybody else and everybody is happy!"

†Translated by Louise and Aylmer Maude.

Then suddenly I heard the housekeeper run in and shout angrily something about a sugar-bowl and Nanny answering indignantly that she had not taken it. I felt pained, frightened, and bewildered; horror, cold horror, seized me, and I hid my head under the bedclothes, but felt no better in the dark.

I also remembered how once a serf-boy was beaten in my presence, how he screamed, and how dreadful Foka's face looked as he was beating the boy. "Then you won't do it any more, will you?" he kept repeating as he went on beating him. The boy cried, "I won't!" but Foka still repeated, "You won't!" and went on beating him.

Then it came upon me! I began to sob, and carried on so that they could not quiet me for a long time. That sobbing and despair were the first attacks of my present madness.

I remember another attack when my aunt told us about Christ. She told the story and was about to go away, but we said: "Tell us some more about Jesus Christ!"

"No, I have no time now," she said.

"Yes, tell us!"

Mitya also asked her to, and my aunt began to repeat what she had told us. She told us how they crucified, beat, and tortured him, and how he went on praying and did not reproach them.

"Why did they torment him, Auntie?"

"They were cruel people."

"But why, when he was good?"

"There, that's enough. It's past eight! Do you hear?"

"Why did they beat him? He forgave them; why did they hit him? Did it hurt him, Auntie? Did it hurt?"

"That will do! I'm going to have my tea now."

"But perhaps it isn't true and they didn't beat him?"

"Now, now, that will do!"

"No, no! Don't go away!"

Again I was overcome by it. I sobbed and sobbed and began knocking my head against the wall.

That was how it befell me in my childhood. But by the time I was fourteen, and from the time my sexual instincts were aroused and I yielded to vice, all that passed away and I became like other boys, like all the rest of us reared on rich, over-abundant food, effeminate, doing no physical work, surrounded by all possible temptations that inflamed sensuality, among other equally spoiled children. Boys of my own age taught me vice, and I indulged in it. Later on that vice was replaced by another, and I began to enjoy women. And so, seeking enjoyments and finding them, I lived till the age of thirty-five. I was perfectly well and there were no signs of my madness.

Those twenty years of my healthy life passed so that I can hardly remember anything about them and now recall them with difficulty and disgust. Like all mentally healthy boys of our circle I entered high school and afterwards the university, where I completed a course of law-studies. I was in the Civil Service for a short time, and then I met my present wife, married, had a post in the country, and, as it is called, "brought up" our children, managed our estates, and was a Justice of the Peace.

In the tenth year of my married life I had another attack—the first since my childhood.

My wife and I had saved some money—some inherited by her and some from bonds I, like other landowners, had received from the Government at the time of the emancipation of the serfs—and we decided to buy an estate. I was much interested, as was proper, in the growth of our property and in increasing it in the shrewdest way—better than other people. At that time I inquired everywhere where there were estates for sale, and read all the advertisements in the papers. I wanted to buy an estate so that the income from it, or the timber on it, would cover the whole purchase price and I should get it for nothing. I searched for some fool who did not understand business and thought I had found such a man.

An estate with large forests was being sold in Penza province.[1] From all I could learn about it, it seemed that its owner was just such a fool as I wanted and the timber would cover the whole cost of the estate. So I got ready and set out.

We (my servant and I) travelled at first by rail and then by road in a post-carriage. The journey was a very pleasant one for me. My servant, a young good-natured fellow, was in just as good spirits as I. We saw new places and met new people and enjoyed ourselves. To reach our destination we had to go about a hundred and forty miles, and decided to proceed without stopping except to change horses. Night came and we still went on. We grew drowsy. I fell asleep but suddenly awoke feeling that there was something terrifying. As often happens, I woke up thoroughly alert and feeling as if sleep had deserted me for ever. "Why am I going? Where am I going?" I suddenly asked myself. It was not that I did not like the idea of buying an estate cheaply, but it suddenly occurred to me that there was no need to travel all that distance, that I should die here in this strange place, and I was filled with dread. Sergey, my servant, woke up, and I availed myself of the opportunity to talk to him. I spoke about that part of the country, he replied and joked, but I felt depressed. I talked about our folks at home, and of the business before us; I was surprised that his answers were so cheerful. Everything seemed pleasant and amusing to him while it nauseated me. But for all that while we were talking I felt easier. But besides everything seeming wearisome and uncanny, I began to feel tired and wished to stop. It seemed to me that I would feel better if I could enter a house, see some people, drink some tea, and above all get some sleep.

We were nearing the town of Arzamas.[2]

1. Located in central Russia in a large, fertile   2. Ancient town in central Russia.
black-earth district.

"Shall we stop here and rest a bit?"

"Why not? Splendid!"

"Are we still far from town?"

"About five miles from the last mile-post."

The driver was a respectable man, careful and taciturn, and he drove rather slowly and wearily.

We went on. I remained silent and felt better because I was looking forward to having a rest and hoped that the discomfort would pass. We went on and on in the darkness for a terribly long time as it seemed to me. We reached the town. Everybody was already in bed. Sordid little houses showed through the darkness, and the sound of our jingling bells and the clatter of the horses' hooves echoed, especially near the houses, and all this was far from cheerful. Here and there we passed large white houses. I was impatient to get to the post-station and to a samovar, and to lie down and rest.

At last we came up to a small house with a post beside it. The house was white but appeared terribly melancholy to me, so much so that it seemed uncanny; I got out of the carriage slowly.

Sergey briskly took out everything that would be needed, clattered up the porch, and the sound of his steps depressed me. I entered a little corridor. A sleepy man with a spot on his cheek (which seemed terrifying) showed us into a room. It was gloomy. I entered, and the uncanny feeling grew worse.

"Haven't you got a bedroom? I would like to rest."

"Yes, we have. This is it."

It was a small square room, with whitewashed walls. I remember being tormented by the fact that it was square. It had one window with a red curtain, a birchwood table, and a sofa with bent-wood arms. We went in. Sergey prepared the samovar and made tea, while I took a pillow and lay down on the sofa. I was not asleep and heard how Sergey was busy with the tea and called me to have some. But I was afraid of getting up and rousing myself completely, and I thought how terrifying it would be to sit up in that room. I did not get up but began to doze. I must have fallen asleep, for when I awoke I found myself alone in the room and it was dark. I was as wide awake again as I had been in the chaise. I felt that sleep would be quite impossible. "Why have I come here? Where am I taking myself? Why and where am I escaping? I'm running away from something dreadful and cannot escape it. I'm always with myself, and it's I who am my own tormentor. Here I am, the whole of me. Neither Penza nor any other property will add anything to or take anything from me. It is myself I am weary of and find intolerable and such a torment. I want to fall asleep and forget myself and cannot. I cannot get away from myself!"

I went out into the passage. Sergey was sleeping on a narrow bench with one arm hanging down, but he was sleeping very peacefully and the man with the spot was also asleep. I had gone out into the corridor hoping to escape from what tormented me. But *it* had come out with me and cast a gloom over everything. I felt just as filled with horror, even more so.

"What foolishness this is!" I asked myself. "Why am I depressed? What am I afraid of?"

"Me!" answered the voice of Death, inaudibly. "I am here!"

A cold shudder ran down my back. Yes! Death! It will come—here it is—and it ought not to be. Had I actually been facing death I could not have suffered as much as I did then. Then I should have been frightened. But I was not frightened now. I saw and felt the approach of death, and at the same time I felt that such a thing ought not to exist.

My whole being was conscious of the necessity and the right to live, and yet I felt that Death was being accomplished. This inward conflict was terrible. I tried to throw off the horror. I found a brass candlestick, the candle in which had a long wick, and I lit it. The red glow of the candle and its size—little less than the candlestick itself—told me the same thing. Everything told me the same thing: "There is nothing to life. Death is the only real thing, and death ought not to exist."

I tried to turn my thoughts to things that had interested me—to the estate I was to buy and to my wife—but I found nothing to cheer me up. It had all become nothing. Everything was hidden by the terrible consciousness that my life was ebbing away. I needed sleep. I lay down, but the next instant I jumped up again in terror. An attack of anguish seized me—similar to the feeling before one is sick, but spiritual anguish. It was uncanny and dreadful. It seems that death is terrible, but when remembering and thinking of life, it is one's dying life that is terrible. Life and death somehow merged into one another. Something was tearing my soul apart and could not complete the action. I went to look at the sleepers again, and once again tried to go to sleep. Always the same horror: red, white, and square. Something tearing within that yet could not be torn apart. A painful, painfully dry and spiteful feeling, no speck of kindliness, just a dull, steady spitefulness towards myself and towards that which had made me.

What created me? God, they say. God . . . what about prayer? I remembered. For some twenty years I had not prayed, and I did not believe in anything, though as a matter of propriety I fasted and took communion every year. Now I began to pray. "Lord have mercy!" "Our Father." "Holy Virgin." I began to compose new prayers, crossing myself, bowing down to the ground and glancing around me for fear that I might be seen. This seemed to divert me—the fear of being seen distracted my terror—and I lay down. But I had only to lie down and close my eyes for the same feeling of terror to reappear and rouse me. I could bear it no longer. I woke the hotel servant and Sergey, gave orders to harness the horses, and we drove off again.

The fresh air and the drive made me feel better. But I realized that something new had entered my soul and poisoned my former life.

By nightfall we reached our destination. The whole day I had been fighting my depression and had mastered it, but it had left terrible dregs in my soul as if some misfortune had befallen me, and I could forget it only for a short time. There it remained at the bottom of my soul and had me in its power.

The old steward of the estate received me well, though without any pleasure. He was sorry the estate was to be sold.

The furniture in the little rooms was upholstered. There was a new, brightly polished samovar, a large tea-service, and honey for tea. Everything was good. But I questioned him about the estate unwillingly, as if it were some old forgotten lesson. I fell asleep, however, without any depression, and this I attributed to my having prayed again before going to bed.

After that I went on living as before, but the fear of that anguish always hung over me. I had to live without stopping to think, and above all to live in my usual surroundings. As a schoolboy repeats a lesson learned by heart without thinking, so I had to live to avoid falling a prey to that awful depression I had first experienced at Arzamas.

I returned home safely, I did not buy the estate—I hadn't enough money—and continued to live as before, only with this difference, that I began to pray and went to church. As before—it seemed to me, but I now remember that it was not so—I lived on what had been previously begun. I continued to go along rails already laid down by my former strength, but I did not undertake anything new. And I took less part in those things I had previously begun. Everything seemed dull and I became pious. My wife noticed this and scolded and nagged me on account of it. But my anguish did not recur at home.

Once I had to go to Moscow unexpectedly. I got ready in the afternoon and left that evening. It was in connection with a lawsuit. I arrived in Moscow cheerful. On the way I had talked with a landowner from Kharkov about estate-management and banks, and about where to stay, and about the theater. We both decided to stay at the Moscow Hotel on Myasnitsky Street and to go to see *Faust* that same evening.

When we arrived I was shown into a small room. The oppressive air of the corridor filled my nostrils. A porter brought in my luggage and a chambermaid lit a candle. The wick was lit and then as usual the flame went down. In the next room someone coughed, probably an old man. The maid went out, but the porter remained and asked if he should untie my luggage. The flame of the candle flared up, revealing blue wallpaper with yellow stripes on the partition, a shabby table, a small sofa, a mirror, a window, and the narrow dimensions of the room. Suddenly I was seized with an attack of the same horror as in Arzamas. "My God! How can I stay here all night?" I thought.

"Yes, untie it, my good fellow," I told the porter to keep him in the room longer. "I'll dress quickly and go to the theater." When the porter had untied it, I said: "Please go to Number Eight and tell the gentleman who arrived here with me that I shall be ready immediately and will come to him."

The porter went out and I dressed hurriedly, afraid to look at the walls. "What nonsense!" I thought. "What am I afraid of? Just like a child! I'm not afraid of ghosts. Ghosts! Ghosts would be better than what I'm afraid of. Why, what is it? Nothing. Myself. . . . Oh, nonsense!"

However, I put on a hard, cold, starched shirt, inserted the studs, donned my evening coat and new boots, and went to find the Kharkov landowner, who was ready. We started for the opera. He stopped on the way at a hairdresser's to have his hair curled, and I had mine cut by a French assistant, had a chat with him, and bought a pair of gloves. All was well, and I quite forgot my oblong room with its partition. In the theater, too, it was pleasant. After the opera the Kharkov landowner suggested that we should have supper. That was contrary to my habit, but just then I remembered the partition in my room and accepted his suggestion.

We got back after one. I had two glasses of wine, to which I was unaccustomed, but in spite of that I felt cheerful. No sooner had we entered the corridor in which the lamp was turned low, and I was surrounded by the hotel smell, than a shiver of horror ran down my spine. There was nothing to be done however, and I pressed my companion's hand and went into my room.

I spent a terrible night—worse than at Arzamas. Not till dawn, when the old man on the other side of the door was coughing again, did I fall asleep, and then not in the bed, in which I had lain down several times during the night, but on the sofa. I had suffered unbearably all night. Again my soul and body were being painfully torn asunder. "I am living, have lived, and ought to live, and suddenly—here is death to destroy everything. Then what is life for? To die? To kill myself at once? No, I'm afraid. To wait for death till it comes? I fear that even more. Then I must live. But what for? In order to die?" I could not escape from that circle. I took up a book, read, and forgot myself for a moment, but then again the same question and the same horror. I lay down in bed and closed my eyes. It was even worse!

God has so arranged it. Why? They say: "Don't ask, but pray!" Very well. I prayed, and prayed as I had done at Arzamas. Then and afterwards I prayed simply, like a child. But now my prayers had meaning. "If You do exist, reveal to me why and what I am!" I bowed down, repeated all the prayers I knew, composed my own, and added: "Then reveal it!" and became silent, awaiting an answer. No answer came. It was just as if there were no one who could give an answer. I remained alone with myself. In place of Him who would not reply I answered my own questions. "Why? In order to live in a future life," I said to myself.

"Then why this obscurity, this torment? I cannot believe in a future life. I believed when I did not ask with my whole soul, but now I cannot, I cannot. If You did exist You would speak to me and to all men. And if You don't exist there is nothing but despair. And I don't want that. I don't want that!"

I became indignant. I asked Him to reveal the truth to me, to reveal Himself to me. I did all that everybody does, but He did not reveal Himself. "Ask and it shall be given you," I remembered. I had asked and in that asking had found not consolation but relaxation. Perhaps I didn't pray to Him but repudiated Him. "You recede an inch and He recedes a mile," as the proverb has it. I did not believe in Him but I asked, and He did not reveal anything to me. I was balancing accounts with Him and blaming Him. I simply did not believe.

The next day I did all in my power to get through my ordinary affairs so as to avoid another night in the hotel. Although I did not finish everything, I left for home that evening. I did not feel any anguish. That night in Moscow still further changed my life which had begun to change from the time I was at Arzamas. I now attended still less to my affairs and became apathetic. I also grew weaker in health. My wife insisted that I should undergo treatment. She said that my talks about faith and God arose from ill health. But I knew that my weakness and ill health were the effect of the unsolved question within me. I tried not to let that question dominate me, and tried to fill my life amid my customary surroundings. I went to church on Sundays and feast days, prepared to receive Communion, and even fasted, as I had begun to do since my visit to Penza, and I prayed, though more as a custom. I did not expect any result from this but as it were kept the promissory note and presented it at the due date, though I knew it was impossible to secure payment. I only did it on the chance. I did not fill my life with estate-management—it repelled me by the struggle it involved (I had no energy)—but by reading magazines, newspapers, novels, and playing cards for small stakes. I showed energy only by hunting, which I did from habit. I had been fond of hunting all my life.

One winter's day a neighboring huntsman came with his wolf-hounds. I rode out with him. When we reached the place we put on snow-shoes and went to the spot where the wolf might be found. The hunt was unsuccessful, the wolves broke through the ring of peasant-beaters. I became aware of this from a distance and went through the forest following the fresh tracks of a hare. These led me far into a glade, where I spied the hare, but it jumped out and I lost it. I went back through the thick forest. The snow was deep, my snowshoes sank in, and branches of the trees entangled me. The trees grew more and more dense. I began to ask myself: "Where am I?" The snow had altered the look of everything.

Suddenly I realized that I had lost my way. I was far from the house, from the hunters too, and could hear nothing. I was tired and covered in perspiration. If I stopped I would freeze. If I went on my strength would fail me. I shouted. All was still. No one answered. I turned back, but it was the same again. I looked around—nothing but trees, impossible to tell which was east or west. Again I turned back. My legs were tired. I grew frightened, stopped, and was seized with the same horror as in Arzamas and Moscow, but a hundred times worse. My heart palpitated; my arms and legs trembled. "Is this death? I won't have it! Why death? What is death?" Once again I wanted to question and reproach God, but I suddenly felt that I dare not and must not do so, that it is impossible to present one's account to God, that He had said what is needed and I alone was to blame. I began to implore His forgiveness, and felt disgusted with myself.

The horror did not last long. I stood there for a while, came to myself, went on in one direction and soon emerged from the forest. I had not been far from the edge, and came out on to the road. My arms and legs still trembled and my heart was beating, but I felt happy. I found the hunting party and we returned home. I was cheerful, but I knew there was something joyful which I would understand when alone. And so it was. I remained by myself in my study and began to pray, asking forgiveness and remembering my sins. There seemed to be only a few, but when I recalled them they became hateful to me.

After that I began to read the scriptures. I found the Old Testament unintelligible though enchanting, but the Gospels moved me profoundly. Most of all I read the Lives of the Saints, and that reading consoled me, presenting examples that it seemed more and more possible to follow. From that time on farming and family matters occupied me less and less. They even repelled me. They all seemed so wrong. What was "right" I didn't know, but what had formerly constituted my life had now ceased to do so. This became plain to me when I was going to buy another estate.

Not far from us an estate was for sale on very advantageous terms. I went to see it. Everything was fine and advantageous, especially the fact that the peasants had no land of their own except their kitchen-gardens. I saw that they would have to work on the landlord's land merely for permission to use his pastures. And so it was. I grasped all this and out of old habit felt pleased about it. But on my way home I met an old woman who asked me the way. I had a talk with her, during which she told me about her poverty. I got home, and when telling my wife of the advantages that estate offered, I suddenly felt ashamed and disgusted. I told her I couldn't buy it because the advantages we would get would be based on the peasants' destitution and sorrow. As I said this I suddenly realized the truth of what I was saying—the main truth, that the peasants, like ourselves, want to live, that they are human beings, our brothers, and sons of the Father as the Gospels say. Suddenly something that had long troubled me seemed to have broken away, as though it had come to birth. My wife was annoyed and scolded me, but I felt glad.

That was the beginning of my madness. But my utter madness began later—about a month after that.

It began by my going to church. I stood there through the liturgy and prayed well, listened, and was touched. Suddenly they brought me some consecrated bread: after that we went up to the Cross, and people began pushing one another. Then there were beggars at the exit. Suddenly it became clear to me that this ought not to be, and not only ought not to be, but in reality was not. And if this was not, then neither was there death or fear; there was no longer the former tearing asunder within me and I no longer feared anything.

Then the light fully illuminated me and I became what I now am. If there is nothing to all that—it certainly does not exist within me. There at the church door I gave away all I had with me to the beggars— some thirty-five rubles—and went home on foot talking with the peasants.

LEO TOLSTOY

Diary for 1855†

23 January, Position on the river Belbek[1]   I lived for more than a month in Eski-Orda, near Simferopol. It seemed dull, but now I look back on that life with regret. But then there's good reason to regret the 14th brigade when you're in the 11th. I've never seen a better brigade in the artillery than the former, or a worse one than the latter. Filimonov, in whose battery I am, is the dirtiest creature you could imagine. Oda-khovsky, the senior officer, is a nasty mean little Pole, and the other officers are under their influence and lack a sense of direction. And I'm tied to, and even dependent on these people! I've been to Sevastopol, got some money, talked with Totleben, walked to the 4th bastion and played cards. I'm very dissatisfied with myself. I must go to the baths tomorrow. I must copy out my plan for the rifle battalions[2] and write a memorandum.

†From *Tolstoy's Diaries*, ed. and tr. R. F. Christian (London, 1985). Reprinted with permission of Athalone Press. In 1854 Tolstoy was sent to the Crimea, where he took part in the defense of Sevastopol. His *Sevastopol Stories* (1855–56) are based on his war experience.
1. A position some six or seven miles from Sevastopol.
2. The plan has not survived.

28 January Played *shtoss* for two days and nights. The result is understandable—the loss of everything—the Yasnaya Polyana house.[3] I think there's no point in writing—I'm so disgusted with myself that I'd like to forget about my existence. They say that Persia has declared war on Turkey and that peace is bound to be concluded.

3, 4, 5 February I've been to Sevastopol. Showed my plan to Kashinsky. He seemed displeased. Didn't manage to call on Krasnokutsky, who had called on me when I was out. The fleet[4] has assembled; something is under way. There's been action at Eupatoria[5]—I asked to be sent there, but in vain.

6, 7, 8 February Played cards again and lost another 200 roubles. I can't promise to stop. I'd like to win everything back, but could get terribly embroiled. I want to win back the whole 2,000. It's impossible, but nothing could be easier than to lose another 400, and then what? It's terribly bad—not to mention the waste of health and time. Tomorrow I'll ask Odakhovsky for another game and that will be the last time. Translated a ballad of Heine's[6] and read *The Misfortune of Being Clever*. I must write tomorrow without fail, and write a lot.

12 February Lost seventy-five roubles again. God is still merciful to me in that there has been no unpleasantness, but what will happen later? My only hope is in Him! A bad business at Eupatoria—an attack repulsed, which is being called a reconnaissance. Time, time, youth, dreams, thoughts—everything is being lost without trace. I'm squandering my life, not living. My losses are forcing me to come to my senses a bit.

14 February [. . .] The thought of retirement or of the Military Academy occurs to me more and more often. I've written to Stolypin to try and get myself transferred to Kishinyov. From there I could arrange one of these two things.

1 March Annenkov has been put in charge of the commissariat of both armies. Gorchakov has replaced Menshikov. Thank God! The Emperor died on 18 February and we've been taking the oath of allegiance to the new Emperor today. Great changes are in store for Russia. One must work hard and be brave to share in these important moments of Russia's life.

---

3. The big house at Yasnaya Polyana in which Tolstoy was born, and which had to be sold, transferred, and rebuilt elsewhere to pay Tolstoy's gambling losses at *shtoss* (an old-fashioned card game).

4. The enemy fleet.
5. Prince Menshikov's plan to take Eupatoria by storm, which was a failure.
6. It is not known which one.

2, 3, 4 March These last few days I've twice worked for several hours at a time on my plan for reorganising the army.[7] It's making slow progress, but I'm not giving up the idea. I took communion today. Yesterday a conversation about divinity and faith inspired me with a great idea, a stupendous idea, to the realisation of which I feel capable of devoting my life. This idea is the founding of a new religion appropriate to the stage of development of mankind—the religion of Christ, but purged of beliefs and mysticism, a practical religion, not promising future bliss but giving bliss on earth. I realise that this idea can only be implemented by generations of people consciously working towards this end. One generation will bequeath the idea to the next, and some day reason or fanaticism will implement it. *Consciously* to work towards the union of mankind by religion is the basis of the idea which I hope will absorb me.

6, 7, 8, 9, 10, 11 March I've lost another 200 roubles to Odakhovsky, so that I've reached the ultimate extremes of embarrassment. Gorchakov has arrived with the whole Staff; I've been to see him and was well received, but there is no news of a transfer to the Staff, which I very much desire. I won't ask, but I'll wait for him to do it himself, or for my aunt to write a letter. Was weak enough to allow Stolypin to induce me to take part in a sortie,[8] although I'm not only glad of it now, but regret not having gone with the assault column. In general this trip from the 9th to the 11th has been full of interesting events. Bronevsky is one of the nicest people I've ever met. A military career is not for me, and the sooner I get out of it to devote myself fully to a literary one the better.

12 March Wrote about a sheet of *Youth* in the morning, then played knucklebones and chatted with Bronevsky. We have a plan to set up a boarding-house.[9] He fully shares this good idea.

13 March Got on with *Youth* and wrote a letter to Tatyana Alexandrovna. The plan for the boarding-house is taking shape. I've failed in so many things that in order to accomplish this one I'll work steadily, diligently and with care.

18 March I've re-read the pages of my diary in which I examine myself and look for ways or methods of improvement. To start with I adopted the most logical and scientific method, but the least practicable one—that of fathoming with the aid of one's reason the best and most useful virtues and trying to attain them. Later on I understood that virtue is

7. Some draft notes have survived about the shortcomings of the Russian officers and men and the loss of morale in the Russian army.
8. An attack on the French positions near Sevas-topol on the night of 10–11 March—the highlight of the "trip" referred to in the next sentence.
9. Nothing came of this.

only the negation of vice, for man is *good*, and I wanted to cure myself of vices. But there were too many of them, and reform on a spiritual basis would be possible only for a spiritual being; but man has two natures, two wills. Then I realised that gradualness is necessary for reform. But that is impossible too. One needs with the aid of one's reason to manufacture a situation in which improvement is possible, in which the will of the flesh and the will of the spirit most nearly accord; one needs certain methods of reform. And I accidentally hit upon one such method—I discovered a standard for determining in what situations goodness is easy or difficult. In general man aspires towards the spiritual life, and to attain spiritual aims one needs a situation in which the satisfaction of the desires of the flesh does not contradict, but rather accords with desires of the spirit—ambition, love of woman, love of nature, art, and poetry.

And so my new rule, in addition to the ones I set myself long ago, is to be energetic, judicious and modest: always to be energetic in pursuit of spiritual aims, to weigh up all my actions on the basis that those are good which aspire towards spiritual aims, and to be modest, so that the pleasure of being satisfied with myself should not turn into the pleasure of exciting praise or surprise in others. I often wished also to work systematically for my own material well-being, but this aim was too diversified, and besides I made the mistake of wishing to mould it independently of circumstances. With my present rule, however, I will work for the improvement of my well-being to the extent to which it will provide me with the means for a spiritual life, and I will only work in such a way as not to run counter to circumstances. My vocation, as far as I can understand from ten years' experience, is not practical activity, and so estate management is least of all compatible with my bent. Today the idea occurred to me of renting out my property to my brother-in-law. In that way I should attain three aims: I should free myself from the cares of estate management and the habits of my youth, impose limits on myself, and free myself of my debts. Today I wrote about a sheet of *Youth*.

20 March For two days I've written absolutely nothing except the rough draft of a letter to Valeryan and two letters to Nekrasov. One is an answer to a letter received from him today in which he asks me to send him some articles about the war. I'll have to write them myself. I'll describe Sevastopol in various phases, and write an idyll of the officers' way of life.

21 March I've done nothing. Received a delightful letter from Masha in which she describes how she made Turgenev's acquaintance.[1] A dear, wonderful letter elevating me in my own opinion and rousing me to

1. In October 1854. Turgenev found her very nice, attractive, and intelligent.

action. But I've been morally and physically ill all day today. On the 24th we're going to Sevastopol.

27 March   The first day of Easter. Went to Sevastopol the day before yesterday; the trip was somehow particularly pleasant and successful. In all my comrades from the South[2] I observed real pleasure at seeing me again—even in the Bashibazouk[3] and Kryzhanovsky. Most pleasant of all for me was to read the reviews in the journals, very flattering reviews, of *Notes of a Billiard-Marker*.[4] It's gratifying and useful because, by inflaming my vanity, it rouses me to activity. Unfortunately I don't yet see any sign of the latter—for five days or so I haven't written a line of *Youth*, although I've started writing *Sevastopol by Day and Night*,[5] and I haven't yet got down to answering the nice letters—two from Nekrasov, and one each from Valeryan, Masha, Nikolenka and Auntie. I've been offered through Neverezhky the post of senior adjutant, and after some hard thinking have accepted it—I don't know what will come of it.[6] Turgenev says quite rightly that we writers need to occupy ourselves with some one thing, and I'll be better able to occupy myself with literature in that position than in any other. I'll suppress my vanity— my desire for promotion and crosses—very foolish vanity, especially for a man who has already found his career. I did nothing today and probably for that reason am in a strange, cold and bad-tempered frame of mind. We're going to Sevastopol not on the 24th, but on the 1st of April.

2 April   Yesterday the battery arrived. I'm living in Sevastopol. Our losses already amount to five thousand, but we're holding out not merely well, but in such a way that our defence must clearly prove to the enemy the impossibility of ever taking Sevastopol. Wrote two pages of *Sevastopol* in the evening.

3, 4, 5, 6, 7 April, morning   All these days I've been so occupied with what has been happening and partly with my duties that I haven't had time yet to write anything except for one incoherent page of *Youth*. Since the 4th the bombardment has eased up, but it still continues. The day before yesterday I spent the night in the 4th bastion.[7] From time to time a ship fires on the town. Yesterday a shell fell near a boy and a girl who were playing horses in the street: they put their arms round each other and fell down together. The girl is the daughter of a sailor's wife. Every day she has been coming to my quarters under a hail of

---

2. Men who served with him in the Danube Army.
3. A. O. Serzhputovsky. The nickname was popularly used of HQ staff officers.
4. Especially the review by Dudyshkin in *Notes of the Fatherland*, No. 2, 1855.
5. The future stories *Sevastopol in December* and

Sevastopol in May.
6. Nothing came of it, since his rank was not sufficiently senior for the appointment.
7. His first night in one of the more exposed positions in Sevastopol, where he was to remain until 15 May.

shells and bombs. My cold is so terrible that I can't settle down to anything.

11 April, 4th Bastion   I've written very, very little of *Youth* or *Sevastopol* in recent days; my cold and feverish condition were the reason for this. Moreover, I'm irritated—especially now when I'm ill—by the fact that it doesn't occur to anybody that I'm good for anything except *chair à canon*, [cannon fodder], and the most useless kind at that. I want to fall in love again with a nurse I saw at the dressing station.

12 April, 4th Bastion   Got on with *Sevastopol by Day and Night* and, I think, it's not bad, and I hope to finish it tomorrow. What a wonderful spirit there is among the sailors! How much superior they are to our soldiers! My lads are a nice lot too, and I enjoy being with them. Yesterday there was another explosion at the 5th battalion: the firing seems to have increased on our side and to have decreased on theirs.

13 April   Still at the same 4th bastion, which I'm beginning to like very much. I'm writing quite a lot. Finished *Sevastopol by Day and Night* today, and wrote a bit of *Youth*. The constant charm of danger and my observations of the soldiers I'm living with, the sailors and the very methods of war are so pleasant that I don't want to leave here, especially as I would like to be present at the assault, if there is one.

14 April   Still at the same 4th bastion, where I feel splendid. Finished a chapter of *Youth* yesterday, and it's not at all bad. Generally speaking my work on *Youth* will lure me on now by the attraction of work begun and nearly half finished. Today I want to write the chapter 'The Haymaking', begin revising *Sevastopol* and begin the soldier's story of how he was hit.[8] O God, I thank Thee for Thy constant protection! How surely Thou leadest me to what is good. And what a worthless creature I would be if Thou were to abandon me. Abandon me not, O God! Help me on my way, not for the satisfaction of my worthless aims, but for the attainment of the great, eternal aim of existence, unknown to me but of which I am aware.

21 April   Seven days in which I've done absolutely nothing except for two rewritten sheets of *Sevastopol* and a proposed address.[9] The day before yesterday we were driven out of the lodgements opposite the 5th bastion, and driven out shamefully. Morale gets lower every day, and the thought of the possibility of the capture of Sevastopol is beginning to become apparent in many ways.

8. The incident comes in *Sevastopol in December*, not in a separate story.
9. A memorandum Tolstoy wrote to the Commander-in-Chief apropos of an officer's proposed patriotic address to the defenders of Sevastopol.

19 May, Position on the river Belbek   On 15 May I was appointed commander of a mountain platoon and moved to a camp on the Belbek, twenty *versts* from Sevastopol. There's a lot to do; I want to attend to the commissariat myself and I see how easy it is to steal—so easy that it's impossible not to steal. I have many plans with regard to this thieving, but I don't know what will come of them. The countryside is delightful, but it's hot. I've done nothing all this time.

31 May   On the 26th Selenginsky, Volynsky and Kamchatsky redoubts were captured. I was in Sevastopol the next day and I'm convinced that it won't fall. My command causes me a good deal of trouble, especially the financial accounts. I'm definitely not capable of practical activity; or if I am capable, then it's only with a great effort, which it isn't worth making since my career is not to be a practical one. [. . .]

31 May   11 p.m. Finished reading *Faust* in the morning. [. . .]

2 June   Got up late. Succumbed to the effect of the sores, *and did nothing* except for reading *Henri Esmond*.[1] Went to see the doctor, who tried to reassure me, but didn't succeed.

8, 9 June   Laziness, laziness. Health bad. Reading *Vanity Fair* all day. [. . .]

11 June   Worked easily in the morning and with great pleasure, but started late and didn't resume in the evening. Apart from that, I twice showed lack of character over the cauterising with lapis, and also in eating cherries. That makes three.

It's absurd that having started writing rules at fifteen I should still be doing so at thirty, without having trusted in, or followed a single one, but still for some reason believing in them and wanting them. Rules should be moral and practical. Here are practical ones, without which there can be no happiness: moderation and acquisition. *Money*.

12, 13, 14, 15 June   Spent two days drilling, went to Bakhchisaray yesterday and received a letter and my article[2] from Panayev. I was flattered that it has been read to the Emperor. My service in Russia is beginning to infuriate me, as it did in the Caucasus. *Laziness*. Vanity, telling Stolypin about my article, and irritability, hitting men at drill. My health gets worse and worse and I think salivation is starting. It's

---

1. Tolstoy's spelling of Thackeray's novel might suggest that he was reading it in French—although his spelling of foreign names was notoriously unreliable and he refers to it later in English as *Esmond's life*. *Vanity Fair* in the next entry is given

its English title and not translated into Russian.
2. The June issue of *The Contemporary*, containing Tolstoy's story *Sevastopol in December*. Tolstoy frequently referred to his stories as "articles."

amazing how loathsome I am, how altogether unhappy and repulsive to myself.

18 June   Finished *Notes of a Cadet*,[3] wrote a letter and sent it off. After dinner I lazed about and read *Pendennis*.[4] [. . .]

24 June   I'm making it a rule when writing to draw up a programme, make a rough draft and a fair copy, but not give a final polish to each section. If you read a thing too often, you make incorrect and unfavourable judgements, the charm and interest of novelty and surprise disappear, and you often strike out what is good and only seems bad from frequent repetition. But the main thing is that with this method you retain enthusiasm for the work. Worked the whole day and can't reproach myself with anything. Hurrah!

26 June   Finished A *Spring Night*;[5] it doesn't seem as good now as it did before. Can't reproach myself with anything.

27 June, Bakhchisaray   Went to Bakhchisaray and read A *Spring Night* to Kovalevsky, who was very pleased with it. My pride was flattered and I was angry with Kryzhanovsky when I learned from Kovalevsky that I had been invited long ago to take part in the Brussels journal.[6] [. . .]

30 June, Position on the river Belbek. 28 June. Use of the day.   Left Bakhchisaray early in the morning, reached my lodgings, had something to eat, gave some orders, wrote a bit of the Diary and set off for Sevastopol. At Inkerman I gave some money to Yelchaninov, visited the Staff officers who are becoming more and more repulsive to me and finally reached Sevastopol. My first encounter was with a shell which burst between the Nikolayevskaya battery and the Grafskyaya pier (next day bullets were found near the library). The second was the news that Nakhimov is mortally wounded. Bronevsky, Meshchersky and Kaloshin are all nice and are fond of me. On the way back next day, 29 June,— the morning of which I spent partly in the officers' battery and partly with Meshchersky—I came across Baron Ferzen at Inkerman and was awfully glad. I really am, I think, beginning to acquire a reputation in Petersburg. The Emperor has ordered *Sevastopol in December* to be translated into French. [. . .]

3. *The Wood-felling*.
4. Here the title of Thackeray's novel is given in Russian, and in abbreviated form.
5. *Sevastopol in May*.

6. The semi-official Russian journal *Le Nord* published in French. Tolstoy only heard indirectly, and not from his immediate superior, that he had been invited to participate.

5 July I'm beginning to be very lazy. The time has only now come when my vanity is being truly tested. I could get on well in life if I were willing to write without following my convictions.

Facts: Soldiers on horseback are awfully fond of singing. Laziness, laziness, laziness.

6 July I hope that today is the last day of the idleness in which I've spent the whole week. All today I've been reading a stupid novel by Balzac[7] and have only just taken up my pen. *Thoughts*: Write the diary of an officer in Sevastopol[8]—various aspects, phases and moments of military life—and publish it in some newspaper. I'm thinking of settling on this idea; although my chief occupation must be *Youth* and *Early Manhood*, the other would be for money, practice in style, and variety. *Reproaches*: (1) Laziness (2) Irritability.

8 July Health very bad, and I can't work. I've done absolutely nothing. I need to accumulate money (1) to pay my debts, (2) to redeem my estate and have the opportunity to free my peasants. I'll copy out rules for play, but only as a means of cutting my losses when I have to play, not of winning. As for the surplus left over from my command of the unit, I'll certainly take it and not tell anyone about it. If I'm asked, I'll say that I took it; I know that it's honest. [. . .]

12 July Wrote nothing all day, read Balzac and have been solely occupied with the new chest.[9] I've decided that I'll keep no government money at all. I'm even surprised how the idea could have occurred to me of even taking what was completely surplus. [. . .]

17 July Health worse. Did nothing. *Three rules*: (1) Be what I am: (*a*) a writer by aptitude, (*b*) an aristocrat by birth. (2) Never speak ill of anyone, and (3) Be economical with money.

19, 20 July Received a letter from Panayev today. They are pleased with *Notes of a Cadet* and will print it in the 8th number. [. . .]

2 August In conversation with Stolypin today about serfdom in Russia, the idea occurred to me more clearly than ever before of writing my four stages in the history of a Russian landowner,[1] with myself as the hero in Khabarovka. The main idea of the novel should be the impossibility of an educated landowner in our times living a just life while

---

7. *Le lys dans la vallée.*
8. A fragment of what may have been the start of this abandoned project has survived (*An Extract from the Diary of Staff-Captain A. of the L. L. Infantry Regiment*).

9. It is not clear whether this refers to the unit's money chest, or to a new type of ammunition chest that was being designed.
1. *The Novel of a Russian Landowner.*

serfdom exists. All its miseries should be exposed, and the means of remedying them indicated.

7 August, Position on the river Belbek I've been to Inkerman and Sevastopol. Won 100 roubles from Odakhovsky and am quits with everyone in the Crimea. Sold Mashtak.[2] Was in good spirits. Decided from today to live only on my pay. I'll play with the money I get from home, and if I lose, then *nec plus ultra* [at the very most] 960 roubles. All that is owed to me and all I receive will be added to the capital I'm accumulating, also what is left from the unit, also everything I win. So far there is only 200 from Rosen. I've behaved well.

25 August I've just been looking at the sky. A wonderful night. O God, have mercy upon me. I am a bad man. Grant that I may be good and happy. Lord have mercy. The stars are in the sky. A bombardment in Sevastopol, music in the camp. I've done no good; on the contrary I won some money from Korsakov. I've been to Simferopol.

2 September Haven't written my diary for a week. Lost a clean 1500 roubles. Sevastopol has surrendered; I was there on my birthday. Worked well today putting my description together.[3] I owe Rosen 300 roubles and lied to him.

17 September Received news yesterday that *A Night* has been mutilated and published.[4] It seems that the *Blues*[5] have got their eyes on me. It's because of my articles. But I wish Russia could always have such moral writers. I can't be a sickly-sweet one, though, and I can't write empty nothings, without ideas and above all without any aim. Despite a first moment of anger when I vowed never again to take up a pen, literature must be my chief and only occupation, taking precedence over all other inclinations and occupations. My aim is literary fame. And the good I can do by my works. Tomorrow I'll go to Karalez[6] and ask for my discharge, and in the morning I'll get on with Youth. [. . .]

19 September, Kermenchik[7] I've moved to Kermenchik; I'm staying with a *secret agent*—a spy. Very interesting. As for women, there seems to be no hope. Wrote a little of *Sevastopol in August*. Did no good to anyone, and no evil. I need at all costs to win fame. I want to publish *Youth* myself. I'll go to the south coast, get some money and apply to return home.

2. A horse.

3. A report for his superior officer on the final bombardment of Sevastopol.

4. *Sevastopol in May*.

5. The gendarmes.

6. The place on the river Belbek where the left flank of the Russian army was temporarily stationed.

7. A village near Bakhchisaray.

20 September   Lots of pretty girls, and sensuality is tormenting me.
[. . .]

21 September   I'll come to grief if I don't reform. Given my character, education, circumstances and abilities, there is no middle course for me—either a brilliant or a wretched future. All my strength of character must go into reform. My chief vices: (1) lack of character—non-fulfilment of plans. Means of reform: (1) to know my general aim, and (2) to think about and note down my future activities and carry them out even if they are bad. My aims: (1) the good of my neighbour and (2) organising myself in such a way as to be able to do this. At the present moment the second is more important than the first, so I must remember all the plans I've made, even if they are contrary to the first general aim. I must prescribe certain actions in advance, at first as few and as easy as possible, and above all ones that don't contradict each other.

My chief aim in life is the good of my neighbour, and its conditional aims—literary fame, based on usefulness and the good of my neighbour; wealth, based on work useful to my neighbour, capital turnover and play, and all devoted towards goodness; and fame in the service, based on usefulness to the country. I'll analyse in my diary what I've done each day to achieve these four aims, and how often I've failed to accomplish what I planned.

Tomorrow, for the first aim, I'll write letters to my aunts and my brother Dmitry, and inquire about the men's food, health and accommodation; for the second I'll draft the plan of an article and write it (or else *Youth*) or as well as *Youth*; for the third I'll do the accounts and write to my headman, and for the fourth I'll study the locality.

23 September   Wrote a letter to Aunt Pelageya Ilinichna, gave advice and promised the Greeks help,[8] which I'll give. For the second aim I drafted the plan of *Sevastopol in August*; for the third, wrote to my headman; for the fourth, rode to our station. Didn't write *Youth*, didn't bother about the men and didn't do the accounts. [. . .]

1 October, Foti-Sala[9]   These last three days I've been constantly busy and on the move; yesterday I even fired two rounds of grape shot. Haven't washed or undressed, and have behaved in a disorganised way. Completely forgot my aims. [. . .]

10 October   I've been in a lazily apathetic, perpetually dissatisfied state for a long time now. Won another 130 roubles at cards. Bought a horse and bridle for 150. What nonsense! My career is literature—to write

8. "Nicholas I's legion" consisting of local Greek volunteers, to whom Tolstoy promised artillery   support.
9. A village near Bakhchisaray.

and write! From tomorrow I'll work all my life or throw up everything—rules, religion, propriety—everything.

21 November   I'm in Petersburg, at Turgenev's.[1] Lost 2800 before leaving, and only just managed to transfer 600 to my debtors. Picked up 875 roubles in the country. It's most important for me to behave myself well here. For that the main thing I need is: (1) to deal cautiously but boldly with people who can harm me, (2) to manage my expenses carefully and (3) to work. Tomorrow I'll get on with *Youth* and write a bit of the diary.[2]

LEO TOLSTOY

Selected Letters, 1858–95[†]

To Countess A. A. Tolstaya[1]

Yasnaya, Polyana,
1 May 1858

*   *   *

Yesterday I rode into a wood which I've bought and am felling, and there on the birch trees the leaves were coming out and the nightingales nesting; and they've no wish to know that they don't belong to the crown now, but to me, and that they'll be felled. They will be felled, but they'll grow again, and they've no wish to know about anyone. I don't know how to convey this feeling—one becomes ashamed of one's human dignity and the arbitrariness one is so proud of—the arbitrariness of drawing imaginary lines and not having the right to make a single solitary alteration to anything—not even to oneself. There are laws governing all things, laws you don't understand, but you feel this curb everywhere—everywhere *He* exists. My disagreement with your opinion about my little piece[2] goes right back to this. You are wrong to look at it from a Christian point of view. My idea was this: three creatures died—a lady,

1. Tolstoy arrived in Petersburg on 21 November. He had been sent as a military courier with a report on the artillery action at Sevastopol and stayed with Turgenev, who had become acquainted with his sister and brother and to whom he had dedicated his story *The Wood-felling*. A plaque now marks the house on the Fontanka near the Anichkov bridge where Tolstoy shared Turgenev's apartment.
2. Perhaps the diary referred to in n. 8, p. 312.
†From *Tolstoy's Letters*, trans. and ed. R. F. Christian (New York, 1978). Reprinted with permission of Scribner's Publishers.

1. The Countess Alexandra Andreyevna Tolstaya (1817–1904) was a relative of Tolstoy's (the daughter of his grandfather's brother). With her close connections at court she was able to assist and protect him. It is likely that had she been ten years younger, Tolstoy would have fallen in love with her. He frequently addresses her in a jocular way as "Granny." She took a particular interest in Tolstoy's spiritual development.
2. *Three Deaths*. Tolstoy must have sent her a manuscript copy, as the story was not published until January 1859.

a peasant and a tree. The lady is pitiful and loathsome because she has lied all her life, and lies when on the point of death. Christianity, as she understands it, doesn't solve the problem of life and death for her. Why die when you want to live? With her mind and her imagination she believes in the future promises of Christianity, but her whole being kicks against it, she has no consolation (except a pseudo-Christian one)—but her place is already reserved. She is loathsome and pitiful. The peasant dies peacefully just because he is not a Christian. His religion is different, even though by force of habit he has observed the Christian ritual: his religion is nature, which he has lived with. He himself felled trees, sowed rye and reaped it, and slaughtered sheep; sheep were born, and children were born, and old men died, and he knew this law perfectly well and never deviated from it as the lady did, but looked it fairly and squarely in the face. Une brute, you say; but how can une brute be bad? Une brute is happiness and beauty, and harmony with the whole world, and not discord as in the case of the lady. The tree dies peacefully, honestly and beautifully. Beautifully— because it doesn't lie, doesn't put on airs, isn't afraid, and has no regrets. There you have my idea, and of course you don't agree with it; but it can't be disputed—it is in my soul, and in yours too. That the idea is badly expressed I agree with you. Otherwise, you, with your fine sense, would have understood it, and I wouldn't have had to write this explanation which I'm afraid will anger you and make you give me up as a bad job. Don't give me up, Granny. I do have Christian feelings, and highly developed ones even; but I have something else too, that's very dear to me. It's a feeling of love and tranquillity. How these two are reconciled I don't know and can't explain; but dogs and cats do lie in the same shed—that's for certain. Goodbye, Granny dear; please write to me about yourself. Give my very best regards, of course, to all your people and don't tell them what a godless fellow I am. You're quite different: it seems to me that you understand everything—you have a chord that responds to everything. Well, come what may: I'm expecting an explosive letter back from you, or even worse, one of gentle commiseration.[3] No, I'd rather you were angry. I'm expecting Mashenka, Auntie and all of them in a day or two.

Goodbye, Granny dear; I cordially press your hand.

Yours,
Count L. Tolstoy

---

3. She replied that his religious views in no way appalled her, that the seed was germinating in him and that God had planted it in too good a soil for it to be choked.

To V. P. Botkin[4]

Yasnaya Polyana, 3 May 1859

Vasily Petrovich, Vasily Petrovich! What have I done with my *Family Happiness*! Only here and now, having come to my senses at leisure and having read the proofs yet sent me of the 2nd part, have I come to see what disgraceful s . . . this loathsome work is—a blemish on me, not only as an author, but as a man. You tricked me into handing it over; now you can be privy to my shame and remorse.[5] I'm now dead and buried as a writer and as a man! That's positive, especially as the 1st part is worse still. Please don't write me a single word of consolation, but if you sympathise with my sorrow and wish to be a friend, persuade Katkov not to publish this 2nd part but to take the money back from me, or consider me in his debt till autumn. I'm keeping my word and I've corrected the proofs with a disgust which I can't describe to you. There isn't a living word in the whole thing, and the ugliness of the language stemming from the ugliness of the idea is inconceivable. But if it's not possible to take away this cup from me, be a friend, look through the proofs and cross out and correct what you can. I can't. I feel like crossing everything out. If, however, you can manage to save me from the still greater shame of having the 2nd part published, burn it, and get the manuscript from Katkov and burn that too. I was right to want to publish it under a pseudonym. I can return the 350 roubles in a week. The end of the story hasn't been sent to me, and there's no need to send it. It's torture to see it, read it and be reminded of it.

Goodbye now; I press your hand and beg you seriously and sympathetically to try to understand what I am writing.

Yours,

L. Tolstoy

I'm sending the proofs to Katkov, but hope that you receive this letter before he does the proofs.

To A. V. Druzhinin[6]

Yasnaya Polyana, 9 October 1859

I believe, my dear Alexander Vasilyevich, that you love me as a man, and not as an editor loves a hack writer who might be some good to

4. Vasily Petrovich Botkin (1811–69), a writer and critic. The eldest son of a Moscow tea merchant, he devoted much time to the study of literature and foreign languages. He was an adherent to the principle of "art for art's sake." Tolstoy first met him in January 1856, and a close friendship was established between the two men. Tolstoy valued Botkin's literary taste very highly.
5. At first Botkin disliked Tolstoy's *Family Happiness*—he found it cold and boring—but he nevertheless advised him to publish it, recognising its obvious merit. However, in reading the proofs of the second part of the work, Botkin's attitude changed considerably; on 13 May he wrote to Tolstoy of its "enormous inner dramatic interest," and he spoke of it as an "excellent psychological study."
6. Alexander Vasilyevich Druzhinin (1824–64), critic, author, and translator. His first work of fiction, *Polinka Sachs* (1847), enjoyed considerable success. He was another staunch advocate of "art for art's sake" and exerted considerable influence over the development of Tolstoy's aesthetic views.

him. As a writer I'm no longer good for anything. I'm not writing, and
I haven't written since *Family Happiness*, and I don't think I shall write
in future—at least I flatter myself with this hope. Why is this? It's a long
and difficult story. The main reason is that life is short, and to waste it
in my adult years writing the sort of stories I used to write makes me
feel ashamed. I can and must and want to get down to business. It would
be good if it could be the sort of thing which would tire me out, which
urgently needed doing and would give me courage, pride and strength—
that would be all right. But I really can't lift a finger to write stories
which are very nice and pleasant to read, now that I'm 31. It's funny
that I should even think about writing a story at all. And so I can't grant
your wish, however disappointing it is for me to refuse.

*   *   *

To Countess S. A. Tolstaya[7]

Saransk, 4 September 1869

I'm writing to you from Saransk, my dear. I've almost reached the place.[8]
It's 46 versts from here. I'm hiring private horses, and going straight on
to the place.

How are you and the children? Has anything happened? For two days
now I've been tormented with anxiety. The day before yesterday I spent
the night at Arzamas, and something extraordinary happened to me. It
was 2 o'clock in the morning, I was terribly tired, I wanted to go to
sleep and I felt perfectly well. But suddenly I was overcome by despair,
fear and terror, the like of which I have never experienced before. I'll
tell you the details of this feeling later: but I've never experienced such
an agonising feeling before and may God preserve anyone else from
experiencing it.[9] I jumped up and ordered the horses to be harnessed.
While they were being harnessed, I fell asleep, and woke up perfectly
well. Yesterday the feeling returned to a far lesser extent during the
drive, but I was prepared for it and didn't succumb, more particularly
as it was weaker. Today I feel well and happy, in so far as I can be,
away from the family.

During this journey I felt for the first time how much I have grown
together with you and the children. I can remain alone doing a regular
job, as I do in Moscow, but when I have nothing to do, as now, I
definitely feel I can't be alone.

*   *   *

7. Sofya Andreyevna Tolstaya, *née* Behrs (1844–
1919), Tolstoy's wife. He proposed and married
her in September 1862. They were very much in
love, shared lofty ideals of family life, and wanted
to have many children. She idolized him as a
writer and assisted him in numerous ways.

8. Tolstoy was travelling to a small place in the
province of Penza in the hope of buying an estate
he had seen advertised in the papers.
9. The incident is described in Tolstoy's *Memoirs
of a Madman*, written in the middle 1880s and
published posthumously.

To G. A. Rusanov[1]

Moscow, 12 March 1889

*   *   *

It's a strange thing—the books I always carry about with me, and which I would like to have always, are the unwritten books: The Prophets, the Gospels, Beal's Buddha, Confucius, Mencius, Lao-Tzu, Marcus Aurelius, Socrates, Epictetus, Pascal. Nevertheless I sometimes want to write, and, can you imagine, it's usually a novel actually—a broad, free one like *Anna Karenina* which could include without any strain everything that seemed comprehensible to me, from a new, unusual, and useful angle. The rumor about a story has its foundations.[2] A couple of years ago I did indeed write a story in rough draft on the theme of sexual love, but so carelessly and unsatisfactorily that I shan't revise it, and if I were to take up the idea again I would start writing from the beginning. There is nobody to whom I write and tell so much about my literary works and dreams as I am now doing to you, because I know there is nobody who has such a warm regard for this side of my life as you have.

Karamzin said somewhere that the important thing is not to write *A History of the Russian State* but to live well.[3] This can't be repeated often enough to writers. I'm convinced from experience how good it is not to write. There is no avoiding it, the job of each one of us is simply to fulfil the will of Him who sent us. And the will of Him who sent us is that we should be perfect, even as our heavenly father, and only by this means, i.e. by our approach towards perfection, can we influence other people—the watering can must be filled to the brim for it to pour—and this influence will work through our life and through the oral and written word, in so far as this word will be a part and a consequence of our life, and in so far as the mouth will speak out of the fullness of the heart. I kiss you and your wife and children.

Yours affectionately,

L. Tolstoy

To V. G. Chertkov[4]

Yasnaya Polyana, 15 April 1891

[18 lines omitted] . . . My wife returned from Petersburg yesterday, where she saw the Emperor and spoke to him about me and my writ-

1. Gavriil Andreyevich Rusanov (1845–1907), a landowner in the province of Voronezh, a graduate of the University of Moscow and a member of various district courts until 1887 when he was disabled by illness. Always a keen admirer of Tolstoy's fiction, he decided after reading A *Confession* to visit him to discuss various moral and religious problems raised by the book, and their friendship dates from Rusanov's visit to Yasnaya Polyana in 1883. Tolstoy respected and trusted his aesthetic sensibility and frequently discussed literature with

him.
2. *The Kreutzer Sonata*.
3. A paraphrase of a passage in a letter to A. I. Turgenev.
4. Vladimir Grigoryevich Chertkov (1854–1936), Tolstoy's most famous and dedicated disciple, was profoundly influenced by his religious and ethical ideas and was responsible for publishing and popularizing many of his works. He was the dominant figure in Tolstoy's life after 1883.

ings—completely in vain. He promised her to allow *The Kreutzer Sonata* to be published, which doesn't please me at all. There was something nasty about *The Kreutzer Sonata*. Any mention of it is terribly offensive to me. There was something bad about the motives which guided me in writing it, such bitterness has it caused. I can even see what was bad. I'll try not to let this happen again if I manage to finish anything . . .[2 lines omitted]

To M. O. Menshikov[5]

Yasnaya Polyana, 8 September 1895

Dear Mikhail Osipovich,

I learned from your letter that our difference of opinion is far greater than I thought.[6] I very much regret this, but I don't despair of removing it. You say that the intervention of reason doesn't contribute to the good, and that goodness depends on the practice of the good and the conditions in which people are placed. This is the very root of our difference of opinion. Firstly, reason and intelligence—Vernunft and Verstand—are two completely different attributes, and it's necessary to distinguish between them. Bismarck and people like him have a lot of intelligence, but no reason. Intelligence is the ability to understand and grasp the worldly conditions of life, but reason is the divine power of the soul which reveals to it its attitude to the world and to God. Reason is not only not the same thing as intelligence, but is the opposite of it: reason releases a man from the temptations (deceits) which intelligence puts in his way. This is the main activity of reason: by removing temptations, reason releases the essence of the human soul—love—and enables it to manifest itself. In childhood there are few temptations, and so the essence of the soul—love—is more evident in children, but *temptations are bound to come into the world*,[7] and so they do, and a return to love is only possible through the removal of temptations, and the removal of temptations is only achieved through the activity of reason. This is the fundamental idea of the Christian teaching, and I have tried to express it in all my writings as well as I could. That's the first point. Secondly, if goodness—love—has only increased, as you say, as a result of inherited characteristics, environment, the conditions in which a man finds himself, the practice of love—also independent of his will—then all our

5. Mikhail Osipovich Menshikov (1859–1919), a journalist who was working at the time for the newspaper *The Week* and who spent a few days at Yasnaya Polyana in 1895. He subsequently turned against Tolstoy and attacked him on several occasions in print.

6. Tolstoy's letter is part of a correspondence concerning his story *Master and Man*. Menshikov had written an article about the story ("Have We Lost the Road?") which badly misinterpreted the doc-

trine of non-resistance to evil which served as the theme of the story. L. P. Nikiforov had seen the article and had written a refutation of it ("Where is the Road?"), first sending it to Tolstoy, who then wrote to Menshikov, trying to clarify his ideas. This is his second letter to Menshikov about the question.

7. Probably a reference to Matthew 18, 7 ("for it must needs be that offences come").

arguments about goodness would be completely useless. If my heredity is not good, my environment not good and the practice of my life not good, then not only do I not need any arguments about what goodness is, but, on the contrary, I need the sort of arguments which would represent my badness as goodness. And so it often happens. If there is no free activity of the reason to remove temptations in people, and thereby release in them the divine essence of their life—love; if every man is the product of the conditions surrounding him and the causes preceding him, then there is neither good nor evil, neither morality nor immorality, and there is no point in our thinking and talking and writing letters and articles, but we should *take life as it comes*, as the saying has it. If my heredity and environment are bad, I shall be bad; if they are good, I shall be good. I don't think that is so. I think that every man possesses a free, creative, divine power (For as the Father hath life in himself, so hath he given to the Son to have life in himself—John 5, 26). And this power is reason. The more this power increases, the more the essence of a man's life—love—is released within him, and the more closely is man united with other beings and with God. The aim of the life of each individual man and of all mankind is this greater and greater unity of people with each other, with the whole world and with God, which is only brought about by reason. And so the activity of reason is the highest activity of man. The Christian teaching which I profess consists in recognising this activity as life itself. That is why I can't agree with you, not only that one can and must prefer spontaneous, unreasoning goodness which constitutes the physiological attribute of certain creatures to the reasonable activity of people consciously striving to follow the dictates of reason, but I cannot even compare the two.

The goodness of a dove is not a virtue. And a dove is no more virtuous than a wolf, or the gentle Slav more virtuous than the vindictive Circassian. Virtue and the degrees of it only begin when reasonable activity begins.

I shall be very upset if my arguments don't remove our difference of opinion. But I can't agree with you, because to do so I would have to renounce all I have lived by these past 15 years, and what I live by now and what I intend to die with.

I'm sending Nikiforov's article. I meant to tone down those passages in it where he, in the heat of the argument, ascribes to you thoughts which you probably never had, but I shan't manage to do so, there's no time. It would be good if you could do it. He gave me carte blanche to change the article and I hand it on to you. It's desirable because it isn't a question of who got the better of whom in the argument, but of making the truth as clear as possible.

I press your hand in friendship.

Yours affectionately,
L. Tolstoy

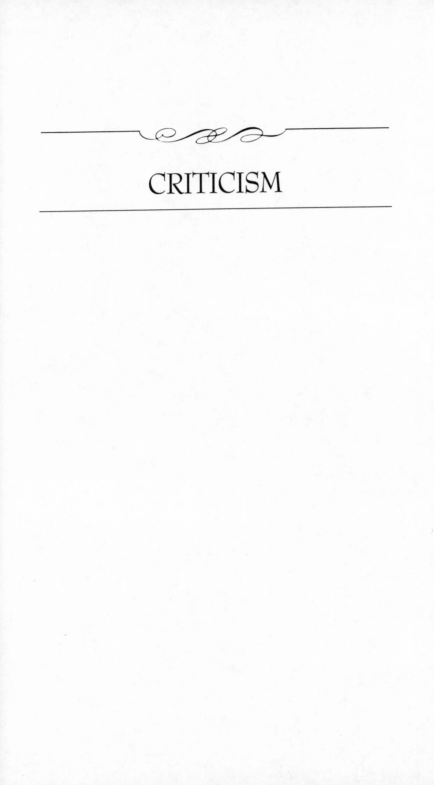

CRITICISM

HENRY GIFFORD

On Translating Tolstoy†

I

One may guess that Tolstoy's readers in the English language are not greatly outnumbered by those who read him in Russian. *War and Peace*, *Anna Karenina*, *Resurrection*, no less than the *Iliad* and the *Odyssey*, have their place in world literature. So it is reasonable to recall Matthew Arnold's classic essay 'On Translating Homer' (1861), not only because the appeal of Tolstoy in his freshness and wide scope is not unlike that of Homer, but because with so many readers depending upon English translation for their knowledge of a very important writer, the question of how to communicate his effect is quite as central for us as that of how to represent Homer was for Arnold. And of all Arnold's 'practical advice to a translator', the most pressing is that Homer 'should be approached . . . in the simplest frame of mind possible'. He recognised that Homer was in many ways remote from the modern age, whereas Tolstoy's milieu still, of course, remains largely accessible to us. The Russian language he wrote is no more strange to the ears of his countrymen today than the language of Dickens, George Eliot or, for that matter, Arnold is to ours. Despite the immense upheavals of political and industrial revolution in Russia, the last five or six decades of the Empire, during which Tolstoy wrote, are more present to our imaginations than the age of Peter the First was to his. At the beginning of the 1870s he was forced to abandon a projected novel on the life and times of Peter. All the characters, as his wife pointed out to him, were dressed and in their places; but they did not breathe.[1] Tolstoy, of course, brings his own time alive for us as no contemporary of Peter's could bring alive that earlier period for him. Yet the historical imagination is hardly needed to call up the world in which Tolstoy lived. The nineteenth century is still part of what we term the modern age.

Arnold required that his translator should not take Homer's text in the wrong spirit. He cites the misunderstanding by Ruskin of two lines from the *Iliad*. Helen has just mentioned her brothers Castor and Pollux who she thinks are alive:

> So she spoke; but them there already covered the life-giving earth
> Away in Lacedaemon in their dear fatherland.

(III. 243–4)

---

†From *New Essays on Tolstoy*, ed. M. Jones (Cambridge, 1978). Reprinted by permission of Cambridge University Press.

1. B. Eykhenbaum, *Lev Tolstoy: semidesyatyye gody* (Leningrad, 1960), pp. 127–8.

Ruskin commented: 'The poet has to speak of the earth in sadness; but he will not let that sadness affect or change his thought of it. No; though Castor and Pollux be dead, yet the earth is our mother still,—fruitful, life-giving.' That kind of sophistication is not likely to arise today when we read Tolstoy: no modern habits of feeling have to be unlearnt.

And yet fidelity to Tolstoy's meaning is not so easily won. He complained about the translators of Homer who gave 'boiled and distilled tepid water' instead of what was really there: 'water from a spring causing the teeth to ache,—with glitter and sun and even with little splinters and dust-specks.'[2] The translations we shall look at are certainly not 'tepid'; but Tolstoy in his own fashion can set the teeth aching, and the translator may often want to discard the 'little splinters and dust-specks'.

When Robert Bridges put two passages from Tolstoy into his anthology *The Spirit of Man* (1916), he allowed himself the same liberties as with Plato, in rendering whom, he said 'I have aimed at pleasing myself'. Nevill Forbes gave him a literal translation; but this compiler who had been 'guided by his own moods' did not hesitate to touch up the description of Prince Andrey and Pierre philosophising on the ferry (*War and Peace*, II.ii.12) so that the general tone would not jar with that of his passages from Plato, Marcus Aurelius or St Augustine. The idiom of all these translations is more deliberately archaising; but the rhythms of the King James Bible played a subtle part in changing the rhetoric of Tolstoy here into one that is not quite the same in cadence:

> Neither have I seen it: nor is it possible for any one to see it who looks upon this life as the sum and end of all . . . in the universe, in the whole universe, truth has its kingdom; and we who are now children of the earth are none the less children of the universe. Do I not feel in my soul that I am actually a member of this vast harmonious whole? . . . I feel not only that I cannot utterly perish, since nothing in the universe is annihilated, but that I always shall be and always was . . .

The original has not the organ music of this which seemed appropriate to Bridges. Pierre says 'the end of all' (*konets vsego*), not 'the sum and end'; and in the latter part of the second sentence he is less smoothly elegant than Bridges: 'and we are now the children of earth, but eternally the children of the whole universe'. He feels that 'I form a part' (*sostavlyayu chast'*), not that 'I am actually a member', of 'this vast harmonious whole'. (Had Bridges somewhere in mind St Paul's saying 'for we are members one of another'?)[3] Finally, Pierre does not seek to vary his phrases: he will say with an awkward insistence, 'I feel that I not only cannot disappear as nothing disappears in the universe, but that I

2. L. N. Tolstoy, *O literature: stat'i, pis'ma, dnev-niki* (Moscow, 1955), pp. 134–5; letter to A. A.   Fet, 1–6 January 1871.
3. Ephesians 4.25.

always shall be and always was.' 'I cannot utterly perish' is surely Biblical, perhaps by way of the Gettysburg address 'shall not perish from the earth'; and 'nothing is annihilated' seems to be invoking a scientific law, whereas Pierre's word 'disappear' (*ischeznut'*) gives the bare fact, shocking the mind which cannot conceive of itself as no longer present.

More may be said about the ways in which Bridges has manipulated the entire paragraph from which the quotations were taken. After Pierre's question 'Do I not feel . . . that I am actually a member', there follows a second which Bridges has rendered 'Do I not feel that . . . I make one link . . .?' But the word he translates 'I make' is the same *sostavlyayu*, 'I form', of the previous sentence. Tolstoy then refers to a 'ladder that leads from plant to man'; but the next sentence, which once again has the ladder, is dropped by Bridges, perhaps as being redundant, and thus he avoids a threefold emphasis on the same image. And his rendering of the previous clauses—'then why must I suppose that it breaks off at me, and does not lead on further and beyond?'—has a deftness not to be found in the Russian words: 'then why do I suppose that this ladder, to which I do not see an end below, it [*sic*] is lost among the plants?' There would be no point in preserving Tolstoy's faulty grammar; but at least the clumsy original should remind us that Pierre's eloquence has its basis in the irregularities of conversation. This oversight makes his voice actual to us, behind the rhetorical cadences.

Bridges was also tempted to poeticise the text. Where Tolstoy notes that now 'the evening frost was covering with stars the puddles at the ferry', the effect is made more ornamental by Bridges: 'the evening frost was beginning to incrust the little pools on the shore with starry crystals . . .', and the closing lines almost transfer the scene to Innisfree: 'The ferry-boat lay drifted along the bank, and only the ripples of the current could be heard lapping feebly against its sides. Prince André fancied that this patter of the water babbled a refrain to Pierre's words "That is sooth, accept it: that is sooth, accept it." ' Tolstoy's description was sturdier and more direct: 'The ferry-boat had long since put in, and only the waves of the stream with a feeble sound struck against the bottom of the ferry-boat. To Prince Andrey it seemed that this gurgling of the waves to Pierre's words kept repeating: "True, believe this." ' The final phrase in Russian, *Pravda, ver' etomu*, plays lightly with onomatopoeia. But it is not a babbled refrain. The rendering by Bridges might conceivably have done for Turgenev, and there was a time earlier in his career when Tolstoy aspired to write in Turgenev's manner. It is not, however, the mood of the scene that counts for him in this passage, but its appropriateness to the metaphysical ideas expressed by Pierre. Prince Andrey would like to believe him, and fancies that the sound of the water has lulled his own doubts.

II

The translator of Tolstoy will find himself in varying degrees wanting to mediate between that 'continuous literary decorum' so much prized by Bridges and the literal text a good dictionary can supply. Arnold would have him 'penetrated by a sense' of the author's eminent qualities, and what these are, in Tolstoy no less than in Homer, should be plain enough. Yet we all make assumptions about style, and may impose them without fully recognising the fact. 'The simplest frame of mind possible' will be complicated by an awareness that the English reader has formed certain expectations, based on what he regards as the appropriate idiom for a modern novel. If Tolstoy seems to him outlandish or pedantic, he will feel let down by the translator. Everyone concedes that the rendering of poetry must be imperfect. Not everyone realises that the rendering of imaginative prose has its pitfalls, and that the great majority of translators, partly through the sheer bulk of their undertaking, and partly through inattention, fail to accomplish what is possible.

There are four translators of Tolstoy ahead of all others in English—Louise and Aylmer Maude, working usually together but sometimes separately; Constance Garnett; and Rosemary Edmonds whose Penguin versions are now widely known. It seems better to leave N. H. Dole and Professor Leo Wiener out of the reckoning. They were pioneers, but nobody is going to argue that the quality of their work has earned them more than a wayside cross. The other four have more solid claims to attention. The Maudes indeed, with their *Tolstoy Centenary Edition* (1928–37), made their bid to establish an Authorised Version. They were not unreasonable in hoping this might be so. The Norton Critical Editions of *War and Peace* and *Anna Karenina* did well to use the Maude rendering. It is the soundest we have, and Tolstoy himself admired their work.

Constance Garnett preceded them in the translation of *Anna Karenina* (1901), *The Death of Ivan Ilyitch, and other stories* (1902), and *War and Peace* (1904), though Louise Maude's *Resurrection* dates from 1900 (revised edition 1902). Mrs Garnett then moved on to other writers—Dostoyevsky and Chekhov (having already translated Turgenev). She has been much praised as a translator, in one respect immoderately so: it is now well understood that her Russian was not dependable. Maude in an appendix to his first volume of Tolstoy's *Life*[4] has pointed out some definite mistakes, and these are not untypical, as any close reading of her work against the original will show. To give a random example (not quoted by Maude): when Levin waits in the hotel before going to Kitty's house as her accepted lover, he overhears the people in the next room (*Anna Karenina*, IV.15). Tolstoy wrote: 'they were saying something about machines and fraud and they were coughing a morning cough.'

4. 'English Translations of Tolstoy' in *The Life of Tolstoy: First Fifty Years* (London, 1930), pp. 456ff.

Mrs Garnett translates: 'they were talking about some sort of machines, and swindling, and coughing their morning coughs.' The first clause is wrong; the second could appear to state that swindling was their activity, not their topic; and the third misses the point of a 'morning cough'—which has a particular sound of its own. 'Their morning coughs' suggest a routine. But Levin in his heightened awareness notices that a morning cough is something different.

The appeal of Constance Garnett consists in her sensibility. She can write with a delicacy of touch which the Maudes, for all their diligence and good sense, seldom achieve. This shows particularly when she hits on some phrase so apt as to seem definitive: ' "When I'm old and ugly I'll be the same", Betsy used to say, "but for a pretty young woman like you *it's early days for that house of charity*" ' (II.4, my italics). Again it seems right that the exclamation used both by Anna and Vronsky in the distress that follows the consummating of their love, *radi Boga*, should be rendered as 'for pity's sake' (II.11); and that (earlier) Anna on seeing her husband at the station in St Petersburg should have found herself saying: 'Oh, mercy! why do his ears look like that?' (I.30). Mrs Garnett muddles at least one of those utterances from Fyodor after the threshing scene which matter so much to Levin (VIII.11); but his final remark comes over in her version with a naturalness not approached here by the Maudes. They put it, stiffly: 'Take you, for instance, you won't injure anyone either . . .' Constance Garnett overlooks the 'either' (*tozhe*); but she catches the rhythm of ordinary speech: 'Take you now, you wouldn't wrong a man . . .' This translation comes alive because it is not cluttered with terms alien to a rustic vocabulary—'for instance', 'injure'—and because there is the sanction of a traditional way of life expressed in that simple phrase 'wrong a man'. The emphasis on 'man' is correct. Fyodor several times uses the word *chelovek*. He expounds a morality in which the due relation with God ensures a proper regard for man. But the precept falls differently in the Maudes' version: it has not been realised, and the insensitivity to rhythm betrays that.

Constance Garnett may also be commended for her refusal to tamper with Tolstoy's syntax. She had an ear for the cadencing of prose to the same degree as Bridges; but she would accept the angularities in Tolstoy and not shrink from his repetitions:

> every day he made ready to talk to her. But every time he began talking to her, he felt that the spirit of evil and deceit, which had taken possession of her, had possession of him too, and he talked to her in a tone quite unlike that in which he had meant to talk. Involuntarily he talked to her in his habitual tone . . . (II.10)

Here it is the Maudes who depart from absolute fidelity to the text:

Every day he prepared himself to have a talk with her. But
each time he began to speak with her he felt the same spirit
of evil and falsehood which had taken possession of her master
him also, and he neither said the things he meant to, nor
spoke in the tone he had meant to adopt. He spoke involuntarily . . .

The many small changes in this may seem preferable to Tolstoy's re-
iterations, which have an aggressive note. Mrs Garnett, however, serves
him better. She has reproduced his mannerism, and yet contrives to
write an English that does not seem uncouth or defiant, as a literal
translation without her modest harmonies probably would.

Aylmer Maude and his wife were qualified in everything except a
creative sense of language to make the ideal translation. They had lived
long in Russia (Louise Maude was born there); they knew Tolstoy intimately, and Aylmer Maude understood, and appraised with an independent mind, the ideas and aims of Tolstoy. Also, as he tells us, they
kept each a vigilant eye on the other's performance. The result is a lucid
and accurate version, at home with the peculiarities of Russian life, and
written in a serviceable prosaic English of the kind we associate with
Mark Rutherford or Gissing. Their work can always be counted on for
those negative virtues which temper a style: sobriety, explicitness, a firm
hold on the argument. However, their resources are limited in range of
tone. They have little sense of colloquial idiom, and certainly not the
inventiveness to match the elliptical and wary speech of the Russian
peasant. In rendering such plays as *The Power of Darkness* they are
competent to give a neutral paraphrase; but the effect is almost that of
the interpreter who explains to the foreign bystander 'What he is saying,
is . . .'.

For the general reader today it is probably Rosemary Edmonds, the
Penguin translator, who represents Tolstoy. Her *Anna Karenina* (1954),
War and Peace (1957) and *Resurrection* (1966) are very widely available.
Like all translations issued by Penguin Books, her work is readable and
it moves lightly and freely; the dialogue in particular is much more
convincing than that contrived by the Maudes. There is a moment in
The Cossacks when Maryana rounds upon Olenin with the indignant
words translated in the Maudes' version as 'Leave me alone, you pitch!'
(chapter 31). It sounds bizarre, and reminiscent of Fluellen; but they
have, with unblinking fidelity, given the sense of *Otstan', smola!* 'Let
go, you wicked man' from Rosemary Edmonds loses the smirching effect,
and faintly suggests a Victorian melodrama, but at least it can pass for
living speech.

In dealing with the many hundreds of pages in a major novel by
Tolstoy, the translator may be expected now and again to slip. Tolstoy
himself was an indefatigable reviser, always prone to jettison whole

sentences in proof. Ideally his translator should approach the text with a similar resolve to make every word justify its presence. Miss Edmonds is sometimes lax about detail—and in Tolstoy's writing detail is always significant. At the close of a chapter to which I have already referred—that describing Levin's visit to Kitty and his future parents-in-law (*Anna Karenina*, IV.15)—he is overcome with tenderness for the old prince on seeing how Kitty responds to her father's embrace and blessing. If we follow Miss Edmonds, it would seem that he noticed 'how fervently and tenderly Kitty kissed his strong hand'. But she kissed it *long*, not fervently, and the hand was *fleshy*. Hands are expressive for Tolstoy—think of Napoleon's, or Speransky's, or the small energetic hands of Anna. Miss Edmonds, and Mrs Garnett too who changes it to 'muscular', presumably did not want the prince to have a 'fleshy' hand.

It is in small but damaging ways like this that a translator can falsify the effect of Tolstoy. These are indeed minute particulars, but they are far from being trivial.

III

At this point we are brought up against those qualities in Tolstoy's style about which the translator, if he takes the advice of Arnold, should be clear in his mind. R. F. Christian's study of *War and Peace* has a chapter that will greatly help him to do this.[5] The first thing that a translator should note is Tolstoy's lifelong preoccupation with different kinds of rhetoric. Christian claims that he used in *War and Peace* 'every device of arrangement and balance known to Cicero and Demosthenes', and shows for example how he would set his clauses in groups of three.[6] The general impression among readers may be that Tolstoy is an exceedingly natural writer, blunt to the point of gracelessness. But he was always a rhetorician, though his style over a span of sixty years did not remain fixed in one pattern. Eykhenbaum emphasises that the opening of *Sevastopol in May* (1855) has the 'exalted and pathetic' style of a declamation, and points out how much in constructing it he had learned from reading verse and particularly that of Lermontov.[7] At the start of the 1870s, between *War and Peace* and *Anna Karenina*, Tolstoy was teaching the peasant boys on his estate, and came to feel more and more dissatisfied with his previous manner of writing. He decided that the language used by the peasants was 'the best poetic regulator. You may want to say what is superfluous, high-flown, unhealthy—the language will not allow it, while our literary language has no bones; so pampered, you may talk whatever rubbish you like—it all resembles literature.'[8]

5. R. F. Christian, *Tolstoy's 'War and Peace': A Study* (Oxford, 1962), chapter 5.
6. *Ibid.*, p. 152.
7. B. M. Eykhenbaum, *Lev Tolstoy* (Munich, 1968), vol. I, pp. 170–2.
8. Letter to N. N. Strakhov, 25 March 1872, quoted by Eykhenbaum, *Lev Tolstoy: semidesyatyye gody*, p. 80.

The stories he wrote for his *ABC* (*Azbuka*) were to achieve that simplicity of outline which he admired in Russian folk poetry and in Homer—like 'pencil sketches without shading'.[9] The supreme example is of course *A Prisoner in the Caucasus* (1872). Soon afterwards the reading of Pushkin's prose tales gave him a fresh incentive to simplicity which can be felt in the style of *Anna Karenina* when compared with that of *War and Peace*. Then at the beginning of the next decade there was another change of manner, arising from his deep spiritual crisis, and resulting in the brilliant expository prose of *A Confession*. In all these phases much persisted from the original character revealed first of all in his diary:[1] the same blend of acute observation and laboured analysis under heads, the working of a mind almost excessively precise, which sought out fixities, the irreducible elements in feeling. He has no patience with ambiguity or with anything that resists definition.

Tolstoy is in one respect easy to translate. Vladimir Nabokov's revised version of *Eugene Onegin* now includes in the commentary what he calls a 'Correlative Lexicon', the purpose of which is to fix in English the exact shade of meaning for the words most often used by Pushkin. Many of these, which express nuances of feeling, are extremely hard to match in another language: *umileniye, skuka, toska, nega* to name merely a few. But Tolstoy is not concerned with this kind of sensibility. More interesting and tangible to him are such conditions as *styd* (shame) and *nelovkost'* (awkwardness), in which his characters so often find themselves. Penetrating though Tolstoy's analysis never fails to be, his moral vocabulary is transparent.

All the same, this definiteness can present problems. These are not in the recognition of terms, but spring rather from his peculiar syntax. More than most writers of prose fiction, Tolstoy would ignore the conventional order of words for the sake of registering his impression more faithfully. *A Prisoner in the Caucasus* might have been considered the very plainest of narratives, offering no difficulties. But extreme honesty— the willingness to see things exactly as they are—calls for the closest attention from a translator. Just before Zhilin is captured, we are told in the Maude version: 'He saw a red-bearded Tartar on a grey horse, with his gun raised, come at him yelling and showing his teeth.'[2] But Tolstoy put it differently: 'He sees—there draws near to him a red-bearded Tartar on a grey horse. He yelps, he has bared his teeth, gun at the ready.' The historical present should be kept. The integrity of the two sentences is important—their separation marks two stages of consciousness. Finally, the order of words is precisely that of Zhilin's taking in the facts; and the climax of all is the sign of imminent danger, the 'gun at the ready'.

In more elaborate writing than this tale, Tolstoy will delay the ap-

9. *Ibid.*, p. 83.
1. B. M. Evkhenbaum, *Molodoy Tolstoy* (Munich, 1968), p. 56.

2. *Twenty-three Tales* (London, 1956), p. 13 (chapter I).

pearance of a noun by a cluster of adjectives or by participial clauses.[3] Here the English language cannot be bent to reflect his purpose. But in another way it can. Christian has singled out the colossally long sentence (above 230 words) describing the futile and contradictory orders of Rostopchin when Moscow is about to fall (War and Peace, III.iii.5). It is preserved in one piece by the Maudes, but Rosemary Edmonds breaks it near the end. Tolstoy's final image in this sentence is of a 'vast popular torrent' that sweeps Rostopchin along in its course; the sentence should be left as a torrent.

It has also to be recognised that Tolstoy is very sensitive to the tone of his characters and their peculiar idiom, whether this reproduces the language of the soldiers in The Wood-Felling,[4] or of independent and old-fashioned aristocrats like Akhrosimova or old Prince Bolkonsky in War and Peace. Both the latter are somewhat intractable. Akhrosimova's speech (War and Peace, I.i.15) is not very far from that of her own peasants, full of quick turns, not a word wasted—but overbearing as they could never be. Prince Bolkonsky talks as a survivor of Catherine's age. He is even capable of modelling a sentence on the Latin-German pattern favoured by Lomonosov. The Maudes render his question to Andrey: 'Well, go on, . . . tell me how the Germans have taught you to fight Buonaparte by this new science you call "strategy"?' The old man's utterance in the original is more contorted. Literally it reads: 'Come on, tell . . . how you the Germans with Buonaparte to fight by your new science, "strategy" named, have taught?' (I.i.23). After his opening words *kak vas nemtsy* the syntax loses all touch with colloquial Russian. It would be difficult to simulate in English, but some indication is needed that he speaks with an old-fashioned formality. So too the translator ought not to let pass his fondness for the diction of an earlier time, as when he uses the outmoded word *propozitsiya* for a proposal of marriage (I.iii.5), or refers to some notes he has made as *remarki* (I.i.25). The Maudes are content to translate this as 'jottings'; so is Miss Edmonds. But some such term as 'memorials' would better convey its antique flavour.

Leontiev said of Pushkin's historical novel The Captain's Daughter that 'the narrative of Grinyov [its hero] is redolent of the eighteenth century'.[5] But Tolstoy did not try to narrate his story of Alexander I's time in the language that would then have been used: he narrates in his own voice, not assuming a *persona* (as Pushkin did for The Tales of Belkin). Nor, Leontiev insists, does Prince Andrey or Pierre really belong to the first decades of the nineteenth century. Their mode of thought and expression is Tolstoy's own in the 1860s.[6] One cannot imagine Tolstoy setting himself to imitate Thackeray's Esmond, in which a de-

3. Christian, Tolstoy's 'War and Peace', p. 156.
4. Eykhenbaum, Molodoy Tolstoy, p. 102.
5. K. Leontiev, Analiz, stil' i veyaniye: o roman-

akh gr. L. N. Tolstogo (Providence, 1965), p. 30.
6. Ibid., p. 118.

liberate patina of archaism is laid on the prose. He was concerned with not the peculiar tone of a bygone epoch, but enduring moral problems; with the laws that govern history, and not its local colouring.

IV

The most remarkable of Tolstoy's talents as a writer has often been noticed—an unfailing ability to penetrate the consciousness of his characters. Except when he dogmatises upon questions of principle in his own person, habitually it is as an impressionist of a particular kind that he sees human life. He does not, like Flaubert and other French contemporaries, satisfy himself with a *pointilliste* rendering of sensations, in which moral concern is so far as possible suspended. Rather he identifies with the character at the given moment, intensely aware of what passes through a mind that may seek to escape from moral issues, but before very long will have to face them. This applies most obviously to the people with whose problems Tolstoy is engaged throughout a story; but even those on the fringes illuminate in some way or other the same problems, however indirectly. Thus each impression, it might be claimed, is a link in Tolstoy's system of linkings; and since the chain is no stronger than its weakest link, the blurring of episodes will diminish the effect of the whole novel. Tolstoy used the expression 'labyrinth of linkings' to account for his method in *Anna Karenina*.[7] There are two aspects of this procedure to be considered.

Tolstoy, as I have said above, sought out fixities. Behind the notation of experience as unpredictably and in manifold form it plays upon the individual consciousness, he looks for the moral values that are to emerge; and these, not surprisingly, are constants. When Levin at the end of his night on the hayrick thinks over what he ought to do, life as led by the peasants seemingly offers him 'that satisfaction, calm and dignity the absence of which he so painfully felt' (*Anna Karenina*, III.12). Two of those three terms, translated here as 'calm' and 'dignity' (*uspokoyeniye i dostoinstvo*), recur with slight modification at key points in the book. Earlier Kitty has admired Varenka at the German wateringplace for 'her enviable calmness and dignity' (*spokoystviye i dostoinstvo*) (II.32), just as Vronsky had regretted that Anna, in her deep involvement with himself, cannot be 'calm and dignified' (*spokoyna i dostoyna*) (III.21). He learns the same day that she is pregnant, and her agitation quickly affects him. 'I cannot be calm', he tells her, 'when you cannot be calm' (II.23); and it is this disturbance that leads him inadvertently to kill his horse, thereby receiving 'the most oppressive and tormenting memory of his life' (II.25). Neither of them will ever attain to the calm and dignity they desire. Levin finds when eventually he does meet Anna that a sudden inexplicable change of feeling comes over her face, 'before

7. See the letter to N. N. Strakhov, 23 April 1876 (Tolstoy, *O literature*, p. 156).

so beautiful in its calmness' (*spokoystviye*) (VII.10); while Kitty on the very last page of the book sees from his face that he is 'calm and joyful' (VIII.19).

It surely matters, trifling though the point may seem, that the translator should emphasise the common element in the words *uspokoyeniye*, *spokoystviye*, *pokoy*, *spokoynyy* which recur so often in *Anna Karenina*. The alternatives they use—'peace', 'calm', 'tranquillity'—are hardly to be differentiated from one another; but when Tolstoy's moral vocabulary is so spare, reduced to the bedrock essentials, something of the novel's steady, even obsessive, preoccupation with certain values is lost should the translator retreat however slightly from singleness of meaning.

The other point is I daresay more substantial. Since the whole process of the novel involves scrutinising a character's thought and feeling at a particular moment, no detail in the registration should be tampered with. The order imposed by syntax, as we have seen with reference to *A Prisoner in the Caucasus*, counts for no less than does the connotation of individual words. Fortunately it can come across in an English rendering with no serious dislocation. The priorities of Tolstoy's syntax in any sentence, its weight, speed and where possible its rhythm, all need to be reproduced. And sufficient to itself as a particular scene may appear, the translator must never forget the linkages to other scenes in the novel, which has been constructed with an internal organisation so close and so richly ramified as to deserve the name 'Shakespearian' (though Tolstoy would doubtless not have cared for it).

Take for example once more the scene when Levin has just been accepted by Kitty (iv.15). 'The whole of that night and morning Levin lived altogether unconsciously and felt altogether withdrawn from the conditions of material life.' He 'felt altogether independent of his body'. So his perceptions are most likely to have the quality of a trance. For him, as for Anna in a totally different scene, the obverse of this, her last journey to the station, common life has revealed itself under a new light of transformation. But whereas Anna can see only its emptiness, the spite and hypocrisy which seem to define all relations between people, Levin is in a state bordering on religious ecstasy. He has that inviolable calm known to Wordsworth, when

> with an eye made quiet by the power
> Of harmony, and the deep power of joy,
> We see into the life of things.[8]

(But this does not prevent him from 'continually glancing at his watch and looking round on all sides'.) So everything that appears before him will be revelatory. The emotion he feels for Kitty is a joy that spreads over the entire scene.

8. 'Lines composed . . . above Tintern Abbey', lines 47–9.

And what he saw then, that afterwards he never saw. Particularly the children on their way to school, the blue-grey pigeons flown down from roof to pavement, and the rolls
sprinkled with flour, which were set out by an unseen hand,
touched him. These rolls, the pigeons and the two boys were
unearthly beings. All this happened at one time: a boy ran up
to a pigeon and smiling glanced at Levin; the pigeon whirred
its wings and fluttered off, shining in the sun between specks
of snow quivering in the air, and from the little window came
the scent of baked bread and there were set out the rolls. All
this together was so extraordinarily nice that Levin began to
laugh and to cry from joy.

In *Anna Karenina* there are two modes of symbolism. One is as it were
conscripted by the story, the other is free. The first mode can be seen
most clearly in the insistent reminders that Anna is to die on the railway,
as when Vronsky's declaration of love in the blizzard-swept station between Moscow and St Petersburg is commented on by the forlorn whistling of the locomotive (I.30). But the blizzard itself belongs, I suggest,
to the second mode. It seems to overcome an obstacle at the moment
he speaks, and the detail of an iron sheet that has been worked loose
and clatters, aptly corresponds to the undoing of a moral structure in
Anna's mind. Here the pigeons and the unseen hand belong to the
second mode. They are no more than Moscow street pigeons, but they
have become, like the boys and even the rolls, 'unearthly beings'—and
the connotations they carry are of human affection—as in Krylov's famous poem, 'Dva golubya'—and probably of divine love. (The Russian
word can mean dove as well as pigeon.) That unseen hand 'works in a
mysterious way'; and it does not seem accidental that the verb immediately following—though not governed by—the hand should be
'touched him'. When the pigeon, impelled by the smiling boy, flies up
into the air it is transfigured among the quivering particles of snow. And
these share in the trepidation of Levin's heart.

The translators have not handled the detail here scrupulously enough.
The Maudes unaccountably omit the pavement to which the pigeons
have descended, and the rolls are not in their translation sprinkled with
flour. They begin specifically with 'two children', following this by 'some
pigeons'; but at the beginning it is not the number of these living things
that interests Tolstoy so much as their epiphany. Rosemary Edmonds
has made them 'silver-grey pigeons', which is inaccurate, and has the
effect of anticipating the way they will shine in the sun. However,
Tolstoy—again like Wordsworth—prefers to show the things as they
normally are, the morning incidents of a Moscow street, before the
vision transforms them. 'All this together'—and 'together', omitted by
the Maudes, is important—harmonises into a mystery. The Maudes
(and Miss Edmonds too) have not the courage of Tolstoy's conviction:

according to the former, the rolls, the pigeons and the two boys 'seemed creatures not of this earth'. However, for Levin unquestionably they *were* unearthly, as Mrs Garnett has recognised. Rosemary Edmonds says 'seemed not of this earth', dropping the idea of 'creatures', but the others translate *sushchestva* in this way. This can be defended, but in spite of the symbolism in the pigeons and the invisible hand, I think that Tolstoy wants to stress the fact of their *being* (as Wordsworth would) rather than their dependence on a creator. This idea would better be conveyed by one of two other nouns: *sozdaniye* or *tvaŕ*.

GARY SAUL MORSON

Tolstoy's Absolute Language†

In the kingdom of words, there are two kinds of subjects. One speaks to other words, the other does not. The first answers what has been spoken before and itself anticipates an answer. Aware of its audience, it knows that it is heard against its social and historical background and evaluated in terms of its speaker's personality. It knows it can be paraphrased, for it paraphrases others constantly. The second kind of word refuses to be paraphrased. It does not say; it is a saying. Admitting no authorship, it condescends to no dialogue. It can only be cited, and recited. When spoken, it belongs to no one; when written, it is Scripture.

This distinction between "dialogic" and absolute utterances—or "words"—as enunciated by Mikhail Bakhtin, forms the basis for his most systematic theory of the novel.[1] It also helps to explain the sense of shock that readers of Tolstoy's novels and stories often experience when they confront one of his absolute truths, expressed in absolute and uncompromising language. In the midst of a fictional context, where the perspective is conventionally novelistic and the language is ironic, qualified, and "multi-voiced," we are stopped short by some of Tolstoy's most famous statements:

> Ivan Ilich's previous life was the most simple and ordinary and [therefore] the most terrible. [*The Death of Ivan Ilich, GSW*, p. 255] [129]

†From *Hidden in Plain View: Narrative and Creative Potentials in "War and Peace"* (Stanford, 1987). Reprinted by permission of Stanford University Press. Page references for quotations from pieces in this Norton Critical Edition are bracketed after the original citations.
1. Bakhtin develops this theory of the novel in "Slovo v romane," *Voprosy literatury i estetiki: Issledovaniia raznykh let* (Moscow, 1975), pp. 72–233. All translations from *Voprosy* are my own. A full translation of this essay, "Discourse in the Novel," appears in *The Dialogic Imagination: Four Essays by M. M. Bakhtin*, ed. Michael Holquist, trans. Caryl Emerson and Michael Holquist (Austin, Tex., 1981), pp. 259–422. I first discussed Bakhtin's theories of language and the novel in "The Heresiarch of *Meta*," *Poetics and Theory of Literature (PTL)*, 3 (1978): 407–27. See also the essays in *Bakhtin: Essays and Dialogues on His Work*, ed. Gary Saul Morson (Chicago, 1986), and Caryl Emerson, "The Tolstoy Connection in Bakhtin," *PMLA*, 100, no. 1 (January 1985): 68–80.

[He] . . . immediately dismissed from his mind this sole solution to all of the riddles of life and death as something totally
impossible.   [*The Death of Ivan Ilich*, GSW, p. 295] [161]

All happy families are alike; each unhappy family is unhappy
in its own way.   [*Anna Karenina*, first sentence]

And indeed, if Eugene Irtenev was mentally deranged, then
everyone is similarly insane. And the most mentally deranged
people are certainly those who see in others signs of insanity
they do not see in themselves.   [*The Devil*, GSW, pp. 348–
49 (first version); p. 351 (second version)]

On the twelfth of June, the forces of Western Europe crossed
the Russian border and war began, that is, an event took place
counter to human reason and to all of human nature.
                                          [*War and Peace*, p. 729]

If we concede that human life can be governed by reason, the
possibility of life is destroyed.   [*War and Peace*, p. 1354]

There is, and can be, no cause of a historical event save the
one cause of all causes.   [*War and Peace*, pp. 1178–79]

The higher a man stands on the social ladder, the more connections he has with people, and the more power he has over
other people, the more manifest is the predetermination and
inevitability of his every act.

    "The hearts of kings are in the hands of God."
    A king is the slave of history.   [*War and Peace*, p. 732]

Bakhtin's theories of language and the novel provide a useful framework for understanding the nature, function, and aesthetic power of
such passages. Bakhtin suggests that the identifying characteristic of the
novel as a genre is its representation of "the concrete life of the [dialogic]
word," which is to say, the exchange of utterances in their social and
historical context. The novel, he argues, represents the drama of speech
reacting to speech, of words struggling to answer, paraphrase, or even
deliberately ignore each other—and of words anticipating how they
themselves will be answered, paraphrased, or ignored. Bakhtin holds,
in short, that language is not only the medium through which the
novelist represents the world, it is also the world he represents. "For the
novelistic genre," Bakhtin observes, "what is characteristic is not the
image of man himself, but precisely the image of language. But language, in order to become an artistic image, must be the utterance of

speaking lips, joined to the image of a speaking person" (*Voprosy*, p. 149).

This purely linguistic description of the novel, according to which characters exist so that words can be spoken, might at first seem a typical example of bloodless Formalism; but the very opposite is the case. Bakhtin's theory was designed in part as a response to what he considered the primary shortcoming of his Formalist predecessors, namely, their failure to pay sufficient attention to history and society. Bakhtin instead contends that the novel is the most sociological of genres, the genre most responsive to the flux of social history, because the dialogic language that the novel represents is itself the most immediate and sensitive register of changing social attitudes. For in the novel as in life, Bakhtin argues, every utterance is necessarily spoken in some "dialect," "jargon," or "speech" (language, according to Bakhtin, is always languages) that carries and implies the attitude of those who characteristically speak in that way, at that time, and in that particular "extraverbal and verbal (i.e., made up of other utterances) milieu."[2] The novelist's art, in Bakhtin's view, is the orchestration of a verbal "polyphony"—or cacophony—that represents the conflict of linguistic subgroups, a conflict that is itself an index to social and "ideological" conflict.

It follows for Bakhtin that language in a novel can never be ideologically neutral or free of social values; it is always someone's language and bears the mark of its speaker's and anticipated listener's unspoken attitudes. Even the seemingly neutral language of a narrator who resembles the author (as in Turgenev) may be used to carry the attitudes of the literate class to which both author and reader belong. Moreover, once placed in a novel, the literary language necessarily enters into complex dialogic relations with the speech of the characters it reports, paraphrases, and selects. In Bakhtin's view, the essence of the novel is to dialogize.

Bakhtin concludes that the novel cannot contain the type of absolute word I described at the outset, inasmuch as absolute words cannot be dialogized. Bakhtin's paradigm of this kind of word is the biblical command: insofar as the command is assumed to have no human author, it bears the imprint of no class and stands above the social and historical flux that novels depict. Inscribed in stone and written in an archaic or foreign language, it precludes dialogue and paraphrase. Placed in a novel, the command inevitably remains inert; it follows for Bakhtin that to the extent that a novel relies on a biblical quotation, it must fail.

As it happens, however, Bakhtin's reasoning on this point implicitly contradicts another of his descriptions of the novel as a genre, according to which the novel differs from all other genres because they are governed

---

2. The citation is from Bakhtin's disciple, V. N. Vološinov, *Marxism and the Philosophy of Language*, trans. Ladislav Matejka and I. R. Titunik (New York, 1973), p. 96. Vološinov's study was originally published in 1929.

by rules and canons whereas it is anticanonic.[3] The novel's essence, he maintains, is to be anomalous, to violate and, indeed, systematically to invert all rules. For Bakhtin, the novel is not a genre but the antigenre; it follows that no sooner do novels begin to develop rules than other novels parody those rules, just as they parody all other literary and social conventions. The novel knows that it participates in the very historical flux it dramatizes, in that its own conventions are historically given and therefore subject to historical change. Thus the history of the novel includes histories of parodies of the novel. By contrast, mock-epic is not in the same way a type of epic.

Bakhtin's second description of the novel suggests the possibility that a novel can successfully violate his first description. For if the essence of the novel is to parody its own rules, then it may also deliberately violate the rule prohibiting unconditional and nondialogic language. That norm could itself become subject to systematic inversion; indeed, it must, if we are to take seriously Bakhtin's second argument that novels are essentially antigeneric. If Bakhtin's second argument is accurate, we may expect some novelists to employ nondialogic language in the midst of a supposedly all-dialogizing context and to take advantage of readers' expectations of novelistic language to shock them with an unexpected contrast. In that case, nondialogic speech could become more effective than it is in contexts where we do expect it: skillfully used, brief sermons in novels may command more attention than long sermons in churches. Considerable literary power could be achieved if, in a context of qualified words reacting to qualified words, of speech struggling to anticipate the objections of future speech, there appeared a sentence that stands above all such petty struggles and pronounces not one man's truth but the Truth. Indeed, this sentence would not only seem to stand above the language of the particular novel in which it appears; it would also seem to stand outside the genre of the novel as a whole. Its absolute, out-of-frame assertions would be read in contrast not only to the particular speech acts that surround it but also to the entire order of limited, purely historical language as such. The novel would be invaded by the non-novelistic, its diction interdicted.

It is important to emphasize that by including nonnovelistic language, an author would not be ignoring novelistic conventions but deliberately violating them. That is, the effectiveness of his strategy would depend on those conventions and would, therefore, bear tacit witness that they are in force. If readers ever stopped assuming those conventions, or if a writer violated them too frequently, the power of nondialogic speech in a novel would begin to fail. The novelist would not be able to violate his readers' expectations, for those expectations would have changed.

As the quotations at the beginning of this chapter suggest, Tolstoy in

---

3. See Bakhtin, "Epos i roman (O metodologii issledovaniia romana)," *Voprosy*, pp. 447–83. An English translation, "Epic and Novel," appears in *The Dialogic Imagination*, pp. 3–40.

fact exploited this strategy. An examination of his use of "nonnovelistic" language can help us to clarify our understanding of the novel in general and the didactic novel in particular. It can also raise fundamental issues about the form and problematics of *War and Peace*, which makes especially striking and frequent use of this technique. After looking at absolute language in Tolstoy's fiction, I will also discuss his use of such assertions in his nonliterary writing and examine some of the questions that Tolstoy's attempt to speak absolutely and nonhistorically raises for his biography.

Tolstoy's Dialogue with the Novel

Tolstoy himself explicitly states the essential difference between unconditional and conditional language in yet another unconditional passage in *War and Peace*:

> If the Deity gives a command, expresses His will . . . the expression of that will is independent of time and is not evoked by anything, for the Deity is not controlled by an event. But when we speak of commands that are the expression of the will of people, acting in time and related to one another, we must, if we are to understand the connection of commands with events, restore (1) the conditions of all that takes place: the continuity of movement in time both of the events and of the person who commands, and (2) the condition of the indispensable connection between the person who issues the commands and those who execute them. [pp. 1430–31]

That is, the language of God is absolute and unconditional in the sense that, unlike the utterance of a person, it is not a function of the circumstances that evoked it, and its meaning is not qualified by an audience whose potential reactions have had to be taken into account. A biblical command can be disobeyed, but it cannot be answered. (Job, for instance, understands well the impossibility of dialogue with God when he challenges God to grant him *an audience* and to answer charges against Him like a defendant in court—a challenge he does not expect God to accept: "He is not a man as I am that I can answer Him, or that we can confront one another in court" [Job 9:32; New English Bible]; "Then summon me and I will answer; or I will speak first, and do thou answer me" [Job 13:22].) Divine speech does not defend itself or allow itself to be limited by particular historical circumstances. No shadow of objectification must fall on it; even when it speaks about history, and even when a particular historical group hears its words, it nevertheless speaks from outside of history.

Proverbs are another kind of absolute language. Like biblical commands, they can be attributed to no particular human author; indeed, it is precisely because they are authorless that they are authoritative.[4] Proverbs are never spoken, they are only cited; and to cite a proverb is to make its nonhistorical statement applicable to, but in no sense conditioned by, a particular historical situation. It is, rather, the historical situation that reveals its conformity to the timeless pattern described by the proverb. It follows that the proverb loses its unconditionality and authority to the extent that we imagine or project a particular source for it. For example, when we identify it as a German or Russian proverb, we tacitly admit the possibility that its wisdom may be the product of the particular experience of a single people and could, therefore, be partial and limited.

Among Tolstoy's absolute statements are those that exhibit characteristics of both biblical commands and proverbs—and of other types of absolute statements as well. He also draws, for example, on logical propositions, mathematical deductions, laws of nature and of human nature, dictionary definitions, and metaphysical assertions. The language of all these forms is timeless, anonymous, and above all categorical. Their stylistic features imply that they are not falsifiable and that they are not open to qualification: they characteristically include words like "all," "each," "every," "only," and "certainly" and phrases like "there neither is nor can be," "the human mind cannot grasp," and "it is impossible that." So frequently does Tolstoy use such phrases that they have become a trademark of his style. Even in sentences that omit them, the very refusal to use a qualifier of any kind can assert unqualifiability. When Tolstoy's absolute statements take the form of syllogisms, the use of the word "therefore" or some explicit or implicit equivalent carries the force of logical inevitability. It carries the same force with Tolstoy's enthymemes, which omit the major premise for the reader to reconstruct. The first of the two examples from *The Death of Ivan Ilich* quoted above, for instance, contains a minor premise and a conclusion of a syllogism; readers themselves must supply the major premise, which would be: "The simpler and more ordinary a life is, the more terrible it is."

In a sense, the entire story of Ivan Ilich's life can be regarded as the minor premise of Tolstoy's syllogism, and the experience of reading the entire novella as the discovery of the timeless truth of which the plot is an instance. It is indeed characteristic of Tolstoy to frame his stories in this way. These absolute principles, either strongly implied or explicitly stated, are not conditioned by the events in the narrative; rather, they pronounce a timeless judgment on those events. Although part of the work, they are part neither of the story nor of its narration; they seem instead to be *cited* from an extranovelistic source and not to be *spoken*

---

4. On the language of proverbs, see Barbara Herrnstein Smith, "On the Margins of Discourse," in Smith, *On the Margins of Discourse: The Re-* *lation of Literature to Language* (Chicago, 1978), especially, "Saying and Sayings," pp. 69–75.

by any novelistic narrator. Indeed, Tolstoy does at times cite well-known proverbs and juxtapose them with proverblike sentences of his own, as in the final example from *War and Peace*.

It is perhaps because these sentences seem both to belong to and to lie outside of the fiction that they frequently occur on the margins of Tolstoy's works—in titles, epigraphs, or opening and closing sentences. This may explain Tolstoy's unusual technique of using complete statements as the titles of his stories, for example: "God Sees the Truth, but Waits to Tell"; "A Spark Neglected Burns the House"; and "Evil Allures but Good Endures." These statements are all proverbs, that is, timeless judgments that may offer a key to a set of events but have not first been uttered in response to them. Tolstoy uses them, as he told Maxim Gorky, because they could not be current coinage.[5] The late tales often use their endings instead of their titles to pronounce an unconditional truth. In some cases, the ending will take the form of a moral and in others (for example, "Three Questions") the form of a solution to riddles posed by the narrative.

The absolute statements in Tolstoy's novels (unlike those in his fairy tales) need not occur in a privileged position like the ending. Although the novels do sometimes exploit their margins in this way, Tolstoy will also interrupt the narration in the middle to include statements from outside the novelistic universe. When statements of this sort occur unexpectedly, as they often do, they command the considerable power of surprise. For example, the absolute statement may form the second clause of a sentence whose first clause is narrative in nature: "On the twelfth of June the forces of Western Europe crossed the Russian border and war began, that is, an event took place counter to human reason and to all of human nature."

Such a statement functions quite differently from seemingly similar ones uttered by characters in the same novel. The "truths" discovered by Levin and Pierre are qualified by the reader's knowledge of the process of their discovery, and what Pierre and Levin believe to be absolutes are sure to prove limited as the narrative progresses. Such limited truths exhibit what we might call an *irony of origins*.[6] No such irony qualifies or limits the truth of judgments cited from outside the narrative. Their anonymous speech center is as "independent of time and . . . not controlled by an event" as is God in the world of the novel's authors and readers.

5. The difference between proverbs and aphorisms according to Tolstoy, that proverbs "are not of today's manufacture," is reported in Maxim Gorky, *Reminiscences of Tolstoy, Chekhov, and Andreyev* (1920; New York, 1959), pp. 9–10. All further references to this book have been amended for accuracy or style by comparison with the Russian version in M. Gor'kii, *Sobranie sochinenii v tridsati tomakh*, vol. 14 (Moscow, 1951), pp. 253–

300. For a more recent version of this essay, see *Maxim Gorky: Collected Works in Ten Volumes*, ed. Nikolai Zhegalov, vol. 9 [*Literary Portraits*] (Moscow, 1982), pp. 92–145 (essay translated by Ivy Litvinov).

6. I discuss "the irony of origins" in *The Boundaries of Genre: Dostoevsky's "Diary of a Writer" and the Traditions of Literary Utopia* (Austin, Tex., 1981), p. 77.

It is probable that all novels are more or less framed by an implicit "for instance."[7] What is characteristic of Tolstoy is that the "for instance" is so often close to explicit. Consider the already "proverbial" beginning of *Anna Karenina*: "All happy families are alike; each unhappy family is unhappy in its own way." This is not a statement in the story, it is a statement *about* the story, a statement spoken by an anonymous voice securely outside the story. It is a fabular moral displaced from the end to the beginning; everything that follows illustrates it but cannot qualify it. Unlike the rest of the novel, this sentence is not conditional and is not the object of any irony: no perspective exists in the novel from which it could be ironic. The effect would have been entirely different and conventionally novelistic if Tolstoy had instead begun: "Anna thought that all happy families were alike, but that each unhappy family was unhappy in its own way" or "it is common knowledge in all of Petersburg that all happy families are alike and that each unhappy family is unhappy in its own way." Then this common belief about the nature of family happiness would have represented the necessarily limited wisdom of some person or social group and would have become the object of increasing irony as the novel progressed. Whether believed by Anna or the society that condemned her, it would have been deeply qualified by the irony of origins, that is, by our knowledge that it was spoken or thought by someone at some time to some real or imagined audience. Its very proverbial quality might, for instance, have become the sign of its naiveté and, as the sign of naiveté, the foreshadowing of tragedy. The novel would have commented on the statement instead of, as it does, exemplifying it.

It is instructive to contrast the first sentence of *Anna Karenina* with the apparently similar first sentence of *Pride and Prejudice*: "It is a truth universally acknowledged, that a single man in possession of a good fortune, must be in want of a wife." Although Jane Austen's opening is also aphoristic, its function is not the same as Tolstoy's. Austen's statement is indirect discourse, and there is clearly a difference in point of view between the paraphrase and the writer who paraphrases. This sentence does not make an assertion, it reports one; and reported speech is already the beginning of dialogue. Considerable irony is implicitly directed at the group that might make such an assertion and identify itself with the universe. The second sentence of the novel, moreover, points to the interests of those who acknowledge the "truth" and to their motives for acknowledging it: we are told it is the neighboring families with marriageable daughters who found this truth most incontestable. The opening sentence of *Pride and Prejudice* is just the sort of ironic and "double-voiced" sentence that Bakhtin says is conventional for novels; the opening sentence of *Anna Karenina*, a sentence that is unironic

[7] On the idea of fictive exemplification, see Smith, "Margins of Discourse." It may be added that novels differ from other fictional genres in that they offer much stronger resistance to allegorization.

and spoken from outside the world of the novel, is not. *Anna Karenina* enters the conventional world of novels only with its second sentence: "All was confusion at the Oblonskys'."

It is important to clarify precisely what does and does not occur when this kind of judgment interrupts the narrative. The essays and lectures on narratology in *War and Peace* function quite differently from the commentary and lectures on plot in *Tristram Shandy* and *Eugene Onegin*, for example. In these novels, the commentary is itself clearly fictive and takes place within the novelistic universe. Few readers, I imagine, doubt that Tristram is himself the fictive, not the actual, author. *Tristram Shandy* and *Eugene Onegin* are novels about the conventions of novel-writing, and they violate those conventions in a way that is both conventional and novelistic. (Pushkin, in fact, cites Sterne as his novelistic predecessor, as Sterne cites Rabelais.) *Tristram Shandy* and *Eugene Onegin* contain fictions within their fiction, and it is only boundaries of the inner fictions that are seriously in question.

Something quite different takes place in Tolstoy's novels. The first sentence of *Anna Karenina* and the lectures on history in *War and Peace* are not spoken by a novelistic narrator at all, not even a "reliable" or authoritative one. Their absolute source lies outside the fictive universe altogether. They are governed, it seems to me, by a set of conventions different from those that govern the rest of the novel, namely, those of nonfictive speech genres. Inserted in a novel, absolute language remains undialogized and—because dialogization is the mark of fictive speech in a novel—nonnovelistic as well as nonfictive. Unlike the rest of the novel in which they appear, Tolstoy's absolute statements claim literal, not literary, truth. The reader is asked to accept them referentially as statements about his own universe, not merely as components of an artistic structure. The reader is expected to believe or disbelieve them; he is asked not to suspend his disbelief but to suspend his suspension of disbelief. In the midst of a novel, which insofar as it is a novel renders all of its language conditional, Tolstoy attempts to make statements that are completely non-novelistic, that is, both nonfictive and nondialogized.[8]

That attempt ultimately fails, as I believe it must. For in the final analysis there is no way to speak completely noncontextually in a novel. The reason for Tolstoy's failure is that, inasmuch as his absolute language derives its rhetorical power from denying novelistic conventions, it implicitly relies on them and therefore honors them in the breach. His absolute statements *polemically* assert their unconditionality and so necessarily enter into dialogue with the genre whose speech they reject. In a sense, Tolstoy's attempt to speak nonnovelistically in a novel resembles Dostoevsky's underground man's attempt to *show* his friends that he is

8. I discuss the problem of literary works containing such heterogeneous elements from a theoretical perspective in *Boundaries*. See especially chapter 2, "Threshold Art."

ignoring them: "I tried my very utmost to show them that I could do without them, and yet I purposely stomped with my boots, thumping with my heels. But it was all in vain."[9] Tolstoy's absolute statements are involved in an analogous self-contradiction. The contradiction lies in the fact that they are implicitly framed by an assertion of their non-conditionality, and yet this very assertion is conditional and conscious of its audience. In short, the very refusal to enter into dialogue is itself both dialogic and dialogizing.

Although Tolstoy cannot make his language nondialogic, he nevertheless does succeed in changing the nature of the dialogue. The kind of context that conditionalizes Tolstoy's absolute statements differs from the kind of context that conventionally conditionalizes sentences in novels. What dialogizes Tolstoy's absolutes is not the surrounding language of the particular novel but the genre of the novel as a whole. It is the reader's knowledge of the novelistic tradition that forces Tolstoy's statements into proclaiming their nondialogicality. There is no immediate contextualization, but there is a secondary, "metacontextualization."

The distinction between contextualization and metacontextualization is an important one. To fail to make it would be to mistake not only the way absolute statements function in Tolstoy's novels but also the relation that particular works bear to their genre. For any linguistic structure in a literary work participates in two contexts: the context of the particular work in which it appears and the context of the genre to which that work belongs.[1] Whereas statements in most novels are dialogized by both contexts, Tolstoy's absolute statements are dialogized only by the second context. Dialogicality is ultimately unavoidable in Tolstoy's novels because—and only so long as—they are read as novels.

CARYL EMERSON

The Tolstoy Connection in Bakhtin†

> About polyphonic music. A voice ought to say something, but in this case there are many voices, and each one says nothing.—Leo Tolstoy, diary entry for 18 December 1899

The juxtaposition of Tolstoy and Dostoevsky is one of the most familiar and time-honored practices in Russian literary criticism. It is hardly surprising, therefore, that Mikhail Bakhtin contributed to the great de-

9. Fyodor Dostoevsky, *"Notes from Underground"* and *"The Grand Inquisitor,"* the Constance Garnett translation revised by Ralph E. Matlaw (New York, 1960), p. 69.

1. Linguistic structures in literary works also participate, of course, in other contexts, such as the broader contexts of literature or of fiction.

†From *Rethinking Bakhtin: Extensions and Challenges*, ed. Gary Saul Morson and Caryl Emerson (Evanston, 1989). Reprinted with permission of Modern Language Association of America.

bate over these two novelists; he was a master at exploiting the polemical frameworks of his time, the better to speak his own unconventional word. To be sure, he left no monograph on Tolstoy comparable to the masterwork *Problems of Dostoevsky's Poetics.*[1] There are only numerous scattered references, prefaces to two volumes of Tolstoy's collected fiction, and several ideological constructs in which Tolstoy plays a crucial part. Despite this low profile, the Tolstoy-versus-Dostoevsky opposition was exceptionally congenial to Bakhtin. In fact, his presentation of the dialogue, explicit and implicit, between these two great nineteenth-century writers can provide a fruitful organizing principle for understanding his work as a whole, both its power and its limitations. It tells us much about the two novelists as well.

First, however, a cautionary note on the general purpose to which Bakhtin puts artists of the word. He is fond of explaining the "spirit of a time" through a single writer: Rabelais for the Renaissance, Dostoevsky for the polyphonic second half of the nineteenth century.[2] But Bakhtin is not primarily interested in the individual novelist as such or in the individual novel as an artistic whole. He does not do the traditional "close readings" of the novels he so admires. Rather, he analyzes small chunks, scenes, patterns, always seeking an artistic imperative more fundamental than the particular structure of any single finished work. In his book on Dostoevsky, indeed, the longer and more complex the work the more fragmentary and synchronic is his use of it. After a lengthy discussion of the early short novels *Poor Folk* and *The Double* and an exhaustive analysis of the brief late pieces "Dream of a Ridiculous Man" and tiny "Bobok," Bakhtin mines the big novels for "new structural elements"—admitting, however, that "we shall spend less time on them" (*Problems*, 237). In his opening remarks to the revised

1. M. M. Bakhtin, *Problemy tvorchestva Dostoevskogo* (Problems of Dostoevsky's Art) (Leningrad: Priboi, 1929). A second and much expanded edition was published in 1963 under a different title: *Problemy poetiki Dostoevskogo* (Problems of Dostoevsky's Poetics), 2d ed. (Moscow: Sovetskii pisal, 1963). An English translation of the 1963 edition is available: M. M. Bakhtin, *Problems of Dostoevsky's Poetics*, ed. and trans. Caryl Emerson (Minneapolis: University of Minnesota Press, 1984). Subsequent references to these editions will be to *Problemy* (1929) or *Problems* (1963 in 1984 trans.).
2. This emphasis constitutes one of the major distinctions between the first and second editions of Bakhtin's book on Dostoevsky. The 1929 original is a monograph on Dostoevsky the novelist; in the 1963 revision Bakhtin sees Dostoevsky as a sort of metaphysical threshold, a watershed in novelistic consciousness. This view is evident, for example, in a fragment from M. M. Bakhtin, "Iz zapisei 1970–1971 godov" (From Notes of 1970–71), 336–73 in *Estetika slovesnogo tvorchestva* (The aesthetics of verbal art) (Moscow: Iskusstvo, 1979), 343:

Pechorin, for all his complexity and contradictoriness, seems integrated and naive when compared with Stavrogin. Pechorin has not tasted from the Tree of Knowledge. No heroes of Russian literature prior to Dostoevsky had tasted from the Tree of Knowledge of Good and Evil. Within the bounds of their novels, therefore, one could still find naive and integrated poetry, lyric, poetic landscape. They (the preDostoevskian heroes) still had access to pieces (little corners) of earthly paradise, from which Dostoevsky's heroes are exiled once and forever.

These notes, written near the end of Bakhtin's life, are now available in English in M. M. Bakhtin, *Speech Genres and Other Late Essays*, trans. Vern W. McGee, ed. Caryl Emerson and Michael Holquist (Austin: University of Texas Press, 1986). Subsequent references will be to "Iz zapisei," and page numbers will refer to the Russian edition. Unless otherwise noted, all translations are mine.

version, Bakhtin acknowledges this aspect of his critical method. "Of course even in this new edition," he writes, "the book cannot pretend to a complete analysis of the questions it raises, especially questions as complex as that of *the whole* in a polyphonic novel" (4).

Bakhtin, in short, is not after specific interpretations of specific novels. He is after the creative force, the generic impulse that a novelist or a novel embodies. He then uses that force as a prism through which to focus a philosophy of language, a hypothesis about authorial intention, or an understanding of a particular cultural period.

What, then, does the "Tolstoyan force" mean for Bakhtin? We should first recall where Tolstoy stood in the Russian tradition—a position that by the 1920s was already almost a cliché.[3] In that tradition, Dostoevsky is a mystic, the apocalyptic poet of the underground, the celebrator of the trap of human consciousness. His characters live on the edge of perpetual crisis, and his plots rely heavily on madness, murder, and suicide. Tolstoy, in contrast, is the teacher of life. His is the realm of *zhivaia zhizn'* ("living life"),[4] an aboveground and exuberant immersion in nature, physicality, and organic process. Bakhtin, in fact, acknowledges this tradition in his theoretical articles of the thirties and forties. There he identifies Dostoevsky with "crisis time" and "threshold space" while defining the Tolstoyan "chronotope" (or time-space matrix) as quite the opposite—as "biological time, flowing smoothly in the interior spaces of townhouses and noble estates."[5] These contrasts are also present in his book on Dostoevsky. But there Bakhtin assigns Tolstoy a harsher and more polemical role. Within Bakhtin's decidedly binary universe, the two great Russian novelists emerge as two rallying points, two poles for opposing tendencies in literature and language.

At the Dostoevsky pole, consciousness is individualized, disunified, made concrete. At the Tolstoy pole, consciousness is generalized, unified, made abstract. When Bakhtin refers to Tolstoy, then, it is not so much to the world of the novelist's writing as to the striving of that world, its outer limit, its fascination with the possibility of "absolute language."[6] Through Bakhtin's lens, Tolstoy is far from being the poet of "living life." He becomes, in fact, the poet of death.

3. Perhaps the earliest comprehensive statement of the Tolstoy-vs.-Dostoevsky paradigm was Dmitri Merezhkovski's *L. Tolstoi i Dostoevskii* (1900), which set up a model that was to have considerable staying power: Tolstoy is the pantheist and pagan, a "seer of the flesh," while Dostoevsky is the great mystical Christian, a "seer of the soul." For an adequate survey in English of the positions of early influential critics, see Vladimir Seduro, *Dostoevski in Russian Literary Criticism, 1846–1956* (New York: Octagon Books, 1969), esp. the sections on Merezhkovski, Rozanov, Vyacheslav Ivanov, and Veresayev.

4. The phrase is from V. V. Veresayev, whose *Zhivaia zhizn'* (1911) was one of the founding-works in the Tolstoy-Dostoevsky tradition. Dos-

toevsky, according to Veresayev, was indifferent to nature, obsessed by the sick and dying, and given to creating characters enslaved by logic. To all this the antidote was Tolstoy.

5. M. M. Bakhtin, "Forms of Time and Chronotope in the Novel," in *The Dialogic Imagination: Four Essays by M. M. Bakhtin*, ed. Michael Holquist, trans. Caryl Emerson and Michael Holquist (Austin: University of Texas Press, 1981), 249.

6. For an excellent discussion of this aspect of Tolstoy's discourse, drawing heavily on Bakhtin, see Gary Saul Morson, "Tolstoy's Absolute Language," *Critical Inquiry* 7 (1981): 667–87, esp. 667–76.

Bakhtin's inversion of received literary canon is characteristically eccentric. But it is more. His Tolstoy-Dostoevsky polemic is, as we shall see, a remarkably selective construct. It emerges as a binary model that can accommodate three of his most insistently recurring concerns: monologism versus dialogism, the relationships of authors to their characters, and the concept of the self.

Bakhtin makes his first detailed case against monologism in the 1929 edition of his book on Dostoevsky. Whereas Dostoevsky, we are told, seeks maximally free words for his heroes, Tolstoy seeks objectified images fixed in words. Dostoevsky's heroes create themselves out of their discourse, but in Tolstoy's characters consciousness and speech are merely two components among many—no more important, say, than a raised upper lip or a plodding step:

> In [Tolstoy's] world a second autonomous voice never appears alongside the author's voice. Therefore the problem of voice linkage never arises, nor does the problem of a special positioning for the author's point of view. Tolstoy's word and his monologically naive point of view penetrate everywhere, into the smallest corners of the world and the soul, subjugating everything to its unity. (*Problemy*, 68)

What matters here is not so much Tolstoy the artist as Tolstoy's "monologically naive point of view." In chapter 3 of this edition ("The Hero in Dostoevsky") Bakhtin develops his concept of monologism, and although he does so at a suitably abstract level, one can easily grasp the real issue he is addressing under cover of Tolstoy, master monologist. Bakhtin's argument is roughly this. Monologism is a brand of idealism that insists on the unity of a single consciousness. It has been the guiding principle in a variety of modern movements, including European rationalism, the Enlightenment, and utopianism. Wherever monologic perception dominates, everything is seen in false unity—as the spirit of a nation, of a people, of history. This unity is false because it is only an apparent oneness; in fact, monologism demarcates, abstracts, excludes, and it is only from within this closed and lopped-off system that everything can be seen as one. Dialogism alone allows for the restoration of a larger, inclusive unity in diversity, through the sort of comprehension of opposites that Bakhtin would later extol in Rabelais. In a dialogic universe, inclusive unity is celebrated by the fact that truth about the world is linked with specific position, with truth for the individual personality.[7]

In a monologic world, truth is impersonal. It is placed in a character's mouth by the author. Characters are not creators of ideas but merely

---

7. The Russian word for unity, *edinstvo* (from *odin/edin*, "one"), has caused Bakhtin's readers and translators some difficulty. In Bakhtin's usage the word does *not* mean unity in the sense of a fusion or conflation of discrete parts; rather, it refers more to the unit-y of something, to the fact that living wholes form an irreplaceable unit from which no part can be extracted or abstracted without violating its integrity (its responsible position in the world).

carriers. The ideas belong to no one. In such a world, an independent idea cannot be acknowledged on its own terms: it is either affirmed (that is, absorbed) or repudiated. Only one individualizing principle is recognized, and that is error. Without any genuine interaction among consciousnesses, dialogue can never be more than "pedagogical."

This question of "pedagogical dialogue" might serve as a useful focus. Pedagogy is crucial to Bakhtin, as it is to Tolstoy; both are fascinated with the image of the ideal teacher. But for Bakhtin, true learning is dialogic and therefore horizontal, an interpenetration of points of view. Interactions become "pedagogical" when dialogue is debased, when the teacher turns out to have known all the answers all along—as happened, Bakhtin claims, in the later Socratic dialogues (*Problems*, 110). For Tolstoy, on the contrary, learning is always and ideally vertical. The revealing document here is Tolstoy's tract on peasant schools: "Who Should Teach Whom to Write, We the Peasant Children or the Peasant Children Us?"[8] That the hierarchy is flipped and Count Tolstoy is now at the feet of his peasants is not significant. The axis has not changed. It is still the omnipresent, monologic *kto kogo* ("who does what to whom")—either I know and teach you, or you know and teach me. Tolstoy's essay might advocate abolition of hierarchy, but it is still cast in what Bakhtin would call a "pedagogical dialogue": "Someone who knows and possesses the truth instructs someone who is ignorant of it and in error, that is, it is the mutual relationship of teacher and pupil" (*Problemy*, 78). For Bakhtin, this mode is inevitable in a monologic world.

Under monologic conditions, Bakhtin concludes, ideas are not represented. They are merely distributed by some higher power or expressed directly, with no distance at all. Distance, of course, is what guarantees voice autonomy in a work: a world where others' ideas cease to be represented is ultimately a world where others' ideas cease to exist. But this insistence on many autonomous voices does not mean the absence of unified truth. And here we glimpse Bakhtin's powerful, veiled, ultimately spiritual relationship with the genuinely authoritative word. The search for a unified truth, Bakhtin insists, need not be carried out under repressive monologic conditions:

> It is quite possible to imagine a unified truth that requires a multiplicity of consciousnesses, one that could not in principle be fitted within the boundaries of a single consciousness, one that is, so to speak, social by its very nature and full of event-potential, one that is born at a point of contact among various consciousnesses. . . . (*Problemy*, 78)

8. The essay was written in 1862, when Tolstoy was deeply involved in peasant schools on his estate. During that year, in the pages of *Sovremennik*, Tolstoy conducted a sharp polemic with Chernyshevsky on the issues of educational hierarchy, preestablished curricula, and the common people's access to universities (and yet how essentially hierarchical Tolstoy's alternative appears). See Boris Eikhenbaum, *Tolstoi in the Sixties*, trans. Duffield White (Ann Arbor: Ardis Books, 1982), 47–71.

Indeed, this seems to be Bakhtin's ultimate task: to make a unified truth compatible with multiple consciousnesses. It is the triumphant accomplishment of this task that in 1929 he ascribes to Dostoevsky, a fellow believer; and it is this achievement he denies to Tolstoy, monologic rationalist.

This fundamental distinction between monologic and dialogic conditions is crucial for another aspect of Bakhtin's image of Tolstoy: the complex relationships Bakhtin charts between authors and their heroes. We must begin with the magisterial protoessay on authors and protagonists that Bakhtin wrote in the early 1920s, a work that permeates (and that was probably composed alongside) the early drafts of the book on Dostoevsky.[9] In this early essay, Bakhtin stresses the fragility of the author-hero relationship and the degree of discipline required to sustain a responsible "outsideness." At this point, Bakhtin has not yet opposed Tolstoy to Dostoevsky; he illustrates his typologies with heroes drawn from the work of both writers, often placing them in the same category. That opposition was to happen only in the late 1920s, when Bakhtin began to see finalization not as a necessary step to art but as a threat to human freedom. The more he came to prefer "unfinalizability" to finalization, the more he exalted Dostoevsky over Tolstoy.

What strikes us in this early essay is the remarkable ease with which Bakhtin crosses the boundaries between art and life. The relationship of author to created character is treated essentially like the relationship of any "I" to any "other." But there is this one distinction: in life we author fragments, "we are not interested in the whole of a person but only in his separate acts," whereas art requires that we assume "a unified reaction to the whole of the hero" ("Avtor," 7–8). Getting the whole of a hero right is an arduous task, Bakhtin admits; how many "grimaces, random masks, false gestures" can result from the whims or caprice of an author (8). But the task is necessary, for only as a conceptualized whole can a hero be released to develop freely within the logic of his *own* reality.

At its most elevated level, of course, authorship is theological—a reenactment, writ small, of supreme authority creating humanity. But here Bakhtin brings the scenario maximally close to our everyday, and continuously creative, experience. To stress the continuity in function between formally aesthetic authorship and its "everyday" real-life counterpart, Bakhtin frequently employs the terms *avtor-sozertsatel'* ("author-perceiver") and *avtor-zritel'* ("author-spectator") ("Avtor," 63–65). Authorship is the problem of one consciousness perceiving another consciousness. "How the other looks from my position," then, is the starting point both for aesthetic perception and for an ethical act ("Avtor," 23).

---

9. Portions of this essay were published posthumously as "Avtor i geroi v esteticheskoi deiatel'-nosti" (Author and hero in aesthetic activity) in *Estetika slovesnogo tvorchestva* (see n. 2 above). A translation by Vadim Liapunov is forthcoming from the University of Texas Press. Subsequent references to this essay will be to the Russian text, "Avtor."

Two individuals are confronting each other, looking into each other's eyes. One can always see something that the other cannot, if only what is behind the other's head (22), if only the other's act of looking. Each is in the process of "authoring" the other, and this is possible because each enjoys a "surplus" (*izbytok*) of vision vis-à-vis the other. Only from the other's perspective can each appear whole; to oneself, there is always an inner loophole, an open-ended potential for change. Whatever stable definitions the "I" possesses are inevitably acquired from the other.

Thus one cannot author oneself: the very fact of expression, aesthetic and otherwise, requires a second consciousness to supply boundaries and impose external integrity. In the visual and literary arts and in real life as well, it is impossible to construct a self out of a single consciousness. Painting one's self-portrait, looking in the mirror or at a photograph of oneself, is always somehow false, the results untrue. "In this sense," Bakhtin writes, "one can speak of the absolute aesthetic need of one person for another, for the seeing, remembering, gathering, and unifying activity of the other, which alone can create his externally completed personality; this personality will not exist if the other does not create it" (34). However abounding or lacking in love, this activity is always beneficial because it always "formally enriches" the object, fixing it in time and space from a point of view fundamentally inaccessible to the object itself. "What would I have to gain," Bakhtin asks, "if another were to *fuse* with me? He would see and know only what I already see and know, he would only repeat in himself the inescapable closed circle of my own life; let him rather remain outside me" (78).

Bakhtin is not suggesting here that we must reject who we are, or that the normal relationship to self is one of self-abasement. But he does claim that we cannot form authoritative images of ourselves from within. An important aspect of our freedom is the fact that inside we are all restlessness, change, movement; whatever temporary stabilizations we enjoy—rest, pleasure, joy, triumph, even the secure sense that something is our own—are gifts bestowed on us by the other ("Avtor," 101, 119–20). To be the other for another is a privilege; "only by being outside another's potential consciousness can we feel its gift-giving, resolving, and consummating potential" ("Avtor," 175).

In *Problems of Dostoevsky's Poetics* this indispensability of otherness emerges with special clarity during discussions of "the word with a loophole" (*slovo s lazeikoi*). In speaking one's idea, Bakhtin claims, one always retains a loophole "in case the other person does not make use of his *privilege* as the other." In *The Idiot*, Nastasya Filippovna, in the wildness of her contradictions, condemns herself and "at the same time insists that the other person, precisely as the other, is obliged to vindicate her" (234). We should not be misled, Bakhtin seems to suggest, by the surface texture of scandal, madness, and eccentricity in Dostoevsky. Underneath them all is a profoundly pluralistic and healing impulse: a faith that the function of the other is not to alienate but to resist our negating ideas of self, to contradict our helplessness by providing new options for the self. Dostoevsky always privileges the other, because it alone can protect individual personality from the awful trap of the final word.

How, then, does the Tolstoy-Dostoevsky dichotomy express itself in the issue of the other's responsibility? In Tolstoy, Bakhtin would maintain, characters exist so that the author can address them, and ultimately the readers, with a truth that transcends them all. Characters have a responsibility toward this truth, and the text as a whole reflects their search. In Dostoevsky, in contrast, a character exists to address an idea to someone else. This other person has a responsibility to challenge (not merely to reinforce) that idea or that concept of self.

Bakhtin's insistence on the validity of a second (and usually dissenting) opinion might explain in part his curious reluctance to engage, in any serious way, the carriers of authoritative discourse. There were, of course, ready political reasons why a literary critic—or any intellectual— might refrain from analyzing "figures of authority" in the increasingly monologic and hero-worshipping climate of the Soviet 1930s.[1] But Bakhtin's reluctance goes deeper than a dialogue with his own time, and deeper than a debate between these two authors. He dismisses the authoritative word in novels wherever he finds it, in Dostoevsky as well as in Tolstoy. "Images of official-authoritative truth, images of virtue, have never been successful in the novel," Bakhtin writes. "It suffices to mention the hopeless attempts of Gogol and Dostoevsky in this regard . . . [as well as] the evangelical texts in Tolstoy at the end of *Resurrection.*"[2] Prince Myshkin, Alyosha Karamazov, and the Elder Zosima can hardly be considered "hopeless attempts" in Dostoevsky's fictional universe. How in fact do characters properly use the authoritative word? What role does Tolstoyan comprehensive truth play for Dostoevsky, and how does Dostoevsky approach and embody such truth?

In a discussion of *The Idiot* Bakhtin briefly suggests one possible mediator, the "penetrated word" (*proniknovennoe slovo*) (*Problems*, 241– 42, 249). The penetrated word, a term Bakhtin adopts from the Dostoevsky criticism of Vyacheslav Ivanov,[3] is linked with hagiographic discourse (although unlike hagiography it need not be stylized) and is

1. Nina Perlina develops this possibility, using Martin Buber to "restore" the theological component of Bakhtin's system that could not receive overt expression under Soviet conditions. See Nina Perlina, "Bakhtin and Buber: The Concept of Dialogic Discourse," *Studies in Twentieth-Century Literature* 9 (1984): 13–28.

2. See "Discourse in the Novel," in *Dialogic Imagination* (n. 5 above), 344.

3. See Vyacheslav Ivanov, "Dostoevskii i roman-tragediia," in *Borozdy i mezhi* (Furrows and boundaries) (Moscow: Musaget, 1916), 5–60; and Iva-

nov's *Freedom and the Tragic Life: A Study in Dostoevsky*, trans. Norman Cameron (New York: Noonday, 1951). In the latter Ivanov says, "Clearly this mode of thought is not based upon theoretical cognition, with its constant antithesis of subject and object, but upon an act of will and faith. . . . Dostoevsky has coined for this a word of his own, *proniknovenie*, which properly means 'intuitive seeing through' or 'spiritual penetration' " (26–27). For an expanded treatment, see the Russian text, 32–34.

informed by authority: it is, Bakhtin tells us, a word without a loophole, without a reservation, confident in its power to mean. Its task is to interfere actively in the interior dialogue of another person and "help that person find his own voice" (242). But unlike the authoritative and authorial discourse that Tolstoy directs toward this end, the penetrated word does not stand above or outside the discourse of the characters. It does not come down but *across*—we recall Bakhtin's distinction between authentic and pedagogical dialogue—and therefore its resolutions are highly context-specific within a given pool of personalities. Bakhtin uses the example of Prince Myshkin. What makes the prince a Dostoevskian and not a Tolstoyan carrier of truth? The prince can, and often does, appeal to one of the voices warring inside another person, and if he reaches an "authentic voice" he can trigger a major moral reversal. But the penetrated word does not last. It can only enter at a specific time and place to work a temporary realization. It is only possible in dialogue, in a specific dialogue with another person; it never accumulates authority and therefore lacks ultimate sovereignty (242). Myshkin's inner dialogue, Bakhtin assures us, is just as active and anxiety-ridden as that of any other character in the novel. The penetrated word makes authority real, but only for the moment; it remains personal, historical, and conditional.

Authority, then, resides only in specific situations. For Bakhtin, and for Dostoevsky in Bakhtin's reading of him, the ideal relationship between personality and authority is embodied in Christ. He is the ideal other, the supreme demonstration of the fact that the one who creates us also saves us—and this fact should be understood on a plane quite separate from questions of religious belief. Christ is a symbol of the necessity for enfleshment. Abstract cognition and pretensions to an ultimate, singular authority cannot embody values; only a view made concrete in time and space, Bakhtin argues, can create a soul within the other and participate in an active relationship. "Even God had to be enfleshed in order to pardon, to suffer, and to forgive" ("Avtor," 113). Resurrection in the flesh is a powerful image, not because it allays our fears of physical extinction but because it emphasizes the inseparability of soul and body ("Avtor," 89), the need for soul to be enacted through a particular and delimited body.[4]

Thus Bakhtin reverses the traditional idea underlying the wonder of resurrection. He stresses the inseparability of body and soul not because the body has a soul but because souls must have bodies; his is a religion not so much of resurrection as of incarnation. Bakhtin therefore does

---

4. It is important to understand that the Russian word *ogranichennyi* (delimited), as it is used by Bakhtin, denotes not the negative sense that "limited" has in English but the hopeful sense of "*de*-limited," outlined in time and space, and therefore capable of having a point of view and generating value (34–35). Elsewhere in "Avtor" Bakhtin develops the familiar distinction between "spirit" (*dukh*) and "soul" (*dusha*): a soul, "I-for-another," is shaped in me and given final form by another, while spirit, "I-for-myself," is my self as I experience it, eternally unfinished and open to change (116–18). "The soul is the gift of my spirit to the other" (116).

not take kindly to all those Tolstoyan gestures that would abstract Christ's words, fuse these words with personal conviction, or erect them into moral systems. Proper unity with authority is achieved not through fusion but by asking a question of the ideal authoritative image:

> [For Dostoevsky] the image of the ideal human being or the image of Christ represents the resolution of ideological quests.
> . . . Precisely the image of a human being and his voice, a voice not the author's own, was the ultimate artistic criterion for Dostoevsky: not fidelity to his own convictions and not fidelity to convictions themselves taken abstractly, but precisely a fidelity to the authoritative image of a human being. (*Problems*, 97)

One does not fuse with an ideal image but chooses, from another integral position, to follow it. Its separateness and unfinishedness—as well as our own—are always paramount. Near the end of his life Bakhtin jotted down this provocative sequence of thoughts: "Dostoevsky's search. . . . The word as something personal. Christ as truth. I put the question to him . . ." ("Iz zapisei," 353). Dostoevsky sees ideal authority present only as relationship. It is an "image-discourse" that is listened to, interrogated, freely followed by the whole person. Tolstoy, in contrast, would not "put the question" to truth, for to do so would too bluntly emphasize the specific time, space, and mortality of the questioner—and of the answerer as well. Tolstoy's impersonal word lies in the realm beyond dialogue; his convictions have become truth as proposition.

In Bakhtin's view, then, the status of authority has close parallels with the status of language. As Tolstoyan discourse strives to rise above specific times and places, it inevitably dehistoricizes language—that is, makes it possible to value a word regardless of when it was spoken and by whom. Bakhtin charges Tolstoy with ignoring, or naively presuming to transcend, the problematic status of language. For Tolstoy, language is not a problem; it is merely a means. His characters all partake of "openly pathetic discourse": either Tolstoy allows a speaker to assume directly the didactic role of teacher, judge, or preacher, or he presents discourse itself as something more solid and impersonal than it is—as a direct impression from life, or as something untainted by ideological preconceptions.[5] In Dostoevsky, on the contrary, it is precisely the ideological preconception that is valued in language:

> It is characteristic that in Dostoevsky's works there are absolutely no *separate* thoughts, propositions or formulations such as maxims, sayings, aphorisms which, when removed from their context and detached from their voice, would retain their semantic meaning in an impersonal form. But how many such

5. Bakhtin, "Discourse in the Novel," in *Dialogic Imagination* (see n. 5 above), 398.

separate and true thoughts can be isolated (and in fact commonly are isolated) from the novels of Leo Tolstoy, Turgenev,
Balzac . . . separated from a voice, they still retain their full
power to mean as impersonal aphorisms. (*Problems*, 95–96)

Impersonal truth is, in Bakhtin's view, a central element in Tolstoy's
monologic world. And it is markedly absent in Dostoevsky, where we
find only "integral and indivisible voice-ideas, voice viewpoints" (*Problems*, 96).

At the end of his early study on authors and their heroes, Bakhtin
asks: What is the author's task? It does not lie, Russian Formalism to
the contrary, in a response to other literary schools and languages or in
a manipulation of devices. The author's task, which Bakhtin calls "god-
like," is "to find a fundamental approach to life from without" ("Avtor,"
166), to define and shape others in a way in which they cannot define
and shape themselves. Crises in authorship come about, Bakhtin suggests, when authors begin to despair of "the right to be outside a life
and to give it final form," when the conviction takes hold that life is
understandable only when lived in the category of "I-for-myself" rather
than "I-for-another," when, in short, there is a fear of drawing boundaries (176). Omniscient narrator-authors, who admit of no barriers between themselves and their created characters, cannot be enfleshed or
delimited. Far from strengthening a moral or evaluative position and
making it more authoritative, such narrators, in Bakhtin's universe,
merely discredit and devaluate that position.

Nowhere does Bakhtin directly confront Tolstoy's theory of art. But
his early writings do offer a potential challenge to the idea of art as
"infection." In the opening pages of "Author and Hero" Bakhtin discusses the proper way to empathize with another's suffering:

> My projection of myself into the suffering person must be
> followed by a *return* to myself, to my own place outside the
> sufferer; only from this place can the material of empathy be
> rendered meaningful ethically, cognitively, or aesthetically. If
> this return did not take place, we would have an instance of
> the pathological phenomenon of experiencing another's suf-
> fering as one's own, an infection by the other's suffering and
> nothing more. ("Avtor," 25)

Later in the essay (55–81), Bakhtin criticizes Romantic "expressive
aesthetics" for much the same failing. Expressive theories of art know
only the doubling act of *co*-experience; they strive to make aesthetic
value real in a way "immanent to a single consciousness; [such theories]
do not permit the counterpositioning of *I* to *other*" (58).

One might contrast Bakhtin's views with Tolstoy's argument in *What
Is Art?*:

A real work of art destroys, in the consciousness of the receiver, the separation between himself and the artist—not that alone, but also between himself and all whose minds receive this work of art. In this freeing of our personality from its separation and isolation, in this uniting of it with others, is the chief characteristic and the great attractive force of art.[6]

The "communication imperative" in Tolstoy's treatise would have appealed to Bakhtin; the implication of fusion, however, would have been rejected. According to Bakhtin, the aesthetic experience should strive not to duplicate another's emotions but, rather, to assume an attitude toward them, to respond to them in a different and supplementary way. It could be argued that in the Tolstoy-Dostoevsky polemic Bakhtin is dealing less with individual authors than with categories of authoring—and, ultimately, with the nature of aesthetic experience.

This observation leads to a final area in which the Tolstoy connection can help focus a major conceptual node in Bakhtin's thought. How much "other" is necessary for the formation of a self? How is an open concept of selfhood compatible with the act of literary authoring, and with the harshly bounded realities of our individual birth and death? Here it is instructive to compare the 1929 and 1963 versions of Bakhtin's book on Dostoevsky. The publication dates of these two editions loosely bracket the years of Stalinism. One might expect a trace of this period in the second edition, some subtext of death and survival that would address Bakhtin's own fate and the general fate of "multiple consciousness" in that troubled and monologic time. One such trace can in fact be found in the expanded polemic with Tolstoy. At issue is the hegemony of the hero's consciousness, and Bakhtin examines it through the severe prism of death.

In the 1963 edition, chapter 2 ("The Hero in Dostoevsky") is greatly expanded. Among the new material is a discussion of Tolstoy's short story "Three Deaths" (69–72)—a model, Bakhtin says, of monologic thinking. In this story, we recall, the three deaths (of a noblewoman, a coachman, and a tree) are connected solely in an external and mechanical way. This externality is not the sort that communes with or interrogates the other. Since the three heroes are not conscious of one another, they can be made meaningful to one another only in the authorial, and authoritative, field of vision that encompasses them all. Noblewoman, coachman, and (of course) tree do not think and talk but

---

6. Leo Tolstoy, *What Is Art?*, trans. Aylmer Maude (New York: Bobbs, 1960), 140. We have secondhand evidence that Bakhtin lectured on "What Is Art" to high school students in Vitebsk (see n. 23). According to Mirkina's class notes, Bakhtin had this to say of Tolstoy's treatise: "In those places where Tolstoy strives to prove the rightness of his own views he is weak, he premeditatedly distorts, and he does not wish to understand the artists he has rejected. But moving on to the theory of empathy, he develops this theory very profoundly, although he discovers anew what had been discovered before him by Lipps" (Mirkina, 265). The German philosopher and psychologist Theodor Lipps (1851–1914) is mentioned several times by Bakhtin as a proponent of "expressive aesthetics" in "Avtor," 56–72.

rather have their thinking and talking done for them by someone who sees more than they could ever see. There are no true dialogic relationships among the characters, and none at all between the characters and Tolstoy, their creator. Whereas "Three Deaths" is a rather primitive example, Bakhtin claims that Tolstoy's longer stories and novels also reflect this basic structure (72).

Bakhtin asks whimsically how those three deaths would have looked if Dostoevsky had written them. But, he quickly remarks, Dostoevsky would never have chosen three *deaths*. His characters could not function if created from that point of view. "Death in the Tolstoyan interpretation of it," Bakhtin concludes, "is totally absent from Dostoevsky's world" (73).

Bakhtin planned more for the Tolstoy-Dostoevsky confrontation than ever got into the final revision of the book. In some posthumously published notes for the second edition ("Toward a Reworking of the Dostoevsky Book") Bakhtin raised this debate on death to a metaphysical level. There the philosophical underpinnings of the Tolstoy-Dostoevsky polemic are, as it were, laid bare:

> In Dostoevsky there are considerably fewer deaths than in Tolstoy—and in most cases Dostoevsky's deaths are murders and suicides. In Tolstoy there are a great many deaths. One could even speak of his passion for depicting death. . . . Tolstoy depicts death not only from the outside looking in but also from the inside looking out, that is, from the very consciousness of the dying person, *almost* as a fact of that consciousness. Tolstoy is interested in death *for the person's own sake*, that is, for the dying person himself, and not for others, not for those who remain behind. He is in fact profoundly indifferent to one's own death as it exists for others. . . .
>
> Dostoevsky *never* depicts death from within. Final agony and death are observed by others. Death cannot be a fact of consciousness itself. . . . Death from within, that is, one's own death consciously perceived, does not exist for anyone: not for the dying person, nor for others; it does not exist at all. . . . Death in Dostoevsky's world is always an objective fact for other consciousnesses; what Dostoevsky foregrounds are the privileges of the other. (*Problems*, 289–90)

These remarks on death invite some expansion. First, Bakhtin suggests that depictions of death can be classified according to a larger literary category, point of view. Because of the brute role played by consciousness, crossing the boundary between life and death is *the* most transparent fictional act, the one event certain to reveal authorial position and the whereabouts of the author's voice. We recall that Bakhtin places Dostoevsky and Tolstoy prominently at opposite ends of a spectrum with regard to authorial position. Dostoevsky, at one extreme, tends to distribute his knowledge among the personalities of his fictional world; what he knows about his characters they know too, or at least have access to—often to their horror. Conversely, what they do not know, Dostoevsky does not pretend to know either. In this respect, Bakhtin claims, Dostoevsky is quite different from Tolstoy, who tends to exploit his privileged position as creator. His totalizing vision reduces the independence of his characters, whose words can be separated from their personalities. Tolstoy's special vantage point permits him to understand a course of events that is still unclear to its participants. In the event of death, he can be on both sides of the boundary.

This spectrum suggests a second and related issue. How the two authors use death is a function of what they expect death to resolve. For Tolstoy, death can be a central event because it accomplishes something; the dying process is bathed in external and internal light, and the great scenes (Ivan Ilych's final agony, Brekhunov's freezing to death in "Master and Man," Andrei Bolkonsky's slow dying after the Battle of Borodino) resolve a question for the victim. This is not to say that all questions are resolved for the reader. But we do sense that the dying person has experienced a necessary resolution, whether or not we can partake of it, and that this resolution closes down and harmonizes the narrative.

The situation is different in Dostoevsky. There, in Bakhtin's words, "death finalizes nothing:"

> Personality does not die. Death is a departure. The person *himself* departs. Only such death-departure can become an object (a fact) of fundamental artistic visualization in Dostoevsky's world. The person has departed, having spoken his word, but the word itself remains in the open-ended dialogue. (*Problems*, 300)

Death resolves nothing because, in Dostoevsky's world, consciousness cannot be present on both sides of the border to appreciate the resolution. The word is immortal, and its carrier has merely "departed." Bodily death as an act can itself be a word—as it is, say, for Kirillov—or it can simply be irrelevant to the word, as in the case of Zosima. But never does it resolve the word or give it finality.

Why is death of no significance to Dostoevsky as an event for consummating personality, whereas for Tolstoy it is of such paramount importance? Again the beginning of Bakhtin's answer can be found in his early essay on authors and protagonists, specifically in his discussion of the connection between genuine otherness and death. My birth and my death, he argues, are events only for others, not for me ("Avtor," 92). Therefore death is the ultimate aesthetic act, a gesture that turns the whole of my life over to the other person, who is then free to begin an aesthetic shaping of my personality (94–95). Only after death, Bakhtin claims, can plot, form, and rhythm begin (103, 115). Death is what makes the other available; it is a gift. But the "gift" is not, of course, free: personal loss is the price we pay for this gift of wholeness from the other. Bakhtin (contrary to some easy readings of him) has great respect for the finished life. But—and this is the crucial point—only the other can bestow this completion on us. We cannot do it ourselves. Thus all the luminescent death scenes in Tolstoy, in which the dying see an inner light, withdraw into themselves and grasp a mystery available to them alone, irritate Bakhtin and strike him as false. In all those instances, the process of dying is marked by an increasing self-sufficiency, by a proud solitude and an indifference to outer context. The dying are completing themselves, and this is not their privilege.

Bakhtin ultimately charges Tolstoy with faulty perspective. No self, not even our own, can be controlled or created from within; we can only be completed from without. In Bakhtin's view, Tolstoy too quickly dispenses with the other. Bakhtin sees this danger already potentially present in the quasi-fictional phenomenon of Tolstoy's diaries, one of Bakhtin's examples of the aesthetic dead end of the confessional form ("Avtor," 124). Confession tries to eliminate the need for the other, to take all the blame on the self. But the other will inevitably appear, either as God (prayer, repentance) or as judge (condemnation). Under such conditions, any positive assessment of self is seen as a further impurity, as a further falling away from the procedures of honest self-analysis. This is the desperate realization of the Underground Man. Solitary confession, Bakhtin argues, is not really open to new birth because it is not open to the purifying effects of the other. Although it can be an ethical act in the world, it resists authentic aestheticization.

In Dostoevsky, the need of the other is absolute. Like any other author he must complete his characters. But he uses his authorial "surplus"—his extra vision—to juxtapose their inner lives, and he submits the whole to a very uncertain ideological resolution. Dostoevsky's "other" comes to represent a relationship among characters, with the author using his surplus to coordinate. Tolstoy's "other," in contrast, represents a relationship between author and character, in which character is infected with author and reader is infected with character. Inevitably, in such situations the authorial surplus is used to instruct.

It is now time to put Bakhtin's vision of Tolstoy versus Dostoevsky into some perspective. It should be admitted at the outset that Bakhtin is not a particularly good reader of Tolstoy. This should not surprise us, however, for Bakhtin does not design his world to accommodate writers like Tolstoy. In it Tolstoy is a loser, the negative example. Bakhtin does make some intoxicating generalizations and insightful comments on certain short pieces. But the longer and more complex the work—that is, the closer he comes to the novelistic masterpieces—the less distinguished his commentary becomes.

Bakhtin is very selective in his sources. He does not, for example, engage Tolstoy's complex and highly self-conscious critique of history, free will, and necessity in the epilogues or draft prefaces to War and Peace. Nor does he confront the many uses to which Tolstoy puts his authorial discourse: Tolstoy's frequent, deliberate undermining of illusions of authority, for instance, or his varied techniques for evading closure. Most telling, Bakhtin shies away from what is certainly the crucial aspect of Tolstoyan discourse: the interaction between the worlds of the characters and the "rhetorical" passages that come, or so it seems, direct from the author's mouth. According to Bakhtin, there is no real interaction. Such authorial insertions simply dry up whatever novelistic contexts they enter and "fall out of the work"—like the evangelical texts at the end of Resurrection and the philosophy of history at the end of War and Peace.[7]

Bakhtin does deal with one Tolstoyan novel in a sustained way, and his treatment is suggestive. In 1929, the year the book on Dostoevsky appeared, Bakhtin also published on Tolstoy. A new edition of Tolstoy's collected literary works was then in production, and for two of the volumes (vol. 11, on the plays, and vol. 13, on Resurrection) Bakhtin wrote the prefaces. In the second of these prefaces, Bakhtin distinguishes between the multiplicity of the earlier great novels and the single-mindedness of Resurrection.[8] Tolstoy's final novel, Bakhtin claims, is in fact a masterpiece of a new genre, the "socioideological novel"—a genre built on a utopian thesis and thus tendentious by definition. Absolutely no element in such a work is neutral; "every word, every epithet, every comparison emphatically demonstrates the ideological thesis" (13:xv–xvi). The preface ends on a reference to Soviet reality:

7. On Resurrection, see "Discourse in the Novel," 344; on the end of War and Peace, see "Problema soderzhania, materiala i forma v slovesnom khudozhestvennom tvorchestve" (The problem of content, material, and form in verbal art), in M. M. Bakhtin, Voprosy literatury i estetiki (Moscow: Khudozhestvennaia literatura, 1975), 6–71.
8. In her work on this topic, Ann Shukman suggests that the Tolstoy prefaces are not single- but decidedly double-voiced. She points out that although these essays are among the most sociological and Marxist of Bakhtin's "own name" writings, they deal with works—the dramas and the novel Resurrection—that embody Tolstoy's most explicitly Christian and anarchic aspects. In an officially orthodox society Tolstoy denounced the church and invited excommunication; in an officially atheist state Bakhtin embraced the church and invited arrest. Shukman sees an overlap between Tolstoy's and Bakhtin's biographies, in the life they led as well as in the life to which they aspired. Both men were faced with the problem of sustain-

ing belief without the institution of the church. She also sees a parallel between Tolstoy's spiritual quest, reflected in the evolution of his peasant heroes, and the fate of Bakhtin himself. For each, the dominant image became that of a wandering ascetic. If read in the guarded light of Bakhtin's religious views, the prefaces are indeed double-voiced and partly parodic texts. The prefaces, while posing as obedient exercises in monologizing Tolstoy, are perhaps also an encoded tribute to the dialogue (at times gracious, at times deadly) that both Tolstoy and Bakhtin conducted with their respective cultures. A later version of Shukman's essay was published as "Bakhtin and Tolstoy," Studies in Twentieth-Century Literature 9 (1984): 57–74, half of which is reprinted in the present volume. Bakhtin's prefaces may be found in L. Tolstoy, Polnoe sobranie khudozhestvennykh proizvedenii (Complete collected literary works), ed. Khalabaev and Eikhenbaum (Leningrad: Pechatnyi dvor, 1929), 11: iii–x, 13: iii–xx, and are translated as an Appendix to the present volume.

In recent times our Soviet literature has been tenaciously laboring over the creation of new forms for the socioideological novel. This is perhaps the most pressing and important genre on today's literary scene. The socioideological novel—ultimately the socially tendentious novel—is a completely legitimate artistic form. Not to recognize its purely artistic legitimacy is a naive prejudice of superficial aestheticism, which we should have long ago outgrown. But actually this is one of the most difficult and risk-laden forms of the novel. . . . To organize the entire artistic material from top to bottom on the basis of a well-defined socioideological thesis, without stifling it or drying up the living concrete life within it, is a very difficult task.

Tolstoy handled this task with consummate mastery. As a model of the socioideological novel, *Resurrection* can be of great use to the literary aspirations of the present day. (xx)

Resurrection becomes the model for the didactic socialist-realist novel; the late Tolstoy becomes a model for early Soviet monologism.[9]

Thus the plea Bakhtin makes for Dostoevsky in the first chapter of *Problems of Dostoevsky's Poetics*—that the novelist should be read for his formal innovations and technical artistry, not for any particular ideology—is inverted for Tolstoy. Tolstoy's artistry is seen precisely as an ally of ideology, and of a singularly tendentious ideology at that. In Bakhtin's world, Tolstoy has only one function: he stands for a single voice coincident with a completed self. Tolstoy is "monologic," Bakhtin would say, because the necessity that rules his novels is of a fundamentally lonely sort; personality, shaped and hemmed in by its unique environment, strives to break through to the author's truth. Dostoevsky, in contrast, stands for selfhood in process. He is "dialogic" because there is no "author's truth"—there is authorial position but no truth outside the context of a specific dialogue among other selves.

Bakhtin's recasting of the Tolstoy-Dostoevsky polemic contains much that is original and evocative. But it does not interrogate Tolstoy on his own terms. Bakhtin closes Tolstoy down, makes his contradictions less provocative, and never satisfactorily confronts the complex issue of personality in the Tolstoyan novel. This issue is worth pursuing, for here, one suspects, an authentic dialogue between Tolstoy and Bakhtin is waiting to be spoken.

In Bakhtin's view, Dostoevsky and Tolstoy demonstrate quite different understandings of the role of the idea vis-à-vis the individual personality. Dostoevsky's method, simply stated, is to use the idea as his basic struc-

9. This point has been ably argued in the West under less trying political conditions. See, e.g., Gary Saul Morson, "Socialist Realism and Literary Theory," *Journal of Aesthetics and Art Criticism* 38 (1979): 121–33, where Tolstoy's aesthetics are reviewed in the context of Soviet official literature.

tural unit and to create plots by passing one idea through many characters. They may commit murder, go mad, hang themselves, create improbable scandals, live always on the unstable edge of society, but the idea each represents is remarkably stable. It is the very durability and inviolability of these ideas, which interact and coexist on a number of planes at once, that produce conflict in society and madness in the individual. The exemplary case here is Raskolnikov, whose great interior monologues are battlegrounds between coexisting personified ideas (*Problems*, 73–75). His interior voice moves quickly from individual biographies to the life positions they represent: "Oh, the Luzhins, the Sonechkas of the world!" (*Problems*, 238). These life positions address themselves dialogically to the unfinished inner core of Raskolnikov's personality (86). Ideas, in short, *use* personality, enriching it, tormenting it, even discarding it once the ideas have been established in circulation. A major character—say, Stavrogin—who generates ideas but then passes through them coldly, unable or unwilling to invest his personality in them, is marked for a meaningless death.

In Tolstoy this relation of idea to personality is reversed. There the dominant and stable force, the major structural unit, is the individual personality itself—perceived not as an ideological position but as an accumulation of life experience. It survives by its flexibility and its capacity to adjust. Instead of passing one idea through many characters—Dostoevsky's route—Tolstoy tends to create his plots by passing many ideas through one personality. The ability to assume and shed ideas, to pass through and remain open to as many life situations as possible, is precisely what defines a major Tolstoyan hero. Tolstoy himself stressed this characteristic in one of his draft prefaces to *War and Peace*:

> It is not a novel because I cannot and do not know how to confine the characters I have created within given limits. . . . I cannot call my work a tale because I am unable to force my characters to act only with the aim of proving or clarifying some kind of idea or series of ideas.[1]

One cannot imagine in Tolstoy an interior dialogue such as Raskolnikov's, one in which a hero refers to "the Bezukhovs, Andrei Bolkonskys, and Konstantin Levins" of this world. Those lives stand for too many things, and Tolstoyan characters are related to one another in a different way. Each identity is "secure" to the extent that it is *not* fastened down to a single idea.

Consider two famous conclusions that focus this difference between Dostoevsky and Tolstoy. The first, also singled out by Bakhtin (*Problems*, 239), is the ending of *The Double*: "Our hero shrieked and clutched at his head. Alas! This is what he had known for a long time would happen!"

---

1. "Drafts for an Introduction" [Draft 3], Leo Tolstoy, *War and Peace*, ed. George Gibian (New York: Norton, 1966), 1365.

The second, which brings *Anna Karenina* to a close, describes Levin's spiritual regeneration:

> I shall still get angry . . . I shall still express my thoughts inopportunely; there will still be a wall between the holy of holies in my soul and other people . . . I shall still be unable to understand with my reason why I am praying and I shall continue to pray—but my life, my whole life—every moment of it, is no longer meaningless as it was before, but has an incontestable meaning of good, *with which I have the power to invest it.*

The Kingdom of God, Tolstoy tells us, is Within You.

Both Dostoevsky's hero and Tolstoy's hero realize a truth. But for Golyadkin, the hero of *The Double*, the realization is that nothing has changed, that the idea has won out over all his attempts to mask or evade it. He is at last forced to confront what has been, for him, always true. For Levin, in contrast, the realization (which, we are told, saves him from suicide) is that his personality can win out over any individual idea that may seek dominance over him—that his personality is in fact validated by the richness and multiplicity of ideas it can accommodate. "Confrontation with the truth," in Levin's sense, means not a face-to-face showdown between carriers and the ideas they represent, but precisely the inability of any single idea at any given moment to be forever decisive or binding on the personality.

This comparison raises some interesting questions about Bakhtin's famous, and far too facile, categorization of Dostoevsky as a "polyphonic" thinker and of Tolstoy as a "monologic" one. Both, it is clear, exhibit a genius for multiplicity. But each writer has a different way of connecting multiplicity with language and with the formation of a self. For Dostoevsky, multiplicity is spatial, coexistent, and—for want of a better word—immortal. Voices are refracted, juxtaposed, but never assimilated or eliminated. Death can be an act in this world, but conflict cannot be resolved through it. Once death occurs, the word that had been embodied returns to the pool of ideas out of which selves are born. The Kingdom of God is located not within you but among you.

For Tolstoy, multiplicity is located elsewhere. It is more linear and temporal than spatial and coexistent. Life is a matter not of seeking external confrontation with other equally and eternally valid ideas, but of processing an idea or a situation at the proper time to guarantee the survival of the organism. For all his robust fullness of setting, Tolstoy is a master at mapping the ways in which people are *not* free. The choices a person can make depend on a very specific and restricted immediate context. Thus Tolstoy's obsession with timing: Vronsky breaking the back of his mare, Varenka and Koznyshev out mushroom picking, the awful last-minute sense of accident in Anna's death, and the horrible casualness with which Petya Rostov is killed in battle. Bakhtin is right, Tolstoy *is* a poet of death—but not because of any special morbidity on Tolstoy's part. This emphasis is, rather, the natural result of a fictive world in which ideological systems exist to serve individual personality, and not the other way around. When the personality is cut off by death, there is an absolute cutoff of one person's unique, unrepeatable accumulation of ideas and interactions. No one but the author is left to step in and fill the gap, with his absolute language and extrapersonal perspective.

The Bakhtinian model, in sum, does not really allow for any investigation of the Tolstoyan sense of self.[2] Bakhtin to the contrary, that self is not consummated through the activity of an unfairly privileged author, sitting above and apart from his characters and completing them from within rather than from without. The Tolstoyan self is simply consummated in another way. Not even the other has power to complete it. Because the self has no single internal point of crystallization, no ideational center, the best it can do is focus, for a while only and at considerable mental effort, on a select sequence of events. These events do not penetrate a given mind "logically." They must confront a highly individualized, contradictory complex of habits, reflexes, and accumulated experience—a complex that is, at the same time, enormously vulnerable to the accidents of the outside world. Just as history, in Tolstoy's construct, has no ultimate coherence, so the *I* does not cohere; thus it can be profoundly and irreversibly moved by random environmental factors. Tolstoy is deadly serious about chance. This fact has led Gary Saul Morson to suggest that *War and Peace*, that unclassifiable work, is closer to satire than to any other genre. Its target, he proposes, "is all forms of thinking that would explain away the randomness, the asystematicity and 'unstorylike' character of history and psychology."[3] Tolstoy's greatest works all explore this ruthless radical contingency, and his successful heroes learn how to build a life within it. In each of these protagonists the absence of an ultimate coherence to the self, along with Tolstoy's failure to endorse a strategy of explanation, constitutes a sort of freedom and terror that Dostoevsky could not have envisioned for his characters.

Dostoevsky, of course, also shows us a world where not everything is

2. For a good treatment of Tolstoy's "expressivist" vision of the self and its origins in Rousseau and Herder, see Patricia Carden, "The Expressive Self in *War and Peace*," *Canadian-American Slavic Studies* 12 (1978): 519–34. For an instructive contrast, see Bakhtin's critique of "expressive aesthetics" in "Avtor," 55–81. For the sort of sensitive and profound attention to language constraints, inner monologue, and dialogic processes in Tolstoy that Bakhtin was unable or unwilling to provide, see Lidiia Ginzburg, *O psikhologicheskoi proze* (Leningrad: Khudozhestvennaia literatura, 1977), 317–68. It should be noted, however, that Ginzburg (as a student of Yuri Tynianov) is sympathetic to the structuralist thinking of mature Formalism; she ultimately defines the Tolstoyan self

as a system organized by a "dominant" and prefers to work with personality types as codes. Both stances were uncongenial to Tolstoy, and (in my view) to Bakhtin as well.

3. Gary Saul Morson, "Structures of Self in Dostoevsky and Tolstoy" (paper presented at the Midwest Slavic Conference, Columbus, Ohio, May 1984), 5. Tolstoy's radical contingency and its governing influence on his understanding of psychology, history, and narrative are the subject of Morson's *Hidden in Plain View: Narrative and Creative Potentials in "War and Peace"* (Stanford: Stanford University Press, 1987). The paper "Structures of Self" is integrated into chap. 7 of that book.

known and where incompatible truths are carried around in individual selves. But for Dostoevsky, the unknownness of the world is a matter of mystery, not of contingency. The accidents and "coincidences" that saturate his work eventually add up to a revelation. To be sure, the revelations may be multiple; in this sense Dostoevsky is truly polyphonic. But such polyphony can increase as well as decrease the authority of the author. As one critic has ably noted, under polyphonic conditions characters

> are neither equally significant nor equally evaluated, but to the extent that it is possible each is confirmed by the writer in his own special truth. . . . What is called "polyphonism" in Pushkin and Dostoevsky imparts a loftiness not only to the heroes, but to the authors as well. It makes the author's view on things maximally broad, objective—the view not only of an artist, but of a wise man, a prophet, as well.[4]

In Dostoevsky, a character cannot explore this prophecy alone; individuals need one another in their pursuit of the mystery. Tolstoy's world is by far the lonelier place. There is no mystery there, only the brute facts of everyday experience. Such a vision was understandably alien to Dostoevsky, and, for other reasons, to Bakhtin as well. In his lectures on Tolstoy to high school students in Vitebsk (1922–23) Bakhtin stressed just this loneliness of the Tolstoyan hero: "Ivan Ilych understood that he lived alone, that all that is most essential took place in solitude. Life as reflected in the consciousness of others was a fiction, a mirage, a falsehood."[5]

It was, in fact, this loneliness that Bakhtin addressed in his 1961 notes toward the new edition of his book on Dostoevsky. "Separation, dissociation, and enclosure within the self as the main reason for the loss of one's self. . . . No nirvana is possible for a *single* consciousness."[6] Bakhtin saw the Tolstoyan self, at its most intense moments, vainly seeking that nirvana, which to Bakhtin was nonexistence.

4. E. A. Maimin, *Pushkin: Zhizn' i tvorchestvo* (Pushkin: life and works) (Moscow: Nauka, 1981), 150–51.

5. Bakhtin's lectures have not survived, but notes on these lectures were made by one of his students, R. M. Mirkina (whose words are quoted here). From her summary, it appears that Bakhtin read a number of Tolstoy's early and late works (but not the great novels of the middle period) in terms of "I-for-myself" and "I-for-another." See R. M. Mirkina, "Konspekty lektsii M. M. Bakhtina" (Notes from Lectures by M. M. Bakhtin). *Prometei: Istoriko-biograficheskii almanach 12* (1980): 257–68, esp. 265.

6. M. M. Bakhtin, "Toward a Reworking," in *Problems* (see n. 1 above), 287, 288.

N. G. CHERNYSHEVSKY

[Tolstoy's Military Tales]†

"Extraordinary powers of observation, subtle analysis of spiritual processes, precision and poetry in depictions of nature, and elegant simplicity—these are the distinguishing characteristics of L. N. Tolstoy's
[literary] talent." Such is the opinion one hears from anyone who follows
the development of our literature. Criticism has repeated this description,
inspired by the common consensus, and in doing so, has been absolutely
faithful to the truth of the matter.

But, can criticism really limit itself to this judgment, which, it's true,
has identified traits in Count Tolstoy's talent that really do belong to
him, but has yet to show the particular ways in which these qualities
are manifested in the author's works such as * * * his "Military Tales"?
Powers of observation, subtlety of psychological analysis, poetry in depictions of nature, simplicity and elegance—one finds all this in both
Pushkin and Lermontov, as well as in Turgenev—it would be fair to
describe the talent of each of these writers using these same epithets,
yet it would be insufficient to distinguish one from another; and to repeat
the same thing about Count Tolstoy still fails to capture the individual
physiognomy of his talent and fails to demonstrate how this splendid
talent differs from other splendid talents. It must be characterized more
precisely.

* * *

* * * Let's take as an example the description of what a man experiences at the moment preceding a blow expected to be mortal, then at
the moment of the final convulsion of this man's nerves resulting from
that blow: [Chernyshevsky quotes a lengthy passage from Tolstoy's "Sevastopol in May" included in the present volume on pp. 14–43, from
the paragraph beginning "Praskukin, who was walking together with
Mikhaylov" and ending with the sentence "He had been killed instantly
by a splinter that struck his chest."]

Without exaggeration this depiction of an interior monologue [*vnu-
trennego monologa*] must be called astonishing. One won't find such
psychological scenes described from that point of view in the works of
any other of our authors. And, in our opinion, that aspect of Count
Tolstoy's talent that affords him the possibility of capturing these psychological monologues constitutes the particular, individual strength of
his talent. We don't want to say that Count Tolstoy will always and
without fail present us with this kind of picture: that depends entirely
on the circumstances he's describing, and, in the final analysis, simply

†From *Pis'ma bez adresa* (Moscow: Sovremennik, 1983) 111–17. Translated by Michael R. Katz. The
review first appeared in *The Contemporary* in 1856.

on his will. One time he wrote "The Snowstorm"[1] consisting of a series of interior scenes; another time, "Notes of a Billiard Marker"[2] in which there's no such scene because the subject of the story didn't demand it. Expressing this idea figuratively, he knows how to play on more than this one string; he can play on it or not, but the very ability to play on it lends his talent that individuality that is constantly evident in everything he writes. Similarly, a singer whose range extends to unusually high notes may not use those notes if the part he's singing doesn't call for them—nevertheless, whatever notes he sings, even those equally accessible to all voices, each of them will have a very special sonority that derives from his ability to reach those high notes, and in every one of his notes the connoisseur will recognize the full extent of his range.

This particular trait in Count Tolstoy's talent that we've been discussing is so original that it's necessary to examine it with great care; only then will we understand its full significance for the artistic merit of his works. Psychological analysis is almost the most essential quality that lends strength to creative talent. Usually this trait has a descriptive character, if one may express it thus; it takes a specific, stable feeling and dissects it into its component parts, giving us, if one may so express it, an anatomical table. In addition to this aspect, in the works of great poets we note yet another tendency, the appearance of which acts on the reader or the spectator in a very striking manner: that is the apprehension of dramatic transitions from one feeling to another, from one idea to another. Ordinarily only the two last links in this chain are presented to us, the beginning and the end of the psychological process—because most of our poets whose talent possesses a dramatic element are primarily concerned with results, the manifestations of internal life, the confrontations between people, actions, but not with the mysterious process by means of which the idea or the feeling is worked out; even in monologues that obviously must serve to express this process more than any other form, a conflict of feelings is expressed and the noise of this conflict distracts our attention from the laws and transitions governing the associations of our conceptions—we're preoccupied by the contrast, not by the forms of their origin. Monologues almost always differ from dialogues only in their external appearance if they contain more than simple anatomical analysis of stable feeling: Hamlet, in his famous soliloquies, seems to be divided in two and arguing with himself; in essence his monologues belong to the same kind of scene as the dialogue between Faust and Mephistopheles,[3] or the argument between Marquis Posa and Don Carlos.[4] The originality of Count Tolstoy's talent lies in the fact that he doesn't limit himself to a depiction of the results

---

1. A short story by Tolstoy written in 1856 and first published in *The Contemporary*.

2. A short story by Tolstoy written in 1855 and first published in *The Contemporary*.

3. Characters from Goethe's dramatic poem *Faust* (1808).

4. Characters from Schiller's drama in blank verse *Don Carlos* (1787).

of the psychological process: it's the process itself that interests him. The evanescent manifestations of this inner life that replace one another with extraordinary rapidity and inexhaustible variety are masterfully depicted by Count Tolstoy. There are painters who are famous for their ability to capture a flickering reflection of a ray on quickly rolling waves, the shimmering of light on rustling leaves, the play of colors in the changing outlines of clouds: it's generally said that these artists know how to capture the life of nature. Count Tolstoy does something similar with respect to the mysterious movements of psychological life. Therein, it seems to us, lies the absolute originality of his talent. Of all our noteworthy Russian writers he alone is a master in this regard.

Of course this ability, like any other, must have been innate to the writer; but it would be insufficient to stop with this overgeneralized explanation. Talent develops only through independent [moral] activity, and in this activity, the extraordinary energy of which has already been attested to by the above-mentioned originality of Count Tolstoy's works, one must see the strong foundation acquired by the talent. We're talking about self-examination, the indefatigable attempt to observe oneself. The laws of human action, the play of passions, the connections to reality, the influence of circumstances and relationships—we can study all this if we observe other people carefully; but all knowledge acquired by this means will possess neither depth nor accuracy if we don't study the most precious laws of psychological life, the play of which is made manifest to us only in our [own] consciousness. He who has failed to study man in himself, will never achieve a profound understanding of people. That feature of Count Tolstoy's talent which we described above demonstrates that he has studied the mysteries of the life of the human spirit in himself very carefully; this knowledge is valuable not only because it has afforded him the possibility of portraying pictures of the inner movement of human thought to which we have directed the reader's attention, but even more, perhaps, because it has provided him with a firm foundation for the study of human life in general, for the understanding of character and the springs of action, the conflict of passions and impressions. We would not be mistaken in saying that self-observation must have sharpened his powers of observation greatly and have taught him to observe people with a penetrating eye.

This quality is precious in a talent, and perhaps the most fundamental of all the claims to fame of a genuinely remarkable writer. Knowledge of the human heart, an ability to reveal its secrets to us—that's the first thing to say in describing any one of our authors whose works we read and reread with amazement. And, in talking about Count Tolstoy, his profound study of the human heart will always impart a very high worth to whatever he writes and in whatever spirit he writes. He'll probably write much that will strike each reader by other, more effective qualities—the profundity of his ideas, the interest of his conceptions, strong traits of his characters, vivid pictures of daily life—and in those of his works that are already known to our public, these qualities have always aroused interest. But for the true connoisseur it will always be obvious—as it is even now—that knowledge of the human heart is the fundamental strength of his talent. A writer can attract readers by his more dazzling traits; but his talent is truly strong and lasting only when he possesses this quality.

✻   ✻   ✻

BORIS EIKHENBAUM

[Sevastopol Stories]†

✻   ✻   ✻

In narrative prose the principle tone is set by a storyteller who in himself represents the focal point of the work. Tolstoi always stands outside of his characters, and therefore he needs a medium whose perception can provide a basis for description. This necessary form is created only gradually. Tolstoi's own tone has a constant tendency to develop apart from the described scenes, to hover over them in the form of generalizations, precepts, sermons[1] almost. These sermons often assume the characteristic declamatory form, with its typical rhetorical devices. Thus begins the second Sevastopol sketch "Sevastopol in May 1855."

> Already six months have passed since the first cannon-ball whistled from the bastions of Sevastopol and blasted the earth on the enemy's embankments, and since then *thousands of bombs, balls and bullets have not ceased flying* from the bastions to the trenches and from the trenches to the bastions, and the angel of death has not ceased hovering over them.
>
> *Thousands* of human conceits have had time to be offended, *thousands*—have had time to be gratified, inflated, *thousands*—to be calmed in the embrace of death. How many pink coffins and linen palls! But *still those same* sounds resound from the bastions, *still in the same way*, with involuntary trepidation and dread, do the French look out from their camp on a clear evening at the yellowish dug-up earth of Sevastopol's bastions . . . *still in the same way*, from the telegraph tower, does the navigating officer look through a telescope at the colorful figures of the French . . . and *still with the same* fervor, from different parts of the world, do diverse crowds of

---

†From *The Young Tolstoi*, trans. Gary Kern (Ann Arbor, 1972). Reprinted with permission of Ardis Publishers.

1. It was not by accident that Tolstoi wrote sermons in 1851.

people, with even more diverse desires, stream to this fatal place. But the question unresolved by the diplomats is still not resolved by powder and blood. (Chapter I)

This is the typical speech of an orator or preacher, with its rising intonation, emotional repetitions, and phrases of a broad declamatory style designed for a large crowd of listeners. This tone runs through the entire thing, returning in the accented portions of the sketch. Thus Chapter XIV, which separates the first day from the second, is written entirely in this style, with the very same devices.

> *Hundreds* of fresh, bloodied bodies of people, a couple of hours ago full of various lofty or petty hopes and desires, were lying with stiffened limbs in the dewy, blossoming valley which separated the bastion from the trenches and on the smooth floor of the mortuary chapel in Sevastopol; *hundreds* of people with curses and prayers on their parched lips crawled, writhed and moaned, some among the corpses in the blossoming valley, others on stretchers, on cots and on the bloodied floor of the dressing station,—but *still in the same way, as on previous days*, the summer lightning flashed above Sapun hill, the twinkling stars grew pale, the white fog extended from the sounding dark sea, and the scarlet dawn lit up in the east, long purple cloudlets scattered along the light azure horizon, *and still the same way, as on previous days*, promising joy, love and happiness to the whole revived earth, there floated out the powerful, beautiful luminary.

The scheme of both "sermons" is identical: "thousands . . . thousands . . . and still those same . . . and still the same . . . hundreds . . . hundreds . . . but still in the same way as on previous days . . . and still in the same way as on previous days . . ." Such sweeping antitheses as the following are also extremely characteristic of oratorical devices: "thousands . . . have had time to be *offended*, thousands have had time to be *gratified*," or "hundreds of bodies, full of various *lofty and petty* hopes and desires . . . hundreds of people with *curses and prayers*." The conclusion is written in the same way, and in combination with the cited pieces forms a complete sermon.

> Yes, on the bastion and on the trench white flags are displayed, the *blossoming valley* is filled with dead bodies, the *beautiful sun* descends to the blue sea, and the *blue sea*,[2] heaving, sparkles in the golden rays of the sun. Thousands of people crowd, look at, talk to and smile at one another. And these

---

2. I italicize those words which link this passage with the preceding one [*Eikhenbaum's note*].

people are Christians, professing the one great law of love and
self-sacrifice . . . etc. (Chapter XVI)

Such is one scale of this sketch—the scale of large proportions. Within
it the divisions of another scale, the "Stendhalian" scale, are marked.
In this scale there appears a series of characters who were not even
present in the first sketch. And remarkably, the first one to appear,
Second Captain Mikhailov, is described with such minuteness that it
seems he will play the role of the main hero around whom the events
must revolve. Not only are all the details of his appearance and dress
made known, but also his recollections of "blue-eyed Natasha," his
thoughts, dreams and hopes. Afterwards, in point of fact, Mikhailov
retires entirely to the background, and this minuteness remains self-
sufficient. In connection with the question of narrative prose and Tolstoi's devices, it is interesting to stop at this point and examine how
Tolstoi describes Mikhailov. As we have more than once indicated,
Tolstoi always regards this with particular attention and concern. In
prose of the narrative type, the tone and the manner of character description is determined by the narrator's tone and the demands of the
plot. Sometimes a character is described at first from a certain distance,
as though the narrator himself does not yet know him, but only observes
him. Personages are often *introduced* in this way so that afterward, when
their role has become clearly defined, a detailed characterization can
be developed in some way. Tolstoi does not recount and does not construct a plot-filled novella. Consequently, he does not *introduce* his
personage but presents him all at once. However, an external description,
or more than that, a description seemingly channeled through someone
else's perception, is a device which Tolstoi usually finds indispensable
(the portrait of Knoring, Kraft, etc.). This problem is resolved in an
original way in the second Sevastopol sketch. First we are given a completely external description:

> A tall, slightly stooped infantry officer, drawing on a not
> completely white but smart glove, came through the gate of
> one of the sailors' little houses built on the left side of Morskaya
> Street, and pensively gazing down at his feet, started up the
> hill toward the boulevard. The expression of this officer's un-
> handsome face *did not reveal* great mental abilities, but sim-
> plicity, discretion, honor and an inclination to proper form.
> He was badly built, not quite agile and seemingly shy in his
> movement. He wore a little-used cap, a thin coat of a rather
> strange lilac color from under which showed a gold fob chain,
> trousers with foot-straps and clean, shining calf-skin boots. *He
> could have been* a German, had his features not revealed his
> pure Russian origin, or an adjutant, or a regimental quarter-
> master (but then he would have been wearing spurs), or an

officer transferred for the duration of the campaign from the cavalry, or perhaps even from the Guards. (Chapter II)

This description is even accompanied by guesses and reflections, so that the moment at which the personage appears actually coincides with the moment at which the author observes him, without knowing who he is yet. But there is no game of illusion here: this is Tolstoi's usual method of description, only lacking in this instance any motivation, even in the person of that cadet who observes Kraft in "The Wood-Felling." Proof of this statement is the abrupt transition from the first part of the description to the next:

> *He was indeed* an officer transferred from the cavalry, and at the present moment, going up toward the boulevard, *he was thinking* of a letter he had just received from a former comrade, now retired, a landowner in the province of T., and his wife, the pale blue-eyed Natasha, a great friend. *He recalled* only one passage from the letter . . . etc.

The description moves from external observation to an account of what Mikhailov thought and recalled. There follows a complete interior monologue: Mikhailov's dreams of receiving the medal of St. George—"and then there will be more action and as a well-known man, I will be assigned a regiment . . . a second lieutenant . . . the St. Anna on my neck . . . a lieutenant . . ." And all these details—this blue-eyed Natasha and the landowner in the province of T., whose letter is quoted here in parentheses (with the naive motivation that Mikhailov *recalled* one passage in it)—all of this develops no further. Different characters appear, among whom Mikhailov not only does not play a prominent role, but on the contrary often fades out completely and yields his place to others.

The dialectic of the soul foreshadowed in "The Wood-Felling" is developed into a complete system here. The second sketch centers on the portrayal of battle scenes. We are given a series of interior monologues exposing the hidden mechanism of each character's psychic life. All of the characters—Mikhailov, Praskukhin, Kalugin, Galtsin, Pesth—pass in succession through Tolstoi's chemical process. Mikhailov is supposed to go with his company to the lodgements:

> *I am sure to be killed tonight*, I feel. And the main thing is that I didn't have to go, but I volunteered. And they always kill the one who asks for it. And what is that damned Nepshisetski sick with? It may very well be that he's not sick at all, and because of him they will kill a man, *they'll kill him for certain*. But if they don't kill me, I will surely be commended. I saw how it pleased the regimental commander when I said: allow me to go if Lieutenant Nepshisetski is sick. If I don't come out of this a major then surely the Order of Vladimir.

374 Boris Eikhenbaum

After all, I'm going to the bastion for the *thirteenth* time already. *Oh, 13 is a lousy number. They'll kill me for certain*, I feel they'll kill me . . . etc. (Chapter IV)

Kalugin goes to the bastion:

"Ah, that's lousy!" thought Kalugin, experiencing some unpleasant feeling; and he too had a presentiment, i.e., a very ordinary thought,—the thought of death. But Kalugin was conceited and blessed with wooden nerves, which is what they call brave in a word. He did not give in to his first feeling and began to encourage himself. (Chapter IX)

But further on the same thing that happened to Mikhailov happens to Kalugin:

He suddenly felt frightened, galloped some five steps and lay down on the ground. When the bomb burst, and it was quite far from him, he got terribly irritated with himself, and he stood up looking around to see if anyone had seen his fall . . . He, who always boasted that he never even ducked, went with quickened steps and almost on all fours along the trench. "Oh! This is bad!" he thought as he stumbled, "They'll kill me for certain." (Chapter IX)

In another passage, when Mikhailov leaves the lodgements with Praskukhin, the monologues of both are given in parallel:

"Damn, how softly they're going," *thought Praskukhin*, continually looking back as he marched beside Mikhailov. "Really, I better run ahead, since I've already given the order . . . But then, no, they might say afterwards that I'm a coward! What will be, will be. I'll walk beside him.

"And why is he walking with me?" *thought Mikhailov on his part.* "How often have I noticed, he always brings bad luck. Here it comes, flying straight at us it seems." (Chapter X)

Scenes of fear alternate with scenes of death and maiming. Interior monologues are developed, peculiar in that they run contrary to reality. The death of Praskukhin is described circuitously, as he himself does not realize he will die:

"Thank God, I'm only bruised! . . . I must have bloodied myself when I fell," he thought . . . Then some red fires began leaping in his eyes, and it seemed to him that soldiers were putting rocks on him; the fires leapt less and less but the rocks they were laying on him pressed down on him more and more. He made an effort to push the rocks off, stretched himself and no longer saw, heard, thought or felt. *He had been killed on the spot by a piece of shrapnel in the middle of his chest.* (Chapter XII)

Here we cannot speak simply of "realism" or "truthfulness," for obviously only the dead could be the witnesses and judges. The material itself commits us to speak of the device. And it is characteristic that Tolstoi does not need the fact of death so much (because the death of Praskukhin has no plot significance) as the process of *dying*. Praskukhin is made an outsider to himself: this is the same device familiar to us in other types of motivation. We note the same external analysis of the psychic life, in this case strengthened by the fact that the true sense of everything observed is entirely different. Tolstoi treats Mikhailov in exactly the same way, but the relationship [of the psychic life to the outside world] is reversed.

> "It's all over, I'm killed," he thought when the bomb exploded
> . . . and he felt a blow and a cruel pain in his head. "Lord!
> Forgive me my sins," he murmured, clasping his hands, rising
> and falling backward unconscious . . . "This is the soul de-
> parting," he thought. "What will I find *there*? Lord! Receive
> my soul in peace" . . . *He was slightly wounded in the head
> by a rock.* (Chapter XIII)

In this contrasting juxtaposition the typical Tolstoian paradox lies hidden, bestranging the traditional "literary" conception of death—especially heroic death. Tolstoi says essentially the same thing he said of the Caucasus: people simply do not die the way it is usually written. Nature is not such as it is portrayed, war is not such, the Caucasus is not such, bravery is not manifested that way, people do not love that way, they do not live and think that way, and finally, they do not die that way. Here is the common origin of the Tolstoian system. There now approaches the most fatal and likewise most inevitable "not such" for Tolstoi—art is not such as people write and think about it. In this sense, Tolstoi is truly the canonizer of crisis: the forces of disclosure and destruction lie hidden in almost every one of his devices. Tolstoi is not an initiator but a consummator. Dostoevsky sensed this very well when he wrote to Strakhov in 1871: "But you know this is all landowner literature. It has said everything that it had to say (magnificently in Lev Tolstoi). But this word, landowner to the core, was the last."

It is not without reason that the second Sevastopol sketch unfolds on the background of a moral sermon. And it is not without reason that at its conclusion Tolstoi looks back over his work in apparent bewilderment:

> Where is the expression of evil which should be avoided?
> Where is the expression of good which should be imitated in

this story? Who is the villain, who is its hero? All are good and all are bad.

Neither Kalugin with his shining bravery—*bravoure de gentilhomme*—and vanity, the mover of all his actions, nor Praskukhin, an empty, harmless man even though fallen in battle for the faith, throne and fatherland, nor Mikhailov with his shyness, nor Pesth, a child without firm convictions, can be either the villain or the hero of the story. (Chapter XVI)

Here we have neither Captain Khlopov nor even Velenchuk. Microscopic analysis and chemical reaction have destroyed even these images. The mechanism of the psychic life has proved to be identical in everyone. The cadet Pesth tells how he stabbed a Frenchman, but Tolstoi, as it were, intervenes in this story and without even bothering about a motivation, straightforwardly and pointedly says: "But this is the way it really was." And instead of an exploit, instead of heroism, something absurd and incomprehensible occurs apart from Pesth's will and awareness, as if in a dream:

Pesth was in such terror that he positively *did not remember*, was it long, where and who, what happened. He walked *like a drunken man*. But suddenly from all sides a million fires flashed, and *something* whistled, crashed. He screamed and ran *somewhere*, because everyone was running and screaming. Then he stumbled and fell on *something* . . . *Someone* took the rifle and stuck the bayonet into *something* soft. "Ah, Dieu!" *someone* yelled in a terrible, piercing voice, and only then Pesth understood that he had stabbed a Frenchman. A cold sweat broke out all over his body, he shook as if in a fever and threw down his rifle. But this continued for only a moment; immediately the thought entered his head that he was a hero. (Chapter XI)

Thus Stendhal's comparatively modest method was developed in Tolstoi's hands. Tolstoi *unmasks* his own characters at every step. This same Pesth tells how he conversed with the French soldiers during the truce, and Tolstoi again intervenes, offering his own evidence:

In fact, though he was at the truce, he did not manage to say anything in particular . . . and on the way back he thought up those French phrases which he was now relating. (Chapter XV)

Kalugin, Prince Galtsin and a lieutenant walk along the boulevard and talk of yesterday's action:

The guiding thread of the conversation, as it always is in such cases, was not the action itself, but part taken by the one

> speaking in the action. Their faces and the sound of their voices had a serious, almost sad expression, as if the losses of yesterday strongly touched and distressed each one; *but to tell the truth*, since not one of them had lost a very close friend, this expression of sadness was an official one *which they only considered an obligation to display*. Kalugin and the lieutenant would be prepared to see such action every day if only each time they would receive a gold sword and major-general, *in spite of the fact that they were fine fellows*. (Chapter XV)

Thus not only the conception of heroes is depreciated, but also that of merely "fine fellows," whose psychic make-up proves both more complex than is usually described and at the same time simpler, in that it is identical in everyone. With good reason Tolstoi compared people to rivers: "the water in all is identical and is everywhere the same." This is Tolstoi's invariable system of *digression*: "people are not like that." And therefore he unfailingly maintains a distance from his personages— he is equally close to and equally distant from them all. In the second Sevastopol sketch his personal role as an author takes the form of a constant intervention in the conversations and actions of his personages, with constant evidence to show what they feel and think *in actual fact*.

After all these disclosures, Tolstoi describes one horrifying scene to put an end to all these "elevating illusions," to contradict them with "the vile truth," and then to switch to his sermonic tone:

> But enough. Better you look at this ten-year-old boy, who in an old—probably his father's—cap, with shoes on his bare feet and nankeen pants held up by one suspender, went out beyond the rampart at the very beginning of the truce and walked through the hollow, looking with dull curiosity at the French and at the corpses lying on the ground, and gathered the blue field flowers with which the valley is strewn. Returning home with a big bunch of flowers, his nose covered against the smell which was carried to him by the wind, he stopped near a heap of transported bodies and for a long time looked at one terrible headless corpse which was nearest to him. Having stood a rather long time, he moved closer and with his foot touched the outstretched, stiffened arm of the corpse. The arm shook a little. He touched it once more, harder. The arm shook and again stayed in its place. The boy suddenly screamed, hid his face in the flowers and ran away at full speed toward the fort. (Chapter XVI)

Stendhal has a similar detail: Fabrizio comes across a soldier's mutilated corpse and at a sutler's suggestion shakes him by the hand. But typical of Tolstoi are these augmentative touches of the child and blue flowers.

In fact, Tolstoi often uses children for disclosure-bestrangement.[3] In this same sketch a little girl takes the bombs to be stars: "The stars, the stars; look how they roll! . . . There, there another rolled down. What's this for, huh, mommy?" (Chapter VI). It is interesting that a little earlier Kalugin and Galtsin also spoke of the similarity between bombs and stars, but there the comparison was reversed: "And that big star—what is it called?—*it's just like a bomb*" (Chapter V).

Tolstoi's compositional devices in both of these Sevastopol sketches are similar to those he has used before, i.e., a series of scenes ordered simply by the progression of time and usually confined to one day, and a frame or ring construction. The first sketch opens with the morning twilight and concludes with the evening twilight. Concomitantly, in the beginning the sounds of voices carry across the water and blend with the sounds of gunfire, while in the end "across the water there come the sounds of some old-fashioned waltz being played by the military band on the boulevard and the sounds of firing from the bastions, echoing them strangely." In the second sketch the composition is more complex. First of all, as indicated above, it is framed by a sermon, and since this sketch encompasses two days (Chapters II–XIV and Chapters XV–XVI) there is a tail-piece on their borderline (Chapter XIV) which repeats entirely the introduction ("hundreds of fresh, bloodied bodies . . ." etc.) and thereby forms a kind of ring. The scenes of the first part of the sketch are kept within the confines of one day. The first of them portrays the boulevard, where "*near the pavilion* a regimental band was playing, and crowds of military people and women leisurely moved along the lanes" (Chapter II). The second part, which in its entirety (there are only two chapters) serves as the conclusion to the sketch, opens with a repetition of this very same scene: "The next evening a chasseur band *again* played on the boulevard and *again* officers, cadets, soldiers and young women leisurely strolled *near the pavilion* and along the lower lanes of blooming, fragrant white acacias" (Chapter XV. Cf. Chapter III: "Below, along the shady fragrant *lanes of white acacias*, secluded groups were walking and sitting").

✳   ✳   ✳

---

3. *Oblichitel'noe ostranenie,* elsewhere translated as "revelatory bestrangement."

GARY SAUL MORSON

The Reader as Voyeur: Tolstoi and the Poetics of Didactic Fiction†

> Of course, I myself have made up just now all the things you say
> . . . can you really be so credulous as to think that I will print all this
> and give it to you to read, too? . . . I shall never have readers.
>
> Notes from Underground

Readers of Russian fiction accede with special haste to Stendhal's dictum that "politics in a work of literature is like a pistol shot in the middle of a concert, something loud and vulgar, and yet a thing to which it is not possible to refuse one's attention."[1] There are countless histories of Russian literature that divide its authors and critics into two irreconcilable camps, those who judge art "in its own terms" and those who insist on a moralistic or political framework external to art. The nihilist's assertion that boots are more important than Shakespeare, Maiakovskii's self-destructive pledge to step on the throat of his song, Turgenev's plea to Tolstoi to remain a belles-lettrist and leave religion to the church—these are the usual landmarks in the history of Russian literature. Attempts to save radical critics like Belinskii from opprobrium usually take the form of arguing that he was not so Stalinist as the Stalinists say; when we praise the late Tolstoi we marvel at the great art he was able to produce *in spite of* his moralistic strictures.

It is an account on which the new critics and the Soviets can agree, although their values are reversed. And yet it is possible that both sides misstate the question. It is simply inappropriate to ask whether great art *can be* didactic; the fact is, that it often is. I do not know many scholars, whether formalists or new critics, who would deny *The Possessed* and *The Death of Ivan Il'ich* the status of "great literature"; and to argue that they are such despite their didacticism is simply to force reality into a theoretical mold. I simply cannot imagine what would be left of *The Death of Ivan Il'ich* or *The Kreutzer Sonata* without their moralism: perhaps something like the *War and Peace* Percy Lubbock wished Tolstoi had written—without the lectures on history and the polemical story of Napoleon. The right question, however, should not be *whether* great art can be didactic, but *how* it can be didactic; what we need (and what

---

† From *Canadian-American Slavic Studies*, 12, No. 4 (Winter 1978), 465–80. For the Russian texts of Tolstoi, I have used the ninety-volume (Jubilee) edition of his works: L. N. Tolstoi, *Polnoe sobranie sochinenii*, 90 vols. (Moscow: Gosudarstvennoe izdatel'stvo "Khudozhestvennaia literatura," 1928–59). The translations cited in the text are from Maude, modified for accuracy when necessary.

1. I am not so much citing Stendhal as Irving Howe citing Stendhal, in *Politics and the Novel* (New York: Avon, 1970), p. 17. Howe asks shrewdly: "Once the pistol is fired, what happens to the music? Can the noise of the interruption ever become part of the performance? When is the interruption welcome and when is it resented?"

formalism and new criticism have prevented us from finding) is a poetics of instruction. Only then can we begin to appreciate Russian literature on its own terms.

There is perhaps no better place to start than with the new critics themselves. "We reject as poetry and label as mere rhetoric," write Wellek and Warren, "everything which persuades us to a definite outward action. Genuine poetry affects us more subtly. Art imposes some kind of framework which takes the statement of the work out of the world of reality. Into our semantic analysis we thus can reintroduce some of the common conceptions of aesthetics: 'disinterested contemplation,' 'aesthetic distance,' 'framing.' "[2] An absolute gulf separates art from reality, for art is framed—as surely as a physical frame surrounds a picture—by an implicit set of conventions which remove it from the world of "is" to that of "as if." Literature is implicitly preceded by what Gregory Bateson has called metacommunicative statements, statements of the type "take this as a joke," "read this as a metaphor," or "this is only a story."[3] We are not asked to believe, but to suspend our disbelief. The reader takes the text which follows as fiction, and does not judge its "truth" in literal (or referential) terms. We must be able to understand this language about language, or we will resemble Dostoevskii's Smerdiakov, who objects to Gogol because his stories are "not true," or like the judge at the Daniel trial who equated fiction with slander on simple literalist grounds. Conversely, the formalist insistence on the absolute, ontological division of fiction from reality also separates persona from biographical author, and text from reader. That is why, indeed, it rejects as "mere" rhetoric (rhetoric is here opposed to art, to "genuine" poetry) works which insist on being evaluated by non-aesthetic criteria. A poetics of didacticism (as distinguished from a study of how ideas can become material for fictive discourse) would seem to be a contradiction in terms.

The present article suggests a model for a poetics of didactic literature, a model derived from a study of the Russian tradition (though not limited to it). I choose Tolstoi as emblematic of that tradition, and "Sevastopol in December" as a fiction in which his devices are most conspicuously "bared." My thesis in brief is that Tolstoi's violation of the principles of "framing" and "aesthetic distance" is strategic; he assumes that his readers expect to read fiction with a set of conventions that separate it from reality and he therefore deliberately encourages those expectations so that he may violate them later. For it is precisely aesthetic detachment that these stories seek to challenge. Their recurrent theme is that the

2. René Wellek and Austin Warren, Theory of Literature, 3rd ed. (New York: Harcourt, 1956), pp. 24–25. On frames and frame-breaking, see also Erving Goffman, Frame Analysis: An Essay on the Organization of Experience (New York: Harper, 1974) and Boris Uspensky, A Poetics of Composition: The Structure of the Artistic Text and Typology of A Compositional Form, trans. Valentina

Zavarin and Susan Wittig (Berkeley: Univ of California Press, 1973).
3. Gregory Bateson, Steps to an Ecology of Mind (New York: Ballantine, 1972), pp. 159–339. See especially "A Theory of Play and Fantasy" and "The Logical Categories of Learning and Communication."

aesthetic experience is itself immoral, that to observe is to act—and act badly. There are not only "speech acts," but also listening acts. These fictions therefore work by morally implicating the reader in the experience which is in process as he reads that very fiction. The reader of the story is culpable *because* he is a reader of the story. He responds by trying to reassert the conventions of fiction, and so to separate the aesthetic experience of the story from the aesthetic experiences he is led to condemn in the story; but he comes to learn that this act of distancing has also been planned and is, indeed, part of the story's strategy of implicating its reader. A series of metafictional devices constantly break frame; and we are allowed to reconstitute the frame only so that it may be broken again. Involuntarily, the reader *of* the fiction becomes an actor *in* the fiction. If the reader still rejects the story's anti-aesthetic, he has nevertheless defined himself in terms of the story's own set of choices.

In other words, these fictions do not ignore literary conventions, they defy them. Structured as patterns of violated expectations, they first ask us to read them as literature and then lead us to reject the conventions on which such a reading is based; and this structure implies that they rely on those conventions every bit as much as Turgenev's works do. Tolstoi's fictions are deliberately paradoxical, and we can only appreciate a paradox if we already hold beliefs that the paradox challenges. Their strategy is both to be and to deny being "mere literature," a strategy that is closely related to Tolstoi's frequent rhetorical device of asserting that his stories are not stories, but reality. In the middle of his fiction "Lucerne," for instance, Tolstoi breaks frame and tells the reader that "this is not a fiction, but a positive fact, which can be verified by anyone who likes from the permanent residents at the Hotel Schweizerhof, after ascertaining from the papers who the foreigners were who were staying at the Schweizerhof on the seventh of July."[4] The reader is trapped between conflicting sets of conventions, as the story alternately insists on being read as fiction and as journalism; and to rest with either side of the contradiction is to misread the work.

Consider, for instance, Tolstoi's first Sevastopol story. No better refutation could be provided to Wayne Booth's assertion that "efforts to use the second person [form of narration] have never been very successful, but it is astonishing how little real difference even this choice makes."[5] "Sevastopol in December" is written almost entirely in the second person, and one need only try to rephrase it in the first or third person to see that it depends for its effectiveness on that form. "The radical unnaturalness"[6] of the narration is disturbing, and is meant to be. For it seems to violate an essential convention of fiction which

4. *Leo Tolstoy: Short Stories*, ed. Ernest J. Simmons (New York: Modern Library, 1964), p. 328.
5. Wayne C. Booth, *The Rhetoric of Fiction* (Chicago: Univ. of Chicago Press, 1961), p. 150, n. 3.
6. *Ibid.*

normally distinguishes it from rhetoric, a distinction succinctly stated by John Stuart Mill: "eloquence is *heard*, poetry is *overheard.*" The speech of fiction takes place within the fictive frame; we, the real historical audience, as distinguished from the implied or fictive one, are mere eavesdroppers. So far as the fictive speaker of the work is concerned, we do not exist at all. (This is the device that is "bared" in the quotation from *Notes from Underground* with which this essay begins.) But the strikingly "unnatural" second person address momentarily seems to break the frame, to be addressed to *us*, as if the author wanted us for once not to eavesdrop, but simply to listen. If we are experienced readers, we try to regard even this address as a literary device, and so to reconstitute the frame, but our effort is never fully successful and our position as audience remains problematic. The strategy is symmetrical to the ambiguous position of the narrator in "Lucerne," who alternately claims to be persona and biographical author, and the reader's uncertainty about his own ontological position becomes a central element of his experience of reading this didactic fiction.

This work is written in the second person because it really is addressed to the second person, its reader. While it is fiction, it is also Mill's "eloquence," Wellek and Warren's "rhetoric." The second-person address constantly threatens to make the reader a character in the story, a participant in an unmediated dialogue with the author—a threat that is the first of the work's many strategies to overcome the aesthetic distance it assumes we "assume." The work is addressed directly to the reader because it is about the reader, and the act of reading. This story is, in Henry Sams' phrase, a "satire of the second person."[7]

To read a text as literature is to apply aesthetic criteria to it: we judge it as performance, we detach ourselves from personal involvement. As Shklovskii observes, "art is thus without compassion, or outside it, except in those instances when the feeling of commiseration serves as material for an artistic pattern."[8] Now, it is precisely this act of distancing, our ability to turn horror into "tragedy," that is the theme of Tolstoi's story. The aesthetic experience stands in opposition to the ethical; and this opposition applies to our apprehension of this work as well. The very fact that its reader is able to appreciate the artistic transformation of an ongoing battle into art makes him morally suspect. " 'Well, you know, I wanted to see * * * ' "[9] Pierre explains his presence as gentleman tourist at Borodino. "Mounting the steps to the knoll Pierre looked at

7. Henry W. Sams, "Swift's Satire of the Second Person," in Frank Brady, ed., *Twentieth-Century Interpretations of Gulliver's Travels* (Englewood Cliffs, N.J.: Prentice-Hall, 1968), pp. 35–40. Sams' essay, which first appeared in 1959, argues that Swift strategically violates his "contract" with his readers, who discover that they, not some "third person," are the objects of this "disingenious" kind of satire.

8. Viktor Shklovsky, "A Parodying Novel: Sterne's *Tristram Shandy*," in John Traugott, ed., *Laurence Sterne: A Collection of Critical Essays* (Englewood Cliffs, N.J.: Prentice-Hall, 1968), p. 79.

9. Leo Tolstoy, *War and Peace*, tr. Louise and Aylmer Maude (New York: Simon and Schuster, 1942), p. 846 (bk. 10, ch. 20).

the scene before him, spellbound by its beauty. . . . the sound of the firing produced the chief beauty of the spectacle. . . . and for a long time [Pierre] did not notice the killed and wounded, though many fell near him. He looked about him with a smile which did not leave his face."[1] The strategy of the second person address in "Sevastopol" is to turn its reader into just such a tourist of death, to make him see the act of reading is an *act* of reading. We learn too late that this is a reflexive fiction and that we are its protagonist. The reader becomes voyeur. This text does not so much have an "implied" reader as an implicated one.

Tourism is the controlling metaphor of "Sevastopol in December." The story is, indeed, a fictive tour guide and that is why it is written in the second person (and second person imperative). As in real tour guides, whose language the story imitates, this form of address works as a set of directions (quite literally) for seeing a museumized world. I quote from George W. Oakes' guide *Turn Right at the Fountain*: "Carrying a rain-coat or umbrella . . . start at *Piccadilly Circus*." "Just past Lloyds . . . you will have an amusing time. . . . As you turn back toward *Traitor's Gate* and contemplate the great personalities . . . you may be in the mood for something out of the ordinary."[2] Here the underscoring of names of places, like the titles of books and paintings, renders them and the people in them (whose "typical" conversations "you will enjoy") into a kind of sculpture: they are "picturesque." The tour guide is a subset of "how-to" books (which are also written in the second person) that tells us how to *see*. It teaches us not simply to look, but what to look *at*. The world becomes theatre (its setting is "authentic") and you have the script; its people are actors in your "play." "From the stream of action," writes Dean MacCannell in his recent study *The Tourist*, "select bits are framed" so that they can be "savored."[3] If MacCannell is right that the quintessential moment of tourism is the "instant replay," then a tour guide is an "instant preplay."

But a walk through Sevastopol is no promenade through Lucerne. The central irony of Tolstoi's fictive tour guide derives from the de-scription of war as one might describe such a promenade, a battleground where men are still dying as a historical landmark. "You" expect to see the site of "beautiful historical legends," and you try to appreciate the "majesty" of heroism in process. But "you are mistaken": there are things to which art is not adequate, events which we must not even try to view with equanimity. The form of a tour guide becomes singularly inap-propriate to the "sights" of this tour, and we must read its descriptions *against* the conventional expectations we have of such forms: "You enter the large Assembly Hall. As soon as you open the door you are struck

1. *Ibid.*, pp. 880–83 (bk. 10, chaps 30–31).
2. George W. Oakes, *Turn Right at the Fountain*, 2nd ed. (New York: Holt, Rinehart, 1965), pp. 21–28. Several of Oakes' walking tours were first published in *The New York Times* Travel Section.
3. Dean MacCannell, *The Tourist: A New Theory of the Leisure Class* (New York: Schocken, 1976), p. 27.

by the sight and smell of forty or fifty amputations and most seriously
wounded cases, some in cots but most of them on the floor." As he
described the smell of the sea, your guide now evokes that of putrefying
flesh. "Now if your nerves are strong, go in at the door to the left; it is
there they bandage and operate. . . . The doctors are engaged in the
horrible but beneficient work of amputation. You will see the sharp
curved knife enter the healthy white flesh; you will see the wounded
man come back to life with terrible, heart-rending screams and curses.
You will see the doctor's assistant toss the amputed arm into a corner
and in the same room you will see another wounded man on a stretcher
watching the operation, and writhing and groaning not so much from
physical pain as from the mental torture of anticipation." Characteristically, in this drama of observation, "you" are made to watch someone
watching, and inevitably to remind yourself that there are observers and
observers; and "you," thankfully, are one who does not have to undergo
what he witnesses. "You" are pleased that for you these deaths are only
objects to be seen; and here the moral problems of watching already
begin to be apparent. *You take comfort* in the fact that for you these
amputations are only sights, are objects, and that you are as detached
from their pain as that arm is from its former owner.

The kind of time in which a tour guide is written also multiplies the
horror of the scene. The tourist simply does not exist in the same kind
of time as the people he observes, and he sees them across this time
difference (it is the consciousness of the separation which frames them).
The present tense of a guidebook does not mean "now," but "whenever."
Its present tense is an absolute present. For the point of a guidebook,
indeed the very possibility of writing one, depends on the sights being
constants. People are not present, they are re-present-ative. Indeed, it
is *because* all the sentences of a guidebook contain an implicit "whenever" that the word may be omitted. A Russian guide (and Tolstoi's
fictive one) is made up of iterative verbs because its action may be
reiterated as often as one likes; its imperfectives point to the possibility
of repeating its actions (as do some future perfectives, e.g., *uvidite*). But
the very idea of repeating this promenade is grotesque, as is the implicit
repeat "performance" of amputation. The effect of the tour guide narration in this case is to juxtapose the specificity of the pain that each
soldier suffers with "your" knowledge that it might be seen at any time.
The author of the guide describes what you would like to believe are
exceptions as utterly unexceptional, so unexceptional that "you" have
come knowing the pain you will witness at each point. The topology of
pain is mapped out with geographical precision.

If this text has a subtext, it is *The Inferno*. There, too, an omniscient
guide shows the way through the house of torments; and this text also
chronicles its "tourist's" reaction: "Now the notes of pain begin to reach
my ears; now I am come where great wailing breaks on me." When he

wonders if he may speak to the sufferers, Tolstoi's tourist is echoing
Dante. "Poet," Dante addresses his guide, "I would fain speak with these
two. . . . 'O wearied souls, come and speak with us if One forbids it
not.' "[4] It is only necessary to rewrite these passages in the second person
and the absolute present to turn Dante's singular account into Tolstoi's
repeatable tour. This difference redefines the reader.

Here we begin to approach a still more significant inversion of the
form of a guide: the relation of its implied reader to its text. For in a
real guide the second person form of address is no more than form: the
text emphasizes not the one who sees, but what he will see. Though it
"plots," it is plotless; though it may be told as a narrative, we understand
that to be a transparent device for rendering the immediate apprehension
of space in the sequence of language. No "story" is in fact being told.
That, indeed, is why a guide may be opened at any point. One may
progress to that page not only by reading the preceding pages, but also
by simply reaching the physical place it is then describing; and guides
are usually written assuming that they will be used that way (thus the
wealth of cross-referencing, the repetition of necessary information, the
division into brief, easily digested sections). But Tolstoi's "guide" is in
fact not a guide at all, but the story of its reader. We learn not so much
about the sights of Sevastopol as about what will happen to "you" when
you see them. The observer changes because of what he observes. One
cannot read the same guide twice.

What the tourist of Sevastopol learns to see is himself. This is a story
of his growing self-consciousness, his rite of "passage." As the journey
progresses the tourist begins to realize that he himself is one of the sights
of Sevastopol, an expected part of the scene for which provisions have
been made and which he must consider in his survey of the battleground.
He begins to watch himself watching, just as he has watched other
watchers. And in the process of growing self-observation, "you" come
to realize that seeing is an action and keeping one's distance a relation.

"You" begin secure in your role as tourist, and your point of view is
unself-consciously aesthetic. As you approach the harbor, you hear "the
majestic sound of firing" and are prepared for picturesque scenes of
heroism and valor. At first, this is what the tour guide seems to promise,
beginning with its initial paragraph's deceptively placid description of
the dawn that will soon make "the dark blue surface of the sea" begin
to sparkle "merrily." But your disillusionment begins early, though at
first on purely aesthetic grounds. "Your first impression [of the camp]
will certainly be most disagreeable: the strange mixture of camp-life and
town-life—of a fine town and a dirty bivouac is not only ugly but looks
like horrible disorder." You are wrong again, however, and as you heed
your guide's command to "look more closely" at the faces of the soldiers,

4. *The Divine Comedy of Dante Alighieri*, tr. John D. Sinclair (New York: Oxford Univ. Press, 1961),
1 (*Inferno*), 77 (Canto V).

your impression of Sevastopol once again changes. Twice mistaken, you now reflect on your errors and on yourself. "Yes, disenchantment certainly awaits you on entering Sevastopol for the first time," the omniscient narrator predicts your inner monologue. "Perhaps you may reproach yourself for having felt undue enthusiasm and may doubt the justice of the ideas you had formed of the heroism of the defenders of Sevastopol, based on the tales and descriptions and sights and sounds seen and heard from the North Side." But of course this re-evaluation will itself soon be re-evaluated in your constant process of learning through a series of planned errors—the "pitfalls" of your guide's uneven tour.

Expectation, disillusionment, self-reflection, and new expectation—this is the pattern "you" constantly repeat. Your tentative expectations repeatedly prove false (and so they become more and more tentative). The narrator then corrects you: "But look more closely," "But you are mistaken," "Do not trust the feeling that checks you." You then reflect upon, and reproach yourself, "you . . . begin to feel ashamed of yourself in the presence of this man," and so learn not only about Sevastopol, but also about "you" who observe Sevastopol. And as the process of vision and re-vision, analysis and self-analysis, unfolds, you become more and more implicated in the horror you watch.

Your painful self-discovery gradually becomes the center of your attention. You see less and less of Sevastopol as you (an unattractive you) enter your field of vision. " 'What matters the death and suffering of so insignificant a worm as I, compared to so many deaths, so much suffering?' But the sight of the clear sky, the brilliant sun, the beautiful town, the open church, and the soldiers moving in all directions, will soon bring your spirit back to its normal state of frivolity, its petty cares and absorption in the present." But do not trust this normal state. As you approach the bastion, and death ceases to be a "remote" possibility, a less self-indulgent "self-consciousness begins to supersede the activity of your observation: you are less attentive to all that is around you and a disagreeable feeling of indecision suddenly seizes you. But silencing this despicable little voice that has suddenly made itself heard within you . . . you involuntarily expand your chest, raise your head higher, and clamber up the slippery clay hill." (p. 128) What you are most closely observing now is you; and when you look at the enemy ("him") that is now the distraction. And it is a welcome distraction, because its very intensity is (perhaps) capable of drawing your attention from the "despicable little voice" to the already "regular and pleasant whistle . . . of a bomb." You try simply to look (just look) to prevent yourself from looking at your self looking. So you go to the bastion, lean out of the embrasure, and stare.

It is here that the climax of the story takes place. For your benefit, the naval officer "will wish to show you a little firing." And the exchange of shells will please you, the narrator predicts: "you will experience interesting sensations and see interesting sights." Distracted from yourself, "you revive and are seized, though only for a moment, by an inexpressibly joyful emotion, so that you feel a peculiar delight in the danger—in this game of life and death—and wish the bombs and balls to fall nearer and nearer to you."

But just as you are enjoying this game, it kills a man; and the "scarcely human appearance" of the mutilated, dying soldier is the next sight on your tour. His death is the last event in the story. The text breaks, and the narrator now summarizes "the principal thought you have brought away with you": the heroism of the soldiers in contrast to "that petty ambition of forgetfulness which you yourself experienced." When the guide ends his tour on a pacific description of the evening, we recognize the apparent parallelism with the story's opening as ironic. Since the death of the soldier, "you" are not the same "you," and cannot take the same aesthetic joy as before.

It is of the utmost importance to understand what has happened in the story's climactic scene: the tourist has literally become implicated in a death, a death which has taken place for his aesthetic pleasure. Looks kill. "Your" story is your growing awareness that (literally and metaphorically) you are responsible for what you look at. It is this growing awareness that may "seem to inspire a dread of offending" the wounded in the hospital by *looking* at them, a dread that makes you want to look away. But that reaction, the narrator immediately corrects you, is precisely the wrong one, for it repeats the moral error by further denying your relation to the sufferer. "Do not trust the feeling that checks you at the threshold, it is a wrong feeling. Go on, do not be ashamed of seeming to have come *to look* at the sufferers, do not hesitate to go up and speak to them. Sufferers like to see a sympathetic human face." The only way to redeem looking is to acknowledge it as an action, to make it a form of relation and not of separation. And that will mean going through the painful process of listening (again like Dante) to the wounded man's litany of pain, a process which "you" wish to cut short as soon as possible. One *bears* witness.

Now, reading is also a form of tourism, and a particularly cowardly form of it, since it distances us all the more. Unlike the reader, the tourist at Sevastopol momentarily enters the time of the soldiers, because he can die in it. But as readers, we take no risks by leaning out of an embrasure. We protect ourselves from ever having to see men in agony and, more important, from ever having to see them watching our tourism and compelling us either to talk with them or show we are only "looking." The key point I wish to make is that we gradually come to learn that what applies to "you" also applies to *us*, that we are simply tourists through the written word. As "you" come to observe yourself while trying to see Sevastopol, we learn equally involuntarily about ourselves

while trying to *read* "Sevastopol." The pattern of reluctant advances and
cowardly resistances that are enacted between this omniscient tour guide
and his tourist is repeated in a similar tension between the author of the
story (Tolstoi) and his historical, real readers. There is "leakage" of the
narrative out of its frame. The story is double; the text creates its own
context. The narrative projects out of itself a second story in which we
are actors, in which we gradually come to realize that as readers we are
implicated in the crime of "disinterested" observation. We resist that
leakage; but that very resistance is simply a form of "looking away" and
implicates us (as it implicates the tourist at the hospital) still more. There
is no way simply to "read about" Sevastopol. As "you" come to look at
the act of looking, we come to look at the act of reading.

The real story, therefore, may be described as the story of our encounter with what we at first *think* we are reading, the story of the
"plotted" failure of our attempt not to apply the "you" to us. Like the
confidence game it is, "Sevastopol in December" exists by making its
audience its unwilling participants.[5] It is primarily for this reason, I
think, that the effects of its passages are lost when rewritten in the first
or third person. (I invite the reader of *this* article so to rewrite the passages
I have cited.) Confined in its frame, the double-level story would turn
into a single-level account.

Consider again the striking form of the second-person narrative. The
address implies the immediacy of direct discourse rather than the me-
diated language of fiction; it threatens to make us listen when we want
to eavesdrop. Precisely because this is not the conventional way to construct a story, we must remind ourselves that the conventions of story-
telling do still apply, that the fictional frame encloses the first part of
the Sevastopol trilogy as surely as the third. This imitation tour guide
constantly seems to alternate with a real tour guide and appears on the
verge of claiming not real*ism*, but reality. This ambiguity of genre, it
seems to me, is the reason for the journalistic title, the documentary
quality of the first two sketches (which footnote linguistic data), and the
original intent to publish the narrative in a new military, rather than a
literary, journal. The fiction constantly threatens to deny its own fictiveness; and to the extent that it succeeds in doing so, we become not
readers of a fiction in the form of a tour guide, but real tourists through
the medium of non-fictive journalism. And as tourists, the condemnation we have made of the immediate observer in the fictive guide
becomes applicable to us, since we are now in the same position.

We therefore try to resist the identification with the implied reader,
to remind ourselves of the story's fictiveness, and so to distance ourselves
from it. We attempt to appreciate it aesthetically, and so to assert a
comforting aesthetic distance. But in so doing, we justify the very ac-

5. My interpretation of the "framing" of a confidence game follows Goffman, pp. 83–122.

cusation whose applicability we hope to deny. Our attempt to look across a fictive frame means we insist on being disinterested, not responsible for artistically rendered pain. " 'Blood' in art," to quote Shklovskii, "is not bloody."[6] In the hospital, the tourist encounters an amputee who describes how he managed to avoid pain. " 'The chief thing, your Honor, is *not to think*,' " he declares. " 'If you don't think, it's nothing much. It's most because of a man's thinking.' " It is advice that the tourist accepts all too quickly to distance himself from his pain of looking, until the wife of the wounded man interrupts to say that her husband was indeed in dreadful agony and to imply that the advice is extended for "your" comfort. And so "for some reason [you] begin to feel ashamed of yourself in the presence of this man." Now, "your" mistake is precisely our mistake. We, too, try "not to think" of the concrete pain of real sufferers, but only of characters in narrative; and the narrative corrects its reader as surely as its character corrects its tourist. Not to think, not to look—this is the natural reaction to other's horror, precisely because it classes it as *other's* horror; and the aesthetic distancing made possible by the classing of a work as "only a story" is simply another way of "not looking."

It is, in fact, a response that the tourist in the story also makes. When pain becomes unbearable, he tries to apply an aesthetic standard, to judge events as if they were performance. When you leave the "house of pain," you will be in this state of mind. "You may meet the funeral procession of an officer. . . . The funeral will seem a very beautiful military pageant, the sounds very beautiful warlike sounds; and neither to these sights nor these sounds will you attach the clear and personal sense of suffering and death that came to you in the hospital." The removal of the personal sense of suffering, is of course, precisely what the aesthetic frame is designed to do; and this is why the narrator interjects his reproach for "your" relief at your spirit's return to its "normal state of frivolity." It is a reproach he repeats several times, whenever "you" attempt to see this tour as tours are usually seen. "Your" appreciation of the "beauty and majesty" of the "sights" betrays you.

But the same process betrays us; we also come to look with discomfort at our initial appreciation of the majesty of the sunrise in the first paragraph. Indeed, our very attempt to read this story as a story, to admire *its* artistry repeats the tourist's error. "Sevastopol in December" contrasts aesthetic and personal approaches to suffering, and is therefore structured to force its readers to experience both in turn. The story plays

6. Shklovsky, p. 79. Aware of Shklovskii's tone of polemical overstatement, Viktor Erlich wisely cautions that "this is not to say that 'blood' in literature is wholly 'bloodless'. . . . As the formalist theoreticians themselves indicated . . . the distinguishing characteristic of poetic language is not that it is 'trans-emotional,' but that its emotional load, along with its acoustic texture and grammatical form, becomes an object of aesthetic contemplation rather than a catalyst of fear, hatred, or enthusiasm; something to be 'perceived' and 'experienced,' as part of a symbolic structure rather than acted upon." *Russian Formalism: History—Doctrine*, 3rd ed. (The Hague: Mouton, 1969), p. 210.

us false. It tells us to read it as fiction, then reproaches us for doing so. The reader is caught between contradictory characterizations of the text he is reading, between "this is a story" and "you are culpable for reading this as a story"; between "as if" and "as if as if." The structure of the reader's experience therefore fits the pattern of what Gregory Bateson has called a "double bind."[7] And the double bind is essential to its strategy to reach beyond the text to "infect" its reader with a personal sense of the pain it describes, to make him present.

The story includes the story of reading it. It works much like Velasquez' meta-painting, *Las Meninas* (here I follow Foucault's interpretation).[8] The canvas portrays an artist painting a canvas, whose subject lies outside the canvas. But we can guess who that is, because a mirror in the back of the painting points to the place where the subject is standing, and reflects a royal couple. Since the place where the subject stands is also the place where the viewer must stand to see the painting, this projection beyond the frame constitutes an elaborate compliment to the viewer, to us. What is happening here is that the position where we must stand to observe the painting has become part of the painting— just as the process we must go through to read "Sevastopol in December" becomes part of it. Crucial differences also obtain. The portrait of us in Tolstoi's narrative is humiliating. More important, since a narrative must be read in sequence and over time, the process of reading can itself be "plotted" in advance. Tolstoi constructs a pattern of repeated humiliations for us, makes us construct the story of our encounter with ourselves as readers. We are "taken in."

The story we think we are reading, therefore, turns out to be an enclosed narrative, and we are the protagonists of the frame tale. Our reading of this outer tale is its central event, and our discovery of it becomes a double discovery of the self. Like "you," we learn (against our wishes) about ourselves. Indeed, this unwilling self-knowledge, this change we have not expected and perhaps resisted, is the goa towards which all instructive literature strives. Didactic fiction is reader-implicating fiction.

Some generalizations about the poetics of didactic fiction are in order. Instruction seeks to change its audience, perhaps to move it to specific action. Fiction, on the other hand, only states in the subjunctive; its "truths" obtain only in possible worlds, but not in the actual one. "The poet is least of all men liar, for the poet nothing affirmeth," writes Sidney; and his statement may be neatly contrasted with the closing line of the second Sevastopol sketch: "The hero of my story," writes Tolstoi, "is the truth."

Didactic fiction, then, is something of an oxymoron, and its best

7. Bateson, *loc. cit.* See especially "Toward a Theory of Schizophrenia," pp. 201–27.
8. Michel Foucault, *The Order of Things: An Ar-*   *chaeology of the Human Sciences*, no trans. (1971: rpt. New York: Random House, 1973), pp. 3–16.

practitioners work not by avoiding but by taking advantage of its necessary contradiction. The didactic story-teller doubly encodes his text as fiction and as truth, and manipulates the reader's experience through code-switching and an ambiguous frame. He realizes that fiction is an effective means of seduction precisely because it is defined as counterfactual, as "only a story"; and so we willingly make ourselves into its implied audience as we might not when listening to a sermon. For the duration of our reading, we suspend our beliefs (not just our disbelief). We allow our expectations to be shaped not by what we think about the real world, but by what the author tells us of his. We give up metaphysics for genre, exchange principles for conventions. The strategy of the didactic fiction-writer is to make this assumption of his view carry over into the reader's real world, and so to abuse convention to induce conversion. He must make orthodox (if disingenuous) use of the opening frame ("this is only a story") but elude, as much as he can, the power of the closing frame. He must, in a sense, not allow the curtain to fall. In this particular sense, the story strives to remain open, as its ontological status seeks to be (in the full etymological sense of the word) indeterminate.

The didactic poet exploits the doubleness of the moment of reading. The plot of his story may unfold in a fictive, infinitely repeatable time, but the reading of the story takes place in a unique time, continuous with the rest of experience. It is this peculiar kind of simultaneity that the poet uses to create "leakage" of text into context: and so, doubleness becomes duplicity. The poet is most of all men liar, for he affirms he is only a poet.

The poetics of didactic fiction, therefore, does not essentially challenge formalist assertions about the autonomy of the literary function. On the contrary, it assumes we necessarily hold these beliefs, however intuitively, in order to read fiction at all. Its violation of our expectations is strategic: if we ceased to understand the fictiveness of fiction, didactic art might be impossible.[9]

Though it seems paradoxical, then, there may be no better formalist text than *What Is Art?* (unless it is *The Republic's* justification for banishing the poets). The perception of art as seduction—and that is the metaphor which controls Tolstoi's *The Kreutzer Sonata*—implicitly affirms that we assume an absolute separateness of art from life. That, indeed, is why those who fear art point out the dangers to which that assumption can lead. Shklovskii and his Soviet censor may have had more in common than either one knew.

We may take the argument one step further. Not only is formalism a fruitful way of studying didactic fiction, but the analysis of didactic fiction can tell us much about the limitations of early formalism—precisely because early formalism is so well suited to it. Briefly put,

---

9. The distinction between instructing and moving to a specific action corresponds to that between simple didacticism and its subset, propaganda.

formalism fails to explain how texts can live when the conventions by which they are originally encoded do not survive;[1] and didactic texts do fail at that point. In its initial concern with the conventionality of literature, formalism insists that texts be read according to the conventions of their times. Implicitly it denies the leakage of signs and ignores the renewal of readability in unexpected ways. A text must die with the wearing out of its "devices," and with the passing of the readership that sustains them—and didactic fiction does in fact die at that point. If the second person form of narration should ever become too commonplace to shock, or fictionality ever cease to be a central category of narrative, "Sevastopol in December" would fail in its plotted instruction. It might, however, survive on other terms. For we do re-author our texts and make them mean in unforseen ways: didactic literature is reread, in that emasculating phrase, "as literature." The final irony will belong to the high culture Tolstoi despised when it can comfortably and un-self-consciously incorporate even *What Is Art?* into its canon.

If the limitations of formalism suggest a model for didactic fiction, we must, nevertheless, take those limitations into account. For in an important sense, there may be no such thing as didactic fiction, just as there is no fiction which is securely framed from context. Shklovskii's *mots*—that literature is always free from life, that there is absolutely nothing that can be learned from a work of literature—are at best useful overstatements. The very opposite may be the case. There is no literature from which we do not learn, and in that sense, all fiction is didactic. I think we must ultimately speak not of a class of texts that are didactic, but of the didactic strategies of all texts. Then we can read stories like "Sevastopol in December" as narratives in which the didactic element is the "dominant," and our explication of them will also serve to make us aware of less obvious, but essentially similar, strategies in even the least "instructive" of narratives.

The false framing of the narrative and the consequent "framing" of the reader—this is the strategy of didactic fiction. *Sevastopol's* duplicitous use of the second person, as both fictive and real reader, may therefore stand as archetype of reader-implicating narrative.[2] For Tolstoi, the reader of fiction implicates himself simply by being a reader of fiction: he is therefore a member of the leisure class and lives the sort of life that allows him to indulge in the artifice of art. As Dostoevskii's underground man tells his readers that they do not exist, Tolstoi tells his that they should not exist (at least, not as readers). Tolstoi wants us to reject Tolstoi as Tolstoi rejected Tolstoi.

1. This problem was, however, addressed with remarkable subtlety and success by later formalists, especially Tynianov and Bakhtin.
2. Socialist realism, it seems to me, uses the inverse of *Sevastopol's* duplicitous strategy. Here the duplicity is that of flattery. The implied reader of the text is the perfect Soviet citizen, and the experience of reading becomes one in which the real reader tries to justify the author's implicit extravagant praise of him. When the curtain fails to fall, he will, hopefully, leave the text with some of the attitudes he has assumed in order to read it.

It follows that we can understand fictions like *The Kreutzer Sonata* best if we treat them as anti-fictions. *The Kreutzer Sonata* is a brilliantly contrived aesthetic masterpiece that teaches us to despise such contrivance and mastery—and that is its duplicitous strategy. Tolstoi's didactic fiction is in a perfect position to manipulate the experience of reading because the object of his attack is the aesthetic experience itself. Even if we are sophisticated enough to understand and still ultimately reject his lesson, the process of reading his anti-fictions at least makes us experience the choices involved in the act of reading fiction—beginning with the choice to read fiction at all.

Tolstoi's characteristic device for implicating the audience of his fiction is to depict an audience in his fiction: the audience in the narrative becomes the reflection of the audience of the narrative. In condemning it, we unwittingly condemn ourselves; too late, we recognize ourselves in its unexpected mirror. So we are invited to *The Death of Ivan Il'ich* as our fictional equivalents are invited to his funeral. As they invoke social conventions to deny the applicability of the death to themselves, we invoke those of fiction. We make ourselves the "proper" audience that art requires. If we are sophisticated—*comme il faut?*—we will frame the narrative "as a story" about Man and his death. That is, in our socially defined role as readers, we will think away the "inappropriate question" of our own death. But Tolstoi's story is not literature, it is anti-literature; and the conclusion of its syllogism is not that "Caius is mortal" but that *you* will die. To the extent that we recognize this breach of literary decorum, we, like Pëtr Ivanovich at the funeral, take this "reproach to the living" as somehow "out of place, or at least not applicable to him." Our reading condemns us. Even if we imagine that we do agree with the story's lesson, the very fact that we are at that moment reading fiction belies us. The only person in the story to whom its lesson does not apply is the one who could not read it, the peasant Gerasim.

The device of the pictured audience is, therefore, deeply metafictional (more specifically, reader-implicating) in Tolstoi. These onlookers are part of his "satire on the second person," and are meant to be understood—but belatedly, only after we have made the error they exemplify—as metaphors for the process of reading the work in which they occur. The tourist of Sevastopol will reappear as Pierre at Borodino; the seduction and rejection of Natasha (which begins as she watches an opera) is a metaphor for our experience as well. Tolstoi is no less a "cruel talent" than Dostoevskii. To enjoy him is to misread him.

But it is possible to read him correctly only if we misread him, as he has planned us to do. Return again to the hospital at Sevastopol. Remember that the tourist is observing a man observing the amputation, and we are observing the tourist. Could I suggest that what we are really observing is the compromising process of observing, and that the pain at one remove is our own. And the doctor—well, let me take the doctor as a metaphor for the author, who is engaged "in the horrible but beneficient work of amputation."

Tolstoi's is an aesthetic that characterizes the Russian tradition. Tolstoi is, of course, only one of a series of writers from Gogol' to Solzhenitsyn to "reject art" (in the narrow sense). My feeling is that many of those "accursed questions" of Russian aesthetics—the inclusion of sermons and essays in fiction, the cultivation of works which lie in the interstices between recognized genres ("notes," diaries, autobiographies, dialogues, utopias) or between fiction and non-fiction altogether—derive from a deep suspicion of the conventions of literature. Poised between meta-fiction and didactic fiction, Russian literature is the literature of frame-breaking. It is, in fact, not so much literature as counter-literature, governed by an anti-aesthetic. The justification of its own existence is perhaps the most recurrent theme of Russian culture, and it is a theme which profoundly shapes its tradition of self-referential and "self-consuming" works. The emblem of this tradition could be Man Ray's *Object To Be Destroyed* and its epigraph (perhaps also its epitaph), Bakunin's aphorism: "The will to destroy is a creative will."

To appreciate Russian literature is, in a sense, to be false to it. Yet one cannot be true to it unless one has first been false to it. It intends itself to be used up—and, unfortunately, it has been—like the propositions of Wittgenstein's *Tractatus*: "My propositions serve as elucidations in the following way: anyone who understands me eventually recognizes them as nonsensical, when he has used them—as steps—to climb up beyond them. (He must, so to speak, throw away the ladder after he has climbed up it.) He must transcend these propositions, and then he will see the world aright."[3] To read Russian literature aright is not to need to read it.

MIKHAIL BAKHTIN

[Tolstoy's *Three Deaths*]†

* * *

The new position of the author in the polyphonic novel can be made clearer if we juxtapose it concretely with a distinctly expressed monologic position in a specific work.

We shall therefore analyze briefly, from the vantage point most relevant to us, Leo Tolstoy's short story "Three Deaths" [1858]. This work, not large in size but nevertheless tri-leveled, is very characteristic of Tolstoy's monologic manner.

3. Ludwig Wittgenstein, *Tractatus Logico-Philosophicus*, trans. D. F. Peats and B. F. McGuiness (London: Routledge, 1961), pp. 150–51.
†From *Problems of Dostoevsky's Poetics*, ed. and trans. Caryl Emerson (Minneapolis, 1984). Reprinted with permission of University of Minnesota Press.

Three deaths are portrayed in the story—the deaths of a rich noble-woman, a coachman, and a tree. But in this work Tolstoy presents death as a stage of life, as a stage illuminating that life, as the optimal point for understanding and evaluating that life in its entirety. Thus one could say that this story in fact portrays three lives totally finalized in their meaning and in their value. And in Tolstoy's story all three lives, and the levels defined by them, are *internally self-enclosed and do not know one another*. There is no more than a purely external pragmatic con-nection between them, necessary for the compositional and thematic unity of the story: the coachman Seryoga, transporting the ailing no-blewoman, removes the boots from a coachman who is dying in a roadside station (the dying man no longer has any need for boots) and then, after the death of the coachman, cuts down a tree in the forest to make a cross for the man's grave. In this way three lives and three deaths come to be externally connected.

But an internal connection, *a connection between consciousnesses*, is not present here. The dying noblewoman knows nothing of the life and death of the coachman or the tree, they do not enter into her field of vision or her consciousness. And neither the noblewoman nor the tree enter the consciousness of the dying coachman. The lives and deaths of all three characters, together with their worlds, lie side by side in a unified objective world and are even *externally* contiguous, but they know nothing of one another and are not reflected in one another. They are self-enclosed and deaf; they do not hear and do not answer one another. There are not and cannot be any dialogic relationships among them. They neither argue nor agree.

But all three personages, with their self-enclosed worlds, are united, juxtaposed and made meaningful to one another in the *author's* unified field of vision and consciousness that encompasses them. He, the author, knows everything about them, he juxtaposes, contrasts, and evaluates all three lives and all three deaths. All three lives and deaths illuminate one another, but only for the author, who is located *outside* them and takes advantage of his *external position* to give them a definitive meaning, to finalize them. The all-encompassing field of vision of the author enjoys an enormous and fundamental "surplus" in comparison with the fields of vision of the characters. The noblewoman sees and understands only her own little world, her own life and her own death; she does not even suspect the possibility of the sort of life and death experienced by the coachman or the tree. Therefore she cannot herself understand and evaluate the *lie* of her own life and death; she does not have the dia-logizing background for it. And the coachman is not able to understand and evaluate the wisdom and truth of his life and death. All this is revealed only in the author's field of vision, with its "surplus." The tree, of course, is by its very nature incapable of understanding the wisdom and beauty of its death—the author does that for it.

Thus the total finalizing meaning of the life and death of each character is revealed only in the author's field of vision, and thanks solely to the advantageous "surplus" which that field enjoys over every character, that is, thanks to that which the character cannot himself see or understand. This is the finalizing, monologic function of the author's "surplus" field of vision.

As we have seen, there are no dialogic relationships between characters and their worlds. But the author does not relate to them dialogically either. A dialogic position with regard to his characters is quite foreign to Tolstoy. He does not extend his own point of view on a character to the character's own consciousness (and in principle he could not); likewise the character is not able to respond to the author's point of view. In a monologic work the ultimate and finalizing authorial evaluation of a character is, by its very nature, a *second-hand evaluation*, one that does not presuppose or take into account any potential *response* to this evaluation on the part of the character himself. The hero is not given the last word. He cannot break out of the fixed framework of the author's secondhand evaluation finalizing him. The author's attitude encounters no internal dialogic resistance on the part of the character.

The words and consciousness of the author, Leo Tolstoy, are nowhere addressed to the hero, do not question him, and expect no response from him. The author neither argues with his hero nor agrees with him. He speaks not with him, but about him. The final word belongs to the author, and that word—based on something the hero does not see and does not understand, on something located outside the hero's consciousness—can never encounter the hero's words on a single dialogic plane.

That external world in which the characters of the story live and die is the *author's world*, an objective world vis-à-vis the consciousnesses of the characters. Everything within it is seen and portrayed in the author's all-encompassing and omniscient field of vision. Even the noblewoman's world—her apartment, its furnishings, the people close to her and their experiences, the doctors, and so forth—is portrayed from the author's point of view, and not as the noblewoman herself sees and experiences that world (although while reading the story we are also fully aware of her *subjective* perception of that world). And the world of the coachman (the hut, the stove, the cook, etc.) and of the tree (nature, the forest)—all these things are, as is the noblewoman's world, parts of one and the same objective world, seen and portrayed from *one and the same authorial position*. The author's field of vision nowhere intersects or collides dialogically with the characters' field of vision or attitudes, nowhere does the word of the author encounter resistance from the hero's potential word, a word that might illuminate the same object differently, in its own way—that is, from the vantage point of its own *truth*. The author's point of view cannot encounter the hero's point of view on one plane, on one level. The point of view of the hero (in those places where the author lets it be seen) always remains an object of the author's point of view.

Thus, despite the multiple levels in Tolstoy's story, it contains neither polyphony nor (in our sense) counterpoint. It contains only *one cognitive subject*, all else being merely *objects* of its cognition. Here a dialogic relationship of the author to his heroes is impossible, and thus there is no *"great dialogue"* in which characters and author might participate with equal rights; there are only the objectivized dialogues of characters, compositionally expressed within the author's field of vision.

In the above story Tolstoy's monologic position comes to the fore very distinctly and with *great external visibility*. That is the reason we chose this story. In Tolstoy's novels and in his longer stories, the issue is, of course, considerably more complex.

In the novels, the major characters and their worlds are not self-enclosed and deaf to one another; they intersect and are interwoven in a multitude of ways. The characters do know about each other, they exchange their individual "truths," they argue or agree, they carry on dialogues with one another (including dialogues on ultimate questions of worldview). Such characters as Andrei Bolkonsky, Pierre Bezukhov, Levin, and Nekhlyudov have their own well-developed fields of vision, sometimes *almost* coinciding with the author's (that is, the author sometimes sees the world as if through their eyes), their voices sometimes *almost* merge with the author's voice. But not a single one ends up on the same plane with the author's word and the author's truth, and with none of them does the author enter into dialogic relations. All of them, with their fields of vision, with their quests and their controversies, are inscribed into the *monolithically monologic whole* of the novel that finalizes them all and that is never, in Tolstoy, the kind of "great dialogue" that we find in Dostoevsky. All the clamps and finalizing moments of this monologic whole lie in the zone of authorial "surplus," a zone that is fundamentally inaccessible to the consciousnesses of the characters.

Let us return to Dostoevsky. How would "Three Deaths" look if (and let us permit ourselves for a moment this strange assumption) Dostoevsky had written them, that is, if they had been structured in a polyphonic manner?

First of all, Dostoevsky would have forced these three planes to be reflected in one another, he would have bound them together with dialogic relationships. He would have introduced the life and death of the coachman and the tree into the field of vision and consciousness of the noblewoman, and the noblewoman's life into the field of vision and consciousness of the coachman. He would have forced his characters to see and know all those essential things that he himself—the author—sees and knows. He would not have retained for himself any *essential* authorial "surplus" (essential, that is, from the point of view of the desired truth). He would have arranged a face-to-face confrontation between the truth of the noblewoman and the truth of the coachman, and he would have forced them to come into dialogic contact (although not necessarily in direct compositionally expressed dialogues, of course), and he would himself have assumed, in relation to them, a dialogic position with equal rights. The entire work would have been constructed by him as a great dialogue, but one where the author acts as organizer and participant in the dialogue without retaining for himself the final word; that is, he would have reflected in his work in the dialogic nature of human life and human thought itself. And in the words of the story not only the pure *intonations of the author* would be heard, but also the intonations of the noblewoman and the coachman; that is, words would be double-voiced, in each word an argument (a microdialogue) would ring out, and there could be heard echoes of the great dialogue.

Of course Dostoevsky would never have depicted three *deaths*: in his world, where self-consciousness is the dominant of a person's image and where the interaction of full and autonomous consciousnesses is the fundamental event, death cannot function as something that finalizes and elucidates life. Death in the Tolstoyan interpretation of it is totally absent from Dostoevsky's world.[1] Dostoevsky would have not depicted the deaths of his heroes, but the *crises* and *turning points* in their lives; that is, he would have depicted their lives *on the threshold*. And his heroes would have remained internally *unfinalized* (for self-consciousness cannot be finalized *from within*). Such would have been a polyphonic treatment of the story.

※　※　※

RENATO POGGIOLI

Tolstoy's *Domestic Happiness*:
Beyond Pastoral Love†

I

In 1856, while waiting for his official discharge from the army, Leo Tolstoy fell in love with a girl far younger than himself. She was a wealthy orphan by the name of Valeria Arseneva, and lived in Sudakovo, not far from Yasnaya Polyana. As a friend of her family, Tolstoy had accepted to act as her legal tutor. We know the full story of this infat-

---

1. Characteristic for Dostoevsky's world are murders (portrayed from within the murderer's field of vision), suicides, and insanity. Normal deaths are rare in his work, and he usually notes them only in passing. [See the eloquent expansion of this idea in Bakhtin's notes for the 1963 edition, "Toward a Reworking of the Dostoevsky Book," Appendix II, pp. 289–91, 300.]

†From Renato Poggioli, *The Oaten Flute: Essays on Pastoral Poetry and the Pastoral Ideal* (Cambridge, MA, 1975). Reprinted with permission of Harvard University Press. "Domestic Happiness" is an alternate translation of "Family Happiness."

uation through the writer's diaries and letters,[1] and there is no doubt in our mind, as there was hardly in his, that in this affair Tolstoy played an undignified role, and made a fool of himself. Tolstoy felt attracted by the freshness and youth of his ward, and thought seriously of marrying her. Valeria attended the coronation ceremonies of 1856, and her tutor reacted with distaste at a letter from her praising snobbishly and glowingly the worldly and courtly splendor of the occasion and of the attendant festivities. Tolstoy finally used Valeria's sentimental friendship for a music teacher as a flimsy pretext for being jealous, and even for insulting her. Although he never proposed, he behaved in such a manner as to make Valeria and her relatives believe that an early wedding was possible, and even probable. Soon enough, however, he brutally put an end to a liaison which had been less than a troth and more than a flirt.

Precisely because he knew that he was not in the right, he sought both solace and revenge by composing a story to prove to his and everyone else's satisfaction that, had he wed the girl, the marriage would have ended in failure, or turned out to be a mistake, and that the bride alone would have been responsible for such an outcome. This story was *Domestic Happiness*, written in 1858 and published in 1859.[2] For a while the author thought of withdrawing, and even of destroying, the manuscript, which in one of his diaries he described as "a shameful abomination." Tolstoy's hesitations were due not only to moral scruples but also to literary doubts, which very few of his critics have shared. Most of the interpreters and readers of that tale have decided otherwise: and their enthusiastic approval is well represented by the opinion of Romain Rolland, according to whom *Domestic Happiness* is as perfect as a piece by Racine.[3] Rolland was undoubtedly right, and it matters little that he mistakenly identified the heroine of the tale with Sonia Bers, Tolstoy's future wife, or that he misread the story to the point of seeing in it "the miracle of love": a definition that would have been more fitting if the narrative had stopped halfway, since the rest of the story deals, at least as much as with the miracle of love, with the lesson of life.

If there is no doubt that the tale is a little masterpiece, it is no less evident that it is, as masterpieces often are, an ambiguous creation. Its ambiguity lies in the antithetical contrast between its two parts, one evoking love before and the other after the marriage. The opposition

1. For the diaries and letters dealing with this episode see the Jubilee Edition of Tolstoy's complete works, *Polnoe sobranie sochinenii* (Moscow and Leningrad, 1928), vols. XLVII, LX. A full account of the episode may be read in the authoritative English biography of the Russian master, Ernest J. Simmons, *Leo Tolstoy* (Boston: Little, Brown, 1946), pp. 139–146.

2. The Russian title is *Semeynoe schastie*. The tale appeared in two installments, in the first and second April issues of the journal *Russki vestnik* [Russian Messenger]. I have followed the text of the

Jubilee Edition, vol. VII. For my quotations I have used the translation of Aylmer Maude, *Family Happiness*, in *The Short Novels of Tolstoy*, ed. Philip Rahv (New York: Dial Press, 1949).

3. The Franco-Swiss writer stated this opinion in his *Vie de Tolstoï* (Paris, 1911). One could say that in Tolstoy's canon *Domestic Happiness* plays the same role that *Bérénice* plays in Racine's and that the relation between *Domestic Happiness* and *Anna Karenina* is not too different from that between *Bérénice* and *Phèdre*.

between the components of this diptych may be summed up by saying that the first is written in the key of a pastoral romance; the second, of realistic fiction.[4] To be sure, the term "pastoral romance" as applied to the opening section of *Domestic Happiness* should be understood figuratively rather than literally, as a reminder that its inspiration is genuinely idyllic. Obviously the author reshaped that inspiration according to modern ideas, values, and tastes, and replaced the formal conventions (but not the inner spirit) of the old-fashioned pastoral with a more concrete feeling for psychological reality, and with a more direct concern with human experience. Yet he tempered likewise the moral and practical realism of the closing section with classical measure, mature detachment, and lucid wisdom. He finally gave a superior unity to the composition by the device of having the story told by the girl, and from her point of view, not only in the first but also in the second part, even though the latter may seem to present the outlook of the masculine partner.

This device seems paradoxical if on one hand we take into account the autobiographical origin of the story, and keep in mind on the other the perspective, and even the bias, of the pastoral vision, which places woman in the foreground just because it is preeminently a man's wishful dream. The very fact that *Domestic Happiness* is the only story by Tolstoy in which a woman speaks in the first person may suffice to suggest the author's stand toward the pastoral or quasi-pastoral conception of love: a conception which he could envision only by projecting it outside of both his own sex and himself. There are good reasons to believe that the psychological motivation that dictated the story combined with a polemical intent: that Tolstoy wrote *Domestic Happiness* also as a protest against the credo of feminine emancipation, which was gaining ground even in Russia, in the wake of the success of the novels of George Sand. It would be remiss to fail to remark in this context that George Sand had often chosen to convey the nobility of passion by describing it in pastoral terms.[5] One could then say that whereas George Sand had the masculine mask of her pen name to proclaim the rights of woman, Tolstoy took on in this story the mask of his heroine to proclaim the rights of man—or that in the two parts of the tale he made Masha speak both for and against George Sand.

4. In the essay "Tolstoy as Man and Artist," *Oxford Slavonic Papers*, X (1962), 25–37, reprinted in *The Spirit of the Letter* (Cambridge: Harvard University Press, 1965), we have already stated that many of Tolstoy's works, including *War and Peace*, are diptychs at least in a figurative sense. *Domestic Happiness*, however, is also literally so. This is made evident by its division into two antithetical and yet symmetrical parts. In a real diptych, neither of the two panels can stand alone, and it was perhaps to emphasize the fundamental singleness of his dual creation that Tolstoy numbered the subdivisions in a single series. The first part is made of five sections, and the second of four, but the latter are numbered from six to nine, as if to indicate that the two parts are linked together and that there is no dissolution of continuity between them.

5. All of George Sand's "rustic idylls" had been published toward the end of the preceding decade: *La Mare au diable* in 1846, *François le Champi* in 1848, *La Petite Fadette* in 1869.

The great business of George Sand was romantic love, which is a more modern and more dramatic, more intensive and more inclusive manifestation of the erotic version of the pastoral dream. We must never forget that in all his life Tolstoy rejected that kind of love with all his being, on instinctual as well as on ethical grounds. It was not only his mind, or even his conscience, but also his sexual temperament that prevented him from accepting and experiencing that kind of love. In his later years, when he tried to liberate himself from what in his old age he was once to define as "the tragedy of the bedroom,"[6] he practiced, or at least preached, abstention and asceticism, which is the Christian but certainly not the pastoral or romantic solution of the sexual problem. Yet, as he proved in so many masterpieces, he was able to understand and to express romantic love in others as few writers have done before or after him. Even so he always selected feminine characters as the only possible vehicles or objects for the representation of that kind of love: as he did in the case of the Valeria-Masha of *Domestic Happiness*, whose girlish psychology he unveiled with uncanny insight. Nor must we forget that in all such situations he used the masculine partner not to convey through him the lesser role which man plays in a liaison of this kind, but the masculine side, the male's conscious denial or unconscious rejection of romantic love. In *Domestic Happiness* this task is entrusted to Tolstoy-Sergey Mikhaylych, even though the latter acts as the willing foil, or plays but an antagonist's role, in regard to his feminine counterpart, who is at once the heroine of the tale and the narrator of the story.

II

Masha starts her tale when she is seventeen years old, which is the perfect age for a maid or a nymph. Shortly before, having been fatherless for a long time, she lost her mother, and now she is an orphan, feeling lonely and afraid before life and the experience of adulthood. In this too we may see a common pastoral theme, that of the young maiden who needs protection and help for being left alone in the world. Although an orphan, Masha is not poor, because even in a modern Arcadia excessive prosperity and excessive poverty are equally unknown. As a matter of fact, both she and Sergey Mikhaylych are members of the leisure class, or, more literally, of the Russian landed gentry just before the end of serfdom. The heroine of such an idyll could not but reside in the country, and she lives indeed on the country estate left by her family to her and her younger sister, with no other companion or adviser than a trusted governess. Both the sister, who is only a child, and the governess, who is an elderly woman, count for little in the story, in

6. In a talk with Gorki, reported by the latter in his *Reminiscences of Leo Nikolaevich Tolstoy*, trans. S. S. Koteliansky and Leonard Woolf (New York: B. W. Huebsch, 1920), p. 17.

which the latter plays the role of a discreet confidante, and the former that of a silent witness. These three women have just spent, closeted in the solitude of their house, a winter of discontent, when suddenly comes springtime, the bucolic season par excellence, bringing in its stride not only the promise of a milder weather but also the stirrings of a new life.

Such visitation coincides with the visits of their neighbor Sergey Mikhaylych, a man thirty-six years of age, or old enough to have been a friend of Masha's father. He had already appeared in the house to assist Masha at the time of her mother's death, and now he reappears regularly to see whether everything is going well with the two girls, whom he considers his wards. Yet he is obviously interested only in the elder of the two, who in turn has no eyes but for him. Masha reports all that Sergey Mikhaylych does and says in her presence, yet she says nothing of his aspect, whether he is good-looking or not. This oversight may be due either to the modesty of the storyteller or to the self-consciousness of the writer, or possibly to both. Since the narrative is partly autobiographical, it is not too indiscreet to remind the reader that Leo Tolstoy was never handsome and that he was painfully aware of his plainness. This, and the fact that masculine beauty is not a pastoral requirement, justifies the surmise that Sergey Mikhaylych must have homely traits, if not an outright ugly face. But besides resembling his creator, morally as well as physically, Sergey Mikhaylych resembles many of the masculine characters that Tolstoy later reflected in the introspective mirror of his art. This is hardly surprising, since one's self-image is the only model that a writer, even more than a painter, has always at hand.

As for what seems to be Masha's self-portrait, it is, as we know, but the fictional likeness of a girl who had posed for the artist, unconsciously and unwillingly, only once in her lifetime, to disappear from his sight forever, and all too soon. For Tolstoy the man Masha was Valeria Arseneva, or a real person, different from any other girl he knew, yet the disguised or masked portrait he gave of her in *Domestic Happiness* foreshadows several of his future feminine characterizations, most of which are also based at least in part on persons no less real and unique. This means that Tolstoy tended to represent the same feminine ideal in many of the fictional women he refashioned or created anew, as he tended to represent the same masculine type, or human ideal, in quite a few variants of a single self-image, hardly changing with the passing of time. In brief, Masha and Sergey Mikhaylych, even though they fail to reproduce themselves in Tolstoy's future works as a couple, anticipate two types that regularly occur in the creations of his maturity. If we compare the hero and the heroine of *Domestic Happiness* to their more familiar equivalents in Tolstoy's two supreme masterpieces, we shall better understand the specific as well as the generic significance of these two prototypes.[7]

7. These two prototypes might be viewed also as archetypes in the Jungian sense of the term; if so, Masha would stand for the *anima*, and Sergey Mikhaylych for its opposite, the *animus*.

Masha resembles Natasha, the heroine of *War and Peace*, as well as Kitty, the lesser of the two heroines of *Anna Karenina*, at least in her virginal longing, in the whole of her maidenly nature. Yet she differs from both at least in this: that before marriage she feels far surer of her feelings than either one of them, but after marriage she loses that sureness, whereas Natasha and Kitty gain it all at once, and in full. If Natasha and Kitty never feel disappointed in their mates, it is also because in their girlhood they had met other men and fallen in love with them; hence their disenchantment with romantic love.[8] If Masha does not turn into another Anna Karenina it is because, until the story is almost over, she never sheds the illusion that marriage and romantic love should or might coincide. The greatest difference, however, lies in their social environment: Natasha, Kitty, and even Anna are surrounded by a swarm of relatives, acquaintances, and friends (in Anna's case, even by cronies), which means that they are part of a large family circle, or of a broad social set. But Masha is an orphan living in utter solitude; except for her sister and governess, she is literally alone in the world.[9] During her betrothal she does not meet, even casually, any other man—had she met one, she would have hardly noticed him. Thus she seems to stand before the man she will marry just as Eve stood before Adam, lonely and intact, in the chaste nudity of her soul.

The man before whom she stands has already reached the threshold of middle age, and lived twice her life span. With slight variations in age, Tolstoy portrayed the same psychological type in the Nikolay Rostov of *War and Peace*[1] and, above all, in the Konstantin Levin of *Anna Karenina*. The type in question is that of an eccentric country squire, reserved and even boorish, embodying within himself the original and natural man. Such a character hates the conventions of the world and denies the values of society; lives following no other norms but the laws of nature, and no other dictates but those of his inner voice: a voice that speaks on behalf of his temperament as well as of his conscience. A character of this kind is not only an idealization of the author's actual personality but also the embodiment of a human ideal the writer had found ready-made outside of himself. He had found it in the works of Jean-Jacques Rousseau, in which it remains all too often a mere ideal, or an object of the writer's abstract preaching, seldom projected into vital fictional beings. Yet the masculine protagonist of *Domestic Happiness* resembles at least one of Rousseau's minor figures, Julie's husband

---

8. Kitty loved Vronsky before marrying Levin. As for Natasha, she was the fiancée of Prince Andrey before marrying Pierre Bezukhov, and during her betrothal to the former she almost eloped with the rake Anatole Kuragin.

9. The splendid isolation of Masha would suffice to prove how wrong Romain Rolland was in surmising that he saw a portrait of Tolstoy's future wife, Sonia Bers. Sonia Bers was one of many sisters, and Tolstoy avowed that at first he had fallen in love with all of them. The writer attributed the same attitude to Konstantin Levin, who, as Tolstoy says, "was in love with the Shcherbatsky household," especially "with its feminine half," at least as much as with Kitty herself (*Anna Karenina*, I.vii).

1. The validity of this parallel may be qualified, but not denied, by the consideration that Nikolay Rostov is more of a portrait than of a self-portrait: his real or main model is Tolstoy's father.

in *La Nouvelle Héloise*. Sergey Mikhaylych is a creature of flesh and
blood, while his model is pale and lifeless; yet in many of his traits,
especially as a wise husbandman of his estate and his passion, he looks
very much like the Rousseauian character bearing the quasi-Russian
name of Wolmar. Needless to say that at first, at least in the mind of
Masha, he plays the same role as Julie's lover, the far younger Saint-
Preux. At any rate, in the atmosphere of *Domestic Happiness* or, more
generally, of Tolstoy's ethos, there is hardly room for a ménage à trois;
in that story there is no place but for a single man and a single woman,
who stand not only for themselves but also for the eternal Adam and
the eternal Eve. If we are not told their surnames, it is because they are
not needed. The man is called also by his patronymic, as if to indicate
that he acknowledges the ties of the family while rejecting the shackles
that bind most of his fellow men to society and the world. As for Masha,
she is always called by her Christian name alone,[2] as if to emphasize
her orphanhood, solitude, and singleness: a state which implies both
danger and freedom, since it allows her to choose her own bonds.

III

The bonds she chooses are, as we know already, those of romantic or
pastoral love. Precisely because the story is told by her, we must accept
her outlook, and describe the initial situation in bucolic terms. The
situation is that of a seventeen-year-old girl falling in love with a thirty-
six-year-old man, and of a thirty-six-year-old man falling in love with
a seventeen-year-old girl. The situation is a typical projection of the
pastoral imagination, so typical as not to admit of the reverse, or of a
liaison having woman as the senior partner. (In this connection it is
worth remarking that Tolstoy made the situation more extreme, and
thus more typical, by aging his hero, or by making Sergey Mikhaylych
eight years older than he was himself at the time of the actual affair.)
According to the erotic code of the pastoral, when the woman is older
than the man, her love remains unrequited: which, far from rendering
the situation pathetic, as it would do in the case of a man, simply renders
it ridiculous, or even grotesque.[3] But when the senior partner is a man,
the liaison is possible, probable, nay unavoidable: love this time will be
returned, although the man, besides being no longer young, is not even
handsome. This is how it should be, since the prime mover of pastoral
love is youthful feminine beauty, which is endowed with such innocent
power and unconscious charm as to entice at all ages the spirit and
senses of man. "You have youth and beauty," says Sergey Mikhaylych
to Masha at least twice, at the very beginning of the tale, thus paying

---

2. Masha is a familiar and intimate form of Ma-   full name is Mariya Aleksandrovna.
riya. Only once in the story are we told that her   3. For this code, see chapter 2, "Pastoral Love."

to its heroine the most obvious of all compliments, so obvious as to have been paid innumerable times by the sons of Adam to the daughters of Eve, and to serve as a fitting epigraph for all love pastorals. Those two qualities, which combine together to make the supreme attraction of a maid or a nymph, cannot be separated from each other, so that youth does not count without beauty, and beauty is of no avail without youth.

So the attraction between the young maid and the older man is reciprocal, and is based on a spontaneous reaction, on a love freely given and freely returned. Feminine youth longs for security and protection, whereas mature manhood seeks virginity and purity and yearns for a fruit fresh and intact, which life has not yet soured or spoiled. This too runs true to the idyllic pattern, since pastoral love often originates from familiarity and friendship. Masha avows to have at first loved Sergey Mikhaylych "from old habit," as a family friend or an older relative, like a father or an uncle. Without implying the slightest suggestion of incestuous feeling, one might say that their love starts with filial overtones on Masha's part and with paternal ones on Sergey Mikhaylych's. What is more significant is that the older partner loves this woman-child for being a simple and natural creature, whom he hopes to reshape in his own image, at his own will. One of the most extreme bucolic views is the rejection not only of manners and conventions but also of fashions and even of clothing, which are viewed as an unnatural disguise, as a kind of makeup hiding the real person under a false mask.[4] Youth must be simple and even bare; beauty, unadorned and unaffected. Hence Masha should not have felt surprised at Sergey Mikhaylych's "complete indifference and even contempt for . . . [her] personal appearance," for the manner in which she was dressed and groomed, even though he would seem silently to blame even more than her ladylike finery her "affectation of simplicity."

The idyll, which had started with the spring, turns by summer into a genuine passion, which, however, on the girl's part feeds not on reality but on dreams. As pastoral life at its best, that passion manifests itself in a constant communion with nature, according to the changing moods of the hour and the varying hues of the landscape. As if afraid to destroy this silent music, to break the miraculous sympathy so established between themselves and the world, the two lovers speak softly and in whispers. It is with the almost mystical term of "wild ecstasy" that Masha tries to define the instants when this feeling of perfect harmony attains its peak. Then physical sensations and spiritual emotions seem to blend into a sense of magic bliss. They seem to obtain such a "wild ecstasy" in the charming episode in the orchard, when the girl climbs on the cherry tree to pick its fruits, while the man watches from below. Without

4. The return to the innocent nudity of the Golden Age is one of the most extreme demands of the pastoral code of free love.

a shade of libertine frivolity, and in an aura of absolute purity, the scene
reminds one of a real-life happening that Rousseau relates in the *Confessions* (iv), and which is known to the readers of that book as "l'idylle
des cerises." In that idyll Jean-Jacques simply shares a basket of cherries
not with a single nymph of his choice but with two maidens met by
chance in the woods. The scene Tolstoy evokes is no less idyllic, but
its inspiration is nobler and deeper: what we witness in these pages is
almost an agape, whereas in Rousseau's we watch little more than a
picnic.

Masha, in a perfect bucolic mood, considers the bliss she is now
experiencing as the natural state of man ("it seemed so necessary and
just that everyone should be happy"), and thus she wants that bliss to
last without change or end in the flux of time ("that . . . [her] present
frame of mind might never change"). This desire to arrest the fleeting
instant is the characteristic trait of a thoughtless bliss: the wish to remain
within the enchanted circle of an everlasting youth is a sign of immaturity, or the symptom of a crisis in growth. What bewitches Masha is
the narcissism of adolescence, or the self-love of a youthful soul. As
such, it is a morbid state, which, when acute and brief, may even
contribute to man's psychic health. But when it outlasts youth and
becomes a chronic ailment it turns into that idolatry of the self that
marked the older Rousseau. Then introspection becomes an irresponsible adoration of all the movements of one's soul, and the person loves
himself just for being what he is.[5] It is self-contemplation and the contemplation of her love that make Masha play in the first part of *Domestic
Happiness* the role of an *Allegra*, enjoying her emotional bliss not only
without doubt but also without thought. Beside and against her Sergey
Mikhaylych seems to play the role of a *Penseroso* simply because he
cannot cast away all his doubts or ignore his thoughts.

IV

The end of the first part brings the pastoral romance to its climax. Masha
has created around herself a kind of magic wall, as if "the world of the
possible ended there." So full of happiness as to be afraid of life, she
goes to the little church to pray, and prepares herself for an early wedding.
Her preparation is only psychological, and it contrasts with the practical
attitude of her governess, for whom preparing for a wedding means
preparing a trousseau, and all the rest is "sentimental nonsense." But
nothing troubles the soul of Masha, and on the morning of her wedding
day she sees a sign of the peaceful serenity of her life in the spotless
purity of the sky: "In the clear sky there was not, and could not be, a
single cloud." This image is but one of the many by which the writer

5. For the connections between the pastorals of love and solitude, see chapter 7, "The Pastoral of the
Self."

develops one of the main motifs of his story: a complex and coherent seasonal symbolism, which unfolds according to a quasi-archetypal pattern. Masha had lost her mother in autumn, the season of falling leaves, and the orphan's sense of dejection had lasted all winter, the season of ice and snow. Her protector, the man to whom she was bound to give her heart, had first appeared briefly in late winter, as if to announce that life was at hand. Spring had then come, and love had silently sprouted in two hearts, one still too young, and the other not yet old enough. That love had bloomed in the glory of summer, joining them with troth's vows. When the wedding takes place, the year's cycle has made a full turn, and we are again in the fall season, which stands for both maturity and decline, thus alluding to the age of the bridegroom, and to the consummation of conjugal love.

During the honeymoon the newlyweds become fully oblivious of the world and find that reality is not inferior to the dream. But the honeymoon ends with the beginning of winter, which brings again to Masha a mood of monotony, sadness, and solitude. "So two months by," says she, "and winter came again with its cold and snow; and, in spite of his company, I began to feel lonely, that life was repeating itself." Business, that great enemy of pastoral mirth, which is founded on leisure, claims again the daily attention of Sergey Mikhaylych. The betrothal had been, so to speak, an outdoor idyll, but the cold season and married life make of Masha a stay-at-home, without a responsibility of her own, since the household runs like a clock under the strict supervision of her mother-in-law. The mistress of the house that Masha has entered as a bride represents the matriarchal or patriarchal order, or a way of life within which, at least ideally, there is no conflict between youth and age, love and marriage, innocence and happiness. When a newly married couple takes its place within such an order, groom and bride are expected to live quietly and to age gracefully in their little corner, and to turn at the end of their lives into another Philemon and Baucis. Before marrying Masha had thought that happiness meant unchangeability: that where and when there is bliss time seems to stand still. During her betrothal she had indeed believed that only in immobility love could last and grow. But now that she is married and settled the motionless bliss of conjugal love turns into a kind of deadly inertia, and she is frightened when she discovers that her love, "instead of increasing, stood still." When the honeymoon is over, married life turns out to be a letdown and a disappointment, especially if compared with the early days of their troth: "To love him was not enough for me after the happiness I had felt in falling in love." Masha's change might be described by saying that once she had confused pastoral and romantic love, whereas now she thinks that they are two different things, and seeks the second in lieu of the first: "I wanted excitement and danger and the chance to sacrifice myself for my love." Now that life seems to flow indifferently past her, Masha resents her husband's quiet acceptance of a mode of being in which life itself seems to be at a standstill. What repels the young wife more than anything else is the patriarchal way of life, based as it is on the forces of tradition and habit: "I suffered most from the feeling that custom was daily petrifying our lives into a fixed shape. . . ."

Masha's restlessness is another sign of immaturity, and youth's immaturity is never so evident as when it claims the rights of adulthood. It is just when Masha declares that she wants no longer "to play at life," but to live, as her husband does, that without knowing it she treats life as if it were a plaything. Sergey Mikhaylych yields to her pressure, as if he knows in his heart that the time has come for Masha to visit the great city, to get into high society, to enter the wide world. Thus he decides that they will spend the season in the capital. Just before Christmas they settle in Petersburg, for a test which for him is a trial, and for her a triumph. Masha looks so "unlike the other women," with the fresh charm of her "rural simplicity," that she wins the acclaim of the worldly, and shines among them like a new, bright star. Her husband, reduced to playing the role of an escort, disappears like a dim shadow in the radiance of her halo. When she stands out in the glamour of her beauty and the splendor of a gorgeous dress, "he effaces himself in the crowd of black coats." And whereas Masha drinks with intoxicating joy the heady wine of success, Sergey Mikhaylych tastes the bitter fruit of disappointment, resentment, and even jealousy.

Yet it is only when Masha forces him to stay in the capital a few days beyond their due for the sake of attending a reception in honor of a foreign prince wishing to make her acquaintance that the hidden disagreement between husband and wife turns, for the first and last time, into an open rift. Sergey Mikhaylych limits himself to avowing, in a few and clear words, the repulsion he has been feeling while watching his wife share day by day "the dirtiness and idleness and luxury of this foolish society"; yet Masha takes that hardly unexpected outburst as an injustice and an insult. Wife and husband return home apparently reconciled, but what seems a peace is but a truce, even though neither party ever dares or cares to break it. From that time on they live morally estranged under the same roof. The husband devotes again all of his time and thought to the management of the estate, while "fashionable life," as Masha confesses, takes full command of her. Even the facts of life, such as the birth of a child and the death of her mother-in-law, fail to disenchant Masha from her infatuation with the false values of the world. After three years she convinces her husband that they should spend the summer abroad. In Baden, the famous German water resort, Masha's vanity is flattered again by the allurements of social success. But all veils fall from their eyes when what had started as an innocent flirt with an Italian marquis turns into an attempted seduction which for an instant brings her to the brink of ruin.[6] She saves herself in time, but the horror and shame at her weakness, which had led her almost to the end of the path of corruption, deprives Masha of her self-esteem as well as of the hope to regain her husband's love or even respect.

V

After tasting the ashes that life's "forbidden delights" all too often leave in our mouth, Masha returns home to wither and languish in the utter loneliness of a silent despair. With no help from her husband, who refuses to intervene either in word or deed, behaving with a discretion so extreme as to look passionless, she slowly realizes that the fruit of good and evil may be picked only from the tree of knowledge. Still tortured by the delusion of her youthful hopes, aware that the affection of her husband has turned into a strange and remote aloofness, fearing that "he had no longer a heart to give" and doubting that she will ever be able to live for others now that she is no longer able to live for herself, Masha finally succeeds in overcoming her dejection after a long, un-planned talk with her husband. It is indeed more a question of a con-versation than of a confession or an explanation. Through this exchange husband and wife are able to communicate again, without wrath or bitterness, and it is with a few quiet words that they seal again the peace of their hearts.

During this talk Masha avows her wrong, while still wondering whether she was fully responsible for it: "Is it my fault that I know nothing of life, and that you left me to learn experience by myself?" In her self-questioning she seems to blame also her husband, at least for having failed to guide her: "Why did you never tell me that you wished me to live as you wished me to?" Sergey Mikhaylych's reply to this query is worthy of Rousseau's Wolmar: "All of us, and especially you women, must have personal experience of all the nonsense of life, in order to get back to life itself." As for Masha's fear that she is no longer able to love, Sergey Mikhaylych reassures her by saying that "each time of life has its kind of love," and that the hour has come for them to love each other as husband and wife, not as betrothed or newlyweds.

The wise Sergey Mikhaylych puts Masha on guard against committing again the same error, which is to confuse times and kinds of love. "Let's not try to repeat life," he tells her, knowing that it can be repeated only in dreams. Yet he forgives Masha in the best possible way, by giving

---

6. Masha is a gentlewoman, yet in the episode she finds herself in the stock situation, and plays the stock role, of the rural lassie about to be seduced by a city slicker. Such a situation is one of the standard episodes in the legend of Don Juan. See the scenes dealing with the peasant Charlotte in Molière's version of the legend, *Dom Juan ou le festin de Pierre*.

her hope, and by sharing her sense of guilt: "Our quest is done. . . ." At this point the adolescent narcissism of Masha disappears once for all. From now on she knows that love is not a passive image reflected in the mirror of the soul but the action or motion of a heart turning toward other objects or beings outside of itself. Her trial is now a thing of the past: from now on she will be the full partner of her husband: "That day ended the romance of our marriage; the old feeling became a precious, irrevocable remembrance; but a new feeling of love for my children and the father of my children laid the foundation of a new life and a quite different happiness, and that life and happiness have lasted up to the present time." Whereas the climax of the first part found its symbol in the serenity of the cloudless sky of her wedding day, the climax of the second part and of the whole story, which coincides with this moment of understanding and self-revelation, is intimated by a sudden rain, or by the purifying tears of nature itself.

VI

Only in the second part is there a story, and this is why it is easier to sum up that part and to quote from it. If little or nothing can be quoted from the opening section, it is because one should quote almost everything. Every one of its phrases is full of poetry, beauty, and charm: every one of its moments is not an event but an *état d'âme*. Reversing Amiel's famous aphorism, one could say that each one of such *états d'âme* turns into a different *paysage*, since it reflects itself within the changing moods of the day, the varying backgrounds of the landscape, the passing phases of nature's cycle. As we have already said, the first part of *Domestic Happiness* is not only a pastoral of love but also an outdoor idyll, wholly dominated by the pathetic fallacy, since all of nature's objects and images seem to reecho or to mirror Masha's every emotion and feeling, even the dimmest and vaguest of them. In the whole of Western literature there is perhaps only one other work evoking with equal bewitchment the experience of sentimental love as rehearsed by a youthful heart, as projected by a self feeling in communion with God's world. This work is Rousseau's *Nouvelle Héloïse*, which Tolstoy certainly took as a model, especially (and this is less strange than it seems) in the letters that describe the idyll of Julie and Saint-Preux as it unfolds not before, but after Julie's marriage to Wolmar.

If not the whole second part, at least its end, which closes the whole diptych, could at first sight be interpreted, like the first half of the tale, in idyllic terms. Its final scene seems indeed to bring about a restoration of the pastoral of innocence after the pastoral of happiness has failed to succeed. If this were really true, *Domestic Happiness* could be viewed as an anticipation of *War and Peace*, a historical novel or prose epos that at least one critic did indeed read as a "heroic idyll."[7] Even so, one should not fail to point out an outstanding difference between this minor, and that major, masterpiece: that the peace regained at the end of *Domestic Happiness* is the peace of the spirit, and that the crisis which for a while threatens that peace is but a war of hearts. Yet their message coincides at least in this: that in both stories it is the selfsame institution, the family, that triumphs over the powers of disorder, over the chaos of either passion or war. Yet even the admission of such coincidence should be qualified by remarking that *Domestic Happiness* views that institution in intimate and private terms, reducing it to its minimum common denominator, which is the tie between husband and wife, whereas *War and Peace* expands the family into the dimension of a clan, extending, so to speak, in space and time, including within itself the representatives of three generations, embracing within its fold serfs and retainers, as well as kindred of other branches. But the most fundamental distinction is that in Tolstoy's later novel the family meets primarily challenges that threaten its existence from without, whereas in the earlier tale it faces challenges that endanger its stability from within. The external factor determining this challenge in *Domestic Happiness* is not the greater world of history but the lesser one of "high life," what the French call simply *le monde* and pastoral poetry embodies in society, the city, the court.

All this notwithstanding, the general curve of *War and Peace* seems to coincide with the idyllic pattern more fully than *Domestic Happiness* does. The reason for this is that in the former the heart's desire of the characters agrees with the demands of life, whereas in the latter, at least in Masha's case, it is at odds with them. Unlike *War and Peace*, *Domestic Happiness* is a fable with a moral. The moral is that life chastises those who think that life is a dream. It is a sign of Tolstoy's artistic stature that despite the personal motivations that dictated the writing of this story, he chose to have Masha chastened by life rather than by her husband, in whom he had portrayed himself. There is no doubt that the lesson of life has something to teach even the older, stronger, and more experienced partner, and this is why, after writing the first part as a temporary victory of woman, Tolstoy refrained from writing the second as man's final revanche. In Freudian terms one could say that the first panel of this diptych evokes the passing triumph of the pleasure principle, whereas the second celebrates the lasting triumph of the reality principle. Since Tolstoy knew Schopenhauer and loved him well, one could con-

7. This critic is D. S. Mirsky. The pertinent passage is worth quoting in full: "The general tone [of *War and Peace*] may be properly described as idyllic. The inclination toward the idyllic was from first to last an ever present possibility in Tolstoy. It is the opposite pole to his increasing uneasiness. Before the time of *War and Peace* it pervades Child- hood. Its roots are in a sense of unity with his class, with the happy and prosperous *byt* of the Russian nobility. And it is, after all, no exaggeration to say that, all said and done, *War and Peace* is a tremendous 'heroic idyll' of the Russian nobility" (*A History of Russian Literature* [New York: Knopf, 1946], p. 268).

vey the peculiar quality and meaning of the first half by saying that it is ruled by the cosmic will, which deludes us into believing that we freely want what a blind and impersonal instinct seeks through us and beyond us, who are but its passive, or voluntary, victims. The second half, on the contrary, is ruled by the active, self-controlling power of the ethical will, which restrains all inner urgings imperiling the safety of our being and the integrity of our soul.

Hence the moral adorning this tale is moral in the highest sense of this epithet and turns the fable into a feminine equivalent of the evangelical parable of the prodigal son. Masha, this prodigal daughter-wife, takes again the place that belongs to her within the family order, without undue festivities, but also without unseemly recriminations. The woman-child has grown into a real woman, and what she has gained from the lesson of life is not a sentimental education but its very opposite, which is ethical growth. Masha has finally diseducated herself from all "sentimental sense," from the fancies of pastoral and romantic love. She now knows that that kind of love is but a make-believe that deludes us into thinking that falling in love and loving are one and the same thing. Now she has learned that love may become stronger and truer by surviving the short-lived honeymoons of the spirit and the flesh. Now she knows with her husband that "each time of life has its kind of love": so there is happiness after all, a happiness suited to the present time of their lives, and to the kind of love that corresponds to it. Thus the youthful, transitory, and deceitful dream of romantic love vanishes forever and will never return, since normally it should appear only once in a lifetime, like one of those pastoral oases that dissolve like mirages just when they seem within reach.

Masha once thought that it was feeling that should guide life; now she discovers that it is life that should guide feeling. At this point the bucolic ends, to be replaced by the georgic, or by a life close to nature in the moral rather than in the sentimental sense. From now on she will accept not only "the days," but also "the works," becoming a full partner of her husband, sharing with him not only the joys of life but also its responsibilities and hardships. So the story, which had begun as a pastoral and unfolded as a romance, closes with the conventional ending of a bourgeois novel, with the implication that Masha and Sergey Mikhaylych lived happily ever after. Masha simply says that she and her husband have lived happily "up to the present time," or up to the very day or hour she has been telling her story. Yet, even if the narrator of the story had been the writer, rather than the heroine, the thought that they lived happily thereafter might have still been left unsaid. It seems indeed that the reader of *Domestic Happiness* should not need the help of anyone else, even the author, to realize that after the end of the story Masha and Sergey Mikhaylych were destined to live as happily as a married couple possibly can—neither more nor less. The story ends on such a note, and its double, paradoxical message is that passion is deemed limitless only as long as man and woman remain within the sphere of pastoral and romantic love, which is but an enchanted circle. But as soon as two lovers go beyond the boundaries of pastoral fantasy and romantic fancies they discover that love can last, and grow stronger and truer, only if and when it is circumscribed.

KATHLEEN PARTHÉ

Tolstoy and the Geometry of Fear†

> . . . Tolstoy is truly the canonizer of crisis: the forces of disclosure and destruction lie hidden in almost every one of his devices.
> —Boris Eikhenbaum[1]

Tolstoy was repeatedly drawn to the crisis of dying because he felt that the traditional literary perception of death was inadequate. Death for Tolstoy was not just another subject; it was an important personal and aesthetic challenge. The critical literature, however, has treated death in Tolstoy only from the thematic point of view, and the devices the author chose so carefully to signify death have been for the most part unexamined and underestimated. Virtually no attention has been paid to the most unexpected of all the devices: the first-person narrator in "Notes of a Madman" ("Zapiski sumasshedshego") experiences the fear of death as "a horror—red, white, and square" (*uzhas krasnyi, belyi, kvadratnyi*).[2]

The goal of this article is to demonstrate that this "square" is more than simply another interesting example of the various ways of fearing death that Tolstoy observed in himself and others.[3] I will attempt to show how this seemingly anomalous image is actually related to a series of Tolstoyan linguistic devices for depicting death, and is in fact the ultimate device in that series. Three kinds of evidence will be offered in support of this argument: other examples in Tolstoy's work, independent observations in linguistic and critical literature, and similar groupings of devices in writers such as Bely and Zamyatin. Finally, the square will be discussed as a type of geometric image, which, along with other mathematical borrowings, enjoyed a rich development among twentieth century artists, especially in Russia.

"Notes of a Madman" is a first-person story, in the form of an extended

† From *Modern Language Studies* 15 (Fall 1985) 4:80–92. Page references for quotations from pieces in this Norton Critical Edition are given in brackets.

1. *The Young Tolstoi*, 109.
2. *Sobranie sočinenij* 12:45–56. There is an En-

glish translation in *The Works of Leo Tolstoy* 15:210–225; I have used my own translations in this article. Tolstoy began "Notes" in 1884, worked on it intermittently over the years; it was published posthumously in 1912.
3. Rilke 2:150.

flashback, by a man who has been judged sane by a court, although he knows that he is mad. The flashback briefly touches on the narrator's childhood, but primarily addresses itself to several shocking confrontations with death. These confrontations took place in a town called Arzamas while he was on a land-buying trip, in a Moscow hotel, and while hunting in the forest. The first confrontation is presented in great detail, and it is here that the square appears. The other incidents are briefly alluded to as being similar in nature.

The "Arzamas horror" is a commonplace of biographical criticism of Tolstoy. In September 1869, Tolstoy was traveling through the Penza province, and spent the night in Arzamas. A few sentences in a letter to his wife indicate that the night was anything but restful.

> The day before yesterday I spent the night at Arzamas and something unusual happened to me. It was 2 o'clock in the morning, I was terribly weary; I really wanted to sleep, and nothing was hurting me. But suddenly I was seized by despair, fear, and terror such as I have never before experienced. The details of this feeling I will tell you later; but I have never experienced such an excruciating feeling, and I hope to God no one else experiences it.[4] [318]

When Tolstoy was beginning work on the story in 1884, he referred to the 1869 incident in his diary: "I thought of 'Notes of a non-madman.' How vividly I experienced them. . . ."[5] Without resolving to what extent this story is a somewhat disguised transcript of the author's own experiences, one can say that in the period following 1869 Tolstoy became increasingly interested in the artistic and personal problems that death presented. The artistic results of this preoccupation are seen in such works as *The Death of Ivan Ilych*, *Master and Man*, and "Notes of a Madman." The personal side of the struggle can be observed in the diaries, *Confession*, and, most dramatically, in the flight from Yasnaya Polyana to his death in the small railway station at Astapovo. It has been said that in this flight Tolstoy was "his own figure" and brought to its dramatic conclusion the soul's struggle with death that he presented in his works (Rilke 19).

The first confrontation in the story begins when the narrator dozes off in the carriage that is racing through the night towards an estate that he wishes to purchase. He awakens suddenly and experiences the vague fear that death awaits him on this journey.[6] He decides to have the

4. In *Sob. sočinenij* 17:332.
5. Diary entry for 30 March 1884 in *Sob. sočinenij* 19:315. See also 12 and 27 April 1884. A number of biographies and critical articles take the story at face value as a transcript of the 1869 experience, e.g. Troyat, Spence, and Shestov. The always colorful Troyat explains the fictional form thus: ". . . fearing his readers' incredulity, he did not dare to present the text as a description of an actual experience" (390). One should note the alternate use of 'non-madman' and 'madman' in the title as well as the fact that Gogol wrote a story called "Notes of a Madman" in 1833–4.
6. A sudden awakening to terror is found elsewhere in Tolstoy, e.g. the ailing mother in *Childhood*, the dying Prince Andrey and his son Nikolenka in *War and Peace*.

carriage stop in the next town, Arzamas, where he hopes that his feelings of uneasiness will vanish. However, the white color of the houses, the sound of his servant's steps, and a spot on the cheek of the man who showed him to his room all reinforced his uneasiness in an eerie, almost Gogolian way. The room itself had an even worse effect on him.

> It was a small, freshly whitewashed, square room. I remember
> how it tormented me that the small room was square. There
> was one window with a curtain—a red one. There was a table
> of Karelian birch and a couch with curved sides. We went in.
> (49) [298]

During the night, the narrator again wakes up suddenly and, tormented by questions of what he is running away from, he briefly leaves the room. Feeling as if he is being followed, he asks himself what he fears, and this time he gets an answer: 'Me,' silently answered the voice of death. 'I am here.' (49) [299] He says that had he actually been facing death, he would have been afraid, but he would not have suffered as much as he did at that moment: "It was terrifying and awful. It seems that it was a fear of death, but when you remember, when you think about it, it was a fear of dying life" (50) [299]. Tolstoy shows here the psychological state of someone for whom death, while not imminent, is still becoming part of his life, his "dying life," a state which has its own special terrors.[7]

As life and death seem to merge before his very eyes, the narrator feels a "tearing" within his body and soul. At this point, neither the red glow of the candle, nor thoughts of the estate he hoped to buy could protect him from the consciousness of death, of that slow ebbing away of life in even the healthiest person. This is a moment of great psychological disorientation and vulnerability.

> Something was tearing my soul to pieces and yet could not
> tear it up completely. Once more I went over to look at the
> others sleeping, once more I tried to fall asleep, but always
> the same horror—red, white, and square. Something was tear-
> ing; it did not get torn apart. (50)[8] [299]

Rilke's writings on Tolstoy and death, while not directly referring to this story, provide ways of understanding the particular literary form the death-fear took. He sees the author as trying to find the external expression for what goes on in the soul (19). The soul's struggle with the fear of death could appear in different forms. It could, for example, manifest itself as fine particles that like an "odd spice" permeate the "flavor of life" (150). But, more terrifying to Tolstoy was the possibility that some-

---

7. Tolstoy discusses this state in detail in chapter 3 of *Ispoved'* (*Confession*) in *Sob. sočinenij* 16:101–5.

8. The sensation of 'tearing' also appears in Dostoevsky's *The Brothers Karamazov* where a number of characters undergo harrowing experiences described (using one of the two roots in Russian that Tolstoy used in "Notes") as spiritual 'lacerations' (Terras 82–3).

where death existed not as particles but in a "pure" and "undiluted" form; undiluted death, at one with the fear it inspired, could be experienced as an animate figure or as a structure (150). The experience of pure death as a square horror in "Notes of a Madman" fits both Rilke's sense of the invisible fears of the soul made visible, and Tolstoy's own observation in *Confession* (104) that such terrifying confrontations with death took place during what seemed to be a brief stoppage of life.

The philosopher Lev Shestov recognized the extraordinary nature of the death-image in this story.

> How are we to apprehend these groundless terrors which so suddenly appear, red, white, and square? In the world which is common to us all, there is not and cannot be a "suddenly"; there can be no action without a cause. And its terrors are neither red, nor white, nor square. What happened to Tolstoy is a challenge to all normal, human consciousness. (158)

Shestov brings us back to the focus of this discussion, the device itself. Its stimulus in the color of the walls and curtain and the shape of the room is deliberately transparent. It is reinforced later in the story by the experience that the narrator will have in Moscow, where the shape of his hotel room triggers a similar crisis.

At first glance, the square seems to be a marked departure from Tolstoy's usual repetoire of devices for signifying death, which consist of personal pronouns (*ona* 'it [fem.],' *ono* 'it [neuter]'), indefinite pronouns (*chto-to* 'something'), demonstrative pronouns (*eto* 'this,' *to* 'that'), and certain third-person verb forms with 'something' or the neuter 'it' in subject position or with no subject at all. Tolstoy relied on various means of grammatical 'masking' available in Russian to achieve the desired effect of namelessness and the appearance of actions (as Shestov said) "without a cause."[9] Indirect signification of death is appropriate and effective because death is difficult to understand, frightening, and taboo.

While there is a general inventory of Tolstoyan devices for scenes where death is in some sense 'present,' the actual distribution and emphasis of the devices is somewhat different for each story. In the description in *War and Peace* of Prince Andrey's death, the most prominent devices are *eto* 'this' and *ono* 'it.' 'This' (*eto*) is supplied with varying subjective definitions in one key passage in order to indicate the slow process of dying first from the point of view of Natasha and Princess Marya, and then from Andrey's own privileged perspective. 'It' (*ono*, a neuter form used to refer to death, a feminine noun) is used to give

9. "Masking" means incomplete, indefinite reference to the agent of an action, the result being a disorienting effect on the reader. Masking can be used when the author wants to hesitate between a natural and a supernatural explanation of unusual characters or events. Several grammatical devices can be used for masking, e.g. "depersonalized" (temporarily subjectless) verbs, indefinite pronouns, and demonstrative and anaphoric pronouns with obscured referents. See Parthé, "Masking the Fantastic and the Taboo."

death an eerily neuter animacy; Tolstoy uses the phrase 'something not human—death' both to define *ono* and to reinforce the effect of this grammatical device. The aggressive, relentless '*it*' (emphasis in original) that in a pre-death dream breaks through a door to get to Andrey is very effective in presenting Andrey's personal psychic experience of dying.[1]

Similarly, in *The Death of Ivan Ilych*, Tolstoy uses the indefinite pronoun 'something' (*chto-to*) to carefully record the stages of Ivan Ilych's consciousness of his worsening physical condition. Combined with a careful choice of verbs, the author is able to emphasize that the 'something' is internal, growing in strength, and getting out of control. When the suffering man finally realizes that he is dying, the pain that is gnawing from within manifests itself outside him as *ona* ('*it* [fem.],' emphasis in Tolstoy), death itself. The *it* presents herself repeatedly before Ivan Ilych, forcing him to look at her and "suffer inexpressible torment."[2] The terrifying recognition of death, the repeated confrontations which are compressed into just a few pages, and the sense of Ivan Ilych's complete isolation make this a bold and harrowing tale.

Some of the grammatical devices used to achieve temporary namelessness appear in "Notes of a Madman" as well. 'This' and 'everything' (*vse*) are used at the beginning to suggest that an important event has taken place, before explaining what it is. 'Something' is used on a number of occasions, e.g. when the narrator first wakes up in the carriage ("I became afraid of something," 48). 'Something' is useful in presenting the narrator's frequent, minute observations of his psychic state.[3]

There is a transition from vague fears and premonitions to a figure that achieves a level of animacy when the narrator first seeks to escape the room.

> . . . I went out into the corridor thinking to escape from what tormented me. But it went out behind me and darkened everything. I was even more terrified than before. (49) [299]

The parallel verbs that are used with the subjects 'I' and 'it' establish a neuter, animate presence:

I went out into the corridor	. . . ia vyshel v koridor
. . . it went out behind me and darkened everything	. . . ono vyshlo za mnoi i omrachalo vse

With the phrase 'it went out behind me' we are made to accept 'it' as a psychological reality for the narrator, while still questioning its nature.

1. See Parthé, "Death Masks."
2. In *Sob. sočinenij* 12:94. See Parthé, "The Metamorphosis."
3. Another example: "I am running away from something dreadful and cannot escape it" (49) [298] as well as the two examples in the 'square' passage. The indefinite pronouns can often suggest something frightening or dangerous without directly naming it. The 'something' plus verb form

has a similar meaning or effect as the same verb form without any subject; both state that an action is taking place (or has taken place) and a specific agent is responsible but the speaker is unable to specify its identity. Knowing that the 'something' has to do with the awareness of death does not help to explain it better; the narrator says that it is now in his soul, poisoning his former life (50) [300].

'It' plus a verb of motion ('went out') produce the effect of nameless, neuter animacy that we have already seen in *War and Peace*. Tolstoy then uses a somewhat trite personification—"the voice of death"—before switching to the more chilling, unapproachable square. The square is the final device for death in the story; the other confrontations are simply referred to as being far worse.

In a thematic sense, the devices for presenting death, or, more accurately, for making death *present*, are all related. In going through the history of these devices in Tolstoy, it is interesting to see what the author sought to achieve at each stage, what he was trying to understand and explain about death. In *War and Peace*, the neuter animate *it* (*ono*) suggested that one might see death as a non-human monster out of a frightening folk-tale. The animate feminine *it* (*ona*) of *The Death of Ivan Ilych* led us to concentrate on the horror that lies just below the surface of ordinary life; *it* forces Ivan Ilych to retreat from the world into one small room, where he and *it* are alone in the universe.

"Notes of a Madman" is frequently treated as an earlier version of *Ivan Ilych*.[4] If this is true, one would expect the devices to be somewhat similar. In fact, the 'voice of death' has some affinity with the *it* that Ivan Ilych sees. The square, however, when subject to more careful analysis, is much more an extension of the idea of 'something not human—death' that first appeared in *War and Peace*. There is the suggestion that the perfect symmetry of the geometric form is not beautiful but is in itself dangerous and threatening. Nothing remains here of the ancient, to some extent comforting personification of death; what could be less human than a square? This 'non-humanness' from *War and Peace* combined with the type of isolation found in *Ivan Ilych* leads to the cumulative power of this device in the first death scene of "Notes of a Madman."

Tolstoy used all of these devices to indicate a high level of psychic disorientation and distress. This disorientation is not surprising, since the characters are faced with the prospect of their own deaths. He described an occult experience, that is, one beyond human understanding, beyond words. Namelessness, whether by means of pronouns, verbs, or a geometric figure, is a stylistic strategy which is consistent with the goals of what Eikhenbaum calls Tolstoy's "new psychological aesthetics" (*YT* 45).

The square, then, has affinities with the Tolstoyan aesthetic system that are more than thematic. Tolstoy uses the square at precisely the moment and in the context where in other stories a non-referential pronoun would be used. The square is less directly referential than a pronoun, but the two devices are not unrelated. A link between pronouns and geometric figures has been noted independently by a number of

---

4. See notes by Rozanova to *Ivan Ilych* in *Sob. sočinenij* 12:474-8.

Soviet and émigré scholars (Zaretskii 17, Vinogradov 323, Jakobson 24, Lotman 195). Zaretskii pointed out that this link had long been noticed by scholars and added:

> The link between pronouns and non-pronominal words is sometimes cleverly compared to the relationship between geo-metrical bodies and physical ones. Maybe one can compare it to the relationship between variable and constant values. (17)

Lotman (195) went further in saying that "the study of the artistic func-tion of grammatical categories is to a certain extent equivalent to the interplay of geometric figures in the spatial kinds of art."[5] A proportion of relationship, which we can extend as Lotman does to an equivalence of aesthetic effect, is thus set up: Pronouns are to Non-pronominal words as Geometric figures are to Physical bodies and as Variables are to Constants.

The common properties of relationship between the different groups have to do with withholding of information vs. disclosure, and with the degree of abstraction in representation. The links between these groups have been noted not in reference to any work or writer, but simply as aesthetic possibilities. In his descriptions of characters facing death, Tolstoy seems not to have chosen at random, but with a sense of the kind of effect that he was seeking, and of the various devices that could achieve that effect. Death is in itself abstract and yet present, and he was able to find a number of ways, from the pro-nominal to the geo-metric, to express that dichotomy.

*   *   *

The main purpose of this article has been to give the unusual image for death found in "Notes of a Madman" a stylistic context and a literary history. However, we should not forget how it functions in the story itself. This strongly resonant image does not transform the story; the author does not bother to relate the subsequent encounters with death in detail at all. By neglecting to do so, he allows the story to peak too soon; expectations are disappointed and all sense of threat and psycho-logical terror is lost. "Notes" becomes a criticism of property, wealth, career, sex, and even marriage and family life, with religion and vol-untary poverty the only cures for the soul's crisis. There is a seemingly quick and easy transcendance of the horror of death at the end when the narrator walks off with the peasants. To some extent this contradicts the beginning of the story (which takes place chronologically after the end) when the narrator announces that he is mad. Shestov understood Tolstoy to mean that the consciousness of death is the path to awareness, but therein also lies the danger of insanity (158–60). Shestov felt that

5. See also Buchanon 18.

Tolstoy's mad vision of death as a geometric horror could be infectious; others would have this experience not while half asleep, but in their waking moments (159). The infectiousness of the vision, or the possibility of it being a sign of change in the aesthetic vocabulary seems to be borne out by Bely, Zamyatin, Andreev, and other writers and artists of the early twentieth century. The time span between the first publication of "Notes of a Madman" (1912) and these works is just a few years (Tolstoy worked on the story as late as 1903), indicating the possibility of a shared artistic climate and shared anxieties.

Most of the work of "Notes of a Madman" was carried out at the same time that Tolstoy was working on *The Death of Ivan Ilych*. Both stories experiment with various configurations of devices to solve the artistic problem of describing death in an accurate and exciting new way. *Ivan Ilych* shows Tolstoy more in control of his style, and the story leaves a unified impression. "Notes" is awkward when seen as a whole; this is worth noting even with Eikhenbaum's caveat that when a writer is concerned with psychological aesthetics, a smoothly written story is a secondary consideration (YT 45). After the scene where the narrator experiences the square and the 'tearing' inside his soul, the story loses its intensity; it seems as if Tolstoy has almost gone too far, has reached the ultimate image for death, and thus has come to the boundaries of what literature can do to make death present. Like Malevich when he painted the white square on white, Tolstoy can go no further in this artistic direction.

One may criticize the vestiges of a nineteenth-century morality tale in "Notes of a Madman," but the story cannot be simply dismissed because it contains a device which, in Eikhenbaum's terms (YT 109), hid "the forces of disclosure and destruction." There is in this unfinished work one mad, alienated, modern vision of death as "a horror—red, white, and square," a vision which stops time and isolates one in the universe, paralyzed by the geometry of fear.

JOHN BAYLEY

[Ivan Ilyich]†

* * *

Nothing, if one comes to think of it, can be more daringly presumptuous on the writer's part than to put himself inside a dying man and describe his last moments of life. Tolstoy does it with Ivan Ilyich as well as with Hadji Murad. But whereas he makes no attempt to explain or to own the latter, the former is his creature entirely. And one of the signs of

†From *Tolstoy and the Novel* (London, 1966). Reprinted with permission of Chatto & Windus/The Hogarth Press.

possession is the determined use of metaphor in his last moments: he is not even allowed to die in his own way. To die is (apparently) to lose the awareness of oneself, and this is what Hadji Murad does, but Tolstoy assumes and retains awareness on Ivan Ilyich's behalf. He is thrust into "the black bag", and "he felt that his agony was due to his being thrust into that black hole and still more to his not being able to get right into it. He was hindered from getting into it by the conviction that his life had been a good one." But at last he fell through the hole, "and there at the bottom was a light"

> What had happened to him was like the sensation one some-
> times experiences in a railway carriage where one thinks one
> is going backwards while one is really going forwards and
> suddenly becomes aware of the real direction.

As he has done before, Tolstoy alternates the metaphor used for the sensations of the dying with description of what the spectators saw. The account makes a great initial impact, but is not, I think, ultimately moving by Tolstoy's highest standards. We are deeply impressed by our first reading of *Ivan Ilyich*, and our expectations, remaining high, are surely disappointed when we read it again. The description is too weighted, the power too authoritative. But the account of Andrew's death—seen as it is by persons whom we have gradually come to know so well because they are involved in the true and yet artificial continuity of a story—increases its power to move us at each reading. And this in spite of the fact that the process of Andrew's death is so like that of Ivan Ilyich in the telling, and, in so far as this is confident and metaphorical, almost equally unconvincing. Andrew's dream, in which he feels death as a monster forcing its way through a door which he tries in vain to hold shut, is surely a nightmare of the healthy and alive, not of the dying? The dream does not seem his but Tolstoy's; the author's metaphors and figures of speech have the property of removing the individuality of what is happening. Perhaps apprehending this, Tolstoy usually distrusts them, as one feels he would have distrusted Turgenev's graphic metaphor in *On the Eve*.

> Death is like a fisherman who has caught a fish in his net and
> leaves it for a time in the water. The fish still swims about,
> but the net surrounds it, and the fisherman will take it when
> he wishes.

How many of us, as individuals, actually feel ourselves in this position? And it is as individuals, not as metaphors, that we die.

So Andrew dies, but Ivan Ilyich does not. Ivan Ilyich is a very ordinary man. Tolstoy emphasises this continually, but he also emphasises that as a result of his approaching death Ivan Ilyich ceased to be ordinary.

And this change is not natural but arbitrary and forced. The background is filled in with pungent and detailed observation in Tolstoy's most effective style—the furniture and decoration of an upper-middle-class flat in the Petersburg of the '80s is brilliantly described—but it is not affectionate detail, like the description of the Bergs' party in *War and Peace*. That Ivan Ilyich should have his slight but fatal accident when adjusting the folds of the curtain on a step-ladder is grimly effective, for interior decoration is perhaps more subject than most human activities to the law which Tolstoy holds here to be typical of all activity except saving one's soul—the law of diminishing returns. When the curtains are adjusted they cease to interest and distract and one must find some other interest and distraction, but Tolstoy ignores the fact that Ivan Ilyich—like most ordinary mortals—is quite capable of finding one. He will not have it that human life, even at its most aimless level, is usually self-renewing. And though we can believe that the sick man would sometimes have hated his wife for being well, he would not have hated her the whole time, "with his whole soul". Sometimes at least he would cling to her as something familiar, human and once physically loved, but Tolstoy became convinced in his later years that what was once physically loved must become for that very reason physically repellent.

It is not so much this, however, nor the implications of the statement that "his life had been most simple, most ordinary, and therefore most terrible" that falsify the tale. No one is more able than Tolstoy to interest and impress us by what he asserts; and there is an almost complete harmony in *War and Peace* between the narrative and didactic sides, as between all the other disparate elements. Nor can we object to Tolstoy's contempt for doctors, a contempt as much in evidence in *War and Peace* and *Anna Karenina* as it is here. No, it is when he imputes all these things to Ivan Ilyich himself that we cease to assent. His death is bound to be painful, but not in this terrible gloating way. In fact, Ivan Ilyich's reaction to his fate has at first the simpleness and naturalness of the great open world of self-conceit which Tolstoy knew so well, the world of *War and Peace* in which solipsism is in reasonable accord with mutuality.

> The syllogism he had learnt from Kiezewetter's Logic: "Caius is a man, men are mortal, therefore Caius is mortal", had always seemed to him correct as applied to Caius, but certainly not as applied to himself. That Caius—man in the abstract—was mortal, was perfectly correct, but he was not Caius, not an abstract man, but a creature quite quite separate from all others. He had been little Vanya, with a mamma and a papa, with Mitya and Volodya, with the toys, a coachman and a nurse, afterwards with Katenka and with all the joys, griefs, and delights of childhood, boyhood, and youth. What did

Caius know of the smell of that striped leather ball Vanya had
been so fond of? Had Caius kissed his mother's hand like that,
and did the silk of her dress rustle so for Caius? Had he rioted
like that at school when the pastry was bad? Had Caius been
in love like that? Could Caius preside at a session as he did?
"Caius really was mortal, and it was right for him to die; but
for me, little Vanya, Ivan Ilych, with all my thoughts and
emotions, it's altogether a different matter. It cannot be that
I ought to die. That would be too terrible."

We remember Nicholas's sensation at the battle of Schön Grabern. "Can
they be coming at me? And why? To kill me? *Me*, whom everyone is
so fond of? He remembered his mother's love for him, and his family's,
and his friends', and the enemy's intention to kill him seemed impossible." It is this sensation, surely, and not "the conviction that his life
has been a good one", that makes death dreadful to Ivan Ilyich? And
we know that this sensation would persist until, numbed by physically
suffering, he would disappear among such scraps of recollection from
his childhood as Tolstoy gives him ("the taste of French plums and how
they wrinkle the mouth up")—disappear without other dignity than the
right and proper one of being himself. That dignity requires that his
death should take place on the same level as "the visitings, the curtains,
the sturgeon for dinner", because these were the materials of his life.
He is not Prince Andrew. We feel for him as we might for an animal
compelled by its master to perform some unnatural trick.

*   *   *

Y. J. DAYANANDA

The Death of Ivan Ilych: A Psychological Study On Death and Dying†

The Death of Ivan Ilych (1866),[1] Tolstoy's great masterpiece in the genre
of the short novel or novella, represents an extraordinary contribution
to the literature of death and dying. Death, not sudden, violent death
but slow inch-by-inch, the moment-by-moment disappearance, or
death, which according to Montaigne is just a moment when dying
ends, has not been sufficiently treated in works of literature even though
it is one of the constants of human society. The reasons for this literary
conspiracy are obvious. *Death like birth is inexperienceable*; you can
observe another's public death or birth but not your own. No novelist

---

†From *Literature and Psychology* 22 (1972):191–
98. Page references for quotations from pieces in
this Norton Critical Edition are given in brackets.

1. Leo Tolstoy, *The Death of Ivan Ilych* (New
York: New American Library, 1960). Future references will give page number only.

has given so complete and so realistic a picture of the process of death, especially of the last agonizing moments of a man's life as Tolstoy. No novelist has dwelt with unsparing detail on the horrors of dying—he even writes in clinical detail about "the odour of the decomposing body"—as Tolstoy.

Recently a growing league of professional psychologists and psychiatrists has been trying to throw new light on the long-taboo subject of dying. Dr. E. K. Ross's *On Death and Dying*[2] (1969) is a remarkable book which developed as the result of the University of Chicago interdisiplinary seminar on death and dying—the first of its kind. Dr. Elizabeth Kubler-Ross, then a psychiatrist at the University of Chicago, is currently Medical Director of the Mental Health and Family Services of South Cook County in Flossmoor, Illinois. At this seminar which was attended by medical and theology students, physicians and clergy, nurses and social workers, approximately five hundred terminally ill patients were interviewed in a one-way mirror set up. Dr. Ross relies heavily on this seminar at the University of Chicago Billings Hospital and these interviews conducted over a period of almost three years for her book. Most of the dying patients welcomed the opportunity to talk and quickly poured out their bottled up feelings and fears before they died. They expressed their real concerns, inmost conflicts and coping mechanisms. It was as if a floodgate was opened. The students on the other side of the mirror sat through these interviews and discussions, sometimes uncomfortably, other times comfortably, but rarely without learning much about the biggest crisis in human life—death. They heard what it was like to be dying from the dying patients themselves.

Dr. Ross has formulated the five-stages theory as a result of these extensive video-taped interviews. All the terminally ill patients go through five stages between the diagnosis of fatal illness and their death. The time interval between these two events varies from a few days up to two years. The stages don't always follow one another; they overlap sometimes and sometimes they go back and forth. The five stages are: Denial and Isolation, Anger, Bargaining, Depression, and Acceptance.

> All of our patients reacted to the bad news in almost identical ways, which is typical not only of the news of fatal illness but seems to be a human reaction to great and unexpected stress: namely, with shock and disbelief. Denial was used by most of our patients and lasted from a few seconds to many months . . . After the denial, anger and rage predominated . . . When the environment was able to tolerate this anger without taking it personally, the patient was greatly helped in reaching a stage of temporary bargaining followed by depression, which is a steppingstone towards final acceptance . . . These stages do

2. Elizabeth Kubler-Ross, *On Death and Dying* (New York: MacMillan, 1969).

not replace each other but can exist next to each other and overlap at times.[3]

In *The Death of Ivan Ilych* Ivan Ilych dies in the first page of the opening section but he goes through the five stages of dying in the remaining eleven sections. It is one of the marvellous strokes of Tolstoy to make the epilogue the prologue, to portray death as an event or moment first and then to portray dying as a process or as a series of stages leading up to that event or moment when dying ends. The novella is a post-mortem examination of Ivan's dying which is a prolonged, complicated and painful process. His dying is more like the traversing of a corridor than the closing of a door.

I intend to draw upon the material presented in Dr. Ross's *On Death and Dying* and try to show how Tolstoy's Ivan Ilych in *The Death of Ivan Ilych* goes through the same five stages. Psychiatry offers one way to a better illumination of literature. Dr. Ross's discoveries in her consulting room corroborate Tolstoy's literary insights into the experience of dying. They give us the same picture of man's terrors of the flesh, despair, loneliness, and depression at the approach of death. The understanding of one will be illuminated by the understanding of the other. The two books, *On Death and Dying* and *The Death of Ivan Ilych*, the one with its systematically accumulated certified knowledge, and disciplined and scientific descriptions, and the other with its richly textured commentary, and superbly concrete and realistic perceptions, bring death out of the darkness and remove it from the list of taboo topics. Death, our affluent society's newest forbidden topic, is not regarded as "obscene" but discussed openly and without the euphemisms of the funeral industry.

I. First Stage: Denial and Isolation. "No, not me."

Almost all patients, when told that they have a fatal illness, react with shock and denial—the "No, not me, it cannot be true" stage. The shock is very great but denial is rarely total. Dr. Ross found that only three out of four hundred maintained this denial to the very end. This initial denial, partial denial at times, does not last long with most patients who learn to drop the denial gradually, though the need for it continues to exist in every patient. In some denial appears and disappears, and exists side by side with awareness of impending death. As Dr. Ross points out:

> Denial, at least partial denial, is used by almost all patients, not only during the first stages of illness or following confrontation, but also later on from time to time . . . Denial functions as a buffer after unexpected shocking news, allows the patient to collect himself and, with time, mobilize other, less radical

3. Kubler-Ross, p. 263.

defenses . . . It is much later, usually, that the patient uses isolation more than denial. He can then talk about his death and his illness, his mortality and his immortality as if they were twin brothers permitted to exist side by side, thus facing death and still maintaining hope.[4]

Ivan Ilych, a member of the Court of Justice, leads a thoroughly artificial and conventional life. But when he is brought face to face with death—the result of an injury in his side which turns out to be the origin of a fatal disease—he reacts with shock and denial. Death is something that happens to others, not to him. He said to himself: "It can't be. It's impossible! But here it is. How is this? How is one to understand it?"[5] [150]

Ivan Ilych moves from success in school to success in profession and in society. He marries the right girl, gets the right sort of friends, has the right kind of house and the right kind of furniture. Everything goes pleasantly and properly until a trivial accident in the trivial business of fixing a curtain occurs. He falls from a stepladder when he tries to show the upholsterer how he wants the hangings draped. From that point on everything goes wrong. The dull pain in his side becomes insistent discomfort and in three months becomes the most excruciating pain. He spends the last three days of life screaming incessantly with pain. It was only just two hours before his death that he stopped screaming and accepted death calmly. It is during these last three months—between the day of his fall from the stepladder and the day of his death—that he goes through the five stages of dying. These stages do not replace each other but exist next to each other and overlap at times.

Ivan's feelings of shock and denial appear again and again, and torment him after his meetings with doctors. Now he thinks it is only a bruise and now he worries about what the doctor had said in scientific and dubious language. His first problem was to find out the exact truth about his condition; he had to depend on clues while doctors and relatives withheld the truth. He was haunted by questions: "Is my condition bad? Is it very bad? Or is there as yet nothing much wrong?" On the one hand he ignores the pain and dismisses more serious thoughts. "Well," he thought, "Perhaps it isn't so bad after all . . . It is a good thing I am a bit of an athlete. Another man might have been killed, but I merely knocked myself, just here; it hurts when it's touched, but it's passing off already—it's only a bruise."[6] [138–43] And on the other hand he is absolutely terrified of death. He had no doubt that he was dying and so he was in despair. He was not at all accustomed to the thought of his own death. On one occasion, after a long talk with the doctor, he came

4. Kubler-Ross, pp. 39–42.
5. p. 132.
6. pp. 116–123.

home and was reviewing the physiological details of the doctor's opinion, and the medicine he had recommended to lessen pain.

> 'I need only take it regularly and avoid all injurious influences. I am already feeling better, much better.' He began touching his side; it was not painful to touch. 'There, I really don't feel it. It's much better already.' He put out the light and turned on his side . . . Suddenly he felt the old familiar, dull, gnawing pain, stubborn and serious. There was the same loathsome taste in his mouth . . . And suddenly the matter presented itself in a quite different aspect. 'Vermiform appendix! Kidney!' he said to himself. 'It's not a question of appendix or kidney, but of life and . . . death. Yes. Life was there and now it is going, going and I cannot stop it. Yes. Why deceive myself? Isn't it obvious to everyone but me that I am dying . . . There was light and now there is darkness. I was here and now I am going there! Where?' A chill came over him, his breathing ceased, and he felt only the throbbing of his heart.[7] [148]

He could never believe that he was dying. Like most people, he thought he was immortal. He had also occasionally thought of death in abstract terms. He had casually thought that everyone should go one day, not that he himself should go. He had learnt the syllogism:

> 'Caius is a man, men are mortal, therefore Caius is mortal.' But it had always seemed to him correct as applied to Caius but not as applied to himself. Ivan Ilych is not Caius, an abstract man, but a man of flesh and blood, of hopes and desires. 'Caius really was mortal, and it was right for him to die; but for me, little Vanya, Ivan Ilych, with all my thoughts and emotions, it's altogether a different matter. It cannot be that I ought to die. That would be too terrible.'[8] [149]

As the pain grows worse and more incessant Ivan's denial becomes more and more partial. Pain and suffering drive him slowly not only to the recognition of his own death, to a knowledge, not merely theoretical but proved on his pulses, of his own mortal condition but also into a state of absolute isolation. One of the best things in Tolstoy's novella—its power proceeds from this—is its marvellous evocation of the utter loneliness of Ivan Ilych; he suffers and dies alone. Even his wife and daughter regard his illness as an annoyance and would not interrupt their social activities to be with him in his agony. His family and his doctors erected a wall of formality and hypocrisy around him. He felt

7. pp. 129–130.   8. p. 132.

his terrible loneliness could not be more complete anywhere—either at
the bottom of the sea or under the earth.

> There was no deceiving himself: something terrible, new,
> and more important than anything before in his life, was taking
> place within him of which he alone was aware. Those about
> him did not understand it, but thought everything was in the
> world going on as usual. That tormented Ivan Ilych more than
> anything else . . . He had to live thus all alone on the brink of
> an abyss, with no one who understood or pitied him.[9] [144–46]

II. Second Stage: Anger. "Why me?"

In most people, Dr. Ross found, denial quickly gives way to anger and
rage—the "Why me?" stage. The dying patients at this stage are hard
to handle, overly critical, nasty and uncooperative. Visitors make their
visits shorter and less frequent, making the patients feel even more
deprived, isolated and rejected. The patient is not really angry at individuals—nurses, doctors, members of the family and other visitors—but
is expressing resentment and envy because these represent all the health
and joy of living which he is in the process of losing. As Dr. Ross says:

> The stage of anger is very difficult to cope with from the
> point of view of family and staff. The reason for this is the
> fact that this anger is displaced in all directions and projected
> into the environment at times almost at random . . . Nurses
> are more often a target of their anger. Whatever they touch
> is not right. . . . He may put the television on only to find a
> group of young jolly people doing some of the modern dances
> which irritates him when every move of his is painful . . . He
> may listen to the news full of reports of destruction, war, fires,
> and tragedies—far away from him, unconcerned about the
> fright and plight of an individual who will soon be forgotten.
> He will raise his voice, he will make demands, he will com-
> plain and ask to be given attention, perhaps as the last loud
> cry, 'I am alive, don't forget that. You can hear my voice, I
> am not dead yet![1]

Ivan Ilych is not very much different from those terminally ill patients
at the University of Chicago Billings Hospital; he shows the same feelings
of anger, rage, envy and resentment. He spent the last three days of his
life screaming which could be heard through two closed doors. His
quarrels with his wife became more explosive and more frequent.

> But this discomfort increased and grew into a sense of pres-
> sure in his side accompanied by ill humour. And his irritability

---

9. p. 125.   1. Kübler-Ross, pp. 50–52.

became worse and worse . . . Scenes became frequent, and
very few of those islets remained on which husband and wife
could meet without an explosion . . . His bursts of temper
always came just before dinner . . . Sometimes he noticed
that a plate or dish was chipped, or the food was not right, or
his son put his elbow on the table, or his daughter's hair was
not done as he liked it, and for all this he blamed Praskovya
Fëdorovna . . . once or twice he fell into such a rage at the
beginning of dinner that she realized it was due to some physical derangement brought on by taking food . . .[2] [141]

When his wife tried to tell him one day about Petrishchev's formal
proposal to their daughter, "he turned his eyes toward her with such a
look that she did not finish what she was saying; so great an animosity,
to her in particular, did that look express. 'For Christ's sake let me die
in peace' he said."[3] [163–64] A moment later he looked at his daughter
and doctor also with angry eyes.

Ivan Ilych's irritability often gave way to envy and resentment. Every
show of health and cheer, whether by his doctor, or his wife or even
his daughter, produced resentment in him. He does not like his doctor
to come in "fresh, hearty, plump and cheerful with that look on his
face that seems to say: 'There now, you're in a panic about something,
but we'll arrange it all for you directly!' "[4] [156] He shows resentment
at his wife, "looks at her, scans her over, sets against her the whiteness
and plumpness and cleanness of her hands and neck, the gloss of her
hair, and the sparkle of her vivacious eyes. He hates her with his whole
soul."[5] [157] He dislikes even his daughter's display of youthful flesh,
"her fresh young flesh exposed (making a show of that very flesh which
in his own case caused so much suffering), strong, healthy, evidently
in love, and impatient with illness, suffering, and death, because they
interfered with her happiness."[6] [158] When he heard one day through
the door the distant sound of a song with its accompaniment, his anger
choked. "It is all the same to them, but they will die too! Fools! I first,
and they later, but it will be the same for them. And now they are merry
. . . the beasts."[7] [148]

III. Third Stage: Bargaining. "Yes, it is me, but . . ."

Following anger, there often comes a brief period of bargaining—the
"Yes, it is me, but . . ." stage. The patient says: "If you give me one
more year, God, I promise you I'll be a good Christian." Dr. Ross writes
about a terminally ill woman who was in intense pain nearly all the

2. p. 120.   5. p. 142.
3. p. 151.   6. p. 144.
4. p. 141.   7. p. 130.

time. The woman asked for only one day without pain so that she could leave the hospital and attend her son's wedding. Through self-hypnosis her wish was granted. On returning to the hospital she said: "Don't forget now, I have another son."[8]

Most bargains are made with God in secret. Some even make frantic promises to offer their kidneys or hearts to secure an exchange for an extension of life. They generally do not keep their promises but this stage undoubtedly gives them an opportunity to relax for a moment and to gain strength for the last few difficult days or weeks. Dr. Ross says:

> The bargaining is really an attempt to postpone; it has to include a prize offered "for good behavior," it also sets a self-imposed deadline (e.g. . . . the son's wedding), and it includes an implicit promise that the patient will not ask for more if this one postponement is granted. None of our patients have kept their promise . . ."[9]

Ivan Ilych makes one last attempt to postpone and to promise during the last few days. He turned to God and "bargained" with Him though he was not at all religious, when he realizes the terrible truth that his whole life was wrong.

> It had occurred to him that what had appeared perfectly impossible, namely that he had not spent his life as he should have done, might after all be true . . . 'But if that is so,' he said to himself, 'and I am leaving this life with the consciousness that I have lost all that was given me and it is impossible to rectify it—what then?' "[1] [164]

He lay on his back and began to review his life. He felt that his whole life was a terrible and huge deception which had hidden both life and death from him. At this time his wife approached him and suggested that he should take communion. After a moment of angry protest he muttered: "All right. Very well."

> When the priest came and heard his confession, Ivan Ilych was softened and seemed to feel a relief from his doubts and consequently from his sufferings, and for a moment there came a ray of hope . . . He received the sacrament with tears in his eyes. When they laid him down again afterwards he felt a moment's ease, and the hope that he might live awoke in him again . . . 'To live! I want to live!' he said to himself.[2] [165]

8. Kubler-Ross, p. 83.
9. Kubler-Ross, pp. 83–86.

1. p. 152.
2. p. 153.

IV. Fourth State: Depression. "Yes, me."

The next stage is usually depression, a time of mourning over things already lost and of grieving over impending losses—the "yes, me," stage. Anger and rage are replaced with a sense of great loss—not only of the past loss of a job or health, or of figure for a woman but also of the impending loss of everything and everybody the patient has ever loved. The patient now shows courage enough to acknowledge that death is indeed at his door. He is naturally very depressed; he often cries silently and alone. Dr. Ross calls this kind of depression "preparatory grief or depression," usually a period of silence in which the patient prepares himself slowly for the final decathexis, for his own separation from the world.

> In the preparatory grief there is no or little need for words. This is the time when the patient . . . begins to occupy himself with things ahead rather than behind. It is a time when too much interference from visitors . . . hinders his emotional preparation rather than enhances it . . . This type of depression is necessary and beneficial if the patient is to die in a stage of acceptance and peace. [3]

During this stage of depression Ivan Ilych wants to be left alone. Most of the time he lay staring at the back of the sofa, living only in the memories of the past. He became very impatient with his wife and her conventional words of comfort. One day he looked at her "straight in the eyes, turned on his face with a rapidity extraordinary in his weak state and shouted: 'Go away! Go away and leave me alone!' "[4] [165] He shouted even at Gerasim, the only person in the world who understood and pitied and helped him during those last agonizing days:

> Till about three in the morning he was in a state of stupified misery . . . 'Go away, Gerasim,' he whispered. 'It's all right, Sir. I'll stay a while.' 'No. Go away.' He removed his legs from Gerasim's shoulders, turned sideways onto his arm, and felt sorry for himself . . . he restrained himself no longer but wept like a child. He wept on account of his helplessness, his terrible loneliness, the cruelty of man, the cruelty of God, and the absence of God . . . 'Why, why dost thou torment me so terribly?' He did not expect an answer and yet wept because there was no answer and could be none . . . [5] [160]

Ivan Ilych continued to weep until he reached the final stage of acceptance. He groaned, tossed from side to side, pulled at his clothing,

3. Kubler-Ross, pp. 87–88.   5. 146–147.
4. p. 154.

and screamed through the last three days—all alone and in a state of desperate depression.

V. *Fifth Stage: Acceptance. "Thy Will Be Done"*

Eventually the depression subsides and the dying patient enters the stage of total acceptance—the "Thy will be done" stage. The patient in this 'dying hour' concedes his readiness to depart—"My time is very close now and it's all right." Dr. Ross describes this period as being a peaceful period in which the dying person, accepting the lost struggle and the inevitable end, is relaxed and ready to depart. He is now neither depressed nor angry about his "fate" but experiences a sense of surrender and peace. He has already expressed his feelings, his envy for the living and his anger at those who are not dying. He has already mourned the impending loss of people and places. He has found his bargaining and his depression of little use. He has finally realized that he is dying and that there is nothing he could do about it; a sense of peace seems to ease the final flickering out. Dr. Ross thinks that this acceptance is not a resigned and hopeless "giving up," a sense of "what's the use?" or "I cannot fight it any longer," though we hear such statements too:

> Acceptance should not be mistaken for a happy stage. It is almost void of feelings. It is as if the pain had gone, the struggle is over, and there comes a time for 'the final rest before the long journey' . . . While the dying patient has found some peace and acceptance, his circle of interest diminishes. He wishes to be left alone . . . Our communications then become more nonverbal than verbal . . . He may just hold our hand and ask us to sit in silence. Such moments of silence may be the most meaningful communication . . . It may assure him that he is not left alone when he is no longer talking and a pressure of the hand, a look, . . . may say more than very noisy words.[6]

Like the majority of Dr. Ross's patients Ivan Ilych too came out of his depression and faced the fact of his own death more calmly for having been through it. He did not go out, as some patients did, fighting all the way. Dylan Thomas speaks of them:

> Do not go gentle into that good night,
> Old age should burn and rage at close of day;
> Rage, rage against the dying of the light.

But Ivan Ilych's dying was not like this; it is W. S. Landor's lines that apply to him: "I warmed both hands before the fire of life/It sinks, and I am ready to depart."

Dr. Ross quotes Tagore's lines to describe this feeling of acceptance:

6. Kubler-Ross, p. 113.

> I bow to you all and take my departure.
> Here I give back the keys of my door—
> and I give up all claims to my house . . .
> Now the day has dawned and the lamp that
> lit my dark corner is out. A summons has
> come and I am ready for my journey.[7]

Ivan Ilych's final stage of acceptance was not a stage of resignation, of defeat and bitterness but of calm victory bordering on ecstasy after a long and gallant battle. He reached this stage at the end of the third day of screaming two hours before his death. Just then his schoolboy son came up to his bedside, caught the dying father's hand and kissed it. That was the moment of truth for Ivan Ilych when he "fell through and caught sight of the light, and it was revealed to him that though his whole life had not been what it should have been, this could still be rectified."[8] [166] He opened his eyes, saw his wife and son and felt sorry for them. "Yes, I am making them wretched," he thought. "They are sorry, but it will be better for them when I die." He did not have the strength to speak. "Besides, why speak? . . ." he thought.

> With a look at his wife he indicated his son and said: 'Take
> him away . . . Sorry for him . . . Sorry for you too . . .' He
> tried to add, 'forgive me' but said 'forgo' and waved his hand,
> knowing that He whose understanding mattered would un-
> derstand.[9] [166–67]

In his final moments Ivan Ilych does not give up saying "what's the use?" but shows a new understanding and acceptance. There is no longer any fear of death. Now he does not even find it hard to die:

> 'How good and how simple!' he thought. 'And the pain?'
> he asked himself. 'What has become of it? Where are you,
> pain?'
> 'And death . . . where is it?'
> 'So that's what it is!' he suddenly exclaimed aloud. 'What
> joy!'
> 'Death is finished,' he said to himself. 'It is no more!' He
> drew in a breath, stopped in the midst of a sigh, stretched out,
> and died.[1] [167]

The study of dying not as a biological but as a psychological event, as an experience, though relatively recent, can tell us something about the treatment of death in literature. It should be clear from the reading of *The Death of Ivan Ilych* in the light of Dr. Ross's *On Death and Dying* that psychoanalysis offers a rich, dynamic approach to some

---

7. Kubler-Ross, p. 112.
8. p. 155.

9. Ibid.
1. p. 156.

aspects of literature. Tolstoy and Dr. Ross agree that the experience of death, however elusive, can be broken down into the specifics—denial, loneliness, anger, bargaining, depression, and acceptance. Tolstoy's novella, like Dr. Ross's study, minutely records the final moments of dying. It is not without purpose that Tolstoy calls his novella *The Death of Ivan Ilych*. Admittedly, as many critics have seen, it is a savage satire on the hypocrisy of conventional life. But the stuff of the novella is dying. Quite simply, *The Death of Ivan Ilych* receives its force and intensity from its uncompromised and penetrating analysis of the greatest human crisis—death. Behind Ivan Ilych's anguish of insurgent flesh and spirit there stands the suffering of every man face to face with death. What gives the novella its dread intensity is its sense of the helplessness of mankind which it conveys. One will search in vain in literature to find its parallel.

VLADIMIR NABOKOV

[Ivan Ilych's Life]†

* * *

Now comes my first point: this is really the story not of Ivan's Death but the story of Ivan's Life. The physical death described in the story is part of mortal Life, it is merely the last phase of mortality. According to Tolstoy, mortal man, personal man, individual man, *physical* man, goes his physical way to nature's garbage can; according to Tolstoy, *spiritual* man returns to the cloudless region of universal God-Love, an abode of neutral bliss so dear to Oriental mystics. The Tolstoyan formula is: Ivan lived a bad life and since a bad life is nothing but the death of the soul, then Ivan lived a living death; and since beyond death is God's living light, then Ivan died into new Life—Life with a capital L.

My second point is that this story was written in March 1886, at a time when Tolstoy was nearly sixty and had firmly established the Tolstoyan fact that writing masterpieces of fiction was a sin. He had firmly made up his mind that if he would write anything, after the great sins of his middle years, *War and Peace* and *Anna Karenina*, it would be only in the way of simple tales for the people, for peasants, for school children, pious educational fables, moralistic fairy tales, that kind of thing. Here and there in "The Death of Ivan Ilyich" there is a half-hearted attempt to proceed with this trend, and we shall find samples of a pseudo-fable style here and there in the story. But on the whole it is the artist who takes over. This story is Tolstoy's most artistic, most perfect, and most sophisticated achievement.

Thanks to the fact that Guerney has so admirably translated the thing

†From *Lectures on Russian Literature* (New York, 1981). Reprinted with permission of Harcourt, Brace and Jovanovich.

I shall have the opportunity at last to discuss Tolstoy's style. Tolstoy's style is a marvelously complicated, ponderous instrument.

You may have seen, you must have seen, some of those awful text books written not by educators but by educationalists—by people who talk about books instead of talking within books. You may have been told by them that the chief aim of a great writer, and indeed the main clue to his greatness, is "simplicity." Traitors, not teachers. In reading exam papers written by misled students, of both sexes, about this or that author, I have often come across such phrases—probably recollections from more tender years of schooling—as "his style is simple" or "his style is clear and simple" or "his style is beautiful and simple" or "his style is quite beautiful and simple." But remember that "simplicity" is buncombe. No major writer is simple. The *Saturday Evening Post* is simple. Journalese is simple. Upton Lewis is simple. Mom is simple. Digests are simple. Damnation is simple. But Tolstoys and Melvilles are not simple.

One peculiar feature of Tolstoy's style is what I shall term the "groping purist." In describing a meditation, emotion, or tangible object, Tolstoy follows the contours of the thought, the emotion, or the object until he is perfectly satisfied with his re-creation, his rendering. This involves what we might call creative repetitions, a compact series of repetitive statements, coming one immediately after the other, each more expressive, each closer to Tolstoy's meaning. He gropes, he unwraps the verbal parcel for its inner sense, he peels the apple of the phrase, he tries to say it one way, then a better way, he gropes, he stalls, he toys, he Tolstoys with words.

Another feature of his style is his manner of weaving striking details into the story, the freshness of the descriptions of physical states. Nobody in the eighties in Russia wrote like that. The story was a forerunner of Russian modernism just before the dull and conventional Soviet era. If there is the fable noted, there is too a tender, poetical intonation here and there, and there is the tense mental monologue, the stream of consciousness technique that he had already invented for the description of Anna's last journey.

*   *   *

DOROTHY GREEN

The Kreutzer Sonata: Tolstoy and Beethoven†

The origin of this paper was a strong impression that there is a closer connection between Tolstoy's novel and Beethoven's music than is usually allowed for in criticisms of the book. The paper is also an attempt to counter a tendency to regard the book merely as an expression of a thesis. Before anything else, Tolstoy's *Kreutzer Sonata* seems to me a complete work of art, as much a thing made and existing in its own right as Beethoven's sonata, obeying the laws of a particular kind of literary form, as the sonata obeys those of a particular kind of musical form.

Criticism of this kind is bound to be impressionistic: it is obviously impossible to prove what a piece of music suggests to the mind of anyone but oneself, but it is hoped that the interpretation will be found to be inconsistent neither with the text of the novel, nor with that of the music. It would be absurd for one knowing no Russian to undertake any kind of verbal analysis and I have tried to draw conclusions which are independent of linguistic knowledge, and as far as possible, independent of a comparison of variant texts. There are nine of these altogether, bearing witness not only to Tolstoy's struggle for artistic excellence, but to the strenuousness of the argument he was conducting with himself. The finished work seems to me a triumphant solution to a dual problem.

Alexandra Tolstoy, in her biography of her father, tells us that he had begun and abandoned a story called *The Murderer of His Wife* in the 1870's. His English biographer, Simmons, says that on a hint given him by the actor Andreyev-Burlak, he had begun this tale of sexual love in 1887 and put it aside. Both agree that early in 1888 in the spring, occurred the incident which gave a new and final impetus to the story. Among the guests at the Tolstoy house in Moscow were the painter Repin, Burlak and Lysoto, a violinist. The violinist and Tolstoy's young son Sergei played Beethoven's *Kreutzer Sonata*, a performance which for some reason particularly moved Tolstoy. As we might infer from the novel itself, Tolstoy responded especially to the first movement and when one considers the ideas that come to the surface in the story, it is not hard to suggest why, as I shall try to show. Under the influence of the music, Tolstoy suggested that Repin should paint a scene inspired by it, a kind of back-drop, and that in front of this Andreyev-Burlak should read the story that Tolstoy would write, based on the sonata, or on the ideas it suggested to him. That is to say, his conception of the total

† From *Melbourne Slavic Studies* I (1967). Reprinted with permission of the author.

experience "Kreutzer Sonata" shaped itself as a kind of miniature drama, with a background of unheard music; in reality, a miniature music-drama. Merezhkovski, who is usually so sensitive to Tolstoy's artistry, complains[1] that the hero is 'reduced' to a voice: "a mere plaintive voice and a pair of eyes, glowing with feverish, half-crazy fire." With all due respect, this seems to me precisely the point, the essential element in Tolstoy's structural intention. The story makes its appeal, and was intended to make its appeal largely through the ear. The voice is the literary equivalent for the instruments; it has to carry the burden of the statement that Tolstoy reads, or hears, in the music. One's attention is constantly being drawn to sounds, for example, to Pozdnyshev's cough, or laugh, "like a sob". (One has to resist the temptation to formulate an analogy here, very strongly). The view that the story was designed to appeal to the ear has thematic justification also: the novel is cast in the form of a "confession". No other narrative method but that of the almost continuous speaker could have approximated to the music embodied in piano and violin, those two voices that strive through the sonata to become one. The main critical problem, then, resolves itself into trying to identify what the music of the story is saying. And this is where I find most of what I have happened to read about the novel in English unsatisfactory. Its relationship with Beethoven's music is ignored, the artistry of the story itself is dismissed and criticism is sidetracked into discussions of the merits and demerits of Tolstoy's ideas about sex, chastity, modern medicine, the relations between men and women and the position of women in modern society. To make matters worse, discussion of the ideas is confused by the publicity given to Tolstoy's personal life. They are never discussed for their own sake, but always in the light of his own application of them and in that of his relations to his own wife. Whether Tolstoy practised what he preached is in the long run irrelevant; a doctrine is not necessarily wrong because its advocate fails to practise it. And it is not at all certain that the intention of the story is to persuade one to follow a doctrine. Some of the confusion in discussion is Tolstoy's own fault. Essays like *An Afterword to the Kreutzer Sonata* distract our attention from the artistic organisation of the tale and encourage the view that he was more interested in propagating a belief than in creating a work of art. When an artist finds his ideas being taken seriously, he is often tempted to become a kind of "doctrinaire-after-the-fact". Before writing the *Afterword*, it is important to remember, Tolstoy insisted to Obolensky that the views expressed in the story were the views of its hero. This seems to me an unassailable fact; there is nothing in the views themselves inconsistent with the dramatic situation set up in the novel. It is true, perhaps, that once he had written the story, Tolstoy became ambivalent in his attitude to it, unable

---

1. See *Tolstoy as Man and Artist*, by Dimitri Merezkowkski (Constable, 1902).

to make up his mind whether he preferred it to be regarded as art or as sociology. Even at the second level, the usual discussions have done less than justice to the ideas in the book and it might be as well to have another look at them before going on to the more relevant artistic questions.

Two of the ideas at least are extremely important and highly relevant to our own situation. The fact that Tolstoy has tangled them up with notions of chastity that seem at first sight rather bizarre has tended to obscure their importance. In the first place, he raises that irritating question *What is it all for?* He is asking: "Do we raise children in order to raise children in order to raise children . . . ?" and so on, ad infinitum. This is a question of the same kind as "Do we train teachers to train teachers to train teachers . . . ?" These are the sorts of fundamental questions which are not supposed to be asked and which are always begged by writers on education or on family relationships. But at some stage in our history they are questions which will have to be asked, even though there must and should be uncertainty about the answer. The mere asking them acts as a corrective. Tolstoy irritates those who are obsessed with processes because he forces us to face squarely the fundamental question of purpose. Not only does he question the whole notion of child-bearing as an end in itself, but he points out the possibility that child-bearing may be an obstacle to the accomplishment of full adulthood; he reminds us that life on this planet must end, whether we subscribe to the religious or to the scientific point of view and that its limitation makes the accomplishment of life's purpose, whatever it may be, more urgent.

> 'You ask how the human race will continue to exist,' he said, having again sat down in front of me, and spreading his legs far apart he leant his elbows on his knees. 'Why should it continue?'
> 'Why? If not, we should not exist.'
> 'And why should we exist?'
> 'Why? In order to live, of course.'
> 'But why live? If life has no aim, if life is given us for life's sake, there is no reason for living . . . But if life has an aim, it is clear it ought to come to an end when that aim is reached . . .'

If the possibility of life on some other scale than the mere animal, life-for-the-sake-of-life, appears idiosyncratic, we should remember that it has been put forward by an outstanding scientist in our own day, Teilhard de Chardin, as an evolutionary possibility. Moreover, scientific materialists who are overtly opposed to teleological views, frequently behave and write as if they held them.

The second idea which is fundamental to the structure of the novel concerns the changing role of women in human history, the full implications of which have hardly yet begun to be seen. Like George Eliot, Tolstoy perceived that this was no simple matter which could be adjusted by a few adroit social and political changes.

> 'If there is to be equality,' says Pozdnyshev, 'let it be equality!' 'Women's lack of rights arises not from the fact that she must not vote or be a judge—to be occupied with such affairs is no privilege—but from the fact that she is not man's equal in sexual intercourse and has not the right to use a man or abstain from him as she pleases—is not allowed to choose a man at her pleasure instead of being chosen by him. You say this is monstrous! Very well! Then a man must not have those rights either. As it is at present, a woman is deprived of that right, while a man has it. And to make up for that right, she acts on men's sensuality and through his sensuality subdues him, so that he only chooses formally, while in reality it is she who chooses.'

In spite of surface modifications, this picture is still substantially correct. Tolstoy goes on to paint a further and more vivid picture of the economy of the western world dominated by female consumer-demand, a picture which, to us, seems more accurate than when he drew it.

Both Tolstoy and George Eliot perceived that the real obstacle to the genuine independence of women lay partly in man's concept of woman and partly in her concept of herself. Tolstoy felt the concept to be the result of sexual drive in the male and held the male responsible. Eliot was perhaps more perceptive in grasping the fact that women are saddled with a physiological organisation ill-adapted to social change. But both pointed to the necessity for a woman to organise a meaningful life for herself without reference to a man. Tolstoy arouses resistance because his way of making his point is repugnant to a generation conditioned by Freudian thinking. The situation will change, Pozdynshev says, "only when woman regards virginity as the highest state and does not as at present consider the highest state of a human being a shame and disgrace." If we substituted the phrase 'single state' for 'virginity', we might feel less resistant, but only to a slight degree. The question Tolstoy is really asking is too revolutionary still for us to contemplate without passion: Is marriage now, as it once was, the best way of organising society, or has it outlived, in its present form, its traditional function? The attempt to commend the notion of woman as a free-living organism brings us up against the ideas about chastity that so many people find repellent and hysterical, especially when they identify Tolstoy too closely with his central character. But what Tolstoy is really doing is pointing out that our attitudes to this question are partly the result of conditioning and education. In this he is anticipating by about eighty years some recent thinking on the subject.[2] It is in fact difficult to know how much of our sexual appetite is innate and how much is the result of tradition and outside influence. It is quite possible that a great many more people could lead happy, purposeful and celibate lives if the propaganda against doing so were not all-powerful at an early stage. Even now, a good many do, for religious reasons. And the lot of those who must do so, for other reasons, would be much easier to bear if they had not already been conditioned to regard it as unbearable. The conditioning of girls for motherhood begins very early. No-one thrusts a doll into a little boy's hands; he is usually asked what he *wants* to be when he grows up. But a little girl is told what she wants to be. The cynical commercial exploitation of sex-drive in our own day by the advertising world is evidence enough of the point Tolstoy is making: that wants and beliefs can be foisted on people to the point where it is impossible to conceive of any alternative.

A third fundamental question raised by Tolstoy, which again anticipates some very recent thinking on the subject is the increase in anxiety-states paradoxically brought about by advances in medical science, particularly in respect of the mother's attitude to her children. In every instance, what Tolstoy is attacking is some subtle form of propaganda, brain-washing, manipulation, or exploitation. Behind the whole argument is the detestation of the idea that one human being should be used by another for his own purposes.

Such, then, are the main general questions raised in the novel and by the novel, but it does not seem to me that these are what the story is about.

For one thing, they are reflections, meditations, the attempts at an intellectual understanding of his situation by a man who has been brought by a catastrophe to question the whole foundation of his life. Pozdnyshev raises the questions, but does not claim he has the answers; he is merely, in trying to make sense of his experience, shaking his and our own basic convictions. We have to try to set aside our knowledge that for a time Tolstoy himself preached complete chastity as the goal for human beings, though he modified his doctrines sensibly enough later on. The conclusions of the novel are Pozdnyshev's and given the kind of man he presents himself to be and the situation he is in, they are the kinds of conclusions which are natural and credible. He presents himself as insanely jealous, and sees the jealousy as the immediate cause of the disaster. The foundation of the jealousy, however, he detects in his 'swinishness'; that is, he attributes the jealousy to his innate sexual drive which causes him to view women as its goal, or object. The drive is 'swinish' because it has caused him to regard a human being as a

2. See *Psycho-analysis Observed*, edited by Charles Rycroft (Constable, 1966); especially the contribution by Geoffrey Gorer, "Psycho-analysis in the World"

thing, a thing which exists only for the purpose of gratifying him. Because he finds that the thing is not his exclusively, but has a being of its own, he kills it in a fit of jealous rage. When he becomes aware of the cause of his state of mind, he wishes naturally enough to obliterate the cause, to discredit the sexual drive.

> "I wouldn't take a young man to a lock-hospital to knock the hankering after women out of him, but into my soul, to see the devils that were rending it! What was terrible, you know, was that I considered myself to have a complete right to her body, as if it were my own, and yet at the same time I felt I could not control that body, that it was not mine and she could dispose of it as she pleased and that she wanted to dispose of it, not as I wished her to."

When a man has been brought suddenly to realise the essential otherness of a human being, the truth that it has a sacred centre of selfhood which has no reference to his own, is it inconceivable that he should wish to destroy that impulse in his nature which has prevented him from recognising this otherness? The tragedy is that Pozdnyshev realised the otherness of his wife only when he destroyed her. Is it inconceivable that his horror at the deed his blindness has brought him to should tempt him to generalise his experience and hold it up as a warning? The generalisation, the articulate moralising, it should be noticed, occur in the story up to Chapter 18, before the advent of the musician into the narrative and the account of the disaster that ensued. That is, they are not allowed to break the unity of the central events, yet they are not only a consequence of these, but a preparation for our understanding of them. It is difficult to agree with George Steiner's objection (in *Tolstoy or Dostoevski?*) that the moral elements have become too massive to be absorbed into the narrative structure. They seem to me to have been placed in the narrative structure exactly where they ought to be.

But to come now to the connection of the novel with the music, to its artistic organisation.

Tolstoy's interest in music had developed early in his life and it is clear that he was particularly open to its influence. He regarded it, his daughter tells us, as a divine manifestation of the human soul; it heightened his creative powers and loosed a flood of images. One would expect Pozdnyshev to be conscious of its voluptuousness, and he tells us that he is. There is a reason to believe Tolstoy responded to music in the same way as his hero.

When he was nineteen, Tolstoy wrote down in his preposterous program of self-education: (8) "Achieve the highest degree of accomplishment in music and painting."

He did, in fact, become an accomplished pianist and made up his mind at one stage to become a great musician and composer. He was carried away by the combination of sounds, and attempted to formulate his own theory of harmony, under the title *The Fundamentals of Music and Rules for its Study*. As far as composers were concerned, Beethoven seems to have inspired in him a kind of love-hate relationship; perhaps he resented Beethoven's power to carry him out of himself. There is no doubt, then, of Tolstoy's response to music, of his initial competence to find something in a piece of music which others had missed. And there is no doubt that he was well acquainted with the formal structure of music.

We must now look briefly at the formal structure which immediately concerns us. The word 'sonata' in general refers to instrumental music arranged usually in three or four movements in different rhythms at different speeds; for instance, fast, slow, fast, sometimes with a brief, slow introduction. As a rule, there is a return during the last movement to the key of the first one. Beethoven's sonatas, according to Scholes,[3] are characterised by strong dramatic feeling, intense emotion, and violent contrasts of moods and emotion. On this last point, Beethoven's appeal for Tolstoy is obvious enough. Violent contrast is the groundwork of Tolstoy's being, as it is of Pozdnyshev's. Like his creator, Pozdnyshev is tormented by the warring impulses of the flesh and the spirit; their nature is a battle-ground; the only defence against the unsubduable flesh is to crucify it, only to find that this cannot be done without injury to the spirit. This constant yearning for a resolution, it seems to me, may have been what Tolstoy heard in the dialogue of piano and violin in the sonata.

As to dramatic feeling, Pozdnyshev's long monologue is dramatic if anything in Tolstoy ever was. This is a quality which is usually denied him; his genius, we are told, lies in his analytic power. But Pozdnyshev's monologue is a whole drama in itself; he is not only there carrying on his civil war in himself, but he evokes his wife, her presence, the tones of her voice, her appearance, as vividly as if she were present in the story as an actual antagonist. Tolstoy's artistic achievement in the person of Pozdnyshev reminds us of the great mimes, or diseurs of the stage. He peoples his setting for us with the figures of the wife, of the violinist Trukhashevsky, the guests, the servants, the children, the people in the railway carriage in his own nightmare journey within a journey. The last is a tour-de-force in atmosphere compression: the device of the journey within a journey doubles for us all the suspense, the sense of impotence, of doom, of suffocating claustrophobia, that the whole marriage relationship has meant for Pozdnyshev. The figure of the passive narrator who introduces the story performs the function of intermediary, distancing us from the central figure, preventing us from identifying with him and from identifying the author with the character. To have

3. See *Oxford Companion to Music*, by Percy Scholes.

Pozdnyshev 'confess' direct into our ears would have meant the loss of detachment which is crucial to understanding.

The value of the sonata form as a vehicle for the expression of strong personal emotion and its relationship to the novel in this respect is too obvious to mention. Its function is analogous to that of the dramatic monologue in verse and the novel is as near to that as it could be without being written in verse. To choose a normal third-person form with the conventional omniscient narrator would have been impossible.

These, it is clear enough, are large general relationships between the music and the novel. But I think there are others. The story seems to me to have three clearly marked rhythmic divisions which deserve the name of movements, and in addition to that, to have three less emphatic, but still marked movements within each of the larger ones. The tempo pattern is the same as that of the sonata, i.e. fast, slow, fast, but the whole is preceded by a short, slow introduction. The first big division in the story occurs at the end of Chapter 12, or with the beginning of Chapter 13. The pause is the more clearly marked because there is an interruption in the narrative. "Two fresh passengers entered . . ." There is still a sense of the outside world. Pozdnyshev has not yet retreated into his own nightmare territory.

The subject of the first movement concerns the general notion of solicitation between the sexes and the particular instance of this in Pozdnyshev's own courtship, wedding and honeymoon. As in the sonata, there are false starts, the subject is introduced, dropped, hinted at, in the reference to the Kunavin Fair, the lady's conversation with the lawyer and so on. Chapters 1 and 2 are a kind of overture or introduction to the theme, laying down the lines of the problem: the old man is the voice of tradition, the lawyer and the lady represent the new thought. These are quickly eliminated, for neither is capable of much insight, and the real subject is then undertaken by Pozdnyshev and his interlocutor. Pozdnyshev at first is dominant, the narrator parries the questions he raises, and Pozdnyshev finally becomes the narrator.

The second movement of the novel concerns the married life of Pozdnyshev and his wife; the begetting and rearing of their children and above all the growth of Pozdnyshev's irrational jealousy, exacerbated by the freedom acquired by his wife when she ceases to bear children. The jealousy motif is the dominant one, reflected in the husband's struggle to impose his will on his wife, in his growing intolerance, his impulses of violence. Each is contending for power, or rather, each is striving to be free from the dominance of the other, like two hostile convicts chained together.

It is important to notice that there are no further interruptions in this movement from the outside world. In Chapter 17, Pozdnyshev gets up and leaves the carriage for a moment, but he returns and the sense of constriction deepens and is sustained until the end.

The movement ends in Chapter 19, with the introduction of the change in the wife's situation, the complete breach between them, the wife's renewed interest in music and the heralding of the entrance of the musician, Trukhachevski.

Before he is introduced to the wife, there is a direct example of the kind of situation prevailing between husband and wife, an episode of violence full of the menace of destruction, which sets the seal on their separation. The final movement is the physical counterpart of the psychic murder enacted here; indeed, in a sense, this psychic murder (prepared for earlier)[4] is the "real" murder, and the physical one an irrelevance, or at least an anti-climax. The delay between the announcement of the musician theme and its full development is a masterly stroke, enabling Tolstoy to re-introduce the notion of death (in the quarrel scene), so that it is associated with the musician theme. 'I wish you were dead as a dog!' Pozdnyshev shouts in a rage. The sentence orients our minds in the necessary direction, and then our attention is distracted by the new interest.

Chapter 20 heralds the prevailing mood of the final movement. The frenzy increases, the tempo is speeded up, there are no more interruptions until just before the catastrophe. The pivot of the movement is the sonata itself. It is prepared for by the discussion on music and its connection in the speaker's mind with the subject of adultery. There is a gradual crescendo of jealousy and the catastrophe in Chapter 27 is the actual murder. In Chapters 25 and 26 occur two more strokes of genius: the effect of the conductor's entering, putting out the candle, without supplying a fresh one and leaving the two travellers in half-darkness releases the unbearable tension for a moment before Tolstoy gives a final twist to the screw. The gesture also has strong symbolic overtones relating to the deed that is coming perhaps, but also relating to the argument itself. The story has been told so far in the semi-darkness of night; what is to follow is told in the half-daylight. That is, confession has gone as far as it can go, the problem has been laid bare, but there is no real illumination, only the half-light possible to a mind that is relieved of a burden, but not renewed in hope. The sense of tension and suspense is accentuated at the beginning of Chapter 26 by the words "At the last station but one, when the conductor had been to collect the tickets . . ." This time, of course, it is Pozdnyshev's journey home that is referred to, not the one he is engaged in at the moment of speaking. The sentence produces an effect of momentary hesitation, the last chance of a change of heart before the final action, before automatism sets in and the agent is swallowed up in the action itself. The same kind of hesitation occurs at the moment of the murder, resolved by the words "Fury has its laws . . ."

4. Compare also the passage in Chapter 13 (*The Kreutzer Sonata*, World's Classics edition, translated by Aylmer Maude) beginning: "They asked me at the trial with what and how I killed her. Fools! They thought I killed her with a knife . . ."

The description of the murder is accomplished with all the uncanny kinesthetic precision of which Tolstoy is the supreme master. Before he has finished, the reader has the physical sensation of having committed the act himself. The scene rivals in this respect the one in *War and Peace* where a young man stands on the window-ledge of a high building drinking a bottle of brandy, a scene which produces an actual sensation of vertigo.

The last Chapter, 28, rounds off the third movement in the manner of a coda. It sustains the violence and passion of the main subject of the movement, comments on it and then returns us to the mood of the opening of the story, the silent grief, the intense isolation, the utterly hopeless loneliness which is Pozdnyshev's inescapable lot. I am not suggesting that the structure of the story corresponds exactly with the structure of Beethoven's sonata, or that the music has any literary meaning. In any case, Tolstoy, or rather Pozdnyshev, was interested only in the first movement, particularly the Presto. But I think it does correspond to the general sonata form. And I think also that the first movement taken alone can be shown to have particular significance for the theme of the story.

It is interesting to remember that the performance that fired Tolstoy's imagination was given by two young men. In the story, the violin is given to a man, the piano to a woman. It is not possible to know what the music of the first movement suggested to Tolstoy, but I do not think it is too fanciful to suppose that it suggested first of all a dialogue between a man and a woman, and I should myself suggest that the dialogue continued into the second movement in the form of an argument, or a struggle for supremacy. In the first movement, the musical dialogue is a kind of mutual solicitation, at first mere flirtation, then developing seriously. The violin opens the movement, slowly and hesitantly; the piano replies in a restrained manner; there are modulations and hesitations, a feeling of suspense is created, then the subject is opened up with sudden determination. It is interrupted, and a fresh start is made. A great deal of use is made of a rising semitone—almost an interrogative—and one is forcibly reminded of the passage in which Pozdnyshev's wife and the violinist play together for the first time. "From the first moment his eyes met my wife's I saw that the animal in each of them, regardless of all conditions of their position and of society asked 'May I?' and answered 'Oh yes, certainly!' " In both Russian and English, the language is used merely to convey the meaning of the facial expression, the interrogation of the eyes, and this meaning is the same in all languages and is a possible way of interpreting the music. The whole of the opening Adagio suggests, or could suggest, the preliminary skirmishing, the retreats, vague fears, agitations and hesitations of a passion which wishes to declare itself and may not, and this situation is the one in which Pozdnyshev's wife and the musician find themselves: the Adagio is recapitulated, that is to say, in the third movement of Tolstoy's story, when the Musician theme is getting under way.

The Presto of the sonata is devoted to a following up of the initial advantage, the violin is the dominating instrument, the inviting instrument; the piano changes key and sidesteps the issue. There is an extraordinary progressive ascending movement at the end, which strongly suggests a dragging away by force; there is a significant silence, a kind of consent, and a haunting passage which could suggest shame, and the movement ends with a burst of passion from both instruments, with the violin in control.

Though it is impossible to know precisely the nature of the feeling the sonata produced in Tolstoy or his creation Pozdnyshev, both were profoundly stirred by the music and reacted strongly to it, while Pozdnyshev, we know, associated this, the noblest of the arts, with adultery, with voluptuousness. In Chapter 23, the playing of the sonata is introduced in this way: "His face grew serious, stern and sympathetic, and listening to the sounds he produced, he touched the strings with careful fingers. The piano answered him. The music began . . ." The overtones of the last two or three phrases are obvious. Then Pozdnyshev continues:

> "Ugh, ugh, it is a terrible thing that sonata. And especially that part (i.e. the Presto). And in general music is a dreadful thing. What is it? I don't understand it. What is music, what does it do? And why does it do what it does? They say music exalts the soul. Nonsense! It is not true! It has an effect, an awful effect—I am speaking of myself—but not of an exalting kind. It has neither an exalting nor a debasing effect, but it produces an agitation . . . it transports me to some other position not my own. I can do what I cannot do."

Pozdnyshev goes on to elaborate its power of sympathetic magic, its hypnotic effect. What is clear about these two passages when they are read in full is that the feeling evoked by the sonata at the beginning changes before that movement ends. What had begun by disturbing and disgusting Pozdnyshev is submerged in a new revelation. In which, the alternative version says, jealousy had no place. It is as though the sonata, while revealing to him the nature of the relationships between men and women, also began to reveal to him that other relationships were possible besides those commonly taken for granted. Debate, argument, dialogue between two instruments can perhaps be fused into one perfect harmonious statement, in which each instrument instead of aping the other, is allowed to speak for itself, just as the two warring impulses in Pozdnyshev himself, the sensual and the aspiring, the earth and the spirit, might perhaps come to a composition, instead of each striving to eliminate the other.

Nothing comes of it, of course. Pozdnyshev has prepared us for the fact. Music belongs to another dimension: 'It makes me forget my real position; it transports me to some other position not my own.' But the suggestion of other possibilities is implanted and it is these presumably that rise to the surface, when in the act of destroying his wife, Pozdnyshev first realises that she has an independent existence.

> "I looked at the children and at her bruised disfigured face and for the first time I forgot myself, my pride, and for the first time saw a human being in her. And so insignificant did all that had offended me, all my jealousy appear and so important what I had done, that I wished to fall with my face to her hand, and say: 'Forgive me,' but dared not do so."

The parallels with the sonata could I think be taken further than I have taken them, but they would require a minute musical analysis, for which there is no space here. Easier to indicate is the parallel of the general effect produced by each on the listener, or reader. And the reader of this novel, should be in a very real sense a listener. We need to remind ourselves again that Tolstoy conceived his story with the living voice of an actor in his mind. That is, it was written, as the sonata was, for an instrument. The first movement of the sonata is disturbing, passionate and at times violent, and so is the story. What Tolstoy's music finally conveys to us is the sensation of torment, of pain, of a cry like St. Paul's: 'Who will deliver me from the body of this death?' The nearest thing in our own literature is the music of *Othello*, a play on much the same subject, the destructive power of a jealousy that comes from concentration on outward appearance instead of inner reality, on what can be received, rather than on what can be given.

But there is no Iago in Tolstoy's story. Pozdnyshev's Iago is an internal one, the terrible misconception in the soul that arises from a preoccupation with the ego and its wants, a misconception whose consequences are far harder to bear than those that flow from having been wrought upon.

A superficial interpretation of the story sees it perhaps as Tolstoy's ritual murder of his wife, an act of revenge committed after twenty-seven years of marriage upon a woman who had borne him thirteen children. His wife apparently saw it as such and never forgave him. But surely, if the story must be regarded as biography, is it not more than anything else an act of confession and reparation? The whole responsibility for his situation is taken by Pozdnyshev and placed upon men and upon himself as a representative man. Right through the story runs an impassioned plea for the inviolability of woman as a human being in her own right—the same kind of plea that Ibsen was making. All the terrible consequences are shown to flow from a failure to make this recognition, and Pozdnyshev constantly lacerates himself for his failure, which, he says, is caused by obsession with his own rights and pleasures. If the hero must be identified with his creator, then a whole identification must be made. The epigraph to the story suggests the lines along which we should think: Christ's words about lust. By extension the words apply to murder. Certainly the story may be regarded as Tolstoy's confession as well as Pozdnyshev's. But if we have read it right, it is a general confession. All of us who seek to use another human being without regard to his separateness are guilty of destroying him.

Most of us escape punishment. Pozdnyshev's, like Othello's, resulted from allowing his hand to execute the imagination of his heart. Both had to face the knowledge that the deed cannot be reversed, that to put out the light is final.

> "Only when I saw her dead face did I understand all that I had done. I realised that I, I, had killed her; that it was my doing that she, living, moving and warm, had now become motionless, waxen and cold, and that this could never, any-where, or by any means, be remedied . . ."

This is the haunting note the music of the story leaves with us, just as the music of *Othello* does. And wild regret and yearning, and tragic human longings occur in the sonata, though they are overlaid in the final movement by the pressures of formalism, dissipated in the con-ventions of the sonata form, just as the pressures of the outside world return in the story. And Pozdnyshev's punishment is that he has to go on living in the real world, possessed of the knowledge that he murdered not only his wife's body, but her essential being as well. Perhaps Othello was more fortunate.

STEPHEN BAEHR

Art and *The Kreutzer Sonata*: A Tolstoian Approach†

For Tolstoi art encompassed more than painting, poetry, novels, music, and sculpture. To his famous question "What is Art?" he replied with an extremely broad definition: art is the product resulting when "one person consciously communicates to others, by means of certain external signs, some feelings which he has experienced" in such a way that "others are infected by them and relive them for themselves" (XXX, 65).[1] In the treatise on art Tolstoi noted that people apply the term "art" to only a small proportion of its appearances and argued that "art, in

†From *Canadian-American Slavic Studies* 10 (Spring 1976) 1:39–46. Page references for quo-tations from pieces in this Norton Critical Edition are given in brackets.
1. All quotations in this article are from L. N.

Tolstoi, *Polnoe sobranie sochinenii, iubileinoe iz-danie*, 90 vols. (Moscow, 1928–1958). Volume and page references to this edition will be given in parentheses following quotations.

the broad sense of the word, penetrates our entire life" (XXX, 66). Although most of his essay discusses the more traditional types of art, Tolstoi suggests that art includes "any activity which communicates feelings" (XXX, 67) and any activity "by which we commune with each other" (*kotorym obshchaemsia mezhdu soboi*; XXX, 67). Tolstoi's definition thus extends art considerably beyond its traditional boundaries.

In *The Kreutzer Sonata* (1887–1889), Tolstoi seems to be exploring, perhaps unconsciously, some of the broad implications of this definition. The story, written while he was still at work on *What is Art?* (1882–1897), seems to extend his concept of art to human relationships, especially marriage.[2] I believe that the basic equation underlying the many parallels between the two works, providing a key to *The Kreutzer Sonata*, is that "life is art." In this paper I will explore these parallels in an attempt to reconstruct a possible "Tolstoian" interpretation of *The Kreutzer Sonata*.[3]

I

Throughout his treatise on art Tolstoi stresses that genuine art cannot be simply sensation and pleasure; he chides the upper classes of his time for their hedonistic "perversion of art" and states that any art that titillates, instead of communicating genuine emotions from one person to another, cannot but be "counterfeit." Tolstoi argues that "the absence of genuine art among the upper classes has had its inevitable consequence: the corruption of the class which has made use of that art" (XXX, 81).[4] In *The Kreutzer Sonata*, he illustrates this corruption by portraying the past life of Pozdnyshev, who is established as a typical member of the upper class, and whose marriage bears many similarities to Tolstoi's conception of counterfeit art. The dire consequences of this "counterfeit" marriage reflect Tolstoi's fears: "Among us people marry without seeing anything but copulation, and the result is either deception or violence" (XXVII,

2. The central role of art in Tolstoi's scheme for *The Kreutzer Sonata* is suggested by the fact that even in the untitled first draft, where the music plays no role, the adulterer was an "artist."

3. Parallels between "life" and "art" had occurred in earlier works by Tolstoi. Some of the clearest examples are in *Anna Karenina* (1873–1877), where the dilettante Vronskii dabbles at life and love in much the way that he dabbles at art, which he misunderstands and perverts; the true artist Mikhailov understands life, and his works thus have "that inexpressible complexity of everything that lives" (XIX, 41). John Bayley in *Tolstoy and the Novel* (New York, 1968) has noticed some of these parallels, observing that "there is a remarkable analogy, whether or not Tolstoy intended it, between his conceptions of what is bad in art and his presentation of what happens to Anna and Vronsky's love" (p. 235) and that "*Anna* puts Tolstoy's

view of art into a deeper and closer relation with the rest of life than does *What is Art?*" (p. 236). Bayley's chapter on "*Anna Karenina* and *What is Art?*" is very useful, although I believe that even more parallels between the two works can be observed. George Gibian in *Tolstoy and Shakespeare* (The Hague, 1957) points to Karenin's fondness for talking about Shakespeare, Raphael, and Beethoven—all of whom were later condemned by Tolstoi (p. 18). In short, the Tolstoian character who misunderstands "art" does not understand life.

4. Tolstoi saw the upper classes as the teachers of other classes and felt that upper-class corruption had inevitably caused the corruption of all classes. This point is made particularly clear in the first draft of *The Kreutzer Sonata*, when the old merchant says explicitly that "it was from them [the upper classes] that we learned it [lust]" (XXVII, 356).

15) [179]. As Pozdnyshev's name suggests, he becomes aware of this result too "late."

The marriage of the pleasure-seeking Pozdnyshev embodies the same three feelings that in *What is Art?* are said to characterize the counterfeit art of the upper classes—"pride," "lust," and "world gloom" (*toska zhizni*; XXX, 87). Like counterfeit art, his marriage is based on "the illusion that beauty is good" (*chto krasota est' dobro*; XXVII, 21) [184]—one of the basic problems which Tolstoi attempts to combat in *What is Art?* Like counterfeit art, the marriage aims solely at pleasure and therefore precludes the emotional communication and infection necessary to make marriage into "art": "Conversation was a Sisyphean task for us. . . . There was nothing to talk about. . . . If we had been animals then we would have known that we *were* expected to talk, and there was nothing to say because what we were concerned with was not the type of thing which gives rise to conversation" (XXVII, 27) [189]. Just as counterfeit art divides people and prevents their unity and equality, so does the marriage of the Pozdnyshevs lead to bitter hatred and mutual attempts to enslave one another.

The parallels between marriage and art extend to the imagery of the two works and are particularly apparent in the many images of sexual perversion and degeneracy used to characterize both counterfeit art and counterfeit marriage. For example, Tolstoi compares the counterfeit art of his time to a prostitute: "Genuine art, like the wife of a loving husband, does not need embellishment. Counterfeit art, like a prostitute, always needs to be embellished" (XXX, 178); in *The Kreutzer Sonata*, Pozdnyshev states that lives of the upper classes are "just one big house of prostitution" (XXVII, 23) [186] and that women of the upper classes attract their prey through sensuous clothes and actions like "prostitutes" (*ibid*). Pozdnyshev frequently calls himself a "lecher" (*bludnik*)—the masculine equivalent of the word *bludnitsa* used to describe counterfeit art (XXX, 178). In the essay on art, Tolstoi also compares counterfeit art to a woman who is unnaturally preventing the birth of a child by misusing her "capacities designed for motherhood" and compares true art to a child conceived in a climax of love (XXX, 178–179). In consonance with the patterns which I have been discussing, Pozdnyshev's wife learns the techniques of contraception and stops bearing children.

One explanation for the many parallels between counterfeit marriage and counterfeit art is reflected in Tolstoi's belief that both spring from a single cause—improper faith. In *What is Art?* he states: "One church father has said that the main problem of mankind is not that they do not know God, but that they have put in the place of God something which is not God. That is the problem with art as well" (XXX, 155). Similarly, Pozdnyshev claims that much of the torment of upper-class life results from the positing of faith not in God but in "priests of science"—doctors. "So when a child is sick, you must take him to the very best doctor, the one who saves. . . . And this is not a faith that is unique to my wife, it is the faith of all the women of her circle. . . . If she were fully a person then she would have had faith in God . . . and would have known that the power of life and death is beyond the control of man" (XXVII, 42) [202].

As the Satanic agent of improper faith, the doctor is the high priest of counterfeit art for Tolstoi. As Pozdnyshev states, "if we just followed their advice, then, thanks to infections (*zarazy*) everywhere, in everything, people could not move in the direction of unity but would be forced to move toward isolation" (XXVII, 39–40) [199]. The doctor thus works at cross-purposes to the best Tolstoian artist, who infects people with religious ideas and brings them together in unity. It is interesting that Tolstoi uses a form of the word "infection" to describe the functions of both artist and doctor. The opposition between these two professions is thus captured through a fitting *double entendre*: while the genuine artist unifies people by "infecting" them with emotion, the doctor moves people apart by *curing* "infection." The doctor thus prevents life from becoming "art."

II

For Tolstoi, esthetics and ethics were inseparable. Thus in *What is Art?* he discusses not only the esthetic categories of "real" and "counterfeit" art but also the ethical categories of "good" and "bad" art. As early as Chapter V in the treatise on art, he acknowledges that real art may be based on "the most varied feelings—the very strong and the very weak, the very significant and the very insignificant, *the very bad and the very good*; if only they infect the reader, spectator, or listener, then they constitute a work of art" (XXX, 65—emphasis mine). The moral quality of real art depends upon the feelings relived and communicated by the artist; when embodied in real art, feelings of little moral worth have as much potential impact on a reader, listener, or spectator as feelings of great moral value. The essay on art reflects Tolstoi's fears that bad art can lead even moral men to commit immoral acts, since, like all real art, it has the power to directly affect actions by infecting a person against his will and disconnecting his powers of reason and judgment.[5]

In *The Kreutzer Sonata*, the sinister power of bad art is illustrated in the performance of Beethoven's "Kreutzer Sonata" by Trukhachevskii and Pozdnyshev's wife—a musical liaison that legitimizes their sexual duets. The choice of a piece so agitating and violent is made by Tru-

5. Tolstoi's fear of the perverse power of bad art recalls Plato's views in *The Republic* (which are mentioned in ch. v of *What is Art?*). But unlike Plato, Tolstoi did not feel the necessity of banning art. Tolstoi believed that bad art would be eliminated when the quality of human feelings improved—an event which he felt would come about naturally. He felt that in a society in which the Church reflected the teachings of Christ, true art could act only morally, but in a society like his own, where the Church had "distorted and perverted" Christ's teachings, certain types of genuine art could do great damage.

khachevskii, who extends the principles of bad art into human life just as Pozdnyshev has extended the principles of counterfeit art. Trukhachevskii is said to be a good musician but an evil person—the perfect combination for the creation of bad art.[6] His powerful but malefic performance—whose central role is reflected in the title of Tolstoi's story—makes Pozdnyshev lose control of himself and causes the agitation which leads him to murder his wife.[7]

Pozdnyshev's description of the "Kreutzer Sonata" recalls Tolstoi's definition of genuine art, which has the power to "merge the [audience] with the artist" to such an extent that any feeling expressed in the art seems to be "the very thing that [they themselves have] been wanting to express for a long time" (XXX, 149). For example, Pozdnyshev states:

> Music immediately and spontaneously transports me into the state of mind of the person who was writing it. My soul merges with his and together with him I am borne from one state to another, but I don't know why I do this. Take the composer who wrote the "Kreutzer Sonata," Beethoven: he knew why he was in a particular state of mind, and this state led him to certain acts (*postupkam*), and therefore for him this state made sense. But for me it makes none. That's because music only rouses the senses, it does not end the rousing (*Muzyka tol'ko razdrazhaet, ne konchaet*; XXVII, 61) [218].

In short, the music clearly succeeds in "infecting" Pozdnyshev. But the central problem in Tolstoi's story is that the piece infects Pozdnyshev with the *wrong* kind of feelings, and makes him act immorally and irrationally, as if in a hypnotic trance.[8] Pozdnyshev comments: "Music makes me forget myself and my true situation; it carries me into a new situation that is not my own. Under the influence of music it seems to me that I am feeling things which I, myself, am not really feeling or

6. Tolstoi's distaste for Trukhachevskii is apparent from the character's name, deriving from *trukha* ("rot"—"the dust of rotted wood"). Gogol' had briefly introduced a character by this name in *Dead Souls* (Book I, ch. vii), calling him one of the "useless" people "who only cumber on earth." Tolstoi's Trukhachevskii has several other strikes against him, including his musical education in Paris (the domain of animals within the scheme of the story) and his "soft white hands" (a trait which he shares with such other negative characters as Karenin in *Ann Karenina* and Speranskii and Napoleon in *War and Peace*).

7. Like Yeats, Tolstoi seems to have had difficulty distinguishing "the dancer from the dance." He has Pozdnyshev attribute the horrible effects of the music entirely to Beethoven, although Pozdnyshev is really describing a *performance*. This reflects a weakness in Tolstoi's theory of art, which fails to give any consideration to the role of the performer in the artistic process. Presumably, Tolstoi is im-

plying that a performer must himself be infected by a work of art to such an extent that he merges with the composer or author and can communicate that person's feelings to others.

The blame for performing the "Kreutzer Sonata" is attributed entirely to Trukhachevskii, who supplies the music and plays the dominant role. Relatively little is said about the contribution of Pozdnyshev's wife.

8. In *What is Art?* Tolstoi had called Wagner's "counterfeit" art "hypnotic" (XXX, 139) but had not pursued the dangers of hypnotism in art. In *The Kreutzer Sonata*, Pozdnyshev does pursue this theme: "In China music is controlled by the state. And that's the way it should be. Can we really permit just anyone to hypnotize another person or many people and then do with them what he wants? And, most important of all, can we permit the first immoral person who comes along to be the hypnotist? If so, a frightening power would be in his hands" (XXVII, 61–62). [218]

that I can do things which I really cannot" (XXVII, 61) [217]. The "new" feelings which grip Pozdnyshev during the first movement of the "Kreutzer Sonata" make the murder (which he had considered before hearing the sonata but had rejected because he "knew that this was forbidden" [XXVII, 59] [216]) seem not only possible and moral but "pleasing."

Although the music is never explicitly linked with the murder, the implicit connections are quite strong. For example, Pozdnyshev states that pieces like the "Kreutzer Sonata" must be played at the right time and place for otherwise they can arouse "energy and feelings . . . that cannot but act destructively" (XXVII, 62) [218]. The destructiveness of this performance is made clear when Pozdnyshev says that "on me at least this piece acted horribly" (XXVII, 62) [218]. He even uses the musical term "crescendo" (the Italian word calling attention to itself in the Russian text) to describe his increasing agitation in the moments immediately preceding the murder. Thus it is probably not coincidental that the word "*strashnyi*" ("terrible," "frightening," "horrible") serves as a frequently repeated *leitmotif* for both the music and the murder or that Pozdnyshev's recounting of his premonition on the night before the murder ("something frightening and very important is going to happen to me") echoes his warning that pieces like the "frightening" "Kreutzer Sonata" must be played only when "important" actions (*postupki*—a word also used for the murder) require completion. In short, the murder illustrates Tolstoi's fear of the power of genuine art to make a person act against his will—a fear that applied especially to music, the art which Tolstoi said possesses by its very nature a "direct physical power over the nerves" (XXX, 117–118). The central action of Tolstoi's story thus illustrates the strong influence of art on human life and indicates why he spent so much effort to improve the feelings communicated by art.

III

Despite Pozdnyshev's damning description of his hellish past, there is a surprising note of optimism in *The Kreutzer Sonata*. Several times in his monologue he expresses distinct hope for the future, frequently using the phrase "the time will come" (*pridiot vremia*).[9] This optimism fully corresponds to Tolstoi's hopes for the future of art, illustrating the idea stated in *What is Art?* that the moral level of a class in any given period corresponds to the level of its art in that period.

Tolstoi believed that an "evolution of feelings" would bring about a new kind of art in the future, providing "a means of transferring Christian and religious consciousness from the realm of mind and reason to the realm of feeling" and thus bringing people together in "perfection and unity" (XXX, 185). Significantly, the function of this true religious art

9. This phrase expresses Tolstoi's hopes for the future in other works as well, including "The Kingdom of God is Within You."

will be "to eliminate violence—something which Tolstoi says that "only art can do" (XXX, 194). According to Tolstoi, art will eliminate "the debauchery of people in the most important concern of social life—the relationship between the sexes" and thus will end "the suicides and murders of lovers about which something is printed in almost every newspaper" (XXX, 174). In short, this new religious art will lead to the elimination of murders such as that committed by Pozdnyshev; it will accomplish this goal by infecting people in such a way that "the feelings of brotherhood and love . . . will become the habitual feelings and the instinct of all people" (XXX, 195).[1]

According to Tolstoi, the best art communicates religious feelings that are on the highest level for a given time; he felt that the best art of his own time communicated feelings of brotherhood and unity. Pozdny-shev's past life clearly destroyed these ideals. But, paradoxically, Pozdnyshev himself is now preaching them. Indeed, the discontinuity between these two very different aspects of Pozdnyshev suggests that we should speak of not one Pozdnyshev but two: the deceived mass man of the past who destroyed all ethical norms (Pozdnyshev I) and the enlight-ened individual of the present who has undergone a "moral transfor-mation" and now sees and preaches Tolstoian truth (Pozdnyshev II).[2] The moralizing Pozdnyshev II attempts to bias the stick-figure narrator (and hence the reader) against the sins of his past by reliving his past feelings with (and for) him. In the process, Pozdnyshev II comes to satisfy all of Tolstoi's criteria for the genuine artist.

Pozdnyshev II's vivid recollections of past feelings so infect the narrator that he copies the words verbatim—a sufficient basis for "genuine art" in Tolstoi's scheme. Like all genuine art, these feelings are "new" (as is reflected in the many comments of the narrator that "all this was new and astounded me"); as in all genuine art, communication results from an "inner need to express feelings" (XXX, 150), as Pozdnyshev II states when he remarks that "it is painful for me to remain silent" (XXVII,

1. Since for Tolstoi the level of art has major im-pact on all social relationships, this new genuine art will presumably lead to the triumph of "gen-uine" marriage. While Pozdnyshev hints the com-ing of such a marriage, he makes relatively few explicit comments about it. However, from his remarks, it is clear that the genuine marriage would be based on a communication of feelings rather than on the pursuit of pleasure and would ideally be a relationship of continence. It would lead to "a unity of ideals, a spiritual affinity" (words used by one of the characters in the initial conversation in the railway car [XXVII, 14]) [179] and "a Chris-tian love, a brotherly love stronger than stone walls" (words used by one of the characters in the first draft of the work [XXVII, 358]). Pozdnyshev says that this type of marriage already exists "among those people who see in marriage something sa-cred, a sacrament that is binding before God" (XXX, 195) and implies that it will become more

widespread as people understand the errors of their pleasure-seeking relationships. Tolstoi saw art as a means of helping people to reach this understanding.

2. Unlike Tolstoi's other works depicting a "moral transformation" (such as "The Death of Ivan Il'ich" and "Master and Man"), *The Kreutzer So-nata* takes place entirely *after* the transformation has occurred. This results in an unusual narrative structure, presenting a simultaneous "double vi-sion" of a character both before and after trans-formation. Although our attention is focused on Pozdnyshev I throughout much of the story, all of our information is filtered through Pozdnyshev II. This "double vision" accounts for much of the ambiguity of the story and has led many critics to see Pozdnyshev as entirely negative—the result of identifying the negative Pozdnyshev I with the nar-rating Pozdnyshev II.

16) [180]. Like the best true art this tale (which the narrator calls a *rasskaz*—which can mean a "short story" [XXVII, 78] [232]) is based upon the highest "religious consciousness" of the time.

In view of the overwhelmingly negative nature of these recollections, it may seem somewhat unusual to claim that they constitute a work of art or that Pozdnyshev II emerges as an artist. But in *What is Art?* Tolstoi clearly indicates that the best religious art can be either "positive" or "negative." Like negative religious art, these recollections express an "indignation, a horror at the destruction of love" (XXX, 159–160); they belong to the "poetry of love for one's neighbor" and the "poetry of abstinence" (*poeziia tselomudriia*) which Tolstoi had named and applauded in Chapter X of the essay on art (XXX, 110).

Pozdnyshev II meets all Tolstoi's criteria for the true artist: he has the ability to "relive" his past feelings and is strongly infected by them himself (as is seen in the strange, choke-like sound that he involuntarily emits at crucial points in the narrative); he is able to recount characteristic details of these past feelings (details which seem almost excessive when judged by non-Tolstoian standards); and he understands the problems of his time. This last criteria is probably the most important for Tolstoi and is stressed frequently in *The Kreutzer Sonata* through comments like the following:

> I do have one attribute. I have knowledge. Yet, it is true that I know things which will not be known by the average person for a long time (XXVII, 40) [200]. Only having suffered as I suffered, only as a result of this have I understood the root of everything, understood what should be and therefore seen the whole horror of what exists (XXVII, 17) [181].

In short, Pozdnyshev II fulfills Tolstoi's dictum that the true artist "must stand on the level of the highest world view of his time, must relive a feeling and have the desire and the means to communicate it, and must have talent for some form of art" (XXX, 119).[3] Unlike Pozdnyshev I, who had been "like all the others of his circle," Pozdnyshev II is described by the narrator as "a man apart" (*osobniak*)—the typical position of the artist; unlike Pozdnyshev I, who had been characterized by the phrases "I did not know," and "I did not understand," the new Pozdnyshev says "I know" and "I understand."

Of course, as readers, we must decide whether to accept the words of Pozdnyshev II at face value. In most modern first-person fiction, the repetition of phrases like "I know" and "I understand" signals the presence of irony. But *The Kreutzer Sonata* is decidely unmodern; there is none of the separation between narrator and character which creates irony. Thus although it is at first somewhat tempting to interpret

---

3. Pozdnyshev possesses "talent" in the Tolstoian sense of the word—"the ability to easily express his thoughts and impressions and to observe and recall characteristic details" (XXX, 119).

Pozdnyshev's comment that he is "something like a madman" (*ved' ia vrode sumasshedshego*) literally and to assume that his claim that he knows the truth represents not art but madness, this solution is not satisfactory.[4] For if he is mad, his madness is "Tolstoian," like that of the character in *Notes of a Madman* (1884), whose madness begins when he rejects his upper-class life and begins to feel love for all men, no matter what their class. Like Tolstoi's other "madman," Pozdnyshev II is a person who feels love for his fellow man in a society where sanity and self-interest are equated. Like the other "madman" the reformed Pozdnyshev II, having once lost his way, has now found the right path. For Tolstoi such "madness" is the stuff of art.

In sum, Pozdnyshev II, driven by an inner need to recount the errors of his past, bears many similarities to Tolstoi's genuine artist and like his prototype becomes, in effect, a teacher, helping others to benefit from his understanding.[5] Like the new Tolstoian artist, Pozdnyshev II is not a professional but simply a man driven by an inner need to spread the "Good News" of brotherly love and unity.[6] His transformation illustrates Tolstoi's hope that just as Pozdnyshev I had once been "like all of the people of his circle," so in the future will all of these people become like Pozdnyshev II and transform their lives into "art."

N. K. MIKHAYLOVSKY

Master and Man and *The Death of Ivan Ilych*†

How does one preserve life without the thought of death that poisons one's existence? How does one burn out, destroy this fear of death that, as we have seen, "is put into everyone?" This is Tolstoy's main task lately. Although it concerned him before, now he is exclusively concerned with it, and all his writings are merely peripheral to it, connecting the various points of his outlook with this fear of death at its center.

---

4. One problem with the conclusion that Pozdnyshev is mad (in the current, pejorative sense of the word), is that he seems to be preaching Tolstoian doctrine. Thus the conclusion that he is mad would either imply the same for his begetter or would indicate that Tolstoi was parodying his own ideas. Neither alternative seems viable.

5. A similar conclusion could be drawn for certain other positive Tolstoian characters. One of the best examples is Platon Karataev in *War and Peace*, who communicates his zest for life to Pierre Bezukhov in such a way as to infect him with a similar zest. Platon has the ability to see something new even in the most familiar circumstances and to clearly communicate his feelings to others. Thus he is able to repeat a familiar tale in such a way that Pierre feels rapture at every retelling (*War and* *Peace*, Book XIV). If life is "art" for Tolstoi, it is not surprising that certain positive characters who understand life satisfy his criteria for the genuine artist.

6. On the new, nonprofessional artist, see ch. XIX of *What is Art?* Like this new Tolstoian artist, the resurrected Pozdnyshev preaches true Christian doctrine, as emphasized by his frequent paraphrasing of Christ's words (especially the precepts of Matthew V and XIX, which are used as epigraphs to the story).

†From *Critical Essays on Tolstoy*, ed. E. Wasiolek (Boston, 1986). Reprinted with permission of the translator, Edward Wasiolek. Originally from *Otkliki* 2 (St. Petersburg: Russkoe bogatstvo, 1904): 63–68. Translated by Boris Sorokin.

All of his discussions of physical labor, about "harness," pure air of the fields and woods, and other hygienic features of his moral doctrine belong here in the first place. However these things merely guarantee health and longevity, death is only postponed, while still remaining the dreadful, inevitable end. Couldn't it be made at least not so dreadful? For this there is a prescription, already worked out to perfection by the Buddhists: without repudiating life, one must reduce its budget as much as possible, so that when one reaches the inevitable end, one can pass without fear and regret into that area of nirvana, which, strictly speaking, is neither life nor death. If this is so, then the end may be not only free of fear but not even inevitable. I refuse to follow the fantastic leap of thought or the just as fantastic crawl of the willowy syllogisms with which Tolstoy arrives at the conclusion that the right kind of life will preserve us from death. I will merely remind the reader of the ending of *The Death of Ivan Ilych*. This ending is, artistically, an unpleasant blot on the story—to such a degree it is arbitrary, unmotivated, lacking in that bright and pitilessly authentic realism Tolstoy is justly famous for. Ivan Ilych didn't do anything particularly bad, but lived his entire life as a limp, shallow egotist and, having fallen ill, began to suffer from the fear of death. But just before the very end, having realized that his wife and son are really feeling sorry for him, becomes imbued with pity and love himself.

> And suddenly it became clear to him that what had been oppressing him and would not leave him was all coming out suddenly, and from both sides, from ten sides, and from all sides. He felt sorry for them, felt the need to do something so that they would not suffer; to free them, and himself as well, from this suffering. "How nice and how simple," he thought. "And the pain?" he queried himself, "Where shall I put it?" "So, where are you, pain?"
>
> He turned his attention to it.
>
> "Ah, here it is. Well, what of it? Let the pain be."
>
> "And death? Where is it?"
>
> He was looking for his former habitual fear of death and could not find it. "Where is it? What death?" There was no fear, because there was no death. Instead of death there was light.
>
> "So that's what it is!" he suddenly said out loud. "What joy!"

I think that this exclamation "What joy!" must strike any artistically somewhat sensitive person as a dissonant note that pains the ear. And if such a great artist like Tolstoy introduced this false chord into his story, then it must have been because he was so very eager to show that death may not be so dreadful after all, that it may not even exist. He is trying to console us as well as himself here. We appreciate it, of course. We thank him, particularly, for saying that in order to conquer the fear of death one needs to practice not just Buddhist asceticism but love, active love, love in the form of good deeds, even though this love might have been presented as having another, more solid and less speculative basis.

Ivan Ilych didn't do anything very bad, he lived more or less like everybody: went to work, played cards, went visiting, and had people come to his house, had a wife and a son with whom he more or less got along. But it was only at the very end that a spark of real love ignited in him that hitherto had had almost no chance to express itself in a good deed. But even that was enough to free Ivan Ilych from the fear of death and make him partake of a joyous death, even an absence of death. In this new story, "Master and Man," Tolstoy apparently makes a considerably greater demand upon one of his protagonists in terms of active love.

I said earlier that the new story reminds one of Tolstoy's peak years of literary production. One newspaper account even had it that "this story is a masterpiece even among the works of the famous writer himself." This, I believe, is going a little too far. The same paper asserted that the story was "almost four signatures long." This is not true: the story is less than two and a half signatures long, and if in reading it someone has felt that it was almost twice as long, then we have here a clear indication of one of the shortcomings of Tolstoy's new work: it is stretched too much with numerous and unnecessary details. It does remind one of Tolstoy's peak years, but that's all it does. The inner suspense of the story is concentrated in the last two chapters, which I shall quote here fully, especially since they are, artistically, the best too. As already mentioned, the master and man went in winter to take care of the master's pretty ordinary, everyday, yet not quite clean business, typical of the sort of man he was. To conduct this business the master, a well fed, rich, self-satisfied peasant-businessman and sweatshop owner who, by the way, was also a church warden, took along a sum of 2,300 rubles belonging to the church. Along the way they got lost and, after a number of misadventures, the man realized that he was freezing to death and was about to submit uncomplainingly to the will of the higher power. Meanwhile the selfish master decided to leave him to perish, while he himself rode away on horseback wherever the horse would take him. But the horse, after having circled aimlessly a few times, brought him back to the same place where his man was slowly freezing to death in the sleigh. In order to get warm, he lies down on the man's body and warms him up in this way. In his own terminal delirium he imagines that:

And he lay on the bed, still unable to rise, waiting, and the waiting filled him with dread and also with joy. And suddenly his joy was complete: the one he was waiting for came, and it was not the policeman, Ivan Matveich, but someone else, but it was the one he was waiting for. He came and is calling him, and the one who is calling him is the same one who told him to lie on top of Nikita. And Vasilii Andreich is glad that this someone has come for him. "I'm coming!" he shouts joyfully. And his own shout wakes him up . . .

And he wakes up, but now he is a different person from who he was when he fell asleep. He wants to get up but can't; wants to move his arm, and can't; his leg, too, would not move. He wants to turn his head, and can't do that either. And he feels surprise but is not in the least worried about this. He understands that this is death, but this does not worry him in the least either. He understands that Nikita is lying underneath him and that he is now warm and alive, and it begins to seem to him that he himself is Nikita, and Nikita is him, and that his own life is now not in him but in Nikita. He strains his hearing and hears Nikita breathing, even snoring faintly. "Nikita is alive, therefore I am alive too," he says triumphantly to himself. And something quite new, a feeling that he never knew all his life, is now descending upon him.

And he remembers all about his money, his shop, his house, buying and selling, and the Mironov millions, and he is now at a loss to understand why this man whom they call Vasilii Brekhunov used to do all those things he was doing. "Well, he did not really know what was what, that's why," he thought about Vasilii Brekhunov. He didn't, but now I know. I know for sure that I *know now*. And again he hears the one who is calling him, and his whole being responds joyfully, "Coming, coming!" And he feels that he is now free and that nothing keeps him back any more.

And indeed, Vasilii Andreich neither saw nor heard not felt anything any more in this world.

. . . .

But Nikita died only this year—at home, as he wished, lying below the icons and with a burning wax candle in his hands. Before he died he asked forgiveness of his wife, and forgave her her affair with the cooper; he also took leave of his son and his grandchildren, and died, genuinely glad that his death relieves his son and daughter-in-law of the need to feed an extra mouth, and that now he really was passing from this wearisome life into that other life which with each passing year and hour had become for him more and more compre-

hensible and attractive. Is he better or worse off in that place
where he awoke after this his real death? Was he disappointed,
or did he find there whatever he expected? That we shall all
soon know.

So there we have two more deaths (not counting the horse) in Tolstoy's
rich collection. The master's death strongly reminds one of the death
of St. Julian the Hospitalier in a well known legend by Flaubert, translated by Turgenev. St. Julian, too, lies down on a dying man in order
to warm him, and, dying himself, also feels "an abundance of happiness,
a superhuman joy." In his terminal delirium the person of the leper
whom he was warming, also fuses with the higher being who, admittedly,
does not call on St. Julian to join him but directly carries him off into
the wide blue yonder. The master is not guilty of any of those terrible
sins and evil deeds that burden St. Julian's soul, but on the other hand,
St. Julian atones for his sins by years of achievement, and his final
selfless deed is merely the last link in a chain, which lends the story a
naturalness insofar as this is possible in a legend. The master, on the
other hand, did not spill any blood, like St. Julian, nor did he kill his
parents, yet he was a crook and probably responsible for the ruination
of dozens of people in order to advance his own well being. Let us say,
all this can be atoned for by his last minutes, but it seems to me that
only one of two things is possible: if the master saved his man unconsciously, inadvertently, hoping to save himself by warming himself with
the man's body, then this is hardly a self-sacrifice, and the moral value
of the master's last few minutes is not great; but if he really did forget
about himself and his only thought was to save the man, then this would
seem to be too sudden a turnaround, too unmotivated an act—since
only a short time before he was ready to betray and abandon the man
to his fate in order to save himself. The "joyous" death that St. Julian
earned, the master got as a real bargain: with an almost unconscious
and in any case semi-conscious deed, the result of which was a rescue
of his fellow man immediately after a heartless deed toward this selfsame
fellow man. And yet his deed is somewhat more substantial than the
terminal flareup of love in Ivan Ilych. As regards the man, Nikita, here
we have an uncomplicated man, hardly a saint, a drunkard, but a
goodnatured one, servile and hardworking, nonresistant to evil and completely satisfied with his lot, as opposed to his master who wants more
and more money, no one knows why. Nikita knows that besides the
"master" in the story he also has another "Master" in heaven, whose
will be done. So, these are, then, the two roads that lead to a joyous
death. . . .

As any other work of Tolstoy, his new story lends itself to drawing
several conclusions from it, besides the main one concerning death;
among others, one may, for example, conclude that it is better to be a

man than a master. This conclusion would not be news for Tolstoy. In one of his fairy tales, "Ilias," the man and his wife, who used to be masters themselves, praise their present status. They say: "For fifty years we were looking for happiness and did not find it, and only now, for the second year that we are left with nothing and live as laborers, have we found real happiness and don't need any other . . . We used to live from one worry to another, one sin unto another, and saw no happiness in life . . . Now we get up, chat a little with each other lovingly, always agreeing, have nothing to argue about, nothing to worry. All we need to think about is how to serve the master." I'm afraid that neither masters nor men will believe Tolstoy.

RICHARD GUSTAFSON

[On *Ivan Ilych* and *Master and Man*]†

*   *   *

The Death of Ivan Ilych (1886), Tolstoy's first major fiction after *Anna Karenina*, is a story of sin and suffering and death, and therefore it is a tale of the loss and recovery of love and a narrative of "mortal life." It is an emblem of dying. The work opens with the announcement of Ivan Ilych's death, but the first chapter focuses on Peter Ivanovich, Ivan Ilych's "closest" friend, the one for whom "everything is too far away." Peter Ivanovich does not know "what meaning this death could have" nor "what he must do." In the face of death he reacts to others in his routine manner: he grasps at the opportunity to fill the "place" vacated by their departure. The task of life for him is the quest for a bigger and better place, regardless of others, and in this he resembles all others. On this resemblance all friendship indeed is founded, for these people are the ones who like each other because they are alike. They share the belief that life must be "pleasant" and "proper," that one does what others do and likes what others like, and life for them is the striving to be alike in order to be liked. They live for others in order to live for themselves. When Peter Ivanovich reads a message of contentment on his dead friend's face, he does not understand that Ivan Ilych has accomplished his mission, because he is solely concerned with his own behavior. When he hears from Ivan Ilych's wife the details of suffering and dying, he thinks not of his friend but of himself and goes off to play cards. Peter Ivanovich is the one who is distant even when close, whose task of life is the quest for another place, not the quest for his task in his place and who, instead of remembering death, plays cards. He does

†From *Leo Tolstoy: Resident and Stranger* (Princeton, 1986). Reprinted with permission of Princeton University Press.

not know how to live or love and death for him is terrifying. He resembles most Ivan Ilych.

Ivan Ilych is not an orphan. He is the son of one whose life is a "career" which leads to a "position" where he can no longer "fulfill any essential duty" but continues "to get fictious places and non-fictious thousands" to "a venerable old age". The father's task of life is just to move from place to place, living by the "inertia of salary," and Ivan Ilych feels called to become like his father. Ivan Ilych's early life, then, is moved by every "change in job": "New institutions appeared, new people were needed, and Ivan Ilych became that new person." His job, he believes, has nothing to do with his "private life." He develops the "device of distancing himself from all circumstances that do not touch his job" and thus separates himself from his task. He is distant even when close. He changes his physical image to fit the new life and gets married because others think it is "correct" to do so and, besides, it is "pleasant" for him.

> The very process of marriage and the first period of married life with its conjugal kisses, new furniture, new dishes, and new linen went so well right up to his wife's pregnancy that Ivan Ilych began to think that marriage would not only not destroy but even improve the mode of easy, pleasant, merry, yet always proper and approved life which Ivan Ilych considered inherent to life itself. But then, from the first months of his wife's pregnancy, there appeared something new, unexpected, unpleasant, difficult, and improper which he had not expected and from which he could not separate himself.

Ivan Ilych's marriage reveals his flaw. He fails to understand what life is; when it appears, it seems the very negation of what he thinks it is. Life understood as a career will inevitably stumble on the facts of life and death. For one whose understanding of life is thus flawed, the facts do not fit the expectations and seem to be the negation and adversary of life. The syntax of this paragraph reflects the theme of the whole work: what seems positive becomes negative and what is expected is the opposite of what happens. The central word here, as in the whole work, is the adversative conjunction "but" (*no*). *The Death of Ivan Ilych* is the story of twisted values that in the end get turned right. The key words "position," "task," "life," and "death" change their meaning in the process, and in the end which is the beginning we see that Ivan Ilych's dying is his position, task, and life, while his conception of this position, task, and life is his death. In this story of conversion, the very words get converted in their meanings.

When the "complex and difficult task" of marriage fails, Ivan Ilych finds himself drowning in "a sea of silent enmity and alienation." To protect himself he becomes "impenetrable" to his wife's emotional outbursts. He returns to his work, which now becomes "his world" (*mir*) and "the whole interest of his life." But then, just when he has worked out the "relationship" to his marriage, his world of work falls apart. The "salary is not sufficient for life" (iii). That year of 1880—the year of Tolstoy's most serious crisis—is "the most difficult year in Ivan Ilych's life." "Everyone abandoned him." "For the first time" he experiences "boredom and unbearable anxiety." He must "seek a new place," a "new arrangement of his life," and "punish those" who have betrayed him. He journeys to St. Petersburg, where his quest is crowned with success. Now "his enemies are shamed," they "envy him his position," and "everyone loves him." Ivan Ilych marks the triumph of his punishment and revenge with a new apartment whose arrangement "grows and grows to the ideal" he has set, and his living room begins to "be like all other living rooms." But then, just when he is hanging the last drapery, he falls from the ladder of his successful arrangement of life. From this point on Ivan Ilych's own world tumbles down upon him, and he becomes ill.

In his illness Ivan Ilych suffers from the arrangement of life he had achieved. "Every spot on the tablecloth . . . annoyed him," and he "suffered from the apartment" he had arranged. As the pain increases, he goes to the doctor, who treats him as he had treated defendants in the courts and diagnoses his illness as a "wandering" kidney and a "blind" intestine. He experiences "doubt," "terror," and "despair," but no one like him understands what is so unlike them and they think that "he is guilty." His wife works out a definite relationship to his illness in which she too sees him "guilty," and at work he becomes the one who is soon "to vacate a place." The life he had arranged with its new furniture, its "device of distancing himself" from his task, its self-protective relationship to his marriage, and its unending quest to fill the vacant place, returns as his suffering, just as his diagnosed illness is the judgment on his blind and wandering life. None of this, of course, does he see. He just suffers from his sins, alone as he always was. But then, at the center of the work, Ivan Ilych looks in the mirror and sees the "changes" (v). He overhears the judgment that "he is a dead man," and he realizes the truth of his dying. From this point on his suffering begins its teaching task.

Suffering shows Ivan Ilych that others "do not know or take pity" on him and that in his dying as in his living he is alone. Suffering shows him that he is indeed like everyone else, like Caius in the syllogism, the mortal who must die. Suffering shows him that the facts of life and death are neither proper, nor pleasant, and that with urination and defecation we must live and die. Suffering shows him that "no one will take pity on him because no one even wants to understand his position," and so they all lie to themselves and others (vii). Suffering shows him that truth comes out twisted, as it does from his wife, because it is all self-centered: "She did everything for him only for herself and told him that she was doing for herself what she was really doing for herself in such an incredible way that he had to understand just the opposite" (viii). Suffering shows Ivan Ilych who he has been and what he has done: draped in the self-protective arrangement of his life, he has lived only for himself, even though he has not known himself. Suffering untwists the truth, but not completely.

What completes the lesson of suffering is the lesson of love. The servant Gerasim, the only figure in the story shown without family or friends, is the one who knows how to live and love because he accepts the facts of life and death. Gerasim knows that "we will all die" (vii) and that in the face of death one can offer solace and comfort but no remedy. Gerasim's presence stays Ivan Ilych's pain and terror, but his absence as a result heightens the dying man's sense of isolation and abandonment. In Gerasim's absence Ivan Ilych "pities himself" and "weeps like a child" (ix). Gerasim's departure, the loss of love, brings Ivan Ilych to the despair which will turn him around. "He wept over his own helplessness, his own terrifying aloneness, over the cruelty of people, the cruelty of God, over the absence of God." But then, he "stopped weeping and breathing and became all attention," listening to the "voice of his soul" which recalls his life of love as a child. "But the person who had experienced that pleasantness no longer exists; it was as if it were a memory of someone else." The course of his life becomes clear: "The further, the deader" but "the further back, the more life, the more good in life, the more of life itself" (x). His life in quest of place after place has in fact been a "series of increasing struggles flying faster and faster toward the end, the most terrifying suffering," the "terrifying falling, shock, and destruction" of death. Gerasim's love teaches Ivan Ilych the ultimate truth that he himself is guilty of destroying his own life. There is no God who is tormenting him. He is tormented because he is not like Gerasim.

What Gerasim knows is that the task of life is not to seek place after place, but to see his task in his place. He lives not by the "inertia of salary" (*zhalovanija*), but by his ability to "take pity" (*zhalet'*) on others. He knows in what way we all are alike and how we all need to be liked, but he does not seek to be alike or liked. Because he identifies with others without needing to be like them or liked by them, he is able to give spontaneously and freely of himself. From Gerasim Ivan Ilych learns that to live does not mean to be loved but to love. The "aloneness in the populous city amidst his numerous acquaintances and family, the aloneness fuller than it could be anywhere, at the bottom of the sea or in the bowels of the earth" (x), Ivan Ilych learns, comes from his deadly life: he isolated himself and then wanted to be pitied by others for his own self-isolation. What must be done is "to take pity" on others. This Ivan Ilych experiences when his hand touches his son's head, his son grasps it and kisses it, and Ivan Ilych feels "pity" for him. The pain and the death disappear in the act of pity which is Ivan Ilych's illumination and rebirth to life. To this concept of "pity" we shall turn in the next chapter.

The Death of Ivan Ilych is an emblematic story of crisis and conversion. Written just before the completion of the major philosophical work *On Life*, this autopsychological prose fiction tells of the discovery of life in the face of death. It is the fictional image of the "arrest of life" (*ostanovka zhizni*) which, as Tolstoy would have it in *A Confession*, was the immediate cause of his major crisis and conversion. All of a sudden the Tolstoyan questions started to rise relentlessly to the surface of his consciousness, and he fell into an arresting despair which led to his illumination (iii). In *A Confession* Tolstoy attempts to articulate this "arrest of life" by this clarifying simile:

> There occurred what occurred with everyone sick with a deadly internal disease. At first there appear trivial signs of indisposition to which the sick man pays no attention, then these signs reappear more and more often and merge into one ceaseless suffering. This suffering grows and, before the sick man can glance back, he becomes aware that what he took for an indisposition is what is for him more important than anything else in the world—death.

The simile then supplies Tolstoy with the metaphor for the first fiction he completed after *A Confession*.[1] The story, therefore, is grounded in Tolstoy's experience, embodies his image of the experience, and reveals the later articulated idea drawn from the experience. *The Death of Ivan Ilych* in this sense represents Tolstoy's art in its most typical form.

* * *

The perfect type of Tolstoy's fiction is *Master and Man*. This late (1895) narrative is an emblematic journey of discovery and a parable of the way to love. Vasily Andreevich Brekhunov, a "local merchant of the second guild," is the one who thinks he is the master (i). He is in a most profound sense, therefore, a liar and a braggart. His name (*brekhun*) suggests both. He "boasts to himself and rejoices in himself and his position" (vi). He certainly thinks he is not like everyone else. "With me it's not like with them others where you gotta wait and then there's bills and fines. We go on honor. You serve me and I'll not abandon you" (i). He believes he is a "benefactor." This kind master lives for all and loves his neighbor as himself. "I desire for you as I do for myself." Brekhunov lives according to his conscience and will do no harm to a soul. "Let the loss be mine. I am not like others" (ii). Brekhunov the

---

1. The parallel between this passage in *A Confession* and *The Death of Ivan Ilych* was first pointed out by Rimvydas Silbajoris in his excellent article "Human Contact and Tolstoy's Esthetics," *Papers* in *Comparative Studies*, The Ohio State University, Columbus, Ohio, Vol. I, No. 1, 1981, p. 39, n. 23.

master has no doubt about himself or his virtue as a master. He knows who he is and what he must do. The church elder, he seems a man of faith.

Because he is the master, Brekhunov is the one to whom the world belongs. But to the merchant master the world that belongs to him is the sum total of his acquisitions. For him, then, to live (*zhit'*) means to acquire (*nazhit'*), and the task of life is to acquire for himself as much as possible. At the center of the story, therefore, he visits with an old man whose son wants a share of his father's land, and Brekhunov gives him his sound advice: "As for sharing, my friend, don't give in. You have acquired it, you are the master" (vi). The master is the one who is removed from human relatedness. The height of Brekhunov's spirituality, as a consequence, "the one thing that comprises the aim, meaning, joy, and pride of his life" is the contemplation of the process of acquisition, "how much money he had acquired and could still acquire, how much money other people he knew had acquired and did have, and how they did and do acquire it, and how he, like them, could still acquire a great deal of money." The emblems of himself, then, are his "house with the tin-roofed barn" and his two fur coats. The contemplation of these acquisitions gives him the confidence of his accomplished mission. "What have I done in fifteen years?" he asks himself, as he limns his possessions. "And how did it happen? Because I remember my task, I strive, not like others, and then the task gets done. . . . Labor and the Lord will give." Brekhunov is content, "satisfied with everything that belongs to him and everything that he has done" (i). The merchant master is the one to whom the world belongs because, he believes, he has accomplished his task. God gives His grace, but Brekhunov believes he is self-sufficient. The master does not need others.

Because he is the one whose task is to acquire, Brekhunov lives off the past and for the future. His mental life consists in summing up the past and calculating the future. He lives by his watch and for a goal. This goal he sees ever ahead of him; he constantly strives for it. Thus he spends his life for some future acquisition which in the future will become his past accomplishment, the sign that he has lived and lived well. His son is not the one he loves and who loves him but the one "who in his thoughts he always calls his heir" (i). Brekhunov is a successful merchant master, however, because, although he is content with his past, he must ever keep on the move. His characteristic phrase is "Forward march" (*da i marsh*). Furthermore, the successful merchant not only sees his task still ahead, he knows the way to it. He could even go it alone, he believes, and he certainly knows how to get there. He definitely has the mind of a master and does not know that Christ teaches us to live in the present.

Master and Man tells the story of a man on a mission of acquisition, removed from the world of human relatedness. Brekhunov and his servant Nikita go off into the snow and cold because the master feels he "has to go" (iii). While the master thinks he knows the way, Nikita is the one whose task is to try to stay on the road. Nikita is the man, the "worker," the "non-master" (i). He is the one who has "no home," but lives out in the world, with people (*v ljudjakh*). He has the sense of human relatedness. He is known for his hard work and, although he does not care for his job, "he has to live until he finds another place and he takes what is given." A drunkard, he does not now drink; a husband and father who provides for his family's care, he silently lets his wife continue her affair with the cooper. Nikita has no possessions or aspirations. He has no past he can live off of and no future he would want to live for. Nikita lives in the present, although he does not know this. He is where he is and lives where he lives and does what he does. At the center of the story, when the master tells the master how to be a master, Nikita drinks his tea and keeps warm. On the journey Nikita knows that he does not know and cannot know the direct path to the goal, but he does trust to his horse and listen to the wind; he tries to follow them. When he fails, however, he is neither surprised, annoyed, or dismayed. He knows he is helpless. Nikita did not want to go on this trip and has nothing to gain for himself, but he is there, and he is his master's servant and his master wants it, so he keeps on trying to stay on the road. Nikita, like his "kind and obedient" horse, is the one who does the will of the one who sends him (v). He is a man of the Lord.

Since he is the one who does the will of the one who sent him, Nikita knows how to live and love. He lives his life, not trying to get to the goal of his desires, but by responding to the needs of the moment, both for himself and others. His characteristic phrase is not "forward march" but the name with which he addresses others, "dear heart." He is known for his "kind" (*dobryj*) nature (i). This kindness is expressed in his treatment of his horse. He feeds and tends her with loving care. When Brekhunov and Nikita are overcome by the snow and the cold, Brekhunov cares for himself, Nikita for his horse. He is guided by one idea: "it will be warmer for you" (vi). When on their journey, they encounter the ones who are celebrating the holiday, racing gaily along to wherever, Brekhunov is buoyed up by their spirits and feels ever more strongly the urge to march forward; Nikita is astounded at those "Asians" who beat their horse so violently (iii). When he believes he is dying, he calls to Brekhunov, asks that his final wages be given to his "boy or his wife, it makes no difference," and then begs forgiveness from the master (ix). He has no fear of death and in the end lives on. Nikita, who knows he is the servant called to do his master's will, even when the master seems to have abandoned him, is the man of faith.

Master and Man is a journey of discovery, not for Nikita but for Brekhunov. The men get lost in the emblematic expanse of nature because Brekhunov keeps thinking he knows the way, seeing his goal just ahead of him. Over and over again—"again" is a key word in the story—Brekhunov espies "something black" which he hopes will be what he is after or a marker on the path to what he is after; what he sees keeps on turning out to be fragments of the lonely, desperate, abandoned world: some vines, an isolated tree, frozen wash on a clothesline, a tall wormwood "desperately reeling in the wind" (viii). Each time they chase after the image of Brekhunov's desired goal, they get lost; often they find themselves back where they started. Because Brekhunov cannot learn from his suffering, the quest for the goal of his desire ahead in the future becomes a crescendoing vicious circle until Nikita realizes they must stop right there and spend the night. At this point Brekhunov becomes overcome by "fear" for his life (vi). He now repents of his past, which for him means regretting he had not stayed with his master friend, where it was "quite warm and merry" (iii), and that he had brought along Nikita whom he sees as the cause of his problem (vi). To stay his fear, Brekhunov does what he always does: he gets busy and moves on; "Forward march." He rides off on the tired horse, abandoning Nikita in search of the goal of his desire. The vicious circle begins again. Brekhunov gets off the tired horse, determined to find the road all alone, but now the horse abandons him and he is "alone," buried alive in a snow drift, pinned down by the weight of his two fur coats (vii). His sin has returned as his punishment.

But Brekhunov is resurrected from his snowy grave. At the turning point in his journey he realizes he has "lost his way." No sooner does he see that he is lost than he again sees "something black," but now he sees, not the image of his desire but of his goal: his horse guided him back to Nikita. His "fear" somewhat past, he busies himself caring for the horse in order to keep his mind off his fear. At this point Nikita calls to him, makes his dying request and begs forgiveness. "Suddenly" Brekhunov starts digging Nikita out of the snow and then lies down on top of him to keep him warm. He even resorts to his usual boasting, "that's how we are," but then "to his great amazement" he can no longer speak, and tears flow from his eyes. Like Karenin in his moment of forgiveness he experiences a "majestic tenderness" but Brekhunov thinks the tears prove that he had "really gotten frightened." He does not view his act as a sacrifice but a "weakness" and therefore sees no great merit for him in it. Because of this he experiences "joy he had never felt before." His dream that follows clarifies this experience of the sudden joy of life: "the one he has been waiting for has arrived," but he is not the one he expected but "someone else," "the very one who called him and told him to lie on Nikita." Now he knows that "he is Nikita and Nikita is him, that his life is not in himself but in Nikita, that if Nikita is alive, he is alive." The merchant master is dead. But there is miraculously born another, who speaks of Brekhunov in the third person, who cannot fathom why "Brekhunov had been occupied with what he had been occupied," who himself "now knows what the task is." In his act of love here and now Brekhunov discovers who he is and what he must do. In a profound sense in his own action, but despite himself, he becomes a man of faith.

Master and Man may well be Tolstoy's most disguised piece of autopsychological fiction, but still, like his other works, it is an image of his experience of life. It is not based on a specific documented event as is *Lucerne,* nor does it work out a moment of encounter with death, as does *The Notes of a Madman,* but it is quite literally a trying out in images of Tolstoy's most profound experience of his faith. Like *The Death of Ivan Ilych,* it gives narrative form to a metaphoric statement of Tolstoy's dilemma. This statement was made in *What Is My Faith?* written some ten years before the story.

> I am lost in a snowstorm. One [person] assures me, and it seems to him so, that warm fires and a village are just right ahead, but it just seems to him and to me because we want it. When we go toward the fires they are not there. But another [person] takes off through the snow. He walks around a bit, comes out on the road and shouts to us, "Don't drive anywhere, the fires are in your eyes; you'll get lost everywhere and you'll perish. The firm road is right here, I'm standing on it and it will lead us out." Now that's not much. When we believed in the fires flashing in our blinded eyes, there was always just ahead a village, a warm hut, salvation, rest while here there's just a firm road. But if we listen to the first we'll surely freeze, while if we listen to the second we'll surely get out.

In this metaphoric statement the one person ("I") lost in a storm which is an emblem of life suddenly becomes two different selves: one who represents his desires, the other the certitude of the way; one who represents the personality, the other the divine self; one who leads to death, the other to the way out of death. In the story these two selves are fleshed out as two separate characters, Brekhunov and Nikita. These characters are given a place in the social and economic milieu of Russian life of the mid-nineteenth century, and they are endowed with a simple psychology based on two opposed moral and religious attitudes to the world. The Tolstoyan drama of the call to true life, of the desire for relatedness and the need to be a Resident, is then cast into the form of a journey of discovery, and Brekhunov, the personality, goes through a series of cumulative awakenings, including hearing the voice of death, until in the end he truly encounters Nikita, the emblematic divine self who is the one who loves, and suddenly Brekhunov discovers the way. *Master and Man* is a parable made from Tolstoy's inner experience of the unceasing struggle to find his way to love, of his continuing discovery of his mission, which is not his teaching, his family, his art, or being the master, but the inner divine call to love his neighbor as himself.

This representation of the self as two different selves embodied in two different and opposed characters, one of whom is called to be like the other, is not new. It is just a fine articulation of a method which underlies all Tolstoy's major fictions. As we have seen, in them, but of course variously, Tolstoy represents his struggle for faith by opposing two sets of characters: on the one hand, Nikolenka, Olenin, Prince Andrew, Pierre, Levin, and Nekhlyudov; on the other hand, Maman and "she," Maryanka, Natasha, Kitty, and Katyusha. The female figures are all emblematic residents who embody and reveal the way to divine love. In the later, short fictions these female figures are replaced by male peasants who serve the same function as do the emblematic figures of the beloved in the genres of the rich and learned. Natalya Savishna is the first such figure, both female and peasant. All Tolstoy's major heroes are representations of the personality lost in life, but on a journey of discovery with or in search of an emblematic self. At the end of the journey, only in moments and just in the moment, they encounter their emblematic divine self and see the way to love. *Master and Man* is the perfect type of this autopsychological and theological prose that I call emblematic realism.

*   *   *

ELIZABETH TRAHAN

L. N. Tolstoj's *Master and Man*—A Symbolic Narrative†

In his essay *What is Art?* (1897), Tolstoj rejects contemporary art as involved, affected and obscure (Ch. X). He attacks the French Symbolists for their incomprehensibility (ibid.) and heaps ridicule on Richard Wagner for his use of myths and leitmotifs (Ch. XIII). Good art, Tolstoj suggests, must express universally valid religious or at least humanitarian feelings, experienced by the author and transmitted through direct emotional infection, as is accomplished in the great religious writings, in folk legends, fairy tales and folk songs. When reviewing his own writings from this critical position, Tolstoj is forced to reject all his literary masterpieces. He can only find two instances of "good" art, two of his *Tales for Children* (1872)—"The Prisoner of the Caucasus" and "God Sees the Truth but Waits."

Today, however interesting we may find the essay on art, we will hardly use it as a basis for evaluating Tolstoj's works. Not "The Prisoner of the Caucasus" or "God Sees the Truth but Waits" but *War and Peace*,

†From *Slavic and East European Journal* 7 (1963) 3:258–68. Reprinted with permission of the author.

Anna Karenina, The Death of Ivan Il'ič, and *Master and Man* are generally considered Tolstoj's best works. Yet, paradoxically, in one respect the bias of Tolstoj's theoretical position seems to have affected most critics. Tolstoj is usually discussed in terms of his "realism" or as a moralist, and is rarely given credit for any formal experimentation. Yet already *War and Peace* (1865–69) and *Anna Karenina* (1873–77) make use of certain formal devices, such as interior monologue, free association, structural patterns based on parallels and contrasts, significant detail, even some symbolic, i.e., open metaphors. *The Death of Ivan Il'ič* (1886), in addition, uses "leitmotifs" very much in Richard Wagner's manner, and contains sensory associations of a directness or subtlety very close to that emphasis on nuances and depth which characterizes Baudelaire and the French Symbolists. Finally, *Master and Man* (1894), one of Tolstoj's last stories, is, as I will try to show, a truly modern symbolic narrative.

The plot of *Master and Man* is simple. Vasilij Andreič Brexunov, the master, and Nikita, his man, set out on a business trip to a village some seven miles away. They are confronted by a blizzard, repeatedly lose their way and are finally forced to spend the night in their sledge. Brexunov freezes to death but saves Nikita by shielding him with his body. Initially a selfish, stubborn bully, he now dies willingly and gladly, with a vision of Christ and a belief in the unity of all life.[1] Nikita's life is saved, and he quietly lives out his lifespan.

The juxtaposition of two contrasting characters and their ways and views of life had been a favorite device of Tolstoj's ever since *Three Deaths,* written in 1858. But only on the most immediate level is *Master and Man* the story of Brexunov and his servant Nikita. While Nikita does not change throughout the story, Brexunov undergoes a complete transformation. The indifferent churchwarden becomes a true believer; the greedy and self-confident egotist, a humble and self-effacing human being. *Master and Man* is actually Brexunov's story, for he emerges as both master and man.

As a tale of moral regeneration and religious consolation, the story is thematically close to many of Tolstoj's popular tales, and to his conception of "good" art. Moreover, the detached, simple folk idiom used— much of its charm is, unfortunately, lost in translation—gives the story the naïveté and wisdom of a folk legend.[2] At the same time, even a superficial reading reveals a certain mysterious, magic quality which

---

1. Though Christ is not named directly, the references seem obvious enough not to require lengthy justifications. To be sure, in one critical study the "Someone" and "He" is interpreted as "Love"; the author was probably unaware of the fact that, in Russian, love is feminine in gender. (See Jacqueline de Proyart de Baillescourt, "La représentation de la mort dans l'oeuvre littéraire de Tolstoj," *For Roman Jakobson,* The Hague,

1956.)
2. Compare, e.g., the ending with its detached, ironic legend style: "Is he better or worse off there where he awoke after this death of his? was he disillusioned or did he find there exactly what he expected? We will all soon find out." (All translations of passages from *Master and Man* are my own.)

suggests additional dimensions. Certain words are repeated like incantations. The howling of the wind and the circling of the snow provide an ominous refrain. The sledge and its occupants move in circles which they seem unable to break through. The number "three" occurs some fifteen times in the story, suggesting a bewitched, alien world. And close attention to the text reveals the presence of metaphors and symbols which not only deepen and transform the surface reality of the plot but which form connected patterns and provide additional levels of meaning. Through these symbols, Brexunov's religious awakening becomes a pilgrimage from the village of *Kresty* (The Crosses) to the Cross, almost a reiteration of Christ's Road to Calvary. The personal crisis of Brexunov, the Liar—*brexat'* is "to tell lies"—becomes the experience of an existential moment, the culmination of man's struggle with nature both without and within. Brexunov's final insight not only bestows meaning upon his existence but, through the correspondence of the symbols used, reveals Brexunov's essence to be a reflection of the essence of that external force which he had challenged.

The setting for the story may have been suggested to Tolstoj by a personal experience. During the winters of 1891–92 and 1892–93, he was engaged in famine relief work in the district of Rjazan'. Mme. Raevskaja, at whose estate he was staying, describes how on February 15, 1892, worried about Tolstoj's long absence during a blizzard, they set out after him and found him crossing a snowy field on foot, left behind by his horse.[3] Once before, Tolstoj had written a story based on his own experience of a blizzard during a twenty-two hour trip in January of 1854. *The Snowstorm* (1856) describes realistically an all-night ride, in which the horses instinctively find their way to safety. If contrasted to the early story, the formal emphasis and achievement of *Master and Man* becomes immediately apparent.

The immediate incentive for the story must have been provided by Flaubert's *Légende de Saint Julien l'Hospitalier.* Tolstoj wrote *Master and Man* only a few months before two introductions, one to the works of Guy de Maupassant, the other to S. T. Semenov's *Peasant Stories.* Both introductions reveal Tolstoj's preoccupation with literary criticism. The criteria stated later in *What is Art?* are here anticipated by Tolstoj's emphasis on the significance and universality of the theme, on the proper relation of form to content, and on the author's "sincerity." In the introduction to Semenov's stories, Tolstoj points to Flaubert's tale as an example of an author's lack of sincerity: "The last episode of the story which ought to be the most touching represents Julien lying on a bed together with a leper and warming him with his body. . . . The whole thing is described with great skill, but in reading this story I am always left perfectly cold and indifferent. I feel that the author would not have

---

3. See E. I. Raevskaja, "Lev Nikolaevič Tolstoj sredi golodajuščix," *Letopisi Gosudarstvennogo literaturnogo muzeja,* Vol. II (M., 1938).

done and would not have cared to do what his hero did, and I therefore have no desire to do it, and experience no emotion on reading of this marvellous exploit."[4]

Tolstoj's criticism of Flaubert's story shows not merely the inadequacy of his criterion of "sincerity" but his lack of insight into Flaubert's approach. A comparison with *Master and Man* again becomes illuminating: *La Légende de Saint Julien l'Hospitalier* was written as a deliberate—and probably eminently sincere—attempt to re-create the mood and spirit of the Middle Ages. It is filled with allegorical objects and animals, miracles and coincidences, set against the backdrop of a medieval, stable universe. The story provides an excellent example of what Erich Kahler calls "descending symbolism"—a symbolism dependent on and determined by a preestablished reality. Tolstoj's story, on the other hand, becomes modern both by its emphasis on psychological character treatment and by its "ascending" symbolism. Here a set of freely created unique forms achieves a consummate representation of the author's vision. In contrast to Flaubert's story, the intensity of the vision now absorbs the communicative purpose, and the story's message can no longer be separated from the work itself.[5]

The comparison of Brexunov and his man, Nikita, is achieved largely by direct description, as well as Tolstoj's long favored devices of parallelism and contrast, often used to reflect ironic ambivalences. But since this comparison forms the story's basis, it must be traced at least briefly before we can turn to Brexunov's psychological development and its symbolic significance.

Initially, Brexunov, Church Elder and Merchant of the Second Guild, views the world entirely in terms of his personal power and economic success. Though his estate thrives, both wife and child are "thin and pale." Brexunov's tone toward his wife is rude and condescending, and his son exists for him merely as a personal heir. Nor is Brexunov's attitude toward Nikita positive, though he considers himself Nikita's benefactor. As shown by his taunting remarks about the cooper and by his attempt to sell Nikita a bad horse, Brexunov is as indifferent to Nikita's feelings and to his financial plight as to his physical well-being.

Nikita's relations with his environment, on the other hand, are harmonious. The master's little boy loves him, the mistress worries whether he will be warm enough, and he pleases everyone by his cheerful and obliging manner. He has the peasant's straightforward simplicity and fatalism, his closeness to nature and animals. Nonetheless, Nikita is no saint. When drunk—and he is called a habitual drunkard early in the

---

4. L. N. Tolstoj, *Sobranie sočinenij* (1928), XVIII, 17–18.

5. For the terminology used see Erich Kahler's "The Nature of the Symbol," the introductory chapter to *Symbolism in Religion and Literature*, ed. Rollo May (New York, 1950). It seems far more satisfactory than the customary, socially oriented and rather rigid division into a "traditional" or "conventional" symbolism as against a "private" symbolism, or the vague psychological distinction of a "literary" or "artificial" as against a "natural" symbolism.

story—he can become a veritable fiend. But while his master freely imbibes both before his departure and in Griškino, Nikita resists all temptation, remains sober and thus more aware of the hazards and necessities of their situation.

Ironically, just as Brexunov's two fur-lined coats do not save him while Nikita survives in his thin coat, so Brexunov's personal energy and business acumen turn out far less effective than the simple reasoning of those around him. Nikita would have chosen the safer road, trusted the horse's instinct and, undoubtedly, spent the night safely at Taras' house. Only upon his wife's nagging does Brexunov take Nikita along. This step might have saved his life, had he paid attention to Nikita from the start. It saves his soul when he finally does. It is similarly ironic that, while Nikita derives real comfort from placing his sins and fate into God's hands, Brexunov, the Church Elder, can find no consolation in religion. Instead, he vainly seeks reassurance in the memory of his own achievements and the excitement of future goals.

We do not know whether Nikita would have survived the night without Brexunov's self-sacrifice; but we know that he was ready for death, without any reproach toward his master or God. It almost seems a reward for his unswerving loyalty that Nikita is permitted to die his own death—*nastojaščaja smert'*—the traditional solemn death of the believer, at home in his bed, surrounded by his family and with a lighted taper in his hand.

Even though the last paragraph is devoted to Nikita, *Master and Man* is not his story. The ending merely completes the comparison between him and his master, beyond their actions and attitudes to their actual death experience. In many ways, Nikita is more positive. His actions and decisions, in contrast to Brexunov's, seem appropriate and "right." By his fatalistic acceptance of life in all its manifestations, he reminds us of Natal'ja Saviš na in *Childhood*, the coachman Fedor in *Three Deaths*, Platon Karataev in *War and Peace*, Gerasim in *The Death of Ivan Il'ič*. All of them are contrasted positively to men of greater individuality who are assailed by doubts, fears, and temptations. In Platon, the type finds its culmination. He is less a person than a symbol, a "personification of the spirit of simplicity and truth" (*War and Peace*, Part Twelve, Ch. XIII). He does not take the center of the stage, but the secret of his happiness is coveted by Pierre Bezuxov as much as that of the peasant—whose name, incidentally, is again Platon—by Konstantin Levin. In *The Death of Ivan Il'ič*, the balance begins to shift. Ivan Il'ič incorporates to some extent Gerasim's humble and joyful submissiveness into his own world view. In *Master and Man*, the change is completed. However "right" Nikita's attitude and however peaceful his death, not he, the just man, is exalted but Brexunov, the repentant sinner, who, after a desperate struggle with nature, submits to it and finds God.

The contrast between Nikita and Brexunov is extended into their attitude toward nature. While Nikita accepts it even in its extreme manifestation—the cold and pitiless fury of the blizzard—Brexunov challenges it as he had challenged everything around him before. But while he had been able to impose his will on men and animals, he suffers defeat when he confronts nature with the same ruthless disregard.

When Brexunov's path is blocked by the ravine, he suffers the first decisive defeat, the defeat of his actions. When he vainly seeks reassurance in memories of the past and dreams of the future, he suffers the defeat of his achievements. Finally, when he, no longer master of himself but driven by fear and the instinct of self-preservation, makes one more attempt at physical escape, he suffers the defeat of his values. But like Dostoevskij's Ridiculous Man who, on his dream flight, is stripped of layer upon layer of the armor with which he had fortified himself against life, so Vasilij Brexunov, facing non-existence in a nightmarish and awesome no-man's land, moves step by step toward the core of his existence. He faces his existential crisis alone, weak, unable to muster the support of any ethical, moral, or religious consolations. But now, untrammeled by shackles of conventions and prejudices, a deep inner strength surges up in him. Brexunov begins to find a new self and new values.

Brexunov's attempt to revive Nikita may initially have been due to his fear of being left alone again, of having to submit to death and acknowledge defeat. But the "peculiar joy such as he had never felt before," the "strange and solemn tenderness," and the "joyous condition" which he experiences, bear witness to the fact that a change is taking place within him. Now his thoughts circle around Nikita and the peasant's image fuses with that of the past. Finally, Brexunov sees himself back in the past, when he is immobile, unable to react to his old environment. That this fact does not fill him with fear or indignation, again shows how profoundly he has changed. Formerly an impatient and irascible master, he is now waiting patiently and joyfully for his own Master. His submission is complete: he acknowledges the merit for the good deed as not his but Christ's and follows Him with humility.

The religious theme which asserts itself so powerfully at the end, is latently present from the very beginning. Brexunov lives in a village called The Crosses and, as it turns out, indeed in the shadow of the Cross. His challenge takes place on the second day of the feast of St. Nicholas, who is not only the saint of all Russia and specifically of peasants, merchants and wayfarers, but also of temperance—and a wonderworker. Nikita, who has taken a vow of abstinence and who successfully resists all temptation on the crucial day, is obviously under the protection of St. Nicholas. But on Brexunov the Saint works his miracle.

Initially Brexunov is a sinner. Though a church elder, he ignores the holy day and desecrates church funds by borrowing them for private gain. In Griškino, he sits down at the head of the table for what becomes his last supper. To be sure, with his "protruding, hawk-like eyes," his three thousand rubles and his greed for gain he is still closer to Judas than to Christ. His answer to the anguished complaints of the old man about his son's greed is unconcerned. Brexunov does not realize that his own test has begun.

It is interesting that a counting of heads reveals the presence of thirteen adults in Taras' house: the old couple, two of their sons and one grandson—Petruša—with his wife, Taras' four daughters-in-law, the neighbor, Brexunov, and Nikita. But though such detailed account is given of all twenty-two members of Taras' household as to suggest a purpose, the allusion is again blurred by the fact that only the men sit around the table.[6]

Several other, similarly marginal references occur. The sledge which Brexunov overtakes is driven by one Simon who, however casually encountered, might have shared Brexunov's burden, had he chosen to accept his help. The man who opens the gate to Taras' house for them and again guides them onto their way is called Peter and, for all his willingness, he turns back at the crucial moment and abandons them, if unknowingly, to their fate. These allusions gain weight, as Brexunov recalls one Sebastian who froze to death. The uncommon name clearly evokes the Saint and the possibility of martyrdom and glory. Even more direct is the allusion to treason when Brexunov thinks he hears a cock crow. Not much later, he abandons Nikita with the sacrilegious words: "He won't grudge his life but I, thank God, have something to live for . . ."[7]

When Brexunov sets out alone for the wilderness—the wormwood becomes its appropriate symbol—his punishment seems imminent. Though there is little resemblance between Brexunov's flight into the snowy waste and Christ's withdrawal into the Garden of Gethsemane, Brexunov, not unlike Christ, experiences supreme anguish. He, too, turns to prayer asking that the cup be taken away from him, only to realize the vanity of such prayer. When Brexunov returns to Nikita, he is ready for his burden. As he lies down on his servant with his arms spread out, he, in a sense, mounts the Cross.

During the moment of extreme anguish Brexunov recalled the recent

---

6. Every detail is blended so skillfully into the story line and setting that a symbolic interpretation may seem arbitrary and far-fetched until the entire pattern is perceived. Therefore, Miss McCarthy is hardly the only one to insist on Tolstoj's unintentional, at best "natural" symbolism (*Literary Symbolism*, ed. Maurice Beebe [San Francisco, 1960], pp. 50–51). Even though "intention" is a highly questionable esthetic criterion and rarely supported by satisfactory evidence, a comparison of the various drafts and proofs for *Master and Man* (thirteen exist; one or two are lost) seems to bear out my suggestion of a deliberate stylization: Almost all symbolic details emerge only in the final drafts.

7. Actually there is a threefold betrayal: first, when Brexunov leaves Nikita outside in the snow while settling in the sledge, a second time when, despite the thought that Nikita might die, he does not get up to cover him. The third instance is, of course, the most striking manifestation of the betrayal and the crucial one.

church service and the tapers which he would sell and resell. Lying on Nikita he again recalls service and tapers, but now their images merge with that of Nikita. In sacrificing himself for this man, Brexunov reiterates Christ's sacrifice, and in his last vision Christ comes for him in person and thereby accepts the sacrifice.

Even though Brexunov's symbolic death is somewhat similar to Billy Budd's he is no Christ figure like Billy Budd or like Prince Myškin. Nor does his wrong-doing approach the scope of that of St. Julien. Brexunov is merely a sinner who through suffering returns to love and through love to Christ. Franz Kafka, in *A Country Doctor*, likewise describes a ride through a blizzard, and the doctor, too, lies down to warm a dying human being. There, however, the symbols are used with savage irony. The country doctor lies down willingly, and attempts to escape as soon as he can—only to find his escape turn into a trap, an eternal pilgrimage through "the frost of this most unhappy of ages." Brexunov's religious development, on the other hand, remains thematically entirely within the framework of traditional Christianity, a fitting illustration of Luke 15:7: "I say unto you, that likewise joy shall be in heaven over one sinner that repenteth, more than over ninety and nine just persons, which need no repentance." The symbolic presentation, however, gives Brexunov's final gesture a scope and significance which by far transcends his actual transformation into a humble and dedicated servant of Christ.

The religious symbolism of *Master and Man* represents only one strand in the symbolic pattern of the story. With its use of allegorical names and its actual depiction of a religious vision, it remains to some extent superimposed upon the story. The nature imagery, on the other hand, becomes so intrinsic a part of the narrative, permeates it so completely and intensively that the story becomes an excellent example of what, earlier, I called "ascending" symbolism.

The circle becomes the key symbol of the story. It is menace and trap, futility and despair, but it also represents the unity of life and death, the Chain of Being. The snow whirls around master and man, the wind circles around them, their road turns into circles. Brexunov, by defying the circle as long as he can, rejects every road leading out of it, until there remains only the one leading into its very center—the heart of nature and the self. Darkness and the abyss provide its signposts. Though Brexunov fails to recognize their deeper significance, they effectively stop his outer journey, and the inner journey to the core of the self can begin. Again Brexunov's quest moves in circles, those of his thoughts, then those of his last trip. Finally Brexunov reaches the innermost circle, in which the I and the Thou merge.

The circular symbol is enhanced by the continual recurrence of the number "three," which also adds a supernatural dimension to the reality of the plot. Brexunov starts out during the third hour, with three thousand rubles in his pocket. Three times they set out. Three times Nikita takes over. Three times they see the same cluster of moaning willows, three times they pass the frozen wash, three times wormwood is mentioned. They have three encounters—with Isaj, the horse thief, the three peasants whom they overtake, and Taras and his household in Griškino. Petruša speaks of three domestic councellors. Three times Nikita climbs out to search for the path, the third time reappearing three sazhens further. Three times Brexunov tries to light a cigarette and, after successfully lighting three matches, he is unable to light the last three.[8]

Other secondary images likewise support and extend the symbolic structure. The frozen wash which "is struggling," "fluttering desperately in the wind," and the white shirt which "in particular struggled desperately, waving its sleeves around"—not only reflect the fury of the storm but become portents of doom, of man in distress, of a shroud, a frozen body, perhaps even a crucifixion.[9] The willows are moaning "dismally" and "desperately," "swaying" and "whistling"; the wormwood which is "desperately tossed about by a pitiless wind" fills Brexunov with utmost terror and seems to him his own reflection, as he "awaits an inevitable, swift and meaningless death." These images call to mind Pascal's *pensée* on man as a reed, "le plus faible de la nature";[1] they also suggest Job 21:18: "They are as stubble before the wind, and as chaff that the storm carrieth away."[2]

A series of frightening sounds provides the aural backdrop for the visual imagery and fills the air with the clamor appropriate for Judgment Day: the wild whistling of the wind, the threatening howl of a wolf, the eerie and pitiful cry of the frightened horse.

The poem which Petruša quotes with such joy at its aptness—it is a colloquialized version of the first stanza of Puškin's *Winter Evening*—indeed expresses the Protean power of the storm:

> Storms with mist the sky conceal,
> Snowy circles wheeling wild.
> Now like savage beast 'twill howl,
> And now 'tis wailing like a child. (Tr. by Aylmer Maude.)

Brexunov dies only thirty sazhens (70 feet) off the road and half a verst (about one-third mile) from the village, trapped by the blizzard in a magic circle which he cannot break through. Nor can man break through nature's circle of life and death; he can only transcend it by leaving the

---

8. Like most symbols occurring in the story, the number "three" can be interpreted on various levels and should not be overemphasized. Yet by its very vagueness and ambivalence it contributes depth to the symbolic pattern.
9. I am indebted to Professor Wellek for calling my attention to the symbol of the cross suggested by Brexunov's dead body with its outstretched arms, and anticipated by the white shirt with its frozen sleeves. It was this starting point that suggested to me the complex structure of religious symbols underlying the story.

1. Tolstoj was a great admirer of Pascal. Cf. his diary entry of 23 Dec. 1895 (*The Journal of Leo Tolstoy, 1895–99*, Knopf 1917, p. 15) and his essay on Pascal in *Krug Čtenija za 1906oj god* (Berlin, 1923). Tolstoj's essay *Life* (1887) uses as its motto Pascal's maxim on man's resemblance to a reed.
2. The entire first part of the story can be read as an illustration of Job. 27:16–20.

realm of nature, of life. And while Brexunov follows *His* call, around his dead body the snowstorm once more asserts its symbol of the circle: "All around the snow was whirling as before. The same snow squalls were circling about, covering the dead Vasilij Andreič's fur coat . . ."[3]

The blizzard has lifted Brexunov out of time and space—the time and space of his everyday life—into the vastness of nature, pure, bare, and invincible, stripped of sham values and comforts, and encompassing both life and death in close proximity. The business trip, begun with a disregard for nature's power, continued as one man's challenge, becomes a desperate struggle against the element until nature asserts itself. It forces Brexunov to acquiesce, to accept death at its hands; but it also enables him to understand its secret and to find his own existence and essence in love. An almost mystical union with nature through a supreme act of love becomes his ultimate fulfillment. "Nikita is alive so I too am alive," is Brexunov's final unreserved and unselfish affirmation of life. This is not merely a creed based on the Christian virtues of humility and brotherly love, but a belief in the eternal flow and transfer of life, a Buddhist rather than Christian concept. Käte Hamburger, in her excellent study on Tolstoj, sees the unique accomplishment of *Master and Man* in this visually accomplished act of love, which by far transcends the token gesture of love made by Ivan Il'ič.[4] Yet even *Master and Man*, if more faintly than Tolstoj's other works, echoes its author's own inner split. Despite his self-sacrifice, Brexunov does not come to terms with death nor does he, in Rilke's words, "die his own death."

Of all of Tolstoj's heroes, only Prince Andrej comes close to dying his own death, aside from such "children of God," as Natal'ja Saviša, Platon Krataev, or Nikita. Prince Andrej turns away from life with the same aloofness with which he had turned away from each successive phase of his life. Neither Ivan Il'ič nor Brexunov dies his own death.

---

3. A comparison of the various drafts for *Master and Man* shows that the symbol of the circle only gradually reached its full impact. In the first draft it emerges only in its main features: the return to Griškino and the circling along the edge of the ravine. In the second draft, we find Brexunov's attempt to reach the village on horseback—of which, incidentally, he informs Nikita, who wishes him Godspeed. Similarly, not before the final drafts is there any mention of Petruša's poem, of the reappearing willows and wormwood, of the frozen wash, nor is there any reiteration of the circling of snow and wind. The number "three" occurs only once, very casually, when Nikita reappears "about three sazhens" from the sled. Nor are there any religious symbols. Brexunov takes no church money; Nikita has made no vow to abstain. The Crosses are, inconspicuously, called Mikolskoe, the Gorjačkin (i.e., Burning Man's) Forest, more prosaically, Pirogov's. Isaj is not a horse thief, merely a peasant. No encounter with Simon and the other two peasants is mentioned, and instead of a Sebastian there is a Egor Fedorovič.

Similarly, Brexunov's religious apotheosis emerges only gradually. In the first version, he merely feels awkward about leaving Nikita outside, and lies down upon him so that both may have room in the sledge. The change in him—"something completely different which cannot even be named"—occurs suddenly, and "he entered into it." In the second version a humanitarian motive emerges. Brexunov turns the horse back to the sledge when he hears a wolf howl. Realizing that Nikita is dying, he feels guilty and sorry for him, lies down on him to keep him warm and is happy. He dies like a traditional believer, following *His* call and finding "that all is well now, thanks be to God." Only the final version contains his insight into the circle of being, the unity of all life and the meaning of self-sacrificing love. (Cf. *Polnoe Sobranie Sočinenij*, XXIX, 295–324.)

4. Käte Hamburger, *Tolstoi. Gestalt und Problem* (Bern, 1950), pp. 139–149.

Ivan Il'ič's dying is awful far beyond the sins of his lifetime, while Brexunov, petty sinner that he was, dies an undeservedly beautiful and glorious death. Nor does either of them—in fact, none of Tolstoj's fictional challengers of death—ever come to terms with it. Even Prince Andrej cannot face death squarely. He turns it from an end into a beginning, "an awakening from life"—an escape. Brexunov's story in many ways parallels that of Ivan Il'ič. Confronted by death, both men face the crisis of their existence, and both are forced to reject the values of their past. Yet neither is able to accept death—they merely dismiss or ignore it. For Ivan Il'ič it "ceases to exist," as the immense relief after an almost unbearable suffering floods his entire being till nothing else has room. Brexunov finds a dual escape from facing death: the Christian consolation of a personal immortality and a—basically contradictory—emphasis on the abandonment of individuality in an identification with all life. In neither case is death accepted as part of life, as its end.[5]

Brexunov is much simpler than Ivan Il'ič. He lives by feelings and urges rather than thoughts, and even his act of love and submission takes place on the same instinctive level, brought about by a moment of overwhelming fear rather than a crisis of consciousness. He rejects his past after he has found new values, whereas Ivan Il'ič dismissed his entire life before he had found anything to take its place. Ivan Il'ič was battered and tossed about by his pain until the last shreds of his strength and dignity were gone. Therefore, his final gesture of love may be weak, and his dismissal of death an escape, yet his courage and his suffering give him a heroic scope which Brexunov lacks.

Ironically, though *Master and Man* was prompted by Tolstoj's effort to demonstrate "sincerity," to achieve a direct emotional infection, the impact of the story cannot compare to the impact of Ivan Il'ič's terrible struggle with death. Tolstoj's own fear of death proved stronger than his love of man or God. However, esthetically, *Master and Man* evokes a serenity and pleasure as none of Tolstoj's other works do. The story not only occupies a unique place in Tolstoj's creative output and points to an unsuspected range of his talent, but, both complex and superbly simple, it becomes the most nearly perfect of his works of art.

---

5. Cf. the following, closely corresponding passage from *Life*, in which Tolstoj expressed his own views: "But if a man could place his happiness in the happiness of other beings, i.e., if he would love them more than himself, then death would not represent to him that discontinuance of happiness and life, such as it does represent to a man who lives only for himself. Death to the man who should live only for others could not seem to be a cessation of happiness and of life, because the happiness and the life of other beings is not only not interrupted with the life of a man who serves them, but is frequently augmented and heightened by the sacrifice of his life." (Ch. XVIII, tr. I. Hapgood.)

GARY R. JAHN

A Note on Miracle Motifs in the Later Works of Lev Tolstoj†

As a writer of fiction Tolstoj seems not to have been partial to the fantastic and supernatural. His early works contain only one notable example: the appearance of the ghost of Polikuška in the story of that name. His "stories for the people," written mainly in the 1880s and 1890s, are the main examples of his introduction of such motifs into his fiction during the later part of his career. These stories were intended for the popular audience, and Tolstoj drew heavily on the themes and motifs of the folk tale and religious legend, including their frequent use of supernatural characters and miraculous incident. Not so in the works which he wrote for the audience of his educated peers. Stories like "The Death of Ivan Il'ič," "The Kreutzer Sonata," and "Master and Man" and his novels—*Resurrection* and *Hadji-Murad*—studiously avoid the fantastic. They are in fact marked by what has seemed to many to be an almost painful realism. The purpose of this note is to draw attention to the presence of at least one sort of supernatural motif in Tolstoj's fiction for an educated audience: the artistic exploitation of the passion and resurrection of Christ.

Many and various are the miracles described in the New Testament. The chief of these, and the foundation of the Christian mystery, is the death of Jesus and his miraculous resurrection from the dead. In this note I will briefly examine Tolstoj's attitude to the Christian miracles and the resurrection mystery as it developed from his youth in the 1850s through the time of his "crisis" in the 1870s and then discuss his use of Christ's passion and other Scriptural motifs in certain of his later (post-1880) artistic works.

As a young man Tolstoj had never been impressed by the New Testament miracles or seriously interested in the intricacies of the various church teachings based on them. As early as the mid-1850s he proposed the development of a version of the Christian teaching which was to be chiefly remarkable for having been pruned of all incomprehensible and unnecessary dogma, retaining only the central core of Christ's teachings about the proper conduct of life.[1] It is hardly a surprise, given this lack of interest in the fine points of Christian theology and, by implication, the miraculous resurrection of Jesus which supports them, to find that Tolstoj makes scant use of Christian miracles and mystery as artistic

†From *The Supernatural in Slavic and Baltic Literature: Essays in Honor of Victor Terras*, ed. Amy Mandelker and Roberta Reeder (Columbus, 1988).

Reprinted with permission of the author.
1. Lev N. Tolstoj, *Sobranie sočinenij*, 20 vols. (Moscow, GIXL, 1965) XIX, 150.

motifs in the fiction of his early and middle periods (1850s through 1870s).

As is well known, Tolstoj underwent a profound spiritual crisis in the middle of the 1870s. His unhappy reflections on the meaninglessness of human life brought him to despair. According to his account of the matter, he was saved from an untimely death by his own hand only by the hope and assurance which he discovered in a careful study of the life and teachings of Jesus. This study inaugurated the career of the so-called "later" Tolstoj, and its first fruit was a ponderous trilogy of works on religion. Prefaced by the autobiographical "Confession," the trilogy consists of an account of Tolstoj's version of the Christian teaching, *What I Believe*, (*V čem moja vera*), a fat volume of Scriptural exegesis and commentary, *Harmony and Translation of the Four Gospels* (*Soedinenie i perevod četyrex evangelij*), and a lengthy polemic against the teachings of the Orthodox Church, *Investigation of Dogmatic Theology* (*Issledovanie dogmatičeskogo bogoslovija*). In the latter work Tolstoj made a formal and conscious break with Church dogma, including those which teach the divinity of Christ and the miraculous nature of His birth and death. With perfect consistency, Tolstoj, in translating the Gospels, excised from the received text every mention of the Advent miracle (the annunciation, the Star of Bethlehem, the adoration of the Magi, and so forth) and of the Resurrection.

When Tolstoj, in the mid-1880s, returned to the writing of artistic fiction, his work was marked by a new-found interest in the Gospel motifs. He often used quotations from Scripture in the text of or, even more frequently, as epigraphs to his stories. The score or so of "Stories for the People" makes free and frequent use of Biblical language, quotations, and motifs. True to the conclusions which he had formulated in the late 1870s and early 1880s, any direct mention of the Resurrection, or the Christian miracles generally, is rigorously excluded. An interesting example of Tolstoj's practice in this respect is provided by a story of 1885, "Where Love Is, God Is Also" ("*Gde ljubov', tam i Bog*"), one of the best known of his stories for the people.

Many of these stories were based upon pre-existing narratives, usually of folk origin, which struck Tolstoj as being suitable for reworking into vehicles designed to pull the weight of his newly elaborated religious beliefs. The source for "Where Love Is, God Is Also," however, was of literary origin.[2] In 1882 a Marseilles journal published a story by a then well-known evangelist named Reuben Saillens; the story's title was "Le Père Martin." Early in 1884 an adaptation of this story to Russian life appeared in the magazine *The Russian Worker* (*Russkij rabočij*); the title

---

2. For further information on what we may call the "Saillens affair" see A. E. Gruzinskij, "Istočniki rasskaza L. N. Tolstogo 'Gde ljubov', tam i Bog,'" *Golos minuvšego*, 3 (1913): 52–63 and

D. E. Mixal'ci, "Mnimyj plagiat L. N. Tolstogo," in *Russko-evropejskie literaturnye svjazi* (Moscow-Leningrad: Nauka, 1966), 213–18.

of this translated and Russianized version of the story was "Uncle Martin" ("*Djadja Martyn*"), but it was published with no indication that the story was a translation and without attribution to its original author. The story itself was unchanged, save for alterations in names and settings needed to adapt it to Russian life. It was this Russian adaptation that served as Tolstoj's source. He was quite unaware of the existence of the French original until some years later, when its author, Saillens, encountered a French translation of Tolstoj's story, recognized the lineaments of his own "Père Martin," and hastened to write Tolstoj a few lines of complaint. Tolstoj replied, contritely begging the Frenchman's pardon for his "unintentional plagiarism."

In fact plagiarism, even "unintentional," is far too strong a word. Tolstoj made numerous changes in writing his version of the story and, at the same time, improved its literary quality appreciably. The change that is relevant for our present purpose is that which Tolstoj introduced in the use of Scriptural allusion and quotation. The French original (and, following it, the first Russian adaptation) had set the story at Christmastime and incorporated St. Luke's Advent narrative (chapter two) into the text. Tolstoj, however, struck out the detail of Christmas (in his version it is simply wintertime) and replaced the advent narrative with a passage which he considered more suitable: the dinner at the home of a wealthy Pharisee during which a woman washes the feet of Jesus with her tears, dries them with her hair, and anoints them with costly oil (Luke vii, 36–38). Besides this, Tolstoj adjusted certain details in the scene in which the protagonist, a cobbler whom he calls Martyn Avdeič, gives succor to a starving widow and her baby. In the French original the cobbler makes much of the child and gives him a pair of shoes, thus suggesting the actions of the Magi in the advent narrative. The text clearly suggests that this baby is the symbolic surrogate of the Christ-child, and this is confirmed by the vision which the cobbler sees at the end of the story. Here, the voice of Christ speaks through the mouth of the child. In Tolstoj's version, however, the baby is just a baby. The cobbler comforts it while its mother eats, and then he turns his attention wholly to the widow and her story. Clearly, Tolstoj treated the Advent miracle as artistically worthless as well as theologically irrelevant.

Given this conscious rejection of the basic Christian mysteries, it is more than a little surprising to find allusions to the death and resurrection of Christ in certain of Tolstoj's later works. Good work has been done in this area by professors John Hagan and Elizabeth Trahan in their respective analyses of the long story "Master and Man" ("*Xozjain i rabotnik*," 1895).[3] They, especially Hagan, have conclusively demon-

---

3. Elizabeth Trahan, "L. N. Tolstoj's 'Master and Man'—A Symbolic Narrative," *Slavic and East European Journal* 7 (1963): 258–68; John Hagan, "Detail and Meaning: Tolstoy's 'Master and Man,' " *Criticism*, 11 (1969): 31–58.

strated that this work contains a sub-text of allusions to the Passion narrative.

"Master and Man" is the story of a well-to-do peasant, Vasilij Andreevič, who sets off through a blizzard, accompanied by his hired workman, Nikita, in order to complete the final arrangements for a business deal in which he is engaged. During the course of the terrible night that these two spend together in the open at the mercy of the storm, Vasilij Andreevič comes to see the error of his materialist and mercantile ways. He undergoes a conversion of sorts, and in the end he loses his own life while saving Nikita's.

That Vasilij Andreevič, in effect, lays down his life for the sake of Nikita is only the most striking of the numerous parallels between his story in "Master and Man" and that of Jesus in the Passion narrative. We cannot fail to note, further, that it is the "master" who gives himself for the "man," and that Vasilij Andreevič lives in a village which is called "Kresty" ("The Crosses"). Numerous other details in the story corroborate the suggestions implied by those just mentioned. Thus, while passing and repassing the entrance to a village, Vasilij Andreevič and Nikita notice that a shirt has been left hanging on a clothesline with its arms outstretched. As Vasilij Andreevič shivers through the night waiting for dawn and the end of the storm, he imagines, on three separate occasions, that he hears the crowing of a cock. As he rushes frantically about searching for the lost road, he encounters a hedge-row of wormwood. Finally, when the two travellers are discovered the following morning by a party of peasants, it turns out that the body of Vasilij Andreevič has frozen solid with its arms outstretched in a cruciform position. The parallel between Vasilij Andreevič and Christ can hardly be missed, and it is obviously the Christ of the passion that Tolstoj has in mind.

The extent of the allusions to the Passion story in "Master and Man" is even more striking if we compare the text of this work with that of its partial prototype, a story called "The Snowstorm" ("*Metel'*"), which Tolstoj wrote in 1856. "The Snowstorm" is based upon the same general situation as "Master and Man"—a dangerous journey undertaken at night through a blizzard. "Master and Man" even repeats many of the details contained in its predecessor: the description of the wind and the specification of its direction, the ability of the horses to find their way home if not misdirected by their drivers, the advice (which goes unheeded) not to travel through the storm, the motif of the village as a refuge, and the repeated refusal of the protagonist to avail himself of that refuge. Yet it is clear that in "Master and Man" Tolstoj has invested this material with a completely different artistic force and suggestiveness. "The Snowstorm" uses the journey through the storm as a framework within which to examine the emotions (mainly fear) of the protagonist and to describe the curious operations of the mind with respect to the evocation of memories of the past through association with the experiences of the present. "The Snowstorm," in short, describes a real storm (Tolstoj himself had an experience of the kind reported in the story) and its potential effects on the psyche of an individual person. "Master and Man," on the other hand, puts this same material to the symbolic purpose of epitomizing man's life story as a whole, the tension between the spiritual and material ego within the individual, and man's ultimate spiritual resurrection "accompanied by the loss of his material being." "The Snowstorm" describes the journey of a particular young officer who is travelling home; "Master and Man" is rather the story of Man's journey to his spiritual home. The story ends with the death of Vasilij Andreevič, but this death is portrayed as a victory, as a resurrection or new birth of Vasilij Andreevič's almost extinct soul. Thus, the story contains not only numerous allusions to Christ's passion, but, in suggesting (by the cruciform position of his arms and legs) that Vasilij Andreevič is a Christ figure, the story draws upon the Christian reader's awareness of Christ's physical resurrection as a confirmation of Vasilij Andreevič's spiritual one. At the same time, of course, the comparison may suggest that the achievement of one's own spiritual resurrection is of greater moment than belief in Christ's physical resurrection.

In any event, Tolstoj's specific and unambiguous rejection of the fundamental Christian mysteries and miracles was absolute only in the context of his writings for the popular audience. In several works written for the educated reader the resurrection of Christ, the central mystery of the Christian faith, became for him a covert source of artistic inspiration and exploitation. Such is the case, for example, with the last work which I will mention in the present discussion: "The Death of Ivan Il'ič" ("Smert' Ivana Il'iča," 1886). This was the first work written by Tolstoj when, in the middle of the 1880s, he decided to return to the writing of fiction aimed at the educated reader. The presence in it of a network of allusions to the motifs of the Passion and to resurrection indicates that the phenomenon which I have been discussing was characteristic of Tolstoj's later work from its very beginnings.

As I have tried to show in an article on the story,[4] "The Death of Ivan Il'ič" is remarkable for the number and density of its subtextual configurations. These include an imbedded pattern of organization and clusters of themes and images which both compete with and complement their counterparts in the surface text of the story. As far as I know no one has yet noticed the sub-textual cluster of allusions to the motif of resurrection and to the Passion narrative which the story, especially its final chapter, contains.[5] Ivan Il'ič is, for example, described at one point as the *"phénix de la famille."* This metaphor is a mere cliché as it is used in chapter II, and it seems to refer to nothing more than Ivan's superiority over his two brothers in intelligence, accomplishments, and

---

4. "The Role of the Ending in Lev Tolstoi's 'The Death of Ivan Il'ič,' " *Canadian Slavonic Papers*, 24 (1982): 229–38.

5. For the text of the story see nearly any edition of Tolstoj's works, e.g. Tolstoj, SS XII, 57–115.

what would be called today "career prospects." In chapter XII, however, this epithet, if the reader recalls it, is likely to seem exactly apt as Ivan's spirit, phoenix-like, escapes the pain and ruin of his dying body.

The story also contains a number of details which seem unremarkable when considered only in the context of the surface text. If, however, they are taken together, they comprise a cluster of allusions to the crucifixion of Jesus. For example: Ivan's final agony lasts three days (chap. XII); in chapter IX he calls out to God, "Why do you torment me?" and weeps at "His cruelty and His absence," an echo of Christ's "My God, My God! Why hast Thou forsaken me?"; Ivan's dying commitment of his son to the care of Praskov'ja Fedorovna (chap. XII) recalls another of Christ's last words, "Woman, behold thy son." The emphatic magnitude of Ivan's physical pain is hardly excessive[6] in the context of an implied comparison to the sufferings of death by crucifixion; both Jesus and Ivan are wounded in the side (Ivan's illness originates from a blow in the side suffered in a fall from a ladder, chap. III). At the end Ivan is sorry for those whom he had, with some reason, grown to hate. He has become aware that they, as he had been, are ignorant of the hypocrisy of their lives. His attempt to say *"prosti"* ("forgive"; chap. XII) may be read as a plea in their behalf as well as his own, suggesting a comparison with Christ's "Father, forgive them for they know not what they do." The family's ill-concealed complaints against the inconvenience represented by Ivan's condition are matched in the Passion account by the taunts directed at Jesus by the crowd. One of these is that Jesus saved others but was unable to save himself (*"sebja on ne možet spasti,"* Mark xv, 31). Of Ivan, too, it is said that he is unable to save himself (*"on ne možet spastis';"* chap. XII). It should also be noted that this is said of Ivan in the context of a comparison between his position and that of someone "in the hands of the executioner," as was Christ.

Finally just before his death Ivan hears "someone above him" say "It is finished" (*končeno*; chap. XII). The echo of the Passion narrative is obvious to the modern reader but was more obscure when the Russian original first appeared because the Gospel text (in the received Russian version of Tolstoj's time) employed the word *soveršilos'* ("it is accomplished"). In his *Harmony and Translation of the Four Gospels*, however, Tolstoj emended the standard translation by replacing *soveršilos'* with *končeno*. The story's final chapter clearly suggests a connection between Ivan's demise and Christ's passion. Since Ivan escapes from the power of death at the end of the narrative, it seems appropriate to extend the comparison beyond the passion to the resurrection, especially as this is also suggested by the earlier comparison of Ivan to the mythological phoenix.

---

6. For an account of the opinion that Ivan's suffering is artistically excessive, see E. Wasiolek, "Tolstoy's 'The Death of Ivan Il'ič' and Jamesian Fictional Imperatives," *Modern Fiction Studies*, 6 (1960): 314–24.

Thus, the mystery of the resurrection, which, like all the New Testament miracles, had no theological significance for Tolstoj and which he specifically excluded from his version of the Gospels, seems at the same time to have had a certain amount of importance for him as a motif suitable for artistic exploitation. It was used to good effect in contributing to the reader's appreciation of Ivan Il'ič's new life in the spirit as artistically justified and aesthetically satisfying. One may wonder, in fact, whether the artist in Tolstoj rebelled at the austere and fleshless abstractness of the thinker's newly constructed system of Christian ethics and sought, albeit subtly and covertly, to reintroduce into some of his fictional elaborations of his new themes the deeds of Christ which had originally given that system the power of its attraction. It is also interesting to note that Tolstoj's artistic use of what he deemed theological irrelevancies (or even falsehoods) is confined to works written for the educated audience, as though he considered it an appropriate technique when dealing with readers of some sophistication, but inappropriate (= dangerous?) for the "people." This, if true, would suggest that his apparent rebellion against the rather simplistic aesthetic doctrines outlined in *What Is Art?* (*Čto takoe iskusstvo?*, 1898) began much earlier than, as is usually supposed, the writing (after the turn of the century) of Hadji-Murad.

DONALD BARTHELME

At the Tolstoy Museum†

At the Tolstoy Museum we sat and wept. Paper streamers came out of our eyes. Our gaze drifted toward the pictures. They were placed too high on the wall. We suggested to the director that they be lowered six inches at least. He looked unhappy but said he would see to it. The holdings of the Tolstoy Museum consist principally of some thirty thousand pictures of Count Leo Tolstoy.

After they had lowered the pictures we went back to the Tolstoy Museum. I don't think you can peer into one man's face too long—for too long a period. A great many human passions could be discerned, behind the skin.

Tolstoy means "fat" in Russian. His grandfather sent his linen to Holland to be washed. His mother *did not know* any bad words. As a youth he shaved off his eyebrows, hoping they would grow back bushier. He first contracted gonorrhea in 1847. He was once bitten on the face by a bear. He became a vegetarian in 1885. To make himself interesting, he occasionally bowed backward.

†From *City Life* (New York, 1970). Reprinted with permission of Farrar, Straus and Giroux.

Tolstoy's coat

I was eating a sandwich at the Tolstoy Museum. The Tolstoy Museum is made of stone—many stones, cunningly wrought. Viewed from the street, it has the aspect of three stacked boxes: the first, second, and third levels. These are of increasing size. The first level is, say, the size of a shoebox, the second level the size of a case of whiskey, and the third level the size of a box that contained a new overcoat. The amazing cantilever of the third level has been much talked about. The glass floor there allows one to look straight down and provides a "floating" feeling. The entire building, viewed from the street, suggests that it is about to fall on you. This the architects relate to Tolstoy's moral authority.

In the basement of the Tolstoy Museum carpenters uncrated new pictures of Count Leo Tolstoy. The huge crates stencilled FRAGILE in red ink . . .

The guards at the Tolstoy Museum carry buckets in which there are stacks of clean white pocket handkerchiefs. More than any other Museum, the Tolstoy Museum induces weeping. Even the bare title of a Tolstoy work, with its burden of love, can induce weeping—for example, the article titled "Who Should Teach Whom to Write, We the Peasant Children or the Peasant Children Us?" Many people stand before this article, weeping. Too, those who are caught by Tolstoy's eyes, in the various portraits, room after room after room, are not unaffected by the experience. It is like, people say, committing a small crime and being discovered at it by your father, who stands in four doorways, looking at you.

Tolstoy as a youth

At Starogladkovskaya,
about 1852

Tiger hunt, Siberia

I was reading a story of Tolstoy's at the Tolstoy Museum. In this story a bishop is sailing on a ship. One of his fellow-passengers tells the bishop about an island on which three hermits live. The hermits are said to be extremely devout. The bishop is seized with a desire to see and talk with the hermits. He persuades the captain of the ship to anchor near the island. He goes ashore in a small boat. He speaks to the hermits. The hermits tell the bishop how they worship God. They have a prayer that goes: "Three of You, three of us, have mercy on us." The bishop feels that this is a prayer prayed in the wrong way. He undertakes to teach the hermits the Lord's Prayer. The hermits learn the Lord's Prayer but with the greatest difficulty. Night has fallen by the time they have got it correctly.

The bishop returns to his ship, happy that he has been able to assist the hermits in their worship. The ship sails on. The bishop sits alone on deck, thinking about the experiences of the day. He sees a light in the sky, behind the ship. The light is cast by the three hermits floating over the water, hand in hand, without moving their feet. They catch up with the ship, saying: "We have forgotten, servant of God, we have forgotten your teaching!" They ask him to teach them again. The bishop crosses himself. Then he tells the hermits that their prayer, too, reaches God. "It is not for me to teach you. Pray for us sinners!" The bishop bows to the deck. The hermits fly back over the sea, hand in hand, to their island.

The story is written in a very simple style. It is said to originate in a folk tale. There is a version of it in St. Augustine. I was incredibly depressed by reading this story. Its beauty. Distance.

The Anna-Vronsky Pavilion

At the Tolstoy Museum, sadness grasped the 741 Sunday visitors. The Museum was offering a series of lectures on the text "Why Do Men Stupefy Themselves?" The visitors were made sad by these eloquent speakers, who were probably right.

People stared at tiny pictures of Turgenev, Nekrasov, and Fet. These and other small pictures hung alongside extremely large pictures of Count Leo Tolstoy.

In the plaza, a sinister musician played a wood trumpet while two children watched.

We considered the 640,086 pages (Jubilee Edition) of the author's published work. Some people wanted him to go away, but other people were glad we had him. "He has been a lifelong source of inspiration to me," one said.

I haven't made up my mind. Standing here in the "Summer in the Country" Room, several hazes passed over my eyes. Still, I think I will march on to "A Landlord's Morning." Perhaps something vivifying will happen to me there.

At the disaster (arrow indicates Tolstoy)

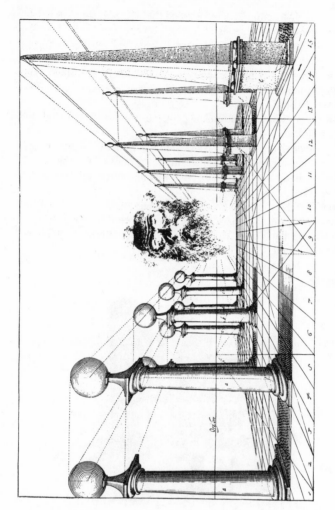

Museum plaza with monumental head (Closed Mondays)

A Chronology of
Tolstoy's Life and Work

1828	Born on his father's estate, Yasnaya Polyana, near Tula, eighty miles south of Moscow.
1830	Mother dies.
1837	Father dies. He is brought up by an aunt.
1844	Enters the University of Kazan; studies languages first, later transferring to the faculty of law.
1847	Leaves the University of Kazan without having graduated; lives on his estate, Yasnaya Polyana.
1851	Goes to the Caucasus; obtains commission in the army; participates in skirmishes with mountain tribesmen.
1852	Completes *Childhood*.
1854	Transferred to Sevastopol; participates in the Crimean War.
1855–56	*Sevastopol Stories*.
1855	Leaves army; goes to Petersburg.
1857	Visits Western Europe; establishes school for peasant children at Yasnaya Polyana.
1858	*Three Deaths*.
1859	*Family Happiness*.
1860–61	Visits Western Europe.
1861	Brother Nikolai dies of tuberculosis.
1862	Marries Sofia Bers.
1863	*The Cossacks*.
1863–69	*War and Peace*.
1873–76	*Anna Karenina*.
1880–82	*A Confession*, describing his spiritual crisis and religious conversion.
1886	*The Death of Ivan Ilych*.
1889	*The Kreutzer Sonata*.

1895   *Master and Man.*
1896–1904   *Hadji Murad.*
1897   *What is Art?*
1902   *Resurrection.*
1910   In late October leaves Yasnaya Polyana to take up residence in a monastery; ten days later, dies in the railroad station in Astapovo.

Selected Bibliography

Books

Benson, Ruth C. *Women in Tolstoy: The Ideal and the Erotic*. Chicago and Urbana: U of Illinois P, 1973.
Christian, R. F. *Tolstoy: A Critical Introduction*. Cambridge: Cambridge UP, 1969.
Shklovsky, Victor B. *Lev Tolstoi*. Moscow: Progress Publishers, 1978.
Wasiolek, Edward. *Tolstoy's Major Fiction*. Chicago: U of Chicago P, 1978.

Articles

Hagan, John H., Jr. "Detail and Meaning in Tolstoy's *Master and Man*." *Criticism* 11 (1969): 31—58.
Jahn, Gary R. "The Role of the Ending in Lev Tolstoi's *The Death of Ivan Ilich*." *Canadian Slavonic Papers* 24 (1982) 3: 229–38.
———. "The Death of Ivan Il'ič—Chapter One." *Studies in Honor of Xenia Gaasiorowska*. Ed. Lauren Leighton. Columbus: Slavica Publishers, 1983.
Olney, James. "Experience, Metaphor and Meaning: *The Death of Ivan Ilych*." *Journal of Aesthetics and Art Criticism* 31 (1972): 101–4.
Pachmuss, Temira. "The Theme of Love and Death in Tolstoy's *The Death of Ivan Ilych*." *American Slavic and East European Review* 20 (1961): 72–83.
Parthé, Kathleen. "The Metamorphosis of Death in Tolstoy." *Language and Style* 18 (Spring 1985) 2: 205–14.
Rahv, P. "The Death of Ivan Illych and Joseph K." *Image and Idea: Twenty Essays on Literary Themes*. Norfolk: New Directions, 1957.
Russell, Robert. "From Individual to Universal: Tolstoy's 'Smert' Ivana Il'icha.' " *Modern Language Review* 76 (1981) 3: 629–42.
Sorokin, Boris. "Ivan I'lich as Jonah: A Cruel Joke." *Canadian Slavic Studies* 5 (1971): 487–507.
Spiers, Logan. "Tolstoy and Chekov: *The Death of Ivan Ilych* and *A Dreary Story*." *Oxford Review* 8 (1968): 81–93.
Turner, C. J. G. "The Language of Fiction: Word Clusters in Tolstoy's *The Death of Ivan Ilyich*." *Modern Language Review* 65 (1970): 116–21.
Wasiolek, Edward. "Tolstoy's *The Death of Ivan Ilych* and Jamesian Fictional Imperatives." *Modern Fiction Studies* 6 (Winter 1960–61) 4: 314–24.
Wexelblatt, Robert. "The Higher Parody: Ivan Ilych's Metamorphosis and the Death of Gregor Samsa." *Massachusetts Review* 21 (Fall 1980) 3: 601–28.